About the a

Graham Oxley was born in 1945 in Weston-Super-Mare and, aside from a year of hitchhiking around Europe in his late teens, has lived there for his entire life.

He went to the local grammar school and left at the age of seventeen with two O-levels to his name. His academic failure at school might have been due to the fact that his mother became ill when he was about seven years old. She died of cancer when he was nine years old. He likes to think that the lack of her guiding hand through his school years was the reason he did not pass exams. However, he does concede that it was probably due to his own laziness and his failure to ever do any homework which caused him to leave school with no qualifications.

He worked at a variety of jobs after leaving school but never found anything which he really liked. Instead, he began studying at home and eventually gained a law degree at a local college. Finally, after several years, he qualified as a solicitor and ended up practising in his home town for about twenty years, before retiring at the age of sixty-nine. It was only then that he began writing seriously and was able to find the time to finish the novel which he had started writing about fifty years before. It's never too late.

A FLIRT WITH JUSTICE

Graham Oxley

A FLIRT WITH JUSTICE

Vanguard Press

VANGUARD PAPERBACK

© Copyright 2021
Graham Oxley

The right of Graham Oxley to be identified as author of
this work has been asserted by him in accordance with the
Copyright, Designs and Patents Act 1988.

A CIP catalogue record for this title is
available from the British Library.

ISBN 978 1 784659 47 9

Vanguard Press is an imprint of
Pegasus Elliot MacKenzie Publishers Ltd.
www.pegasuspublishers.com

First Published in 2021

Vanguard Press
Sheraton House Castle Park
Cambridge England

Printed & Bound in Great Britain

Acknowledgements

Firstly, I wish to give an acknowledgement to Helen Charnley. Many years ago, my then wife Gillian and I had a baby girl whom we named Suzanne. In the same year, Helen had a baby boy who was called Patrick. As we both lived near each other, our children went to the same school and my wife and Helen became friends whilst they stood together outside the school gate. We were invited to their house for dinner one evening and before we left home, my wife told me that Helen was a writer and had had some poetry published. At the same time, I had just started writing this book. That was about thirty or so years ago, and afterwards I kept meaning to get back to my book and finish it, but I was always diverted by my work, family or pastimes, mortgage, etcetera. In the meantime, Helen went on to publish many books, most or all of which I would purchase and promise myself that I would resume writing my own. Helen published her books under the name of Helen Dunmore.

It was not until I retired that I thought I should resume my writing. It was then that I read an article in the *Sunday Times Magazine* saying that Helen was suffering from cancer and not expected to live long. That article determined me that I should finish my book. We both had started our writing careers at the same time and she had been hugely successful whilst I had achieved nothing. I retrieved my file of scribbles and finished the book, and wish to acknowledge Helen's part in inspiring me to do so.

My second acknowledgement is to my friend, Noel Sweeney, who is a barrister who has practised in criminal law for many years. He is also an expert in the law concerning animals. He has also written several books himself. Noel is the most erudite man that I have ever met and has been a good friend to me. Although I worked as a lawyer, I have never felt wholly confident of my own abilities in respect of things legal. Any legal points upon which I was unsure, I would check with him, so if there are any glaring mistakes in this volume, Noel is the one to blame.

Chapter One
The Office

"What's in a name?" said the Bard: the implication being that it is the man behind the name that is important not the name itself. That may be so, but might it not also be the case that a person's name can affect his status in the community?

For example, when searching the telephone directory for a taxi firm how many people would be likely to choose the firm called 'Drat and Co' in preference to the more usual 'Speedy Cab Company etcetera?

The reflection can be extended to cover the general appropriateness or otherwise of names or titles to professions which they represent. Everyone has heard of some humorous examples of such situations. There are undertakers called 'Death', bank managers called 'Stingy', coal merchants named 'Black' or builders called 'Bodget' etcetera.

Mr Arnold Pigg could certainly be excused for regretting his own name. Whether or not his character was in any way attributable to his unfortunate title it is impossible to say. What is certain is the fact that he behaved as if he were trying to live it down. His manners always exuded great pomposity and though one always felt that this was a veneer, one never got the chance to see behind it.

It was as if Mr Pigg feared that his name alone opened him to ridicule and that might well have been the case. To invite further ridicule by allowing the mask of his own self-importance to slip away one felt was something which Mr Pigg had taken a conscious decision to avoid. Ironically it was when he was at his most pompous that he looked most ridiculous but Mr A Pigg Esq seldom, if ever, realised this himself.

At what age he adopted his lifetime role one cannot say. Probably it was at no single time but rather a habit carefully acquired over a number of years. Whenever it was, it must have been after his voice had broken, because part of his act was to shout very loudly in a deep voice. It would have been too absurd a thing for a boy soprano to attempt and so a beginning to A Pigg's metamorphosis was to this small extent possible to pinpoint.

His deep manly voice, a complete accident of nature, was in fact the only aspect of his role that lent any credence to the character he tried to portray. But for this natural gift he would have appeared totally preposterous. The voice was always a surprise to those who had never met him before, both because of its fine quality and its unnecessary volume. A Pigg inevitably spoke to everyone he met as if they were all stone deaf.

His physical appearance did not accord with his mature voice. Though middle-aged, he had a full head of hair, almost jet black, without a hint of grey. His features were almost boyish, with cheeks slightly puffed like a classic painting of a cherub. The irony was that Mr A Pigg was one of those individuals who never behaved childishly, even as a child. He was born with an adult sensibility, which grown-ups sometimes find endearing and which his contemporaries always found infuriating. At school it was always Porky (for such was inevitably his nickname), whose shoes retained an immaculate shine when the footwear of all about him was scuffed and scratched. It was always Porky who counselled ordered behaviour in teacher's absence when all his classmates were intent on creating mayhem. And it was inevitably Porky's hand which shot up first when teacher asked for a volunteer for anything. In short A Pigg was a creep!

Mr Pigg's chosen career was one for which a cynical observer might say he was admirably suited, being an insincere, pompous and intensely officious little man. He was a civil servant. Not that anyone in the Civil Service could be said to have chosen their career. Except perhaps those who enter directly into the rarefied atmosphere of the upper echelons of that official body. It is suggested that, generally speaking, people drift into the Civil Service for want of anything else to do. One cannot imagine for example, that youngsters leave school with a vocational urge to be counter clerks in Social Security offices. Rather, they take such jobs because they can find no others at the time.

Mr A Pigg however was a born bureaucrat. He possessed that characteristic lack of imagination and ability to give painstaking attention to insignificant details, whilst overlooking important points, which bureaucracy so admires and rewards and which men of action find so infuriating. He had no ambition of ever being the author of an original thought but much preferred to implement the set of rules laid down by the department for whom he worked. The fact that this set of rules was not, indeed could not be, totally comprehensive, never concerned him. He followed the rules to the letter. He was a man who worked by the book.

The book by which he worked was a huge compendium of rules and regulations, all kept together in a loose leaf binder system. Each office in the department had such a volume and each manager of each office was exhorted (ironically by periodic reminders included in the body of the rules and regulations), to keep his rulebook up to date.

Keeping the rulebook up to date meant extracting the old rules and substituting the fresh ones, as and when they were delivered from the rule-concocting nerve centre of the department. Such amendments of the rulebook had to be carried out in accordance with the instructions contained within the volume itself.

Mr A Pigg was a manager and as such he was in charge of the small office, which employed a dozen or so people. In Mr A Pigg's mind, the book occupied the sort of importance that the ship's log or Bible would have held for the Pilgrim Fathers.

The irony of Mr A Pigg's rulebook was that it was updated at regular intervals in accordance with its own regulatory contents. This meant that the task of extracting and destroying the old rules, and of substituting the new ones, was delegated to the most junior member of staff. The beauty of this concept was that it left the more elevated members of staff such as Mr Pigg himself, to get on with more demanding work.

In Mr Pigg's office the most junior member of staff was a wafer thin youth with acne called Vincent, who genuinely believed that the only worthwhile pursuit in life was listening to rock 'n' roll music. This he did at every available opportunity, travelling around the country in his spare time, attending concerts and pop festivals and invariably returning home extremely late. Consequently he was always semi-conscious at his desk and constantly destroying rules which he ought to have retained, and keeping those which he ought to have destroyed. At the same time he managed, inadvertently, to muddle the contents of the rulebook. Thus it was that the revered manual, by which Mr Pigg set so much store, his own Holy Grail, without whose advice he seldom took any step of consequence, was both out of date and out of order.

It mattered little. The contents of the rulebook consisted mainly of regulations, enactments and statutory instruments all of which were printed in that unmistakable Whitehall prose, which is more effective than mustard gas. Each regulation contained therein was cross-referred to several others. When one added to this the fact that the general public were not allowed access to this publication (which was classified as a confidential document), it was hardly surprising that the inaccuracies in Mr Pigg's edition did not deter from the smooth running of that gentleman's office.

So it was that Mr Pigg prided himself on the efficient way in which his office was organised. He was firmly of the opinion that it was his own adherence to the edicts laid down in his rulebook which guaranteed this success. The book itself which Mr Pigg so admired was contained in a stiff binder coloured green consequently it was generally referred to as the 'Green Book'.

On a wet windy March day George Davies arrived at Mr Pigg's office. He had been selected for his duties by a Board of Regional Management whose function was to interview aspiring candidates and allocate them to the various offices within its region. George had undergone a written test and an interview and was very pleased to have received a congratulatory letter from the board telling him of his success and asking him to report to Mr A Pigg at nine-thirty a.m. on Monday morning.

It was a typical government building (or so George felt), red bricks on the outside and tiled floors and walls on the inside. It was the sort of Victorian construction which some regard as a monstrosity but which others, more kindly, referred to as 'possessing character'. Certainly the imitation marble which was everywhere, together with the draughty old windows made it a difficult place to heat.

George followed the cardboard signs, in the shape of pointing fingers, which led him along the tiled corridor to a room marked 'Enquiries'. He entered and found a small room which had obviously been a part of a larger room but which had been partitioned off to form a small waiting room. The larger room, from which the waiting area had been segregated, was only separated by a wooden partition of waist height, topped by a frosted glass screen which reached head height. Between the top of the screen and the ceiling of the room was a clear space across which drifted the conversation of those working on the other side of the screen.

"How did you get on last night, Mavis?" enquired a female voice.

"Oh it was awful," came the response. "You wouldn't believe what a disaster it was."

"Why what happened?" asked the first voice eagerly.

"Well, first of all he didn't turn up until nearly nine-thirty p.m.!" said Mavis with great finality as if that in itself were enough to shock the listener. "Nine-thirty p.m.!" she repeated with great emphasis. "I was just about to take off my make-up and go to bed. Seven o'clock I was ready to go out and he turns up at half past nine."

"Why was that?" asked the first voice.

"Oh! He said he'd been to visit his mother in hospital," responded Mavis with a suspicious edge to her voice.

"Oh no! You didn't believe that, did you?"

"Not unless they serve beer down at the hospital!" said Mavis cynically. "He stank of it."

"So what did you do?" enquired her colleague.

"He took me out to that pub on the moor. You know, the one miles from anywhere, near where they're building the motorway."

"Oh no!" said the other. "That's miles out."

"I know," said Mavis. "I reckon he is either married or engaged and he took me all the way out there because he didn't want to risk being seen with me around town."

"Oh no, do you really think so?"

"I wouldn't be at all surprised," said Mavis. "Anyway, he needn't worry about that any more because he won't be seen out with me again."

"Was it that bad then?" pressed her friend gently.

Mavis took a deep breath. "Well I sat in that cold pub right out in the middle of nowhere until way past closing time, while he played darts all night with the motorway construction workers. It was dreadful. They were all filthy dirty and covered in mud and the language was even dirtier."

"Oh dear," said the colleague.

"He must have drunk six pints of beer in that pub," estimated Mavis, "and that on top of whatever he'd already drunk earlier in the evening. Then he drove back along the narrow country road at about ninety miles an hour. I was terrified."

"Didn't you tell him to slow down?" questioned the other. "I know I would have done."

"I did," insisted Mavis, "but he just laughed and went even faster. He reckoned he was a better driver after a few drinks because he was more relaxed."

"That's rubbish!" said the other emphatically.

"I know. I told him that," said Mavis, "but he just laughed all the more. I think he was so drunk he didn't care what he was doing. Anyway, on the way back, he parked on that piece of waste ground by the factory and tried to get me into the back seat with him."

"What! On the first date?" asked her colleague with indignation.

"Yeah, the dirty devil, he was all hands. He laddered a brand-new new pair of tights that I only put on that evening. But that's not the worst of it. When I told him he could cut that sort of thing out and insisted that he take me home, the blessed car wouldn't work."

"Oh no!" exclaimed the other sympathetically. "What happened then?"

"Well, he'd parked in some mud and the wheels kept spinning. Guess what silly bugger had to get out and push the damn thing?"

"Oh no!" repeated the other, even more sympathetically.

"Yeah," said Mavis, much aggrieved. "And ruined a perfectly good pair of suede shoes."

"Oh no!" reiterated the second girl who appeared to be astonished by everything Mavis reported.

George had listened with fascination to this dialogue and had delayed pressing the bell-push (provided for inquirers), for fear of curtailing the conversation. Eventually he felt he had to announce his presence otherwise if he were discovered without pressing the bell he would be regarded as an eavesdropper. He pressed the button and a noise which can only be described as a loud raspberry sounded in the office somewhere. George heard Mavis's voice again.

"I'll go," she said and he heard the sound of high heeled shoes upon the tiled floor. The frosted glass screen was slid noisily back and George found himself face-to-face with an attractive dark haired young lady of about twenty years of age.

"Yes?" she enquired in a manner as frosty as the screen she had just opened. George felt like a naughty schoolboy and nervously produced his appointment letter from the Regional Board. Mavis took it and read it briefly, her features all the while displaying the sort of expression with which a bishop might regard a pornographic magazine.

"Take a seat, please," she said with equal disdain. "I'll let Mr Pigg know you are here."

The glass screen was replaced and Mavis's footsteps retreated to the point in the unseen area from which they had come. George heard her whisper fiercely to her companion, informing her of who it was at the public counter and what his business was.

"What's he like?" demanded the other in an equally audible whisper. George heard no definite reply to this question but discerned a brief "mmm" with an upward lilt which indicated, at best, that Mavis was not definitely 100% on his side. It was obviously accompanied by a gesture which, together with the remark itself, would have given the listener a reasonable idea of Mavis's impression of George. He found this very frustrating, hidden as he was behind the screen.

"One thing's for sure," intervened a male voice loudly. "If he is prepared to work in a place like this, he can't be over intelligent."

"Oh, dry up, face ache!" responded Mavis irritably and then, much more reasonably, clearly now addressing the other female, "I'm just going to tell Mr Pigg that he's here."

Isolated behind the screen, George had listened attentively to the conversation occurring on the other side. He was intrigued by the fact that those behind the screen should think that their remarks could not be heard by him. He was also slightly perturbed by the reference to his own intelligence and wondered why the speaker held his place of work in such low esteem.

After a while he heard Mavis return to her desk. Her conversation with her colleague resumed.

"He's still at it you know."

"What's that?" asked the other.

"Those chart things of his. He's still filling in those graphs and things with all those coloured crayons."

"Oh no!" cried the other. "He was doing those all day yesterday. What an incredible waste of time."

"Little things please little minds," chipped in the same male voice as before. This observation provoked no comment.

"Did you ask him about that special day off you wanted?" asked Mavis's colleague.

"Yes, but he says I can't have it."

"Oh no! Why not?"

"Well," said Mavis petulantly, "he said if it was allowed in the green book then I was welcome to have it but when he looked it up of course there was nothing there."

"Oh no!" said the other, predictably.

"Hmm," said Mavis thoughtfully. "I'm sure it used to be allowed because I remember Agnes claiming a special day off before she was transferred to head office a couple of years ago. Anyway, he checked the book and there was nothing there."

"You know why that was don't you?" said the male voice.

"Why?" said the other female.

"Because that cretin Vincent has destroyed the wrong pages in the green book, that's why."

Their conversation was interrupted by a commotion which erupted further within the building. There was a banging and crashing of doors followed by much shouting and what sounded like the deep throated maniacal laughter that generally precedes the arrival of the genie in a pantomime. George couldn't imagine what was happening but observed that the upheaval was getting closer. Suddenly the glass screen was thrown back and a voice like a megaphone caused him to jump out of his skin.

"Mr Davies isn't it? Sorry to keep you waiting. My name is Pigg. P. I. Double G."

George leapt to his feet and shook the hand that was proffered across the counter. Mr Pigg gripped George's hand in what he believed was a manly style and pumped his arm up and down as if both their lives depended upon it. George felt as if he were in an arm wrestling contest and was astonished at the length of time Mr Pigg continued this formality.

"I'm very glad to see you" he bellowed. "We sorely need another pair of hands. We've been understaffed for a long time. Come on through anyway."

Lifting up a flap at the end of the counter he led the way through the office in which Mavis and the others worked, down a corridor towards a door marked 'A Pigg Manager' beneath this sign was a movable device which when operated, revealed the word 'Engaged'. With great ostentation Mr Pigg moved this sign to indicate to all that he was in conference.

He led George into the room. "Take a seat," he shouted. "I won't keep you a moment, I will just find your papers."

George sat down whilst Mr Pigg busied himself in the filing cabinet seeking a file which was obviously missing. It gave George the opportunity to observe his surroundings. The room had a very Spartan aspect. The filing cabinet, some metal cupboards the size of wardrobes and Mr Pigg's desk were all painted the same dull colour: battleship grey. There was a carpet on the floor the colour of gravy but it looked like an afterthought because it only fitted the centre part of the room. A surrounding area of floor, some six feet in any direction, revealed linoleum of the same uninspiring colour. There was an odd odour in the room.

On the desk in front of him were two framed photographs. One was a picture of a woman (presumably Mrs Pigg) standing on a beach somewhere on a sunny, yet windy day. The weather conditions were deduced from the fact that the woman was squinting badly and her hair was blown half across her face. The second photograph was of a small boy (presumably Master Pigg) holding a chocolate ice cream, whilst asleep. Clearly the boy had blinked just as the photograph was taken!

George found these pictures intriguing. He wondered privately what sort of woman it was who would voluntarily change her name to Pigg. He also wondered how it was that such technically bad photographs should be chosen for exhibition in such a fashion.

"Aha! Here we are," said Mr Pigg waving a buff-coloured file triumphantly. He sat down behind the desk and studied the papers for a moment.

"I see you were born in this area," he said. "Have you always lived here?" Mr Pigg asked this with an emphasis which George found mystifying. "Have you got your P45, please?" George handed over all his documents and Mr Pigg began filling out forms. "Married?" he asked.

George said he was not.

"Good good!" responded his new boss. "Young single men with ambition is what this department is looking for. I can assure you there will be plenty of overtime here if you're interested." He smiled encouragingly and George smiled back because he felt it was expected. In truth, he did not feel encouraged by the prospect of lots of overtime but did not wish to appear anything but eager.

"Have you any objections to moving away from this area?" demanded Mr Pigg unexpectedly.

George was baffled by this question and was consequently undecided as to how he should respond. He looked quizzically at Mr Pigg who placed his fingertips together to form a tent shape and rested his own nose upon them in what he fondly imagined was an intellectual pose. "For example," he boomed, "do you have any aged or infirmed parents living here?"

George said he did not.

"Good, good. I'll mark you down as mobile then," he said with obvious pleasure. "That's the secret of success in this job; mobility!" Mr Pigg thrust his tongue into one cheek and simultaneously raised his eyes to the ceiling. This grotesque gesture was his way of indicating that the information he was imparting was both important and confidential. He examined George's file once more and asked, "What made you choose this department, George?"

"I didn't," said George truthfully. "I requested a different department actually but they posted me here instead." His voice dwindled away as he realised he had said the wrong thing.

Mr Pigg gave a carefully measured "Hmmm," and wrote something in his file. "I see from your records that you have two A-levels."

George affirmed that this was correct.

"Of course," Mr Pigg added, "nowadays the real openings in the department are for degree holders who come in on a direct entry basis. Still, there is room for ambitious young men who are mobile." He thrust his tongue into his cheek again then lowered his voice slightly (but only slightly). "This is an expanding department," he said. "I see you play a lot of sport," he said, continuing to scan George's personal file. "Cricket, squash, football. Don't you find all that a bit time consuming?"

"Not really," said George. "I don't really do anything else with my spare time. Besides I don't play any of these games at a high level, so I don't find it very demanding."

Mr Pigg opened his desk drawer and took out a large black briar pipe, the inside of which he began to ceremoniously scrape with a sharp knife designed for just that purpose. He tapped out the pipe noisily into a metal waste bin, then filled the pipe with tobacco which he took from a plastic pouch which he kept in his drawer. As he applied a lighted match to the results of his labour the room was filled with clouds of blue pungent smoke. George then realised why the room smelt so odd when he had first entered.

Mr Pigg leaned back in his chair and puffed contentedly. When obviously satisfied that the tobacco was properly ignited, he took the pipe from his lips and holding it by the bowl, he pointed the stem at George, saying, "Sport can be a useful asset in many occupations. In the services for example it is very useful to be able to play sport well but that is not the case in this department I'm afraid. There is, I feel, a tendency nowadays to overemphasise the importance of sport it's not, after all, everybody's cup of tea. Take for example young Pete Powell who works in this office. He plays rugby for the local club and by all accounts is a bit of a star but he does tend to allow it to occupy all of his time. So much so that he is unable or unwilling to work any overtime. Now don't misunderstand me overtime is not compulsory here. However, I do think it speaks volumes for a chap's motivation if he is prepared to work on one or two nights a week, don't you?"

George said he did because he couldn't think of anything else to say.

"Good, good!" boomed Mr Pigg. He leaned forward conspiratorially. "Mobility and motivation: those are the keywords in this department."

With great ceremony he tapped his pipe out against the inside of the metal waste bin. The result of this activity was twofold. In the first place the noise it made was so deafening that the further information which Mr Pigg offered on the subject of the department (for he continued speaking all the while), was quite lost to George's ears. In the second place, the burning remains of his pipe tobacco smouldered against some waste paper already deposited in the bin and caused a small fire. Mr Pigg flapped nervously for a few seconds then decided to stamp out the burning paper and temporarily got his foot stuck in the bin and hopped around the room trying to extricate himself and making even more noise. With George's help, he got his foot and the fire out and tried desperately to recapture the poise and authority which he felt he had possessed before the incident.

"Well now," he said, clearing his throat loudly. "I'll take you round and introduce you to everyone." He led the way out of his own room and down the corridor. He crashed open the door of the room adjacent to his own and loudly invited George inside.

The room contained two ladies, one young, the other much older operating typewriters. Each had a pile of files on her desk which were being worked upon and on the floor beside each of them was a similar pile which represented work just completed. That aside, it seemed that every other horizontal surface in the room supported a pot plant of some kind. There were plants on window sills, plants on shelves and plants on cupboards. There were plants in pots fixed to the walls and plants descending from pots hanging from the ceiling. There were plants which climbed out of pots on the floor, entwined themselves around bamboo canes and even insinuated themselves into the cupboards on one wall. The whole room had the steamy atmosphere of an equatorial rainforest.

"These are our typists," yelled Mr Pigg superfluously. Then he added with ostentation, "Ladies, permit me to introduce Mr George Davies our new member of staff."

George said his hellos to the two women whom Mr Pigg identified as Penny and Mrs Balstaff. It was not explained why the latter was not referred to by her Christian name but one look at her was sufficient to allay curiosity on that point. She was an imposing woman both in size and demeanour and it was undoubtedly a bold man who would dare to address such a personage in anything other than a formal manner. She was tall and bulky, probably thirteen stones and her hair which had a blue grey rinse was piled up upon her head by the ingenious use of grips and was held together by a carved wooden device which had the appearance of a tribal dagger. She wore dark-rimmed spectacles which had a thin chain attached to prevent them slipping from her head. When they were not in use they were allowed to hang down upon her enormous bosom. Mrs Balstaff examined George critically over the top of these glasses. Her companion was *very* much younger and appeared to be quite the reverse in character. She was a mousy little creature in her mid to late twenties with short cropped hair, almost like a man, and a thin whippet-like physique.

"We rely very heavily upon these good ladies," said Mr Pigg with a deferential tilt of his head in Mrs Balstaff's direction.

"In fact," he continued, "without these two Trojans I am sure we would all be in a complete turmoil." Again one gained the impression that although his words were praising both women, it was the elder of the two with whom he wished to ingratiate himself.

"Well, it is nice to be appreciated," responded Mrs Balstaff in a matter-of-fact manner which seemed to indicate that she was used to being complimented and furthermore that it was no more than she deserved. "Are you perhaps related to Mr Davies the consultant surgeon at the local hospital?" she asked.

George said that he did not think he was. Mrs Balstaff appeared disappointed. "He's a very nice man," she informed him. "His wife and I play bridge together you know. Do you play bridge, Mr Davies?" George said he did not. Again, Mrs Balstaff seemed disappointed. "Bridge is an excellent pastime, you know," she said. "You meet a very nice class of person playing bridge."

This last statement seemed to beg a response but no one in the room was able to produce one and so an embarrassing silence ensued. This was finally broken by Mr Pigg who noisily cleared his throat. "Well," he boomed "we must press on and introduce George to the rest of the staff."

George said his farewells to Penny and Mrs Balstaff.

As they proceeded down the corridor Mr Pigg informed George that the two ladies he had just met were 'first class workers'. He added with an air of great confidentiality, "Mrs Balstaff has immense experience."

George could offer no response to this remark and so they continued along the corridor until they reached a large room with about ten people working in it. This was the room through which George had passed when Mr Pigg had ushered him through from the waiting room.

Although a large room, it was divided into two smaller areas, each approximately the size of an average room, by the way in which cupboards and filing cabinets were arranged. On the side of this division, closer to the frosted glass screen, sat Mavis and her companion (whose voices George had listened to whilst he was seated in the waiting room) together with a young man of about twenty-five years and another of around sixty years.

George could not see who was seated on the other side of the room because the filing cabinets obscured his view. Mr Pigg did not pause to introduce him to anyone in the room but led him directly to a section at the far end which was partitioned off from the rest of the room by glass panels. It was roughly ten feet square and was, in effect, a room within a room. George learned later that this room was referred to as 'the glasshouse'.

Seated inside the glasshouse was a short grey-haired man with a pencil moustache and half-moon glasses. He was studying some papers and his brow was knitted in a tight frown. He was evidently engrossed in what he was doing because he failed to see or hear their approach. Consequently when Mr Pigg crashed open the door of his compartment he jumped nervously.

"Don't get up, Bill," said Mr Pigg loudly in a reassuring manner. "I just wanted to introduce George Davies who has joined our staff today. This is Bill Butler who will be your section leader, George. You will take all your instructions from him."

George shook hands with Bill who had shown no inclination to stand up until Mr Pigg urged him not to. He indicated a seat to George and they both sat down. Mr Pigg however declined to sit. There was a momentary silence during which Bill regarded him over the top of his glasses. His examination was not as severe as that of Mrs Balstaff but nevertheless George felt embarrassed. Bill made no attempt to speak but seemed to be waiting for Mr Pigg to say something more.

The latter meanwhile was staring out through the glass at something in the outer office which had caught his attention. He took a pen from his jacket pocket and tapped loudly upon the glass with it and then waved his arms in an aggressive gesture. He turned, scowling, to re-focus his attention upon George and Bill. "Have a word with Vincent, will you, Bill," he said curtly. "Try and make sure he's fully occupied all the time will you?"

"Now, George," he continued, "Bill here will make certain you are fully grounded in all aspects of this department. If you have any problems then Bill is the man to see. He is a very experienced officer who has been a valued member of the department longer than anyone else in this office." Though the words uttered were complimentary, Mr Pigg somehow contrived to make them sound vaguely insulting. "A department such as ours is necessarily run according to a set of rules" continued Mr Pigg. "These rules have been formulated over a long period by very able men who have an intimate knowledge of the department's functions." Mr Pigg spoke these words as a priest would a prayer. Though a listener could not doubt that the speaker sincerely believed in what he was saying, one still gained the impression that the speech was not being made for the first time. Confirmation of this was the glazed look in Bill's eyes.

As he spoke, Mr Pigg placed his hands behind his back and began to walk up and down. The glasshouse was not really big enough to permit this and George, eager to assist, tried to move his chair back to give the speaker more room. He attempted to do this by applying a steady pressure with his foot upon Bill's desk. At first this pressure produced no result, then suddenly Bill's desk jerked an inch or two. His mug of tea, which was quite close to the edge of the desk, spilled half its contents which spread rapidly across the paperwork on the desk and dribbled off the edge into Bill's lap. Bill muttered, "Shit!" and leapt to his feet. He swiftly applied his handkerchief to his trouser leg and his paperwork in that order.

Mr Pigg seemed not to have noticed this incident for he continued with his rehearsed speech on the rulebook. "You see, George, experience has shown that without proper guidelines one cannot hope to achieve the sort of smooth running—"

Here he was interrupted by the telephone. Bill reached for the receiver and in so doing knocked over the remains of his tea. "It's head office for you, Mr Pigg," he said and then began salvaging what papers he could from his desk.

Mr Pigg stiffened visibly at the words 'head office', almost as if his instinct had been to stand to attention. He picked up the telephone and said, "Pigg speaking," in a military manner, listened for a moment then said again "Good morning to you, sir, I'm very well thank you. I think if you will allow me, sir, I'll just transfer this call to my own office so that I can talk to you in private."

He then pressed the button on the telephone itself and said, "Penny, I'll be taking this call in my own office. Could you transfer it through please?" Having organised this, he turned back to George and Bill. He said to Bill, "That's personnel on the phone, Bill, so I'd better take it in my own room." He thrust his tongue significantly into his cheek after imparting this information as if to imply an obvious point of confidentiality. The point seemed lost on Bill whose face still wore the expression it had adopted throughout his monologue on rules and regulations.

As soon as Mr Pigg left the glasshouse, Bill appeared to come alive again. The glazed expression on his face was replaced by one of human interest and he asked George a few questions about himself. George apologised for spilling his tea and he said it did not matter. He became almost paternal and George warmed to him. He asked him what had prompted him to join the department and George told him honestly that he had applied for the post because he thought the prospects were good. Bill winced slightly at this but did not make any comment.

Bill revealed that he had a lad of about George's age and that he (Bill) was concerned about his future and that the boy's mother wanted him to get a job in the Civil Service. "I'm not really certain that this type of job would suit him," he confided.

George felt slightly alarmed at this and offered, "But I thought the Civil Service was a good career, I've always been led to believe so anyway."

"Well," responded Bill very slowly, "it's not quite what it used to be. Oh I know it's always felt to be totally secure and a good cushy job with plenty of prospects and the pension at the end but times are changing you know. Nowadays, all the big outfits such as banks, insurance companies etc all pay more than the Civil Service and they all have their own pension schemes. They also give better conditions to work in and often extra advantages like cheap mortgages for employees. The other big drawback here is that since the recession all departments are cutting back on expenditure and staff. "That means there's virtually no promotion any more except when someone up above retires. It's a case of dead men's shoes. No..." he said slowly and with a disappointing finality, "this is not the career it was."

Bill in that brief few moments appeared to be a vastly disillusioned man with very little enthusiasm for his own job. As if suddenly becoming aware of this impression which he was presenting he shook himself out of this mood and said encouragingly, "But don't let me put you off, there's still plenty of opportunities for bright young men like yourself. Let me give you a word of advice. This particular department is contracting. There are rumours that it will be phased out altogether one day and those of us who remain will be absorbed into other departments. Consequently, they are gradually cutting back on the work. Despite what Mr Pigg may have told you and this is strictly entre nous, this office is not particularly busy. Therefore you should be able to cope with whatever work I give you without much trouble. But do concentrate on getting it right. If you're not sure, ask. I shan't be chasing you if you go slowly so long as what you do is correct. The only time I shall be chasing you is when you make mistakes. OK?"

George nodded and Bill gave him a broad wink. "Right let's go and introduce you."

He led George out into the outer office and introduced him to everyone. George was allocated a desk near Mavis and her companion. He noted that Mavis was not as pretty upon closer examination as his first impression of her had indicated. Her dark hair which had looked attractive at a glance was clearly the result of the application of a dye. She was rather too heavily made up and clearly inexperienced in her choice of colours. Her eyes were very heavily blackened and she wore artificial eyelashes which looked incongruous in an office environment. Her lips were bright vermilion which definitely did not suit her. She was a heavy busted girl with a large bottom to match. She wore a tight skirt which was very short and shoes with heels so high that she had difficulty walking. George reflected to himself that she looked a little like mutton dressed as lamb. She accentuated this image by constantly chewing gum. When she was not doing this she smoked king-size menthol cigarettes. Nevertheless, beneath all the paraphernalia there was in George's opinion a pretty girl.

Her companion was almost the exact opposite. She was a long beanpole of a girl with a flat chest and legs like an ostrich. Her hair was long, lank and unkempt and she was the kind of person who looked untidy even when wearing smart clothes. She wore no make-up and had a pasty pallor and looked altogether most uninviting. Her attire was an extremely grubby nylon jumper, green corduroy slacks and sandals. She smoked as many cigarettes as Mavis but unlike the latter she preferred a standard brand. Her name was Helen. George thought that anyone less like the legendary beauty, whose face had launched a thousand ships, was hard to imagine.

Both Mavis and Helen, as far as George could determine, spent most of their time smoking cigarettes and talking to each other. Or rather they spent most of their time discussing Mavis's romantic adventures. Not surprisingly, Helen did not appear to have any dealings with the opposite sex in a romantic capacity and she seemed content to vicariously enjoy those which Mavis experienced which, judging from the overheard conversations, were a great many.

The older man who shared the side of the room on which Mavis and Helen and now George worked, was called Tom Richards. He was approaching retirement age and worked in the Civil Service simply to supplement his Army pension. He had spent much of his service life in the Far East and no doubt it was the harsh sunshine in that area which accounted for the colour and quality of his skin which looked like an old walnut.

The younger man in George's section was called Pete Powell and it was he whom Mr Pigg had criticised for not volunteering for overtime. He was a handsome young man with curly blonde looks like a classical Greek hero, with a physique to match. He had astonishingly blue eyes which gave a hint of the capable intellect behind them. They also sparkled with a readiness for humour which George found particularly interesting. He liked Pete on sight and felt a reciprocal spirit which flowed towards him.

Pete, unlike many of his colleagues, had that enviable knack of looking smart no matter what clothes he wore. At a glance, he looked a really snappy dresser but when one looked more closely one realised that his garments were neither flashy nor expensive. No, when one reflected on his appearance, one had to admit that clothes just seemed to hang well upon him. He was easily able to cope with his daily quota of work by lunchtime each day. George noticed that unlike his workmates who preferred to spend their time in conversation, he busied himself in the afternoons by studying the files of the department.

On his first day in the office George was taken under Pete's wing and instructed in the geography of the storeroom. It was more than a room, it was a series of rooms which originally formed the cellars of the Victorian building. They contained acres of dusty confidential files, each with its own individual buff -coloured wrapper. "This is the only perk there is in this job," said Pete when they'd reached the far end of the storeroom. He pressed the button which started the motor on an ancient photocopying machine which stood against the wall. Whilst the machine warmed up he moved to one of the nearby wooden racks and reached down a file. "In these," he waved the file and winked conspiratorially, "is all the information that's worth knowing about anyone who's anyone in this area."

George looked bewildered as Pete flipped through the information contained in the file.

"Nothing much of interest in this one," he said rather matter of factly. "Now let's see who's next." He moved along the rack and, missing out a few files, triumphantly alighted upon a second one of interest. "Aha!" he said and hurriedly opened it to peruse the contents. "Now that's interesting." Moving over to the photocopier he ran off copies of several of the pages in the file. "This bugger is one of the meanest old bastards in town and look how much property he owns."

George still didn't understand and said so. Pete slid the pages into a briefcase he brought with him and then put the file back in its place on the rack. "All the information in this room is worth a fortune," he said waving his arm expansively around the cellar. "I make sure I make use of my time here." As he said this he tapped his own head. "And in case I can't remember it all, I take some of it home for future reference." He indicated the briefcase and winked archly.

"But," said George naïvely, "I thought this was all confidential information. I mean, what about the Official Secrets Act and all that?"

"Oh, bollocks to that," said Pete. "If you don't take your opportunities when they come you will end up like the rest of those lemmings upstairs." He lifted his eyebrows contemptuously to indicate the cellar ceiling. "Anyway, I look at it this way: in every job there is some perk or other isn't there? If you work as a salesman you get a free car don't you? If you work for a bank you get cheap mortgage. If you work in a shop you get discount on the goods don't you? So what do they offer in this job? I'll tell you, sweet F. A. Well this is my perk."

"But what if you get caught?" asked George, again somewhat naïvely.

"Fat chance!" replied Pete. "They are all so thick and bone idle in this place that they'll never know." Pete said this with the utter certainty with which bank robbers dismissed the possibility of detection by the police. He added more realistically "Anyway, that door at the far end of the cellar makes so much noise when it opens that there is no chance of being found out. In any case I always put the waste bin behind it when I come down here so anyone coming in knocks it over as they open the door. It makes a hell of a noise and that gives plenty of time to hide the old briefcase. Besides," he added, "it's not as though I give the information to anybody else, I just keep it for my own use. Anyway," he added finally, as if to justify his actions beyond any reproach, "the Official Secrets Act is only really designed to protect state secrets. Not this sort of stuff."

George spent most of that first afternoon at work down in the storeroom with Pete ostensibly filing and tidying documents but in reality browsing through the confidential information in the department files.

Chapter Two
The Meeting

"Well that just about wraps things up for this morning. And for all you people still driving to work, its nine o'clock and you're late!"

The light-hearted banter of the disc jockey on the car radio applied directly to Simon Nibble who was still some ten minutes' drive from his nine o'clock appointment in the City. He tapped his fingers in time with the radio programme's signature tune and smiled a contented smile.

His was not just an ordinary smile. It was more than just a facial expression which he himself controlled. His was an involuntary thing which seemed to start deep down inside him and which fought its way to the surface like a young seedling in a barren soil. The smile was like a sneeze. It started as a slight impulse and always ended as an overwhelming desire. He sometimes had difficulty preventing himself from laughing out loud. It was only his sense of decorum which enabled him to contain his own mirth.

His smile was triggered off by many things. At the one end of the scale it was just little things. These were the equivalent of that tiny tickle in the nostrils which precedes the sneeze itself. Such things were the thrill Simon felt when for example, he caught a glimpse of himself in a mirror and obtained confirmation of the fact that a really expensive hand-made suit looks exactly what it is. The special thrill he always felt when booking seats for the opera or ballet and paying for them simply by quoting his charge card number. The feeling of well-being which accompanied the giving of a generous tip to a waiter even if the man did not deserve it, and the luxurious feeling of always travelling first class.

At the other end of the scale there were the more important things such as the pleasure of operating the electric gates to his luxury home from inside his expensive German car. There was the immense thrill of attending important social functions and of being seen talking to well-known people. There was also the comfortable feeling of knowing that once children's school fees are being paid for by a tax-saving scheme specially worked out by one's expensive city accountants. Such things made him smile. He couldn't help it: no matter how he tried he just could not experience these situations without smiling.

He reached the part of the road which developed into dual carriageway. He pulled into the outside lane, dropped the car into fourth gear and pressed the accelerator pedal to the floor. The vehicle responded quietly and immediately. Simon glanced in the rearview mirror and watched the line of slowly moving traffic diminishing in his wake and he smiled.

When he reached the city centre he made his way to the Grand Hotel. He did not park in the car park at the rear of the hotel even though it was quite convenient to do so. Instead he pulled up on the double yellow lines immediately outside the hotel entrance. A uniformed doorman hurried forward and opened his car door. Simon retrieved his leather attache case from the rear seat and stepped out of the vehicle. The car keys he left in the ignition.

He smiled at the doorman who looked quizzically at him. "Hello," he said. "Simon Nibble, I've got a room booked for a conference, I'm quite late already, it's a very important meeting, could you park the car for me? I'd be most grateful, must rush, leave the keys with reception would you?" And swept through the revolving door into the hotel foyer before the doorman could respond.

As he felt the thick pile of the hotel reception carpet beneath his feet and reflected on the knowledge that the doorman would be bound to park his car for him regardless of whether or not it was convenient, Simon smiled his own special smile.

He was still smiling when he reached the reception desk. The young lady behind the desk looked up from what she was reading and more than matched his smile. Hers however, was a different kind of smile. Unlike Simon's smile which was prompted by an impulse from within, hers appeared to have been stuck on from the outside like an adhesive label.

She had platinum blonde hair which was swept upwards and backwards in an elaborate style which included calculatedly careless ringlets which hung down in one or two places. She wore very large earrings, gold in colour, and an expensive-looking, cream coloured silky blouse with a collar which was deliberately turned up at the back the result of which was to give her the appearance of having a stiff neck. Her face was very heavily made up so much so that her complexion had the appearance of a waxwork model. She looked unreal, with a glossy varnished appearance and she exuded an overwhelming odour of perfume.

Simon Nibble stated his business and gave some last minute instructions regarding arrangements for the presentation of the bill and also ordered coffee. During the conversation the young lady's smile never wavered but the longer it remained on her face the more obvious its artificiality became, rather like the facial expression adopted by a ventriloquist during his act. When Simon moved on, she returned to reading her woman's fashion magazine.

He made his way to the first floor and found the small conference room easily. He marched in purposefully, apologising for his own lateness and placing his antique leather briefcase on the table. He surveyed the room generally and those in it and smiled. He walked over to the coat stand near the door and deposited his overcoat. When he turned back into the room he noted the enormous fireplace with a gas log fire blazing and the huge mirror in its ornamental gilt frame above the fireplace. He also noted the heavy flock wallpaper and the large old-fashioned sash window with the generous velvet curtains which descended from ceiling to floor. He smiled again feeling now the overwhelming urge to laugh out loud. He suppressed this urge by observing "This is a nice room, isn't it?"

Despite his efforts, his words hinted at his own relish of the sumptuous surroundings. He crossed to the window and gazed out across the city rooftops. "I've ordered coffee you know," he said and then added, "Oh by the way, Mr Carter, I've arranged with reception for the account for this room to be sent to you." He mentioned this in the matter-of-fact way in which a housewife would add at the end of a shopping order, "Oh and a bag of sugar, please."

As if realising too late that this was perhaps a little presumptuous, he pressed the point by saying, "After all, it saves us all the bother of having to pay separately and then my eventually billing you for it. Oh and by the way, I can't keep calling you Mr Carter. It's Ken, isn't it? You must call me Simon. I'm not one of those old-fashioned solicitors who insist on all the formalities. Much better to do a good job and leave all that sort of thing to the older members of the profession, don't you think?" he asked smoothly.

"I suppose so," responded Mr Carter in a down-to-earth earth tone which indicated that he was far from convinced. He was nearly twice the age of Simon Nibble and had an instinctive mistrust of young men with smooth voices and expensive suits. "I'm blessed if I can see why it was necessary to meet in this place." He continued. "My family have dealt with Duffy Fry and Co the biggest firm in this town for more years than I care to remember and they never once called a meeting in a posh hotel."

"Yes," said Simon slowly. "Duffy Fry and Co. We call them Stuffy Dry and Co. Here he chuckled archly and when he realised that his little joke had fallen on stony ground he added seductively, "They haven't served you too well in the past have they? After all, good professional advice is an essential ingredient for the modern commercial outfit."

"My firm's financial problems have nothing to do with good or bad professional advice," retorted Mr Carter. "My problems stem mainly from the fact that oil prices have quadrupled in the last ten years whereas the price I charge for my goods has remained the same. I can't put my prices up because those bastards in the Far East are making the same thing for half the price, shipping it halfway round the world and still undercutting me. The reason they are able to do it is they pay their workers a bowl of rice per month whereas I have to pay mine the top whack or the union calls them all out on strike."

"Yes, quite so," said Simon in a tone which seemed to imply that he had just been saying the same thing himself. He added gravely, "We all know how difficult the last few years have been for businesses like yours and we also know that successive governments have hardly been sympathetic." He was nothing if not adaptable and he had sensed that his initial attitude had been a little too flippant for Mr Carter and therefore he had immediately changed his tack. He often indulged, quite unashamedly, in these rather obvious tactics which he himself regarded as subtle (like an angler playing a salmon he chose to think) and which experience told him was usually a successful ploy.

"Well actually it was my idea that we meet here," intervened the other man in the room. He was stationed with his back to the fire, hands behind him and legs wide apart. He looked, or perhaps hoped to look, Napoleonic in his pose. He was a small man in his forties whose inflated waist-line indicated his own love of food and drink. His hair was receding badly at the front and in desperation perhaps, he had allowed his locks at the rear to grow longer and longer until his collar was hidden. It was not a style which suited him for his hair had a lank greasy appearance. He wore a flamboyant shirt which was about twenty years too young for him and loud trousers which looked as if they belonged on a golf course. The shirt was opened at the neck at least one more buttonhole than was necessary, revealing a gold medallion hanging on a thick-linked chain.

This was Mr Edward Sharpe (known to everybody as 'Sharp Eddie'), a man of dubious background who, despite a limited education had, on the face of it at least, done very well for himself. This conclusion was a natural one to draw for he always appeared to be financially well-off or well-connected. Eddie was a man who revelled in the luxury of having lots of money. Or perhaps it is more accurate to say that he enjoyed the feeling of giving everyone the impression that he had lots of money. The truth of the matter is that he often owed more money than he had, but he had long ago learned that the ability to brazen things out rather than to give into one's creditors was a useful asset. This skill when possessed by a member of their own ranks is what the upper and middle classes refer to as 'confidence' in matters financial. When people like Eddie display it they are generally described as 'brash'. He was not bothered by this apparent unfairness for he knew his own limitations.

Indeed he often mentioned the fact that he had been 'born on the wrong side of the tracks'. Usually though he only boasted of this fact at a moment when he was exhibiting his own apparent wealth. He liked to describe himself as a property developer though in fact he was simply a buyer and seller. Primarily, he bought and sold land or houses and generally re-sold them on at a handsome profit without achieving any development whatsoever. He was always ready to buy or sell anything if he could sense there was a profit in it. His talent was to sniff out the sick and the lame and to make use of them whenever and wherever he could. He was a commercial hyena who, like his natural counterpart, had a very loud and raucous laugh.

Eddie had a nose for a struggling business and it very rarely let him down. His nose had told him that Mr Carter's business was struggling and he sensed there was an opportunity for a quick profit. His nose also told him when a business or property was a good investment. It was a large hook nose rather like one of those which can be seen carved upon Red Indian totem poles. It was not an attractive nose but for the above reasons it was an irreplaceable aid to Eddie's business operations. In Mr Carter's case Eddie's nose signalled the dual alarm. It told him there was a struggling and a successful business connected with the same person. As far as Eddie was concerned these sensations were both exciting and nerve tingling. It was for him as stimulating as for example the big break through opportunity for an up and coming actor. The situation combines the feeling of elation with the nervous anxiety that the big chance might be more than one can handle.

Eddie's nose had not let him down. Mr Carter did indeed have a struggling business. He also had a very successful one. Both had been passed on to him by his father. The two businesses were run in a nearby town. His father, previously a military man who had spent much of his early life in India, had purchased an existing business and lavished much love and money upon it. Despite this attention the business was not destined to thrive in the modern time and almost as an afterthought he had started a new business alongside the old one. The second business was a brick works which made full use of the local product (a rich red clay) and which quickly made much more money than Mr Carter senior ever expected. When the time came for him to hand over the reins of office to his son, the brick works made more than enough profits to subsidise the glue factory (for such was the original business). Mr Carter was reluctant to close down the first business because of the sentimental feelings which his deceased father had always held for the factory.

Mr Carter senior left his business concerns to his son and daughter. The latter took no interest in the business and left the affairs completely in the hands of her brother who was currently the managing director of both private companies.

The sister, though always dearly loved by her father, nevertheless had been a disappointment to him. She had never shown any desire to join the family business in any capacity. Not only that, but she became involved with and subsequently married, a man of Maltese origin whom she had met whilst on holiday with her father. He had been a waiter in their hotel and had flirted with her outlandishly which flattered her immensely and outraged her father. She was completely captivated by his dark Latin looks and he had been equally attracted by her apparent wealth. Her father had no doubts about the man and disliked him on sight. He recognised him as a lazy good for nothing who would not have looked twice at his rather plain daughter had she been penniless. He made it perfectly clear to Giovanni (this was the name of her olive-skinned Romeo) that he understood what it was he was up to and as far as he was concerned his daughter should have nothing to do with him. He forbade his daughter to see him, an order which she totally ignored and he cut their holiday short by a week in order to take her back to England where she would be out of the clutches of her lover.

He underestimated the man's tenacity however, for having identified his meal ticket he was not about to watch her sail away forever. He followed the pair to England and resumed his hold over the daughter whose infatuation with him grew and grew. Eventually despite intense resistance from her father the girl married her Maltese sweetheart who had, from the first moment he had set eyes upon her treated her as if she had been a rare and delicate orchid. From the wedding day onwards this attitude changed completely and she realised the truly chauvinistic attitudes which are bred into many of the Latin males.

He quickly spent most of her money and rarely gave her any of his own (though he worked so infrequently that he seldom earned much money). He did very little work around the house and always expected her to wait upon him hand and foot. He frequently went out at night with various drinking companions, coming home very late and if she ever dared complain he would fly into a terrible rage which would always terrify her. If on the other hand she ever wished to go anywhere by herself he would jealously interrogate her endlessly to discover who she would be with etcetera. Eventually she found such episodes so discouraging that she gave up going out. Gradually she lost touch with her friends and became a lonely woman.

Her husband Joe (for that was his nickname amongst his drinking comrades) pressed her continuously to sell her shares in the family business in order to raise capital for various enterprises which he had in mind from time to time. These varied enormously but a common denominator was usually the suggestion that Joe should purchase and run some sort of establishment such as an Italian restaurant which would, in theory, make huge profits which would allow him to return for several months each year to his beloved Malta and simultaneously start some sort of tourist-connected business there e.g. holiday apartments. None of his ideas were ever thought out properly. Each was a vague pipe dream which Joe regarded as entirely feasible and if his wife raised the smallest criticism of his plans he would explode with anger and accuse her of not loving him.

One of his drinking companions was Sharp Eddie, who soon realised the potential involved with Joe's wife's inheritance. He quickly persuaded Joe that he would offer a good price for the wife's shares and Joe soon got to work on his wife. This was the influence that Eddie had with Mr Carter. Having purchased his sister's shares he had some say in the running of the Carter family business. He was admittedly only a minority shareholder but it was a sufficiently large minority for Mr Carter to attend when the meeting had been called.

Mr Carter did not like Edward Sharpe whom he regarded as a spiv and a wide boy. He had been outraged to learn that his sister had sold her family shares to Eddie without informing him but had not been surprised that this transaction had been at the instigation of her husband Joe of whom he held the same low opinion as his late father.

He also did not care for Eddie's solicitor who made him feel uneasy. His previous experience of the legal profession had been gained wholly from the visits to Messrs Duffy Fry and Co a long established, somewhat old-fashioned firm with a traditional attitude to their own professional status. Mr Carter was used to the Dickensian style chambers, walls lined with law reports, dusty old files in corners and quaint old manners. He was used to solicitors of the old school who wore dark pinstripe suits and who always spoke guardedly on any subject and very rarely committed themselves on any matter without a great deal of consideration but whose advice was always sound.

Compared to that experience Simon Nibble, as far as Mr Carter was concerned, was a flash Harry. As far as he was concerned proper solicitors did not wear light-coloured suits, pink shirts and pig-skin shoes. They also did not call meetings in expensive hotels and address their clients by their Christian names on their first meeting.

There was a knock at the door and a waiter entered with a trolley upon which was laid out coffee cups and plates and biscuits. The waiter wheeled the trolley into the centre of the room and was about to pour out the beverage when Eddie intervened. "All right, leave them there, we'll pour them ourselves. You can buzz off." The poor waiter hurried off like a scalded pup and Eddie watched him go with a smirk.

"Sylvia can be mum, can't you?" he said to the other member of the group who had so far said nothing. "After all," he added, "no point in keeping a dog and barking yourself, eh?" He gave a long lewd laugh which rang round the room and then left an embarrassed silence. Only Sylvia herself seemed unconcerned and behaved as if she were used to such remarks from Eddie. He always introduced her to everyone as his 'girl Friday', an expression which he regarded as chic and fashionable. The title was a suitable euphemism for the term 'mistress', which was her true function. Eddie himself would never have dreamed of describing her thus however. The word 'mistress' holds connotations which could never truly be associated with a man like Eddie. The expression carries with it implications of romance, delicacy and illicit passion, none of which Eddie had any knowledge or experience of. His needs were basic and uncomplicated. He had been married for twenty years and his wife had long ago denied him all access to her bed and only remained married to him so long as he could provide her with all the material things in life which she had learned to appreciate. At one time she had reached the stage where she had actually loathed her husband but since she had ceased to have any physical relationships with him some years earlier her attitude towards him had softened to mere toleration. Both went their separate ways and found it infinitely more convenient, for a host of separate reasons, to remain legally married than to undergo the indignity of divorce.

Eddie in particular knew that he did not dare to attempt to jettison his spouse because she knew so much about his financial affairs, especially the numerous suspect deals that he had been involved in throughout his married life. He was an acquisitive creature who could not bear the thought of handing over any of his possessions to another. He preferred therefore to retain an expensive wife in name only rather than to release any of his hard-earned, (or so he liked to think) assets. In addition he was fearful that if he even fell out with his wife she would inform on him to the Inland Revenue who would undoubtedly be very interested in a number of transactions which so far he had kept a well-guarded secret.

For her part, his wife knew and accepted that Eddie satisfied his baser instincts with Sylvia and was content with the situation so long as her husband continued to make money. She had occasional flirtations herself, usually with younger men, (she was not unattractive for her age) and felt no resentment towards Sylvia for whom she felt a certain amount of gratitude for catering to her husband (whom she herself regarded as physically repellent) on a level which she was unable or unwilling to match. It was a constant source of amazement to her that her husband could be regarded as even vaguely attractive to any member of the opposite sex.

And so an uneasy truce existed between Mr and Mrs Sharp. Sylvia lived rent-free in a flat owned by Eddie and tried her best to fulfil the official function of secretary/assistant to her sugar daddy. This was no easy task for one who could only type with two fingers and who hadn't a brain in her head. Eddie compensated for her lack of ability in this direction by employing a real secretary (an ageing spinster with a sharp tongue and a jaundiced eye which saw straight through Eddie) who was an organisational genius.

Sylvia busied herself with the coffee cups which stood upon the low trolley. As she bent down she made sure she kept her legs straight. The short tight skirt she wore rode high up her thighs and revealed two of her greatest assets. The others watched admiringly. When the drinks were served they all seated themselves around the huge mahogany conference table and Simon Nibble began shuffling his papers in a preparatory fashion.

He sipped his coffee, savoured the flavour of fresh ground Colombian beans and smiled his usual smile. "Mmm, nice coffee," he observed. "So much nicer than the usual instant stuff, don't you think?" he enquired of the room in general.

"I like my coffee the way I like my women," volunteered Eddie, "hot, sweet, and filthy." He followed this remark with his usual coarse laugh, totally unaware of the insult he had just offered to Sylvia.

"Can we get on with the business in hand?" asked Mr Carter irritably.

"Yes, yes, of course," said Simon condescendingly. "Now as you know, Ken, Eddie here has acquired a minority shareholding in your business."

"One of my businesses," interrupted Mr Carter, still irritable.

"Both companies," interjected Eddie smugly. "The share certificates are there." He pointed at the bundle of papers Simon Nibble had in front of him and then added with a faint hint of desperation, as if he were not absolutely sure himself, "It's all legal and above board. That's right isn't it?"

The question was directed at Simon who smiled blandly. "You are both right of course. Eddie bought your sister's shares in the family business which consisted mainly, though not entirely, of shares in Sodford Cellophane Ltd and a few more nominal shares in Sodford Bricks Ltd."

"Yes and he wouldn't have got those shares if it hadn't been for that worthless brother-in-law of mine," said Mr Carter very bluntly, making no secret of the fact that he did not care for Eddie and certainly did not welcome his involvement in his family business.

"We've been through all this before," said Eddie with a tired expression. He referred to the explosive arguments that had followed the announcement of Eddie's purchase of his sister's shares. Eddie knew Mr Carter did not like him and he did not particularly mind this. He was not a man that needed to be liked and he certainly had not got where he was by worrying about other people's feelings. He felt however slightly injured by the ferocity of Mr Carter's opposition to him thus far but preferred not to reveal this. He knew that if Mr Carter had possessed any spare cash he would not have permitted the sale of his sister's shares but would have purchased them himself. Alternatively, he would have arranged something with a bank to enable her to obtain a loan in preference to selling her only assets. It was the knowledge that Mr Carter's financial position and influence was so weak that he had been unable to prevent the transaction, which so pleased and intrigued Eddie. He felt sufficiently secure to adopt what he himself regarded as a friendly disposition towards Mr Carter, rather than to reflect the resentment which the latter radiated towards him. From Mr Carter's position Eddie's attitude looked more like smugness which infuriated him all the more. He glowered like a sulking child and said no more.

Chapter Three
The Stroke

Bill Butler arrived at the office before everyone else. He always did. The reason for this was twofold. In the first place he had custody of the key to the outside door and also the keys to several of the more important cupboards in the office. Without Bill's attendance the rest of the staff would be unable to start their work. Bill felt this responsibility very keenly and never arrived late. In the second place he enjoyed getting up early. He had done so all his working life and only ever remained in bed later than six-thirty a.m. when he was ill. Each morning his routine was the same. He rose around six a.m., washed, shaved, and dressed himself and then went downstairs to make a pot of tea, sitting alone in his kitchen while he smoked a cigarette. He listened to the early morning news and farming reports on the radio. Although he had no connections with the land and the price of pork or lamb or wheat etcetera, had no direct influence on his life he nevertheless found it strangely comforting to keep abreast of this daily information. All the while he sat listening to the radio the ginger cat, who had arrived at his house many years before, rubbed itself against his legs purring loudly, knowing that he would eventually rise from his chair and prepare breakfast.

After feeding the cat Bill would take in the milk bottles from the front doorstep and draw back the lounge curtains. Then he would make a second pot of tea and place two cups on a tray and go back upstairs and wake his wife, pausing on the way to pick up any letters which may have arrived. Whilst his wife sat up in bed drinking her tea Bill would sit at the foot of the bed and drink his second cup. Bill's wife drank her tea with plenty of milk and no sugar whereas Bill preferred his tea strong and sweet.

Each morning they would sit together drinking their tea and discussing their mail and various domestic items (usually concerning their children). Both of them treasured this moment of each day without expressing that fact to each other.

When their tea was finished Bill would kiss his wife goodbye and take the tray back downstairs and then leave the house for work. He lived only a mile or so from the office and walked to work every day, come rain or shine. He visited the same newsagents on route and bought the same paper each day. He then opened the office, went inside, unlocked the essential cupboards and then went into his glasshouse and read the sports page.

When he'd done this he would start work and it was usually half an hour or more before the next member of staff put in an appearance. This was invariably Tom Richards who, like Bill, rose early each morning, a habit he had acquired in the Army. The two of them would usually sit and discuss the contents of the sports page and smoke a cigarette together before commencing work. The amount of work they achieved, in these moments of solitude was usually greater than could be achieved later in the day when distractions such as telephone calls reduced the effectiveness of their efforts.

The rest of the staff would arrive intermittently. The last to arrive was generally Mr Pigg. He was not last because he had trouble getting up in the morning or because he had transport difficulties. Nor was it the case that he worked especially late at the end of the day to make up the lost time. No, Mr Pigg arrived late each morning by design, though he himself never regarded his own arrival as being in the least bit tardy. His own timekeeping was always immaculate. He always arrived a half-hour hour after the official starting time. He felt that this was a privilege of his own rank and that in some small way his late entrance enhanced his own status.

In all other circumstances he was a great believer in punctuality and was quite severe with any member of staff who tried to follow his example with timekeeping. This attitude was not appreciated by all the staff and there were often undercurrents of discontent in the office especially amongst some of the younger ones who found themselves unable to get to work on time every day. Young Vincent was the worst offender and sometimes even arrived later than Mr Pigg himself. More than once he had been on the gravy coloured carpet in Mr Pigg's room for a lecture on the virtues of punctuality and if it had not been for Bill turning a blind eye to Vincent's frequent late arrivals the young man would have been sacked long ago. Bill knew in his heart of hearts that Vincent deserved to be reprimanded but he felt sorry for him because he knew he had no father and lived alone with his mother who was not very well off.

Mr Pigg always made a deafening arrival, crashing open the outer door of the building and usually bawling out his greetings to everyone before entering the general office on his way to his own room. This always gave everyone the chance to adopt the appearance of great industry when he finally burst upon them. He always carried with him a battered old briefcase which always bulged with files. This was his unspoken gesture to the rest of the staff. It implied that he had taken work home and had worked long and hard during the previous night and thus recompensed for his late arrival. In reality he rarely did any work at home but had long ago developed the habit of giving the impression that he did.

Most of the staff were aware of his subterfuge and often amused themselves by checking the identity of the files in his case when he was out of the office. It was a standing joke that many of the files remained in the case for many months with no action being taken on them. Whenever a file was missing for any length of time everyone knew it was probably in Mr Pigg's briefcase.

Tom Richards, who saw every aspect of life whilst in the Army, referred to Mr Pigg as 'the General'. This title was meant in a derogatory way and showed that Tom regarded his boss in the same way as he regarded those notorious generals in the First World War who had preferred to lead their troops from the rear. It showed also that Tom, who had never risen above the rank of sergeant in a thirty-year career, had little respect for those in authority unless they exhibited a charismatic ability to lead and inspire those around them in the true military sense. Thus, he often talked nostalgically of his own personal experiences with Field Marshal Montgomery and others whom he admired and frequently compared their leadership qualities with those of Mr Arnold Pigg. Inevitably the latter was found wanting in such comparisons.

There were two basic reasons why Mr Pigg's department functioned in a reasonably efficient manner. The first reason was that there was little work to be done due to the policies implemented by the Whitehall mandarins. The second reason was that most of the hard work in the office was done by Bill Butler. By the time Mr Pigg arrived each day Bill had opened all the post and sorted out all the important items and had usually dealt with most of them before his boss put in an appearance. Even those items which, by definition, had to be dealt with by the manager, Bill organised and presented to him in such an orderly fashion that they only required a signature.

Arnold Pigg was in effect a mere figurehead and was blissfully unaware of the exact amount of hard work which his second in command put in.

Mr Pigg had very definite ideas on how his office should be run. These ideas were not his own but he firmly believed in them nonetheless. It has been said previously that he seldom took any official steps without reference to the Green Book and as far as he was concerned all references in that noble volume to the function of management were implemented without question. The instruction manual, however, was primarily concerned with the mechanics of the department's business and only touched briefly upon the question of management. The style of leadership in each of the department's separate offices was left to its individual manager to ensure some form of national uniformity.

The department organised periodic management courses to which the office managers were invited. At these meetings they were guided and instructed on the methods of management and urged to develop their own personal approach. Usually the meetings included lectures by guest speakers, often eminent professors who were chosen, not only for their knowledge on the subject but for their ability to speak both entertainingly and, convincingly. In an effort to offer variety the course organisers strove to provide a different lecturer at each meeting. Naturally, each guest speaker had his own individual views on the art of management and the idea was that the audience could absorb all the various opinions and implement those which most appealed to them.

Unfortunately, Mr Pigg had not grasped this concept. Consequently he regularly attended management courses, made feverish notes and always returned to his office freshly indoctrinated with a new set of ideas on the style in which his office should be run. Only he himself seemed unaware of the transparency of his own 'new ideas' so readily adopted from the views or opinions of successive guest speakers. The enthusiasm with which he adopted each new scheme and his total inability to note his own change of role both amused and amazed those around him. Staff in his office had been subjected to such a variety of different styles of management that those who paid any attention to their boss were thoroughly confused. They had seen Mr Arnold Pigg the ruthless leader who drove his workers unmercifully, convinced that only thus would he achieve the respect that his position demanded. This role was born out of the ideas put forward by one guest speaker who had spoken for far too long about some of the sadistic training methods used by the French Foreign Legion.

This style was unsuccessful mainly because of the small amount of work which the department was required to do. Since his staff were well able to cope easily with their work allocations Mr Pigg's bullying tactics were of little use and served only to provoke ill feelings amongst the staff particularly because of the fact that he confined his verbal attacks to a certain section of his employees. Some members of staff, notably Mrs Balstaff and Tom Richards would not have tolerated any such tactics and Mr Pigg at least had the sense to realise this. In the end he confined himself to occasional tirades against Vincent and these continued from time to time long after he had abandoned his aggressive role.

They had also experienced Arnold Pigg the benign dictator who, having learnt that 'a wise leader knows the hopes, fears and problems of his followers' spent the next few weeks personally interviewing each member of staff in an effort to obtain as much information as possible about their personal lives. This again was a failure and hardly surprisingly created a similar feeling of resentment amongst his staff. Once more, principal objectors were Mrs Balstaff and Tom Richards who refused to answer any of his personal enquiries and persuaded a number of others to respond in like manner. Mr Pigg was forced to abandon this approach as well but not before spending two full days listening in fascination to the account of much of Mavis's love life.

There had also been Mr Pigg in his Napoleonic pose, attempting an inspired yet reservedly detached form of leadership. This was by far the most successful of his roles to date because it consisted mainly of long periods during which he shut himself in his room and searched his own soul, and the contents of the Green Book for the answer to current problems. This gave the rest of the workforce the chance to get on with their jobs and Bill Butler the opportunity to run the office without interruption.

For a brief period there had been the 'born again' Arnold Pigg who, impressed with the astounding success of evangelical leaders, such as Billy Graham, had sought to lead his office in prayers each morning. This method failed because of his inexperience in matters clerical and his total inability to put together any words remotely resembling a prayer. Perversely, this style of leadership was the only one to receive the wholehearted support of Mrs Balstaff whose father had been a lay preacher.

The current bee in Mr Pigg's bonnet was the system of daily briefings so popular among military commanders, the purpose of which is to keep the troops fully informed as to the latest information and to encourage participation by all in the discussion of whatever problems exist. It might have been supposed that this method of leadership would have received some sympathy from Tom Richards but the latter, having experienced wartime briefings from Field Marshal Montgomery, had nothing but disdain for Mr Pigg's meagre efforts. After participating in one of the office 'talk-ins' he had thereafter refused to take part in any other and simply withdrew to the far end of the room and got on with his work.

It was not long after George had started work in the office when he experienced one of Mr Pigg's briefings. These usually commenced around mid-morning (by the time Mr Pigg had arrived at the office, signed the more important items of his outgoing post and enjoyed his morning coffee, that was the earliest time which could be arranged) and continued until lunchtime.

The only notice anyone received of the ensuing session was a great deal of banging and crashing in the corridor. Mr Pigg entered the general office wrestling with an old-fashioned blackboard and easel which he set up at one end of the room. He then retired to his room for a few moments and then re-emerged carrying several large pieces of cardboard which had graph paper stuck on them.

A general groan went up amongst the staff who realised what was afoot and all of them continued to pretend to be working and not to have noticed the presence of their boss in the vain hope that he might go away. The only member of staff who had not noticed the preparations was Tom Richards who was rather deaf.

Mr Pigg cleared his throat loudly and shouted to his workforce, "Can I have your attention please. If you'd all like to gather round I think we can all learn something of interest."

This announcement was followed by a loud stage-whispered oath from Tom Richards who had just understood what was to happen. With great deliberation he picked up his papers and retired to the far end of the office much to the delight of the rest of the staff. Mr Pigg tried to pretend that he had not heard Tom's remark and busied himself straightening the easel and selecting the first of his graphs for exhibition.

"Vincent," he shouted, "go and ask Penny and Mrs Balstaff to join us will you. This concerns everybody, and I'm sure we'll all gain by it." As he made this last remark he shot a malevolent glance at Tom Richards who clearly did not agree. Tom meanwhile caused even more amusement amongst the others by ostentatiously removing from his pocket two rubber ear plugs which with great ceremony, he pushed into his own ears. As a gesture it was effective but it was not really necessary for one so hard of hearing as Tom.

Penny and Mrs Balstaff duly arrived and there followed a great deal of scraping of chairs and moving of desks before Mr Pigg was satisfied that the assembly was in order. He organised a desk at one end on which he placed his graph boards and around which were placed three chairs. At the side of this desk was the easel with the first graph already upon it. Seated at the desk were himself and Bill Butler (who had already assumed that glazed expression which close proximity to his boss seemed to induce in him) and strangely, Mrs Balstaff who as far as anyone present knew, had no special right to be seated at the front desk alongside the boss and his deputy. The rest of the staff had their desks and chairs arranged in a U shape so that they could all see the easel and their boss. George found himself at one end of the U shape wedged between Mavis and a filing cabinet.

It was a strange picture that the occupants of the top table presented to their audience. Mr Pigg already on his feet and prepared to speak, gripped his own lapel with his left hand in a manner which he had once observed a famous barrister affecting in a television film. He had been influenced at the time by the dramatic gesture so much so that he had not taken in the words which the actor uttered. He had made a mental note to adopt such a posture himself on any occasion he was required to speak in public convinced that by so doing he would automatically acquire the gift of oratory. In his other hand he held his briar pipe by the bowl, ready to use the stem to indicate items of interest on the blackboard.

Alongside him sat Bill Butler who looked like an automaton. Clearly he switched off mentally whenever Mr Pigg was present and took the opportunity to indulge in various mental exercises. His favourite pastime on such occasions was to mentally catalogue his stamp collection. Bill had been collecting stamps ever since he was a boy and had by now a sizeable collection. He loved to sit and look at them in the evenings and had done so on so many occasions that he was able to recapture in his own mind any page in his album and picture the exact position of each stamp thereon.

Bill had not previously been a daydreamer by nature. He had always been the sort to get on with whatever work had been at hand and had always immersed himself totally in the activity. His periods of mental preoccupation had coincided with Mr Pigg's arrival at the office. Bill soon found that he liked the sound of Arnold Pigg's voice a lot less than that gentleman himself and so developed the enviable knack of retiring into his own world of mental solitude where Mr A Pigg was persona non grata.

Finally there was Mrs Balstaff looking large, imposing and slightly haughty. Her attitude was one of amusing contrast. Clearly she was pleased to be occupying the top table and yet she contrived to look uncomfortable and disdainful. She reminded one of a lady mayoress attending an official function in a slum area of her borough. She had acquired her privileged position at the top table during Mr Pigg's evangelical period, due to her extensive knowledge of prayers, and had shown no inclination to relinquish her place after the practice of daily prayers was abandoned.

Mr Pigg cleared his throat loudly once more and opened the meeting. He indicated the graph which was on the blackboard and easel and informed those present that it was an analysis of the progress of the office in one aspect of its work so far this year. As far as George could see it was nothing more than a zig zag line on the paper. There was no explanation as to how and why the progress of work had been translated into a single line on a page. The only noticeable thing about the graph was that the line dipped downwards at the end. The graph was replaced by a different one which looked exactly the same as the first. This second graph, according to Mr Pigg showed the exact progress of another aspect of the department's work. The line on this graph turned upwards at the end in an optimistic fashion but apart from this George could discern no difference between it and the previous one.

Mavis leaned across to whisper in George's ear. "He spends all his time making out these graph things and no one understands them."

As she whispered to him her large firm breast pressed into his arm and George received a waft of exotic perfume which lingered on his nostrils for several seconds. He leaned towards her in response and she readily reapplied her breast to his arm.

"I'm not sure he understands them himself," he whispered. "I'm sure that one he's pointing to now is upside down."

Mavis giggled quietly and placed her hand on his thigh momentarily. The brief physical contact aroused George instantly. Her hand lingered a moment too long on his leg or was it just his own imagination? He had not sat next to her deliberately nor had he any such thoughts concerning her until they had touched. She had not retired to the exact previous position and now their shoulders and arms were touching and he could feel the burning excitement which that contact produced. He could also smell her perfume continually now instead of in brief whiffs. His heart began to pound and out of the corner of his eye he chanced a surreptitious glance towards her. Was he mistaken or was her bosom heaving with the excitement which she too felt? It really was a magnificent bosom he had to admit. His eye moved downwards and was further excited by the view of her legs exposed as they were by the inadequately short skirt which she wore.

His heart continued to pound until the sound of it seemed to blot out everything, even Mr Pigg's voice. His angled stare was still firmly fixed on the rounded hose covered thighs which seemed so inviting and which were so tantalisingly close to his own. He wondered if he dared move his own leg to touch hers and tried to anticipate the exquisite feeling which such a contact would produce. He also wondered if, having done so, she would permit their limbs to remain touching or whether she would move away.

He tried gingerly to move his own leg but seemed incapable of moving it at all. With a great deal of mental effort he eventually overcame the paralysis and managed to inch his leg towards hers but this progress was instantly curtailed by a violent involuntary twitching in the leg itself. Try as he might he could not control this spasm and his leg jerked up and down. Cursing inwardly he stretched the leg out and up, flexing the foot in an attempt to calm the offending nerve. He replaced the leg in its original position and slid his own hand along it and gripped it tightly in an effort to control the jerk if it returned. He forced himself to pay attention to Mr Pigg, who by now had moved on to graph number four, hoping that a change in the focal point of his concentration would calm his own nerves.

Immediately his concentration was recaptured as the warm silken thigh of Mavis rested gently against his hand and remained there. The contact was like an electric shock for George who being afraid to look, remained staring at Mr Pigg who droned on and on about his assessment of the achievements of the department since his own arrival. His whole arm seemed to grow numb and for what seemed a long time, though in reality must have only been a few seconds, he tried to discern whether or not he was imagining this exquisite sensation.

He attempted to move his fingers but a millimetre to assure himself that he was not dreaming and sure enough the creamy soft thigh was still there. He was further aroused by the gentle reciprocal pressure. The blood pounding in his own head seemed thunderous and gently, oh so gently, he stroked the silky flesh with one exploratory finger.

The response was more than he would ever have dreamt of for in one lazy expert movement which appeared to require no shift of position in her upper body, Mavis eased her leg downwards and towards him, tucking her own knee under his. This meant that George's hand now rested completely upon her thigh and this she now covered with her own left hand and gently slid her right hand onto his own leg.

George experienced many levels of erotic pleasure as Mavis's nimble and expert fingers massaged his manhood beneath the office desk. He hoped to be able to respond in equal manner but was hampered by the physical difficulty that his chair was slightly closer to the desk than hers. Consequently he could only comfortably reach an inch or two above her knee without shifting his chair and body around and this he dared not do for fear of drawing the attention of the others in the room.

He was also troubled with an increasingly painful cramp in his shoulder which he was only able to tolerate due to the pleasurable sensations which were taking place under the desk. He was aware that his own attempts to fondle Mavis were less than adequate and that compared with her accomplished efforts seemed clumsy. His only worry (apart from the shoulder which was in danger of seizing up) was that he could not, in the face of such heights of eroticism, maintain a blank exterior. He yearned to cry out with joy or at least to moan with pleasure and was terrified that at any minute he might do just that.

The cry, when it came, was not from George's lips but those of Bill Butler. In fact it came out rather like a low groan of disappointment which, due to the unusually dull entertainment content of Mr Pigg's seemingly endless lecture, was received with silent approbation by all those present except Mr Pigg himself. He paused only momentarily to shoot a disgruntled glance at Bill before continuing with his subject.

Bill, his eyes now fixed upon the ceiling, clutched his chest tightly and let out a similar sound which this time had a little more volume and urgency about it. Mr Pigg turned in great annoyance to face Bill who was now the centre of attention. For a short period of suspended animation everyone in the room was watching him closely and saw the colour drain from his face and the pain register in its place. Slowly, slowly, Bill slid off his chair and slumped to the floor.

There was a second or two before anyone reacted and then a sense of panic seemed to invade the room, most of the women either screamed or burst into tears and many present began to instruct others on the correct steps which should be taken. There were cries of "loosen his clothing," or "lift his feet" and "fetch a glass of water someone." Above all other voices was raised that of Mr Pigg who, in tones of extreme desperation, urged everyone to keep calm.

It was Tom Richards who had the presence of mind to telephone for the ambulance which must have been halfway on its journey before any of the others thought of summoning one. It was he also who applied some basic first aid which was probably enough to keep poor Bill alive until the ambulance men arrived at the office.

No more work was done that day by anyone in the office with the exception of Tom Richards. Whilst everyone else sat around in a state of shock discussing the unfortunate events of the morning he buried his head in his work as if very little had happened. Of all the people in the office Tom was probably closest to Bill. Their early morning chats before others arrived had bred close friendship.

In the moment of crisis it was Tom who had been most help to Bill, in a practical way and when the emergency had passed he appeared to be the least interested.

He was however a pragmatic character with a very practical attitude to all things. Once Bill had been confined to the care of the ambulance men he adopted the point of view that there was nothing more that he himself could do for the moment. He could see no benefit accruing to Bill by endless discussions of his heart attack with the other members of staff. He therefore got on with his work quietly. It was not only his military training, but his own character which prompted this course of action.

Mr Pigg spent the rest of the day making telephone calls. The first call was to Bill Butler's wife to break the sad news. This was not an enviable thing for anyone to have to do but Mr Pigg felt and rightly so, that it was his responsibility. He was, he felt, at his paternal best carrying out such onerous duties. After all, he argued to himself, he was chosen for leadership and those who chose him must therefore have judged that he had the required amount of sympathy and diplomacy for such delicate situations.

Secure in this knowledge he announced to Mrs Butler, when she answered the telephone cheerfully, that he had "some very very grave news to impart concerning Bill. "When her voice, naturally enough, took on a tone of distress he diverted the conversation by enquiring if there was a chair nearby for her to sit upon. When she thus became more agitated he enquired about a friend or near relative that she could perhaps call upon to be with her at such a moment. By delaying the awful announcement by this and other means, quite unwittingly, Mr Pigg raised Mrs Butler to a fever pitch of anxiety until she was certain in her own mind that he was leading up to a report of her husband's recent death.

When eventually he related the actual events of the morning it came as a slight relief to her to know that husband was still alive. Mr Pigg went on to inform her of the prompt action that had been taken and that undoubtedly Bill's life had been saved. Warming to his task he went on to emphasise what a thankless job he had in being the one to break the news to her but assured her that he was not one to shirk from such a necessary duty and was certain that she would not have wished to hear the news from any other person.

His pomposity was lost on Mrs Butler whose mind was understandably elsewhere. Quite unnecessarily she apologised to him for the 'thankless job' which her husband's illness had thrust upon him. She concluded the conversation by tearfully thanking him from the bottom of her heart for personally saving her husband's life.

On the whole Mr Pigg considered that the conversation had gone rather well. He then made numerous other telephone calls to various offices in the department starting with the regional office, then the personnel department, the welfare office, the sickness and benefits pay section at head office and finally a number of colleagues in other offices who had no need to be officially informed of the events, but whom Mr Pigg felt might be interested.

By the time he had made his third telephone call the seed, which Mrs Butler had planted in his mind, had flourished. During the subsequent calls it reached full maturity so that by the time he had finished all his telephone conversations the whole region had learnt how Mr Pigg had personally saved the life of his second in command. Mr Pigg was now a hero.

George, meanwhile, was experiencing mixed feelings of annoyance and shame. He was annoyed at Bill Butler for curtailing one of the most enjoyable experiences of his life and then gradually as his more basic instincts subsided he began to feel thoroughly ashamed of himself. He thought of poor Bill and remembering the ashen pain-wracked face realised how selfish his thoughts were.

He glanced across the room at Mavis who had now resumed her usual station next to Helen. As she puffed her King size menthol cigarette and simultaneously chewed her gum he wondered how he could have felt so strongly attracted to her. A moment later he recalled those delicious moments when her fingers had worked their wicked magic on his thighs. He appraised again those generous breasts and experienced afresh the feelings of sexual arousal. Although he glanced at Mavis many times throughout the rest of the day his gaze was never returned. She appeared to have immediately dismissed the matter from her mind and chatted happily with Helen and the others. Her apparent indifference was very puzzling for George.

As the day wore on it seemed a generally accepted thing (by all that is except Tom Richards), that in view of the extraordinary happenings that morning no further work should be done. Occasionally, in between telephone calls, Mr Pigg popped out into the general office to inform everyone of his progress and to report generally on the complicated nature of his responsibilities in this difficult situation.

Someone began a collection for flowers and fruit for Bill and incoming telephone calls and visitors at the public counter were minimal which contributed to the general atmosphere of casualty. Towards the end of the day, when the immediate memories of poor Bill's discomfort had passed the office took on a light hearted holiday spirit which no one (bar again Tom Richards and if he thought so he did not say), appeared to regard as inappropriate.

George ended up having a long conversation with Pete who this afternoon had forgone his usual visit to the storeroom and was eventually persuaded by him to turn out for the local rugby team, just to make up the numbers.

Chapter Four
The Old Sods

George took the road out of town and followed the signpost for Sodford. He was surprised and disappointed to notice that the sign read twelve miles. "Just past the interchange, turn left at the Plume of Feathers, straight on for a couple of miles and you can't miss it," Pete had said. The directions had seemed simple enough but he'd taken the wrong turning at the interchange and it was several miles before he realised. By the time he had retraced his steps and found the correct road he was much later than he had intended to be.

To add to his problems the petrol gauge on his car was indicating that he was either completely out of fuel or had only a quarter of a tank left. The needle on the gauge was always as steady as a rock until it crept into the red danger zone. Thereafter it behaved like a metronome and only settled permanently on the empty pin moments before the car began to splutter. George knew if he didn't find a garage immediately he would never reach the ground in time.

George hated to be late. It upset his whole system if he wasn't on time. He didn't consider himself to be a fastidious timekeeper. Not like some people who made it a sanctimonious virtue to be always on time. No, with George it was subconscious. He invariably arrived early for any appointment without being aware of having made a positive effort to do so. It was only on those rare occasions when fate contrived to make him late that he ever consciously reflected on his habit of preferring to arrive early. Now he was in a sweat because he knew he was going to be late. It worried him that he was late. It also worried him that he was worried. He wished he could sometimes be less conscientious and arrive late for appointments with a carefree attitude.

He reached the Plume of Feathers and duly turned left. In the lingering September sunshine the brightly whitewashed walls of the pub adorned with hanging baskets and window boxes, full of fuchsias, geraniums, and nasturtiums many of which were still sporting a profusion of blooms, made such a splash of welcome colour that it took willpower to drive past. Certainly the care taken over the exterior of the premises led one to suspect, even to fervently hope, that the interior matched up. George made a mental note to return there at the earliest opportunity.

Sodford was by no means a picturesque town. All the houses therein were built with dull red bricks manufactured from clay dug locally and baked at the Sodford Brick Works Limited whose headquarters stood alongside the approach road to the town, a dull red monument to its own product.

Adjacent to the brick works was the glue factory. This edifice made an immediate and lasting impression on any visitor to the town. Immediate because from its centre rose a single tall chimney built of red bricks, which overlooked the whole community like a totem pole in a Red Indian encampment. Lasting, because emanating from the mouth of the chimney, twenty-four hours a day was a yellow haze which inevitably descended upon the town causing it to be permanently pervaded with an odour of something akin to bad eggs.

The town consisted of a single long street lined with shops and houses, built of red bricks, in a natural hollow. On one slope overlooking the street was a large council estate built entirely of the red bricks, presumably occupied by the work-force of the Sodford Brick Works and the glue factory, and on the other slope more favourable because of its south facing aspect nestled a few larger residences where lived presumably the employers of the occupants on the north facing slope. These latter houses were also constructed entirely of the ubiquitous red bricks.

In the centre of the street stood a small square with a monument, made of red bricks, with a brass plate attached which bore an inscription which informed the reader that the construction existed to remind the citizens of Sodford of the heroic activities of their young men during the two great wars. On the back of the monument was a message achieved by the non-artistic use of an aerosol can which reminded the same citizens of the activities of their present-day youth.

George took an instant dislike to the town even before the ozone from the glue factory entered the heating system of his car. Gratefully he spotted a garage and pulled into the forecourt. An aged attendant wearing a grease smeared apron was leaning upon a 'No Smoking' sign and puffing urgently on a large pipe. He completely ignored George until the tobacco was well alight to his satisfaction, then he hobbled arthritically across to the car and began to dispense the petrol.

"Fill her up, please," he said and then backed cautiously as far away from the attendant as he thought decently possible, having noticed that the man was still puffing on the pipe whilst peering closely into the filler cap to check the level inside. To George's enormous relief the car was filled with petrol without mishap. Whilst settling the bill George asked the man where the rugby ground was situated.

"Old Sods," said the old fellow and his eyes lit up. George was unsure if this was a question or a statement and looked bemused. "The Old Sodfordians," continued the other. "Pitch is up t' other end of the street." He indicated with his pipe. "Behind the chapel, you can't miss it. You playin' or watchin?"

George told him that he had been invited along to observe but had been asked to bring his kit in case the team were short.

The older man laughed. He removed the pipe from his mouth the more to savour the joke. His laugh was not a normal one. It was more of an asthmatic exhalation. As he enjoyed his private joke hugely he exhaled long and hard several times. To George it sounded as if his old lungs were made of antique leather. With each breath a squeak and a wheeze came forth.

"They'll be short all right," he assured George. "They'm playing the Army today," he added as if this statement needed no further amplification. George continued to look quizzical. "They'm always short here for the Army match," explained the old man. "Tha's why they have to scratch around for a team."

George's experience in the noble game was not vast but he rather resented the older man's implication that his inclusion in the team today would not be based on any considerations of his ability. More particularly, George did not like the sound of the fact that a team was consistently difficult to field against opponents from the Army. He could imagine that a service team would be both well-disciplined and ruthless. His mind offered a glimpse of huge paratroopers, physical fitness fanatics who, behaving as one immaculately trained unit, swept all before them.

The attendant put his mind at rest on this score by explaining in his rustic manner that the Old Sodfordians had three teams. An annual fixture was arranged against the Army camp based some ten miles away. Teams one and two travelled away to the base whilst team three entertained the Army's third team at home, the Old Sods only possessing two pitches. George learned that the fixture was regarded as something of a needle match. This he ascertained was due to the local resentment felt by the young men of the district for their service counterparts. This appeared to be based mainly upon the fact that the service men snapped up all the young ladies in the neighbourhood. An incidental and perhaps more influential aspect to the day's proceedings was the fact that the Army catering unit always provided an enormous free spread after the game, and the drinks in the bar were free of duty. Apparently these incentives were traditionally available to both players and supporters alike. Consequently, there was a mass exodus from the town the first Saturday each September.

"They'm all gone off already," stated the attendant, his pipe indicating the council estate with a broad sweep. "They'll be in some state when they gets back," he muttered reflectively and then began wheezing again. "They'm a dirty side though," he confided. George presumed he was referring to the service men. The old man wheezed again uncontrollably, so much so that he was forced to remove his pipe. "No, no" he squeaked. "The Old Sods. They'm scared to play us" he boasted. "But Mr Carter," his pipe directed George's gaze towards the choicest of the residences on the south facing slope, "from the brick works, he's a friend of the C. O. up at the camp. They was in the war together. He were a good player in his day," continued the attendant reflectively. "Killer Carter they named him," he recalled and wheezed again shaking his head as if he still could not believe the stories of Mr Carter's exploits on the rugby field.

George thanked the old man and set off to follow the directions given. He drove to the end of the main street and turned at the chapel. The narrow road was flanked on one side by a red brick wall surrounding the chapel grounds, and a high hedge on the other. The sides of this narrow highway were coated with red dust deposited by lorries from the Sodford Brick Works as they passed daily with their loads. The grass verges bore the scar marks of the wheels of the lorries.

The entrance to the rugby ground was a few hundred yards on the left-hand side. A large ornamental wrought iron gate was ajar permitting access to cars. Each side of the gate was a large brick pillar. Fashioned in iron in the centre of the gate were the letters O.S.R.F.C.

George eased his vehicle tentatively into the large car park his tyres crunching over the red gravel which close inspection would have revealed to be finely crushed bricks from the local works. The clubhouse on the slope above the car park was made of the by now tediously familiar bricks.

He scanned the parking area for a space. To avoid driving onto the grass area before the clubhouse he manoeuvred around the outside of the cars to the far end of the red gravel at the rear of the building. As he made his way to the clubhouse a car horn sounded loudly. Pete's car entered the ground at breakneck speed scattering red chips onto the other cars. He screeched to a halt on the grass which George had preferred not to spoil. The hood of his sports car was down which permitted him to climb out of the seat without opening the door. "Hi," said Pete, "you found it all right then? Come on in I'll introduce you."

A wooden plaque set into the wall by the door had inscribed on it in golden letters some information regarding the source of both the cash and the red bricks without which the Old Sodfordians new clubhouse would never have been built. The Sodford Brick Works Limited, (for such was the generous source of both money and building materials), had also donated the land upon which the clubhouse was standing, as 'a gift in perpetuity for the recreation purposes and in the interests of social welfare, and more particularly the furtherance of the game of Rugby Football amongst the inhabitants of the town of Sodford in accordance with the Recreational Charities Act 1958'.

George had no time to study these details as he followed Pete through the main door. He swept confidently down a long corridor pausing briefly to indicate a door on his left. "Bar on your left," he offered in the manner of an estate agent optimistic of an approaching sale. George just had time to catch a glimpse through the eyelevel glass panel of the large room with a highly polished wooden floor and a bar running the entire length of one side.

"Bog on your right," continued Pete, pointing to a door on the other side of the corridor which bore a black silhouette symbol of a man. In fact the silhouette was not unmistakably that of the man. It could for example have been the silhouette of the stick insect though this being an unlikely possibility a viewer would automatically assume it was a man. And perhaps who, being fitted with a surgical collar because of some spinal damage necessarily behaves as if every joint in his body is stiff. Above the symbol, perhaps a tacit admission of its inadequacy, was printed the word 'Gentlemen'.

"In here" said Pete pushing open the next door along the corridor. George followed him into a changing room which was bursting with Sodford manhood in various stages of undress. Three sides of the room contained benches all of which were fully occupied by players struggling to get socks on or off or furiously rubbing their legs or rummaging about in large kit bags. The other wall had no bench against it nor did it contain any pegs and in the centre there was an opening which led to a shower area.

Pete's arrival was greeted good-naturedly by the others. He glanced quickly around the room. "Where's Gorgon?" he asked. "There's someone outside asking for him."

"Who?" demanded a deep voice which seemed to come from a huge pair of buttocks covered in dark hair in the far corner of the room.

"Oh there you are," said Pete in mock surprise. "I dunno who it is, she wouldn't give her name."

This information, that the enquirer without was a female, produced hoots and jeers from the rest of the team.

"Who is this then?" they sneeringly asked.

"Dracula's mother," suggested a lad with buck teeth, who probably immediately wished he'd said nothing.

"No, Bunny, can't be," countermanded another. "Your mum said she was going shopping this afternoon." More laughter.

"Can't be Bunny's mum anyway," shouted another. "She's taking her teeth back this week for a four thousand gallon service." More guffaws.

Gorgon had straightened up now, he was immensely big, approximately six feet eight inches, and probably eighteen stone in weight. He was a Neanderthal type, with a large flat nose which appeared to have been broken several times. Except for his shoes and socks he was naked, and his entire body was covered in dark curly hair. He looked puzzled. "Well, what did she say?" he asked.

"Nothing," responded Pete. "She just asked for you." More jeers and hoots.

"Perhaps it's lady, Wyatt, come to do a bit of slumming," quipped one player.

"Perhaps," shrieked another, "it's big Molly come for a bit more meat." This last suggestion brought the house down though the joke was lost on George. Gorgon continued to look bemused.

Pete took the initiative, though he appeared completely unconcerned. "Please yourself," he said disinterestedly. "I just told her I'd give you the message. He shrugged and turned to look in his kitbag. Gorgon appeared to be applying his intellect to the situation but was unable to come up with a solution. Eventually he wrapped a towel around his naked midriff and lurched ponderously out of the door.

"I thought he'd never go," confided Pete archly in a stage whisper and immediately busied himself transferring Gorgon's kitbag and gear from the bench to the concrete floor on the empty side of the room. He paternally ushered George into the space alongside him which he had created.

"It's no good changing over there," Pete informed George, indicating the bare side of the room. "All your clothes get wet when they all come out of the shower."

The assembled company appeared equally divided between admiration for Pete hoodwinking the unfortunate Gorgon so successfully and sympathy for the latter. All, however, seemed to regard the incident as an amusing diversion.

Gorgon lumbered back into the changing room. The expression on his face showed that he had failed to solve the problem of the mystery woman. The sniggers of his team mates helped him to conclude that he had been sent on a wild goose chase but he evidently had not worked out why.

"Find her then?" asked one amusedly.

"Give her a quick one, did you, Gorgon?" sniped another.

The victim of the joke stood undecided his primaeval brow furrowed. Eventually he spotted his clothes where they had been dumped and with the speed of a retarded dinosaur he realised that he had been duped by Pete.

"Get out of my place!" he bellowed and started towards Pete angrily.

He was intercepted by the oldest member of the team, a man with very little hair on the top of his head but with a healthy growth around his chin. Though he barely came up to Gorgon's shoulder he lacked no confidence in dealing with the young giant. "Now cut it out," he snapped. "Save it for when we get on the field. Get over there and shut up."

He banished Gorgon to the empty side of the room. "Serves you right anyway," he rubbed it in. "You should know by now what he's like."

Gorgon threw a malevolent, "Bastard!" over his shoulder in Pete's direction and then retired sulkily to his newly allotted place.

The intervener was Arthur the team captain. None of the team knew his exact age and nobody dared to ask him. He might have been as young as thirty-five or he might have been as old as fifty-four. His body bore the ravages of time. The skin was an unhealthy white which looked as if it had never had the benefit of being exposed to the sunlight. Here and there, especially on his legs, blotchy marks of small veins close to the surface showed through. Though short, he was a thickset man but time had transformed an evidently once muscular frame and given it a flabby rounded appearance. The once steel-hard torso had not fallen away with the years but merely lost its firmness, so that now his chest was reminiscent of an old native lady with flat sagging breasts which contained no milk. His belly was swollen, obviously due to a regular intake of beer, and because of the lack of firmness in the old muscles, appeared to have dropped, like the stomach of an aged cat. Indeed it appeared to lack any support except that inadequately supplied by the blood-stained jockstrap into which its lower part was plunged. Like its owner's tired muscles, the jockstrap seemed to have reached the end of its usefulness. The previously strong elastic within the garment which in earlier days had gripped so tightly now strained to encompass the flesh which had expanded.

Arthur was a prop-forward, a position on the rugby field which many, who claim to know about the game, have dared to suggest requires no fleet footed athletic ability, no skilful expertise, nor even intelligence. What is most certainly required is great physical strength, mainly in the neck and shoulder area, and a dogged determination not to be intimidated by one's opponent however strong he might be. Arthur being no exception to the general rule, possessed none of the former qualities but had an abundance of the latter. Like many of his ilk he had played the game at a higher level and as nature tipped the scales against him, by ageing him, she evened things up by endowing him with a wily ability to employ all his experience to somehow survive each game, however tough. Like many old-timers throughout the land Arthur turned out year after year in all winds and weathers long after his contemporaries had hung up their boots. His indomitable spirit made one think of Dunkirk and feel that here was someone who epitomised all that was best in the British character and resolution: a true bulldog breed.

Sadly, Arthur's vocabulary, though in a rustic way typically British, did not exemplify what was best in the language of the world's greatest bard. Having dispatched the rumbling Gorgon with such ease he turned upon his persecutor. "You're bleedin late again!" he remonstrated.

"Yes, I'm sorry, Art," apologised Pete. "I had to show George here the way. George, this is Arthur, the skipper," he added.

Arthur pumped George's hand energetically. "Nice to meet you," he beamed. "Thanks for turning out. Have you played before?"

George was about to admit that he had only ever played the game at school many years before and had not acquitted himself too well, when Pete interjected. "He's played a lot, Art. He is good, very versatile, he'll play in any position, won't let you down."

"Great," purred Arthur with a confidence which implied that he had expected no other answer. "You'll be playing on the wing today, OK?" George nodded and Arthur patted him affectionately on the shoulder.

"Good lad," he said and winked confidentially. He turned to address the room in general. "Right, let's start thinking about it," he ordered. "This is not just any game of the season. It's not just another team we're playing today. This is probably the most important game of the year so let's start to think about it!"

As he exhorted his colleagues thus Arthur, who was bad on his feet, hobbled back and forth across the room still clad only in his worn out jockstrap. George had great difficulty in restraining his own laughter at the absurd spectacle of the team captain's Napoleonic toing and froing in such a ridiculous attire.

"Has your wife been borrowing your jockstrap again, Art?" demanded Pete, interrupting his skipper's flow. Arthur raised his eyebrows in query.

"Well, it looks from here as if she's left her understains all over it," Pete continued coarsely. George laughed heartily at this along with the others, partly because he found the remark amusing but more particularly because he was able to expel the pent-up mirth that had been gathering during Arthur's speech.

"That must be the blood of that bloke Art kneed in the chops last season," observed one team member nostalgically. Those present who had witnessed the incident all grimaced at the recollection of the event and agreed that Arthur was one of the dirtiest players in the county.

Arthur, who for an instant had been displeased with Pete's remark, was now gratified that the subject of his own violent reputation upon the pitch had been raised. His face glowed with pleasure. "Well, the bastard was off side," he emphasised and then, in response to Pete's original quip he announced chauvinistically that, "The only time my missus sees this bleedin thing," (he twanged the elastic on the jockstrap), "is when she washes it each week." Everyone laughed and George reflected how much he was enjoying himself, being one of the happy bunch of fellows.

A large wicker basket was opened in the centre of the room and the shirts were taken from it and passed around. In keeping with most of the things George had already seen in Sodford, the shirts were coloured brick red. George's knowledge of the game was so sparse that he did not know which shirt number he should wear. He felt that, had he the experience and ability which Pete had falsely attributed to him, he would be expected to know which shirt was his. He decided to wait until all the other shirts were taken and then to take the remaining one.

This ploy proved unnecessary for a small wiry fellow wearing a flat cap, who had been smoking since George entered the room, and who was in the process of lighting a fresh cigarette from the spent end of the previous one, asked George which wing he preferred to play on. When George answered that he did not mind the other informed him that he would be playing on the right flank as he (the smoker), preferred to play on the left. He then threw George the appropriate shirt which he donned gratefully.

Mild consternation broke out amongst the team as Gorgon took off his shoes and socks. "Phew, you rotten bugger!" remarked one.

"You ought to see a doctor about those," advised another.

George caught a whiff of the offending objects and had to admit to himself that they were the strongest smelling feet he had ever come across. He felt sorry for Gorgon, however, who was subjected to a brief barrage of rude remarks concerning personal hygiene. The latter worked on a pig farm and there were various opinions offered as to how he contrived to bring the smell of his trade with him.

"It's not my fault," he mumbled in a rueful bass tone and then as if to verify that the odour was not as bad as the others maintained, he gently massaged one foot and then raised his fingers to his nostrils. George was reminded of a large gorilla he had once seen in the zoo which had unashamedly poked and prodded various parts of its own anatomy before methodically licking its fingers much to the ghoulish fascination of the assembled crowd.

The team's reaction to Gorgon's self-examination was a mixture of amusement and disgust. George had initially supposed that the giant owed his nickname to his own monstrous appearance but after savouring the aroma given off by those huge feet he quietly reflected that the title might be a diminutive for 'Gorgonzola'.

As the general laughter and groans died down Arthur decided it was time to assert his authority. "Right!" he shouted, "gather round and listen. We've all had a little joke and enjoyed it, the next time I want to hear anybody laughing is when we are back in this changing room after winning this game. Sid, put that bleedin fag out," he ordered severely and then added as an afterthought, "and take that bleedin 'at off! Now then," he continued authoritatively, "this is the first game of the season and we all want to get off to a good start. Now some of us who haven't started training in earnest yet, (here Arthur paused briefly and glowered around the room in the hope that those who were not fastidious about their training would feel their consciences pricked by his remark), will be a little rusty. But," assured the skipper with confidence, "we'll soon run that off. Now we've got a good pack out today. It's the same pack that we finished with last season so you all know each other and should play as a unit. I shall be leading the pack," he added with some relish, "so...." he threatened, "if I hear any voice but mine out there I'll have something to say," not realising the absurdity of his own words.

"We are fortunate to have Pete Powell playing at scrum-half today. As you know, Pete is normally a first-team player so any ball which the pack wins we can expect him to do something constructive with it. Now remember, he'll be too bleedin quick for this lot." Here Arthur's balding head indicated the room next door. "So if he makes a break I expect everyone to go with him and anyone who's dawdling will feel my boot up his arse!""

"We are also lucky to have John here playing on the wing for us." Arthur indicated George and moved across to him.

"George," interrupted Pete. "George Davies."

"Right," affirmed Arthur, as if he knew all along and was merely testing the others. "George Davies," he repeated and rested one white flabby limb on the bench beside George. He placed one elbow on the leg and stared into George's face. "A good Welsh name," observed the skipper. "With a name like that he is sure to score plenty of tries for us."

George could not follow the logic of this but wisely decided to say nothing.

"This is the first game for a long time," announced Arthur momentously, still staring George straight in the face, "that we've had anyone on the wing with genuine pace so I want to see the ball going out to him."

George felt embarrassed that his talents should be so wildly exaggerated but again felt that the moment was not right to speak. He reflected briefly on how Sid the smoker would have taken the news that until this day the team had not possessed a quality winger. He felt doubly embarrassed on this account and would have stolen a glance at Sid but for the fact that Arthur's face was no more than two inches from his own. Arthur's stare was like that of Svengali and George felt most disconcerted.

"This game," continued the skipper slowly in an almost inaudible whisper, "is the most important game of the season. It's bigger than that," he corrected. "It's the most important game you have ever played." Arthur uttered the words deliberately and with great gravity. "This game is the big one every year," he informed them but this year it's more important than ever." His voice began to rise as he continued. "This year is more important because we haven't lost this fixture for the last five years in a row. That's important," he emphasised, "because it proves we can beat 'em and it means we must beat 'em. If we don't we'll be letting the club down and all those players who have fought hard in previous seasons to set up that record. And most of all if we don't win today I shall feel let down."

Here Arthur poked himself in the chest. He went on with a new ferocity in his voice. "If we don't win today, I personally will feel let down! If we lose today…" he revealed, his voice now raised to shout, "I shall feel too ashamed to set foot in this bleedin place again."

George felt that Arthur was perhaps setting too much store by what was, after all, just a game but once more he deemed it wise not to voice his opinion. Arthur had paused, either to allow the importance of his own remarks to be digested or because he was thinking of what to say next. His eyes meanwhile were still fixed firmly on George.

One of the younger players who had been drinking in Arthur's words, as a member of the Hitler Youth might have received a speech from his Feurer, began punching his left palm with his right fist. "We'll show the bastards, Art."

"Shut up!" barked Arthur with such ferocity that a small amount of spittle was deposited on George's face. So intimidating was the look on Arthur's face that George felt unable to wipe it off until Arthur had released him from his mesmerising gaze.

Arthur's tone returned to a mere whisper. "We are not," he hissed, "going to lose this match today. It is…" He uttered the words extremely slowly and deliberately, "a matter of pride. We are not," he continued, just as deliberately his voice rising gradually, "going to lose to these poofter soldier boys. Remember who it is we will be up against today," he added with more severity. "These aren't real soldiers," he informed them contemptuously. "They are just wet-nosed kids. But remember," he said still staring fixedly at George, "these kids are the ones that come down here on Saturday night poncing around as if they own the joint. They are the ones that try to chat up your girlfriends." He paused as if searching for some offence provocative enough to instil the right degree of hatred into his team. Triumphantly he offered them, "They are the ones who made your sister pregnant!"

George was somewhat bewildered by all this. Although he knew that Arthur's remarks were addressed to all those in the room he could not avoid the feeling (introduced by Arthur's hypnotic stare) that the words were aimed specifically at him. This made the situation more ludicrous for not only was this his first visit to Sodford, but he had no sister. Despite this, George without realising it, had allowed Arthur's attempted indoctrination to have some influence on his feelings. He was already dimly aware that his attitude towards the, as yet unseen Army team had turned from complete indifference to something approaching smouldering resentment.

To George's enormous relief Arthur withdrew his gaze. He took his foot off the bench beside George and turned to survey his little brood. It was as if he had divined that George's would be the final vote which he would canvass. Having sensed that George had been won over, Arthur was now satisfied. He swaggered across the room, his red shirt strained tight over his ample middle. Glancing up to the ceiling he announced firmly, "We..." he reverted to his favourite device of uttering the words with extreme deliberation, "are going to stuff 'em." by now he had reached the door. He turned and asked of the rest, "What are we going to do?"

"Stuff 'em!" replied the team in unison.

"I didn't hear you," shouted Arthur, making his way back to the centre of the room. "And neither," he added, his voice now building to a frenzy of excitement, "Did they" his shiny head once more nodding in the direction of the opposing team's dressing room. "Now then," he shouted. "Once more what are we going to do?"

"*Stuff 'em!*" roared the whole company with great gusto. Arthur was immensely satisfied with his little team talk. As an afterthought and somewhat reluctantly one sensed, he informed all those assembled that the game itself was the most important thing and that as long as everyone present enjoyed themselves that was what really counted.

In the last few minutes before leaving for the field of play the team busied itself rubbing quantities of strong smelling embrocation onto legs and necks and smearing thick grease from a communal bowl onto their ears. Some strapped up fingers with Elastoplast and suede bandages around their heads in the style of Apache warriors. George who had declined any of these cosmetic aids, sat quietly waiting. The smell of the liniment mingled with the odour of Gorgon's feet and George longed to be out in the fresh air.

As a final preamble to the coming game Arthur insisted that the rest of the team, (he himself was busy applying a final handful of grease to the inside of his jockstrap) indulge in a physical warm-up. They all ran up and down on the spot, their boots clattering loudly on the concrete floor. This went on for some two or three minutes, the pace quickening until it culminated in a twenty-five second burst with all players loudly counting the footsteps. The combination of the deafening sound of the studs on the concrete floor together with the lusty cries of the Old Sods echoed throughout the building. George realised that this was partly the idea and felt as though he were a primitive warrior intending to instil fear into an opposing tribe by making a fearsome noise. Significantly there were no answering cries from the room next door.

Finally the referee made his appearance, like a call boy in a theatre, to inform everyone that there was one minute to go. Arthur shook his hand warmly and said how nice it was to see him again. He was a small man with white hair and kind eyes and said a few words about wishing to see a "good clean game." Arthur wholeheartedly agreed and requested ten seconds chat with his team before their exit. The referee obligingly left.

Arthur removed his teeth and placed them ceremoniously upon the bench. "Right, listen!" he said urgently. "We all know this little bleeder can't organise an orgy in a brothel. We'll get no protection out there from him so it's every man for himself today. If any punches start flying I want everyone to get stuck in. OK? Right!" he concluded. "Now get out there and enjoy yourselves."

As they clattered out into the corridor their exit coincided with that of the Army team. George was surprised to note how young some of the faces were. He also noticed that some of those faces were very pale. Presumably the war cries had taken their toll.

On their way to the field George chided Pete for misinforming Arthur about his footballing ability. Pete pooh-poohed him and gave it as his opinion that Arthur was a silly old so-and-so who knew very little about the game apart from how to foul others when the referee wasn't looking.

"You'll be all right," he said reassuringly. "If you get the ball just run straight towards the opposite goal line, and if you look like being tackled look inside for someone to pass the ball to. Bunny's playing centre alongside you—he's a good safe player, I'll have a word with him, he'll look after you."

George felt somewhat foolish being wet nursed in this fashion but he was genuinely grateful to Pete whose knowledge and experience of the game was more extensive than his own. As they emerged into the sunlight and took to the field of play George breathed a huge sigh of relief at having left behind the stench of the changing room. Immediately he was reminded that the rugby field was less than a quarter of a mile from the glue factory and he began to wish that he had used just a small amount of the liniment himself.

Both teams took to opposite ends of the pitch and began idly limbering up in front of their own respective posts. The Old Sodfordians were tossing a ball around for practice and George managed to drop it each time it came in his direction. This did nothing for his confidence but at least none of the others made any comment. Soon the referee appeared and took his position in the centre of the pitch and blew his whistle to summon the two captains. Arthur hobbled forward pompously his head shining in the September sun. His opposite number came forward too. Though obviously younger than Arthur, he did not appear to be in a better physical condition. George judged that he too was a prop-forward. Like Arthur his body was bulky and flabby. His gait was reminiscent of a weightlifter. His ample thighs appeared to rub together uncomfortably with each stride. He walked as if a metal girdle was concealed within his shorts. His head was swathed in a dirty bandage which was kept low to protect his ears. Unfortunately, it was so low that it crept down over his eyes and caused him to throw back his head in order to see ahead. Unlike Arthur his skin was pink and he was already sweating profusely.

George noticed that Pete was having a quiet word with Bunny. The latter was nodding in a very serious manner. When Pete had finished he gave George the thumbs up and Bunny revealed his large buck teeth in what presumably was intended to be a confident smile. George's response was somewhat weaker and he felt now a few butterflies in his stomach as the contest approached.

The audience for the coming spectacle consisted of two mothers who were seated comfortably on the grass in the far corner of the field engaged in conversation and knitting. Around them gambolled four small children. None of them appeared to be interested in the players. They gave the appearance of being present merely to enjoy the sunshine. The other member of the public present showed even less interest in the game. He too was enjoying the warm sunlight. He was stretched out luxuriantly on the grass surrounding the pitch near the halfway line, one black front paw crossed over the other and presumably dreaming of exciting chases through long grass with the scent of rabbits in the air. Occasionally his black nose twitched.

The Army team kicked off and the ball went spinning across from the centre spot, was lost momentarily in the sunshine, and then landed out of play on George's side of the pitch. Both packs of forwards, who had converged on the spot where the ball ought to have landed then turned and trudged back to the spot from whence it had come. George meanwhile retrieved the ball and kicked it back to the centre of the field. This was to be his first and last touch of the ball for the next half hour.

There followed a fifteen-minute period of the game which for George was most uninteresting. The play was confined almost entirely to the two packs of forwards who heaved and grunted and sweated in scrums and lineouts. Despite the apparent mammoth physical effort applied by both sides no definite pattern of play was established and neither side appeared to have gained any advantage over the other. Indeed, by the end of this period both packs were still camped upon the halfway line. By now, of course, they were all very hot and short of breath and Arthur's head had turned the colour of a Sodford brick.

The skipper had so far unselfishly contrived to ensure that his own physical contribution to the game had been economical enough to enable him to retain sufficient breath to shout continuous instructions to his teammates. In fact Arthur did not confine himself to mere orders. His constant verbal output was more in the nature of a scathing commentary on the opposition's inability to penetrate the Old Sodfordians ranks. Evidently he regarded as paramount this part of the captain's responsibility. A spectator might have been excused for thinking that Arthur had, at some time in the past, set himself the task of reading a do it yourself manual on 'propaganda techniques'. The same spectator would also be excused for assuming that he had not progressed any further in that task beyond the section devoted to 'demoralisation of the enemy'. The two mothers, having by now gathered up their knitting and their children and moved away, the only spectator remaining to notice these aspects of Arthur's attitude towards the game, still slept soundly near the halfway line, still presumably dreaming of rabbits.

Arthur meanwhile dreamed only of the total confusion amongst the Army players brought about mainly by his own penetrating observations. "They are getting tired," he informed his own team loudly during one of the interminable pauses caused by the ball being kicked out of the ground. "They're a ragged bunch," he continued with great conviction, his voice echoing round the ground. "Five years in a row," he boomed, reminding his colleagues of the outcome of the fixture in previous seasons, "and this lot aren't good enough to stop us making it six."

He continued with this critical appraisal throughout the first half. Many of his remarks were of a more personal nature presumably calculated by Arthur to dishearten the other side or at least to antagonise them into an injudicious loss of temper from which the Old Sodfordians might hopefully benefit.

An observer might have been puzzled by Arthur's persistent monologue. Puzzled firstly by the manner of its delivery which was due to the fact that Arthur had left his dentures in the changing room. This meant that despite the volume of his voice, most of his words were muffled and accompanied by a hissing or spitting sound rather like a badly tuned radio. Puzzled secondly that Arthur should bother to continue with his commentary when its effect on both sides appeared to be non-existent. This could have been partly due to Arthur's imperfect diction or it may have been that both teams were too pre-occupied with the game to attempt to interpret the words issuing from the Old Sodfordian skipper's toothless gums. It may also have been that both sets of players were exercising great self-control and not allowing Arthur's persuasive arguments to influence their attention to the game itself. Finally, it might also have been the case that nobody really cared what Arthur thought or said. Certainly an observer would have been compelled to admit that his remarks were biased, and for that reason, if no other, they deserved to be ignored. His constant references to the inferiority of the Army side and the near-exhausted state of its players were clearly shown to be incorrect by the fact that they had not given an inch of ground to the Old Sodfordians. The only potential observer present was clearly uninfluenced by Arthur's rhetoric. His unconcern was quite evident as he sleepily stretched one black leg and twitched his nose.

George was able during the frequent pauses in the game to sum up the opposition back division. Like George and his team mates they were lined up in redundant fashion. Due to the stalemate situation between the two packs, very little action was being seen among the three quarters. Both sets spent most of the first half of the game stretched out like sentries at regular intervals eyeing each other warily.

George's opposite number was a Negro. George was not encouraged by what he saw. The man was the same height as George, that is five foot ten inches but he was very much heavier. Like so many black men he appeared to be naturally endowed with a muscular athletic body which is an obvious asset in a physical game such as rugby football. In fact from George's viewpoint he appeared if anything to be over endowed for as well as a powerful torso, George could see that his thighs were so large that his shorts were strained to encompass them. In addition, his face bore a rugged uncompromising expression which filled George with misgiving.

If George was discouraged by the sight of his opposing winger he was even less happy with the centre who was playing alongside him. This man was over six foot tall and just as muscular as the Negro. He had a bullet shaped head with closely cropped fair hair, a strong bull-like neck and a large barrel chest. His thighs were equally as powerful as the Negro's and if the latter's expression was uncompromising then this man's expression could only be adequately described as downright malevolent. He had a large square resolute jaw and steel grey eyes. To George those eyes appeared to have a glint of eagerness in them as if relishing prematurely a physical contest which they knew they could not lose. George was reminded of a fresh bull released into a bullring full of indignation and pent up fury, sizing up the situation and full of confidence. He would not have been surprised if the man had snorted and begun to paw the ground. The only difference, he reflected was that there were no picadors available to slow the beast down and he himself was by no means an accomplished matador. In any case, the parallel was not really accurate because the function of a matador was to avoid the oncoming creature. In this situation one was required to stop it in full flight. George shuddered slightly at the thought and was glad at least that it was the buck-toothed Bunny who would be required to tackle this man.

The stalemate situation was eventually ended by Pete, having put the ball into his own scrum, collected it quickly from between his number eight's legs, dummied a pass to his stand-off, cut inside two covering players, changed direction and sliced through the opposition ranks at such speed that he left everyone, including his own team far behind. He side-stepped his way around the flailing full-back and scored under the posts. A simple conversion taken by Pete himself put the Old Sodfordians seven points ahead.

Arthur, who though he had not shown it, must have had doubts before that moment that the Army side was really as incompetent as he had consistently maintained, was now jubilant. True to his tendency, (already remarked upon), to criticise the opposition in preference to offering praise to his own team, he was at great pains to point out to his own side and to anyone else within a hundred yards or so that all his previous assertions regarding the various weaknesses of their opponents were now entirely justified. He gloatingly remarked to everyone in the ground that the "Bleeders were rattled."

As the only ones within earshot of Arthur, (apart from the members of his own team), were the Army players and the still soundly sleeping black mongrel and as the latter had so far expressed no interest in the proceedings whatsoever, one might have supposed that his exultation was a little overdone. Certainly if Arthur had ever taken the trouble to read more of his manual he might have discovered that the morale of a group can often be inversely proportionate to the volume of propaganda to which it is subjected. 'The Bleeders' may well have been rattled, but from their countenances when they returned for the kick-off and their added ferocity in the ensuing moments it was apparent to all except presumably the triumphant Arthur, and the sleeping dog, that they were determined to turn the tables.

Eventually the moment came which George had both hoped for and dreaded. The ball was cleanly won by the Army at a set scrum inside the Old Sodfordians half and whipped smartly out along the line. The bullet-headed P.T. instructor (for George had decided that no one within a military set up, with such a physical appearance could be allocated any other function) with his first touch of the ball, appeared to run straight through the 'safe' Bunny. He then eluded two further tackles and tossed the ball out to the Negro winger who ran round George with consummate ease and touched the ball down in the corner.

It was now the Army's turn to triumph. Copious back slapping accompanied by cries of "Good try, Winston" directed to the Negro and "Well done, Sarg," to the bullet-headed PT instructor displayed the obvious pleasure which the Army team felt. Winston accepted congratulations with great delight his perfect white teeth gleaming in contrast to his coal-black skin. As he trotted confidently back to the halfway line his grin alighted on George. To George it seemed that the grin momentarily became a pearly sneer. It seemed to say that Winston had tested George and found him to be wanting and from now on the owner of the sneer was going to enjoy himself.

The resumption of play was delayed while the unfortunate Bunny was given medical attention. This entailed one of the players rushing off to the side to fetch a bucket of water and a sponge. Bunny was completely winded and croaked hoarsely for a minute or so like an old bullfrog with whooping cough. All the colour had drained from his face so that his skin was as grey as the bullet-headed PT instructor's eyes. The respite was appreciated by everyone, except Bunny of course, for the weather was very hot. Arthur took the opportunity to advise George to mark 'the black bleeder' closely.

The Army failed to achieve a conversion of Winston's try and so the Old Sodfordians led by the narrow margin of seven points to five. Now that both sides had drawn blood the pace of the game began to quicken. Straight from the kick-off the ball was passed swiftly out along the Army line towards the bullet-head.

Both Bunny and George were advancing on their opponents as quickly as possible in order to restrict their mobility. Bunny who was obviously still smarting from his previous encounter with the bullet-head and who presumably wished to re-establish his reputation of being a 'safe' player was, with a look of grim determination bearing down at breakneck speed on the bullet-head. It seemed inevitable that the latter would receive both man and ball simultaneously. Such a moment is a vulnerable one for any rugby player. It requires an ice cool nerve and a keen eye which must not be diverted from the ball despite the intimidating presence of the on-coming player. The bullet-head had two very keen steel grey eyes which never wavered at all. At the very last moment, with what seemed to be a mere shiver of the hips, he contrived to step artistically inside his opponent. At the same time he reached out with his right hand to scoop up the ball which appeared to be flying past his rear. In one synchronised movement he gripped the ball safely to his chest with the right hand and shot out a ramrod left hand into the face of the by now over-committed Bunny who was promptly pole-axed.

He then sped majestically on towards the Old Sodfordians' goal line, adroitly weaving his way in and around opponents, changing pace and direction with ease.

"Go on, Sarg," urged his team mates, "All the way, don't stop."

Sarg it was obvious had no intention of stopping. His long meandering run had taken him diagonally across the field ever nearer to the home side's goal line. He appeared to be happy to show his paces, like a young colt joyfully stretching its limbs in a fresh meadow and he disdainfully ignored any of his colleagues who were in a good position to receive a pass from him. It was apparent that Sarg was fully confident of his ability to score without the assistance of his team mates.

He paused momentarily, his flint grey eyes appraising the situation. Those eyes seemed to signal that so far anyone watching had only witnessed the graceful side of Sarg's game. They indicated that there was a harder edge about to be revealed. They alighted on the opposition goal posts and as if reminded thereby of the simple geometric fact that the shortest distance between two points is a straight line, they flashed the message to Sarg's legs. These responded with another change of direction and Sarg's route to the goal-line straightened. Gathering speed as he went, he bludgeoned his way through four tackles until only the massive Gorgon stood between him and success. One might have expected that the irresistible force had finally met the immovable object that, in so doing, one would have underestimated Sarg's resolute nature. With a final Herculean effort he hurled himself at the giant. His brawny shoulder struck Gorgon in the chest knocking all the wind out of him. With a startled grunt Gorgon was bowled over backwards and Sarg triumphantly touched the ball down between the posts.

Like a true conqueror he picked his way proudly through the debris of the vanquished enemy to receive the acclaim of his fellows. His try was converted seconds before the half time whistle was blown. The Old Sodfordians trailed by five points.

The half time interval was prolonged in order to allow further medical attention to be given to the luckless Bunny. He had remained motionless for a very long time on the spot where Sarg had so clinically deposited him. Eventually he sat up, clutching his mouth protectively and ignoring any enquiries as to how he felt. The referee was most concerned and flapped nervously around him, holding up his hand in front of Bunny and insisting that he count the number of fingers displayed. As Bunny couldn't or wouldn't reply, he convinced himself that the player was suffering from concussion.

The referee was a small middle-aged man. He was passionately interested in sport and had played a bit in his time. He was a school master by profession and though he didn't have too much trouble maintaining discipline at work (it was after all only a junior school so the eldest children were only ten years old) he was if he was honest with himself, always a little nervous when graduating to the big boys on Saturdays. Sometimes he felt inadequate when tempers began to fray. Keeping these beefy adults in order was not the same as controlling young children. In some respects it was easier that was true but even when things were going smoothly he always had that nagging doubt that one day he would be called upon to referee an ill-tempered game which would develop beyond his control. That feeling was always stronger when he had the misfortune to be allocated a game involving a Sodford team. They had a reputation for violent behaviour both on and off the field and none of the referees enjoyed a fixture involving the Old Sods.

It was when he had a Sodford game to referee that he thought of retiring. The game he felt had changed during the period in which he had been involved with it both as a player and an official. When he had started playing it was a game played almost entirely by gentlemen. Now it seemed any old riff raff played and the rotten apples in the bunch infected all the rest. There was much more violence in matches nowadays and players regularly questioned his decisions, a thing never heard of in his playing days and occasionally some openly defied him. He felt it was unfair: after all he willingly gave up his Saturdays in order, he felt, to put back into the game itself a little of the pleasure he had derived from it over the years. But these days, each club had its thugs who spoilt the friendly atmosphere of each game. Men like the present skipper of the Old Sodfordians who always tried to take advantage of his own mild nature. He was a man who liked to be liked and he always got the feeling that the Old Sods despised him. He found Arthur to be very intimidating. He secretly thought of him as being the original Old Sod from whom the club derived its nickname.

The referee was worried at the moment for the injured Bunny. The lad did not seem to know where he was and was unable to focus on his fingers. He had attended a recent course for tuition of referees and great emphasis had been laid upon the dangers of concussion and the referees attending were urged to take every safeguard before allowing a player to continue in a match after a knock to the head.

He felt that he ought to apply the first aid knowledge that he had acquired on the course but this stupid lad paid no attention to him. On the course it had looked simple. The instructor would hold one finger before the eyes of the supposedly injured player and ask how many fingers he saw. If he saw one finger only then he was fit to play on. If he failed to respond at all then he was either dead or unconscious and arrangements should be made to remove him from the field of play immediately. He remembered they had all laughed of course when the instructor had said this. That was all very well but what was to be done now? This lad was obviously unwell, wouldn't allow anyone to help him and now he was crawling about on the floor. He continued to hover nervously around Bunny still preoccupied with the possibility that he was suffering from the dreaded concussion. He voiced his thoughts to those around.

"Concussed!" snorted Arthur "He ain't concussed, he's looking friz bleedin teeth." Sure enough, as the referee was to observe when the patient finally got to his feet, the collision with Sarg had deprived him of the very items without which he would not have been nicknamed Bunny. His two front teeth had definitely been knocked out.

It is a strange thing how the alteration of a single feature can change the appearance of a person. For example, if a man shaves off his moustache he can look most peculiar for a while until those who meet him grow accustomed to it. Bunny certainly looked peculiar now without his crowning glory.

A large black hole now showed where those huge teeth had been. One or two of his colleagues were cruel enough to see the funny side of Bunny's predicament. Their mirth was encouraged when Bunny tried to give them a piece of his mind. His rearranged mouth uttered a sharp whistle each time a word, containing the letter S was spoken.

You rotten buggersss," he complained "You'd all laugh at a cat with its arsssse on fire."

Arthur was not interested in the comic qualities of the situation. He was more concerned with the fact that the Old Sodfordians were in danger of losing the match. It had not escaped his notice that the Army side in general and the bullet-headed Sarg in particular, were more than a match for his side. He was beginning to accept the fact that his psychological warfare of the first half had made little impression on the Army players. He decided to apply them to the referee.

"Look at the bleedin state of 'im" remonstrated Arthur indicating the injured Bunny. For once his basic vocabulary was appropriate and the referee had to admit that Bunny did not look too well. Having failed to persuade him to count fingers he was reduced to simply asking him if he was well enough to continue to play. Bunny whistled in the affirmative though he now looked anything but a 'safe' player.

"Of course he'll play on" insisted Arthur. "It takes more than the loss of a couple of bleedin teeth to stop one of my team," he boasted exposing his own naked gums as he spoke, implying that he had lost his teeth in a similar manner.

"That's not the point though " he continued. "I'm concerned with the protection of my players and if I was referee today I would have sent off the bastard who did that." Here Arthur prodded poor Bunny in the mouth to be sure the referee knew what he was talking about. Bunny squawked with pain, a reaction which seemed to satisfy Arthur. "See?" he shouted at the unfortunate referee his voice full of high dudgeon.

The referee reminded Arthur that as far as he knew there had been no foul play by the Army players and, unfortunate as it was, Bunny's injury was just one of the normal hazards of the game. The top of Arthur's head grew a shade redder as he seethed openly. He had already convinced himself that his team's deficit was due solely to the doubtful tactics of the opposition. Now he did his best, with all the righteous indignation he could summon up, to convince the referee. The latter, despite his eagerness to placate the wrathful Arthur, was in no position to reverse the score so long after the incident had occurred. He avoided the issue by looking officiously at his watch and muttering something about the time already lost and then alerted the two teams with a shrill blast of his whistle. Arthur permitted himself a final intimidating glare in the referee's direction before taking up his position for the second half.

The Old Sods kicked off and after a ten minute period during which very little occurred, the Army team took up where it had left off in the first half. Sarg was again the destructive element. Gathering the ball inside his own half he rounded the wary Bunny (by now a shadow of his former self and anything but safe), drew the remaining defence and timed a perfect pass to Winston who, having taken the ball at top speed, was able to ground it directly under the posts thus virtually ensuring that the conversion would be made. Sure enough it was.

Being twelve points adrift the morale of the Old Sods was beginning to disintegrate. This fact was discernible from the readiness on the part of many of the side to apportion blame for the latest score by the Army side. Poor Bunny was the one who was elected scapegoat and it was suggested in some quarters that he was unsafe. He responded somewhat half-heartedly that it was not all his fault and demanded that the wing forwards take some of the blame.

To Arthur this petty wrangling must have been particularly galling since his master plan had been to demoralise their opponents. He grudgingly admitted that both Sarg and Winston were a talented pair but roundly condemned the ethics of the Army selectors in fielding two such players (obviously first team standard) in a third team game. To George his comments savoured of sour grapes when he recalled how pleased Arthur had been to announce first team Pete's inclusion in the side. Arthur by now had abandoned his attempts at psychological warfare. Presumably he would burn his manual when he got home. He had now decided to adopt plan B which included warfare of a more down to earth variety. His tactics were twofold. Firstly he switched the unsafe Bunny to the opposite flank where he replaced the side's usual scrum half. The latter had been moved from his usual position to allow the more skilful Pete to shine. He was returned to his usual place and Pete was moved to replace Bunny because it was felt that only Pete had sufficient speed and skill to combat the rampant Sarg. Secondly Arthur announced that it was time to "slow em down a bit." He did not elaborate on the remark that accompanied it with a significant facial expression which would have filled the referee with misgivings had he seen it. He finally reminded his three quarters that, should they be fortunate enough to get their hands on Sarg they were at all costs to hold him down until the forwards arrived. "We'll do the rest," he assured them with a further expression which would have sapped the referee's confidence utterly if he had been privy to these exchanges.

But that gentleman was fortunately out of earshot near the halfway line. He dutifully recorded in his notebook the fact that the Old Sods were now twelve points down and prepared for the kick-off. He silently wished that the score line was reversed for experience told him that when the Old Sods were losing, discipline went by the board.

Arthur had just time before the play was resumed, to once more exhort George to "Keep tight on the black bleeder." Thereafter the game began to liven up. Officionados of the sport will recognise this expression as a euphemism for violence breaking out. The sun by this time was sinking low over the hillside. This meant that the Army team and the referee were temporarily blinded as the Old Sods kicked off. As the ball descended full advantage was taken of this situation. A loud crack of bone meeting bone was clearly audible. After this mayhem broke out and both sets of forwards fought toe to toe in a brawl the like of which is common place in Hollywood Westerns. The referee scurried to and fro like a demented hen whose brood was threatened, continually blasting on his whistle. Nobody took any notice of him, his worst fears regarding the outbreak of trouble were now realised. He felt like a small groom trying to manage a group of lively horses barely coming up to the shoulders of most of the struggling forwards. He fervently wished that he was anywhere but the Sodford Rugby Club this Saturday.

Eventually the violence subsided and the referee was able to convince himself that he had regained some control. He was unable to decide who had been responsible for the outbreak of the trouble and eventually compromised by ordering a scrum down. As the brawlers reluctantly disengaged themselves one body was revealed motionless on the ground. He wore the Army colours and his head was wrapped in a bandage. It was Arthur's opposite number. He appeared to be sleeping very peacefully and an observer might have been excused for thinking that there was the beginning of a slight smile on his lips. Certainly, there was no mistake about the smile on Arthur's face. Winking hugely to his team mates and with his back to the referee, he cradled his own fist and grimaced with mock pain to indicate that his had been the hand which had laid out the Army captain. The gesture was superfluous for no one in the Old Sods' ranks was in any doubt as to who had been responsible for the fight.

The Army side was in temporary disarray for when their skipper finally awoke, he was in no condition to continue playing. He was escorted to the clubhouse where he was allowed to continue his sleep on a changing room bench.

Play resumed and the Old Sods pressed home their advantage and gained possession of the ball which was swiftly passed out to George on the wing. Remembering the advice given to him earlier by Pete, he tucked the ball under one arm and ran straight at his opponent as fast as his legs would carry him.

Although the whole incident took only a few seconds, George was able to note in detail one or two of the circumstances as if the whole thing were occurring in slow motion. He noticed in the first place that his immediate opponent (Winston), was barring his way and was poised ready to spring. George was reminded of a waiting puma about to leap upon its victim; the sleek beauty of the dark predatory beast belying the awesome power which it possessed. George also noticed, as he approached ever nearer, that Winston had adopted the same immaculately white sneer which he had sported after scoring his first try. The confidence which the sneer exuded filled George with misgiving. If that were not enough, he observed with alarm out of the corner of his eye that Sarg was moving across the pitch at full speed on what was obviously destined to be a collision course with himself and Winston.

The prospect of being struck by Sarg when travelling flat out was more than George cared to contemplate. His nerve cracked and he applied all the brakes he could muster. Simultaneously he heard Pete's shout from just behind him and without looking, he flung the ball inside and by sheer luck it went directly to Pete's outstretched hands.

The alteration of pace by George allowed sufficient time for the already committed Sarg to hurtle past and hit his team mate with a brawny shoulder and bundle him off the field of play, thus leaving a wide gap in the Army ranks which the fleet-footed Pete gratefully exploited. The Old Sods were now only five points in arrears and George was applauded for his undoubted talent. No one except George himself had any idea that his success had been entirely accidental.

Arthur was beside himself with glee and rushed over to shake George's hand. "Great side step, John!" he boomed and then made his way delightedly towards that area of the field where Sarg and Winston were laid. It was by way of being a bonus for Arthur when he discovered that the two key players on the other side were injured. With great difficulty he suppressed the urge to smile and contrived try to look suitably sympathetic. It transpired that at the moment of impact, which George had barely managed to avoid, the bullet-head had dislocated his shoulder. As he and Winston tumbled off the field of play Sarg trod heavily on the tail of the sleeping black mongrel. The latter erupted in a flurry of anguish and fury and savagely bit the nearest part of its attacker. This turned out to be Winston's left buttock and the mongrel's indignation at being so painfully awakened showed itself in the determination with which he clung on to his quarry.

As Winston and Sarg were assisted away by their fellows, George heard a wheezing sound nearby. He turned to see the garage attendant whom he had met earlier and who now stood on the side lines and appeared to be enjoying himself immensely. Eventually an ambulance was summoned and the two Army players were taken away for treatment. The rest of the service team were now no match for the Old Sods and very quickly the game was put beyond doubt. George managed to score three times, thanks mainly to the generosity of Pete alongside him and even the chain-smoking Sid on the other wing scored once. It was noticeable that as soon as it was apparent that the Army side were bound to lose, Arthur's attitude changed. The more points the Old Sodfordians amassed the more magnanimous he became and was even seen on one occasion to assist an Army player to his feet. The most relieved person on the field was the referee who welcomed the change in atmosphere and was secretly not sorry at all that Sarg and Winston had retired hurt. With great satisfaction he eventually blew the final whistle happy in the knowledge that there were no disciplinary reports to make out.

Arthur shook everyone by the hand warmly, including the referee, and was benevolence personified as he wiped the sweat from his scarlet head with the sleeve of his soiled shirt.

"A bleedin good game,," he affirmed with every hand he shook.

The two teams left the field together and then lined up in turn to applaud each other up the steps to the clubhouse. This seemed to to be a very sporting gesture especially in view of the animosity generated during the middle part of the game. An observer might have been excused for thinking that the whole of the game had been conducted in the same sporting manner. Apart from the pipe-smoking garage attendant, who had arrived late and who had never been under any illusions regarding the sporting nature of any Old Sodfordian team, the only non-participant on the field throughout the major part of the game had now retired to the other end of the town to nurse a bruised tail. And so there were fewer spectators to watch the teams exit the field of play than there were to witness their arrival.

In the changing room the Old Sods were in noisy good humour, everyone reminding each other of this or that incident during the game and everyone laughing a good deal. Arthur did a small war dance wearing just his boots and socks and looked quite absurd. Sid selected his first Woodbine for nearly an hour and a half and sucked in the smoke as an underwater swimmer would the oxygen from an air pipe.

Everyone agreed that George's debut had been a remarkable success and Arthur went so far as to refer to him as "a bleedin miracle" when the incident concerning the collision between Sarg and Winston was recalled for the umpteenth time. They were all agreed that the dog bite which poor Winston had suffered, had been the highlight of the afternoon. As Arthur so colourfully put it in between splutters of mirth, "The look on that black bleeder's face when that dog sunk his teeth in was something I'll never forget."

Arthur delegated to George the duty of collecting the weekly subscriptions from all the players. He led George to believe that this was quite an honour and implied that George's powers on the field had made him the natural candidate for this job. Pete later revealed that the responsibility was Arthur's but that any time he could offload it he was always pleased to do so." Don't let Sid slide off without paying," he advised confidentially.

Everyone repaired to the long wooden floored bar room where huge aluminium jugs were filled with beer and passed around. A trap door in the wall was opened to reveal a small kitchen next door in which two old ladies could barely be seen through clouds of steam. A strong smell of curry emanated from the trap door along with the steam.

Arthur acquired some tokens from a beer mug on a shelf behind the bar. These he handed out to all the players in turn who immediately queued at the hatch and exchanged them for platefuls of hot curried stew with thick chunks of buttered bread. They all sat down at the table and ate their food, talking and laughing loudly. The ale jugs were continually refilled and passed around and George felt himself becoming more and more, good humoured. "Bleedin good curry this," remarked Arthur with the air of one who knows a good curry when he sees one.

Shortly after the meal had been consumed the door of the bar opened and a general commotion followed with the arrival of a group who had left the nearby Army camp earlier and returned to their own clubhouse. Great jubilation followed the mutual announcement that all Sodfordian teams had triumphed on the field of play. At the instigation of a middle-aged man, who wore a tweed jacket with a yellow rose in its buttonhole, a man who all the players appeared to respect greatly, the jugs were replenished anew and the festivities commenced in earnest.

Arthur took it upon himself to play the role of host and took personal charge of the ale jugs. He spent most of his time moving from table to table refilling any glasses that he saw that evening. He totally ignored protestation from anyone who might have felt that he did not require any more beer and kept refilling glasses as if it were his life's mission. The glass he refilled more regularly than any other was his own. Probably it was because of this that he gradually became less steady on his feet. His speech became slurred and although he remained steadfastly cheerful throughout the evening, he nevertheless became more belligerent in his insistence that others consume as much ale as himself.

The gentleman in the tweed jacket who paid for most of the beer which Arthur so lavishly dispensed was identified by Pete as Mr Ken Carter, the owner of the local factories. George was introduced to him by Pete. Mr Carter's handshake was vice like and George could tell immediately why this man was respected by everyone in the club.

As they were exchanging pleasantries Arthur staggered by with a fresh jug of ale and interrupted their conversation. He flung one arm around George's shoulder and leaned heavily upon him for support. "Mishter

Carter, shir," he said drunkenly, "this boy is a bleedin genius. Three times he shcored and laid on another beauty." As he spoke he indicated George with his free arm which held the ale jug and managed to slop beer over his own feet without noticing.

"He'sh got a wonderful shideshtep, Mishter Carter," he continued and then went on to describe at great length the incident in which George had evaded the on-coming Sarg and had managed to pass the ball to Pete at just the right moment.

"I'll never forget the look on that black bleeder'sh face," repeated Arthur, wiping the tears from his eyes and the beer foam from his bearded lips.

George tried desperately to deny the talents which Arthur sought to attribute to him but gave up in the end. He felt doubly fraudulent because he realised that any denial sounded like false modesty after Arthur's glowing report. Luckily for him everyone else was used to Arthur's ways and took with a pinch of salt the prop-forward's description of events.

Later on the gathering became more noisy. A number of games were organised, mainly by Arthur, which seemed to be enjoyed by nearly everyone judging from the raucous laughter which the various competitions evoked. Each game was different in its content but the common factor was always the fact that the unfortunate loser was obliged to pay a forfeit which was always the same and entailed the swift consumption of a drink of some kind, usually a pint of beer. Arthur always oversaw the forfeit payment and was quite ruthless in this respect. Each forfeit was exacted to the precise measure and no loser was allowed to escape his responsibility.

George always shunned such infantile games: even as a child he had not enjoyed that sort of activity and had never joined in with pass the parcel or musical chairs. He shrank away from the main group and joined the few older men standing at the bar near Mr Carter. He watched the antics of the other players, gradually growing more oafish as the beer worked its way into their systems. Amidst the general uproar of the Old Sodfordian clubhouse he was vaguely aware that nearby Pete was talking earnestly with Mr Carter.

Chapter Five
The Office Without Bill

It was less than twenty-four hours before Bill's absence took effect. The following day when Mr Pigg arrived at the office, his normal half hour late, he was alarmed to discover the staff queued up outside.

At first he was angry with his workers for hanging about so aimlessly. This feeling was immediately tempered by the realisation that he himself had the only key to the outer door of the building. His annoyance was quickly transferred towards poor Bill whom he silently cursed for being the cause of this untidy start to the day. He felt some guilt at harbouring such a thought and the knowledge that it was as much his own fault that the staff were locked out made him no less annoyed.

He approached the waiting group who had the appearance of a picket line or an unemployment queue, with suppressed anger. He disliked the disarray which they all presented, casually leaning against the wall and gossiping to each other. He noticed with silent horror the misunderstanding which could be given to passing motorists by the sight of Mavis stood on the corner in a microscopic leather skirt and black stockings, smoking a king-sized menthol cigarette. "Why does that girl have to stand with her legs so far apart?" he asked himself.

To make matters worse Vincent was actually sitting on the pavement. Slumped against the wall of the building he was swaying his head in time with the most awful cacophony which Mr Pigg had ever had the misfortune to hear which was issuing from a small radio which was beside him on the pavement. Mr Pigg could hear the heavy rock music from the other end of the street and inwardly cringed. He was appalled by the sight which his staff presented and feared that this might reflect upon himself. Just as this fear entered his mind he passed Mr Norton the manager of the nearby building society. Despite his young age (he was after all no older than Mr Pigg), he had a magnificent head of silvery white hair which Mr Pigg regarded as very distinguished and envied greatly. He was always most particular about his own standing with other prominent members of the local business community, like Mr Norton, and was mortified to notice the amused grin which that gentleman displayed on seeing the department's staff queueing outside the office door.

As he drew near there was a stirring among the ranks as they spotted him and the critical raising of eyebrows and the general comments made (none of which could be heard above the strains of rock music coming from Vincent's machine), annoyed him even more. He took his anger out on the unfortunate Vincent. Delivering a sharp kick to the latter's legs, he informed him that his posture was not what he expected of one of his employees. "Switch that bloody thing off," he commanded and unlocking the door, he led his staff inside.

His ill-temper was not improved by the realisation that the morning's mail had not been opened and sorted. The day had started badly and got worse as the morning progressed. There were, or so it seemed to Mr Pigg, a great many more telephone calls and visits from the public that day which needed his personal attention and these constant interruptions did not permit him to get down to the real work of the day which was of course the collation of facts and figures and the translation of these into graph form. In reality he found himself dealing with all the innumerable daily queries which Bill Butler normally sorted out.

By lunchtime he had had enough. He was determined that the following day should not start as disastrously as the present. Although he did not wish to admit it he was beginning to appreciate the amount of work which Bill Butler usually coped with. He decided to telephone his Regional Office in order to request a relief officer to replace Bill. He realised that if he over-emphasised Bill's importance then the rather mediocre reports which he had previously given concerning his second in command might be shown to be inaccurate. He wanted to balance this impression with the other one which he always sought to give his superiors, namely that he himself was a dynamic leader of men who could cope with any problem.

The approach he adopted was to stress the pressure which the office was under. This was not really true but he was damned if he would struggle on unaided if help could be arranged. He likened his own position to that of a ship's captain without a first lieutenant. He had borrowed the analogy from a film or T.V. play but he could not remember which one nor was he sure if he had correctly quoted the naval rankings but it seemed to do the trick. He was rather pleased with himself and made a mental note to use the quotation again and even before the telephone conversation ended he was starting to believe that it was his own creation. The man at the other end of the telephone was less impressed than Mr Pigg had imagined but he was well aware of the latter's ability to talk at length on the telephone. By coincidence there was a relief officer on his books who was surplus to requirements. Preferring not to enter into any discussion whatsoever with Mr Pigg, who had on numerous previous occasions managed to waste a great deal of his time, and the department's money in telephone bills, he readily acceded to the demands made.

Mr Pigg was not to know this but congratulated himself, after replacing the telephone receiver, on his newly acquired persuasiveness. He had to admit even to himself, that in the past obtaining the approval of his Regional Office to some of his requests had often been difficult. On reflection he recalled many long telephone conversations during which he put all his points (he modestly felt with accuracy and painstaking detail) and had not been afraid to persist with his own side of the argument and even, where necessary, repeating word for word the same points several times over to ensure that the listener fully understood. If he were honest with himself and might it not have been possible on such occasions that the voice at the other end of the telephone had succumbed to his request with an exhausted sigh? Possibly, he mused to himself.

He gently smoothed his moustache with an exploratory finger and reflected on his new-found skill with words. Now he thought about it there was certainly much to be said for using analogies. For painting a picture with words. After all he thought Jesus had spoken in parables and look how important he'd become. This thought reminded him of the daily prayers which had been banned in the office some time ago much to the obvious relief of all except Mrs Balstaff. He wondered if he ought to try to re-introduce the practice and tried to think up a modern day parable which he could try out on the staff. He was totally unable to think of an original however and each time he tried the phrase 'wise and foolish virgins' kept leaping into his mind and he realised how inappropriate such stories would sound when addressed to an audience, composed of people like Mavis.

After lunch George had a message that Mr Pigg wanted to see him in his office. He made his way along the corridor and knocked on his manager's door.

"Come in," bellowed Mr Pigg from the inside. George entered and made his way to the gravy-coloured carpet. Mr Pigg was pouring over one of his beloved graphs and looked up reluctantly. "Ah, George," he shouted, so loudly and so suddenly that it made George jump. "Sit down, sit down," he commanded and so saying rose from his own chair and promptly left the room.

George was temporarily bewildered until he realised that he had gone outside the room in order to change his door sign to read 'engaged'. As he returned to his seat he must have noticed the bewilderment which was still registered on George's face. "Don't want to be disturbed, eh?" he said indicating the door with his pipe stem. He added, "I like to put the sign up when I've got someone with me. It saves other people being disappointed."

While George was figuring that out, Mr Pigg moved his graph onto the floor and replaced it with a buff-coloured file which he opened with some ceremony.

"Now, let's see, George, you've been with us a few weeks now; how are you settling in?"

George said he thought he was settling in quite well.

"Good. Good!" he said at full volume. He paused and read the file for a moment then continued, "How are you finding your colleagues? Getting on all right, are you?"

George replied that he was and that he thought they were generally a good bunch but that Bill's heart attack had been a very sad event.

Mr Pigg did not move his head but simply peered out from under his eyebrows at George. He smiled a grim smile which seemed to acknowledge the sentiment yet at the same time bore a triumphant glint which seemed to indicate that George had fallen into a well laid trap.

"Well, I'm glad you mentioned that," he said, "because I've got a special favour to ask of you." He reached for his tobacco pouch and stuffed some leaves into the black briar. He struck a match and applied it to the bowl and puffed urgently until the match burnt down. When the air was heavy with smoke he seemed satisfied and leaned back in his chair. "I see you have your own car," he said pointing with his pipe at the file on his desk.

George realised then that the file was his own personnel folder and wondered what Mr Pigg was leading up to. He confimed that he had a car.

"What sort of car is it?" asked his boss. George told him it was an old banger and he looked slightly pensive at this news.

"Have you got it with you today?"

George told him he did and wished that he would get to the point.

"Good good," he responded and then had another long meaningful look at George's file. Eventually he tore himself away from the file and closed it all together. It was as if this man found it infinitely more interesting to read a file about someone than to actually talk to that person and George found this a little disconcerting.

He leaned back in his chair again and sucked on the pipe and nodded sagely. "Yes" he said "that was a very sad business with poor old Bill." George nodded and waited. " Yes."

he repeated again " Very sad. Anyway, life must go on eh?"

George nodded again.

"Well, George, I'll tell you frankly, I don't want to have another incident here like there was this morning."

George's face registered bewilderment again.

"I refer of course to the unedifying sight of the whole of my staff littering the pavement first thing in the morning."

George's expression remained unchanged.

Mr Pigg continued. "If I didn't know better I'd have thought it was a Ban the Bomb demonstration. And that terrible noise Vincent was making with that machine of his, well! Quite honestly, George, I expected better of some of my staff and that includes you. I'm expecting great things of you, George," he confided conspiratorially. "Anyway," he went on, "I'll overlook it this once but I don't expect to see it again, OK?"

George nodded numbly, wondering what had been expected of him.

"Good," said Mr Pigg. "As long as that is understood. Now I made arrangements to collect Bill's key so that there wouldn't be any problem tomorrow morning. I think I'll hand it over to Tom Richards who seems to be the first to arrive each morning. Now I've made arrangements," he continued, "for you to collect Bill's key."

George's expression changed at last. His face now registered surprise.

"Yes," confirmed Mr Pigg, "I'm asking you to do this because, quite frankly, I think you are the right man for the job. Normally, of course, it should be the office junior who runs errands of this sort but to be perfectly honest I don't consider that I can trust Vincent with this sort of task."

George felt some sympathy for Vincent, who clearly was not a favourite of Mr Pigg and also felt slightly flattered that he should have been chosen.

This feeling was soon dispelled as Mr Pigg went on. "Now I have spoken to Bill's wife on the telephone but Bill's key is still with him in hospital. She is visiting him this afternoon and as she can't drive herself, I told her you would pop round and drive her to the hospital. You don't mind, do you?"

George said he did not but reflected that as Vincent did not possess a car then he could not seriously have been considered for the task. He marvelled at his boss's colossal nerve in imposing upon Mrs Butler's period of private tragedy rather than arrive at work half an hour earlier each day.

Half an hour later he pulled up outside the Butler house, an attractive semi- detached house forty years old. The property was in excellent condition, its paintwork having been lovingly restored each year by Bill. The garden was also in beautiful order and much bigger than the average sized garden supplied with a modern day property.

Mrs Butler was in the garden doing some last minute weeding. She was a cheerful looking woman, somewhat plump and red-faced like a farmer's wife. She thanked George for coming to her assistance and sang Mr Pigg's praises for thinking of her. "I'm terribly sorry about the office key," she volunteered, "but everything's been so topsy turvy these last couple of days that we never gave it a thought."

George, with conviction, said that he thought it wasn't that important. He thought Bill's health was much more important and enquired how he was.

"Oh quite well," she said optimistically. "He's really very comfortable and the hospital staff are very pleased with him.

George said he was glad to hear this and assisted her into the car.

When they arrived at the hospital they found Bill's daughter waiting in the corridor outside the ward among the crowd of relatives waiting for visiting time to start. She was a young lady in her late twenties who looked very much like her mother although not so plump. Her hair was dark brown whereas her mother's was grey and her figure, though not so round, already bore that rounded shape which was obviously a family trait.

She had with her her three-year-old daughter who, still endowed as she was with puppy fat, looked surprisingly like her mother and grandmother. She had the same ruddy complexion and jolly disposition. As mother and daughter greeted each other and concentrated their attention on the grandchild George was able to observe the similarities in the three generations of the Butler family. The generally cheerful disposition of the women radiated to George. Their persistently optimistic attitude gave him no indication of what was to come.

When they went into the ward the atmosphere was more depressing than he had expected. All the occupants of the beds were older males who reclined against well-plumped pillows each wearing a tired, worn expression. One bed only had screens around it and ominously this was Bill's bed. They stepped inside the screen and Mrs Butler and her daughter kissed Bill whilst George arranged chairs for them to sit upon.

Only when he sat himself down did George actually have a chance to look at Bill properly. It was a great shock. The face bore almost no resemblance to the paternal friendly one that he had looked at across the desk in the office a day or two earlier. The previously bright intelligent warm eyes were now sunk deep into dark sockets. They now looked out at the world with a dull stare and gave the appearance of complete exhaustion. The features of his face were lined and his hair, previously grey, had turned white overnight. His mouth sagged on one side in a grotesque permanent grimace and at the corner was a dribble of saliva. A tube emerged from his arm and connected to a drip feed bottle above the bed which helped to emphasise the serious condition of the occupant. George realised in one glance that Bill would not be returning to work very soon or even at all.

During the whole of their visit the patient never moved nor spoke. All the time his sad eyes were fixed upon his grandchild who, like her mother and grandmother, was quite unaware of how ill her grandfather was. Bill's wife and her daughter prattled away to each other including him in their conversation from time to time though never talking directly to him. Towards the end of the visit the women whispered earnestly to the grandchild who then stepped forward and grasped Bill's limp hand and softly muttered, "I lub you, Grandpa." The tired strained face for a second brightened up. A faint lopsided smile appeared temporarily and his hand gripped the child's tightly for a moment. A second later his face resumed the resigned defeated expression which it previously wore.

George said his goodbyes to Bill's wife in the hospital corridor. As he left she was beginning a conversation with the ward sister. "We are very pleased with your husband's progress," said the sister.

"Oh yes," she responded with her usual cheerfulness. "He is fine, isn't he?"

Chapter Six
Huw Roberts & Co

The brass plate on the door said 'Huw Roberts & Co. Solicitors'. The building was originally a three-storey Georgian town house which had seen many changes since its original inhabitants had left. The affluent days when they and their neighbours could afford to occupy such an elegant house in the small spa town had long since passed.

The once grand hallway and reception rooms which had once welcomed gentlemen and their ladies who stepped from horse drawn carriages, now accommodated a cross-section of humanity who waited nervously to see their legal advisers about all manner of daily problems.

Little remained of the former glory of the property. Viewed from outside the original charm had been lost due to the fact that the once charming brickwork had been painted over. The delightful Georgian windows with their numerous thin glazing bars had long since perished and were now replaced by modern all-weather PVC double glazed units. All that remained of the architect's original conception was the solid oak front door, but even this was now a mournful aspect. Its original handsome appearance of grained and stained natural wood with a sheen which only a latter day craftsman could achieve and with an ornate polished knocker to set it off, was now, concealed by successive coats of black paint.

Inside, nothing remained of the former elegant times save the fine staircase but here too the polisher's art had been covered by modern gloss paint. The once deep mahogany-coloured banister rails which when first installed must have reflected the warm glow of gas mantles, were now a clinical shade of white.

Gone were the chandeliers and the ornate fireplaces, which once sported large mirrors and original oil paintings in guilt frames but now only boasted a few lifeless prints and a poster advertising a local church bazaar.

On the first floor, the former master bedroom was now occupied by a struggling certified accountant whilst two of the other former bedrooms were now the studios of a professional photographer. The top floor rooms which had once housed the servants of the house, were now used as storerooms by the solicitors who occupied the ground floor, except for one which was the business premises of the 'Chivers Detective Agency'. These rooms, as in the early days of the building, were the dingiest of all.

There was a gloomy air which emanated downwards from the dusty upper floor it was as if the house itself had feelings of melancholy over the glorious days gone by. One felt that the house resented its present occupiers. Perhaps it remembered its former guests, perhaps bankers, possibly industrialists, or even titled persons who entered its portals dressed in their finery. Today it gloomily watched over a succession of petty thieves and battered wives who daily attended in the waiting rooms idly reading the unlikely magazines which were provided for their temporary diversion.

The first person a visitor would meet when entering the building was Mrs Sargent the receptionist who occupied her own individual place behind a high counter with a sliding glass screen upon it. Receptionists generally come in two classes. There are those who feel it is their function to be friendly and helpful towards those who approach them. Such persons may or may not be competent at their jobs but one definitely feels a warmth which radiates from this class. They see it as the main part of their duty to assist the public and such people are always highly regarded by those fortunate enough to be helped by them. The other type of receptionist is the one which is most often observed in professional establishments, very often in doctors' surgeries. This class regard their own jobs as being primarily guardians of their principals. They jealously protect their bosses from direct contact with the public as much as possible. Mrs Sargent belonged most emphatically to the latter category. She always contrived to throw open her sliding glass screen in the most intimidating manner. Her icy "Yes" was always calculated to discourage the most determined of inquirers. If that was not enough her manner of raising one eyebrow in a degree of complete disbelief made any visitor feel very unwelcome. She prided herself upon the fact that during her fifteen-year career with the firm no caller had gained access to her principal without her prior approval.

Mrs Sargent had joined the firm on its opening day. Mr Huw Roberts had moved into the town from South Wales and opened his one man business in a room above a local newsagent. Mrs Sargent had started with him and for the first two years had been his secretary, book keeper, telephonist and messenger. Due to the tenacity of Mr Roberts and his capacity for painstaking care for any case on which he was involved, the firm thrived and eventually moved to its present premises.

As the firm expanded and took on more staff Mrs Sargent's position in the hierarchy naturally improved. Regardless of ability or qualifications, she made it perfectly clear, by her attitude towards each new arrival that his or her position at the firm was a junior one compared to her's. The only exception to this rigid rule had to be the present boss of the firm, Simon Nibble. Since he owned the firm and paid her wages Mrs Sargent grudgingly had to pay lip service to his obvious superiority, though it was on many occasions that she reverted to the attitude which she had previously displayed towards him when he had been Mr Huw Robert's humble articled clerk.

Not that Simon Nibble had ever been humble himself even whilst occupying a traditionally humble post. Mrs Sargent had witnessed his arrival with her usual suspicion and very little about him escaped her eagle eye. She was thus able to judge immediately that he was a very ambitious young man. She noticed how he was able, somehow, to offload much of his work on to those around him yet, contrived to take the credit for any success that these others might achieve.

She noticed also the direct contrast in his entire attitude to the job compared to that of his principal. The latter was, as has already been said, of the old school. This meant he had certain standards below which he dared not fall. He approached no task with anything less than a wholly professional manner. He always addressed those around him in formal tones and never used first names for staff or clients. Every case he worked on was meticulously prepared even if it meant Mr Roberts working into the early hours of the morning, a habit which he maintained until the end. He was, in short, a man with a vocation rather than job, and as such was revered by other members of the profession. Mrs Sargent observed from the start that Simon Nibble was everything which Mr Roberts was not. This was not a wholly bad thing for Mr Roberts had had one or two traits which were not generally known by the rest of his profession or the general public. He was for example a very mean man and obtaining a wage increase from him was as difficult as robbing the Bank of England. He was also extremely fastidious and prone to irritability with his fellow workers who did not match his own impeccable standards. The cheerfully bland Mr Nibble paid his staff quite well and Mrs Sargent was always the first to admit this.

Simon's arrival at the firm of Huw Roberts & Co coincided with two very important events. The first event was a sad one, for Mr Roberts became ill and was diagnosed to be suffering from cancer.

The second event was almost equally as sad, from Mr Roberts point of view, but for everyone else it had its ludicrous side. The '& Co' part of Huw Roberts & Co, a junior partner of the firm's founder and a younger man, carefully chosen by Mr Roberts because of his strong church connections, unexpectedly packed his bags and ran away with one of his clients (a striptease dancer whom he had defended in the local magistrates court on more than one occasion), to start a new life in a different part of the country.

It was difficult to judge which of these two events had a more devastating effect on Mr Roberts. His illness was no surprise to him, for he had known of it secretly for a long time but to his own detriment had preferred to soldier on hoping that he would shrug it off. What was a shock of course was the information that it was a fatal illness and perhaps even more shocking the specialist's opinion that he would be dead within one year. As is often the case, the doctor's estimation was wildly inaccurate and took no account of his patient's hardy Celtic ancestry. As things turned out the malignant growth inside him took three and a half years to finish its grisly job.

From an onlooker's point of view the news of his partner's elopement was more of a body blow to him. To say that he was disappointed by the news was more than an understatement. He was totally shattered by it and never really recovered. By far the worst aspect of the scandal was the moral side, for he felt tainted by the goings-on about which he himself had known or suspected nothing.

To make matters worse, his partner and the stripper were both married already. The deserted wife, who attended the same chapel as Mr Roberts and his wife, immediately threw herself and her family upon that gentleman for assistance and was a constant visitor at his home where she obtained much tea and sympathy from Mrs Roberts.

The practical side of the problem presented itself to Mr Roberts very shortly in the form of an approach from his former partner (now in need of funds to support his new companion as well as his old one), to be bought out. Mr Roberts' initial reaction was to tell the man to go to blazes, but the moral problem for him was that such a solution would mean the inevitable destitution of the man's wife of whom Mrs Roberts was very fond.

In any event he knew he would have to pay him off sooner or later and so he had to borrow from his bank to do so. This was contrary to his natural instincts and was very worrying for him, particularly since his working days were numbered. From this time on Mr Roberts' aim in life (what was left of it), was to leave his own wife secure. He was reasonably successful in this direction because he owned the building in which the firm operated. He immediately conveyed this into his wife's name knowing that the rent would be a steady income for her. He also increased that income slightly by letting one of the storerooms, on the top floor to the 'Chivers Detective Agency'. Mr Chivers, the sole proprietor of this business did little or none of the work which his title implied. He was a short man with a bloated face and a dishevelled appearance. Whatever the weather he always wore an incredibly filthy gabardine raincoat and he financed his frequent visits to the nearby public house and betting shop by serving writs or divorce papers on unsuspecting people.

Perhaps the most damaging part of the whole scandalous affair from

Huw Roberts' point of view was the doubt it cast upon his own ability to judge others. Until this event he had never doubted his own ability to do this. After the dust settled he was no longer sure. His partner had been a member of his own chapel, an apparently steady man without a hint of impulsiveness in his character. If such a person could surprise and disappoint him where did that leave him in his judgement of others?

It was here that Simon Nibble scored. Before his partner's elopement Mr Roberts had his own ideas about Simon both as a person and as a lawyer, and in neither respect did he measure up to Mr Roberts' high standards. After the scandalous affair broke Simon increased his efforts to be personable and effective within the firm. Previously Mr Roberts would have seen through his rather transparent attempts to curry favour but now he was no longer sure. After all, he had been wrong about his partner so why could he not be wrong about young Nibble?

As the months went by the strength slowly drained from Mr Huw Roberts like the sand which pours through an egg timer. At first he lost his vigour and appetite, which he had previously possessed, for his chosen career. Though he still put in long hours the quality of his work was not what it had been before and he began to make mistakes. He also lost his hunger for the job and the obsessive urge to retain control of the cases he was working on. Files which he passed to Simon for some action to be taken before being returned to him, never came back. Previously he would have retrieved them himself and insisted on keeping his finger on the pulse but as his frailty became more noticeable he allowed Simon to take on more and more of his work. Gradually Simon's influence increased and as his principal's declined he introduced various innovations into the firm's procedures, much to the annoyance of Mrs Sargent. He also introduced some new clients to the firm notably Mr Eddie Sharp and one or two of his business acquaintances. The work which these clients brought to the firm was extremely lucrative but more often than not rather shady.

Mrs Sargent viewed these new clients with her usual suspicion and alarm and clicked her tongue loudly whenever Mr Sharp or his associates were ever mentioned. She took the view, some might say illogically, that people like Mr Sharp should only be represented by solicitors in their capacity as criminal lawyers. She somehow felt it was wrong for the firm to act for such a man in any other area. She knew that the criminal clients were wrong doers but felt that at least one knew where one was with a 'good honest crook'. With people like Sharp Eddie one never knew what the real truth was. She knew also that Mr Roberts, when he had been fit and healthy, had similar principles though he would have been able to express them more eruditely. As his health declined so it seemed did his concern for the strict ethics of his profession.

Eventually, inevitably perhaps the announcement was made that Simon Nibble was to become a partner of the ailing Mr Roberts. This announcement which, if it had been made twelve months earlier, would have astonished everybody, was quietly accepted as a natural thing.

Huw Roberts struggled on for another year or so always hoping that he could defeat the internal foe which was sapping his vitality and observing with a bitter irony the advantages which his new partner was taking of his own weakness. Thus it was that before the death of its captain the ship known as Huw Roberts & Co felt itself being steered into darker more dangerous waters.

So the firm dealt more often with commercial matters, particularly the buying and selling of land and property and the setting up of companies for various purposes. Since work of this nature was, on the whole, more profitable than any other, the dissatisfaction which some of the regular clients felt concerning the service which the firm offered after its founder's departure did not concern Simon Nibble. It always concerned Mrs Sargent however who expressed her concern with her single raised eyebrow and her clicking tongue.

A few days after the meeting in the hotel Sharp Eddie called to see his solicitor. "Hello Agnes, how's your love life?"

This enquiry was addressed to Mrs Sargent. She responded with a raised eyebrow which was usually sufficient to put the average caller in his place. With Eddie however it had no effect. His skin was thicker than that of the average client or even the average rhino.

"Good morning, *Mr* Sharp," she said, and the manner in which she pronounced the title somehow made it sound like a term of contempt. Her emphasis on the word Mr also implied that she disapproved of his use of her Christian name. "If you'd like to take a seat, I'll see if Mr Nibble can see you," she informed him.

"Oh, he'll see me," said Eddie with the confidence of a man who knew the amount of business which he brought into the firm. His confidence was not misplaced.

Simon Nibble sat behind a huge expensive desk with a leather top. He sat in an equally expensive matching chair which both swivelled and rocked at the whim of its occupant. The chair was large like the desk and he looked like a small boy sat in it. The cost of the desk and chair had appalled Mr Jenkins the accountant who occupied part of the first floor when he had been shown the invoice. Huw Roberts had always used Mr Jenkins to prepare his accounts, partly because he was so handy, being in the same building, and partly because he wished to give business to a man who was paying him rent. The financially careful Mr Roberts liked the idea of the money he paid to his accountant indirectly finding its way back to his own pocket. When Jenkins pessimistically informed Simon that, "The Inland Revenue will never wear this," meaning the expense of the desk and chair being set against the office expenditure account, he promptly looked elsewhere for an accountant and was gratified to find a firm who assured him that his expenditure was wholly justified. The fact that the cost of this advice was nearly four times that offered by the parochial Mr Jenkins did not seem to bother him.

"Morning, Eddie," said Simon bestowing upon his visitor the smile which indicated the anticipation of costly litigation.

"I want to sort out this business with Ken Carter," said Eddie, getting down to business straight away.

"Certainly, Eddie," said Simon, still smiling sweetly. "Let's have a coffee first, shall we?" Without waiting for a response he pressed the button on his intercom. "Can we have two coffees in here, please?" he asked the female voice at the other end of the machine. "We can't get down to real work without some lubrication, eh?" It was always Simon Nibble's policy to provide coffee for his more important clients. This was, he felt, only proper considering the business they brought to the firm. He also knew only too well that the size of the bill he would inevitably be submitting would be less of a shock if the time they spent at his office was longer. His experience told him that clients generally equated the size of the bill with the length of their interview with their adviser. It was his practice therefore in cases where a large bill was anticipated, to prolong the interview by any means possible.

The coffee arrived and was brought in by the latest employee of the firm. She was a young school-leaver whose function was trainee-typist and general dogsbody. She was the latest in a long line of such workers who seemed to come and go at regular intervals. There were several reasons for this not the least being that Simon Nibble who always assumed full responsibility for recruitment, was particularly inept at this aspect of commercial life. His priorities on such occasions were always to ensure that the potential employee was prepared to work for little or no wages and that she should be physically attractive. The former qualification he generally insisted on in order to maximise his own profits from the business, and the latter because of his desire to be surrounded by things of beauty.

Inevitably he ended up with young inexperienced workers who were very often totally unsuited to the job required of them. This never bothered him for the training of these young hopefuls he left to the capable Mrs Sargent. From a technical point of view this was good policy for that lady had forgotten more about the general administration of a law firm than Simon had ever learnt. Her abrasive character however did not endear her to anyone who was unfortunate enough to be working in a subordinate position to her.

Although then it was dislike of the low wages in general and Mrs Sargent in particular which persuaded the staff to seek their fortunes elsewhere, for reasons mainly of courtesy most gave as their explanation for leaving, that they had received the offer of a better post elsewhere. Simon Nibble was therefore blissfully unaware of the true reason for his regular turnover in personnel. To compound the misunderstanding Simon had long ago convinced himself that his firm was a breeding ground for competent young legal secretaries.

Eddie slurped his coffee noisily and watched the latest recruit reaching across Simon's large desk to retrieve some dirty cups left over from a previous interview. He belched loudly and appraised the young girl's legs from the rear rather as an expert on furniture would examine a valuable piece; critically but appreciatively. As if she were a piece of furniture he said to Simon, "Who's this then?"

"Oh, I'm sorry," he responded. "This is Mr Sharp, and this is our latest arrival, Alison."

"Alice," corrected the girl, blushing slightly.

"Yes, of course," said Simon, smiling blandly. "Mr Sharp is one of my best clients. That's right, isn't it, Eddie?"

"I should bloody well hope so, the amount of money I pay you each year," retorted Eddie. "Most of my friends call me Eddie," he confided to young Alice, who hovered with the tray of dirty cups.

"If I said you had a lovely body would you hold it against me?" Here he laughed loudly and was joined in a polite but restrained fashion by Simon. Alice turned crimson and tried not to feel too stupid but felt she had not succeeded.

Simon relieved the situation by coughing diplomatically. "Yes, well, thank you, Alison, that will be all."

Eddie watched the nubile body leave the room. "I don't know where you keep finding them all," he told Simon. "Pity her tits aren't a bit bigger. Still, give it time, eh?" he concluded with a lewd grin.

They got down to business after the coffee was finished and Eddie gave Simon a quick summary of his requirements. "I've gained an interest in Carter's businesses by buying out his sister's share at a rock bottom price. Now as far as I'm concerned he's got a thriving business, the brick works, and a white elephant alongside it. Now I know the bastard can't stand me and would fight tooth and nail to keep me out of the brick works. In any case I don't know anything about running a brick works and I'm too heavily committed to fight a stubborn bloke like Carter. What I want is an agreement drawn up for me to have the glue factory and Carter to keep the brick works for himself. The value of the land is more than the value of shares but I reckon he'll be glad to sign in order to be rid of me. What I plan to do is demolish the factory and build houses on the land. Now I know he won't negotiate with me so I want you to talk to him for me and persuade him. What I also want is some kind of clause put in the agreement to enable me to purchase bricks cheaply from him but I don't want him to know what my plans are."

Simon Nibble breathed in deeply to indicate that what Eddie was demanding was a tall order indeed.

"And don't give me any crap about it can't be done, just do it!" said Eddie abruptly.

Simon breathed again and smiled his special smile. He knew very well the difficulties involved but he also realised the commercial potential of the proposals Eddie had in mind. Already he had done a mental calculation of the conveyancing fees for a large housing estate on the land under discussion and he was as eager that the idea should succeed as Eddie.

"Let's take this one step at a time," he suggested cautiously. "Now the first thing that bothers me is the manner in which you acquired these shares. I do wish you'd consulted me instead of doing it all by yourself. You see there are certain notices which have to be served in accordance with the Companies Act. From what I've seen of the paperwork these were not served and although I told Mr Carter at our recent meeting that everything was legally tied up that does not appear to be strictly the case."

"Well that's no problem," retorted Eddie. "Draw the bloody things up now and I'll sign them."

Simon smiled paternally. "It's not that simple, Eddie. You see the notice should pre-date the acquisition of the shares and should also bear the signature of Carter's sister, eh, let me see, Mrs Pettaccini isn't it?"

"Don't worry about that," said Eddie irritably.

"I'll get Joe her husband to sign in her place and you can back-date the bloody thing. After all, he's done it before several times to my knowledge. In fact his signature is probably on more documents than hers. I'll bet he's signed more of her cheques than she has. If she signed one herself the bank would probably think the signature was a forgery."

Simon drew in his breath yet again. "I am an officer of the Supreme Court, Eddie, and as such could never be party to—"

"Don't give me that holier than thou shit," interrupted Eddie aggressively. "Just ask yourself whose work it is that brings all the money into this firm. Without me you wouldn't be where you are today. Besides, you've done things like this before. What about those land deals last year? All those nominees appointed to hold those plots. Who do you think they were? None of them exist and don't tell me you didn't know, you can't be that stupid." Here Eddie's eyes acquired a glint. "Get these documents drawn up or I'm walking out of here now and all my business goes with me!"

Simon smiled. "Now, now, Eddie, don't be hasty. Don't do anything we'll both regret. I didn't hear what you said just now and as far as I'm concerned those deals last year were all above board. The best thing I can do I think is to get these documents drawn up in blank and leave you to get them signed and dated. I will process any documents, in good faith, if you assure me that they were all properly executed. Anyway, they'll have to be witnessed."

"No problem," said Eddie, who had re-assumed a friendly air. "I'll leave all the paperwork to you, that's what I pay you for, just let me have them as soon as possible and I'll make sure they are signed and dated."

He rose to leave. He was well pleased with his morning's work. He had cracked the whip when necessary and Simon Nibble had jumped. As a parting gesture, just to emphasise who was the boss in this relationship, he added, "Bring the papers round to my house this evening, will you?"

Simon nodded and mentally added another fifty percent to the bill which he had already calculated in his mind.

Chapter Seven
Pete Powell

Pete Powell was a young man of amazing capabilities. He had a razor-sharp brain which he could turn to any problem. Surprisingly he had not done well at school in an academic sense. In every other respect he had done very well. Always a popular figure with fellows and some, though by no means all of the teachers, he had excelled at sports. He had been the captain of the school first fifteen and set school records at athletics. He had represented the school in various sporting events at county level and established an enviable record which gave him an elevated position among his peers. This reputation was very much enhanced by his individual achievement of being the only pupil in the school's history to bed one of the teaching staff. The woman in question was a young trainee gym mistress whose physical attractiveness was emphasised by the fact that she was seldom seen around the school dressed in anything other than a short skirt and singlet. Unwittingly she made herself the central figure in the erotic fantasies of every boy in the school. Only Pete Powell achieved what all the others dreamed of doing and because of this he was the school hero.

His exploits on the sporting field coupled with enthusiastic involvement in one or two other extra mural activities in which the school specialised made Pete one of the most, if not the most successful pupils to leave the establishment with virtually no academic qualifications.

This shortcoming never worried Pete himself. He came from a poor background in which there was no history of academic success nor was there any expectation of such. Pete's achievements on the sports field were regarded much more highly by his family and friends than any favourable exam results would have been. Pete lived by his own set of rules and had little regard for anyone else's. Not that he deliberately flouted the rules of others. He merely paid them lip service so long as they coincided with his own code of conduct.

As a youngster he had been interested by stories and films concerning detectives or secret agents and had always hankered after the idea of being such an agent himself. He visualised his own success as a relentless pursuer of master criminals or spies gradually piecing together the various scraps of clues available and eventually tracking down his quarry.

He didn't get the job he would have liked for two reasons. Firstly the qualifications required for anyone who wished to become a detective or a special agent were more than Pete had obtained at school. Secondly the preamble required to achieve such a position (eg several years on the beat as an ordinary police constable) did not appeal to him. He was essentially a loner who liked to achieve things by himself and preferred to keep to himself the knowledge which enabled him to do so. Although he had always wished to be a detective of some kind he had no illusions over the picture portrayed of such people by the books and films which he read and watched as a boy. In these stories, which he rightly judged to have little connection with the real world of detection or espionage, there appeared to be little emphasis upon the sort of painstaking investigative work which is surely, he felt, the requirement for a successful career in this field. The heroes, it seemed to Pete, never gathered the information to prove their cases but simply proceeded on intuitive hunches which miraculously always seemed to be correct, and merely bullied their quarries into pathetic admissions. If he were in their position he knew he would behave differently. He would use his intelligence to collate all the information he could gather. He was not interested in joining the sort of organisation which offered this sort of career however because he did not care for the discipline of such outfits or the restraints which they necessarily imposed upon their staff. He preferred to work alone and make his own decisions and not to be answerable to others.

He already practised his craft and was grateful to have a job which allowed him the time and opportunity to do so. As he had revealed to George, he had access to all the department's confidential files and he had already amassed a number of interesting dossiers on many of the more important members of the local community. These were compiled not just from the information contained in the department's files but from any source from which he could obtain details, whether legally or otherwise. He had friends and acquaintances all over the area, many in positions which gave them access to confidential information and Pete was often able to persuade them to part with snippets of information which in themselves were not particularly important, but when added to that which Pete had already gathered from elsewhere helped to build up an accurate picture of the unwitting victim.

One of the dossiers which Pete had already prepared bore the name of Eddie Sharp. The file had not been prepared for any specific purpose but Pete always knew his research would be rewarded one day. The recent conversation he had with Ken Carter in the rugby club bar, when Eddie Sharp's name was mentioned, confirmed to Pete how useful the compilation of his dossier had been.

Now he was determined to expand his file and find out all he could about Eddie. He wanted to do this for Ken Carter, a man whom he admired and was glad to assist if he possibly could. He was also happy to do it just for the satisfaction which the project held for him. At last he had a genuine assignment rather than a theoretical exercise. He had promised himself and Mr Carter that he would find out more about Eddie Sharp without alerting the latter to the fact that he was being investigated. This was how he came to be parked outside Eddie's house in the early evening.

He was not sure what useful purpose was served in surveying Eddie's house but as he had a few hours to spare he could not see that it did any harm. Something interesting might be learned. As he sat there waiting he read the file which he had previously prepared. It informed him that Eddie was a married man. It told him where he lived and what his official income and outgoings were and gave details of his assets and the amount of tax he had paid (or rather failed to pay) in the last ten years. These facts were all gained from the department's files.

In addition he had learned from a friend in another department what the official valuation of Eddie's home was. He also discovered when Eddie had purchased it and how much he had paid for it. Fortunately for Pete the property was registered land and so his friend was able to enquire of the Land Registry if there was a mortgage registered. Pete thus found out how much Eddie had paid for his house and with whom he had a mortgage and how much it was for.

Interesting though these facts were they did not tell Pete the kind of man Eddie was. This was why he was watching the house. He wanted to get the feel of the case and to size up the man in question.He waited for about an hour but observed nothing very interesting. Eddie Sharp's Victorian residence offered no great information other than the obvious fact that it consumed a great deal of electricity. Pete deduced this from the lights blazing in every room and floodlights in the garden.

Just as he was about to give up and go home a car pulled into the Sharp driveway. It was a large expensive German car. It drew up before the front doorstep and a young man in a well cut overcoat got out. He was carrying some papers and was immediately admitted. Shortly afterwards he left without the papers and Pete, having already noted the registration number of the vehicle, followed at a distance. The trail led him to an even more impressive residence only a few miles away.

He watched with interest as the electrically operated gates of the property opened automatically at their owner's approach. He parked discreetly nearby, got out of his car and walked to the gates and noted the name of the property. The house itself was not observable from the road.

The driveway curved round behind a bank of protecting trees. There were extensive lawns which were beautifully manicured. Pete had no doubt that the house was an expensive one. He also knew he had access to the details of its value etcetera through the department's files. He determined to delve a little into this matter which his instinct told him would prove most enlightening.

Thus Pete's dossier on Simon Nibble was opened. During the next week or so he found out many interesting facts concerning his subject. He played rugby with a burly Cornishman who was in the local police force. He drove a motorway patrol car and often spoke about his job to Pete in the bar after training sessions. Pete was the only one interested enough to listen and in return the Cornishman displayed a genuine interest in Pete's tales of his own romantic escapades. Some of the stories which Pete told were exaggerated but most of them had a foundation in the truth. Even if Pete did embellish his accounts of his love life, it was still a love life of infinitely more variety than that of the Cornishman whose experience with the opposite sex was very limited indeed. He relished Pete's adventures and obtained a vicarious pleasure from every salacious detail which Pete revealed to him.

Pete telephoned the Cornishman as soon as he got home and gave him the registration number of the vehicle he had seen arriving at Eddie Sharp's house. He hinted that the driver of the vehicle was an attractive female who he wished to track down for romantic reasons. The Cornishman chuckled archly and promised to run the number through the police computer. The following day he informed Pete that the vehicle was registered in the name of Huw Roberts.

"Who is that?" asked Pete.

"It's a firm of solicitors," explained his friend. "Simon Nibble is the chap whose car you spotted. It must have been his wife you saw driving. Was she a ginger haired piece?"

Pete said it was and the Cornishman enlarged on the subject of Simon Nibble solicitor. "Simon Nobble they call him down at the station," he said. "He's the local bent brief who represents all the well-known villains. All the C.I.D. hate him."

Pete also checked the local electoral list at his local town hall. He did this on the telephone and was informed that Mr and Mrs Nibble were listed as living at the address he was interested in.

He also called at the office of the district valuer which was in the same street but on the opposite side of the road. The two departments had a tradition of liaison and staff from each office was often visiting the other. Pete sought out an attractive female clerk with whom he had previously had a liaison of quite a different sort.

He persuaded her to show him the file concerning Simon Nibble's house and to permit him to photocopy the contents. He discovered that the property was registered at the HM Land Registry and telephoned another of his contacts, a clerk at the registry, with whom he was once at school and with whom he also played rugby. This person gladly assisted him, even though it was strictly forbidden to release the information requested. He checked the register and gave Pete a brief indication of the contents. He learned that Simon Nibble had a mortgage with a certain local bank in which Pete had yet another contact.

Pete's contacts were usually either men who he had been at school with or with whom he played sport, or women with whom he had slept with or whom he was still sleeping. His contact at the bank was the local manager's secretary. He had met her at a recent dinner dance organised by the local cricket club to which he also belonged. She had been a guest of one of the committee; Pete had spotted her vulnerability instantly. She was not glamorous in an obvious sort of way and yet neither was she plain. She was also very definitely not a tarty sort of girl and obviously came from a good background. She was well-dressed in the sense that her clothes were not cheap or grubby and she was neat and tidy in her appearance. Despite this however she contrived to look unfashionable and rather dowdy.

She looked a bit of a wallflower at the cricket club function which was overwhelmingly attended by men who were drinking heavily and shouting to each other loudly about their own exploits on the cricket field or on their views of other people's exploits.

There were a fair few other females present some of whom were more popular with the cricketing males. These were of a more dizzy, eye-batting variety who tended to wear rather more make up than necessary and whose necklines were very often more daringly low.

Jenny, (for that was her name) was not immediately vivacious and so at such a function her company was not so readily demanded. The other males including her committee member escort, all congregated around the other females or merely propped up the bar talking to each other. There was a depth of character to Jenny which made her more attractive, in the whole sense, than the obviously glamorous females near the bar who presently commanded the attention of the beer swilling club members.

One of Pete's talents was that he was able to recognise a girl who was capable of great sensuality when no one else, even the girl herself, had ever realised such a possibility. He was the sort of character whom women found so stimulating, both sexually, socially, and intellectually that once they embarked on a relationship with him their lives were never quite the same again.

Jenny was such a girl. She stood near the wall in the cricket club lounge bar. Pete saw her and assessed her potential at a glance. His instinct informed him that beneath the drab grey outfit was a nubile body capable of responding to his. He knew too the advantages of wooing a girl early on in the evening at such an occasion. Most of the men, he found, usually concentrated on beer consumption during the early part of the evening, and only turned their attention to the ladies present when the effects of the beer gave them the courage required to say the things which ordinarily they could not bring themselves to say to the opposite sex.

It required no courage on Pete's part to converse with women. It was something he did quite naturally and extremely well. He told them generally, though not exclusively (his approach was flexible and could be altered to meet any situation) what they wanted to hear rather than that which was the strict truth. He had an unerring instinct which always told him what it was they wanted to be told.

He certainly said the right things to Jenny that evening. She spent the whole evening talking to him and quite forgot her original escort. Pete took her home and eventually made love to her. It took a long time, by his own amorous standards but eventually he persuaded her. He was the first man to do this. For him it was a challenging and amusing conquest. For her it was an amazing and unique occasion.

Her position at the bank was an added bonus as far as Pete was concerned. But for that the relationship would probably have been no more than a one night stand. The sexual challenge was quickly replaced by a far more intriguing one. He realised that she was a girl of fundamental integrity and set about the task of undermining that character trait with all the wiles at his disposal. He found this struggle more stimulating. Certainly the victory took longer to achieve but in the end, after several weeks she had given herself fully, both body and soul to Pete and was prepared to betray her employer's confidence for her newly formed loyalty. He for his part, during the interim period before the conquest, came to appreciate that there was more to the character of this young woman than even he had supposed. Though he never loved her at all, let alone as intensely as she came to love him, he nevertheless grew to be very fond of her. It was this fondness which persuaded him not to break off their relationship. He did not see her daily or even weekly on a constant basis but he did at least continue to see her regularly. His instinct would have been to dump her but he did not obey his instinct this time.

When the occasion arose that he should need information he was pleased that he had done the right thing. Both Simon Nibble and Eddie

Sharp used the bank for whom Jenny worked and Pete was supplied with photocopies of all records and correspondence. He rewarded her by giving her the night of her dreams. His sexual drive had always been high and that night he felt particularly stimulated. He entered her and took her energetically to the edge of ecstasy a dozen times. She for her part climaxed three times for every one of his and felt throughout the whole night a delicious wantonness which she had never before experienced. It was like an Arabian night for her.

The following day during his lunch time break Pete strolled to the offices of Huw Roberts & Co solicitors to satisfy the curiosity that he now had in the affairs of that firm's senior partner. He observed the same car parked outside the office that he had seen visiting Eddie Sharp's house and satisfied himself that he had traced the right person. He examined the brass plates on the wall by the front door. He noticed that the solicitors occupied the ground floor primarily and that an accountant was on the first floor. What really interested him was the announcement on another plate that the top floor of the premises was occupied by 'The Chivers International Detective Agency'.

Chapter Eight
Lionel Witherspoon

Since Bill's illness Mr Pigg had noticed with considerable annoyance the number of unscheduled interruptions there were to his working day. These interruptions were mostly incoming telephone calls and visitors at the public counter. All such matters were previously dealt with by Bill but were now all pushed through to him.

He did try unsuccessfully to persuade his staff to divert many of these callers and get someone else to deal with them. He was thwarted in this attempt however. All incoming telephone calls were received by the typists who then transferred the caller to the correct extension. Mrs Balstaff had decided unilaterally that each incoming call which was of a type previously handled by Bill could not, by definition, be delegated downwards. It followed therefore that such calls had to be put through to Mr Pigg. When he queried the number of calls he was receiving that lady informed him in superior tones that, "I only ever transfer to you those calls which could not possibly be dealt with by someone of a lower grade."

This reply played upon his own vanity and he felt he could not authorise a delegation of responsibilities without also impliedly admitting that his own position in the department was less important than he had previously given everyone else to understand.

The callers at the public counter were met initially by Mavis. When tackled by Mr Pigg about the increasing number of people he was being expected to interview she wickedly responded by telling him that all callers who were referred to him had personally requested an audience with 'the man in charge'.

This was totally untrue but again Mr Pigg was trapped by his own vanity. Mavis knew this and delighted in referring all visitors to him regardless of whether or not an interview with the manager had been requested. This mischievous procedure was humorously observed and approved by all the staff who knew that while Mr Pigg was talking to members of the public in his room he could not be bothering anyone else.

Relief came for him sooner than he expected and in the cadaverous form of Lionel Witherspoon. Though a comparatively young man he looked prematurely old due to his spectre-like appearance. His gaunt bony face had a permanent grey pallor with darkened eye sockets which made him look a little like a skeleton. In addition the exceedingly short haircut which he favoured gave him the appearance of a concentration camp inmate.

Mavis was the first member of staff to meet him since it was she who met all callers at the public counter. The shock of his physical appearance, which usually put people off, had an immediate impact upon her. It awakened in her feelings both maternal and heroic which until this moment had lain dormant. She felt a strong instinct to clasp him to her bosom. She saw in him that which she had seen many times before in characters in films, (she went to the cinema regularly). He reminded her of the tortured hero who escapes, or is finally released from imprisonment, and is unable to adjust to normal life. Eventually he meets, or is reunited with, the girl of his dreams. With the help of the overwhelming love which flows from this extraordinary woman he is able to make that difficult adjustment and then lives happily ever after. Mavis observed all this in a single glance.

She hoped that the tremendous feeling of passion which she was experiencing was being communicated to him.

What he saw was an attractive dark haired girl with big tits and a peculiar look in her eyes. He announced himself and rather ostentatiously produced an identity card. His hands were unusual to say the least. The fingers were extremely long like those of a concert pianist and his nails were like talons. To anyone else those hands would have been a disconcerting sight, but for Mavis they merely added to the forlorn, romantic atmosphere that surrounded him.

Mr Pigg was informed of his arrival and came crashing through the general office and greeted him as though he were the second Messiah. He gripped his claw-like hand and pumped away enthusiastically. Into that handshake Mr Pigg put all his energy. It was more than just a handshake: it was his expression of all the relief he felt that he would now be able to delegate all those wretched telephone calls and interviews to somebody else and get back to the really rewarding aspect of his job namely the preparation of graphs. Witherspoon felt as if his shoulder had been caught in a machine and his facial expression bore a shell-shocked look which added to his general grotesque appearance.

"My goodness," boomed Mr Pigg gleefully. "You're a sight for sore eyes."

He then led him into his office for a confidential chat leaving the staff in the general office free to discuss the new arrival.

"Who was that?" asked Helen as soon as they had gone.

"New deputy manager," replied Mavis. "He's here on temporary relief from regional office, apparently. His name is Witherspoon. He looks young for a deputy grade, doesn't he?"

"He looks emaciated," intervened Pete.

This observation prompted Tom Richards to say, "When we went into Singapore after the war we released chaps who looked like that from the Japanese camps."

"He looks like Phil Campbell," said Vincent.

"Who on earth is Phil Campbell?" asked someone.

"He plays lead guitar for Green Gilbert," responded Vincent in a tone which indicated that he felt everyone should have known that fact.

"Well I think he looks weird," said Helen and she reflected momentarily upon the newcomer's appearance and gave a little shiver.

"Oh I don't know," offered Mavis thoughtfully. "In a way he's rather dishy."

Helen nearly choked in astonishment and said, "In a really weird way, of course."

"Well anyway," responded Mavis defensively, "he looks an interesting person."

"Phil Campbell is a very interesting person," said Vincent.

"Oh shut up, Vincent," they all chorused.

"Well I don't think he looks a bit interesting," said Pete. "In fact I think he looks like a wimp."

"Oh no!" retorted Mavis. "That's not so, is it, Tom?"

Tom Richards shrugged his shoulders. "I don't think so," he said. "It didn't seem to me that he had a limp."

"Take those bloody ear plugs out!" said Pete.

Shortly after a general commotion was heard in the corridor outside and this heralded Mr Pigg's re-appearance with his new deputy.

"May I have your attention, please," he bellowed.

The staff put down their pens and looked up.

"You'll all no doubt be as delighted as I am to learn that a replacement for Bill has been appointed. I'd like to introduce Lionel Witherspoon." Here he clapped a hand on the bony shoulder of his new deputy who stood beside him. "Lionel here has spent most of the previous five years working on an undercover basis for the 'Black Economy' section. This of course has given him a vast experience of the tricks of the trade which our tax payer friends can get up to given half a chance. He's just been transferred to this department and this is his first permanent posting and so I want you all to make him very welcome. As I say, he has considerable experience, gained with the 'Black Economy' section and I think it must be safe to say he'll be able to answer any questions you may feel you want to put to him."

This was Mr Pigg's way of saying, "Don't bother me with your queries."

And so saying, he retired to his room to pore over his beloved graphs which he had been forced to neglect in recent days.

Lionel Witherspoon installed himself in the glass house and began reading through the pile of files which poor Bill had left unresolved. It did not take him long to understand that his methods differed greatly from those of his predecessor. The content of Bill's files, and in particular the letters which he wrote, did not meet with Lionel's approval. As far as he was concerned Bill was far too friendly. They contained (as far as he could tell) too many understanding phrases and expressions of sympathy. He determined that a few changes would be made.

He looked out through the glass to the general office and found himself being stared at by most of the staff. Immediately they all pretended to get on with their work. All except the girl he had first met on arrival. She continued staring at him and grinning like an imbecile.

"There is that dark-haired girl with the big tits," he thought. "What's the matter with her, for god's sake, why is she leering like that? She must be retarded, but surely Mr Pigg would have mentioned it if she was." He held up a bony digit and beckoned her into his glasshouse.

Mavis was irresistibly attracted to waifs and strays and she had collected many of them in a life which was short yet jam-packed with experience.

A psychological explanation of her behaviour probably would make reference to a latent desire to care for or to mother the men she had met. Such an analysis would have been lost on Mavis herself. She only knew that she always felt an overwhelming desire to be nice to people who somehow (she never tried to define it) appeared to be in need of her bounty. That was why she had been temporarily attracted to George. As a new arrival he had looked lost and shy, like a little orphan boy, and so she had been only too pleased to stroke his leg for him the other day but he was not really her type she thought.

Now the new arrival, Lionel Witherspoon (what a romantic name! Like an old time movie star such as Basil Rathbone or Douglas Fairbanks), he appeared to be something really special. He had that sallow, wistful expression rather like that character, what's his name, in that famous film where he nearly dies of fever and the heroin nurses him back to health and then they marry and live happily ever after.

Both she and Helen watched Lionel Witherspoon poring over Bill's files in the glasshouse.

"Well I don't care what you think," said Helen. "I reckon you must be mad if you can see anything sexy in him. He gives me the creeps."

Mavis drew deeply on her king-sized menthol cigarette. "Oh I can't explain it. I just know when I saw him I felt all peculiar. I think he looks dreamy, just like Clark Gable without a moustache.

There came a snort from Pete who had been eavesdropping nearby. "He doesn't look anything like Clark Gable. He looks more like Ghandi or old man Steptoe," he observed.

Just then the focus of their attention looked up and gazed back at them through the glass partition. All except for Mavis looked away and pretended to be getting on with their work. She continued staring at Lionel with what she fondly hoped was a languid yet sexually smouldering look. He stared back for a short while and Mavis gave him one of her sexiest smiles. In the manner of a ventriloquist she held that smile and informed Helen with teeth clenched that, "He's watching me."

Helen kept her head buried in her work and whispered, "Well get on with your work instead of staring at him and he'll probably look the other way."

"Oh my God!" hissed Mavis without moving her lips or the direction of her gaze. "He wants me to go in there."

With some difficulty she maintained her alluring smile as she rose and made her way to the glasshouse. She felt as if she were crossing the room in slow motion or as if she were drifting on a cloud or crossing a frozen river on skates. "This is how it must have been for the heroine, what's her name, when she met Trevor Thingummy in *Brief Encounter*," she thought. She opened the glasshouse door and entered, still smiling serenely.

Lionel Witherspoon looked up in an irritated fashion.

"Wretched girl," he thought to himself. "What is the matter with her? She must be simple."

"What's your name?" he asked in a matter-of-fact voice.

"Mavis," she replied breathlessly.

"Well, Mavis," he said, "I want you to move all these files out of here please." He pointed to the piles of files which lay knee deep upon the glasshouse floor. "Send standard letter number four on every file then mark them all for bankruptcy proceedings."

"But bankruptcy proceedings aren't really appropriate for most of them, Lionel," she said. "Bill always sends them a personal letter and gives them a telephone call. He says bankruptcy proceedings are too drastic and—"

"Yes well, never mind what Mr Butler used to do. I'm here now and I'm telling you to get these files through to the typists. Get that lad out there to help you," he added, pointing towards Vincent. "And by the way, it's Mr Witherspoon to you."

Chapter Nine
The International Detective

Charlie Chivers, international detective, slurped down the remains of a lukewarm cup of instant coffee, minus milk, and belched quietly. He sat at his desk and stared zombie-like at the calendar on the wall ahead of him.

The picture on the calendar was that of a bare-breasted young girl who smiled proudly back at him. Though she could be no more than fifteen years old her breasts looked as though they had been inflated with a foot pump and it was clearly this fact that caused her to look so pleased with herself. Ordinarily the sight of this picture was guaranteed to awaken Charlie from any reverie. This day he was preoccupied. He reflected ruefully on his current financial position which was little short of desperate. The trouble was, he told himself, no quality work was coming in through the door. All he ever seemed to get was process serving which really was the fag-end of the job. Serving divorce petitions or non-molestation injunctions on errant, or sometimes violent husbands at the nearby council estate was neither lucrative nor inspiring.

What he really needed, as every self-employed inquiry agent would confirm, was a decent proportion of the more interesting type of investigative work. More specifically he required the sort of job which offered him more opportunity to charge a higher rate for his services. The sort of job that really paid well was the kind where one was asked to find out all one could about somebody and then report back. Perhaps also to give a financial status report or perhaps a security reference on a person. Jobs like that could take as little or as much time as one cared to spend and the only restriction was the amount of money the client was prepared to spend. Thus, if one was checking up on a subject and the financial limit of one's investigations was say £200 then it followed that that was the amount the punter would have to pay regardless of the time spent in obtaining the information. He knew that he could often discover a great deal about a quarry without moving from his own desk. It was more of that kind of work that his business needed.

Serving papers on council house yobos was not the sort of work which tested an international detective.

Charlie did not appear to appreciate how bizarre his grandiose title sounded in view of the modest premises which he occupied. What he did appreciate however was one of the prime rules of the advertising world, namely that one should immediately attract the interest or curiosity of the public. The general public he felt just did not realise the nature of the everyday work which private detectives had to carry out. He knew that when most people thought of private detectives they conjured up images of Sherlock Holmes or Philip Marlow type characters who consistently solve crimes which always baffled the top brains in the police force. The reality of the profession was far removed from these fictional images. He spent most of his time carrying out mundane tasks which could be performed by the local postman. He always resented what he regarded as a terrible waste of his own talent.

He continued to stare at calendar girl's breasts without really seeing them. He had a wistful glazed look in his eye. He reflected on his own wasted chances in life and his former wife Beryl came into his mind. She had once had a bosom like the calendar girl he recalled. In fact, in retrospect he realised that it was her breasts, not her, that he had fallen in love with. It became immediately apparent to him, after they had married, that he liked very little else about her.

When they had married he was a uniformed policeman but shortly after their marriage he had transferred to the C.I.D. It was there that he found his true vocation in life which was frequenting the bars in most of the inns and public houses in the area in an attempt to make contacts and pick up items of information concerning the activities of criminals. He worked day and night at this particular aspect of his trade and was fairly successful. It did however put a severe strain upon the marriage and in what later proved to be a naive gesture to patch things up, he and Beryl decided to start a family. They had a little girl whom they named Dorothy, after Beryl's sister. The arrival of the baby increased rather than relieved the tension between them. She was a fractious baby who suffered from colic. Beryl had post-natal depression and was physically exhausted by the difficult birth and the demands of an equally difficult baby.

He continued to stay out all day and each evening and always returned late at night and often drunk.

Beryl would be at the end of her tether when he finally returned each night and they would then shout and scream at each other and eventually wake the baby who would then join in with the screaming. Beryl did not understand why he could not be of more help to her in her period of strain, and he could not understand why she did not appreciate that he was only doing his job and earning lots of overtime money.

The marriage dragged on for a year or so and eventually Beryl returned to live with her parents in a different area of the country. She took Dorothy with her and later divorced him from a distance. He did not defend the petition, partly because he had no wish to and also because the police force did not encourage its members to be parties to any court proceedings.

After Beryl's departure his lifestyle went from bad to worse. In addition to his day time and evening visits to public houses he began to frequent night clubs into the early hours of each morning. He never paid Beryl any maintenance, not because he refused to do so but because his affairs were in such a mess. Beryl's parents supported her for a while until she eventually met another man, a hard working self-employed businessman who was able and willing to support Beryl and Dorothy. They soon married and no further contact, beyond Christmas cards sent for only the first couple of years, was maintained.

After that his life had been a downhill slide for several years. His excessive drinking and one or two other problems had caused him to be drummed out of the force. Of course he had not been sacked. He had been 'persuaded to leave'.

He recalled the expression used at the time which was a typical police euphemism rather like, 'helping the police with their enquiries'. He had only himself to blame and even at the time he had acknowledged this fact. But even after the passage of time he still felt resentment over the treatment he had suffered.

He reflected wistfully that Dorothy, whom he had not seen since the day her mother had taken her away, would now be eighteen years old and he wondered what she was like now.

His mind returned to the present and his eyes slowly re-focused upon the object in his line of sight, the calendar girl's breasts. He gave a silent lustful grimace and then dug deep into his inside pocket and came up with a packet of Manikin cigars. He opened the packet carefully and removed from it the butt of a partially smoked cigar. He lit this and remained seated, still in reflective mood and still staring at the calendar girl.

Yes, he thought, one way or another he had had a raw deal in life. There had been a number of body blows from which he had never really recovered. The first had been the marriage breakdown of course. Beryl had never properly understood him or the nature of his job. The divorce proceedings had forced him to sell the house and give her all the proceeds. After that he had moved into a small dingy bed sitting room in which he still lived. The next big problem in his life had been losing his job in the police force. His drinking, poor timekeeping and the number of debts which he had managed to run up with local bookmakers, were listed among the reasons for his proposed dismissal. He knew however that basically the problem had been a personality clash between himself and that bombastic inspector who had done his utmost to have him thrown out of the force and had finally succeeded. In the end he had agreed to resign in order to salvage a reduced pension. Life had been cruel it was true. Here he was, a fifty-year-old with no prospects, struggling to make a living. All he owned was a few sticks of furniture in the pokey bedsitter which, for the want of a better expression he called home. In fact his dusty office premises were more like home to him since he spent most of his time there. Many nights he slept on the old sofa in the corner of his office in preference to returning to bedsit land. He preferred the absolute solitude which the office premises offered at night.

He also liked to take advantage of the privacy which the moonlight hours afforded and appraise himself of any useful information which might be contained in the files of the accountant on the floor below and those of Huw Roberts & Co solicitors, his landlord. He felt slightly guilty about peeping into the accountant's files, but after all it was a dog eat dog world and he had to obtain his information (the tools of his trade), from whatever source he could. He had no qualms however about inspecting Simon Nibble's confidential records since he regarded his landlord with considerable contempt.

His dislike of the man was instinctive and, if he were honest with himself, contained more than a little jealousy that one so young should do so well materially whilst he himself was virtually penniless. He would not have minded so much if it had not been for the supercilious attitude of the man. He remembered Huw Roberts himself, after whom the practice was named, and recalled with fondness his friendship with the man. Quite often Huw would ascend to the office on the top floor, usually under the pretext of searching out a document from the storeroom, and engage Charlie in conversation. This would usually be in the evening when the rest of the workers had gone home. They would talk together for a long time and inevitably Huw Roberts would inform him that he had some work for him. In those days he carried out all the enquiry work which the firm had. When Huw Roberts died and Simon Nibble took over, the amount of work which the firm passed up to the top floor reduced dramatically.

Charlie Chivers knew that Simon Nibble used another enquiry agent. In fact he had seen the evidence of this in Simon's own files. He had been told by Simon that the amount of suitable work of that kind had reduced since the death of Huw Roberts due to the fact that he (Simon Nibble) had decided to lay more emphasis upon conveyancing work which was more lucrative and less troublesome.

There was some truth in this explanation, but it did not convince Charlie who deeply resented the reduction in the instructions received from down below. He made no secret of his dislike of Simon Nibble who generally only sent work upstairs which required urgent attention. Usually it was the sort of work which no one particularly wanted and it was clear that the cream of the firm's work went elsewhere.

Charlie had long ago acquired for himself a set of duplicate keys to all the rooms in the building and so at night was free to delve into all the files and records thus available. He was always careful to wear a pair of washing-up gloves whilst doing this in order to avoid leaving fingerprints. He had not been in the police force and learned nothing. He was entirely undisturbed during these night time sessions and was secure in the knowledge that the building itself was equipped with a burglar alarm. Thus he knew that if any occupant of the building returned unexpectedly late and entered the premises the alarm would sound. He also knew that whilst whoever it was who had entered the building was making their way to the alarm control box (situated in a broom cupboard at the rear of the ground floor), he would have the opportunity to retire unseen to the top floor. In fact he had never been disturbed.

His nefarious inspections of Simon Nibble's files had confirmed what his instincts had already told him. The solicitor had few scruples and was prepared to indulge in any skulduggery which promised a profit for himself. The files also showed that he was extremely good at covering his own tracks. The International Detective however had amassed photocopies of all incriminating documents. This acquisition had gone on for a number of years and was a common continuing process. He regarded it as his own insurance policy.

He was glad to have this form of insurance since he did not trust Simon any further than he could throw him. He knew that the lease on his office would be coming up for review within another year and he also knew that his landlord would have no qualms about evicting him if he could. Huw Roberts had always assured him that as long as he (Huw Roberts) was alive, then Charlie Chivers was assured of a place to work. He had no illusions that his present landlord would honour this promise. He took a last long drag on his Manikin and made a decision:

"Ah well," he said, presumably to the calendar girl, "time to go down the pub I think."

Chapter Ten
Changes in the office

There were a number of changes brought about in the office as a result of the arrival of Lionel Witherspoon. The effect he had upon the office environment varied according to which opinion one canvassed.

If one asked Mr Pigg what effect Lionel's presence had made one would receive a firm and positive response, for that gentleman was genuinely convinced that Lionel had arrived in the nick of time. It was not just the fact that Lionel's presence allowed Mr Pigg more time to be with his beloved graphs and also more time to chat on the telephone with colleagues in other offices. After all, Bill had achieved all that before him and shielded Mr Pigg from the bulk of work and responsibility.

What Lionel did, which Bill could never hope to achieve, was to match in character what Mr Pigg regarded as the archetypal revenue man. In other words he was an absolute bastard.

This affected the rest of the staff in a variety of ways. Mr Pigg as we have already learned was favourably impressed by the new arrival. He felt that he possessed the required amount of steel inside which was always lacking in Bill Butler. He was also strongly of the opinion that a hard edge was what his department lacked and so Lionel Witherspoon's arrival was fortuitous as far as he was concerned.

Also he secretly felt that Bill Butler had become a little stale and had not provided him with the sort of dynamic support he felt was appropriate. True, he always did the bulk of the donkey work leaving him (Mr Pigg) to deal with the more important issues and to take decisions where necessary but he had always felt that a little more was needed. He had never known exactly what until Lionel arrived but now in retrospect he was able to realise that what he had always needed was a ruthless lieutenant to supply that added something to the persona of the office. If he were completely honest with himself he was glad to see the back of Bill Butler but he was wise enough not to say so. As far as the typists were concerned Mr Witherspoon's arrival had a great effect upon their working day. Mrs Balstaff was a changed character since his arrival. She deplored the change in the type of work which she and Penny were required to carry out. Under Bill Butler, in her eyes, the work had been interesting and varied. Each letter on each file had been different and individual and gave interest to the job.

Since Lionel's arrival no individual or specific correspondence was issued any more. Every file which entered the plant-infested room was marked 'standard letter 1' or 'standard letter 2' etcetera. The standard letters were pre-printed to a large extent and required only the insertion by the typists of the name and address of the tax payer, the reference number, and the details of the subject matter of the letter.

Mrs Balstaff correctly felt that this reduced not only the volume but the quality of the work. She rightfully perceived that she had become no more than a name and address inserter whereas previously she had been a chronicler. The reduction in the volume of work left her spare time in which to reflect upon the alteration in the quality of duties she was required to carry out. She thus had time upon her hands which she used partly by paying more attention to the plants in the room (a task previously neglected when Bill Butler dictated letters) and more particularly by haranguing Penny as to the deplorable drop in standards at the office since Lionel Witherspoon's arrival. She went on at length day after day about job satisfaction in general and Lionel in particular.

Mrs Balstaff regarded Lionel as a loathsome young man without finesse or style and she may have been correct in this judgement. If she were it mattered little to the man himself who was single minded to a degree which even Mr Pigg himself could not aspire.

Penny was also greatly affected by the changes but not in the exact same way as her companion. If she were totally honest with herself (which she was not) she would have admitted that she did not mind the reduction in the individually dictated letters from Bill Butler. In truth she rather preferred a job which required her merely to operate almost as an automaton. If she were honest and frank the quality of the work mattered little to her and job satisfaction (apart from the satisfaction of taking home her pay cheque), did not concern her.

But Penny was never brutally honest with herself let alone with her colleague who was, after all, a much stronger character than herself. She was totally unable to resist the opinion and reaction of Mrs Balstaff to the change in procedures and found herself daily listening to, and agreeing with, the strongly expressed criticisms of Lionel and everything he stood for. The older woman regarded him as vulgar and insensitive and 'lacking in breeding'.

Mavis was greatly influenced by Lionel's arrival. In all her young life she had never before experienced complete indifference to her own overt sexuality. She was used to men tiring of her after a short while: of men who initially purported to be interested in her or something other than her obvious sexual attractions and later losing interest in those merits. She never fooled herself into thinking that she was an intellectual giant but she at least, at a very early age, learned instinctively what it was that men liked and yearned for which is something that most women go a whole life without beginning to understand. What she understood was that most men like to be pampered and made to feel like a man rather than an insignificant worm which the majority of women insist upon. Mavis learnt very early that if she offered her obvious assets in an obvious way (most men she found were not too subtle) she was appreciated and desired more than her contemporaries.

What she had no experience of however was being completely ignored by a man. Even Pete Powell, who was too good looking and desirable to be expected to fall under any sort of spell which Mavis was capable of casting, had succumbed to her sexuality and had several times treated her to a romantic experience in the cellar below the building, the like of which she had rarely enjoyed anywhere else despite her vast experience. Pete of course was extremely muscular and also possessed of great experience in sexual affairs and knew exactly how to please, a woman.

Lionel however appeared to be completely indifferent to her considerable assets and it was undoubtedly his indifference which fuelled Mavis's interest in him. Whether she realised it or not it was his lack of interest in her which fascinated her and she resolved to seduce him out of his state of disinterest. This she contrived to achieve by constantly managing, whenever Lionel looked out of his glasshouse, to be gazing back at him with a dreamy heavy-lidded expression which Lionel was supposed to find sexy. In fact he became more and more exasperated by the fact that every time he looked up she appeared to be doing no work.

Poor Vincent was affected most of all by Lionel's arrival. Previously he had always enjoyed the sympathetic indulgence of Bill Butler who, although spotting Vincent's shortcomings had chosen to ignore them so long as the smooth running of the department was guaranteed. With the quantity of work continually diminishing it was difficult for anyone, even someone of Vincent's unique abilities, to totally disrupt the smooth flow of the department's business. On that basis Bill never saw any point in taking Vincent to task for each and every mistake made but would confine himself to quiet fatherly chats with him on the few occasions when Vincent had done something, or failed to do something, which could not be ignored.

Lionel Witherspoon was less pragmatic and also had less sensitivity. It did not matter to him that the office was well able to carry an incompetent such as Vincent whilst the work of the department was contracting. All he could see was inefficiency and he was quite unable to overlook it. Consequently not one day passed following Lionel's appointment when

Vincent was not summoned to the glasshouse and given a severe reprimand for some error or oversight. Lionel's method of inviting people into his glass domain was to bang on the glass with his own spectacles and then to point to the person who he wished to talk with. Vincent was the person most frequently summoned in this way and unfortunately Lionel never thought to close the door to the glasshouse when reprimanding him. Thus, all staff members in the outer office were able to overhear the conversations in the glasshouse and the discomfort of Vincent was witnessed by all.

Even Pete Powell who was far too intelligent to be discovered in an error by the likes of Lionel found that his activities were somewhat curtailed by the latter's presence. Whereas, under Bill Butler's regime Pete had total freedom to come and go as he pleased he found that Lionel was less easy-going and so his visits to the cellar/storeroom for research purposes were not so frequent.

Only the aged Tom Richards was completely unaffected by Lionel's presence.

Chapter Eleven
The Jubilee Inn

Just around the corner from the office of Huw Roberts & Co solicitors was a narrow road, called somewhat appropriately Small Street, which at first glance appeared to be a dead end street. A closer look showed that the fenced off area at the end was in fact the boundary of a small public park. Tucked away in the far corner of the street was a small wicket gate which led into the park.

The main entrance was in another part of the town. The geography of it made the park and the surrounding buildings in Small Street a busy pedestrian thoroughfare. On each side of the street leading away from the park were half a dozen or so small terraced Victorian houses which had previously been allowed to decay but which in recent years had received the kiss of life in the form of local government improvement grants. Next, after the private houses, on one side of the street was a small ironmongers' premises and on the opposite side a betting shop. Next in turn came a wool shop which faced a newsagents and tobacconists. Finally on opposite corners of the street were a greengrocers and the Jubilee Inn.

Many people walked down Small Street for more than one reason. A great number who did so probably used it as a short cut to the other end of town. If they did they were probably glad they had done so for the floral displays in the park were always a joy to behold.

Charlie Chivers seldom if ever got further than the corner of Small Street. More precisely, the threshold of the Jubilee Inn. If he ever did manage to pass the doorway of that establishment it was only to visit the betting shop.

The interior of the Jubilee Inn, of which Charlie had an intimate knowledge, was not an awe-inspiring sight. The single bar-room was very cramped. Its low ceiling was stained a rusty brown colour by years of tobacco smoke. The few seats which occupied one wall were velvet covered. The velvet, once bright vermillion was now the colour of old port wine with the shine of old age upon it. Matching heavy velvet curtains hung at the windows, blocking out any of the daylight which would otherwise have penetrated the unwashed glass in the small windows.

The licensee was a short rotund man with a shiny red complexion not unlike the appearance of his own velvet cushions. His name was Hubert

Reginald Partridge. He was known to one and all as Reg. Judging from the evidence of all the interior walls of the Jubilee Inn, Reg was known to a great many people. Upon the walls were many photographs all of which had one thing in common. They all depicted Reg Partridge himself in companionable poses with a variety of well-known people.

At first glance a casual observer would be unlikely to realise that Reg was featured in each and every photograph. This was due to the fact that the pictures covered a considerable period of time; Reg Partridge's lifetime in fact.

A non-regular could hardly be expected to realise for example that the small freckle-faced boy in khaki uniform shaking the hand of Baden Powell himself was none other than the licensee of the premises. Similarly, it was unlikely that anyone, even the most sharp-eyed observer, would recognise the man who now pulled their pints, among the throng of 'desert rats' grouped, around a tank atop of which stood Field Marshall Montgomery.

The more recent photographs all revealed the unmistakable presence of Reg Partridge licensee. The portly features, the crimson bald head the benevolent 'mein host' expression all indicated a man who was at home in the company of others, especially if those others were well known.

A closer inspection of the pictures also showed that many of them had messages written upon them. 'Best wishes, Reg. You're no dummy. From Peter Brough and Archie Andrews', written upon the photograph of Reg shaking hands with a ventroliquist's dummy.

There were pictures of Reg with famous people from just about every walk of life. Mainly there were show business or sporting personalities, but there were also politicians and many others. In each and every picture the rosy red corpulent features of Reg were to be seen beaming at the camera lens. This amazing collection of photographs was a never-ending source of interest to the patrons and their landlord at the Jubilee Inn. For every picture Reg could recount a fascinating anecdote concerning his meeting with a well-known personality.

Reg had an easy going manner and ability to converse with anyone from whatever social level. He also had an infectious laugh which he would employ frequently during his own stories. The result was that any tale he told usually brought the house down. His character was thus admirably suited for his profession and his modest establishment brought him more than a modest living. He had a great number of interests which included membership of many clubs and societies, and he frequently took the odd day off from the bar of the Jubilee Inn to attend various functions. Invariably he returned with a new photograph for the wall and an anecdote to cheer his regulars.

It was to this cheerful atmosphere that Charlie liked to repair during the early part of each evening. When everyone else went back to their homes and families he joined that little band of twilight tipplers who met whilst the rest of the world enjoyed their evening meal. He always convinced himself that this was a preferable time to have a drink because the pub was less crowded than at the latter end of the day. He usually intended to merely have the one, or possibly two, drinks and then retire early, but inevitably this resolve weakened in the face of invitations to have one for the road.

"Evening, Charlie," called Reg cheerfully as he entered the bar. "Usual is it?"

"Yes, please," he replied and held the door open for a young man who had followed him in. He took a place upon a high stool at the bar and so did the young man.

Reg pulled a pint of best bitter for Charlie and whilst he served the young man he continued to converse with the detective. As the landlord spoke Charlie took an enormous swig of his beer which half emptied his glass. He belched silently and wiped the froth from his mouth with the back of his hand. He began tapping his pockets, searching for something. After some trouble he located it in his inside jacket pocket. He dug into it and came up with his packet of Manikins. He slowly opened the packet and looked inside with the same amount of care which a scientist would exhibit when examining a slide under a microscope. He produced another cigar butt and ceremoniously licked it. He then discarded the packet and ordered another from Reg.

"Yes," said Reg as he handed the fresh packet over and accepted the money.

"I decided to take the day off and take the wife to see her mother, and that's why I wasn't here yesterday. After all," he added, "I'd promised to take her for months and quite honestly I'd run out of excuses for not doing so. In any event I managed to get another snapshot," he said, indicating a photograph on the wall behind him which depicted Reg shaking hands with someone who Pete vaguely recognised but was unable to identify.

"Who's that then?" asked Charlie, who also seemed unable to recognise the man shaking hands with Reg.

"That," said Reg, "is your local M.P. and shame upon you for not knowing him. No wonder the country is going to the dogs when locals don't even recognise their own representatives."

Pete studied the photos on the wall and actually realised that they were all pictures of Reg together with someone at least moderately well known. He gave a sigh of recognition and began pointing at the photographs.

"These are all pictures of you," he said. "I was mistaken. At first I thought they were all simply pictures of famous people but now I realise that they are all pictures all famous people being bored to death by a short fat chap with a bald head."

All the regulars laughed and so, to his credit, did Reg. It is an essential requirement of a successful publican that he should be able to laugh at himself. Reg was a successful publican and his amusement in response to the young man's unexpected attack, was genuine.

"Seriously though," added the young man, "you have certainly met some well-known people. It's an impressive gallery. Isn't that Barry John?" he asked, pointing out one particular photograph.

"Yes, that's right," confirmed Reg. "Are you interested in rugby then?"

"Well, yes, you could say that. I do play for the local club."

Charlie clicked his fingers loudly and pointed at the young man. His eyes narrowed until they were almost closed to indicate that he was involved in some mental calculation. "Powell," he said finally. "Yes, you play stand-off, don't you? I often watch the local side."

Pete Powell nodded. "Not quite in his class though, I'm afraid," he said, indicating the picture of Reg with Barry John.

"Now there was a player " said Charlie with fervour. "Finest fly-half I've ever seen."

Pete said he agreed with him and offered to buy him a drink. Charlie said he didn't mind if he did and Reg gave him another pint.

The conversation centred upon rugby football for a while since it was apparent that the subject was one of the international detective's favourites. Later they discussed the photographs which festooned the walls of the Jubilee Inn and marvelled, like so many before them, that Reg could have managed to meet and be photographed with such a number of well-known people. Pete expressed doubts that the photographs were genuine but Charlie assured him that they were.

"Yes, I've had a good look at them and they're definitely not doctored," he assured Pete. "I was in the police force for a number of years and I know all about the methods of falsifying photographs and believe you me those are genuine. Actually, the number of pictures is not so surprising once you know that Reg is keen on amateur drama and helps out backstage at the local theatre. Sooner or later anyone who is anyone in show business comes to this town's theatre and when they do Reg gets them snapped."

"So you were in the police were you?" asked Pete, glad to have the opportunity to turn the conversation to the detective's profession.

"That's right," replied the detective. "Twenty years' service. Then I decided to branch out on my own." He plunged his right hand into his left-breast pocket of his sports jacket and produced a card which he handed to Pete. The latter studied the card carefully. He did not return it to Charlie but put it in his own back pocket.

"Let me see," he said, casually quoting the address of the detective's office. "Isn't that just around the corner from here?"

"That's it," said Charlie, "my office is up above those of Huw Roberts & Co solicitors."

"Huw Roberts," repeated Pete very slowly, as if trying to remember something about the name. "What sort of solicitor is he?"

"Was," corrected Charlie. "He's dead now, but when he was alive he was a bloody good one. Which is more than can be said for the young smart-ass who took over from him."

"Another drink?" enquired Pete and reached for the detective's tankard.

Charlie produced another Manikin which he lit and then gulped down a third of his ale. He took a deep drag upon his cigar and expertly blew some smoke rings. As he gazed at the wall behind the bar he was suddenly reminded of something. "That's definitely my favourite," he said, pointing to a photograph of Reg arm in arm with a scantily clad model girl whose bosom could only be described as enormous.

Pete could see what it was that the detective found so interesting in the picture but he did not wish to change the subject.

"You were saying," he said in an effort to divert his attention away from the model girls breasts.

Charlie reluctantly transferred his attention back to Pete. "I could tell you things about that firm that would make your hair curl," he imparted confidentially, and took another deep draft of his ale.

Pete listened attentively to all that his new drinking companion had to say. There was a good deal which he had to say, much of it concerning his years in the police force and his resentment towards that authority. He learned a good deal about the methods employed by a private detective. He learned also a good deal about the disappointments of an estranged husband and father. He also learned a considerable amount about the character of the detective who, it turned out, was a philosopher by nature.

"Par for the course," he observed after relating to Pete his unfortunate report of the last twenty years of his life.

In amongst all the items of information Pete also learned a great many things about Simon Nibble. He was much too canny initially to press for any information on that particular subject. For a long while he allowed the conversation to range over a wide variety of subjects including rugby football, large-breasted girls (Charlie's favourite subjects) and the police force with its shortcomings, and the difficulties of serving legal documents on people resident in non E.E.C. countries. Pete skilfully brought the conversation back to matters legal and lawyers in particular on many occasions without the detective realising. Each time he would learn a little more about Simon Nibble.

Charlie Chivers was a man who had always been able to hold his liquor. Such an attribute is something a great many men are often proud to boast about and he was no exception. It was not however a strictly accurate boast. Many years of habitual daily drinking had given him the ability to with stand, temporarily, the effects of alcohol. In other words it took him longer to get drunk because he was more used to the stuff. In that sense he could certainly hold his liquor. In the strictly literal sense however he could not.

He had suffered for many years with a weak bladder which meant that he was totally unable to hold much more than an egg cup full of any liquid in his own body for more than a few minutes without visiting the toilet.

This complaint was, to a small extent, a contributory factor in the breakdown of his marriage. His weak bladder would cause him to wake several times each night in order to visit the bathroom. Each time he returned he would find himself aroused by the sight of his sleeping wife and would attempt on each occasion to encourage her into some sexual foreplay. She was not a particularly sensual person, especially whilst half asleep in the middle of the night, and invariably refused to respond and the couple usually ended up arguing.

With such a physical problem it seemed ridiculous that he should choose to drink pints of bitter every night but it never occurred to him that this was illogical. He simply regarded his own frequent visits to the toilet with a philosophical air, never stopping to question the necessity of these journeys. Pete took full advantage of these constant departures by disposing, on each occasion, of the contents of the glass he was holding. Whilst the detective was out of sight he managed each time to pour some of his drink into Charlie's glass and dispose of the rest into a giant earthenware jar which stood next to him and contained a sorry looking aspidistra. Thus, each time the detective reappeared he had a full pint to consume whereas Pete had apparently just finished his own.

It seemed no time at all before Reg was calling last orders and exhorting his regulars to, "Go home to your wives or your loved ones."

Charlie stared myopically at his wrist watch in apparent astonishment and disbelief. "Ish it that time already?" he asked the room in general.

"It certainly is," confirmed Reg, who was wiping down the bar and collecting empty glasses. "Now come on, Charlie, drink up or you'll get me into trouble; you know the law as well as I do."

Charlie gave an ironic snort and searched his pockets for some money. He pulled out a ten-pound note. "Give us a small bottle of whiskey, Reg," he implored. "It's too early to stop drinking."

Reg sold him the bottle and Charlie stepped off his bar stool and stumbled and fell down. Pete helped him to his feet but Charlie waved him aside.

"I'm not drunk," he assured his helper and his landlord ,who had leaned across his own bar to observe Charlie on the floor.

Despite Charlie's protestations Pete insisted that he would help him on his way and Reg nodded reassuringly.

"Ah well," said Charlie with a resigned air. "If you insist. We'll finish this bugger off, eh?"

He held the whiskey bottle aloft. With Pete's assistance he made his way from the Jubilee Inn to the offices of Huw Roberts solicitors just around the corner.

Chapter Twelve
Charlie and Pete Compare Notes

Charlie Chivers fumbled for his keys. He had some difficulty in locating the keyhole and when he did the key did not work. He swore under his breath and tried two or three keys before the lock yielded. "Follow me," he grunted and pushed open the door. Pete followed him in and was immediately startled by the wailing of the burglar alarm. Charlie made straight for the broom cupboard and threw the alarm switch. "Thash better," he muttered and then re-set the alarm. He fingered his nose and whispered, "Shan't be dishturbed now, eh?"

He led the way to his own office on the top floor. Once inside he crossed to the window and pulled down a wartime blackout blind. He then switched on his desk lamp and indicated a chair for Pete to sit in. He moved across the room to a door which led into a small toilet. After a few moments there was the sound of a flush being pulled and Charlie re-emerged carrying two chipped mugs which he placed on his desk. He opened the whiskey bottle and poured two drinks and passed one to Pete. He took the other drink and walked over to the couch and stretched himself out. He produced a Manikin which he lit, took a huge swig of the whiskey, put the mug down on the floor beside him and leaned back. He drew hard on his cigar and blew a smoke ring towards the ceiling.

Charlie gave a long sigh which seemed to indicate that he was exhausted. Pete surveyed the dingy dusty office and lied unashamedly. "Well, I must say this is a very nice place you've got here."

Charlie remained flat on his back and continued to stare at the ceiling. He gave another long sigh but otherwise made no comment.

"It's very handy for the shops," Pete continued, "but I expect the rates are pretty steep in this area."

Charlie still stared at the ceiling and took another deep drag on his cigar. "Yeah it suits me," he said non-committally.

After another long silence Pete tried again. "And how do you get on with those downstairs?" he enquired casually.

Charlie took another deep draw upon his manikin and blew yet another smoke ring. "Like I said before. I wouldn't trust them with my cat." He took a last puff of the cigar and sat upright. He stubbed it out against the sole of his own boot and tossed the butt into a nearby waste bin. "And I haven't even *got* a cat," he added with emphasis.

Pete realised that he didn't sound or appear to be as drunk as he had been earlier in the evening. He persisted however with the subject of Huw Roberts & Co solicitors or more particularly Simon Nibble, and whilst not being especially informative Charlie at least did not appear to mind discussing his landlord.

After a while Pete considered that he had hedged around the subject for long enough and decided to come straight to the point. "It's quite a coincidence, you being a private detective and working at this particular address," he observed.

"Oh?" said Charlie. "And why is that?"

"Well," began Pete tentatively, "I happen to know someone who would be very interested to learn one or two facts about Mr Nibble and his affairs and who might be prepared to pay you to supply those facts."

"Meaning Ken Carter, no doubt?" enquired Charlie, looking Pete straight in the eye for the first time that evening. The remark was like a well- aimed arrow which struck deep into the heart of the listener. It came like an electric shock and internally Pete was completely non-plussed. Externally however his icy cold blue eyes never wavered and he returned Charlie's inquisitive gaze with apparent indifference.

"My god, but you're a cool one," observed Charlie nonchalantly. "I spent umpteen years of my life interrogating villains but I never met one with your nerve."

Pete's features were unchanged as he continued to meet the detective's gaze without flinching. Gradually a tentative smile appeared on his lips. It was not however a smile of admission but a smile which contrived to express amused curiosity.

Charlie was not taken in and he let Pete know.

"Oh come on!" he cried with more than a hint of contempt in his voice. "You must think I was born yesterday."

Pete now managed to look slightly bemused but Charlie was having none of it.

"I'm not as green as you think," he informed Pete. "You needn't think I didn't notice that you kept topping up my drink over at the Jubilee. And don't think I was unaware that you kept turning the conversation back to Simon bloody Nibble. Oh, I'm not saying you were not reasonably good at it, but you seem to forget that being devious is my job and has been all my life. Don't try to teach your granny how to suck eggs, lad."

Pete by now had completely regained his composure and smiled again. This time his smile was more genuine. He recognised a kindred spirit and was not at all abashed by Charlie's assessment of him. All he was really interested in was finding out how Charlie had discovered that he was snooping on behalf of Ken Carter.

He assumed that he himself must have inadvertently dropped a clue during the evening although he was certain he had said nothing to indicate such a fact. If he had it must have been a very obscure clue and Charlie must be amazingly intuitive. His assessment of Charlie would need to be drastically revised. Having spent the evening with the detective he had, wrongly it seemed, put him down as a man of limited intelligence. Clearly he would have to change his opinion for Charlie Chivers had put his finger right on the button.

Pete's mind worked feverishly as he recalled the contents of their conversation throughout the evening but this only confirmed in his own mind what he already knew. He had not given anything away and there was no possible way that the detective could know that he was making enquiries on behalf of Ken Carter. Nobody knew, not even Mr Carter himself. Pete was simply doing a bit of sleuthing by himself and had informed no one. And yet this seemingly average little man had discovered his secret mission quite effortlessly. Pete was both impressed and exceedingly curious.

"You're wondering how I know," Charlie informed him matter of factly.

Pete remained poker-faced but inside he burned with curiosity.

"It's not that difficult," said Charlie, taking another swig of whiskey. "After all, you play rugby for the local team and it's well known that Carter is the president of the club. There's an obvious connection."

Pete's brain continued to click and whir like a computer but the input was insufficient to enable it to come up with a satisfactory answer.

"There's more," said the detective, rising unsteadily from his position on the sofa. He moved to the wall which faced Pete and opened a small cupboard. "See this?" he indicated. "It's what they call a dumb waiter. They were installed in all the old houses like this. It was a way of sending stuff up and down to and from the kitchen without carting it up the stairs. Mind you, the people who lived in houses like this when they were first built never carried their own trays of food upstairs anyway. Oh no," said Charlie with more than a hint of irony, which indicated where his political sympathies lay. "They all had servants to wait upon them hand and foot. Still, I suppose these things helped to get the food upstairs quickly whilst it was still hot, eh?"

He began tugging on a sash cord which operated the dumb waiter and eventually the shelf appeared. On the shelf was a tape recorder attached to which was a long length of wire. The detective lifted the recorder from the shelf and gathered up the wire, the end of which was plugged into an electric socket adjacent to the dumb waiter.

"This room is directly above Nibble's room which is two floors below," Charlie said as he placed the recorder on the desk. "This thing," he said, indicating the dumb waiter, "comes out just behind his desk." He pressed a button on the machine which began to rewind its tape.

Pete was fascinated by what the detective was revealing. "But what," he asked, "if he opens the door downstairs and discovers the tape recorder going full blast. How would you explain that away?"

"Ah!" said Charlie in a very meaningful way. He tapped the side of his nose with his index finger and smiled as if to indicate that he was glad Pete had asked that question. He didn't answer the question immediately but instead checked the device, pressed the stop button, and grunted with satisfaction. "Right, that's ready," he said, more to himself than to Pete.

"Now let's have another drink first, shall we?"

He poured himself another whiskey and also replenished Pete's mug. He then rummaged about in his own pockets for his Manikins and finally lit up. He puffed happily for a few moments and then as if startled out of a daydream he said, "What if he should open the door downstairs, you ask. "Aha!" he said, again with obvious satisfaction. "I've made bloody sure he won't. I discovered this little device long ago and I realised the potential of it straight away. At that time, it was Huw Roberts himself who occupied the office below and although I always got on well with him I could still see how useful this thing might be. Business is business after all," he added defensively. "Anyway, the first thing to do, I realised, before any recording devices could be dangled down this shaft, was to make sure the door at the other end could not be opened. I worked evenings or weekends," he explained. "But I was always helped by the fact that the door was never used downstairs. First," he explained with some pride, "I had to make absolutely sure that it could not be opened. I managed this by fixing bolts on the inside. That was not easy. Do you know I had to sit inside this bloody thing and haul myself up and down with these sash cords."

Charlie moved over to the dumb waiter and opened the door to show Pete the size of the space which he had occupied. "Not much room, eh? Believe you me, you need to be practically double jointed to be able to sit in there. I was scared to death the bloody cord would snap because they're not meant to take all this weight." Charlie patted his beer paunch. "Anyway, as well as bolting the thing from the inside, I filled in the cracks all around the door and painted it all so that anyone who thought about opening it up would just assume that it had been stuck with paint. I did it during one Christmas holiday when everyone was away downstairs so that the smell of paint had gone away by the time they returned."

Having explained all that the detective moved back to the table and pressed a button on the recorder. After a slight pause the voices of Simon Nibble and Eddie Sharp could clearly be heard in conversation. The subject of the conversation was Eddie's interest in Mr Carter's businesses. The references to pre-dating share documents and other fraudulent aspects of the proposed dealings were audibly captured for posterity on Charlie's machine. Pete listened carefully to the recorded conversation. When it ceased Charlie pressed the stop button and lit another Manikin.

"What did you think of that then?" he asked triumphantly. He knew already the value of the information they had just overheard but could not resist the enquiry. He felt rather like a journalist revealing the contents of a scoop to his editor.

What Charlie did not know, of course, was the particular interest which Pete had in the two rogues who had just been overheard plotting their particular business. He had to make a decision there and then whether to reveal this interest or whether to keep it to himself and hope that further information would be forthcoming.

He made up his mind on the instant to tell Charlie of his connection with Mr Carter. He explained his researches into Sharp Eddie and Simon Nibble and also admitted frankly that he had not just accidentally bumped into Charlie that evening but had followed him into the pub.

"Oh, I know that," said Charlie with a gesture of dismissal. He drew deep on his cigar and puffed the smoke out in rings. "You don't think I was a copper for God knows how many years without being able to spot when I was being shadowed and pumped for information do you? Mind you, I'll say this for you, you were quite good at it. In fact a bloody sight better than some local C.I.D. I could mention, but you were spotted, laddy. But don't be disappointed; the only reason I twigged you was because I've done the self- same thing myself a thousand times. But one small word of advice."

He gestured at Pete with his cigar to emphasise the point rather as a school teacher would point with his chalk. "Don't overdo the topping up of the drinks while the other guy is not looking. If you're going to add a drop to the other fellow's drink, make sure you don't fill his glass right up to the top. That's a dead giveaway, that is." He gave Pete a wink. Pete gave a wry smile and realised he had met a kindred spirit. Someone who did for a living what he, as a boy, had always wanted to do. He told Charlie where he worked and the sort of information to which he had access and explained his hobby of collecting data on local people who interested him.

As Charlie listened his eyes acquired a sort of glaze which is probably similar to the look worn by a prospector who has just struck gold. He realised that he himself had struck a rich vein in Pete Powell. A source of information inside the Inland Revenue is every private detective's dream. As the two talked on they began to appreciate how much they could help each other.

Chapter Thirteen
No Smoking

The office functioned nearly the same in the absence of Bill Butler as when he had been there but as previously mentioned the presence of Lionel Witherspoon in place of Bill meant a vast difference in atmosphere depending on whose viewpoint one took.

The early morning attendance and opening of the office was carried out by Tom Richards who sorted all the incoming mail as Bill had previously done. He would use the early morning time period, before the arrival of others to study the sports page of his newspaper whereas before he used to talk to Bill. Lionel would usually be the second to arrive but there was no interaction between the two of them. Lionel would occupy his glasshouse position and study the Financial Times before everyone else arrived. He regarded the pink newspaper as the only truly informative daily journal which gave him all the information, he felt, that anyone could need in life. He also felt utter contempt for the fact that Tom Richards studied the Daily Mail each day.

Tom, who had spent a lifetime in the services had equal contempt for Lionel whom he instantly discerned was not a team player. His career in the Army had taught him to recognise someone whom he knew would not watch his back when danger lurked and therefore Tom had written off Lionel before he even got to know him. Tom was secure in his judgement of Lionel because he had the lifetime of Army service as experience and knew also that his assessment of fellow soldiers had never been wrong. He had always been taught and instinctively always knew, that without mutual trust between men in a unit their chances of functioning successfully together were virtually zero. Tom did not trust Lionel even though he had no clear evidence to say why: he simply felt it in his water. However, since he had already, concluded his career with honour and satisfaction, and since his present position was merely an adjunct to his lifetime's military career and since also he knew that he was not far away from full retirement he did not allow his instinctive mistrust of Lionel to worry him but simply decided that, unless it was absolutely essential, he would never speak to him.

Lionel on the other hand was completely unaware of Tom's attitude towards him and misinterpreted Tom's silence as a business-like competency born of military training. In fact he rather admired Tom's apparent devotion to his work and would have preferred that most of the other staff in the office would take a leaf out of Tom's book and spend a little less time gossiping with each other. On that subject he had noticed particularly that Mavis and Helen were talking to each other far too much and from time to time he would rap on the glasshouse window and glower at them in an effort to curtail their gossip. Each time he did this Mavis would bestow one of her sultry looks upon him which made him wonder more and more about her.

He was also unimpressed with the way that Mavis and Helen continually smoked cigarettes in the office. Although it was still accepted behaviour in places of work he had read recently in the Financial Times that there were moves afoot in America to introduce a blanket ban on smoking in all buildings including work places. For Lionel this could not come soon enough. He had been contemplating lately the possibility of introducing a no-smoking ban in the office and regarded such a move as a flexing of his own muscles. The only problem of course was that Mr Pigg was a pipe smoker. Nevertheless Lionel was certain that the move would be a positive one and that, provided he tackled it in the right way, he might be able to get Mr Pigg on board with the idea.

As it happened it was much easier than Lionel had envisaged for Mr Pigg himself had already been considering giving up smoking his pipe. This was due partly to the pressure applied by Mrs Pigg at home for that good lady had already imposed her own smoking ban at the family home and Mr Pigg had for some months been restricted to smoking his pipe in the back garden. Also he had decided that a cleaner, healthier image would suit him better. It therefore only required a casual mention by Lionel that in the Financial Times there had been reports that a forward looking USA was considering national no-smoking areas for Mr Pigg to instantly take up the cudgels on behalf of clean living.

He retired to his own office that very day, confined his pipe and the remains of his tobacco pouch to the dustbin and wrote out the 'No Smoking' signs which he then put up in the office, including the area where the public attended. Before these signs had been erected Mr Pigg had convinced himself that the idea was entirely his own and began telephoning colleagues in other offices to advise them of his forward looking notion and also the fact that, by coincidence, the same policy was being advocated by none other than the Financial Times. Mr Pigg began to borrow Lionel's edition of the pink journal each morning after Lionel had read it, and became familiar with the names of the columnists therein whose names he began to quote frequently to colleagues on the telephone.

Thus, accidentally almost, Lionel discovered how to effect changes in the office without ever suggesting to Mr Pigg that such changes should be made. He would merely mention casually to Mr Pigg that a certain policy was being advocated by someone somewhere of which the pink Journal approved and within twenty-four hours a similar policy would be introduced into the office by Mr Pigg. The latter would then inevitably inform all his colleagues on the phone and urgently suggest that they introduce similar policies in their offices. Thus, gradually he acquired a reputation for being dynamic and forward thinking and became a leading light in policy thinking throughout the region.

Some of the ideas which Lionel vicariously introduced were better than others but he was content to allow Mr Pigg to appear to be the author of each and every one. Like his predecessor Bill Butler, he thus took over the effective management of the daily routines of the office without appearing to usurp any of Mr Pigg's duties.

The introduction of the no smoking ban was by far the most life-altering change brought about by Lionel. Firstly because of the benefit it bestowed upon the non-smokers in the office, namely Pete Powell, Mrs Balstaff, and Penny but secondly because of the inconvenience it caused to the confirmed smokers primarily Mavis and Helen who were, after the introduction of the ban forced to go outside and stand in the street if they wished to have a cigarette. This curtailed greatly the number of cigarettes they could enjoy daily due to the fact that arising from their desks (invariably together) and walking out of the room, drew attention to the fact that they were intending to smoke. This unexpected reduction in their daily intake of cigarette smoke brought about an improvement in both their lungs and their purses. Initially however they were unable to appreciate these improvements and blamed Mr Pigg for introducing the ban and were constantly complaining to each other and those about them of his high handedness. Pete Powell told them that he was thankful that they were no longer clogging up his lungs as well as their own, with their toxic smoke. Mr Pigg was perhaps the biggest recipient of benefit from the ban. From a personal point of view he benefited immediately from the lack of pipe tobacco in his lungs. His breathing felt better and his clothes and his persona no longer reeked of the stale pipe tobacco odour. This endeared him more to Mrs Pigg who had for years disliked the smell of his clothes. Further, the news of the smoking ban which he had introduced to the office had reached the ears of Mr Pigg's Regional Controller (Mr Jenkins) who had long ago decided that of all the office managers in his region, Mr Pigg was the least likely to ever be considered for promotion. He had always judged him to be a pompous, small-minded windbag of a person who had somehow managed to gain promotion to a position at least one step beyond his own level of competency.

Mr Jenkins was a dynamic personality who had always had a natural ability to lead others and to obtain the best from them with a fair minded yet ruthless quality. He had always been a keep fit addict and also admired any attempts by others to improve their own health, for example by taking exercise. Similarly Mr Pigg's introduction of the no smoking ban (the first office in his region and perhaps in the whole country), had captured Mr Jenkins' imagination. He himself had considered introducing such a ban at the Regional HQ building and intended to keep a very close eye on Mr Pigg's office to note the outcome of his experiment. He had noted also the rumours of some other policy changes which Mr Pigg had organised and he determined to keep an eye on these too. Further, he had heard indications that Mr Pigg was an avid reader of the Financial Times which frankly was the last thing he would have expected to hear. Mr Jenkins himself read that pink journal daily and was always impressed to hear of anyone else who did so. He was now seriously thinking that he might have to reconsider his opinion of Mr Pigg.

Chapter Fourteen
Pete and Sandra

Charlie Chivers the International Detective and Pete Powell met frequently after their evening together in the Jubilee Inn. More than once they met in that very hostelry and Pete was able to marvel again at the many personalities the landlord, Reg Partridge had been photographed with. On each occasion they were able to exchange and compare information which each possessed concerning Eddie Sharp and Simon Nibble.

Intriguing and informative as the information which Pete offered was, it was nowhere near as explosive as the tape recordings which Charlie was able to produce. These were actual recordings of personal and private conversations between the two when neither of them thought they were being overheard.

In addition, Pete had the private information illegally acquired, from Eddie's bank, care of the secretary whom Pete had bedded. Further, Pete had also had a relationship with an attractive young reporter on the local paper. She had interviewed Pete once to obtain information about him in support of a piece about him in the sports section of the paper.

Pete was the star of the local rugby team and had also played cricket for the local side. As a schoolboy he had played rugby for a young England team and had also played both rugby and cricket for the local area. A long article in the local paper was of some interest to readers and the young lady journalist who got the job was well equipped to write the article. She had been born and brought up in the area and had also played sport locally, both netball and swimming at a reasonable level. In the time required for writing the article she met Pete on several occasions during which time she found herself becoming infatuated with this personable and handsome young man. She and Pete became romantically involved and their steamy affair lasted for several months. Somehow or other the young journalist managed to write an interesting and informative biography of Pete even though they were both heavily involved with each other.

During their affair Pete discovered that her strongest interest in her chosen profession was for carrying out in-depth enquiries in respect of suspect people (often criminals) and exposing them in flamboyant exposure stories in the paper. This form of journalism was often dangerous work but she loved the combination of detective work and exposure journalism involved in stories of this type. She much preferred it to covering local weddings or shopping centre openings.

Pete, who also enjoyed the thrill of detective work, gave her a ring to enquire if she had ever come across either Eddie Sharp or his solicitor Simon Nibble.

She responded that she had heard of Mr Sharp (who hadn't) but she had never heard of or obtained any information about him that would invite some investigative journalism. Simon Nibble she said she had seen when attending the local Magistrates Court to report on criminal matters for the local paper. She had no reason to ever have taken a professional interest in Simon Nibble who seemed to her to be average for a local solicitor, perhaps a little whimsical in his defence speeches on behalf of clients but in no way suspect. She was however entirely happy to meet with Pete and discuss both people further and perhaps trade any information with him.

Accordingly they met in a local pub one evening for a chat. It had been several weeks since they had last met and Pete immediately reflected that she was a very attractive young woman. Their affair had never ceased for any particular reason and there had been no explosive disagreement. Pete himself realised that she liked him slightly more than he liked her but this was not an unusual situation for him. Many girls fell head over heels in love with him and although this was surely a compliment for him he also found that it brought with it a responsibility for which he was not quite ready.

The young lady, Sandra, was a blond haired attractive creature whose beauty was enhanced with a pair of honey coloured eyes which gave her a limpid allure. Although she was besotted with him she was also, completely immersed in her own profession and therefore suffered little or no adverse effect when their affair appeared to run its course. When Pete had failed to contact her she simply got on with her job which occupied all her waking thoughts.

Now that they were in each other's company again she felt an immediate resurgence of her feelings for him and Pete for his part appreciated once more how pretty she was. She was also eternally happy looking and he referred to her in his own mind as 'Sunny Sandra'. During their conversation she informed Pete that she had recently been approached by a T.V. company who were interested in employing her as a T.V. presenter. He reflected on how entirely suitable for such a position Sunny Sandra would be.

They both drank a little more than they originally intended and perhaps inevitably they both ended up the evening in bed together at Pete's small flat in the centre of town which was situated above a thriving Italian restaurant. Sandra thought she had died and gone to heaven and Pete was not so very far behind her. Both of them wondered how and why they had allowed the relationship to lie fallow for a while. Sandra was grateful that her overwhelming interest in her own profession had prevented her from having any maudlin reflections on her own love life or lack of it. Pete similarly had been distracted, working and always playing sport and also had no real opportunity to dwell upon his own feelings for Sandra. All he did know was that he found her to be a very attractive girl and enjoyed her company.

She had been able to offer Pete some advice on the strength of the evidence which he had already gathered against Eddie Sharp and his solicitor. "Some of the information gathered by you," she suggested, "could be gathered by me from certain sources and therefore could be used in any article published in my newspaper. For example, values of properties owned. Other information might be more difficult to print due to the fact that its voracity could only be confirmed by reference to national files information from which, if obtained, could only be acquired illegally." She basically warned Pete that his position, if it was discovered that he had broken the Official Secrets Act, would be serious.

She also warned him that the tape recording produced by Charlie Chivers could not be used in a court of law because it was also obtained illegally. She also doubted if it could be quoted in an article in her paper since there was nothing to reinforce the truthfulness of its contents. In view of the fact that one of the parties was a lawyer and the tape appeared to confirm that fraudulent acts had been committed by both parties nothing less than a rigorous defence could be expected.

She did say that she would discuss the matter, without mentioning names etc, with the newspaper lawyer who might be able to give some indication of how far an investigative article concerning the pair would be able to go.

Chapter Fifteen
Sharp Eddie at Home

The house in which Eddie Sharp lived was built on a hillside overlooking the town. It was a Victorian built mansion of a house originally intended as a home for a well to do family. The house was approached by a winding driveway bordered on each side by mature rhododendron bushes which, for a short period during the end of May each year, were a sight to behold when the flowers were in bloom. For the rest of each year they were left unattended and each successive year the bushes or trees became more leggy. The soil in which they grew was a mixture of sand and peat which was natural to the hillside on which they were sited. Eddie had no interest in horticulture except to take any credit for the beautiful sight which the plants offered each year in May. When he had purchased the house some ten years ago the plants were in situ and Eddie offered them no feed or attention whatsoever and now the plants looked very much as they had looked when Eddie first viewed the property.

The house was very ample in size having been built for occupation by a large family with extra rooms provided as living quarters (either at cellar or attic level) for domestic servants. Originally the property must have been sumptuous with many tall rooms, each with artistically corniced ceilings some of which contained candelabras dangling from the centre of each room.

Eddie had made no attempt to preserve the beauty of the Victorian property and had got a builder in to give every room a dash of magnolia paint to freshen it up. The only compromise he had made with the notion of improvements had been to install in the corner of the old original Victorian lounge room a cocktail bar which was adorned with fairy lights and from which he himself loved to dispense glasses of all manner of cocktails whenever guests arrived. Eddie was very proud of one cocktail which he had invented himself and which bore the name 'a dirty weekend'. He would always hand this drink over to its recipient and explain its title with a lewd laugh.

The only other attempt by Eddie to make any improvement to the family home had been the installation of a snooker table in one of the downstairs rooms along with an enormous T.V. screen attached to one of the walls. This afforded, for Eddie, the opportunity to combine two of his main hobbies in life, namely playing billiards or snooker, and watching horse racing on the T.V. A cynic might observe that by fitting a separate refrigerator into the same room Eddie had provided for himself a chance to indulge another of his hobbies, drinking beer, which he stored in the fridge, but in truth Eddie never regarded beer drinking as a hobby. To him it was more a way of life.

Eddie's wife was called Doris. She was an only child who had been born to a couple who ran a large furniture shop in the town which had been inherited from Doris's grandparents. Although the business was no longer growing it was still the only furniture shop in town and as such had enjoyed a reputation for many years of selling good quality furniture. In addition, the shop was in a central position in the town and came as an unencumbered, freehold premises, the value of which rose each and every year. Consequently, Doris's parents without being particularly gifted business people nevertheless were comfortably well off and socially regarded in the town. They were a church going couple who had little or no interests in life other than their business and their daughter Doris on whom they lavished all their money and attention. It was their greatest disappointment in life therefore when their beloved daughter decided to marry Eddie Sharp.

In truth Doris had not so much decided to marry Eddie so much as she had decided, when she discovered that she had become pregnant, not to have an abortion. Despite the enormous disappointment that Doris's parents experienced with their daughter's choice of partner they nevertheless supported her in that decision. From that moment on however they transferred all their affection and financial investment in the resulting granddaughter who became the apple of their eye. It was therefore the case that the only visual evidence of any meaningful investment in Eddie and Doris's home was provided by Doris's parents who financed the decoration of the grandchild's bedroom and a downstairs room now referred to as 'the music room' in which they installed a grand piano in the optimistic hope that, when she became old enough, the granddaughter would receive and enjoy personal tuition (paid for by themselves) and become as musically talented as they had hoped Doris would be.

Doris herself was in no doubt that her union with Eddie had been a huge mistake but she also shared her parents' resolve that her daughter, when she grew up, would vicariously become the accomplished and sophisticated creature that she herself ought to have been. She was also in complete agreement with her parents that all and any wealth which they might ultimately bestow should be channelled directly to the grandchild because she, Doris, (like them) could not bear to think that by transferring any of their wealth or assets upon herself they might someday find their way into Eddie's hands.

Eddie was relaxing in the sports room on Saturday morning. He was practising a few shots on the snooker table whilst simultaneously watching the horse racing on T.V. On a side table stood a half-finished pint of beer. The doorbell signalled the arrival of someone but Eddie made no attempt to answer it himself. Eventually Doris entered the room followed by a swarthy looking individual who clutched her hand and kissed it several times uttering the word 'bellisimo' repeatedly. She regarded him with barely concealed contempt and then left the room.

"Morning, Joe," said Eddie cheerfully. "Care for a beer?" Joe accepted the beer which Eddie took from the refrigerator in the corner of the room and seated himself on the leather Chesterfield while Eddie continued to pot balls. After a couple more shots he put down his cue, took up his own part-finished glass and asked," So, have you got the papers?"

"Si," responded Giovanni, and took some papers from the inside pocket of his jacket. "Are these okay?" he asked, handing them over to Eddie who examined them carefully.

"Of course they are," he responded, still studying the papers. "They were drawn up by my solicitor. Of course they are okay. Your wife has signed them, hasn't she?"

"Si si," assured Joe and gave Eddie a conspiratorial wink and then raised his eyebrows questioningly.

"Well, that's okay then isn't it," said Eddie and then folded the papers and placed them in the drawer of a small desk.

"I will give these back to my solicitor in due course," he assured Joe and then picked up his cue again re-setting the balls on the table. "Do you play, Joe?" He asked and when the latter nodded Eddie smiled and said, "I hope you brought some money with you."

Chapter Sixteen
A Visit from the Controller

Mr Pigg was surprised and excited to receive a telephone call from Mr Alan Jenkins the Regional Controller. When the call was put through to him, he reflected momentarily that it was fortuitous that he had made an effort that morning to arrive at the office on time instead of being his customary fifteen minutes late. His Regional Controller had already been at work for two hours or more and as usual, had cleared his desk of the normal daily paperwork. This left him free to monitor and contact the offices in his region and to plan his week ahead.

Thus, he telephoned Mr Pigg at nine a.m. for a brief discussion. "Good morning, Arnold," he said, "I'd hoped that I wouldn't be too early to catch you. I expect you are dealing with your morning's paperwork?"

"Yes, I've just finished all that," lied Mr Pigg. "I like to start early. I always enjoy an early start," he lied again.

"Aha you are a man after my own heart," responded Mr Jenkins, who had half-doubted whether Mr Pigg would be at work at this time of the morning.

"There is no substitute for an early start to the day," he continued.

"That's what I always say," lied Mr Pigg again, and then, warming to his task he said, "There is nothing like being alone in the office early in the morning before the troops arrive. It gives one the chance to think and plan ahead." He did not know why he had said this but just felt that it was the right thing to say at the time and was exhilarated by the response it provoked.

"Exactly," said Mr Jenkins, emphatically. "I can see that you and I are similar in nature, Arnold. Have you a busy day in front of you?" Mr Pigg paused for a second he was flummoxed by the question and wasn't sure if it was a trick question. If he answered that he was very busy could this be interpreted as meaning that he was unable to cope? Alternatively, if he said that he was not too busy could this be interpreted as meaning that he was not very industrious. He pondered momentarily, panic stricken as to how to answer the question. He glanced at the only piece of paper on his desk, which was yesterday's edition of the *Financial Times* and a headline that, 'The Chancellor was concerned about the state of play in the financial markets in Hong Kong'.

"I was just reflecting," he blurted out, "the state of play in the financial markets in Hong Kong." Having said this he was rather at a loss as to how to continue and ended up reading out loud a quotation from the newspaper column and somehow managing to express it as if it were his own thoughts rather than that of the *Financial Times'* columnist. His words were met with complete astonishment from Mr Jenkins who had never previously credited Mr Pigg with the intelligence or acumen which his words had indicated that he might possess.

"Well I must say," said Mr Jenkins, who was genuinely impressed by what he had heard. "I was reading something along the same lines only yesterday. How uncanny! I really had no idea that you were an F.T. man."

Mr Pigg had absolutely no idea what this meant but was at least smart enough not to say so. He coughed confidentially and indicated that they were just some trivial thoughts that had occurred to him.

"Well, I think you are being far too modest, Arnold," said the other, "but actually I was telephoning to enquire if you had any appointments today because I was thinking of paying you a visit after lunch for an hour or so." Mr Pigg received this information with a mixture of delight and anxiety. He assured Mr Jenkins that he 'could always find the time to be available for a meeting with the Regional Controller' and confirmed that the office would be ready for an inspection.

"Not an official inspection," assured Mr Jenkins, "More a social visit." Mr Pigg confirmed that he would be honoured to receive him. After replacing the telephone receiver, he reflected on the implications of his Regional Controller's unexpected visit later that day. He still had no idea why Mr Jenkins was coming. Nevertheless, he was experiencing extreme stage fright. He decided to advise his staff and to give them some instructions as to what to expect and how to behave.

There followed the usual crashing and banging as Mr Pigg left his room, slamming the door behind him, and making his way along the corridor to the general office. Once there he immediately made his presence felt (as if no one had heard his noisy arrival), by taking his, by now redundant, pipe cleaner from his pocket and tapping it loudly on the nearest desk and shouting loudly, "Can I have your attention please." This announcement was greeted generally with barely discernible groans and a universal raising of eyebrows by all the staff who looked up from whatever they were doing. All, that is except Tom Richards who continued writing and without deigning to even look up to see what it was that Mr Pigg had to say to everyone.

"I just wanted to say," opened Mr Pigg in his loudest tone, "That there will be a visit this afternoon by our Regional Controller Mr Jenkins."

This news was greeted with complete silence. It was not certain what response Mr Pigg had been expecting but for some reason he obviously regarded the silence as a disappointment. He paused for a second and then, as if the silence had been an expression of hostility, he continued, "I can assure you all that this visit will not be an official inspection. Think of it more as just a social visit by Mr Jenkins. I would remind you that you should all be on your best behaviour for the duration of this visit."

Here he paused to flash a malevolent glance in Vincent's direction. And then, with a final "do I make myself clear?" he promptly left the general office and returned to his own room to make a few telephone calls to colleagues in other offices. His exit was followed by further more audible groans from the staff who began to talk amongst themselves over Mr Pigg's announcement. Eventually the general chit chat was interrupted by Lionel tapping loudly on the glass wall of his room and glaring generally at everyone.

"What's he coming here for?" Hissed Mavis to Helen. Both kept their heads down pretending to work.

"I've no idea," responded Helen. "Perhaps it's something to do with Bill's heart attack?" She continued inquiringly.

"Surely not," mused Mavis. "Why would that warrant a visit from the Regional Controller? After all, we've got Lionel here now so what more is required?" she added with an affectionate glance in Lionel's direction.

"Hmm," responded Helen with obvious contempt. "I hope he gets moved on as soon as possible. He is nowhere near as good as Bill was."

"Oh, I don't know," responded Mavis, bestowing a further admiring glance towards Lionel. "I think he may have a certain something."

"Oh my God!" exclaimed Helen, then, in a John McEnroe style continued, "You cannot be serious."

Their conversation was cut short by a tapping on the glass followed by a beckoning bony finger from Lionel. Mavis eagerly rose from her seat and went into the glasshouse in response to the summons. As she walked towards the glasshouse Mavis, contrived to move in what she thought was a slinky manner. Her previous experience taught her that generally men found this to be irresistibly sexy. She dared to hope that Lionel would be no different from all the other men she had known.

Lionel for his part watched her as she approached his office. His reaction was not what Mavis herself intended. As he watched her, he could not understand how awkward and ungainly was her gait. He regarded her as far too plump and not at all desirable. In truth he never had any feelings of desire for many women at all and certainly not curvaceous ones like Mavis. Lionel's preference was always for very thin females preferably without breasts or bottoms. Although he would never admit it, even to himself, let alone to others, the only females he ever felt attracted to were pre-pubescent young girls. Thus, it was of course a mission impossible on which Mavis was currently engaged.

She entered the glasshouse trying to look demure. Lionel had a file on his desk and he pointed a bony finger at an entry and demanded, "What's this?"

Mavis came around the side of his desk to look over his shoulder at the entry. She also leaned forward and gently rested one ample breast upon Lionel's shoulder. He jumped sideways as if he had just been stung by a wasp. He then pushed the file towards her so as to allow her to read the entry without having to stand too close to him.

"Oh, that's a kind of shorthand that Bill used to employ to remind him of the person involved."

"But what does it mean?" demanded Lionel who was studying an entry which read GEWV.

"Umm," murmured Mavis for a second…. "Oh I know, go easy wartime veteran."

Lionel was astonished, "What has that got to do with anything?" he demanded.

Mavis paused, "Well, Lionel," she began, "Bill was in the war and I think he always wanted to treat others who were similarly placed, with great care and sympathy."

As she said this, she placed her hand on her thigh and slowly and deliberately eased her skirt up her leg and tentatively enquired, "You don't think my skirt is too short do you, Lionel?" She had supposed that when she did this Lionel would be overcome with lustful feelings.

Instead, he looked at what she was displaying as if it was a rotting corpse. "Of course it's too short!" he uttered, contemptuously. "And I told you before, it's Mr Witherspoon to you. If you think I'd be interested in what you have to offer you are sadly mistaken. Now get back to your desk and get on with some work."

Mavis took a deep breath which appeared to inflate her bosom even more and, with a poisonous look at Lionel flounced out of the glasshouse twice as quickly as she had entered. She had no idea how the politics of the office would work out but she did know that sooner or later Lionel would be very sorry that he had scorned her.

Chapter Seventeen
Transfers

The brass plate on the wall by the entrance to the offices of Huw Roberts & Co shone brightly having been lovingly polished by Mrs Sargent early that morning before any of the other occupants of the building arrived. By mid-morning when Eddie Sharp arrived at the offices the plate still shone brightly reflecting both the morning's sunshine and the image of anyone who stepped over the threshold. Eddie's reflection showed that he wore a pair of red and white chequered trousers reminiscent of Rupert the Bear and a lilac-coloured polo shirt. These garments were worn by Eddie when he was playing golf.

He had little love for the game but played it regularly in order, he thought, to elevate himself socially. He also felt that it afforded him a means of regularly coming into contact with people he could do business with.

Inside the building he was met as usual by Mrs Sargent who raised one eyebrow before giving him her customary, "Good morning, Mr Sharp, how can I help you?"

"Morning Agnes," responded Eddie. "I need to see Simon if I may?"

"Do you have an appointment?" demanded Mrs Sargent, suspiciously, purporting to check her diary as she asked.

"No, I'm sure he'll want to see me," said Eddie. "I've got something for him."

Mrs Sargent gave a sharp intake of breath whilst still examining the diary and all the while shaking her head. In truth Mr Nibble had no immediate appointment but she was always reluctant to allow anyone to see her principal without previously having made an appointment.

"I'll just see if Mr Nibble can spare a moment to see you." she said in a tone that seemed to indicate that this would not be likely. As an afterthought she added, "I could fit you in for ten minutes later this afternoon if that would be all right."

"No, sorry Agnes, I'm just on my way to play golf so I won't be around for the rest of the day."

Frostily Mrs Sargent contacted Simon Nibble on the telephone who agreed to see Eddie straight away.

When he entered Simon's room, he found his solicitor studying an ultra-modern computer screen which was placed on one end of an elaborate horseshoe-shaped desk. Simon was seated in an equally impressive leather swivel chair which resembled the seat of an aeroplane pilot. He swivelled around to face Eddie and with excessive cheerful fullness said, "Good morning, Eddie. How are you this morning? Would you care for a coffee?"

"Don't mind if I do," responded Eddie. While Simon ordered the coffee on his telephone, he took the documents which he had been carrying in the back pocket of his Rupert Bear trousers and placed them on the desk.

"And these are?" enquired Simon Nibble glancing at the documents as he spoke.

"They are the transfer of the share certificates you printed for me" said Eddie. "Joe brought them to me." he continued.

They were interrupted by a knock at the door which opened immediately to reveal Alice the office gopher with a tray containing two coffee cups. Eddie instantly brightened up on her arrival and shamelessly ogled her as she entered the room. As before, he openly admired her legs as a stock breeder would examine an animal.

"Well, hello," he said meaningfully patting her bottom affectionately. "It's Alice, isn't it?"

The girl turned crimson and timidly avoided Eddie's reach. She placed the cups on the desk and started to reverse out of the room whilst Eddie still leered at her.

"Thank you, Alison," said Simon blandly as she closed the door. Then he said to Eddie quizzically, "I presume these have been signed by Carter's sister?"

"But of course," assured Eddie with a conspiratorial wink. "Joe is not entirely stupid you know."

Simon studied the papers further and then noted, "There are no witness signatures on the documents."

"Well," said Eddie, "That's a technicality which you can take care of isn't it."

Simon smiled blandly, "There is no way I can sign these documents now. They should have been witnessed at the time they were signed by Carter's sister."

"Oh, don't give me that," said Eddie aggressively. "I just paid Joe £20,000 for those shares and I'm not prepared to lose that money. You can get someone in your office to sign them. No one will ever know."

"Carter's sister will know," said Simon Nibble and she might decide to deny that she has been to this office to sign documents."

"Oh come on.," said Eddie, "She does exactly what Joe tells her and she is generally so addled with the booze she drinks to be able to remember what she did or did not do. In any case, her own husband would be able to give evidence to say that she did. Anyway he could not deny it having already taken the money. No you can find a witness otherwise you will have to forego the enormous fee that you are already anticipating."

With that Eddie rose from his chair and left the room to go to the golf course. Simon Nibble picked up the telephone and asked Mrs Sargent to send Alice up to his room.

Chapter Eighteen
Mr Jenkins Arrives

Mr Pigg had not had much time to spend in preparation for the visit of his Regional Controller Mr Jenkins. In truth he had done no work at all today. By the time he had announced the visit to his staff and then spent half an hour or so in conversation with Lionel Witherspoon in the glasshouse, he barely had time to converse on the telephone with the majority of his fellow managers throughout the region when Mr Jenkins' arrival was announced.

Mr Pigg hastened to the public counter area with the usual commotion and welcomed Mr Jenkins with great ceremony and much hand shaking. They retired immediately to Mr Pigg's office and two cups of tea were ordered, and produced by Mrs Balstaff who contrived to behave in a manner quite unlike her normal imperious self. In the presence of the revered Regional Controller, she became more ingratiating and almost adopted the persona of a shy young maiden being introduced to a grand duke.

"Well, it is nice to see you again, Mrs Balstaff said the Regional Controller. "And how are things with you?"

"Oh, very well indeed," she responded shifting nervously from one foot to the other and inserting her index finger between her teeth to affect a coy attitude.

"Splendid, splendid," said Mr Jenkins in a genial manner, which somehow seemed to terminate the meeting.

At the last second however, Mr Pigg chose to intervene with the observation that, "Mrs Balstaff is of course one of the mainstays of this office and we rely heavily upon her." With this he inclined his head ingratiatingly to towards her and she almost blushed in response.

"Wonderful," said Mr Jenkins loudly. "We won't trouble you any more then, Mrs Balstaff." She then retired from the room still bearing the flush on her face but otherwise looking very pleased with herself.

"So," said Mr Jenkins getting down to the business of the day. "You have a good little team here which seems to cope well with the business of this office. A shame about poor Bill Butler though. What is the prognosis?"

"Not so good, I'm afraid," replied Mr Pigg, who went on to detail the medical information he had received from Mrs Butler, and the hospital.

"Oh dear," responded Mr Jenkins, who had always had a fondness for Bill who was personable and diligent. He knew that Bill had no aims for promotion and had not been too far away from retirement age. Nevertheless, he was not unaware of the worth of the man who had clearly been the lynchpin of the office. Despite this and his previous, as he saw it now, erroneous opinion of Mr Pigg's abilities he still knew that Bill virtually ran the office.

"I have been looking at the figures since Bill left us and I have to say that despite his absence the results produced by your team do not appear to have diminished in any way. That of course is undoubtedly due to the efforts of your good self, but I presume some of the credit must no doubt go to Mr Witherspoon who has been with you for a while now. How do you see him Arnold?"

Mr Pigg coughed confidentially and assured his Regional Controller that he felt that Mr Witherspoon was very efficient and appeared to handle his position very well.

"Hmm," said Mr Jenkins questioningly, "Very diplomatic I'm sure, Arnold. I am aware that he has the ability to be competent in the post but tell me how does he handle the staff? Is he popular? Is he a leader?"

Mr Pigg was non-plussed and realised instantly that he had no idea what the answer to the question was. He himself had not observed Lionel's relationship with those around him.

"Well," he said. "It is still early days of course," and then paused wondering how on earth to proceed.

"I sense that there is a BUT in there somewhere, Arnold, but you are much too canny to come out with it. I will be very frank with you, Arnold, inside these four walls and this is for your ears only. Mr Witherspoon has all the brains and qualifications to be handling a position of at least one grade above his present job. His only downside is the way in which he deals with fellow members of staff and whether or not he has the ability to inspire those around him. In effect, Arnold does he have great powers of leadership? You yourself clearly know the difficulties of handling and leading others."

Mr Pigg's chest puffed slightly and he modestly offered, "Well, I like to think I do certainly."

"Precisely," said Mr Jenkins, as if Mr Pigg's own admission proved the fact beyond argument.

"But Mr Witherspoon is a bit of a conundrum, Arnold. Again, strictly between you and me," Here, Mr Jenkins lowered his voice slightly as if to ensure that there could be no eavesdroppers listening. "There have been a couple of occasions in the past when he has not shown powers of leadership shall we say, and that does bother me a little. Has he got over these slight misdemeanours and moved on? I ask myself. What do you think, Arnold?"

Mr Pigg was yet again non-plussed for he really had no idea what his Regional Controller was talking about.

"Well," he said carefully, "I would say that he appears to have settled in fairly well, and has certainly not blotted his copy book as far as I am concerned." Here, Mr Pigg inserted his tongue into one cheek and contrived to look as though he were implying great wisdom into his own words.

The gesture appeared to work for Mr Jenkins, slapping his own knees, rose from the chair and said, "There is more wisdom in you than at first there appears to be Arnold. I think you've more or less helped me to make up my mind. Well let's go and have a little chat with your people, shall we?"

Mr Pigg rose also and accompanied his Regional Controller into the general office and as they walked together, he wondered what it was that Mr Jenkins had been talking about and how it was that he himself had somehow given the impression that he knew and also understood everything that had been troubling the man.

In the general office Mavis and Helen were whispering together. The latter had noticed, when Mavis returned from the glass house that she was not in a good mood. She had immediately interrogated Mavis as to what had gone on. For her part, Mavis was only too pleased to explain things to Helen who quickly realised that her companion was seething volcanically and could barely contain the anger which she felt towards Lionel.

"He said my skirt was too short!" she told Helen as if the suggestion was preposterous. "Didn't stop him from taking a good look though." she continued, with great venom. He's got to be the most despicable man I've ever come across."

Helen, who had never liked Lionel from the first, was only too happy to encourage Mavis in her critical commentary. "He's so unattractive, in so many ways," she offered encouragingly.

"Too right," agreed Mavis, who was still beside herself with outrage.

Their conversation was interrupted by the noisy arrival of Mr Pigg and his guest who conducted a brief tour of all the desks exchanging greetings with the Regional Controller who, like the efficient leader that he was, had remembered the names of everyone together with personal details which he had briefly memorised before leaving his offices earlier that day.

Mr Pigg and Mr Jenkins both entered the glasshouse and after a brief conversation Mr Pigg retired to his office to leave the Regional Controller alone with Lionel Witherspoon. After about twenty minutes Mr Jenkins returned to Mr Pigg's office. "Well, I have to hand it to you, Arnold," he volunteered. "Your assessment of Mr Witherspoon, was spot on. There is a ruthlessness there that has convinced me that he would be able to run an office like this. Also, I notice that he too is an F.T. man like yourself."

Mr Pigg smiled deprecatingly but still had no idea what the expression F.T. meant. Nevertheless, he was astute enough to nod wisely in agreement with what his Regional Controller was saying.

"In fact, I am convinced that not only could he run any office but I have decided that I will promote him to run this office," he continued.

Mr Pigg's smile remained on his face but began to take on a frozen appearance. He was now totally confused but continued to nod his head as if this information was exactly what he had expected to hear.

"I am sure that news will be extremely gratifying for Lionel," he offered even though the information had still not sunk far enough into his brain for Mr Pigg to ask the obvious question.

"I know what you are thinking," said Mr Jenkins, once again over estimating Mr Pigg's intelligence. The latter remained static with the same frozen smile and could not, in truth think of any question to pose.

"What's going to happen to me, you are thinking?" continued Mr Jenkins, with a more relaxed smile on his face. "Well, I'll tell you, Arnold," he said. "I have created a new post for you. I've been very impressed lately with the innovations you have introduced and I believe your time would be more effectively spent roaming all the offices in the region and observing procedures and making suggestions for any improvements. At the same time, you could carry out some of the more mundane inspection procedures which I normally carry out which would free up some time for me. Your new position would be that of mobile Assistant Regional Controller. You would be answerable only to me and you would be based in the Regional Office HQ, but spend most of your time on the road each week. Well, what do you think of that? Do you think you would be able to handle it?"

Mr Pigg as usual was completely dumbfounded but after a second or two the realisation of what was being offered dawned upon him and he reacted with all the enthusiasm he could muster. He grasped the hand of his Regional Controller and shook it vigorously and assured him that he would not be disappointed with the decision he had just made.

"I sincerely hope not, Arnold," said Mr Jenkins.

"But I have to tell you that this time last year I would not have felt that you were ready for such a change. Recently, as I said, I was impressed by some of the decisions you made and the changes you introduced and frankly, Arnold, I was pleasantly surprised. For example, the smoking ban in the office. How has that been received?" Here, Mr Jenkins sniffed the air and said, "It certainly smells a lot fresher in here. Have there been any objections from the staff?"

Mr Pigg confirmed that there were none and then went on to explain that the ban had been favourably received by the majority of the staff. He also added that he himself had foregone the pipe smoking and felt much fitter.

"Splendid," said Mr Jenkins, rising from his chair.

"Well, official letters will be issued to both you, and Mr Witherspoon, in the next day or so and the new arrangements will commence from the first of next month. I will leave you to inform Mr Witherspoon and the staff and say goodbye and look forward to working with you more closely from next month onwards.

Chapter Nineteen
Changes

The staff in the general office were not feeling too work-ish following the visit of the Regional Controller. It was nearly the end of the working day and so most of them were not inclined to do any further work. Instead, they were discussing Mr Jenkins and generally wondering what the reason for his visit had been. Everyone knew that the Controller normally only visited the office once a year and since he had already done so a few months earlier no one could see any reason why he should visit them again so soon after.

George Davies, being a newcomer had no knowledge of the usual procedures and had not met Mr Jenkins before. He was impressed by the detailed information the Regional Controller appeared to have about himself, and without the aid of any written notes. He had to assume that this information had been passed on by Mr Pigg.

He asked Tom Richards, with whom he was sharing a table what his own opinion of the visit was. Tom almost closed his eyes to a squint as if to register the fact that he was giving the matter some thought. When he fully opened them again George noticed how watery the eyes were, as if they had been painted in watercolours which had now faded with age.

"No," confirmed Tom, who in his military career had experienced innumerable visits from senior officers.

"It didn't really make any sense. Perhaps it had something to do with him." Here he indicated with a wrinkled old finger the man in the glass house.

"I think the sooner he moves out of this office the better," observed Mavis with some contempt."

I wish poor Bill would return. He was so nice.

"Here, here," said Helen who was still fascinated to know just what exactly Lionel had said or done to upset Mavis so much.

"He's such an odious man," continued Mavis. "Why would anyone wish to visit this office just to see him."

"He is a prat," agreed Pete, "But why let it bother you so much? At least he keeps himself to himself: he's not an old woman like our beloved leader."

Their conversation was interrupted by the usual commotion which accompanied the arrival of Mr Pigg. That gentleman entered the room in his usual manner and loudly demanded, "Can I have your attention please."

He commanded Vincent to kindly fetch Mrs Balstaff and Penny, who he felt sure, would like to hear this announcement.

There then followed the usual scraping of chairs and tables in order to arrange a semicircle shape around the table at the end of the room which Mr Pigg was occupying. He paused long enough to allow for the arrival of Mrs Balstaff and Penny and also Lionel Witherspoon who joined Mr Pigg at the head table.

Everyone took up the same positions as they had previously occupied which meant that George found himself close to the cupboard with Mavis beside him. She snuggled up close to him and whispered in his ear, "I wonder what this is all about. At least he hasn't got any of those stupid graphs this time."

George was slightly surprised that Mavis was apparently only too willing to resume where she had previously been with George. He had not been able to understand why she had ignored him after their previous encounter.

"Tom thinks it might be connected to Lionel," whispered George, to her. As he leaned towards her Mavis also leaned in to him to hear him and in so doing her breast cushioned itself against George's upper arm and her hand gently rested upon his thigh. As before, George's heart and eardrums beat fiercely as he once again found himself under the sensual spell afforded by close proximity to Mavis.

The absent members of staff arrived and when everyone was assembled Mr Pigg opened proceedings, "I have asked you all to come together because I have an important announcement for you," he began. The usual response to such an opening volley from Mr Pigg was a low groan of disappointment from the staff but on this occasion they all seemed genuinely interested in what he had to say.

"As you know," he continued, "Our Regional Controller Mr Jenkins came to see us earlier today and he has made a decision which will I think affect all of us here."

He paused to clear his throat and was gratified to see the anticipation on the faces of those in front of him. The normal reaction to anything he said was a glassy eyed stare from everyone. Today was not such an occasion and that was the reason for the pause which added a touch of drama to the occasion.

"Mr Jenkins has decided to create a new office in the region: that of trouble shooting mobile Assistant Regional Controller with a responsibility for introducing new methods of procedure." Mr Pigg allowed a moment for this information to be absorbed and then added, "the Regional Controller has seen fit to offer this new prestigious post to myself and so, as from next month, I will no longer be in this office although of course I will be visiting from time to time in my new roving capacity." Mr Pigg allowed a further moment for this item of news to sink in and then finally delivered the coup de grace. "You are, no doubt, wondering who will be filling my place here and I can announce that the new manager of this office from next month onward will be none other than our current stand-in deputy, Lionel Witherspoon. Congratulations Lionel."

"Oh God," uttered Mavis, in more than a stage whisper and her sentiments were echoed almost universally by the rest of the staff in the form of a low moan of disappointment.

George gently laid his hand upon that of Mavis, which was still resting upon his thigh and quietly whispered in her ear. "Would you like to go out for a drink this evening?" As he uttered these words, he amazed himself by gently kissing Mavis on the ear. This was something he would never normally dare to do but the result was a beaming smile and a vigorous nod of the head.

Chapter Twenty
George and Mavis go for a Drink

The Jubilee Inn at seven p.m. extended its usual welcome to the early evening regulars. When the velvet curtains were drawn and the lights were switched on it afforded an old-fashioned atmosphere to all who were willing to enter.

Charlie Chivers the International Detective was already seated at a table when Pete Powell arrived with a file of papers under his arm.

Reg Partridge was behind the bar looking pink and benevolent and recognised Pete who purchased a pint of bitter for himself and a pint of whatever Charlie was drinking. After a brief glance at some more of Reggie's pictures on the wall behind the bar Pete joined Charlie at the table and passed the fresh pint of beer to him.

As they greeted each other Pete unfolded the papers which he had brought with him and allowed Charlie to survey these whilst he sipped his beer. Charlie raised his new pint, just received from Pete, and took a long draught whilst perusing the papers.

"Hmm, very interesting," he observed, "Does sharp Eddie really own all these properties? And

none of them with a mortgage? So where did he get all the money to buy them?"

"That's a very good question." responded Pete. "According to his returns he should never have had enough money to purchase all of these properties so that is an unanswered question."

"Well, he's certainly making a lot of money somehow which is definitely not on the official landscape." said Charlie. "There can't be many ways to make big money quickly, it must be either drugs or sex. I think I might give one of my mates in the CID a ring and see if he is of particular interest to them. Course he might want a quid pro quo."

Pete understood and explained that all he really wanted was to help Mr Carter. Any information flowing to the local C I D which might result in the prosecution of sharp Eddie or his solicitor could only help Mr Carter.

"Well," said Charlie, "I got another very interesting tape of the pair of them admitting further fraudulent activity. I am sure my former colleagues would be very interested in that. The only trouble is their friends in the Crown Prosecution would not be too pleased to hear about the way the information was gathered. Equally, the information in your files would be difficult to use in a court of the law of without you being involved in a breach of the Official Secrets Act." Pete was only too aware of that technicality.

"But what if my information, and yours too for that matter was revealed anonymously to the press or T.V. who followed it up with investigatory stories or programs which revealed the truth about them to the world at large?" asked Pete.

"How would they answer or defend that? They'd be in some difficulty wouldn't they. And your friends in the C I D would have more than a reasonable cause to question them about matters that were all over the newspapers or TV wouldn't they?"

Pete went on to explain about his journalist colleague Sunny Sandra and her interest in the stories which Pete had to tell, about Eddie Sharp and Simon Nibble. Charlie was very impressed with this information and suggested that Pete should introduce him to Sandra. Charlie then got up to get another drink for himself and Pete.

Whilst Charlie was at the bar Pete occupied himself by glancing again at the papers, he had brought with him. His back was to the bar and so he did not see the couple who passed by him to occupy the table next to the one which he and Charlie occupied. He felt a tap on his shoulder and turned to see George Davies who was just pulling out a chair for his companion who for a brief moment Pete did not recognise. A second later he realised of course that it was Mavis. Initially he felt that his failure to recognise her instantly was due to the fact that he had never anticipated that he would ever see them out together. However, he now discerned that there was something physically different about her and he struggled momentarily to understand what it was. Gradually he realised that she was no longer wearing the heavy make-up which she always wore to work. Her face looked fresher and much prettier than usual especially since she was also not wearing the usual dark heavy eye make- up. He even noticed a few freckles on her nose which he had never before been aware of. Altogether, thought Pete, she looked much more attractive than usual. In fact, she looked like a fresh English rose. She wore a light floral designed dress instead of her normally very short skirt and looked quite lovely. She also looked quite happy which Pete found quite endearing.

They said their hello's, and Pete heard himself asking, "What are you two doing in here?"

Mavis responded in a chirpy way, "Well, we could ask you the same thing." Pete was slightly flummoxed by this but did not show it.

Just then Charlie returned to the table and placed the two fresh drinks down. Pete was a bit embarrassed about the situation but again did not show it.

"This is Charlie," he announced. "These are George and Mavis my colleagues from work."

They said hello to each other and Charlie then sat down and fixed his gaze upon the bosom of Mavis which to him gave the appearance of possibly being about to burst out of the thin almost diaphanous covering afforded by her dress.

"Well," remarked Pete in a friendly way, "You two are dark horses. I didn't expect to see you both out together."

"No," said Mavis with a cheerful smile reaching out her hand to grasp George's, as if to reinforce their togetherness. "And what do you do Charlie?" she asked pointedly.

"Charlie is an investigator," offered Pete, "We were just discussing something private."

"Ooh, ooh," said Mavis continuing her friendly smile. "Sounds intriguing."

"Not really," replied Charlie his eyes still fixed upon Mavis' breasts. "Generally speaking, it's quite boring work but it does have its moments."

George had noticed the papers on the table in front of them and recognised the file cover in which they had been carried as one from work and immediately put two and two together.

"Well," he said "We'll leave you to get on with your private business." He then turned his chair slightly to be facing Mavis more directly and they both began to talk quietly together.

Charlie and Pete continued their beers and their conversation. Charlie pursed his lips and indicated Mavis by slightly inclining his head in her direction but while still looking at Pete who smiled at Charlie's appreciation of his work colleague. He had to admit to himself that he had never before seen Mavis looking so lovely.

"I'll have a word with Sandra and see what more she has to say," said Pete. "And what about your former colleagues? Is there anyone you can really trust?"

"Yes," said Charlie, "I've got a friend who used to be a sergeant with me. He's now a D I He'll take any case I can give him and he's got a good nose for villains."

They finished their drinks and decided to leave. They both said their goodbyes to George and Mavis and then left the pub.

Mavis and George watched them go then looked at each other. "Well," said Mavis, "What did you make of that?"

"I'm not really sure," said George. "How do you mean?"

"Well," said Mavis, "What is an investigator exactly?"

"I don't know," said George, "A private detective, I suppose."

"But why would Pete be talking to a private detective?" wondered Mavis.

"I'm not sure I know that either." replied George even though he had a fair idea having remembered what Pete had told him in the cellar/basement at work. Obviously, he figured, Pete was passing on, or selling, information acquired from work. Why and to whom, George did not know.

"Well anyway," concluded Mavis, "It was interesting to see them. I've never actually met a private detective before. Do you suppose he was a member of MI5?"

"I shouldn't think so for a minute," said George. "He didn't look like a spy catcher. He looked too ordinary."

"But isn't that exactly how they are supposed to look?" said Mavis. "After all, if they all looked odd in some way, they couldn't really carry out work for the secret service could they?"

George had to admit that she had good point there but couldn't offer any other ideas upon the business which they had together.

"Anyway," said Mavis looking at her watch, "They must have been here early. Pete must have come here straight from work. I nearly didn't make it myself. My mother held me up and I never had time to put on any make up. I must look a sight," she added shamelessly fishing for a compliment.

George instantly responded without thinking. "But you look so beautiful, I thought you had taken ages to get ready." He realised as he said it that it may have sounded a bit corny.

"I, umm, I've never seen you out of the office," he added apologetically. "I mean that you just look, well, umm, lovely."

Whatever he was trying to say and however much he felt that he was stumbling in an embarrassing way to express himself it certainly did the trick for Mavis who found herself completely won over by his schoolboy awkwardness.

"What you mean is I look better without make-up than with it," she said in a motherly way. "Well, I think I will take that as a huge compliment," she continued and leaning forward gave him a soft kiss on the lips.

George, still reacting in the schoolboy role, blushed furiously and wondered why he was experiencing this feeling when, not too long ago in the office together they had assumed a sensual and physical closeness that seemed so far away from their present awkwardness. To him it was as if Mavis without her make-up and short skirt was a different person from the one he had known at the office. Although he still found her to be attractive it was no longer in a sexy obvious way. To him she now looked like a childhood sweetheart rather than a desirable call girl type.

"It's just, you look slightly different," he stumbled. "When I first saw you at work, I thought you were very attractive, but... I... didn't think you were as beautiful as you are now." He stumbled again, he could not have been more wrong. He was really embarrassed now and was totally unpractised at complimenting women and felt that he was digging himself into a hole from which he might never emerge.

He could not have been more wrong for Mavis watching him clumsily tripping over his own words yet still managing to express his own honest opinion of her was utterly conquered by his embarrassment which she found completely endearing. She realised again what it was that had originally drawn her towards George. It was his persona of the little lost boy which she found so attractive. She could not believe that she had temporarily transferred her interest or attention to that odious Lionel Witherspoon. She gazed at George and looked and felt so happy. She instinctively felt that here was someone who liked her for herself and who found her to be pretty and not just someone with whom he wanted to have sex. At the same time, she did not wish to dissuade George from such feelings because she was a girl who had always loved to have sex but she felt that here was someone who might want her for more than that and it made her feel extremely content.

George for his part could not believe his own naivety and had thought at one point during his rambling that Mavis might have walked out on him. He was so relieved that she had not responded negatively and as they chattered away, he felt more and more enamoured with her.

When it was time to leave George walked her home and they walked along together holding hands. He felt as if he was walking on air. While they were on their way, they discussed the latest office news. Being a newcomer George had less knowledge of Mr Pigg or Lionel although Mavis reminded him that she also had little knowledge or experience of Lionel. Nevertheless, she did have a fixed opinion of him though she did not mention to George her recent contretemps with Lionel in the glasshouse. She merely confirmed that she found him to be a disagreeable personality and unsuited to be in charge of the office. George agreed with her on the final point.

His opinion of Mr Pigg was less critical than that of Mavis who admitted that she had always regarded him as pompous and incompetent although she did concede that now that Lionel had been appointed as manager, she would prefer that Mr Pigg was still in charge. She lamented the ill fortune that had befallen poor Bill Butler.

George suggested that he had thought of visiting Bill again and wondered if she would like to come with him. Mavis was really touched by this offer and expressed her appreciation by giving George another affectionate kiss telling him that she thought he was" a very nice person." George said he would take her to the hospital the next day or to Bill's house if he was no longer at the hospital. He reminded Mavis that he had already been to Bill's house to take Mrs Butler to the hospital.

When they reached the house where Mavis lived with her parents, they stopped to say goodnight to each other. They kissed goodnight on the doorstep but the kiss involved no lust but simple affection. George was quite happy about this and found Mavis to be a very attractive girl but felt that there would be plenty of time in the future for physical aspects of their relationship. He just did not wish to force himself upon her at an inappropriate moment. Mavis seemed to sense this and found George to be even more sweet as a result.

Chapter Twenty-One
Simon Goes to Court

It was a dry sunny morning. One of those days when it made a chap pleased to be living in England. Birds were singing in hedgerows and the magnolia tree was in full blossom in the garden.

Simon Nibble reversed his large BMW out of the garage and eased it gently down the driveway. He smiled as the automatic electric gates opened for him at the end of the driveway. He thought how nice it was to have a day away from the office and how appropriate it was that the weather was good.

He switched on the car radio and smiled again as the surround sound was introduced. The automatic gears on his car eased gently up to a comfortable speed and Simon allowed himself a moment to reflect upon the day to come. He was destined for a day in the Crown Court for the trial of one of his regular criminal clients, a habitual thief who used to be represented by Huw Roberts himself when he began trading in the town. He represented the client, Jimmy Pearce for crimes of dishonesty on countless occasions. He had recognised Pearce as a congenital offender who would never change his ways. He was always content to represent Pearce in the magistrates' court generally and advised him to plead guilty and then usually did a good job of mitigating for him and always knew that inevitably Pearce would be in trouble again and require the same services from Huw Roberts.

Simon Nibble inherited Jimmy Pearce from Huw and had represented him also in the magistrates court several times. Although Jimmy was not as completely impressed with Simon Nibble as he had been with his predecessor, he was happy to be represented by him. He realised that Simon did not possess the same amount of experience or respect in the magistrates' court as Huw, but he had noted that he was less rigid in his attitude towards him and often quite happy to run a not guilty plea when all evidence appeared to invite a guilty plea.

In today's case the entry of a 'not guilty' plea Jimmy knew would not have been tolerated by Huw Roberts. The distinction between the charges that Jimmy was facing today (the theft of a bottle of whiskey from a local trading store), and previous similar charges which he had faced, was the element of violence allegedly involved. Jimmy was accused not only of stealing the whiskey bottle from the store but, when challenged and chased by the shop assistant who tried to apprehend him in the street, of attacking and injuring her. This aspect elevated the charges, usually a relatively minor theft, to which Jimmy would plead guilty, to robbery with violence a charge which, with his previous record, would end inevitably with a prison sentence.

Simon was only too pleased to encourage Jimmy to plead not guilty and was now looking forward to a day in the Crown Court. His receptionist/office manager, Mrs Sargent had not been pleased to learn that he was planning to take a day at the Crown Court sitting behind counsel. She had argued, probably correctly, that this was a waste of his valuable time and that the job could be delegated to someone less important or perhaps employ as an agent a junior from a firm of solicitors close to the court. Simon however would not countenance this and assured Mrs Sargent that, "He," meaning Jimmy Pearce was "an awfully good client, Mrs Sargent. He is always getting into trouble. I could not, consign him to a junior."

Thus, Simon was driving his BMW towards Bristol for the trial of Jimmy Pearce in the Crown Court. He arrived fairly early in the morning and parked his car in a multi-story car park close to the court. His first port of call however was Clifton Chambers one of the many barristers' chambers in the town. Here Simon had a pre-trial conference arranged with the barrister he had instructed to act in the defence of Jimmy.

The counsel in question was Algernon Phillipson who had been at Clifton Chambers for a number of years. He was well versed in criminal law and altogether an experienced counsel who was well known to all the judges on circuit.

Algernon was quite senior at Clifton Chambers having been there for a number of years. He commanded a middle to high fee for his appearances which reflected his experience but this did not bother Simon who had arranged legal aid for Jimmy in view of the serious charges he was facing.

When he arrived at Chambers Simon found Jimmy already seated in the waiting area. Despite regarding Jimmy as "an awfully good client" Simon did not think enough of him to offer him a lift to court in his car.

"Morning Jimmy," he said cheerily, "How are you feeling this morning?"

"A bit nervous actually Simon," replied Jimmy who would never have dreamt of calling Huw Roberts anything but Mr Roberts. Simon's general attitude seemed however to invite conversations on first name terms.

"You've got nothing to worry about today," Simon assured him. "We've got a very experienced counsel for you. There're not many defendants that Mr Phillipson doesn't get off. I'm sure that we will get a successful verdict this morning."

Jimmy said he hoped that would be the case but still looked very nervous. "I hope so," he said, ""I admit I've done a few things in my time but never any violence, Simon, they have to believe that, Simon. My record shows that after all."

"Yes, well," observed Simon, "The jury will not hear anything about your past record unless or until they have made their decision on today's charges."

Just then they were joined in the waiting room by Algernon Phillipson himself who bade a good morning to them both.

"Nice to see you again, Simon," he said shaking hands. "And this I presume is Mr Pearce?"

Simon confirmed that it was and Jimmy stood up and reached out his hand to shake as Simon had done. Algernon declined to take Jimmy's hand but assured him that it was nice to see him.

"I wonder if you would mind waiting here for a brief moment while I have a word with your solicitor, Mr Pearce," he said and with that whisked Simon away before Jimmy could respond.

Once they were ensconced in Algernon's private room he said, "Well, it's been a while Simon. We don't always meet but I always appreciate the cases that you send me."

"Not at all, Algie," responded Simon who always preferred to be on first name terms with everyone. "I've just bought an apartment in Tenerife," he announced with some relish. "If you and Philippa want to go out there just give me a ring."

Mr Phillipson was slightly surprised and diverted by this announcement. Although he knew Simon Nibble moderately well, he did not feel that he knew him well enough to stay in his Tenerife apartment. He was also not particularly pleased to be referred to as Algie by him.

He paused for a moment long enough to brush a speck of dust from the lapel of his pinstripe suit. The reference to Philippa had concerned Mrs Phillipson who was a fellow barrister in the same chambers. She was considerably younger than Algernon and specialised in cases concerning divorce, separation, adoption and horses. She seldom received any instructions on the latter but always included that detail in her official description of tasks which she was willing to undertake. Both she and Algernon lived in a picturesque village a few miles from chambers where they had some stables on the land attached to their property. Philippa had always been passionate about horses and when she married Algernon, who had considerably more money than her, she was able to realise her childhood dream of owning some horses. Presumably she must have thought this was a fair trade for changing her surname to Phillipson but in reality, this was no embarrassment because the tradition in barristers' chambers was for females who married to continue to practice under their maiden name.

"I thought we would have a quick private chat before I see Mr Pearce in conference," said Algernon." Your brief was... well just that... Brief."

"I just wanted to fill in one or two gaps that occurred to me." Simon smiled hopefully.

Algernon rifled through the papers he had received from Simon and stroked the Neville Chamberlain lookalike moustache which he wore. Like his hair it was flecked with grey streaks which as well as indicating his age also lent an atmosphere of wisdom or sagacity to him. Simon thought that jurys would definitely be influenced by his appearance.

"I'm a bit worried about the evidence in this case," sai d Algernon. "The CTV from the store appears to show your client in the shop, taking the whiskey bottle and yet Mr Pearce is pleading not guilty. What is the basis for that plea?"

"I agree" said Simon but the CCT.V. only shows the interior of the shop not the roadway outside. Jimmy Pearce does not deny that he was in the shop but does deny that he took the bottle outside the store. When he was accosted by the shop assistant, he was shocked and when attacked he attempted to shake her off and unfortunately, she fell and hit her head on the concrete plinth of the next-door building. The prosecution has no independent evidence of any..."

"I'll be honest with you," he said. "Today we are in front of Judge Fallow, who does not suffer fools gladly. Your client has to be made aware that if he persists with a 'not guilty' plea and the jury find him guilty then he will impose the maximum sentence. Now, I discern that the basis of your defence is that the shop assistant was completely mistaken and had challenged your client without having any good reason for doing so. Does your client fully understand the outcome of today's trial if the evidence of the shop assistant is believed by the jury?"

Simon shrugged his shoulders and raised his hands palm upwards." Jimmy is adamant that he did not take the whiskey bottle out of the shop and the CCT.V. does not show him doing this. The alleged violent attack was simply a misunderstanding and as such is merely Jimmy's word against that of the shop assistant.

Algernon looked extremely sceptical but accepted what Simon said. "Very well," he said. "Let's get him in and see what he's got to say for himself." With that he picked up the telephone and requested his reception to show Simon's client into his room.

There followed a thirty-minute conference in which Jimmy was interrogated vigorously by Algernon concerning the occurrence at the store. Jimmy was experienced enough to stick to his story but often, when answering, appeared to be looking to Simon for help. Algernon continued to look sceptical and left Jimmy in no doubt that if he felt uncomfortable being questioned by him that was nothing to the discomfort he would feel under the gaze and interrogation of Judge Fallow. The conclusion of the meeting was that Jimmy fully accepted his dire history of offending and also agreed that, if absolutely necessary, would be prepared to enter a plea of guilty to attempted theft but emphasised his innocence in respect of the alleged violence.

Algernon remained sceptical but did at least note one thing in Jimmy,s favour was his angelic appearance. He realised that this might sway some members of the jury. It did not cut the mustard with Algernon though who had already seen the record of Jimmy's past offences and had no doubt in his own mind that the man was guilty.

He paused again and breathed in deeply and then exhaled long and hard through half closed lips, making a noise not unlike that made by Philippa's horses. "Very well then," he said, "Not guilty it is so let's make our way over to the Crown Court and do our best."

They all then rose and walked through the streets together to the Crown Court building which was situated only a short distance from Clifton Chambers.

Chapter Twenty-two
The Gallows Court

Judge Jeremy Fallow Q.C. was a tall and distinguished looking man whom many observers likened to the Duke of Edinburgh. He was good looking and, like the Duke had a ram- rod straight back which, added to his six feet two-inch frame made him look even more impressive. Like the duke, Judge Fallow suffered no fools gladly and he also had a wry sense of humour.

He was born in the Cirencester area to a well to do farmer and his wife. His mother who in her youth had been a well- connected debutant / society girl had doted on Jeremy as a child. He was the first born and naturally demanded as much attention as his mother could afford. When his younger brother Roger was born some three years later Jeremy continued to demand the same amount of attention from his mother as he had been used to before the birth of his brother.

Roger, as a small child had to amuse himself and occupied himself alone quite often for his mother was not able to spare as much time for him as she managed for Jeremy. The latter was a clever child who always excelled academically. He was also hard working and diligent and never had to be nagged or reminded to do his homework. Roger on the other hand preferred to play outdoors and seldom if ever did any homework unless his mother forced him to.

Both children were educated at a private school near their home. Jeremy, to his mother's unlimited joy was a complete success at school. He passed all exams and was always top of the class throughout his school career and was appointed head boy in his final year. He was also prominent in the school drama society and often took the lead parts in the annual school play.

Roger however showed no great inclination for study per se even though he was not unintelligent. He excelled on the sports field and also showed some promise in the music classes mastering both the violin and the cello. After leaving school he managed to earn a living as a batsman playing for Gloucestershire Cricket Club. He was never regarded as a formidable talent but nevertheless was known locally as a workman-like opener who seldom gave his wicket away cheaply. In his spare time, he joined a quartet of like- minded musicians who played Bach, Beethoven or Mozart to anyone who was prepared to listen. They played at schools, nursing homes and charitable events throughout the West Country.

Jeremy, although academically gifted, had no great skills to match his brother's ability with a cricket bat or musical instrument. After school he chose to study law at Bristol University and not surprisingly acquired a first-class honours degree. From there, despite some offers from private law firms, he decided to enter the police force. He entered under a system of entry which had just been introduced for graduates who entered the force at inspector level. Jeremy learnt quickly and was soon promoted and destined for a lofty rank but after a few years he decided upon a change of course. He elected to study once more and took the Bar examination and thereafter joined the Crown Prosecution Service as a barrister and quickly gained a reputation as being a hard-working and talented prosecution barrister who was eventually rewarded by being appointed as a Queens Counsel. During his time at the Bar he was often to be seen seated at the County ground at Bristol watching his brother playing cricket. Invariably there were few other spectators during matches played in the mid-week especially if the weather was inclement. This never bothered Jeremy too much since his knowledge or appreciation of the game of cricket was not too detailed and since his presence was more than 50% due to the involvement of his own brother. Also, he always had papers to study.

Eventually he was recognised by the system as being worthy of promotion to the bench and finally appointed as a Crown Court Judge in the city in which he had spent his working life. He brought to the bench an ability to administer trials with a meticulous and stern authority. It was hardly surprising to anyone that Judge Fallow should reveal a preference for the prosecution in any trial in which he presided. With his history of being in the police force and the Crown Prosecution it was inevitable that such a criticism should be levelled at him. On occasion his interventions during trials which appeared to favour the prosecution led to the nickname jocularly afforded to him by barristers' clerks generally and sometimes amongst the members of the local bar as 'Judge Gallow'.

Whether Jeremy himself was aware of this nickname or not he was always careful during summing up procedures or interventions to use stock phrases such as" but that members of the jury is something for you to decide."

This morning Judge Fallow was seated in his chambers glancing at some papers and savouring a cup of fresh coffee which had been made for him in an expensive coffee machine that was perched on a table in the corner of the room. The person who had made the coffee for him sat on the other side of the desk from him. She was his chief clerk Shirley Kemp, a middle-aged woman with two children and a husband who was a self-employed plumber. She was an experienced court clerk who had been with the judge for some time. They were both quite fond of each other and whilst they were in his chamber the judge always called her Shirley. In open court he referred to her as Mrs Kemp. She never referred to him in anyway but Judge.

"So what have we this morning Shirley?" he asked between sips of coffee. "This doesn't look much of the case does it?" he added glancing at some of the paperwork before him. "How long is it listed for?"

"Three days, Judge," said Shirley who had herself doubted that a case such as this could last that long in the court of such a decisive judge as himself.

"I see we've got Mr Phillipson acting for the defendant," he said. "Procedurally he's quite reliable, although he does waffle on a bit sometimes."

"Only when you let him," quipped Shirley with a wry grin. "And that's not very often."

Judge Fallow also grinned and then said, ""Who is this acting for the prosecution, a Mr Sabin? I've not seen him before."

"No," agreed Shirley. "Apparently, he is newly qualified but you might be seeing some more of him in the future."

"Well, I hope he is procedurally correct otherwise he'll be feeling the wrath of my tongue."

"He is new and young," said Shirley. "So be kind and gentle with him. He is probably terrified of appearing before you so early in his career."

"I'm not terrifying surely?" It came out as a statement posing as a question but did not fool Shirley.

"Not a bit of it, Judge. Just be gentle with him."

They both chuckled a little together and then Shirley rose to leave the chamber and the judge said he would be out in a few moments.

In court outside all parties were assembled as Shirley took up her position on the lower bench at one end. Behind her was the raised desk at which the judge sat. After checking with both counsels that everything was ready Shirley popped back through the door from which she had just appeared and a second later came back again calling loudly as she came, "All stand please."

With that Judge Fallow came through the same door with his robes and wig on and occupied his place above and behind Shirley. "Good morning, everyone." he said. "Please be seated." Then looking in the direction of the prosecution Counsel. "Yes, Mr Sabin."

The latter rose to outline the prosecution case and although he had practised his few lines over and over again, he still felt very nervous. As a relatively newly qualified barrister he had already appeared in lower courts to hone his style but today he was definitely feeling out of his depth in the court of Judge Gallow. He was the son of a couple who had immigrated to the UK from Pakistan a few years before he was born. They were not well off but made a modest living and were enormously proud of their son who had recently joined the bar in the country they had chosen to live in.

Mr Sabin was more than halfway through his opening speech and beginning to feel that it was perhaps going slightly better than expected when the judge intervened. "Do you have the CCTV evidence available in court this morning, Mr Sabin?"

"Yes, you're honour," was the reply.

"I presume you have seen this Mr Phillipson?"

Algernon got to his feet and almost without thinking hooked his thumb into one side of his robe. "Yes, I have your honour although the defence does have an issue with the importance which my friend appears to attach to it."

Judge Fallow nodded sagely and glanced at the defendant who, though pale with anxiety still managed to look like an accused choirboy.

"Very well, proceed, Mr Sabin," continued the judge and sat back in his seat and looked around the court. It was then that he spotted, in the front row of the viewing gallery his brother Roger who was listening intently to what was going on. The judge quickly wrote a brief note which said, "When I adjourn stay in court."

He then reached down to Shirley and gave her the note which he had folded and and whispered a soft instruction. She then beckoned the court bailiff over handed him the note. The bailiff then went into the gallery and handed it to Roger who read it.

Mr Sabin had nearly finished his opening speech and was beginning to almost congratulate himself that things were going better than he had hoped when Algernon got to his feet to challenge a point which he had made. Once again, he had his thumb hooked under his robe in a classic orator pose.

Before Mr Sabin could respond the judge intervened again. "Where exactly is this going, Mr Phillipson?"

"Well, Your Honour," answered Algernon sententiously," I wonder if I could have a quick word with my friend regarding this point. I am hoping it may be of some assistance to the court."

"Very well," said the judge looking at his watch. "Shall we adjourn for half an hour?" he raised his eyebrows as though there might be someone in the court who could object. Both counsels nodded in agreement so the judge advised the jury that there would be a half hour adjournment and they were then ushered back to their waiting room.

The judge retired to his chamber and in a few moments his brother Roger was escorted into the room by Shirley. "Hello, Roger," said Jeremy, "I never expected to see you in my court."

"No," agreed Roger, who seldom ever attended his brother's court. "I was at a loose end and thought I would pop down. The game we were playing finished a day early so I've got today off. I thought I'd see some action but nothing much has happened so far."

"No." said his brother, "and if the defence have got something up their sleeves then perhaps nothing will happen."

"Well," said Roger, "the defendant looks a nice enough chap. I'm surprised to see him in court at all."

"Oh, please," said the judge with disdain. "Don't they all look the same? Honestly, Roger, you can be so naïve sometimes."

"Well, each to their own," said Roger philosophically, "he looks innocent to me."

His brother tut-tutted and invited him to return to court in a moment or two and then he would see whether or not the jury agreed with him.

"We are playing Somerset at home tomorrow," said Roger. "If you are free then come along."

Jeremy raised his eyebrows with interest. "Well, that depends on whether or not this case folds," he said. "If it does then I might be tempted. I will see at lunchtime when I next adjourn."

Roger then returned to his seat in the viewer's gallery. When the court case resumed and before the jury returned Algernon sent a message to the judge via Shirley asking for a five-minute conference in his chambers. Both counsels were ushered in and as soon as they were seated the judge said, "Gentlemen."

Algernon took the reins as the senior counsel present and advised the judge that both sides had come to an agreement that the charges would be amended so as to read that Jimmy was now charged only with attempted theft to which he would be pleading guilty. All reference to violent assault were to be dropped.

The judge raised his eyebrows but did not speak. Algernon continued and referred to the lack of solid evidence in respect partly of what went on in the shop and definitely as to what happened outside. He then went on to labour the condition of the witness who had been the shop assistant and emphasised that she had been quite badly injured in the fracas. Algernon reminded everyone that the lady had received an injury to the head which would necessarily affect her memory as to what had happened. He himself had seen her seated outside the court this morning with bandages on her head and one arm in a sling. He further argued that no one would want to see this poor woman put through a harrowing interrogation in the court.

Once more Judge Fallow raised his eyebrows. "What do you say, Mr Sabin?" he enquired. Before he answered the question the judge thought to himself that when he had worked as a prosecution counsel, he would never have agreed to reduce charges in this fashion. On the other hand, he had to admit that he had not meticulously examined all the evidence. He also had to admit to himself that a day watching his brother playing at the County ground would be most enjoyable.

Mr Sabin coughed diplomatically and re-iterated what Algernon had said. He also emphasised that this solution would save discomfort for the unfortunate victim and also confirmed that there was no CCTV evidence of what went on outside the shop. He also shrewdly reminded the judge of the money that would be saved by terminating the proceedings two days early.

The judge agreed and both parties returned to the court and awaited the return of the jury. Jeremy caught Roger's eye and smiled and gave a slight nod of his head. He also noticed the defence solicitor who had been seated behind Mr Phillipson. The man was whispering with the defendant and both were grinning triumphantly. The judge noted that the solicitor was wearing a cream-coloured Armani suit which though beautifully tailored did not really look appropriate for a court of law.

Mr Sabin was greatly relieved that the first occasion in which he had appeared in the court of the fearsome Judge Gallow had not been a disaster. His ready-made response to any criticism of the result when he returned to the office would be that the whole thing had been supervised and overlooked and approved by Judge Fallow. He knew that no one in the Crown Prosecution offices would dare to challenge that.

After the jury were advised of the diminishment of the charges against Jimmy the judge thanked them for their assistance and then told them that their services were no longer required. They were then led back to their waiting room where they waited to see if they could go home or whether another trial would be found for them.

Both Simon and Jimmy were cock-a-hoop over the outcome which frankly had been better than either of them could optimistically expect. Simon assured Jimmy that it was exactly what he had expected and reminded him that the result was exactly what he had predicted.

Algernon Phillipson could hardly believe what had been achieved and felt that perhaps he should pinch himself to make sure it was true. As they all said goodbye to each other in the street outside the Crown Court building he said, "Well, Mr Pearce, I can assure you that you are a very lucky man. I think I can say that on any other day the result could have been very different."

Jimmy repeated his thanks to both men and moved off down the street with a spring in his step. Algernon and Simon said their goodbyes and Simon reminded Algernon of his offer for him and his wife Philippa to visit Simon's newly acquired apartment in Tenerife.

On his way back to the office Simon enjoyed the surround sound of his car radio and smiled to himself.

Chapter Twenty-three
George and Mavis Plan a Visit

The following morning was a nice sunny day and the mood of everyone in the office seemed to reflect this. Tom Richards was in early as usual, and had dealt with the normal daily procedures such as unlocking cupboards and transporting files to desks etc and by the time that Lionel arrived he had settled down to read the Daily Mail. As usual neither of them spoke to each other and Lionel went straight to the glasshouse and began reading the Financial Times.

Gradually the rest of the staff arrived and Pete noticed that Mavis appeared to have foregone make up again. He reflected that, as in the Jubilee Inn the previous evening she looked particularly bright and pretty. The few freckles which he had noticed before at the top of her nose were still there but he also noticed a mere sprinkling of some more at the top of each arm. Not too many he thought but just enough to add a light touch to the overall effect. She no longer looked tarty which was how he had always seen her, but pretty like an English rose.

Helen also noticed the change in appearance and immediately remarked, "No make-up this morning, did you wake up too late to apply any?"

"No, no," said Mavis in what was intended to be a pensive mood. I just thought it was time for a change."

"Well, it suits you I must say," remarked Helen. "And I like that dress."

Mavis beamed, "Oh, thanks. It's an old one I haven't worn for a long time." The dress was similar to the one that she had worn the previous evening. It had a pink floral design almost exactly like the other. She had been so gratified with the effect which the other dress had lent to her appearance that she had retrieved this one from the back of her wardrobe and tried it on first thing this morning. When she looked in the mirror, she was gratified with what she saw and was delighted that Helen also liked it. There was a sparkle in her eyes which prompted Helen to ask, "Go out did you last night?"

"Hmm," nodded Mavis looking immensely pleased with herself but saying no more.

"Come on, then," said Helen impatiently. "Where did you go and who did you go with?"

Mavis smiled and lowered her head and leaned towards her companion and whispered virtually inaudibly, "Went out with George," she almost mimed indicating, with an inclination of her head and eyes, their colleague at a nearby desk. Helen looked or feigned complete amazement and covered her nose with both hands. She looked as though someone had just informed her that she had won the lottery.

"Really?" she responded in a whisper to match that of Mavis who nodded emphatically. She mimed to Mavis, "Was it OK?"

Mavis answered this by raising both eyes to the ceiling and miming the word, "Dreamy."

Helen was beside herself with vicarious delight as she always was with any tale of the love life of her companion. "Where did you go?" she asked, still in a whisper but this time slightly louder.

"The Jubilee Inn," Mavis replied at her normal volume. "It was quite nice," she added. "We saw Pete in there, didn't we?" she said inviting a response from either Pete or George who were listening at the next desk.

"Yeah, that's right," responded Pete. "And whether it was the general atmosphere of the place, or Reg the landlord or the pleasure of bumping into me I'm not sure but Mavis looked radiant," he said mischievously.

Mavis blushed instantly and Helen uttered a sustained, "Oooh." Which seemed to imply that she had understood perfectly every nuance of the previous evening.

One of the telephones began to ring and Mavis was glad to answer it so as to avoid embarrassment or discomfort.

Later Pete and George found themselves in the cellar/basement area which gave George the opportunity to question Pete about his meeting in the Jubilee Inn. The latter was not at all phased by George's interrogation and gave him the gist of what he had been doing. He fingered his nose and said to George, "But this is strictly between you and me?"

George nodded vigorously and Pete then changed the subject.

"So how did you get on with our Mavis then? It seems to me that you hit it off very well."

George confirmed that was the case and confided with Pete that, although it was early days in the relationship, he was quite smitten with Mavis. Pete said that he was extremely pleased for them both and added, "You certainly look good together and I must say you have a good effect on her. I've never seen her looking so attractive. You, lucky bugger." he chuckled good naturedly.

George then told him that he and Mavis planned to go and visit Bill to see how he was but were not sure which evening to go. Pete said, "Evening? No, go in the daytime! It is office business after all! Go and see Piggy and say that it would be a welfare visit. He'll say yes and then tell everyone it was his idea." George thought that this was quite a good idea and resolved to do so.

Later that morning George knocked on Mr Pigg's office door. "Come in," bellowed Mr Pigg and George entered nervously.

"Yes, George," said Mr Pigg indicating a chair. George noted when sat himself down that the room no longer smelled. He then appraised his boss of the idea which he and Mavis had of visiting Bill and wondered if this would be allowed in office hours.

By coincidence, and unknown to George, Mr Pigg had earlier been wrestling with the subject of Bill's welfare. He had some office forms which required Bill's signature and he also needed to collect or receive from Bill or his wife the medical certificate which was required by the personnel department at the Regional Office. Although such matters, were strictly speaking, the duty of the office manager, he had no inclination to visit Bill in person and felt that as George had visited him in hospital that it might look only natural to delegate a further visit to George. He felt also that the presence of Mavis might add a feminine touch. He reflected that no one in the office looked more feminine than Mavis. "Yes," he said, "As it happens there are some papers that I needed Bill to sign and also I need to collect his latest medical certificate."

With that, he picked up his telephone and buzzed through to the room next door in order to speak to either Penny or Mrs Balstaff. "Ah, Mrs Balstaff, my good lady," he loudly uttered. "I wonder if you would be good enough to get hold of Bill Butler's wife on the telephone and put her through to me. Thank you so much, Mrs Balstaff."

After a brief moment his telephone rang and he picked up the receiver. "Thank you so much, Mrs Balstaff. I don't know what I would do without you," he added unnecessarily. Then he spoke again. "Hello, Mrs Butler. How are you? Good, good. Yes, I am very well, thank you. More particularly how is Bill?"

Mrs Butler reported that Bill was very well thank you and only yesterday he had been released from hospital and was now at home. As usual she was very optimistic as to her husband's progress.

"Oh, that is good news," shouted Mr Pigg as if there was a large audience who needed to applaud. He went on to tell her the purpose of his call and that he would be sending George and Mavis round to see Bill and to deal with some paperwork. "Not at all, not at all," he bellowed, as Mrs Butler uttered her grateful thanks, for everything he had done for her.

When the call terminated Mr Pigg confirmed that everything was in order. "Now you know where Bill lives, don't you?" he said and George confirmed that he had already been to his house. He thanked Mr Pigg and said he would be on his way and just as he was leaving the room Mr Pigg said as an afterthought, "You'd better check that it's OK with Lionel, before you go. If he can spare you then it's all right, Otherwise, we'll have to make other arrangements."

George concurred and returned to the general office where he passed on the news to Mavis who began to gather together her handbag and jacket. Tom Richards put his hand in his pocket and took out a ten-pound note which he passed to George. "Take this, and buy some flowers for him and give him my best wishes."

"Oh, that's so sweet," said Mavis.

George then went to the glasshouse to have a word with Lionel who was talking to Pete about something. The door to the glasshouse was wide open so George did not feel as though he were interrupting anything too private or personal. He explained the situation and the fact that Mr Pigg had OK'd the visit and that he had suggested that George check with Lionel that it was fine.

Lionel leaned back in his chair and curled up his nose as if he had just discerned a bad smell. "Firstly," he said haughtily, "When I'm having a conference with someone, I do not expect to be interrupted by you and secondly do you seriously think that I can spare two people to go out of the office on a jaunt just when they feel like it?"

Pete stepped forward and placed his muscled forearms on Lionel's desk and leaned forward until his face was close to him. He fixed him with a steely gaze and said very slowly and deliberately, "These two are going to pay a visit to a sick man, who is worth ten of you. It's OK with Mr Pigg, and it's OK with the rest of us. This office can manage for an hour or two without them and as far as we are all concerned..." Pete paused here and Lionel could see the muscles in his jaw clenching. With great venom he finished his sentence. "You can stick it up your fucking arse!"

With that he ushered George out of the glasshouse before Lionel could respond. George thanked him for sticking up for him but wondered if he had perhaps gone too far and made a bad enemy in Lionel.

Pete snorted with derision and simply said, "I don't give a shit about him."

Lionel was still seated at his desk and feeling shell-shocked by the words that Pete had uttered. He could feel himself trembling with the fear he experienced when Pete had leaned in close to him. It was not so much the ferocity of the words uttered or the profanity of the language used. It was the physicality which Pete had exuded when he was up close to him.

Lionel had never been a physical person and when confronted thus he had no experience to call upon to enable him to deal with it. He remained speechless at his desk for quite a while before the trembling dissipated.

Chapter Twenty-four
The Visit

George and Mavis left the office and made their way to George's car. Once they were on their way, he told her about the incident in Lionel's glasshouse and also about how supportive Pete had been in response to the information that he and she were an item.

"Yeah," said Mavis guardedly, "Pete's OK."

She presumed that Pete had not told George about his previous relationship with her. She sincerely hoped that he never would and she certainly had no intention of telling him herself. She knew that she had a bit of a reputation for being a girl of easy virtue but had never previously allowed that to trouble her. She had a sensual side to her and enjoyed the company of men and enjoyed lovemaking. She was never troubled that people should see her as that sort of girl but strangely since the commencement of feelings for George she no longer felt proud of that side of her nature.

George told her exactly what Pete had said to Lionel and she laughed.

"Serve him bloody right," she said. "He's a horrible man." She did not reveal to George the exact reason why she had said this. She would never tell him that, perversely, she had once thought of him as attractive partly because she was ashamed of this and partly because she did not want George to see her as a girl with loose morals.

They soon arrived at Bill Butler's house and rang the doorbell which was answered by Bill's wife who looked just as plump and red-faced as the last time George had seen her. He thought, as before that she looked like Mrs Bunn the baker's wife.

He introduced Mavis and they were led into the lounge where Bill was lying on the sofa wrapped in a blanket. They presented the bunch of flowers which they had purchased at a petrol station on the way, and Mrs Butler went off to find a vase.

Bill was pleased to see them and thanked them for calling to see him. George noticed that his mouth still drooped to one side but he appeared to have more shine to his eyes than the last time he had seen him. His speech was slightly affected by the drooped mouth, caused by his stroke, but he was able to talk nevertheless. George would not have thought this was possible when he had seen him in hospital.

"You look really nice," Bill said to Mavis, who brightened up considerably at the words. He had never before complimented her on her appearance although he had always been kind to her. Mavis patted his hand in appreciation of his kind words.

Bill explained that for a few days following the stroke he had felt really bad but said that he was getting better by the day and that the doctors were very pleased with his progress. He said that only a few weeks before he had felt very pessimistic but now, he was feeling much better and was even looking forward to returning to work in the near future.

This came as both a shock and a pleasant surprise to George and Mavis who had both been led to believe that Bill would never be returning. They looked at each other both of them wondering what to say.

Mavis took it upon herself as one who had worked in the department longer than George to recount to Bill what had happened in the office since his departure. "What!" cried Bill in surprise. "They can't do that. On what basis do they presume to replace me? Nobody said to me or confirmed to them that I would not be returning."

Mavis told him that Mr Pigg had announced to everyone including the Regional Office that he (Bill) would not be returning to work because he was too sick to work again.

"What!" said Bill again. "That man couldn't organise a booze up in a brewery let alone take on a promotion. I used to run the office not him."

Mavis had never before heard Bill say anything disrespectful about Mr Pigg and although what he said was true it was still a shock to hear him say it. "Well, I know my rights," continued Bill. "And if they think they can pension me off that easily they can think again."

"That's the spirit," said Mavis who could not wait for Bill to return and for Lionel to be ousted. She mentioned him to Bill and assured him that he was nowhere near as good as him and also that none of the staff liked him.

Bill toyed with the name, "Witherspoon," he pondered. "Thin and weedy with glasses?" George and Mavis nodded.

"Hmm," he said. "I remember a few years ago he was at another office and there was a bit of an incident."

George and Mavis were all ears. Bill searched his grey matter for a moment. "There was a rumour that he'd tried it on with a young woman in the office though nothing was proved."

Mavis could not believe this following Lionel's rejection of herself and all her charms. She felt vaguely insulted.

"Really?" she said. "I know he is loathsome but I find that difficult to believe."

"Yes," said Bill slowly still struggling with his own memory,

"Oh, I know, she was a young trainee straight out of school, very young and who was anorexic I believe. Apparently, he took her under his wing and was trying to groom her but her parents made a fuss and she was dismissed upon medical grounds. She was supposedly suffering from mental problems. He was then transferred to the Black Economy Section."

"Well!" said Mavis, with astonishment. "Would you believe that?"

She already felt vindicated with regard to her own sexual charms and felt that someone who would reject them had to be suffering from some disorder themselves. "Wait until I tell Helen," she said with some glee.

"Oh, but nothing was ever proved or admitted," added Bill with some trepidation, "So don't go saying too much."

"Of course not," said Mavis who couldn't wait to get back to Helen.

They then had a cup of tea thanks to Mrs Butler and passed on the good wishes of all the staff to Bill before leaving. Bill surprised them by walking them to the front door even though he was wearing just a dressing gown.

George was pleasantly surprised by the vast improvement to Bill's health since his visit to the hospital and was wondering how he was going to explain this to Mr Pigg.

On their return journey they both discussed what had been revealed at Bill's house. Both were astonished by the rumour about Lionel and Mavis in particular was ecstatic about the possible return of Bill. They pondered as to how they should announce this to Mr Pigg.

"I know," said George suddenly. "We don't have to say anything definite about his condition other than that he is on the mend. The medical certificate which he has just given to us should say everything which is relevant. Have a look at it."

Mavis took the certificate from her handbag where she had stored it and perused it. "It doesn't say anything other than a one-month duration."

"Well, that's it isn't it?" said George. "We'll just hand it in and he can do what he likes with it."

They drove a little further and George reflected on how wonderful it was being in her company on such a lovely day. "This is so nice," he said glancing over to her. She smiled and reached across placing her hand on his thigh. She gently began to massage him and he quickly developed an erection which her fingers stroked.

"Yes, it is nice isn't it?" she murmured flirtatiously.

"Oh god that is so wonderful," exclaimed George, "but I don't think you should do that while I'm driving, I can't concentrate."

Mavis laughed openly and removed her hand. "But seriously," she said, ""it would be nice for you and me to be together in that way wouldn't it?"

"Absolutely," said George emphatically.

Chapter Twenty-five
The Barn

Near the centre of town just a stone's throw from the rugby ground there stood a used car lot which stretched for about seventy-five yards along the road and partly around the corner of a quiet cul-de-sac in which were situated half a dozen or so industrial units. One sold and fitted plastic windows, another sold cheap furniture, another sold second-hand goods and specialised in house clearances. There was a car valet service in another which was closely related to the car sales on the corner. There was also a mechanic shop which appeared to specialise in fast cars, and this establishment was also linked to the car lot on the corner.

The sign above the car lot read, 'Eddies Motors'. Other signs promised, 'The best cars in the country' or 'guaranteed perfect runners'.

This car lot and the valet service as well as the garage although they had separate names, were all owned and run by Eddie Sharp who also owned the freehold land on which they were all situated. Eddie earned a useful rental income from each of the units in the cul-de-sac. All that is except for the property at the very end. This was an old barn of a place which looked as if it might have belonged to a small-holding which existed in the area many years before. The fields had been gobbled up to provide houses and the industrial units and only the barn was left. This was owned together with the freehold land on which it stood by a gentleman by the name of Jim Wild.

Jim was a man in his late fifties who had always been a hard worker. As a small boy, he had risen early every day, to do a paper round and on weekends, when school friends played, Jim would be carrying out deliveries by bicycle for a local grocer's store. This was in a time before the advent of supermarkets in abundance and when housewives would order their supplies from the local neighbourhood store. Jim had a special bicycle like one of those used by postmen, with a specially constructed basket at the front in which all the groceries would be loaded.

When he left school, he went to work in a local factory where he operated a machine for many years. All his working life he saved. He seldom had a holiday and never bought a car and had only one interest or hobby which was boxing. As a young schoolboy he joined the local boxing club which was run by an enthusiast at the premises known as 'The Barn'.

Jim loved boxing and was a favourite with the instructor/teacher who also owned 'The Barn'. The owner had been a serviceman in his younger days and boxed for the Army. He was a tough as nails individual who passed on all his knowledge of the sport to Jim who enthusiastically took up the sport and would be seen pounding the streets daily in training for amateur competitions. He also joined the local rugby club not to play the game of rugby but to be involved in their training sessions which Jim always regarded as second to none.

He had quite a successful career and represented the club in many prestigious tournaments and was locally famous for being a real scrapper in the ring. His ethos was one of never knowing when he was being beaten. Many contests in which he was involved ended with a victory for Jim even though in the early part of the fight it appeared that he was going to lose. His grit and determination nearly always saw him through.

When the time came for the owner of 'The Barn' to retire Jim purchased the place lock stock and barrel spending almost all of his lifetime's savings which he had amassed. It was a bargain made in heaven for both men. For Jim it was the culmination of all his life's dream to own his own gym and for the seller it made perfect sense to pass the business over to his number one member or student.

After the change of ownership Jim gave the outside of the building a fresh lick of paint and erected a new sign above the doorway which read 'Jim's Gym'. Despite this all the locals still referred to the place as 'The Barn'.

Pete Powell was a member of the Barn and usually went there twice a week to do some weight training for strengthening purposes to improve his fitness for his duties as fly half at the nearby rugby club. He was one of Jim's favourite members for a number of reasons. Firstly, there was Jim's connection with the rugby club. He still went there for the fitness training sessions as well as lifting weights in his own premises on a daily basis. For his age Jim was a very fit man and he recognised in Pete a kindred spirit who enjoyed not only playing a game but also enjoyed the practice and training that went into it. Also, Jim was a keen supporter of the game of rugby both at a local and a national level. He often watched the local team when they played at home and admired Pete's skills on the pitch.

Although Jim had freshened the place up with a coat of paint when he took it over it was still very old fashioned in many ways. Although there were some modern exercise machines installed and some exercise classes organised for ladies in an upstairs room, the main area of the Gym still operated as a 'grunt and groan' outfit. In one corner there was a boxing ring and on the opposite side there were many weights and the machinery for lifting them. Traditionally, the premises appealed primarily to male members who strived to build their bodies up rather than to female members who wished to keep their weight down.

Pete arrived on a Sunday morning for a session with the weights. He was accompanied by Gorgon the giant lock forward from the rugby club. They usually worked out together at the Barn. When lifting weights, it is always useful to have someone with you. Pete often did a session with Gorgon whose real name was Jacob. He worked for his father who owned a nearby dairy farm. Although he was slow and ponderous, he was extraordinarily gentle with the herd of cows at the farm.

Pete and Gorgan were like chalk and cheese. Pete was quick witted and intelligent and very good looking whereas Gorgon whilst not ugly per se was by no means what one would describe as a ladies' man. He was slow witted but not completely unintelligent. Although he could never match the nimble wit of Pete, he could appreciate the humour involved when Pete habitually mocked him in a good-natured way. Indeed, it was often Gorgon himself who laughed most heartily when he was the target of Pete's satirical jokes. Perhaps it was the fact that they were such opposites that brought them together.

It was Pete who had nick-named Jacob as Gorgon and although most of the rugby club members had not a clue what the name meant the nick-name stuck. He was extremely fond of Jacob and had been grateful to him on the rugby pitch on more than one occasion when the giant had protected him from predatory players on the other side

The gym was not very busy this Sunday morning. Pete wondered to himself if all the weightlifters were in church. There were just four young men standing around in the weight lifting area when they arrived and they certainly did not look like church goers. Pete had seen them before and did not like the look of them. To him they all looked like whippets who had been pumped up to look like bulldogs, It was clear that they had all worked hard to increase the size of their shoulders and biceps but they still had puny legs. Instead of working hard they appeared to be standing around chatting. Pete noted that two of them were twins each with a similar quiff in their hair. He had noticed before that they preferred to loiter around looking to intimidate anyone who attempted to use the weights with which they were occupied or make snide jokes to each other about any other Gym members or ogle any of the ladies from the upstairs exercise classes who were injudicious enough to come in.

When Pete and Gorgon arrived, they stood back respectfully from the weights and all leaned nonchalantly against the window sill on one side of the room. Predictably they did not tidy away the weights they had been using and some of these remained on a bar which was positioned above a bench.

The first thing Pete and Gorgon did was to load an extra one hundred and fifty kilograms on the bar. Gorgon then lowered himself onto the bench and pressed the bar upwards twelve times with consummate ease. The onlookers grimaced to each other at the enormous power displayed by the lock forward. When it was Pete's turn to lift, he had to reduce the weight on the bar a little but still lifted more in his set of bench presses than the lounging spectators had managed. Both of them worked the weights vigorously for about forty-five minutes while the others continued to hang about.

When they were leaving, they both paused in the entrance way to pass the time with Jim. "Good session?" asked Jim who was doing some paperwork at the front desk of the building.

"Yeah, pretty good," said Pete mopping his brow in mock exhaustion. "Who are those blokes in there now?" he asked Jim.

"Oh, them!" replied Jim with disgust. "They don't know the meaning of the term 'work out', they are just posers." he said.

"Who are those twins?" asked Pete. "I think I remember them from my schooldays but they were very skinny then. Do they spend much time in here?"

"Yes, unfortunately," said Jim. "Not that they are a great deal of trouble. I just don't like them. But they pay their money like everybody else so I can't say much. The twins are called Gibson," he continued, "They come from the rough end of the council estate."

"Gibson," repeated Pete slowly, "Yeah, I think I remember them now. Never liked them! I see there are a few flashy cars out the back, do they belong to them?"

"Hmm, yes," said Jim with a similar amount of contempt. "They work I think for the car lot on the corner. At least they are always hanging around there when they're not in here. Not that they ever look as though they are doing any work."

"Hmm," said Pete with some interest. "So they work for 'Eddie's Motors', do they? That's very interesting."

"Yes," confirmed Jim. "That's why they're in here all the time. Not that they work hard when they are in here. I'm pretty sure that they use steroids rather than hard work to develop their muscles. Not that I've any proof but I did find a needle in the toilets once. But if I had any evidence of drug taking, I would ban them straight away."

"Well," said Pete. "If you ever get any trouble from them just give a shout to the Rugby club and we'll get a few bodies over here to give you a hand."

Here he clapped his companion across the shoulders, "They wouldn't want to mix it with Jacob here, would they, Jake?"

Gorgon smiled modestly and Jim could believe, looking at him that nobody in their right mind would want to risk a contretemps with him.

"Well, thanks lads," he said, ""but I think I can handle them."

Chapter Twenty-six
Charlie meets Des

Charlie Chivers the International Detective made his way to the Jubilee Inn. He had a meeting arranged with an old colleague from the police force. Charlie reflected as he approached the Jubilee that its lounge bar was in effect the conference room of his business.

He entered the pub and was greeted by Reg Partridge the landlord. "Morning, Charlie," he said, ""Your usual is it?"

Charlie said hello and also said yes to a pint of his preferred beer.

"Don't see you in here very often at lunch times," said Reg. "No work today?"

Charlie said he had arranged to see someone and ordered himself a packet of crisps. Whilst he was waiting to be served, he glanced idly at the photos of Reg behind the bar. He pointed to one of the photographs which he had not previously noticed. "Who's that?" he asked.

Reg looked and said, ""That's Bob Dylan."

"Really?" said Charlie, "He looks so young. Where was that taken?"

"I met him on the Aust ferry a few years ago. Before the Severn bridge was built. I think he was on his way to Cardiff." He selected a different photograph which pictured Reg kissing Shirley Bassey. "Which is where that one was taken," Reg said proudly.

Charlie shook his head in apparent disbelief and said, ""Well I never. You are amazing, Reg."

The landlord looked pleased and Charlie seated himself at a table to await his appointment. He thought back to a time many years ago when he had attended a police recruitment college many miles away. There he had encountered and become friendly with a fellow recruit who was the same age as him. This young man's name was Des Onions and they struck up a firm friendship which lasted through the years. Des in recent years (having served in many places) returned to the local area and was no longer P.C. Onions. He was now known as Detective Inspector Desmond O'Nighons. Charlie chuckled when he thought about this and reflected to himself,

"You'll always be Des Onions to me."

Soon Desmond arrived and bought himself a sandwich and a drink and joined Charlie at the table. They reminisced for a while and then got down to business. Charlie explained about Eddie Sharp and Simon Nibble and described in general terms the information that he had in respect of both of them and also how that information had been obtained.

Charlie and Des had served together when they started their careers and they both knew and understood each other well and also trusted each other implicitly. Charlie did not pussyfoot around but told Des exactly how he had obtained the tapes he had and the exact information contained on them. He trusted Des completely not to reveal to anyone how this information had been obtained. He also told him about the information Pete had given him but did not reveal Pete's details.

Des assured Charlie that if the contents of the tapes were exactly how Charlie had described that he (Des) would be very interested. He admitted to Charlie that receiving such evidence which seemingly would lead to a conviction in respect of a well-known business man and his respected solicitor would be a feather in the cap of the local CID.

"Sounds like a real nest of vipers," he said and Charlie confirmed that was the case.

"I kid you not, Des," he said, ""these tapes are mustard. The only thing as I see it is how the evidence would stack up when they are first approached. I can't for the life of me think that they are going to hold up their hands and say it's a fair cop."

"No, I agree," said Des, "but let me have a nose about in our records and see if something else comes up which might prove useful."

"OK," agreed Charlie who felt encouraged, "And what about the Nark fund? Is there a chance of any sort of financial reward?"

"Definitely," said Des "don't you worry about that."

Chapter Twenty-seven
Lionel's Last Purchase

Lionel Witherspoon was the last person to leave the office as usual. After locking the doors he made his way to the car park where he had left his car early in the morning. He placed his money in the ticket machine and as usual was astounded at the daily fee imposed. He looked forward to next month when he would begin to receive a manager's salary.

Being a single man who had little ability to cook and no partner to look after him and /or cook for him he had two alternatives at the end of each day:

1   Eat out at a restaurant or
2   Buy a ready-made meal.

The former was too expensive for him so he usually purchased the latter either on a daily basis or occasionally in bulk on weekends when he had the time to visit a supermarket.

Today he knew he had nothing at home to eat and so he determined to visit a store which he had used before and which was conveniently on the road home. The store was situated approximately halfway between the office and the house where Lionel lived in a small village on the main road. It was a small shop cum supermarket which was in effect a village store. Lionel knew that they stocked the ready-made meals which he usually chose to purchase.

He was also aware that at this time of evening a young girl, presumably the daughter of the shopkeeper was often serving behind the counter. Lionel was attracted to her and usually extended the time he spent in the store, by purporting to decide what to buy and then inevitably changing his mind and examining the goods again. All the time he would be observing the young girl while pretending to look at the wares.

The store was on the right side of the road so Lionel had to park on the left-hand side of the road and walk across to the store. This he did and entered the store and was excited to see that she was indeed on duty near the till. She was a very slender girl of approximately thirteen years of age with long dark hair. She had skin of a light brown hue and Lionel guessed that one at least of her parents must be of eastern extraction, perhaps Indian or Pakistani. She wore a school uniform, a short blue skirt with a top of matching colour and long white socks and black shiny shoes. She looked up when he entered but took little or no notice of him. She had earphones on and was seated on a stool with one foot on the top bar and the other leg on the bottom bar. The result was that her upper leg, being higher, exposed all of her thigh right up to her knickers. She seemed unaware of this and nodded her head in time with the music she was listening to.

Lionel was not brazen enough, to stand and stare and so had to busy himself apparently examining the contents of a freezer chest. Occasionally he peeped round the side of a display unit, noting that the young girl was still positioned in the same erotic way. He was overcome with excitement and kept bobbing back and forth for as long as he could decently manage without being too obvious.

Eventually he chose one or two items and made his way slowly to the checkout planning to himself that he might engage her in a harmless conversation and see how things developed. Just as he reached her and she looked up to serve him, a door opened behind her and a man came out. As he had shrewdly guessed the man was of Indian or Pakistani appearance. Seeing Lionel with his items he allowed his daughter to serve him and give him his change and waited to talk to her.

Lionel had no alternative but to leave the store and he turned when he was outside to see what was going on. He waited in case the father would return to the inner room or whether he would stay in the shop area. He planned, if the man vacated the shop quickly, to return to the store under the pretence that he had forgotten to buy something.

As it turned out the father was obviously replacing the girl at the checkout and he watched as she moved to the connecting door. With a sigh he stepped off the pavement to cross the road and get back to his car.

There was an engine roar followed by a screech of brakes. Lionel was struck broadside by a heavy lorry the driver of which had no time to stop as Lionel stepped out without looking. He was lifted off of his feet and travelled about sixty feet in the air but he was already dead before he landed.

The sign on the side of the lorry that struck Lionel said, ""Sodford Brick Works Ltd."

Chapter Twenty-eight
Bad News

The following day Tom Richards was the first to arrive at the office as usual. He went through all the normal procedures, unlocking cupboards etc then made himself a cup of tea and settled down to read the *Daily Mail* for a while expecting Lionel to arrive shortly.

By the time everyone except Mr Pigg had arrived Tom was fairly confident that Lionel was not going to turn up.

"I wonder why he's not here?" said Helen when everyone was present. "Were there any telephone calls, Tom?"

Tom Richards shook his head gravely. "No," he said. "Perhaps he has had a problem with his car or perhaps he is sick."

Everyone agreed that sickness was unlikely because the previous day he had looked quite well. They took the opportunity to discuss the visit of George and Mavis to Bill Butler's house. They reported what had happened and everyone was pleasantly surprised to hear of Bill's improvement but shocked that his condition had been so poorly assessed. They all agreed that Bill's comments as to his ability to return to work should not be reported. They thought, as had George and Mavis, that the medical certificate should be handed over to Mr Pigg and leave him to draw conclusions.

"It stands to reason," observed Tom Richards, "that as the certificate is only for a month then Bill is required to return to work when that time expires unless a further certificate has been issued. It's all down to the doctors so let us leave it to them."

Everyone agreed that was the correct position but nevertheless none of them could believe that Mr Pigg could have been so incompetent.

Eventually this topic of conversation was terminated with the arrival of Mr Pigg himself. Initially he went straight to his room and stayed there for approximately half an hour. When it finally became clear to everyone that he was not coming out they elected Tom Richards as the appropriate member of staff to go and tell him. This Tom duly did and after ten minutes or so he came back to his desk.

"He is checking his file," he reported, "to see if there is a telephone number he can ring. Otherwise we'll just have to wait for Lionel to check in."

There was very little post that morning and therefore no immediate problem with Lionel's absence.

Later in the day Pete and George retired to the basement where they had a chat. To begin with Pete asked how the journey to Bill's house had been and how things were going with Mavis. George confirmed that everything was well and that he still felt the same about her. Pete nodded and was happy for him.

Pete then asked him if he would like to do him a favour. George said of course and how could he help. Pete sucked his teeth and then grimaced a little and said perhaps he would be asking too much. George pressed him and insisted that he explain what he was thinking. Pete then told him of the people he had seen in the gym and what their connection was with Eddie Sharp whom he had already spoken to George about. He was wondering if someone could make enquiries at the gym about the possible supply of steroid drugs.

"But how will I know who they are?" asked George.

"That's easy," said Pete. "There're about four or five of them and two of them are twins named Gibson. You can't miss them."

"But what do I ask them for?" said George.

"You simply have to attend the gym, do some work with the weights and ask anyone there if they know of anyone who can supply something to make you a bit more muscular. They will probably contact you if they hear you. I couldn't do it myself because they know who I am. They don't know you. If they offer to sell you anything and or do hand anything over then let's hope they will leave fingerprints on it and you could give evidence to say they were dealers. If they sell it to you at the car lot so much the better."

"Sounds straightforward enough," said George, "but I'm really ignorant about drugs. It's not dangerous is it?"

"Not really," said Pete, "you simply ask if anyone knows anyone and leave it to them to then propose something to you. I'm pretty sure they use it themselves but it's just a question of whether or not they are prepared to deal with others. I bet they are. Jim who owns the gym has found a needle or two in the toilets and I'm sure it can't be anyone but them. Anyway," he said, ""Gorgon and I will be just around the corner when a deal takes place."

George said he would be willing to give it a try. Pete said he would give the owner of the gym a ring to ensure that George could gain an entry on a trial basis.

The two of them returned to the general office just in time to hear the buzzer go off in the public waiting area. Mavis went to answer the call and after a brief conversation she returned and walked through the general office on her way to Mr Pigg's office. On her way through she whispered fiercely, "It's the police."

A few moments later she re-emerged followed by Mr Pigg who made his way to the public counter. "Oh really, my goodness," they heard him yell. "Do come through." He then returned followed by a male and a female police officer in uniform. All three went into Mr Pigg's office and shut the door.

The rest of the staff looked at Mavis who was looking quite shocked. "It's about Lionel," she said. "They had his name and information and wanted to know if he worked here. Do you think he's done something wrong?" she asked. "No," said Tom. "I think it may be something different."

After ten minutes or so the police came out again and Mr Pigg escorted them to the outside door. He then came back into the general office and stood for a moment without speaking. He took a deep breath and then announced, "The police have just informed me that Lionel was involved in a road accident yesterday evening. He was killed I am afraid."

The information was a complete shock to the whole office. Mr Pigg when he recovered spent the rest of the day on the telephone to the Regional Office and thereafter to all the other offices in the region. In the circumstances it did not occur to him to pay attention to the medical certificate from Bill which George and Mavis had given to him.

Chapter Twenty-nine
Sunny Sandra

The following evening Pete and Sandra met again. He had booked a table for them at the Italian restaurant situated below the flat where Pete lived.

As usual the restaurant was quite busy and the owner, Filippo, Pete's landlord, was on duty and escorted them to their table. As he handed them a menu he said to Pete, "Eetza nice to see you again, Pete."

"Good to see you too, Phil. This is my friend Sandra," he said.

Filippo grasped Sandra's hand and planted a flamboyant kiss upon it in typical latin style. "Bella," he declared. "Whatta can I getta you to drink?"

Pete ordered a beer and Sandra asked for a glass of wine. Filippo left to get the drinks and the couple studied their menus. When the drinks arrived and they had ordered their food they chatted casually. "You look nice tonight," said Pete who genuinely meant what he said.

"Well, thank you," Sandra's honey-coloured eyes seemed to sparkle.

"Do you want to hear my latest news?" she added excitedly. Pete nodded vigorously. "I got that job!" she almost shrieked, "Can you believe that?"

"You mean the job on TV?" asked Pete.

Sandra nodded. "Yes, I'm so excited and the first investigatory story I intend to run is the one you've given me," she said, "Can you give me an update?"

Pete told her about his latest piece of information which he had gleaned at Jim's Gym. He explained that the gym low-life were apparently employees of Eddie.

Sandra thought this was very interesting and confirmed that she would definitely look into it. Pete enquired about any research she had carried out on the matter of the quality of the evidence which he had given to her. She poo-pooh'd it and stated firmly that both the lawyers for the newspaper and for the T.V. company were quite optimistic about things.

"Their attitude is, that generally, they are unafraid of any threats of legal proceedings. So long as there is a grain of truth in any allegations, they are happy to publish and be damned. They are quite gung-ho. Not many people want to risk court action against a newspaper or a TV company. Mostly because they cannot afford it. The newspapers however can and even if they lose the case, they sell more papers.

"Now tell me some more about these body-building drugs."

Pete said that he knew little about the drugs themselves or how people came by them. He knew they were illegal and connected with sport but although he had always been involved in sport in one way or another, he had never come across anyone who took them. "It's only the top athletes or the bodybuilders who are interested in taking them." he said.

"I certainly wouldn't want to take any. They may build muscle but as far as I understand they affect nearly every organ in the body including the brain. You can ask Jim at the Barn. He knows a lot more about them than me. He has found some needles in the toilets at his gym." he said.

"The Barn?" enquired Sandra. "I thought it was called Jim's Place or something?"

Pete explained about the name of the gym and exactly where it was situated. He described again the low life of the weights section of the gym and mentioned the twins. "But be careful of these people," he urged. "They do not look very nice."

Sandra said that she was fine and had interviewed hundreds of scumbags in her career so was not bothered.

"You have the incisive mind of a journalist, and the face of an angel," he said. "You will be perfect on TV. Oh, and also you have the legs of a chorus girl."

Sandra laughed, but appreciated the compliment.

"What was the name of the Italian chap who you said married Mr Carter's daughter?" she asked. "Perhaps your friend, Filippo, knows him?"

Pete admitted that was a possibility. He knew how ex-patriots tended to know everyone from their home country.

Pete chose a pizza and Sandra opted for lasagne. When these arrived Pete ordered a bottle of Chianti to go with it.

By mid-evening the early rush died down and during a slight lull in proceedings, Fillipo took the opportunity to join them at their table. Pete offered him a glass of wine which he graciously accepted.

"You are a beautiful couple," he announced. He patted Pete on the leg and said to Sandra, "He's my favourite. He is a good tenant and a wonderful sportsman." Fillipo was a fanatical sports' fan, particularly football and rugby.

"He's a star player you know," he said proudly. Sandra smiled and said she knew. She explained that she worked at the local newspaper and had interviewed Pete for the paper.

Pete added, "And now she's been offered a job on TV."

Fillipo said, ""Mama mia! you will be perfect on TV, you are so beautiful."

Sandra blushed and smiled.

"You are right there, Phil," said Pete.

"Ask him about that chap," urged Sandra.

"Oh, yes," said Pete. "Do you know a man called Giovanni... eh... what was his name...? Oh yes, Pettacinni. I presume you know all the Italians who live locally? He is married to the sister of Mr Ken Carter the chairman of the Rugby club."

"Si, si," confirmed Fillipo, "but he's not Italian. He comes from Malta. When he first come to this country I give him a job here as a waiter but he did not stay too long."

"Was he no good as a waiter?" asked Pete.

"No, no, he was OK, but a bit lazy. Once he marry into the money," here Fillipo rubbed his fingers with his thumb, "He no longer want to work. But he was a gambler. Always around the corner in the betting shop. He likka the horses."

Shortly after Fillipo returned to work leaving Pete and Sandra to chat further. When they had finished their meal, Pete settled the bill and they went upstairs to his flat. Pete put on some music and they sat together on the sofa.

"Phil's right," he said. "You will look wonderful on TV. I'm so pleased for you that you got the job."

"Yes," she said, and the sparkle was still in her eyes. "I am so thrilled about it."

They kissed at first in a romantic formal way but after a second or two their contact became breathless and lustful. Pete's hand which had been holding her face, descended to her neck and then began to undo the buttons on her blouse. He pushed the blouse aside from her shoulders and then slipped his hand into her bra and fondled her nipples which immediately became erect.

She in the meantime began to undo the buttons on his shirt as he pushed up her bra to reveal her bare breasts. She whispered in his ear, "Shall we go to bed?"

Chapter Thirty
The Barn Again

A few days later George spoke to Pete at work and told him that he thought he might go to the gym that evening. Pete asked him what time he was thinking of going and said he would give Jim the owner a ring to OK it for him.

The work in the office did not appear to have suffered as a result of Lionel's absence but everyone (except for Mr Pigg himself) knew that there was not enough work to keep all the staff going flat out. The economic law which stated that 'work expanded to meet the time allotted to it' definitely applied in Mr Pigg's office. However little work there was it still took the staff all day to do it.

Mr Pigg himself was not too concerned about the day-to-day tasks of the office which he had always habitually left entirely to Bill Butler and latterly to Lionel. The staff were experienced and managed quite well by themselves.

As boss Mr Pigg was wholly concerned with telephone contacts with other offices in the region. These conversations were almost entirely unnecessary and unofficial but Mr Pigg himself always regarded such contacts as essential. He had also had conversations with the welfare department to determine what information was in place regarding Lionel's next of kin who needed to be advised of his death. Mr Pigg was relieved to hear that this department had the necessary details and would be dealing with the matter of Lionel's untimely departure.

He had a long telephone conversation with Mr Jenkins the Regional Controller who was quite shocked to hear of Lionel's unfortunate death. "I shall have to give this some consideration Arnold," he said. "Obviously, these circumstances must postpone your intended promotion to this office until suitable arrangements can be made. I must let the dust settle before making any rash decisions. Until then you will remain in your present post, Arnold."

Mr Pigg indicated that he entirely understood and would await further instructions from him.

"Good man. Arnold," said Mr Jenkins decisively and then hung up.

George arrived at the Barn at the allotted time and signed the attendance book at the front counter. The person at the counter was a middle-aged woman and so George assumed that Jim the owner was elsewhere.

He went into the changing room and then into the gymnasium area which was sparsely occupied by just a few men. In the corner which accommodated the majority of the weights there were four or five men of about twenty-five years of age. They all looked extremely muscular in an unnatural way and although they looked as though they had done a lot of weight lifting in the recent past, they were certainly not doing much when George walked in.

He insinuated his way past them to find some barbells of a modest weight and began exercising his biceps. He noticed that these fellows were observing him with barely concealed disdain and he also noticed that two of them were twins. He knew that this must be the group that Pete had spoken of.

He worked his way around some of the machines on the premises testing out the strength of various muscles in his body. The group of men occupied their time, when they were not watching George, by singly lifting the odd weight or two accompanied with a great deal of grunting and then returning to their fellows who would all from time-to-time stand flexing their muscles in front of a floor to ceiling mirror.

George determined that the best way to proceed was to feign complete ignorance of weight lifting in order to enlist some help from them and maybe thereafter engage them in conversation. He thought to himself that he did not really need to feign anything. He was indeed a rooky at this sort of thing. He made a bit of a song and dance about the particular exercise he was attempting and looked appealingly towards the closest person to him who smiled contemptuously and stepped forward to take some weight off the bar George was trying to lift.

"First time?" he asked disdainfully, and George said that it was.

"It's much harder than it looks," he said to the man, comparing his bulging muscles to his own. "How on earth do you get that big?" he asked. "Does it take years? What age did you start?"

"Oh," he replied, inflating his chest slightly and taking a glance at the mirror. "I've been doing it for a while."

George puffed and sighed a bit to indicate that he was already exhausted, which was not the case and tried to extend the conversation. "How many hours per day do you have to do to look like you?"

The other paused and once again glanced at himself in the mirror. "Oh, a couple of hours per day, at least." He informed him with fake modesty.

"But I could never spare the time to manage that," said George. "I only have a couple of hours a week. Is there no other way of building muscle?

What about these food supplements I've heard about? Would they do the trick?"

The other shook his head emphatically. "No" he said, ""supplements are OK, but they don't build muscle. You have to lift weights for that. There are other things of course but they are not sold on the open market."

"Really?" said George, "that sounds interesting. How can one get hold of those?"

"Well… said the other tentatively.

Just at that moment the door opened and all eyes turned to look. A stunning blond girl in a very fetching lilac tight vest and black leggings strolled in. All the eyes of the weight lifters were out on stalks and they all appreciated the view. The young lady smiled broadly and went straight to a running machine and commenced pounding. The men were all watching her buttocks working hard and it was a wonder that they did not salivate.

She worked her way around the room all the while listening to music on her earphones, trying various machines until she had worked up a bit of a sweat, and then walked over to the group and said, "So, you boys are so big, aren't you?"

"Yeah, we're big everywhere," said one of the twins, with lewd intent. The others sniggered.

She seemed entirely unabashed at this and said, "Do you go in for competitions?" she asked, adjusting her earphones.

"Occasionally," said another flexing his bicep and looking at himself in the mirror.

"Hmm," said the blond appreciatively. "Very impressive. And which one of you boys usually wins?" she enquired coquettishly.

"There're different categories," said one of them churlishly.

"Oh, I see," she said, although the other had not explained or defined what this meant.

"And do you all manage to look like this without any artificial aid?" This was met with a dumb silence from the group.

"Oh, come on," she exclaimed. "I bet you can't look the way you do without some steroid enhancement. You can't fool me," she said archly laughing. "Are you trying to tell me, you've never even tried it?" she held up her finger and thumb and said, ""Not even a tiny bit eh?" and laughing again.

The men guffawed and one or two jokingly admitted that they might.

"Aah, aah!" she cried triumphantly, and then turned on her heel and left the room.

After she had gone, they all exchanged remarks about her and all heartily agreed that they would not mind lifting a few weights with her.

"I wouldn't say no to a few bench presses with her," said one of the twins and everyone laughed including George who found himself now to be a part of the group.

He managed to isolate the man that he had been talking to before and said, "But seriously though, she was right, wasn't she? Could you get hold of any of that stuff for me perhaps?"

The other man grimaced slightly and sucked his teeth as if he were talking about something distasteful which in some ways he was. He looked both ways even though it was obvious that the room was empty apart from his friends and George. "You'll need to talk to the twins" he said and pointed at them as if there were more than one set of twins in the room.

They sauntered over and one of them asked, "Who's looking to buy then?"

"I just wanted something to give me a bit more muscle," said George hopefully.

"Not seen you here before," said the other twin suspiciously, "where do you come from?"

"I'm new to the town," said George, "I've just joined the gym today. If you can't manage it, that's OK. I just wanted to look like you lads." he added gratuitously.

The first twin said, ""It's two hundred quid cash. Same time same place next week, in the car lot at the corner. Come alone!"

George said OK, and that he would see them next week with the money. He went to the changing room to don his clothes. Then he made his way out and paused at the counter to sign himself out. This time there was an older grey-haired man at the desk talking to the blond who had been in the Gymn. The man stopped talking to the blond, to allow George to sign out. "Aagh," he said, ""You must be Pete Powell's friend. How did you get on?"

"Fine thanks," replied George, and made his way outside.

The blond followed him out. "Excuse me," she said to him. "Did I hear that you are acquainted with Pete Powell?"

George said that he was and waited. "Do you mind if I ask what your relationship to Pete is?"

"I'm George Davies," he said, ""I work with Pete." He looked into the honey-coloured eyes of his inquisitor.

"My name is Sandra," she said, ""I'm friendly with Pete. Were you talking to those guys in there?"

George said he had, and gave a bit of a grimace and smiled. Sandra smiled also and said goodbye and went to her car.

Chapter Thirty-one
La Scala

The next day Tom Richards was the first to arrive at the office as usual. He opened up and did all the normal things which he did every day and then settled down with his cup of tea and the Daily Mail.

The next person to arrive was George who seated himself next to Tom as usual. As they awaited the arrival of all the others they chatted. Inevitably the main subject of discussion was the news of Lionel's death and the effect it might have on office life.

"It seems," said George "that Mr Pigg will not be leaving us now. At least not for the moment."

"So it would seem," agreed Tom who took any information about Mr Pigg with a pinch of salt.

"You don't like him very much, do you?" said George.

"Well let's say I'm not his number one fan," said Tom. "I worked under commanding officers all over the world throughout the whole of my in the Army," added Tom,

"But I never served under anyone like him." Tom said this almost with a sneer. "I understand that you are courting Mavis" he enquired.

George was surprised by Tom's use of the old-fashioned term. He had not thought of his

relationship with Mavis as being courting.

"Do you think that's silly?" asked George. Tom exhaled long and hard and said,

"It's nothing to do with me. You must do what you want to do of course. One thing I will say is that there is much more to Mavis than appears on the surface. There is a lot more to her than the obvious charms she displays. She is a lovely girl."

George was surprised and impressed by Tom's opinion of Mavis. He himself had already come to the conclusion that much of what Tom had said was true and that Mavis had hidden depths.

One by one the others arrived and there was only Mr Pigg left to come.

Mavis arrived looking exceptionally bright and cheerful and once again wearing only a minimal amount of make-up. Once again, she wore a bright and flowery dress. Everyone thought that she looked fresh and lovely again but only Helen expressed that feeling in words. "You're looking nice again," she said. "Is that another new dress?"

Mavis looked down automatically at the dress itself and smoothed her hands downwards across her breasts. "Oh, this," she said modestly. "I bought this in Marks and Spencer's sale last year, but this is the first time I've worn it."

"Well, it really suits you," said Helen. I think it's about time I bought myself something fresh but I dare say it wouldn't look as good on me as it does on you?"

All the men in the room silently agreed with her. Helen wore one of her usual dowdy outfits and it was the contrast with this that emphasised the freshness of Mavis.

Mavis announced that for a few weeks now she had been going to exercise classes and perhaps this had some influence on how she looked. She proudly said that she had lost a few pounds.

"Well, it certainly agrees with you," said Helen mournfully looking down again at her own unfashionable appearance.

"And you've given up smoking," she declared in mock frustration. "I don't stand a chance now."

Again, the men in the room secretly agreed but said nothing.

"How long is it since you stopped smoking?" asked Pete.

"Ever since Piggy introduced the smoking ban," answered Mavis. "I just couldn't be bothered to go all the way down to the street every time I wanted to have one and I soon realised that I didn't really need them. They were so expensive and I feel so much better!"

"It's the best thing you've ever done," said Pete who had always been in favour of the anti- smoking ban.

Mr Pigg finally arrived and busied himself on the telephone as usual. Due to the fact that there was no one in the glasshouse he had to spend some of his day in there signing documents etc in place of Lionel. Pete and George had little time therefore to retire to the basement. They did find one moment in the day when they could talk alone and George explained what had gone on at the gymnasium the previous day. When he mentioned the appearance of the blond girl with the honey-coloured eyes, Pete's forehead creased with concern.

"She certainly was a looker," said George. "All the blokes had their tongues hanging out. And she was flirting with them all. Apparently, she knows you."

Pete nodded thoughtfully and said that he thought he knew who she was. "I think it's time we made up a foursome," he said.

"How do you feel about Italian food?"

"Great," said George rubbing his hands together. "I love it."

"Good," said Pete, "so how do you feel about you and Mavis having a meal together this evening in an excellent Italian restaurant. It's downstairs from my flat."

"And who is the other member of the party?" said George expectantly.

"She's called Sandra," said Pete. "I'll book the table, OK?"

George said that was wonderful and he went to whisper the details to Mavis.

When George and Mavis arrived at the Italian restaurant at the agreed time, they were greeted by Fillipo in his customary welcoming manner. He showed them to the table where Pete was sat with an attractive young lady.

George was shocked to realise that it was the same girl that he had met at the Barn the other day. Everyone was introduced and served with the drink of their choice and then while they were glancing at the menu Pete described what Sandra did for a living and also the fact that she was soon to be working on TV.

"Oh, that is so cool," observed Mavis. "You must be so clever. And we all work for Mr Arnold Pigg." she said downcastedly and then they all laughed.

"You certainly had that bunch of yobbos eating out of your hand," said George to Sandra. "If Pete had been there, I'm sure he would have been eaten up with jealousy," he added.

Sandra smiled and Pete patted her hand paternally.

"Yes, well, perhaps it was just as well I wasn't there," he said. "Anyway," he continued, "I didn't know she was going to go there that soon." He still held Sandra's hand and said, "I would have preferred to be nearby and perhaps with Gorgon as a back- up. I just don't like the idea of you seeing them alone," he said patting her hand again.

"Oh, really," Sandra replied, "I was OK. In any case if you had been there, they would have recognised you."

Fillipo returned to take their order and Pete immediately ordered his favourite pizza and persuaded George to order the same. Sandra assured Mavis that the lasagne was very good and so they both plumped for that. Pete also ordered a bottle of Chianti and Fillipo hurried off to place the order. Soon he returned with the bottle and after presenting it to Pete for approval. He opened it with great ceremony and poured some into each glass.

"I avva to say, eets not often that I serve two prettier girls than you." he said in the romantic way which only an Italian could get away with. The girls both smiled and thanked him and Mavis said that she bet he said that to all the ladies who dined there.

"Well at least he never says it to the men," said Pete and everyone laughed, including Fillipo.

They all enjoyed their meal and it was clear that Mavis and Sandra liked each other. When they had finished the meal and settled up Pete invited everybody upstairs to his flat. Once they were settled down Pete asked George to go over again the incident at the gymnasium which he did.

"So, we want someone there to photograph the deal," said Pete, "who do we know with a camera?" he added

"No problem," said Sandra. "I can get my cameraman from the TV programme to do it. He will get a good video film of the whole thing. He's a professional. He'll photograph the money, show it being placed in an envelope then film it being handed over. We also photo graph the numbers of the bank notes which will later be evidence if found in their possession."

"I should be there with Gorgon," said Pete, "just as a back-up."

"Definitely not," responded Sandra. "If you show up, they will be alarmed. My cameraman is a professional. Leave it to him."

"Well, I think I'd better talk it through with Charlie. He has contacts in the police who might wish to witness the hand- over."

"Well, OK," agreed Sandra, "so long as they don't get in the way or compromise my cameraman."

"OK," said Pete. "So long as he gets a clear film of the deal taking place and then pans out to show the premises on which it is taking place. That should give us solid evidence against the twins and a definite possibility that, because it would be happening on his premises, Eddie Sharp was involved in the deal."

"Eddie Sharp?" echoed Mavis who had been quiet throughout, "I know his wife, Doris."

Everyone was surprised to hear this and Pete asked how she knew her.

"I've been going to exercise classes with her for a few weeks," she said. "At the Barn, we hit it off and so each time we go we always go for a coffee and a chat afterwards. She is really quite nice. Her parents own the furniture shop in town. They've always been quite well thought of."

"So how does someone who comes from a nice family marry a sleaze-ball like Sharp Eddie?" asked Pete with genuine astonishment.

"I know," said Mavis. "She admits it. Says it was the biggest mistake of her life but she has a sweet daughter out of it. Actually, I shouldn't be telling you this, but she is thinking of divorcing him."

"I'm not surprised," said Sandra. "What took her so long?"

"Yes, I know," said Mavis again. "We just went for the first cup of coffee and she started sobbing and then it all came out. She's been unhappy for years and was frightened to do anything because she thought she would lose everything and her daughter. I persuaded her to go and see a solicitor and just to encourage her I said I'd go with her for support. We are going to see someone at Duffey Fry & Co next week. We have become quite good friends doing the exercise classes together and talking about her troubles. She is so unhappy and she just unburdened herself on me and we have become really good friends. Isn't it silly." Mavis reflected. "Mavis and Doris perhaps we were thrown together because we both had old fashioned names," she said with a wry smile.

Everyone was amazed by this revelation and George thought yet again how true Tom Richards' words had been when he said that there was more to her than met the eye. When they walked home hand-in-hand he felt really proud of her and he told her as much. She responded by standing on tip toes and kissing him passionately on the lips and told him it was mutual. George felt very happy.

Chapter Thirty-two
Mavis Helps a Friend

Pete got in touch with Charlie Chivers as soon as he could and told him of the recent developments at the gym close to Eddie's car lot. He detailed the agreement struck by George with the muscle- bound Gibson twins and the time and date of the intended transaction. He also told him that the deal, when it took place, would be recorded by a professional photographer.

The International Detective was very interested to hear this and said he would immediately contact his colleague in the local CID to see if he was interested in being involved.

Later he telephoned Pete back to confirm that his contact was very interested and wanted to have a meeting with himself, George and Pete as soon as possible to discuss details. He also asked Pete to bring Sandra with him.

Accordingly, Pete George and Sandra were sitting in the lounge bar of the Jubilee Inn when the International Detective strolled in with a companion who was introduced as Detective Inspector O'Nighons.

They all discussed the intended meeting between George and the Gibson twins. Des Onions told them that he and his colleagues were well aware of the existence of the Gibson twins who each had a record for minor criminal offences including possession of drugs and a number of assaults.

He admitted that they had never been charged with dealing in drugs which was much more serious than mere possession but he was sure that they had been dealing for a while but there had never been sufficient evidence to charge them.

He was very gratified to be able to gather definite evidence of their dealing and particularly if this were to take place on the premises of Eddie Sharp's car lot. He admitted that they had not yet gathered all the evidence that he felt they needed for a full case against Eddie and Simon Nibble and so he did not want this relatively small matter with the Gibson twins to raise the alarm for all concerned.

He had decided therefore that he and some other officers would attend to observe the deal with George who would then hand over the drugs to the police where they would be finger-printed and stored along with the video evidence of the transaction and that a further deal should be arranged later when they were ready and able to co-ordinate a mass arrest of Eddie and his solicitor and the Gibson twins all at the same time. He was very confident that the Gibson twins when presented with the incontrovertible evidence of their guilt would be only too pleased to give evidence against the other two in the hope of saving their own skins.

This was agreed by all and Des Onions made it clear to Sandra that this operation was entirely under his control and warned her of the seriousness if she or her cameraman went outside of the boundaries discussed. Sandra said she understood. It was then agreed, and not before consulting Des Onions, that Sandra would be free to attempt to interview publicly both Eddie Sharp and Simon Nibble and make available to the police any evidence contained in the TV film.

Although all these terms had been agreed Sandra never mentioned to Des Onions that when she had spoken to the men in the gym she had been wearing a tape recorder and not a music maker. Therefore, she had recorded their admissions of taking steroids even though there had been an element of humour in their admission.

Eddie Sharp's wife and Mavis were seated at a table in a coffee shop in town. They had just finished their exercise class and were having their usual chinwag.

"How are you feeling?" asked Mavis.

Since they had met and become friends Mavis was always slightly concerned to enquire about her friend's situation not because she was unsympathetic, but because she found that every time she enquired, she seemed to touch another nerve which produced more sorrow. She had realised that Doris unburdened all her troubles upon her because she had no one else to confide in. Doris had told her that she had no close friends and that she had never felt able to discuss her matrimonial problems with her own parents.

"Oh, all right," she said in an unconvincing way.

"What's the matter today?" said Mavis. "Has something else happened?"

"No," said Doris, "Ive just been worrying about going to the solicitors. I'm scared that Eddie might find out and what he will do."

"Well," said Mavis taking her friend's hand gently. "He won't know will he. In any event he's going to find out eventually isn't he when the divorce papers are served upon him. You are still going through with it, aren't you?"

"Yes," said Doris with a long sigh, "it's just all such a worry. The lady at the solicitors told me on the phone that I had to write down details of all the times when Eddie had behaved badly and bring the notes with me. I,ve been writing for days but still hadn't finished."

"Has he ever hit you?" asked Mavis sympathetically.

"Yes, but not recently. I told you we hadn't slept together for some time and he's now got that girl Sylvia who he carries on with and things have settled down a lot even though the atmosphere is still intolerable."

"Well couldn't you just divorce him for adultery with Sylvia? Why does the lady want all the details of all the other things?"

"I'm not sure," said Doris. "But anyway I have no proof that Eddie is having sex with Sylvia. He's sure to deny it and simply say that she just works for him. But it's not just that that worries me," she said, her eyes filling up with tears.

"She wants me to provide her with details of Eddie's income and resources with written proof of anything I can find. The truth is I don't know anything about his finances or his business and I have no idea what properties if any he owns or what savings he may have. There is no way he will tell me anything and there is no way I can find out. I don't even know if he's got an accountant. She then began to sob and Mavis put an arm around her shoulder and patted her until she pulled herself together.

She breathed in deeply and forced a smile for Mavis. "So, there we are," she summarised, "I live a wretched life with a pig of a man who I cannot stand. I have absolutely no savings of my own and nowhere else to live. I have not had sex with anyone for years and I don't know any details about my husband's financial affairs and I don't know anyone who does."

"You might not know anyone but I sure as hell do," thought Mavis to herself. She told herself that she must stay strong for her friend and patted her on the shoulder again.

"You are still an attractive woman," she assured Doris. "As soon as you get rid of Eddie you will soon find someone else. There are plenty more pebbles on the beach. As for his financial situation I'll see what I can find out at work."

Doris brightened up considerably and thanked Mavis for her support and asked her if she was still able to come with her to Duffey Fry & Co and Mavis confirmed that she would. She wondered to herself how she would feel if she had not had sex for a number of years and she felt so sorry for Doris.

A day or two later Mavis found Pete in the basement area at work. He was standing at the photocopying machine reading through some papers. "I thought I'd find you down here," she said. As she spoke, she looked over his shoulder at the papers he was photocopying. "Anyone I know?" she asked with a wry smile.

Pete smiled too. "I doubt it," he said.

"You know we were talking about Eddie Sharp the other day and I mentioned that I was friendly with his wife?" she asked in a tentative way.

"Yes..." said Pete, slowly raising his eyebrows. "Well... um... I was wondering if you had any information on his financial affairs etc, because his wife needs to show stuff to the divorce solicitor, except she has no idea about any of his affairs. She doesn't know what bank or building society accounts he has or what properties he owns. I thought .... eh ...." she added coquettishly, that you might be able to help .... What do you say... pretty please."

Pete smiled ironically and reached down into his briefcase which was stood next to the photocopier. He sorted out some papers and then photocopied them and handed them over to her. Mavis quickly scanned the pages and could see at a glance how comprehensive they were.

"It's only because we've, erh, known each other for a while," he said. "And it's just between you and me, OK?"

Mavis stood for a moment and then quite unexpectedly burst into tears. She threw herself against his chest and murmured,

"Thanks Pete, you're a star. That woman is so unhappy. This will mean the world to her."

Pete put his arms around her and patted her back and felt somewhat compromised by the fact that her body was so close to him. "Look," he said paternally, "We've had some fun down here but it wouldn't do for George to come in and find us like this would it?"

Mavis shook her head but still made no attempt to withdraw. "I am really fond of him," she said, with tears still streaming down her cheeks.

"You won't ever tell him about you and me, will you?" she entreated. Pete took her by the shoulders and held her at arms-length. "Mum's the word," he assured her. "He'll never find out from me. He's a great bloke and you and he look really good together. So go back upstairs and dry your eyes before anyone misses you."

Mavis planted a big kiss on his cheek and with a final, "thanks again," disappeared out of the basement. Pete watched her go and smiled to himself

Chapter Thirty-three
Alice Helps

Simon Nibble also smiled to himself as he finished dictating an invoice addressed to Eddie Sharp in respect of the share transfers and land acquisition. The invoice was for an astronomical sum considering the normal charging rates for a high street solicitor's office.

He was not bothered by this however since he already knew that the firm's client account already held a massive amount of money previously deposited by Eddie. The invoice which Simon had just dictated was not one that would be delivered to his client but was simply put in place to allow him to transfer the funds across from client account to office. That was why he smiled. After all he thought I have just incurred considerable expense purchasing the seaside apartment in Tenerife. Again, he smiled.

There was a knock at his door and he called, "Come in."

The door opened and his junior, Alice, came nervously into the room wondering why she had been summoned. "Ah, come in, Allison," he said, "take a seat."

"Umm, actually it's Alice," she said, and sat down.

"Of course," said Simon leaning back in his chair. "Now how long have you been with us?" he asked.

Alice felt very nervous, and feared she might be in some kind of trouble. "I haven't done anything wrong, have I?" she asked.

"Why no," said Simon smiling benevolently at her. "Quite the opposite I can assure you. I've heard good things about you, from Mrs Sargent, and I see that you've settled in very well. How are you liking it here?"

Alice said that she was quite happy and found the job interesting. What she did not tell him was that she had been looking for another job because the wages he paid were so low. As if by magic or osmosis Simon said, "I was thinking that it was about time that we arranged an increase in salary for you. After all, you've been here long enough to become really useful. And if I may say so..." he added, with an extra smile, "You are quite a decorative addition to the premises."

Alice was astonished because not only had Mr Nibble never flirted with her before but he had clearly hardly been aware of her existence. She could not begin to fathom what was happening. Nevertheless, her ears pricked up at the mention of a salary increase.

"And perhaps, we'll give you some money with which you can buy some new clothes," he said in such a way as to imply that this was not unusual. "Not of course, that I mean that you don't look smart already. You always look very pretty. But a smart lady around the place is rather like an adornment, don't you think? It's good for business. Think of it as a uniform."

Alice did not know what to say. Mr Nibble had hardly looked at her and now he was being so nice. She still did not understand.

"While you are here, I should just get you to sign a document for me," he said almost matter of factly. "You know Mr Sharp, of course?"

Alice confirmed that she did although she did not like him but she did not say this.

"Well, I have some documents here that I would just like you to sign as a witness if you'd be good enough," he said, shuffling some papers on the desk. "Do you have a boyfriend or fiancé perhaps?" he enquired, whilst looking at the papers. Alice said she did have a boyfriend who worked in a local factory. She said they were not engaged yet but were hoping to marry eventually.

"It's just that I expect you both struggle to afford a good holiday, don't you?" he suggested. "I've just purchased a beach apartment in Tenerife" he said, as if it were the most natural topic of conversation between them. How would you feel about a week's holiday there, in the sunshine, with your boyfriend? Nothing to pay and the week includes the aeroplane flights to and fro. Doesn't that sound nice, eh?"

Simon then produced a brochure from under his desk and showed her a page. "This is the apartment here," he said pointing a finger. "Doesn't it look nice? I believe the weather is perfect there at this time of year. What do you think?"

Alice was dumbfounded and quite overcome. The picture of the apartment in the brochure looked beautiful to her. She was already imagining how wonderful it would be to go there with her boyfriend. She smiled hopefully.

"Let's just sign these papers a moment and then you can have another look at this" he said, replacing the brochure with the papers for signature.

"As a bona fide member of staff your signature is valid. Just sign here, here, and here," he said as he indicated the places on the pages. Alice was totally bemused but happily signed the documents as Simon had assured her that it was completely in order.

Simon took back the documents and smiled at her. He handed her the brochure of the Tenerife apartment again. "Do have another look at this and decide when you would like to go out there. You show it to your boyfriend and let me know when you would both like to go then I can book the flights for you, OK?" Alice was overcome with delight and nodded enthusiastically.

"Oh, just one thing," added Simon by way of an afterthought, "Don't mention this to any of the other members of staff. I am sure you understand that there could be some jealousy among some of them and it would not be possible to accommodate all of them. Shall we let it be our secret?"

Alice again nodded and found herself thanking him profusely. She took her leave of Simon who smiled as she left the room.

Chapter Thirty-four
Preparation

Mavis and Doris met outside of the offices of Duffey Fry & Co ten minutes before the appointment time. Doris was very nervous and breathing deeply and expressing to her friend her overwhelming doubts about the whole idea of even attempting to dump Eddie. Mavis tried hard to instil some confidence in her friend and kept telling her that everything would be fine.

Without the presence of her friend Doris knew that this was the time when she would have lost her nerve if she had been on her own. "Thank you so much for coming," she said clutching the hand of Mavis. "I would not have been able to do this by myself."

Mavis took her arm and marched her into the office and they announced themselves to the receptionist and then sat down to await their turn with Mrs Robinson who was a legal assistant who specialised in divorce work.

When they were admitted to her room, they found Mrs Robinson to be a friendly, sympathetic middle-aged woman with plenty of experience. She also had a reassuring manner which put Doris at her ease.

She spent the first five minutes or so making written notes regarding the standard items which would be included in the divorce petition when it was lodged with the court. She asked Doris to supply the full names and addresses of herself and her husband, their dates of birth, the full name(s) and age(s) of any children, the date of the marriage etc. She asked Doris if she had her marriage certificate and this was handed over.

She then asked Doris if she had made notes on the behaviour issues between herself and Eddie. Doris produced the notes which she had made, which ran to about five pages. They sat in silence while Mrs Robinson read through them pausing only to ask Doris one or two questions.

She then moved on to the question of the financial affairs of Eddie and here Mavis produced the papers which Pete had copied for her. Mrs Robinson asked how she came by this information and Mavis told her where she worked. Doris asked if this information could be used or would it perhaps be disallowed because of where it came from. Mrs Robinson said it did not matter and that the court would accept almost any information as long as it was truthful. Clearly none of the facts listed in these papers could be challenged by Eddie since they were patently true, some of the documents even signed by Eddie himself.

In any event, she offered, once the other side saw the quality of the evidence offered against them, they would not waste time and money challenging it. Any competent lawyer, she assured them would advise Eddie to settle reasonably as soon as possible.

She was able to assure them that the papers produced by Mavis were dynamite. She was able to guarantee that Doris would be able to retain the matrimonial home where she could live with her daughter and obtain a substantial lump sum payment together with maintenance for the daughter.

"It is not very often in a divorce case that one gets such comprehensive evidence of a respondent's financial position. There are however some aspects of the information you have given to me that slightly concern me," she said.

Both Doris and Mavis raised their eyebrows with surprise.

"Don't misunderstand me," she said. "You have a very strong case and I can assure you that you will be financially secure when all this is finished. There are some aspects, as I said, which are unusual and I would like to refer this to a barrister who specialises in divorce work. I think this would be advantageous to you."

"Oh, I'm not sure about that" said Doris. "I don't have much money. What will it cost?"

"Not to worry," replied Mrs Robinson. "You've already given me a payment to cover standard costs for a divorce case and that expense will be recouped from your husband in the proceedings. So too, will any costs or expenses incurred in respect of the barrister's involvement. The one I have in mind for you is called Phillipa Fry. She operates from Clifton Chambers in Bristol and she is very experienced and well thought of. I will arrange a meeting with her and let you know as soon as it is arranged. Now I have your telephone number but of course I note that you still live with your husband and I am wondering if a telephone call would cause any difficulties for you.

"Yeah, no problem," said Doris. "He's usually out every morning playing golf or drinking in the pub."

They said goodbye and then left the offices. Outside they paused for a chat. "Well, she seemed very nice, and quite professional," said Mavis, and Doris agreed.

"Shall we have a quick cup of coffee?" she suggested and Mavis agreed.

In the nearby coffee shop, they sat down together at a table and Doris confirmed that the interview had not been anywhere near as bad as she had anticipated. In fact, she admitted that she had been really encouraged by the attitude of Mrs Robinson. "All the same," she noted, "I'm not entirely sure about the involvement of this barrister she mentioned and God knows what will happen when Eddie gets served with the papers." Mavis as always was encouraging and offered to go with her to Clifton Chambers if she wished. Doris said she definitely would be glad if Mavis could accompany her.

Mavis was not the only one attending a meeting that day. At the same time Pete was in conference with Ken Carter. They met at the Plume of Feathers public house and Pete brought him up to date with what had been going on with Eddie Sharp and his solicitor. Mr Carter was very grateful for the time and trouble and interest which Pete had spent trying to help him. "I just need to know that both of them can be exposed as the crooked pair they are and that somehow I can reverse what has gone on with my business fortunes and be rid of the couple," he said.

"Well," said Pete, "There appears to be sufficient evidence to show that all his involvement with your business was fraudulent and criminal. My friend Charlie has admissions from the pair of them which will stand up in court. They will both go to prison so you really will be rid of them. There is slightly less evidence against your brother-in-law although he has definitely played a part in the frauds.

"That does not surprise me one bit," said Mr Carter. "I've always known him to be a crook and a sponger. My biggest problem was getting my sister to realise it. With her on my side I am sure I could dispose of him very quickly. However, she has always been besotted with him and could never see any wrong in him. But lately I sense that she is turning away from him and perhaps coming back to my point of view. Perhaps I had better work on her a little bit more."

After this they spoke for a few minutes about rugby (a favourite topic for both of them) and then bade each other farewell. Pete promised to keep in touch and let him know if he gained any further information.

A couple of weeks after his Crown Court case Jimmy Pearce could still not stop pinching himself following the result. He could still recall the woman who had chased him from the mini-market in an attempt to retrieve the whisky bottle which he had stolen. She had been surprisingly strong and determined and though he struggled manfully she would not let go. It was only when he had struck her over the head with the whisky bottle that her grip loosened. Then he was able to dash her against the wall of the building and delivered a well- aimed kick at her. He remembered with satisfaction the effect which the kick had had upon the woman and could still hear the grunt of pain which it produced. "Stupid bitch," he thought. "It was only a single bottle of whisky. Why was she making such a fuss? It wasn't even as though the shop belonged to her. She was just an employee.

He pulled his van into the car lot and got out. He lit a cigarette and stood looking at some of the cars on display. "All right, Jimmy?" called a voice across the lot. Jimmy turned to see the Gibson twins walking towards him. "What's on then?" said one of them.

"I came round to see if you wanted any more stuff?" he replied.

"Depends on the quality, Jimmy. Let's have a look."

Jimmy dug into his pocket and produced a sealed plastic bag and handed it to one of the twins who ripped open the corner of the bag with his teeth and tipped some of the powder into the palm of his hand. He licked a finger and dipped it into the powder and tasted it suspiciously.

"It's good stuff," Jimmy assured him. "A mate of mine from London has got it. All the way from Holland. A good batch. Fifty quid a bag: he's got five hundred of them going spare. You interested?"

"That depends," said the other twin, "We'd have to run a deal like that past Eddie. Leave it with us."

"What happened in that court case of yours the other day?" asked the first twin. "I heard you were a certainty to go down for that."

"I got off almost scot free," boasted Jimmy. He then went on to give an account of his Crown Court case. "That guy who took over from Huw Roberts got me off." he said. "We went up to the Crown Court and he got me a barrister and I was found not guilty. The Crown folded and I got off thank very much," he gloated.

"I don't know," said one of the twins, "you are a complete loser Jimmy. You must be making a fortune passing off all this stuff and yet you still run the risk of getting caught over a single bottle of whisky. You're a complete fucking nob head. I'm not so sure Eddie will want to deal with a loser like you."

Jimmy was not pleased to be insulted but knew better than to trade insults or anything else with the Gibson twins. Those your cars?" he asked, looking across the lot at the two expensive vehicles. The twins nodded, "You two aren't doing so bad then?" he said sarcastically.

"Yeah well..." sneered one of the twins looking across at Jimmy's van, "at least they're a bit better than that heap of shit you're driving."

Jimmy winced because he knew they were right. He lit another cigarette and drew deeply upon it, "Anyway," he said as he moved towards his van, "give us a shout when you've talked it over with Eddie. It's good stuff." he repeated.

Chapter Thirty-five
Arnold Remains

As usual Tom Richards was the first to arrive at the office and, as usual, he opened all the cupboards and made himself a cup of tea and settled down to read the Daily Mail

As seemed to be the habit now George was the next to arrive. He joined Tom at the table and they began what had become their regular early morning conversation. They were not expecting any company because it was still early. Tom was just explaining to George the efficacy of Tiger Balm ointment a popular cure-all medicine in the far east, when the door opened and Mr Pigg burst in.

He bellowed his "good morning" and went straight on through to his own office and shut the door.

Both Tom and George were surprised to see him at this time of the morning. "Well," said Tom "I thought I'd seen it all!"

Gradually the others arrived one by one the last being Vincent who had clearly been out late the night before and could barely keep his eyes open. Each of them was warned that Mr Pigg was already in the office although nobody could understand why. Mavis took the opportunity to inform George and Pete of her visit to the solicitors the previous afternoon. They were both interested to hear her story, particularly Pete who had supplied some of the evidence for her. Mavis told them what the lady at the solicitors had said and that Doris had been relieved or encouraged. "I'm so gratified that I went with her" said Mavis.

"Well," said Pete "It was very good of you to give up an afternoon's holiday for her."

"I will have to give up another one soon because I will be going with her to see the barrister: isn't that exciting?" she said. Both George and Pete said it was.

Just then Mr Pigg came crashing into the room yelling as he did so for everyone to remain seated. No one had thought to stand up in any case but they all looked up to see what he wanted.

"As you all know Lionel died the other day and it seems that he had very few relatives. The Head Office Welfare department have seen fit to ask me to go to his property and box up any paperwork or belongings of any importance and to bring them back to this office to be held to be passed on to any relatives that may be found."

The room was silent for a moment." But shouldn't that be done by his family or friends?" said Mavis voicing everyone's thoughts.

"Well, that's the point Mavis," said Mr Pigg irritably. "There doesn't seem to be any relatives that we can find. Apparently, Lionel lived in a rented property and the landlord wants any valuable possessions to be moved immediately. Any possessions that are not moved will be taken to the rubbish dump. The police, who as you know were involved, have decided that we are the appropriate people to sort this out and Head Office have agreed. Now let me think, have you brought your car this morning George?"

George said he had.

"Good," said Mr Pigg. "Then I would ask you kindly to assist by following me out to Lionel's place, where I have to meet one of the police officers who will let me into his property, and then boxing up any valuable items which can be brought back here for storage. Now, um…. who can I ask to kindly go with you?" Mr Pigg asked himself out loud his eyes searching round the room. They alighted on Mavis who was holding up a finger and smiling.

"Yes, eh Mavis, I wonder if you would be so kind."

Mavis said she would be happy to do so and secretly was delighted to go for a ride with George.

"You'll be able to claim expenses for your petrol. Usual rates." confirmed Mr Pigg. He then checked his watch and told them to be ready shortly and follow him up the road. Pete assisted George to collect a few storage boxes from the basement area and helped load them on the back seat of his car. With a wry smile he reminded George not to do anything which he himself wouldn't do.

"Pretty open page then?" said George and got into the driving seat. Mavis then arrived and sat in the passenger seat. Soon Mr Pigg's arrival was heralded by much honking of his car horn and George moved off in pursuit.

Mavis fastened her seat belt and then turned smiling broadly to George and said, "Well, this is nice isn't it?"

"Absolutely," confirmed George,

"I think I've died and gone to heaven. Just think, I'm getting paid to go for a drive with you." They both laughed.

As they drove along Mavis re-told her report about the meeting at Doris's solicitors. She detailed in particular the way Pete had provided her with such comprehensive detail of Eddie's financial affairs. George said he hoped that, as he put it, when the shit hit the fan that Eddie wouldn't inflict any violence upon Doris.

Mavis said she was anxious about that possibility as well and had thought to herself, that perhaps Doris ought to move in with her parents and take her daughter with her.

They eventually reached Lionel's property which turned out to be the top floor of a dingy semi-detached house in a rather tired street. The policeman was parked outside and he produced the door key which had been found on Lionel's person by the police after the accident.

They entered the property led by the policeman who was followed by Mr Pigg. George and Mavis went in last. What they found was a very disappointing one-bedroom apartment which consisted of a kitchen dining area, a bedroom containing a double bed and a wardrobe, a toilet and a bathroom. They all looked around and found that the flat was very Spartan in appearance. There were no photographs or pictures on the walls. There was a single TV set but it was quite small.

The policeman handed the door key to Mr Pigg and bade them all farewell. When they were alone, they all began to search drawers and cupboards and to decant anything of interest into the boxes which George had brought with him.

Mr Pigg soon tired of the search and excused himself saying that he had to get back to the office. He told George and Mavis to check all items and to box up anything of any interest or value and to bring it back to the office. He reminded them to lock the door when they left and bring the key back to him. With that he left the building.

For about thirty minutes George and Mavis loaded up the boxes and were nearly finished. There was very little of any value or of importance. "Oh my god" exclaimed Mavis who was in the bedroom. George was in the living room at the time at the time so he went into the bedroom to see what she had found. She was thumbing through a magazine which she had found in a bedside cabinet drawer. With a grimace she showed it to George who took a look and found that the magazine contained pictures of child pornography.

"Well!" exclaimed Mavis who secretly thought that her own sexuality was vindicated by this discovery. "I always knew there was something weird about him" she said, "Ugh."

George put his arms around her and gave her a paternal hug. They both realised simultaneously what a lonely desperate life Lionel must have led. As they stood there with their bodies in close contact George reflected that on any other occasion and in any other place, his mind would have been firmly on matters sexual. He was surprised that although he was pressed against her, he had not achieved an erection.

214

Obviously, Mavis had the same abhorrence of the place because she said, "Do you mind if we get out of here as soon as possible." George agreed and they loaded the boxes into the car, and drove away.

As they drove back to the office George said, "If someone had told me earlier that today I would find myself alone with you in an empty apartment with a double bed and not have sex with you, I would have told them they were mad."

Mavis smiled and gave him a kiss. She said, "Thank you for not trying to have sex in there."

George smiled and said "But I still want to do it."

"So do I," said Mavis and kissed him again.

The next day Tom Richards had already finished his cup of tea and had reached the sports page of the Daily Mail by the time George arrived.

"I see the Arsenal won again" he said as George seated himself next to him. They both chatted for a while until the others arrived and Tom folded his paper and put it away.

Mavis' cheeriness seemed to be a given nowadays and when Helen appeared, dressed in turquoise cardigan she happily announced, "Wow that's lovely, is it new?" Helen confirmed that it was but expressed some misgivings about her choice of colour, Mavis poo-pooed that and assured her that it looked nice.

"Well, I thought I'd better try something" said Helen. "You've been putting me to shame lately." As she said this, she noticed that Mavis was wearing yet another new dress, this time a canary yellow one. "Well," said Helen almost with regret, "that looks fabulous on you. You've done it again and made me look drab."

Mavis smiled and thanked her for the compliment but assured her that was not true and yet all the men in the room silently shared Helen's opinion.

Aside from Mr Pigg, Vincent was the last to arrive. He looked terrible and sat down at his desk half asleep and when anyone spoke to him, he seemed to have trouble focusing his eyes on them. Although he had some work in front of him, he was clearly not doing anything except occasionally nodding his head. Eventually he left the room to go to the toilet.

Everyone looked at each other and Helen said, "Looks like he had a rough night. I'd guess he has one hell of a hang-over."

"Hmm…" pronounced Tom with the wisdom of age, "I'd say it was a bit more than that. He looks the same way the coolies used to look out east when they'd been on the opium."

"Oh, surely not" said Mavis with great concern. "Where would he get hold of that? No, I don't believe it. But he did look awful didn't he. Pete, go and check on him would you."

Pete duly did as he was told and when he entered the toilet area, he found Vincent slumped on the floor completely unconscious. Pete gently shook him and urged him to wake up but it was some while before he did so. Pete helped him to his feet and assisted him to the wash hand basin and ran the tap. Vincent splashed his face and looked at himself in the mirror and gasped.

"What were you on last night?" asked Pete, "You're not a drinker are you?"

Vincent shook his head and splashed some more water on his face. "No" he murmured "I had a little sniff of something which I think did not agree with me. I think it must have been a duff batch."

"Jesus Vincent!" exclaimed Pete. "What are you doing for Christ's sake. Where did you go?"

Vincent continued splashing his face and peering in the mirror. "God," he muttered, "I've got such a headache."

"But where did you go to get this stuff?" asked Pete.

Vincent gave a long sigh and looked in the mirror again and groaned. "It was in a club in the High Street. It hasn't been open that long. It's owned by some foreign bloke, Italian, I think. They play lots of cool music there. That's why I go there. It's a nightclub called The Nite Club."

"But you can't afford to get into that sort of habit," said Pete. "How do they allow that sort of dealing to go on openly. Haven't they got any security to weed out people like that?"

Vincent looked in the mirror again and gave a wry smile then held his head with one hand and grimaced. "Oh yeah, they've got plenty of bouncers there but they are the ones peddling the stuff."

"What?" exclaimed Pete again. "You should stay clear of the place and tell them to piss off. Don't have anything to do with them."

"Oh," responded Vincent, "these are not the sort of blokes you say 'piss off' to. They are seriously big and strong: like body builders. The two who usually work the door are twins."

Pete pricked up his ears at this and asked Vincent for a few more details. "Come on Vincent," he said taking his arm. We don't want Piggy finding you in this state. You can go straight home and get some sleep. We'll tell him you were taken ill with a tummy upset and you might come back tomorrow if you are well enough."

He helped Vincent to the door and watched him as he weaved his way along the pavement looking like a drunkard. He then went back to his desk and picked up the telephone and called Charlie Chivers. The International Detective was studying page three of the Sun newspaper when his telephone rang. "Chivers!" he cried into the receiver and waited for a reply but heard none. "Chivers," he repeated with a bit more volume. He then realised that it was Pete at the other end and that he was talking very softly. He listened very attentively and then said to Pete, "That's very interesting, Pete. I'll pass this on to Des who I'm sure will be fascinated to hear it. I'll be in touch."

Pete replaced the receiver and announced to the room that he had sent Vincent home and that he was going to advise Mr Pigg, when he arrived, that Vincent had a tummy upset.

Mavis who was seated closer to Pete than the others, had managed to hear some of his telephone conversation with Charlie even though he had been whispering, said to Pete in a soft voice, "Are those the same people that you and George met at the gym?" Pete nodded but said no more because at that moment Mr Pigg arrived.

Shortly after work that evening Charlie Chivers the International Detective strolled into the Jublee Inn. As he ordered a pint of his favourite beer and a sandwich he glanced at the pictures on the wall behind the bar. He spotted a picture tucked behind two optics on the wall. He moved along the bar to study it more closely. The picture showed Reg Partridge the landlord with his arm around an ample breasted lady in a low-cut dress both smiling at the camera. "Who's this?" he asked as Reg handed him his pint across the bar. The latter turned to look and then said, "Oh that's Jayne Mansfield. A lovely girl eh? The wife put it there out of sight."

"Now, that's what I call a woman!" declared Charlie looking wistfully at the bust of Miss Mansfield.

Just then Pete and George arrived and they all settled down for a chat. Charlie confirmed that he had told Des Onions about the new nightclub in the High Street, called The Nite Club, and the possibility of drug dealing at the premises. Des apparently had checked with others at the station and discovered that the Gibson twins had been under observation by the CID for some time. One of Des's colleagues knew quite a lot about them. He had told Des that they worked as bouncers at the club but that they did not appear to do any other work. Instead, they spent most of their daylight hours hanging around Eddie's car lot or loitering about in the Barn. They both drove very expensive and flashy cars but there appeared to be little or no income to show how they could afford to buy such vehicles.

Des when he arrived, was able to tell them that the nightclub had been opened recently by one Giovanni Pettacinni who was a man who apparently had no experience of running a licensed premises, but he had a tame employee whose name was on the license. Des assured them that the police were intending to keep a firm eye on the place.

No one was surprised to know that Mr Pettacinni was married to Ken Carter's sister. Charlie Chivers sucked his teeth and said, "The common denominator in all this, is Eddie Sharp, of course." The others agreed.

Chapter Thirty-six
Mavis meets Phillipa

Mavis and Doris travelled on the train to Bristol together. They were on their way to the conference with the barrister, Phillipa Fry, which had been arranged by Mrs Robinson of Duffey Fry & Co. They enjoyed each other's company immensely and on the journey, they prattled away and barely gave any concern to the approaching meeting but when they arrived outside Clifton Chambers Doris began to experience collywobbles and was grateful for Mavis's presence. She was still slightly confused as to why she was there but only hoped that it would be all worthwhile.

When they were shown into the room of Miss Fry, they met an attractive young thirty something lady with dark hair swept back from her forehead and tied up neatly into a ponytail which emphasised her youthful appearance. Her eyes were beautifully made up and she wore a pearl shade of lipstick.

Mavis could see at a glance what she had previously never been able to appreciate. The art of sophisticated make up. She realised in that single glance what she had never understood before. The subtlety of cosmetic enhancement. When she looked at Phillipa she saw everything that she had intended for herself but never achieved. In addition, there was an intellectual je ne sais quoi about her which was probably enhanced by the thick black-rimmed spectacles which she wore.

"Good afternoon, I'm Phillipa Fry. Do sit down," she said in a cut glass accent which made Mavis feel like a yokel. "Now," she said forcefully, "It's not very often that I see such a comprehensive set of details about the financial affairs of a respondent. And this information includes, (she emphasised with relish), tax return forms signed by your husband, bank and Building Society statements and many more items which are seldom ever available in situations like this. I propose that we issue proceedings based on a multi-factual basis." Both Doris and Mavis looked mystified. Phillipa continued, "Our petition will say that your husband has committed adultery with this young lady umm Sylvia, and also, that he has behaved unreasonably on all the occasions as listed in the schedule of events which we will attach. Although we only need one substantial item of misbehaviour to convince the court that a divorce would be appropriate, we nevertheless will enhance our accompanying application for financial settlement with the seriousness of the allegations contained therein."

Mavis wondered why she used so many long words but at the same time was so impressed with the overall effect of the way that Phillipa delivered the words. Also, she admired her make-up so much.

"In short," said Phillipa, "We are going to take your husband to the cleaners Mrs Sharp and secure you financially for the rest of your life."

The manner of her delivery and the immaculate diction convinced both Doris and Mavis of the certainty of the outcome of her proceedings. Phillipa then assured Doris that all the papers would be ready for service upon Eddie in a mere day or so. She enquired about the possibility of Doris moving to a place of safety eg. her parents' house along with her daughter. She did assure her that it would probably be only a short time before she would be returning to the matrimonial home.

Both Doris and Mavis left Clifton Chambers with great hope and confidence and both confirmed on the way home that they could not have been more pleased and impressed with Phillipa Fry.

Eddie Sharp pulled into the car lot in his top of the range Mercedes saloon car. He glanced at the two eye catching sports cars already parked in the car lot. He got out of his car to be greeted by the Gibson twins who had been waiting for him. "I must be paying you too much," he sneered indicating the twins' cars. "Haven't you two got the brains to realise that these draw attention to you?" The twins shrugged and waited to see what else their boss would say.

"So what's this you have to tell me about Jimmy Pearce?"

"Well it's like I told you on the phone," said one of the twins. "Here is a bag of the stuff he's offering. He's got a contact in London who gets the stuff from Holland. He says it's good stuff. Reckons it's worth fifty quid a bag but he's full of bullshit. I reckon we could get it from him for twenty-five quid a bag. He says there are five hundred bags which means a profit of somewhere in the region of half a million."

"Oh yeah," said Eddie sceptically, "but Jimmy is such a little prick isn't he. He cannot be trusted to do anything properly, can he? No, my instinct is to stay clear of anything which involves Jimmy Pearce."

"Well, it's up to you," replied one Gibson twin who appeared to be the more decisive of the two, "But the stuff does appear to be OK and there are plenty queueing up to buy it. As for Jimmy he's not really any trouble to us. He wouldn't dare try to cross us because he knows that we would break his back for him."

"Well, OK," said Eddie without too much enthusiasm. As long as you are sure. So long also that you let him know that this is a one-off deal. I don't want to get sucked into doing regular deals with him because if we do sooner or later, we'll come a cropper."

"I think we can make a real killing with this batch," said Gibson. "the big question of course is how one can hide the gains. You can't simply stick it in a bank or building society because the Old Bill can trace it can't they. You can't stick huge sums of money under the mattress, can you?"

"No problem," said Eddie. "I can give it all to my solicitor who will stick it in his client account. It's all confidential and secret. And nobody's going to suspect a solicitor and when the dust has settled you can just get him to write you a cheque. Who is going to suspect that a cheque from your lawyer is dodgy?"

"Is that the same chap who got Jimmy off the charge in the Crown Court recently?"

"Yes," confirmed Eddie, "Simon Nibble."

Chapter Thirty-seven
The Judge leaves Chambers

Jeremy Fallow QC stood before the tall sash window looking out at the park across the road. He could see an old man walking a reluctant dog along the path and a young mother pushing her baby in a pram. Not far beyond, beneath the lofty chestnut trees, was a kiddies' playpark with some swings and a slide and roundabout. In the foreground was a goldfish pond with lillies on the surface.

"What a delightful view," he reflected to himself, "This is one thing I shall miss about Clifton Chambers…"

Since achieving the office of Crown Court Judge he had decided that he could no longer continue to be Head of Chambers and, in all honesty could no longer give the office the time which it deserved. He had returned to the chambers today to vacate his room and he took the opportunity of enjoying the view from the window which had the best outlook in the building. He mused that his private chamber in the newly constructed multi-story Crown Court building across the city was nowhere near as stately with virtually no outlook whatsoever.

There was a knock at the door and Phillipa Fry looked in. "Jeremy," she said, "A little bird told me that you might be in this morning."

"Come in Phillipa please," he said effusively "How very nice to see you."

Phillipa was Jeremy's favourite barrister in the chambers. If he was honest, he would admit that he was more than a little charmed by her. He found her to be a damnably attractive young woman and often told himself that were it not for the vast difference in their ages he might find himself making a move for her. He certainly felt that she was far too good for Algernon Phillipson.

"I was just admiring the view for the last time," he said I had just popped in to pick up a few things."

"Oh Jeremy," sighed Phillipa giving him a big hug. "We will all miss you so much you darling man."

"Do please sit down," he said proffering a chair as he seated himself behind his desk. He watched as she seated herself and crossed her legs ostentatiously. He had always admired her legs which were extremely shapely. Her skirt was encouragingly short and her top leg was positioned so as to give him a generous view of her thigh. "You do have lovely legs Phillipa," he said thinking to himself that they spent more time wrapped around a horse when they could be doing other exciting things.

"Oh, do you think so?" she said in mock surprise. She rose from the chair and gently raised her skirt as if to check on what he had said. As her skirt came up it revealed that she was wearing black stockings and suspenders. She held the skirt aloft for a moment to give Jeremy a full view and then lowered it. Jeremy's lower jaw had opened. "You know you really are a dog," she said with mock severity lowering herself onto the chair again and crossing her legs once more.

She had always known that Jeremy found her attractive and she enjoyed teasing him in this way. She habitually flirted with him shamelessly and was always gratified by the attention he gave her. Being a barrister, she was a born actress. She had an inborn sense of theatre. As a schoolgirl she had taken part in drama as had Jeremy himself but she had never been given interesting parts to play. She had found that the role plays between herself and Jeremy gave her the sort of satisfaction that such parts would have provided. She had always thought that if she ever strayed (matrimonially), it would be with someone like Jeremy. She did not find the age gap to be a disincentive. He was still a good-looking man and so erudite with an intellectual twinkle in his eye. Quite unlike Algernon who really could be quite dull at times.

"I had an interesting case the other day," she said and then detailed many of the facts contained in the divorce case for Doris Sharp. She gave no names but gave Jeremy a gist of the information obtained. "Now, you are a prosecution man, aren't you?" she said "And if I'm not mistaken you were quite an expert in the field of fraud. Now would you reach a verdict of guilty on those facts?" she enquired.

"Most assuredly," replied Jeremy.

"And would you?" she enquired in a flirtatious way, "accept as evidence in your court a copy of a divorce petition with all those details contained therein?"

"How could not accept anything from one such as you," said Jeremy smiling lasciviously.

Phillipa returned the smile in equal proportions and then said, "I just popped in to invite you and your good lady to our country cottage for an evening meal next Saturday. It would be so nice to have an intimate chat with you over a good glass of claret." She pouted wantonly.

Jeremy gulped and said, "That would be lovely, Phillipa. I will look forward to that."

"Rumour has it, that you have the deciding vote for who will replace you as Head of chambers. As you know Algie is standing and I was hoping that he would be able to count on your vote Jeremy. Perhaps when you come round, we can get Algie to show your good lady around the grounds and the stables whilst you and I can inspect the bedrooms."

Jeremy gulped again. "That sounds wonderful, Phillipa. How can I say no to you?"

She looked into his eyes with as much sensuality as she could muster and said, "You don't have to, Jeremy."

Jeremy gulped one more time as he watched Phillipa's bottom leave the room. He knew of course that all this was mere horse-play grossly over emphasised by her but nevertheless he did find it to be so stimulating.

Chapter Thirty-eight
The Deal

An hour or so before his appointment time with the twins George, along with Pete and Sandra together with her cameraman, met Des Onions and Charlie Chivers in the coffee bar of the local library. George had considered it to be a strange meeting place until he got there and found it to be an enormous mausoleum of a place. The coffee bar area was about the size of a tennis court. All of the tables were empty and so they were all able to occupy a table and discuss matters in complete privacy.

Before attending George and Pete had been to the local bank to obtain the money which had to be paid to the Gibson twins. Conveniently the twenty-pound notes in the bundle were new and consecutively numbered. They were laid out on the table alongside the front page of the day's Times newspaper and the cameraman took photographs.

Des, who had been wearing thin plastic evidence gloves when he laid the notes out gave a pair of driving gloves to George. "Put these on," he said, "I presume you touched these notes once but just the top and the bottom note in the bundle. Is that correct?" George nodded.

"Well," said Des, "we want to keep the number of prints to a minimum so that once they are handed over to the twins most of the prints on them will be theirs. So let's be clear about this," he continued, "my men are already in place watching the car lot. You," (he indicated the cameraman), "will go to the place we decided and film the whole procedure and when the deal has been done you will hand the film over to us. You, (he indicated George), will meet them, hand over the money and collect the drugs, without removing your gloves, and then hand them over to us in due course. There will be no TV interviews today, understood?" As he said this, he looked meaningfully at Sandra who nodded.

Then they all left the coffee bar and made their separate ways to their appointed positions. George went to his car and waited for about fifteen minutes and then drove slowly round to the car lot. When he arrived, he could not see anyone anywhere including the twins. He parked his car opposite the lot and surveyed all the vantage points nearby to see if he could spot anyone. There was no one that he could see. So after another five minutes he got out of his car and walked casually across the road. He wondered as he approached the lot, what would happen if the twins insisted on doing the deal inside the car lot premises or even drove him to an alternative meeting place. He decided, if possible that he would always remain in the outside area of the lot where he could be easily observed by everyone.

As he waited on the forecourt of the lot, he saw the twins get out of an expensive looking Porsche car. He stayed where he was and they approached him.

"Got the money then?" said one of the twins holding out his hand. George dug into his coat pocket and held out the bank notes which one of the twins eagerly snatched and began counting. He nodded to his brother who then took a packet from his pocket and handed it to George who looked at it.

Feeling rather stupid he said, "How do I take this?"

"Instructions on the packet," said the second twin. "And you keep this to yourself and you tell no one. Do you understand?" George nodded. "Otherwise we come looking for you," he said flexing his bicep as he spoke the words.

"So this will do the trick will it?" asked George, "Put a bit of muscle on me?"

The twins looked at each other and rolled their eyes. One said, "What a plonker! No, this is just one course. You still have to lift the weights like fury and you will need more of this."

This was what George had hoped they would say for he had been instructed by Des Onions to make a further appointment as soon as possible. Tentatively he said, "Same time in two weeks' time, same price?"

The twins nodded and watched George as he walked back to his car.

Charlie Chivers the International Detective had not been idle. For the last few evenings, instead of retiring to the lounge bar of the Jubilee Inn he had remained in his office and when everyone else in the building had gone home, he had availed himself of the opportunity to re-examine Simon Nibble's files. In particular he studied carefully again the file in respect of Eddie Sharp and made a painstaking note of the most interesting entries. He also made a number of photocopies of various documents which he passed on to Des Onions.

He also conducted covert observation of one Jimmy Pearce who it seemed was very active recently. On one particular occasion he trailed Jimmy who got on a train and went all the way to London. Charlie followed him to an address in the Soho area where he observed him to meet a foreign looking gentleman who came out of the property Charlie was watching and walked down the street with Jimmy to a pub where they began talking to two other fellows who also appeared to be foreign.

. Charlie could not get close enough to hear their conversation but his experienced ex-police officer nose told him that they were all villains. When they had finished their conversation, they all rose and left the pub at the same time. Jimmy and his friend took the direction from which they had come and Charlie assumed they were returning to the property he had been previously watching. The other two men walked in the opposite direction so Charlie opted to follow them. They were not aware that he was following them and eventually they led him to an address which was a first floor flat above an estate agent's office. Charlie made a note of the address and the estate agent and then returned to Paddington station for the homeward journey.

All the information that he discovered Charlie passed on to Des Onions who immediately got on the telephone to his London colleagues to advise of the addresses and the occupants thereof.

Chapter Thirty-nine
Developments

Tom Richards had unlocked all the cabinets and decanted the various files to their appropriate tables. He had made his cup of tea and was settling down to study his Daily Mail when George arrived.

They both seated themselves together at their table for their early morning chat during which George told him about his adventure with the Gibson twins and their supply of steroids etc. He did not really know why he had confided this information to Tom and deep down he knew or felt that he should not have divulged this news. He felt however that he had come to be a friend of Tom and that their early morning conversations had made him a confidante. He also knew that Tom, as an older wiser man, was shrewd and experienced enough to be discreet.

"You be careful of people like that," he said after George had described the twins. "People like that are volatile and dangerous. You stick close to Pete. He's a natural. He'll watch out for you."

Mavis and Helen arrived almost simultaneously. Mavis, unlike recent days, had applied some make up this morning. It was nowhere near as heavily applied as in the past but her eyes were quite dark and heavy. Helen noticed immediately though, in truth, the men had barely noticed at all. Helen said, "Aah, a little make up this morning I see."

Mavis conceded and nodded to her but gave a slight grimace and said, "Yes….but I'm not sure myself."

Helen said, "Oh no it looks fine. Don't be so self-critical." Mavis grimaced again and said, "When I went with Doris to Bristol and we saw Phillipa Fry she was just so amazing. Not only was she extraordinarily beautiful but her make-up was fantastic. She was also super intelligent. I just wish I could get my make up right so that I could look as attractive as her."

"But," said George instinctively, "you are beautiful anyway."

"Oh, thanks George, you are so sweet but I know that I just don't compare with her."

"That's crap, Mave," said Pete "you are as good as anyone. You only admire them because they're so posh. They've all got a hole in their arse you know."

"Oh, trust you," said Helen with a look of disapproval. "But you are as good as this Phillipa whatsit. You are beautiful!"

"You are what you are," announced Tom Richards "beauty is in the eye of the beholder."

There was no time for further conversation because, with a crash and a bang Mr Pigg arrived. With a hearty "Good morning, all," he went straight to his room and shut the door.

Later in the day George was summoned to go into Mr Pigg's office. Whilst he stood on the gravy-coloured mat, he wondered what Mr Pigg wanted.

"Aah, George," he said, "I've just had the Welfare section on from the Regional office asking about Bill's condition. What can you tell me about him?"

"Well, he seemed a little better," said George tentatively.

"But how well is he?" asked Mr Pigg. "Did he say anything to you?"

"Um, erh, well he did talk about coming back to work."

"But why didn't you tell me?" said Mr Pigg with annoyance.

"Oh well, there was all that business about Lionel that seemed to overtake everything."

"Yes, well, did he look well enough to return to work?"

"Well... .he looked better than when I saw him at the hospital. If he improves any more I'm sure he'll be in perfect health by the end of the month. Anywa,y Mr Pigg doesn't it all depend on what the doctors say and the information in his medical certificate?"

"Medical Certificate?" said Mr Pigg. "What medical certificate?"

"The one we brought back from Bill's house," said George, "I gave it to you when Mavis and I came back. Don't you remember?"

Mr Pigg appeared to be paralysed for a moment. Then he jumped up and began searching in his filing cabinet. Eventually he found what he was looking for, and spread out Bill's medical certificate on his desk. He stared at it for a long silent moment then said, "A month! he'll be back in a month!" George shrugged his shoulders.

"But won't that be OK? After all Lionel is no longer here and no one knows better than Bill how to do the job."

Mr Pigg thought about it for a moment. "That's right" he said.

His telephone then rang and he was soon involved in a conversation. George rose from the chair and excused himself with a hand gesture. He returned to the general office where everyone was still chatting.

It was Mavis who was the first to notice. "Where is Vincent?" she exclaimed. "Did he come in this morning," she asked of Tom who shook his head.

"So how was he yesterday when you found him in the toilet?" she asked of Pete who shrugged.

"Well, he wasn't too good but when I sent him home, I thought that he only needed a good sleep to get over the effects of whatever he had taken the night before."

"Well, I hope he's feeling better this morning," said Mavis "Does anyone have a phone number for him?" No one knew of a telephone number for Vincent.

"Does anyone know where he lives?" continued Mavis. No one knew where Vincent lived.

"Perhaps he's gone to the doctor this morning." suggested Helen.

"I'm a bit worried about him." said Mavis "We ought to find out how he is. Perhaps Mr Pigg has some details on his file. If we could just find a telephone number, we could discover how he is.

As soon as Mr Pigg finished his telephone call Mavis went into his office to advise him that Vincent had not turned up. "I am a bit worried about him." she said, "He did look bad yesterday."

"Yes, well, if he didn't stay out half the night getting drunk and had a good night's sleep instead he would probably feel much better." said Mr Pigg uncharitably.

"But Vincent isn't a drinker" said Mavis defensively, "he must have taken something."

"What!" exclaimed Mr Pigg, "You mean drugs? That's even worse. No wonder he always looks half asleep."

Mavis wished she had not mentioned it now but could not unsay what she had said. Mr Pigg found Vincent's file and wrote down his address and telephone number and gave it to her.

"Give him a ring," he said, "And tell him to get back to work as soon as possible."

Throughout the course of the working day Mavis tried to telephone Vincent but on each occasion the telephone was not answered.

"I don't understand it," said Mavis "There's no answer-phone facility so the phone just rings and rings."

"Well perhaps he's gone out." suggested Helen.

Mavis reflected and said, "But he lives with his mum and dad doesn't he. Surely they should answer the phone."

Nobody could suggest a satisfactory answer. At the end of the working day Mavis persuaded George to give her a lift to Vincent's house. As they got into George's car Mavis took the scrap of paper, on which Mr Pigg had written Vincent's details, from her handbag. She studied it briefly and said, "I think it's up on the council estate at the end just past the roundabout. Do you know it?"

George admitted that he did not but Mavis assured him that she would direct him.

Each road that took them closer to Vincent's address looked more and more dingy. There were some three or four storey blocks of flats with concrete exteriors which had been covered with graffiti some of it obscene. They passed some dumped vehicles one of which was burnt out.

When they reached the road in which Vincent lived, they could see that the houses were just single storey prefabricated structures which had been thrown up during or just after the second world war and which had only been intended as temporary housing. None of the properties had proper walls or fences but were only separated from each other by the occasional concrete pillar with wire mesh in between.

George parked outside Vincent's house and they walked up the path to the front door. The front garden, which perhaps had at one time contained a lawn, appeared to resemble the town dump. Sticking out of the ground there appeared to be the top half of a child's pushchair. Mavis grimaced to George as she rang the bell.

The door was opened by a tired looking middle-aged woman wearing a pinny. She had straggly blond hair turning grey. She had kind eyes which were sunk well back into her head and on one side of her face she had a lived bruise.

"Mrs Hudson?" said Mavis hopefully. The woman nodded warily. "We are from the office where Vincent works." said Mavis "We were wondering how he is. Is he at home?"

"No" she replied, "He's out. I'm not sure where he is at the moment. It's just my husband and I here at the moment."

"Who's that?" came a roar from inside the house. Vincent's mother screwed up her face. "It's all right Ted I'll deal with it. '"

"Who is it?" the voice bellowed again. There followed the sound of footsteps and there
appeared behind Mrs Hudson a large pugnacious looking man wearing grubby overalls.

"It's just some people from Vincent's office." she explained "I'll help them."

"What do you want?" he asked them aggressively, "What's he done now?"

Mavis explained diplomatically that Vincent hadn't been well the day before and they were merely here to check on his health.

"Well, he's not here," explained the step-father. "He's probably gone off to another of those fucking pop festivals. He's not been home for days."

"Yes, yes, all right, Ted. I'll see to this. You go and finish your tea."

said his wife.

He turned to go back in and then said, with a malevolent look over his shoulder.

"When he does come home, he'll feel the back of my fucking hand!"

Mrs Hudson looked embarrassed and said, "I'm very worried about him but I don't know what to do. My husband gets very upset about him. He often stays away for a few days and then comes home but he doesn't get on with his step-father very well."

"Perhaps he might be staying with a friend?" suggested Mavis. "Perhaps a girlfriend?" she further suggested.

"No, I don't think he's got any girlfriends. He never brings anyone home here." she added.

Well thank you so much, Mrs Hudson," said Mavis "If he does come home please tell him we called."

They walked back to the road and the parked car. Mavis looked back at the dingy little house and felt her eyes welling up with tears. She turned and buried her head in George's chest and sobbed.

"Poor Vincent," she cried "I had no idea. None of us ever took much interest in him. He must be so unhappy."

Chapter Forty
Still Looking

The International Detective positioned himself behind the bar at the Jubilee Inn so as to be able to see the photograph of Reg with Jayne Mansfield. Having purchased a beer he took a swig and began thumbing through the papers he held. These were the photocopies of the documents he had recently made in Simon Nibble's office.

DI Desmond O'Nighons soon appeared and they both took a seat at one of the tables. "So how was the video?" asked Charlie, "Was everything OK?"

"Yeah, brilliant," said Des. "We got the Gibson twins banged to rights for supplying the steroids. We just need to get them tied up for supplying the other drugs at the club and we could mop up that Pettacinni guy along with sharp Eddie and his solicitor."

"Well, these should help on that score," said Charlie pushing the papers across the table. "These show him to be fully involved with Eddie and Nibble in all the fraudulent deals over the land and Company share deals."

"Excellent" said Des perusing the papers for a moment. "You've come up trumps here Charlie. I reckon we could get not only a conviction on this guy but an order for deportation as well."

"Pretty good then?"

"Absolutely," said Des still reading.

"So what about the Nark Fund?" asked Charlie.

"Yeah definitely: no problem," Des replied, still reading the information supplied. "But it is of course subject to a conviction. So it cannot be paid out prior to a guilty verdict. But then you know that anyway, don't you?"

"Yes, I know that," said Charlie, "but I've put a lot of hours into this and incurred quite a few expenses you know. Like for example having to travel to London the other day. Is there no way you can see your way clear to an advance Des?"

"Oh well, you know the rule as well as I do Charlie. No conviction, no access to the fund. However…." he said fishing into his pocket and bringing out some money, "Here's a hundred quid from me personally just to show good faith. I'll take this back from the fund money when it comes. The good news Charlie is that those fellows you traced Jimmy Pearce to are being watched closely by the Special Branch and if and when we round them up at the same time as our villains there will be a separate Nark Fund payment to you from the Met."

This cheered Charlie up considerably. "Thanks Des" he said "but will I still have to give evidence at the trial? My days of standing in the witness box are far behind me and I can't guarantee that young George will do a good job either."

"No problem" said Des, "You probably won't need to give evidence at all nor your man George. The only witnesses, I hope, will be our boys who will give evidence, in the case of your recordings, that they planted the listening devices, and that George was video'd receiving the goods but not as part of the gang. CPS are OK with that. In any event, the evidence will be so overwhelming that they probably won't be able to plead not guilty. Anyway, if they did plead not guilty and challenged the evidence offered by police officers who would believe them?

"The International Detective pondered the question and had to admit that Des had a point. "So what's the next step?" asked Charlie, "Do you need any further evidence?"

"Not really" confirmed Des, "we are all set up to observe the second handover to George in a week or so and we intend to pounce on everyone then. We'll get warrants to search Eddie's house and his business at the car lot and the solicitor's office. Not that we really need a warrant for the latter because we've already got copies of the incriminating documents from you, but we'll go through the motions of a search and find the original documents when we go in."

Charlie was happy with that and agreed to keep in touch with Des and keep him informed of any developments at his end. He thanked him again for the advance which Des had given him and bought himself a small bottle of whisky to take home with him.

All the staff listened avidly whilst Mavis described what she and George had found the previous evening. "It was so distressing." she told them as she herself recalled the sight of Vincent's grubby pre-fab property. "And that step-father of his looked like such a brute. I had no idea his home life was so awful."

Everyone commiserated with Mavis who was nearly as upset as she had been the previous day. They felt sorry for Vincent and Mavis but did not really know what to do about it.

"He hasn't come in again this morning." said Helen, "Perhaps he's still sick."

"But where is he?" asked Mavis. "We've got to find him. He might be really ill."

"But we wouldn't know where to start looking," said George, "his mum didn't have a clue where he might be and she didn't know any names of any of his friends or indeed if he had any."

"What about your friend Charlie?" said Mavis to Pete. He's a private investigator, isn't he? Couldn't he find Vincent?"

Pete shrugged his shoulders and said, "Well, I don't know where he would even start to look. And in any case, he would expect to be paid for any work he did so who would pay that?"

"Well, somebody has to do something," responded Mavis defiantly. "If nobody else can do it then I'll have to make enquiries on my own."

"If you are going to start asking around you will need a photograph of him to show people." suggested Pete.

"What about his warrant card for delivering and accepting post etc." offered Tom. "Mr Pigg must have a copy of that on file. Perhaps he would let you take a copy."

Mavis thought that was a good idea and determined to tackle Mr Pigg about it when he arrived. "But I wouldn't know where to ask about him" reflected Mavis. "I really know very little about him or his habits so where could I ask?"

"Well," said Pete cautiously, "you could start at that night club where he bought the drugs which made him feel bad but I wouldn't recommend that you go there by yourself."

"I'll come with you," offered George. So it was decided that Mavis and George would visit the place that evening purporting to be a normal couple having a good time, while Mavis would make some surreptitious enquiries about Vincent.

When Mr Pigg finally arrived, he was surprisingly helpful towards Mavis. Having heard her description of her visit to Vincent's address and the fact that his parents did not know of his whereabouts he was only too keen for somebody to track him down. He supplied Mavis with a photocopy of Vincent's warrant card which had a photograph of Vincent on the front. "But remember," he said, as Mavis was leaving his office, "these enquiries are all unofficial. I cannot authorise any travel expenses or night club entrance fees. Is that understood?"

Mavis said it was and thanked him for the copy ID. Back in the general office she felt as though she was doing something positive for Vincent who, for all she knew, could be in deep trouble. She was also looking forward to spending an evening in a nightclub with George.

They met that evening near the High Street and walked together to the nightclub. George thought she looked particularly attractive in a lacy blouse and short skirt with a warm jacket over the top. "You look nice," he said as they walked along. "Thank you," said Mavis, "and you look good as well."

They reached the nightclub doorway which was roughly midway down the street. The door was open and inside was a staircase which led up to the first floor. At the doorway on the street level there were two or three bouncers who all wore black shirts who were casually conversing with each other. It was early evening and probably not a time when people coming in were vetted too meticulously by the door staff. In any event, a girl and a boyfriend did not attract any attention. George noticed that one of the Gibson twins was in the group at the door. He gave George a curt nod as they walked through the doorway but he could not be sure that he had recognised him.

When they reached the entrance desk towards the top of the stairs they had to wait a moment for a group of girls who were just paying their entrance fees. They each wore skirts even shorter than that of Mavis and since George and Mavis had to queue a couple of steps below them, he tried to pretend to himself that he was not looking up their skirts. Mavis smiled at his embarrassed look. They paid their entrance fee which was half the normal fee because it was early in the evening. This was a common ploy amongst nightclubs to attract business early in the evening and to avoid an impatient queue at the door when all the pubs closed.

When they first entered the dancehall area the lighting was so dim that they had difficulty in seeing anything. Gradually their eyes focussed and they were able to make out a central dance floor surrounded by tables and chairs. At the far end was a bar which ran the length of the wall.

There were very few people in the club probably because it was still early. They walked to the bar and ordered a couple of drinks. The bartender looked very young but seemed efficient at dispensing the drinks. Mavis immediately produced the copy of Vincent's ID card and asked him if he knew him.

The bartender studied the picture for a moment and then said, "I don't think I recognise him but the photograph is not that clear. I only work two nights per week so perhaps on another evening someone might recognise him." He indicated a barmaid who was serving someone else. "Perhaps Mary will know him" he said and took the photo over to her and showed it to her.

She had just finished serving so wandered across. "Yes, I recognise him," she said, "What's the problem?" Mavis then explained that they worked together and that he had been unwell and had seemingly disappeared. Could the girl help she wondered.

"Well," she said "I do recognise him as I said but I don't really know much about him. He usually comes in on his own and seems to enjoy the music but he generally keeps himself to himself."

Mavis wondered if Vincent had a regular girlfriend or a group which he habitually spoke to etc but Mary shook her head. "No not really," she said "I think he might be a bit of a loner. He did often speak to the DJ though."

They took their drinks to a table and sat down. One or two of the girls who had queued in front of them were gyrating on the dance floor and they watched them for a while.

"I think I'll try the DJ," said Mavis and crossed the room to where the man was seated at a desk containing all the paraphernalia of record decks and CDs etc. She showed the photo of Vincent to the man and he nodded positively and then shouted something in her ear. Mavis nodded and returned to the table.

"He knows Vincent," she said. "But the music was too loud over there that it was difficult to talk. He's going on a break in a moment so he'll come over." George nodded and they continued to watch the young women who moved in an alluring way.

Eventually the music stopped and the DJ announced a brief pause. He left some music playing softly and came across to their table. He confirmed that he knew Vincent and that the latter was a music officienado who had more knowledge on the subject than him. He said that Vincent used to sit with him on occasions to observe his style and technique. He said that Vincent was a nice lad, and in his opinion, had the knowledge and personality to make a first-class DJ.

"He didn't really have a group of friends that he would hang around with, but I do remember there was a girl he would often talk to. She would usually dance by herself. Vincent didn't dance very often. He nearly always sat with me when he was here."

"What was her name?" asked Mavis.

"I don't know her name," he said, "but what I can say is that she always wears tartan designed Doc Martins and she lives near the library. Oh, and she wears glasses. That's all I can tell you. Oh-oh, that's the boss's wife: I'd better get back to my desk." He then scuttled back to his den.

George and Mavis turned to look at the person who had caused the DJ to jump back to his desk. "Why that's Freda?" exclaimed Mavis with surprise. The lady in question, who had just come into the room, looked across when she heard her name being spoken. She paused momentarily and then came across to their table to say hello. "What are you doing here?" she said.

Mavis said she was there to have a drink with her boyfriend. She introduced George who judged her to be a thirty something year old attractive lady with a broad smile. Mavis explained that she and Freda were friends from the same exercise class as she and Doris attended at the Barn.

Freda sat down beside Mavis who then confessed to her that she was there partly to try to trace her work colleague Vincent. She showed her the photograph but Freda explained that she only came to the club occasionally and therefore knew none of the clientele. "I only came in to see my husband," she said, "he's supposed to be running this place but as usual he doesn't seem to be here." She went on to have a good moan to Mavis about the myriad of faults of her husband Giovanni Pettacinni. She admitted that she had been besotted with the man since she first set eyes on him. She had even married him against the wishes and advice of her own father. Lately she admitted she had become disenchanted with him and was tired of his misbehaviour of every variety.

Mavis told her of some of the marital problems experienced by Doris and the fact that she had accompanied her to the solicitor and then the barrister. "Her name is Phillipa Fry" she told her, "she is absolutely brilliant. She is going to tie her husband up with a ribbon and serve him on a plate. If you're interested, I can give you her details. You should have a coffee with Doris and me after our next class."

Freda said she might well be interested and would see both her and Doris at the next class. She then said she had to go home since her husband was not where she thought he was. She wished goodbye to George and said she had been pleased to meet him and she gave Mavis a farewell kiss and promised to see her soon.

After that the evening belonged solely to George and Mavis who spent much of the time moving rhythmically on the dance floor to the DJ's music. Although George liked music with a heavy beat, he had to admit to himself that he preferred the few brief moments when slow soft smooch numbers were played. On these occasions he was able to get really close to Mavis.

The following day everyone was entertained by a further descriptive passage from Mavis concerning the evening at the nightclub.

Helen was particularly interested in the account of Vincent's possible girlfriend who lived near the library. "You say she wore Doc Martins with a tartan design?" she remarked, "well they shouldn't be too hard to spot."

"Well, yes," agreed Mavis, "but I don't suppose she wears them every day of her life. I could hang around near the library but if she went by wearing a different pair of shoes, I would never know it was her. It would have been much better to have had a name or an address."

Helen said she supposed that was right. "Just suppose she never wore the shoes again. You would have no hope of tracking her down."

"Yes, thanks very much," said Mavis disconsolately, "that's very encouraging."

"Well, I'm only saying," replied Helen, "I mean, even if you did manage to find her, she might not have seen Vincent for weeks." Mavis had to concede that Helen had a point.

Pete was more interested in the fact that Mavis knew the wife of the man who owned or ran the night club, Ken Carter's sister. "You certainly keep surprising us," he said to Mavis. "Who else have you got in your exercise class, Lord Lucan's ex-wife?"

Mavis shrugged, "I didn't know that much about her," she said, "It was a big surprise to see her in that place. And her circumstances are not that different from that of Doris."

"Well," said Pete, "that will not be a disappointment for Ken Carter. But is she actually going to divorce him?"

"I don't know," said Mavis "but what I can say is that she is thinking about it. I told her about Phillipa Fry who's acting for Doris and she did seem to be interested."

"So what will you do now?" asked Helen, "just hang about near the library?"

Mavis nodded. "I suppose so, there's not much else I can do. I might be lucky and see her straight away. On the other hand, even if I find her, she may not know where Vincent is."

When Mr Pigg arrived Mavis updated him on the enquiries she had made the previous evening. He noted what she said and agreed with her that the only action to be taken was to try to locate the young woman in the vicinity of the library. "Well, do your best," he urged "and let me know how it goes." Mavis said she would. Later she persuaded George to go with her to the library area after work.

Chapter Forty-one
Vincent is Found

Jeremy Fallow QC was far from happy about the outcome of his chambers vote for a new Head. The two contenders were: Algernon Phillipson who had the undoubted advantage of being married to Phillipa Fry who was perhaps one of, or the most able barrister in the chambers. Despite her own abilities she had never once considered standing for Head of Chambers and in a male dominated profession that would perhaps have been a step too far even for the talented Miss Fry.

She preferred to put her energies behind Algernon's election bid and certainly succeeded with one or two of the chambers' notables, Jeremy Fallow being one of them. However, her efforts on behalf of Algie with some of the other members of the chambers, notably most of the female barristers was not so effective. There was an overwhelming vote in favour of Algernon's opponent, Augustus Samuel, who had already occupied the room previously used by Jeremy.

Augustus had been at the bar for a number of years and had previously specialised in cases involving admiralty matters. He cut his teeth on cases involving piracy on the high seas but in recent years such cases had almost dried up thanks to the increase in patrols by naval vessels in a number of countries particularly off the east coast of Africa. He reverted to straight forward criminal law and in recent years had made himself a bit of a name defending minor celebrities.

He was known to everyone in the bar as Humphrey. He obtained this nickname due to his habit of commencing any meaningful address to a court by taking a large breath and then making a throat clearing sound akin to "Humph ". he had a reputation for bullying prosecution counsels who might be on the timid side and occasionally, excessively lenient Judges. This reputation was partly responsible for his popularity with the minor celebrities he represented. He found that nothing pleased a defendant more than witnessing his counsel harassing the prosecution counsel or the Judge.

Jeremy Fallow had never liked Augustus Samuel from the moment he entered Clifton Chambers. He regarded him as a blusterer who never paid any attention to detail in his preparation for a case, preferring to indulge in tempestuous outbursts in court rather than rely on irrefutable items of evidence. On a number of occasions in the past Jeremy had won cases against Humphrey due to his own meticulous attention to detail rather than any emotive bombast.

Phillipa Fry called to see Jeremy one lunch time at his new chamber in the Crown Court building. Shirley Kemp the judge's clerk served both a cup of coffee and then retired to leave them alone.

"Oh, Jeremy," said Phillipa in a downcast manner, "that election was the most outrageous, the most preposterous pantomime it's ever been my misfortune to witness. I mean, Algie is not perfect, but I ask you, Gus Samuel! Who could be less suitable?"

"I quite agree. Humphrey is most unsuitable for the position of Head of Chambers. The vote was quite unexpected. I was unable to use my casting vote."

"I know," said Phillipa tearfully, and you would have used your vote for Algie wouldn't you?"

"Oh, absolutely. But I would have used it for you rather than Algie."

"Oh, you are such a sweetie," she said, rising and coming round the desk to give him a cuddle and a kiss on the cheek. "You are always so supportive Jeremy." She gave him one more kiss which left a lipstick mark on his cheek. "You don't mind me popping in to see you do you?"

"Not at all, Phillipa. It is always especially nice to see you."

They kissed again more formally on alternate cheeks and then she left the room with an evocative swing of her hips.

George and Mavis met after work at the library. Although it was late in the afternoon the coffee bar was still open and so they decided to have a cup of coffee whilst they figured what to do. Inside they found that the place was almost empty. Mavis chose a table to sit at and George went to the counter to order and pay for the coffees. The young lady behind the counter told him to take a seat and that she would bring the coffees over to him.

They sat together at the table looking out the window at anyone who passed by. "We can't just sit in here waiting for someone to walk past wearing tartan Doc Martins can we?" said George.

"No, I suppose not," replied Mavis, "I was wondering how many houses there are nearby and whether or not we could go door to door showing the photograph of Vincent?"

George watched the girl come out from behind the counter carrying a tray with their coffees upon it. "What, for example would that investigator chap Charlie do in this situation?" asked Mavis.

"Well…" said George watching the coffee cups on the tray held by the girl who was wearing tartan Doc Martins, "I think he would use his brain and sit tight." As he said this, he pointed to the feet of the waitress who was meanwhile placing their coffee cups on the table.

Mavis gave a startled double take and produced from her handbag the photograph of Vincent. "I was wondering if you had seen a friend of mine recently in this area. You see I work with him and he hasn't been at work recently and I am quite worried about him." She showed her the photograph of Vincent. The girl looked at it for a moment without speaking. "His name is Vincent. Do you know him?" she said. The girl nodded but still did not say anything. "Well, do you know where he is?" asked Mavis. The girl nodded again but still did not answer the question.

Eventually, after some consideration, the girl said, "Vince is at my place, which is just around the corner. I'm just about to close up here, if you wait, I'll take you to see him."

Mavis was beside herself with joy. "I can't believe how fortunate that was. We just came in here for five minutes and she appears. This private investigation business is easier than I thought."

George smiled and said, "It's just a matter of luck. I'm sure that if Charlie Chivers had been here, he would have walked up and down the street for hours and then gone home empty handed. You are just lucky."

Mavis gave a smile of delight and mentally patted herself on the back. The girl was ready to leave the premises and so they followed her out into the street. She led them to a street about two blocks away which contained three storey terraced houses which once must have been quite grand. Now however they all looked a bit run down and had all been turned into small flat-lets or bed-sits. What was once a rather grand and sedate terrace had turned into an overcrowded slightly jaded street.

On their journey the girl told them that her name was Lizzy and she had known Vincent since schooldays. She said he had been unwell and was resting in her place because he had not wanted to go home seemingly under the influence of something.

The house in which she lived, like all the others in the street, was obviously divided into flats or bed-sits judging by the number of bell pushes by the front door. She led them up the stairs to the very top of the property, to a flat- let which had been built into the roof space.

Lizzy ushered them into the living room which was quite small. There was a sofa on one side of the room on which Vincent was reclining. He looked pale but Mavis reflected that he never looked ruddy or sun-tanned. He may have been surprised to see them but he did not express any surprise at all. he gripped the bridge of his nose and with a grimace said, "I've got such a headache.

Lizzy gave him a cup of take away coffee which she had brought with her from the library. Vincent gratefully tucked into it and had swallowed half of it before taking a breath. "Aah, that's better." he said.

"So, how are you?" asked Mavis.

"Oh, OK," he replied "Just the headache now."

"Will you come back to work tomorrow?" enquired Mavis. "We'll have to tell Mr Pigg that we've found you and you appear to be OK. Have you been to the doctor?"

"No, but I'm feeling a bit better now, so I'll be in work tomorrow. Don't want to upset Piggy."

"Well, that's great," said Mavis "but why have you been living here? Your mother is worried about you."

"Yeah, I know," he said, "but I didn't want to go home looking or feeling under the influence of anything. I take it you've been round to my mum's place? Did you meet my step-dad?" Mavis nodded making a face.

"Yeah, well," he continued, "that says it all. He is a real turd and I couldn't go home while he's there."

"So does that mean that you've left home?" asked Mavis.

"I don't know, I'll have to wait and see."

"But what made you get into drugs in the first place?" asked Mavis "It's such a mistake."

Vincent shrugged and said, "I first did it at one of the music festivals I went to. It was so easy that I kept doing it. Then I found this local guy who could supply stuff and bought some off him. But I fell out with him and then began to get stuff at the Nite Club."

"What do you mean when you say you fell out with him?"

"Well, he sold me some stuff once and it made me feel bad. I was supposed to pay for it in instalments but next time I saw him I told him he could whistle for the balance, and if he didn't like it, I'd go to the police and report him. He didn't like that."

"But wasn't that dangerous?" said Mavis, "These drug dealers can be violent."

"He didn't look like a violent person. He was quite thin. Nearly as puny as me," he added with a sneer. "A chap called Jimmy Pearce from the council estate near my mum's house. He's nothing."

"All the same," said Mavis, "It never pays to upset these people."

The following morning Tom Richards opened the office as usual and unlocked the cupboards and dispensed all the files onto the various tables. He then made himself a cup of tea and settled down to read his *Daily Mail*.

George, as usual, was the second to arrive and sat with Tom and told him about the success he and Mavis had with their visit to the library and subsequent discovery of Vincent in Lizzy's flat.

"So how did he look?" asked Tom.

"Well...." said George, "a bit pale and fragile I suppose but to be honest he always looks a bit that way."

"Yes, I suppose so," said Tom. "what he really needs is a sunshine holiday. Is he coming in today?"

"I think so," said George. "Though if Mavis hadn't been there to buck him up and insist that he return I don't suppose he would have bothered."

"She's a girl isn't she?" said Tom.

George smiled and replied, "Yes, she is, but I'm not a hundred per cent certain that her entreaties will be sufficient to persuade Vincent."

The others arrived in due course and were appraised of George and Mavis's success of the previous evening. Vincent was the last in time to arrive much to the delight of Mavis in particular. "Are you feeling better Vincent?" she asked and Vincent confirmed that he was.

Tom announced that in the Daily Mail today it was reported that a young man of about Vincent's age had died after recently taking a cocktail of drugs which had been purchased in a nearby town.

"The police are looking for the person or persons who peddled this lethal cocktail to the young man" he read. "They are urgently asking for anyone who may have purchased drugs recently to come forward and assist them. They will not be prosecuting anyone who assists them. They merely wish to receive any information which may be available."

"Maybe you should tell the police what you know." said Helen to Vincent.

"Not really," said Vincent. "I don't want to get involved with anything that would bring those twins and their friends down on me."

"I see your point," said Pete, "but they are already on the police radar for the steroid drugs they supplied to George here. As far as the police are concerned they would rather get them for the more serious stuff."

"A mixture of cocaine, cannabis and ketamine apparently," said Tom quoting again from the *Daily Mail*. "Also," he added, apparently, they pad it out with crushed aspirin, talcum powder and ground down bath salts, which makes the stuff go further."

"You have to help," said Pete, "both the police and me and Gorgon will be there to help and assist you. If we can achieve proof of a more serious matter against them, they will be put out of circulation for quite a while so they would not be bothering you. We've already got them banged to rights for the supply of steroids to George. The extra charge for supplying the stuff that you bought would put paid to them for some time. It would also ensure that plenty of others like yourself would be protected from the possibility of suffering what you had to put up with."

Everyone looked at Vincent who still seemed uncertain and anxious. "You know it makes sense" said Tom Richards. "It's the only way to deal with people like that."

The conversation was cut short by the arrival of Mr Pigg who immediately retired to his office. He had clearly noticed Vincent in the general office but did not speak to him directly. In his room he busied himself with a telephone call to the Regional Office Welfare section concerning Bill Butler. He was able to confirm to them the details of Bill's medical certificate a copy of which he had sent to them. It was, as he had already advised them on the telephone, a one-month duration after which, in theory, Bill would return to work.

When Mr Pigg was asked about Bill's current condition, he was able to say that that it was as good as could be expected in the circumstances. The person on the telephone at the Welfare Office demanded, "But have you carried out a welfare visit to be certain that he is in reasonable health and in need of nothing?"

"I have," confirmed Mr Pigg. "I visited him in hospital just to make sure that he was all right."

"Well yes of course" said the voice from the Welfare Office as if to imply that this was something that was naturally expected would be done. "But have you visited him since then? To monitor his improvement?"

Mr Pigg said yes, he had. He developed the white lie about the hospital visit and assured the voice that he had visited Bill at his home and had found that he was vastly better than he had been during the hospital visit. He also confirmed that Bill had been talking in terms of returning to work by the beginning of next month.

"Well," said the voice with some satisfaction, "That is good news indeed, I will pass on that information to Mr Jenkins, who I am sure, will also be pleased. And may I say Mr Pigg that your personal visits to check on Mr Butler's welfare are much appreciated. You might be surprised to hear that in some offices we deal with, the managers would not trouble to visit their staff at all in circumstances such as this. I am sure that Mr Jenkins will be especially pleased with you." Mr Pigg's chest puffed out and he modestly stated that it was the least he could do.

After he put the phone down, he requested George to come to his office. "Well, George," he said, "I see that you and Mavis managed to track down Vincent and that he has returned to work this morning. Do you know is he really well enough to come back to work."

George was slightly surprised at the question because Mr Pigg had never previously expressed any interest in Vincent's well-being. "He seems all right," was all he could say.

Mr Pigg, who had almost been caught out by the Welfare Office call concerning Bill Butler's welfare did not wish to be exposed as an uncaring boss. "Well I'm glad to hear that, George. You know I'm always interested in how you all are and I will have a word with Vincent later. In the meantime, I believe it is time for me to pay a visit to Bill Butler to see exactly how he is and to see if there is anything he might need. Perhaps you could give me directions to his house."

While Mr Pigg was out of the office it gave Pete the time to work on persuading Vincent to agree to assist the police in respect of the suspect drugs which he had purchased from the twins at the Nite Club. Finally, Vincent agreed and Pete then arranged for a meeting to take place with himself and George to be present. He set up the meeting on the telephone with Charlie Chivers.

Chapter Forty-two
La Scala Again

The International Detective was sitting in his office when the telephone rang. He listened to the information which Pete had to offer concerning his work colleague Vincent.

"OK," he said, "Sounds really good, give me five minutes and I'll see what I can arrange." He replaced the receiver and then dialled the number of Des Onions and stared distractedly at the calendar girl's breasts as he waited for the number to connect. "O' Nighons," said a voice and Charlie said. "It's me Des, I've got more info on those dodgy drugs which has hit the news recently. It's a work colleague of Pete and George the two lads who are already on board in connection with Eddie Sharp and his solicitor and the Gibson twins. Apparently, he bought some of the dodgy stuff from the twins at the Nite Cub and it made him ill for the best part of a week but he's now able to give evidence and/or testify concerning the drugs. Can we set up a meeting so you can have a look at him?"

Des said OK and they agreed to meet in the Jubilee Inn that evening. Charlie phoned Pete back to get him to bring Vincent to the pub later that day. In the early evening therefore, Pete and George took Vincent to the Jubilee Inn where they found Charlie Chivers seated on a barstool gazing at the photograph of Reginald next to Jayne Mansfield. They all purchased a drink and while they were waiting for Reg to serve them, they all surveyed the mass of pictures on the wall all of which featured a smiling Reg. Vincent, who had not been inside this pub before, immediately spotted a picture of Reg with the DJ, Tony Blackburn.

They all seated themselves at a table and awaited the arrival of Des Onions who soon put in an appearance. Vincent was introduced to both Charlie and Des and the latter quizzed him as to how and when he had acquired the drugs and from whom he had bought them. Vincent told Des that he was not in the least bit interested in making statements or giving evidence in court against the twins or their friends.

"I would be too scared," he admitted. "OK, you might get a conviction and they might be put away for a while, but if they see me giving evidence and then in a few months' time they come out, my life won't be worth shit."

"No, no, no," said Des shaking his head with assurance. "You will not be giving evidence in court nor will your friend George here. The only people giving evidence in court will be police officers who will say that the drugs were supplied to them by the twins or whoever not realising that they were Police Officers."

"But they will know, won't they," responded Vincent, "and they can say that they never supplied anything to your officers."

"Yes," said Des, "and who is going to believe them? They are criminals, aren't they?"

"Hmm, I don't know," muttered Vincent who was far from convinced. "they are scary people you know."

"They are nothing," acclaimed Des, "they are just tuppeny ha'penny trash, who don't know what they are dealing with. We already have video evidence of them supplying steroids to George on one occasion and another video will be all tied up in a day or two. Ideally we would like a further video of them supplying you with these other drugs and they won't be going anywhere for quite a while."

"What!" exclaimed Vincent in alarm, "You want me to be filmed buying more drugs off them so that they can be convicted in court of supplying. They'll know I'm involved then if you show the film in court won't they?"

"No, no, no," said Des again shaking his head almost in disbelief. "There won't be a trial in court for them because they will be pleading guilty to lesser charges and giving evidence against their boss and his crooked lawyer. They'll be so stitched up that they won't be thinking of giving you any trouble because we'll have so much hanging over them that they'll do as they are told. You will be in no physical danger because we will have plain clothes officers everywhere watching you."

"Oh, I'm not sure," said Vincent, "You can't be watching me all the time."

"I assure you we can." said Des Onions.

"Anyway," said Pete, "I'll be there to keep an eye on you together with a couple of mates from the rugby club."

"This will be our operation." said Des "I don't want any amateurs interfering with our business."

"We won't," Pete assured him. "We will simply be there at the Nite Club for a drink or two enjoying ourselves and keeping an eye on Vince."

"Well, make sure you do." reiterated Des "Because once it all kicks off, I don't want anyone interfering with my officers. Got that?"

"Sure," said Pete.

"Right," said Des, "I'll be in touch with Charlie here to specify the time and date when all this will take place. There will be a number of officers involved and this will mean it is an expensive operation so I do not want anything to go wrong, understood?" Here Des looked meaningfully at Pete again who nodded emphatically.

Mavis and Doris met at the coffee shop after their latest exercise class. This time Freda was with them having been persuaded to join them by Mavis. Their conversation started lightly because although they all knew each other from previous classes neither Mavis nor Doris knew Freda as intimately as they did each other.

After a few minutes of polite conversation Doris grasped the nettle and announced, "I have moved myself and my daughter out of the family home and gone back to live, temporarily at my mum and dad's place: Mrs Robinson at Duffey Fry & Co has told me that the divorce papers are ready to be served on Eddie so upon her advice I decided to be out of the way when the papers are personally served upon him."

"Wow," said Mavis excitedly. That didn't take very long did it. We only went to see Phillipa Fry about a week ago. Have you read the papers?"

"Yes," said Doris rolling her eyes as she spoke. "That's what prompted me to move out. He is not going to like it when he reads it all."

"Was it good then?" asked Mavis almost overcome with curiosity.

"Phew," said Doris, with another roll of her eyes. "Talk about comprehensive. She left nothing out. It even amazed me and I already knew everything before I read it. He will be livid."

"I told you she was brilliant." said Mavis. "She will take him to the cleaners. Don't you think."

"I certainly do now that I've read what she has written about him."

Doris fumbled in her handbag to pull out a copy of her divorce petition and accompanying papers and passed it to Mavis to peruse. "So," said Doris to Freda, "I understand that your husband is no better than mine."

"Well, yeah," she replied "He's done all the usual annoying things like getting drunk, gambling, not letting me go out without cross examining me about who I might see etc. etc. But recently he's overstepped the mark by playing around with another woman I believe, although I can't be certain."

"That sounds just like mine." said Doris, "of course, if they go in for all the other peccadillos then eventually, they are bound to try adultery. In any case it seems, the positive proof of actual adultery doesn't appear to be required any more if you add all the other items, it seems you can't fail to get a divorce. Have a look at that." she added indicating the papers which Mavis was reading. Mavis passed them over to Freda who read through them quickly.

"It looks like Joe and me," she said, "like looking into a mirror."

"Well, there you are," said Mavis encouragingly. Why don't you go and see Phillipa Fry and she can do the same thing for you? You can't lose with her on your side." Freda admitted that it was tempting and she said she would give it some thought.

"Well, don't leave it too long," advised Doris. "The longer you wait the more he'll do. My advice is that you write down all the things that he has done and see what the list is like when you've finished. For me it was therapeutic, just writing it all out. When I'd finished the list I thought to myself, "why have I put up with all this for so long and who reading this would not say, Get rid of him.""

"Perhaps I'll do that," said Freda thoughtfully. "If you need any help or support, I can be with you" said Mavis "I helped Doris, didn't I?"

"She certainly did," confirmed Doris. "I could not have done it alone. Mavis was so helpful and she got information against Eddie from her place of work which was really helpful." As she said this Doris realised that she might have revealed too much and put her hands over her mouth saying, "Oh, I am sorry, Mavis, I shouldn't have said that, should I."

"Oh, that's all right," said Mavis "I was only too pleased to help. Anyway, the information was all true so it's difficult if not impossible for Eddie to deny it."

"Well, I certainly know a number of things about Joe," said Freda "a lot of the things which I know he doesn't know that I know if that doesn't sound too Irish."

They all agreed to meet again soon when Freda would present them with her list of Joe's misdemeanours for their scrutiny.

The next morning when George arrived at the office Tom Richards had already drunk his cup of tea and had reached the sports page of his Daily Mail. He regaled George with the information that Arsenal had beaten Tottenham Hotspurs in an evening game yesterday. Tom had always been an Arsenal supporter and he knew that George had a fondness for the Spurs.

"Too good for you last night," he announced triumphantly. George nodded but reflected to himself that he wasn't that big a Spurs fan so the result didn't really bother him. The others gradually arrived and began chatting as usual. Mavis recounted to Helen what had gone on the afternoon before with Doris and Freda. She had already described to Helen who Freda was when she had told her about their adventure at the Nite Club in search of Vincent.

"She seems to be in an identical fix to that of Doris with her husband Eddie. All the same sort of symptoms. We told her about Phillipa Fry and how brilliant she is and she's thinking of using her to get rid of her husband."

This information raised everyone's eyebrows especially Pete who then began to pay particular attention to what Mavis was saying.

"Doris showed us a copy of her divorce papers which Phillipa Fry had drawn up. Absolutely brilliant!" she continued. "She's stitched him up like an oven-ready turkey."

"So Freda's going to do the same thing?" said Helen.

"Well, she's thinking about it." said Mavis "I told her that I didn't mind helping her, you know going to the solicitor and or the barrister with her, just as a support. I wouldn't mind going back to see Phillipa Fry again. She is so marvellous." Pete's eyebrows raised again at this further information.

Helen said, "Well if you go to see her again you might be able to get some more info on her perfect make-up."

"Well actually…" said Mavis, fishing about in her handbag, "I bought this magazine which is really informative." She produced what turned out to be a very expensive looking journal full of fashion tips and advice with particular emphasis paid to make up and eye liners etc. "There's this section here," said Mavis, pointing out a page with information on eye make-up, "that I think has the same sort of effect that Phillipa Fry was wearing. I think it looks wonderful, don't you?"

Helen admitted that it was good but looked at the price tag on the back of the magazine and winced.

"I know," said Mavis, "but it is only a one-off purchase. I'm going to experiment and try to get the same effect instead of using the cheap stuff I've always used before."

"Well, it certainly looks beautiful," agreed Helen.

Mr Pigg then arrived with a crash and a bang and without a word went straight to his room. Everyone wondered whether he would tell them what had happened at Bill Butler's house or whether he would stay in his room all day.

"He hasn't done any more of those stupid graphs lately," said Mavis. "Well that at least is a blessing," responded Helen.

"Perhaps he's mapping out a plan of campaign," remarked Tom who could never cease to harp back to the old days when he was in company with Field Marshall Montgomery and the like.

"Yeah," sneered Pete, "perhaps he's planning how to invade Poland."

Whilst everyone was sniggering, Mr Pigg's door opened and he came into the general office. "Can I have your attention, please," he bellowed. "Vincent, go and fetch Mrs Balstaff and Penny, if you would."

Vincent did as he was told and came back with the pair who took places in readiness for a public announcement. Penny sat amongst the others and Mrs Balstaff took her place at the end of the room alongside Mr Pigg who then addressed them all.

"Now, as you know I went to see Bill Butler at his home yesterday to ascertain how well he is recovering from his illness. I am pleased to tell you that Bill is making good progress and should be well enough to join us again within the next two to three weeks. I am sure that this will come as good news to you all." Everyone nodded and smiled and looked relieved, especially Mavis and Vincent.

"But I want you all to remember that Bill suffered a serious stroke and may wish to settle back into work as gently as possible so please try to help him as much as you can." Everyone nodded again and said of course they would, and most of them reflected that the one who should help the most was Mr Pigg himself but they all doubted that that would be the case.

Later that afternoon Mavis found Pete in the basement again. She sidled up to him and asked if he would mind if she requested a small favour from him.

"Over there" he said pointing to some papers lying on the top of the photocopier.

"What?" she said moving over to the machine to have a look.

"Information on Giovanni Pettacinni," replied Pete. "That's what you were going to ask for wasn't it?"

"Oh, you are a brick," exclaimed Mavis scanning the paperwork quickly.

"Yeah, well, I've already given all this information to your friend's brother Mr Carter." he said, "so it's not that confidential any more."

"Thanks, Pete," said Mavis. "How's your friend Sandra? Would you like to have another meal with George and I at the Italian restaurant?"

"Sure," said Pete. "We were going to go there this evening anyway. If you and George want to join us, I'll book a table."

George and Mavis arrived at La Scala the Italian restaurant at approximately seven thirty p.m. This was considerably earlier than the last time but they had remembered that on that occasion Pete and Sandra were already seated at the table waiting for them.

They were greeted at the door, by Fillipo, who was as effusive as ever. "Eetza so good to see you again" he told them. He grasped the hand of Mavis and kissed it greedily. "Aah" he said with a smile, "so beautiful, you are a very lucky young man," he said to George. "I could get used to this," sighed Mavis as he led them to their table. They were surprised to note that despite their own punctuality Pete and Sandra were already seated.

They greeted each other and ordered a drink each which Fillipo scurried off to collect. Both Mavis and Sandra were happy to meet each other again and felt the same connection as before. They were soon chattering away happily.

When Fillipo returned with the drinks he brought them a bowl of crisps to munch on whilst deciding what to choose from the menu. They all studied the menu carefully and almost inevitably each of them made the same choice as the last time they had been there.

"I feel guilty about choosing the same thing again" said Mavis. "But it was so delicious that I must have it again."

Sandra said she felt the same.

"How is your new job going?" asked Mavis. Sandra said it was very interesting and rewarding. She explained to Mavis some of the things she had been doing since they had last met. "It has taken a bit of practice to get used to talking in front of the camera but I think I have mastered it" she said. "I am quite used to interviewing people already from my days at the newspaper."

"I think you must be so clever," said Mavis. "I know that I couldn't do it."

"Oh, it's only practice," said Sandra modestly. "So, what have you been up to?"

Mavis instantly went into a long explanation of her now possible involvement in the divorce proceedings of Freda Pettacinni and also how she had managed to track down Vincent who had gone missing from the office. These were items of information which appealed to Sandra who was herself an investigative journalist.

"She's turned into an amateur sleuth," remarked Pete and Sandra agreed that Mavis certainly had. Mavis smiled modestly and declared that she found private investigating to be quite exciting and much less difficult than she had first supposed. Both Pete and George laughed at this for different reasons. George recalled how fortuitous Mavis had been in finding Lizzy at the Library coffee house and Pete was amused by the fact that most of the information which Mavis had acquired about both Eddie Sharp and Freda's husband he had supplied. Mavis blushed, as if she had read his thoughts and admitted to Sandra how helpful Pete had been.

"Nevertheless," said Sandra, "You pieced it all together and worked everything out. You remind me of me." Mavis blushed again and felt hugely complimented to hear what Sandra had said.

"And what about you?" Mavis asked, "Have you started on your story about Eddie and his crooked solicitor?"

"Oh, yes," said Sandra, "I've done quite a lot of research, much of which has been kindly donated by Pete, and have quite an impressive file in readiness. I am planning to try to get interviews with them but I'm not hopeful that either of them will talk to me."

"What I would like to find out on behalf of Freda," said Mavis "is who the woman is that her husband has been playing around with. I just need a name to give to Phillipa Fry."

"Well," said Sandra with a glance to Pete, "perhaps your friend Fillipo might have some idea."

Pete nodded and made a note to catch the eye of Fillipo as soon as he could. Eventually the Italian saw Pete trying to attract his attention and came over to their table. Pete decided that it would be an appropriate moment to order another drink for everyone and the order was made. When Fillipo returned with the drinks Pete asked him to take a seat for a moment and he drew up a chair.

"Giovanni Pettacinni?" said Pete, "Do you have any idea who is the woman he has been playing away from home with?" Fillipo was momentarily caught out by the manner of the question which his grasp of English did not allow him to instantly understand.

"Aah," he said at last, "si, when he worked for me he would slip out to the betting shop whenever he could. He was not going there just to put money on the horses. There is a lady who works there who he was always sneefing around."

"What is her name?" asked Mavis

"I can't remember," said Fillipo, scratching his chin "but I think it was Molly or Dolly or something like that."

"We can check the list of employees tomorrow," murmured Pete. "Thanks Fillipo."

Eventually, when the meal was over, they all retired upstairs to Pete's flat. Mavis and Sandra sat on the sofa and began to chatter away whilst Pete and George went into the kitchen to prepare some coffee. "They do get on well, don't they?" said George nodding his head towards the lounge where the girls were talking.

"Yeah," said Pete "they're like soul mates aren't they."

When the coffee was made the boys joined the girls in the lounge. Mavis was showing Sandra the fashion magazine which she still carried in her handbag. "Yes, I really like that" said Sandra indicating the page on eye make-up. "I see that you've mastered it already."

"Oh, thank you," said Mavis "I think I have more idea now but I've still a long way to go before I can match Phillipa Fry."

"You look just as nice as her," said George defiantly.

"You've never seen her, so how can you judge?" said Mavis "but thanks anyway."

George wanted to say that as far as he was concerned there was nobody anyway who could look nicer than Mavis but he did not say it because he thought it might sound a bit too cheesy. Pete said, "I think it must be your new found talent for investigation which has brought out the best in you. It has given you a sparkle in your eye which looks good on you."

"I agree," said George, "You are much prettier now than when I first saw you."

Mavis blushed. "I'm going to feel embarrassed in a minute with all these compliments flying about. I'm afraid I can only allow you both another thirty minutes and then I will have to say no more compliments. Anyway, Pete you should be saying nice things about Sandra not me."

"I don't need to," said Pete "she knows how I feel about her."

"That's as maybe," said Sandra jokingly, but I would not object if you gave it a try."

Everyone laughed.

Chapter Forty-three
The Car Lot

The following Saturday morning George arrived at the car lot equipped with more brand new twenty-pound notes, to deliver to the Gibson twins for a further package of steroid drugs. As before, the hand over was pre-arranged with Sandra's cameraman hidden nearby and also the officers of the local CID as hidden witnesses.

The twins were there looking left and right up the road to be certain they were not being observed by anyone. As before, George wore his driving gloves so as to minimise the fingerprints on the bank notes he handed over.

One of the twins said, "Got the money then?" George handed over the cash and the receiving twin quickly counted it.

The other twin meanwhile examined George and with contempt said, "Doesn't seem to have made any difference to you. You do realise that you have to keep lifting the weights?"

George said he had been busy lately and had not found the time to do much exercise but was intending to get round to it. The twin handed over the package and George went on his way.

A short while after Eddie arrived at the car lot and the twins came out to see him. One of them was carrying a sports bag which was full of something. He handed the bag to Eddie who unzipped it and glanced inside. The bag was full of bank notes of various denominations.

"One week's worth," said the twin proudly, "not bad eh?"

"Have you taken any share?" asked Eddie.

"No," said one twin defensively.

Eddie took two bundles of bank notes from the bag and handed to each of the twins. "Right" he said "I'll go and hand the rest of this over to my lawyer who can stick it into his client account for me."

"This is really lucrative" said one of the twins. "I believe that Jimmy Pearce is expecting another delivery from his contact in London soon so we thought you might want to do the same again? If so you might want to hold some of that back?"

Eddie sucked his teeth and thought for a moment. "I wouldn't trust Jimmy Pearce further than I could throw him. The more deals we do with him the more certain it is that we all get caught."

"But it's so easy," said the twin "and so profitable. Just one more delivery?"

Eddie thought for a moment then said, "OK, one last transaction but after that no more deals with Jimmy. He can't be trusted. Take five grand out of here" he said handing back the sports bag. One of the twins counted out the bank notes and then handed back the sports bag to Eddie who got back into his car and drove off.

Later, he arrived at the offices of Huw Roberts & Co solicitors. As usual Mrs Sargent was at the reception desk when he entered. "Morning, Agnes," he said. "Ok to go up?" he said this without waiting for a response and was already making his way up to Simon Nibble's room before Mrs Sargent could give her permission.

When the door to his room opened suddenly Simon Nibble was surprised to see Eddie carrying a sports bag. "Hello Eddie," he said in surprise, "What are you doing here on a Saturday morning?"

"I just came to deposit this," he said, "Ten grand, OK?"

"Oh, I'm not sure Eddie. That much cash is difficult to justify."

"Oh, bollocks!" retorted Eddie, "Just stick it in your client account and stop moaning. You charge enough for God's sake. Can't stay, I'm off to play golf." With that he hurried out of the room and left Simon Nibble looking at the sight of all that cash in the sports bag. He smiled.

DCI Desmond O' Nighons was cock ahoop. Seated in the Jubilee Inn with Charlie Chivers he confirmed that the second sale of steroid drugs to George had been successfully captured on film and the drugs themselves had been gathered in evidence bags and fingerprinted. "We are nearly there," he confirmed to Charlie. "In fact we already have more than enough to secure a conviction against the Gibson twins but I would like just a little more before swooping on Eddie Sharp and his solicitor. If we could just do the same thing at the Nite Club and gather more evidence against them, this time for supplying the dodgy class A stuff then that would put us in an even stronger position."

"Well," said Charlie, "that operation does depend upon the work colleague of Pete and George, uhm, Vincent I think his name is. I don't know about you but I think he is a bit flimsy and certainly needs handling carefully."

"I know, I know," said Des, "but we will saturate the place with plain clothes officers who should be able to control things. What's the latest on that little toe rag Jimmy Pearce?"

"Well, I'm keeping an eye on him but nothing much has happened since I last reported to you but that's not all bad news, in one sense because it confirms that his main or only source of distribution for the stuff is via the twins. I'm certain that his only source of supply is from the chap in London that you say Special Branch are keeping an eye on. It's been a month or so since he went to London so I guess he does not have any more of the stuff at present. He must have off-loaded

the whole caboodle on the twins because I've not noticed him moving anything else. In any event, I doubt whether he would have the nerve to try anything underhand with the twins. What have you heard from your London contact?"

"They are certain that something may happen soon. Their counterparts in Amsterdam are expecting another batch any day. If we get the tip off for that we can scoop them all up together and listen to them sing. Jimmy Pearce will be the first to trill like a canary. He is a self-serving little gobshite who will immediately betray everyone else to further his own ends."

"So when are you thinking of doing the raid on the Nite Club?"

"Possibly this coming Friday evening," said Des, "but I will let you know."

"Will you be in the club?" asked Charlie.

"No," confirmed Des "I will be waiting outside. I'm too old to go into the Nite Club without sticking out like a sore thumb."

"OK," said Charlie "There is no way now that I could get away with it either. Leave it to the Youngsters, eh?"

On the same day Mavis, Doris and Freda all met in the coffee shop following an exercise session. Freda announced that she had completed her list of faults by her husband Giovanni. She produced two copies of her list and handed a copy to both Mavis and Doris.

"Almost the same as my list," said Doris. "You will have no trouble with this. The question is are you willing to go ahead with the divorce or do you want to stay with him?"

"No, I don't," confirmed Freda. "You were right about the list making. It is therapeutic. By the time I had finished the list I knew that I no longer wanted to be with him. I am cured. I can no longer see what I ever saw in him."

"Good for you" said Mavis "Will you go on the same route as Doris? Duffey Fry & Co solicitors and Phillipa Fry the barrister?"

"I 've already telephoned for an appointment. I've got a meeting with Mrs Robinson tomorrow. Would you like to come with me to give me some support?"

Mavis nodded enthusiastically, "Certainly, what time do we meet?"

Tom Richards opened the office and the filing cupboards as usual and settled down to drink his cup of tea and read the Daily Mail. When George arrived, he was halfway through his paper and was able to tell George that another report in the newspaper concerned the suspect drugs which had affected Vincent the week before. This time, apparently a young man in a nearby town had suffered and had spent a few days in hospital. The police were "looking into it" said the Daily Mail.

"They are a bit behind the times" said George "but I suppose that's just a standard report like" helping the Police with their enquiries." Tom Richards agreed.

Mavis and Helen arrived next and the former announced that she was hoping to take the afternoon off in order to accompany Freda on her visit to the offices of Duffey Fry & Co.

"You are like a knight in shining armour, aren't you?" said Helen "I expect you are just hoping to get another interview with Phillipa Fry eh?"

"I certainly would," confirmed Mavis.

Pete arrived next and told George that he had been advised by Charlie Chivers that the raid on the Nite Club was organised for Friday next. Mavis was quite excited by this and said that she thought that she ought to go to the Nite Club with George to keep an eye out for Vincent. George was trying to find a reason to refuse but had to admit that he would look much less obvious at the Club if he were accompanied by Mavis.

When Vincent arrived, he was advised of the same information. He was not especially pleased to hear it but at the same time he knew that sooner or later the moment would come when he would have to go through with it. That day had now arrived or rather would shortly arrive on Friday.

There followed some conversation as to how the drugs deal would be financed. Vincent was asked how much the last consignment had cost him and he told them it was one hundred pounds. He also explained that for that much money one obtained a very small amount of drugs, approximately a thumb nail size pack.

Not surprisingly Vincent informed them that he had no money and would not therefore be able to pay for the drugs. Pete told him not to worry. He said he would talk to Charlie Chivers and the DCI Des Onions to arrange some money for the deal.

Mr Pigg arrived last as usual and buried himself in his office for a while, trying to decide what he would do today and who he could telephone and what he could say to them. He was interrupted from his reverie by the telephone. It was Mr Jenkins the Regional Controller who always phoned early.

"Good morning Arnold," he said in a cheery manner. "How are you this morning?"

"Good morning to you," replied Mr Pigg endeavouring to emulate the cheeriness of his caller, "I'm very well thank you sir."

"Good, good," said Mr Jenkins. "I've been hearing good reports about you from the Welfare Department. I understand you have made several visits to see Bill Butler."

"Umm, yes sir, I have," said Mr Pigg warily. "Excellent!" exclaimed Mr Jenkins. "Going the extra mile as usual eh? That's what I like about you Arnold."

Mr Pigg puffed up a little and realising how the land lay said to his controller, "I couldn't just sit on my hands, sir, I had to get out there and assess things for myself. It would have been easy enough to send somebody else but that's not the way I do things. I had to go there myself and see how Bill was."

"Excellent, Arnold," repeated the Controller, "and how exactly is Bill doing?"

"Oh, very well indeed," said Mr Pigg, "he should be back to work within two or three weeks. When I called to see him, he was very eager to return. I have to say that we need him back here. Since Lionel's unfortunate demise we have missed him terribly."

"I am sure you have, Arnold, but I'm hoping that you will be able to hang on for just a couple more weeks until Bill returns. I have been reviewing my files and I believe that my overall impression of Bill Butler has been raised since his absence from the office. Initially I thought that his enforced absence, with Lionel replacing him, was a fortuitous occurrence but now I am not so sure. Now I believe that Bill's return will be the fortuitous occurrence. But more of that later Arnold. You just hang on for two weeks or so and we shall see."

Later the same day Mavis met Freda outside the offices of Duffey Fry & Co solicitors. "Thanks for coming with me," said Freda, "I would have felt intimidated on my own."

"Not at all," said Mavis "Now, did you remember the items I mentioned, the marriage certificate and your list of faults that you prepared." Freda confirmed that she had brought the items. "Well let's go in then" she said. They both entered the offices and were soon both seated together in Mrs Robinson's room. The latter took details from Freda and then asked for the marriage certificate which Freda handed over together with her list of faults.

When Mrs Robinson asked for details of Mr Pettacinni's finances she half glanced at Mavis and was not at all surprised when the latter produced the pages which Pete had supplied. Mrs Robinson read these carefully and when she had finished, she said, "Well, I have to say that you have come up trumps again. This is utterly comprehensive and completely damning.

Speaking to Freda she said, "My advice to you is exactly the same as that which I gave to the last lady which your friend brought to me. There are some details of your situation which I feel require the attention of an expert in matrimonial matters. That is a barrister by the name of Phillipa Fry who I am confident would be happy to take over your divorce and ensure that you would achieve the best and most secure outcome of these proceedings." She cocked an eyebrow in the direction of Mavis as if to say,

"Is not Phillipa Fry the right woman for this job?" Mavis nodded her head emphatically.

"Right," said Mrs Robinson with great assurance, "I will prepare a brief and send it to Miss Fry who will no doubt wish to see you following which she will prepare your divorce papers and supervise the whole process. How does that sound."

Freda said she thought that sounded all right and Mavis had trouble containing herself and not clapping her hands with joy.

Chapter Forty-four
Petition Served

Charlie Chivers the International Detective was alone in his office when he received the telephone call from Duffey Fry & Co solicitors. Would he be willing to personally serve divorce papers on one Eddie Sharp?

Charlie confirmed that he definitely would be willing to do so, at the normal rates. He agreed to call around at their offices to collect the papers in the next hour. He stared vacantly at the calendar girl's breasts, and reflected upon the irony of this his latest task. It was a ten-minute stroll from Charlie's office to those of Duffey Fry & Co. After collecting the papers, he made his way to the local newsagents and purchased a daily paper and a fresh packet of Manakin cigars. He then returned to his office and settled down to read the divorce petition which he was about to serve upon Eddie Sharp. He lit a fresh Manakin and leaned back in his chair to peruse the documents. As his eyes made their way down the page, he gave a low whistle. Most of the facts therein he was already aware of due to his collaboration with Pete but there were a few facts of which he was unaware. More than that, it was the style and quality of the narrative which impressed him.

"Well, Eddie my boy," he muttered to himself, "that's you trussed up and hog tied. Get out of that!"

With a last fond glance at the calendar girl's breasts he gathered himself up and left the office to go and visit Sharp Eddie at his home. In a further ten minutes he was walking up the driveway to Eddie's house. He eyed the property with some approval as he approached the front door. There was a step up into a porchway that had its own tiled roof and floor with waist-high stone walls to match those of the house and above that panels glazed with leaded windows of various coloured glass panes.

Charlie pressed the doorbell inside the porchway and unzipped a briefcase which he was carrying.

The door was opened by Eddie himself who looked suspiciously at Charlie. "Yes?" he said.

"Good morning, Mr Sharp," he said in an ultra- cheery tone, "I've got a little parcel for you here," he added, still poking about in his briefcase.

"Who are you?" demanded Eddie even more suspiciously. He had in his lifetime experienced many attempts by people to serve him with court papers and was already in the course of closing his door on Charlie.

The latter continued with his cheerful persona and said, "Charlie Chivers, Mr Sharp. I'm the local agent for the lottery winners' department. We are trying to trace missing winners."

Eddie was somewhat puzzled by this and paused long enough for Charlie to take advantage. "Aah here we are," he said and handed over the papers to Eddie who unfolded them and glanced briefly at what he was holding.

"What's all this?" he asked with further wariness.

"It's a divorce petition hereby served on behalf of your wife Mr Sharp," said Charlie continuing the cheeriness of his demeanour. "Good morning to you" he chirruped and retired down the driveway whistling softly to himself as he went.

He then returned to his office and typed up an affidavit of service document which he immediately took downstairs to the offices of Huw Roberts & Co solicitors. At the front desk he explained to Mrs Sargent that he had a document to be sworn and she immediately granted him access to one of their legal clerks who duly witnessed Charlie's signature thereon. Charlie paid the fee in cash and left the office bearing a receipt. He then went straight to the offices of Duffey Fry & Co to present them with the evidence of due service of Doris petition.

The International Detective chuckled to himself at the irony of the situation whereby the firm of Huw Roberts & Co solicitors had witnessed the affidavit of service in respect of Simon Nibble's most important client.

The door to Huw Roberts & Co solicitors crashed open and Eddie Sharp stormed in like a tropical hurricane. "Morning, Agnes, is he in?" he said addressing Mrs Sargent who, having seen him coming, had raised one eyebrow.

"I'm afraid not, Mr Sharp," she responded. "He is in court this morning so won't be back here before two o'clock."

Eddie expelled breath noisily and looked frustrated.

"Was there anything we could help you with in the meantime?"

"I very much doubt that, Agnes. This is a personal matter which is extremely confidential."

"Everything between a solicitor and his client is confidential," she advised him. "Nothing goes beyond these walls without the client's approval." Mrs Sargent's eyebrows seemed to show that what she had just said was obvious and self-apparent and hadn't really needed to have been said but that lady was of course unaware of the nocturnal activities of the International Detective upstairs.

Eddie breathed deeply and said, "My wife, who must have taken leave of her senses, has served divorce papers upon me, and I want Simon to put a stop to this nonsense immediately."

Mrs Sargent's eyebrows appeared to indicate that Eddie's wife had finally come to her senses and made the first sensible decision for many a year. "Mr Nibble does not deal with divorce law, Mr Sharp," she said, "we have a clerk here who deals with the matrimonial cases. Would you like to have a word with him?"

"No, I bloody wouldn't," said Eddie forcefully, "I don't want a clerk, I want the top dog, that's what I pay you for!"

Mrs Sargent's eyebrows said that here was a very discourteous man who was incapable of understanding plain English. "Of course," she said through gritted teeth, "You are entitled to the best advice which your money can buy. That is why I have already told you that Mr Nibble does not do matrimonial work. It is not that he can do it but refuses to do it just to be awkward, but because he has no experience in that area of law whereas someone who does have experience could do a better job for you."

Eddie was still not satisfied, "I'll be back at two o'clock," he said firmly and marched out. The eyebrows of Mrs Sargent, who watched him go, expressed the opinion that if she were Mrs Sharp, she would do exactly the same.

At precisely two p.m. Eddie returned and gained immediate access to Simon Nibble's office. "Hello Eddie," said Simon blandly. "I understand you have received some papers."

"Yeah," said Eddie producing the copy of his papers. "My fucking wife has decided that she wants a divorce and I've just received these," he said throwing them on the table with distain. "What are you going to do about it?" he demanded. Simon held up his hand whilst still reading through the divorce petition and attached papers. When he had finished reading, he looked up at Eddie and smiled. "What would you like me to do?" he asked.

"Well put a fucking stop to it of course," he responded "she can't be allowed to say all that shit about me and get away with it surely?"

Simon continued to smile. "But she has said it, hasn't she? There is no way that it can be unsaid except if the whole petition is withdrawn by your wife and those representing her and I doubt if that is possible anyway. But in any case, Eddie, all this is just a means of obtaining a divorce from you. If you don't oppose it then it will all go through on the nod and no one will be any wiser. It won't be reported in the local paper or anything. It might cost you some money because you will have to settle with her financially. But I'm sure you can afford it?" Again, Simon smiled blandly as if to say what's all the fuss about.

"So why does Agnes say that you can't deal with it?"

"This firm can deal with it of course," said Simon still smiling. "It's just that I have no experience of dealing with divorce cases so I always delegate that to someone else." As he said this Simon picked up the telephone and dialled a number. "Hello, Chris, I have a gentleman with me who is a very important client. He has just received a divorce petition. Would you please pop up here for a few minutes just to have a look at it and give him a bit of advice?"

He replaced the receiver. "Chris is coming up," he explained, "have you had a word with your wife? What does she have to say?"

"Nothing at all," said Eddie, "she left home a few days ago and has gone to live at her mother's."

"So you have spoken at least?"

"No. She left a note telling me not to contact her."

There was a knock at the door. A face looked in expectantly. The face wore a ginger moustache and pebble glasses.

"Aah come in, Chris," said Simon. "This is Eddie Sharp our most important commercial client, who has just received these divorce papers from his wife." He handed over the copy papers which Chris began reading. When he had finished reading, he nodded and looked up.

"Hmm," he said still nodding. "Pretty standard stuff though colossally over the top although quite stylish in it's narrative. No disrespect but it is the kind of thing which normally one would only see in respect of a marriage breakdown for a well- known celebrity. It is pretty well belt and braces stuff to make sure that the court will definitely grant a divorce."

"But what can I do about it?" pleaded Eddie.

"Well not much I would suggest," offered Chris. "Generally one has two choices. The first is to fight the divorce and to challenge all the points made in the petition, or to accept the position generally and allow the divorce to go through. The former is extraordinarily expensive and, I would suggest not sensible in a case like this. I would guess that even if you could deny or challenge some of the points raised there are probably some others which you would have to accept as being true. In any event what the court would have in mind is that to uphold a challenge to this petition would, in effect, force the two parties to remain living together when clearly a document like this shows that that would be an intolerable situation. All you have to do is file a reply form with the court and thereafter negotiate a financial settlement with your wife. Quite straightforward really."

"And you of course would be able to help Eddie do that" said Simon.

"Oh yes of course," confirmed Chris.

Simon smiled as if all problems had just been solved. "So, there you are," he said. "You go downstairs with Chris, and he'll sort it all out for you."

Eddie appeared to be far from completely satisfied but reluctantly went downstairs with Chris to give him the information for the reply forms.

Chapter Forty-five
The Flirtation Begins

Jeremy Fallow QC was in his chambers at the Crown Court building. A case on which he had been presiding had unexpectedly terminated by lunchtime. The jury had come to an almost instant guilty decision on the case of a man who had caused the death of another by dangerous driving.

The smart money had been in favour of at least a five-day trial with perhaps thereafter anything from one to two days for the jury to make its decision. Due however to the constant interruptions during the proceedings by the judge himself, clearly on behalf of the prosecution, the jury came to a guilty decision.

Jeremy had adjourned the case for one week for sentencing but had warned the defendant to expect a custodial sentence. Thus, he was now in his chambers drafting a speech sentencing the unfortunate defendant to a three-year custodial sentence. The rest of the day was one in which Jeremy was free and that was why he was endeavouring to spend his lunch hour drafting his sentence speech in the hope that he might be able to take the afternoon off and might even be able to pop up the road to watch Gloucester playing against Yorkshire. He dared to hope that his brother might be batting this afternoon.

Shirley Kemp the Judge's clerk came in from the outer room which she occupied. "Can I get you a cup of coffee, Judge?" she asked, gathering up the cups and organising the coffee machine in the corner of the room.

"Yes, Shirley, thank you very much. Have you got anything you have to do that cannot wait until tomorrow? As the trial finished unexpectedly early, we both have a free afternoon. Why don't you go home early? You stay late on other occasions so why not take advantage of this occasion. I'm just finishing the draft of my sentencing for today then I thought I would pop off early."

"Well, thank you, Judge, I'd like that," and glancing at his notes she added, "I'll type those up for you in the morning."

"Yes, thank you, Shirley. Have a nice afternoon."

Shirley went back to her room and Jeremy sipped the cup of coffee she had made for him. He was deciding whether or not to visit the county ground to watch some cricket when Shirley popped her head around the door to say, "A visitor for you, Judge. I'll let myself out and see you in the morning."

"Yes, thank you, Shirley," he responded and with that Phillipa Fry eased herself into his room.

"Hello, Jeremy," she said in a husky tone, "I was in the matrimonial court and I heard that your trial had finished early so I thought I would pop over to see you."

Jeremy could not have been more pleased to see anyone and his face showed it. "What a nice surprise," he said "would you like a coffee? Shirley has just made some," he said, indicating the cups and the coffee pot.

"I don't mind if I do," said Phillipa, who went over to the corner of the room to help herself. Jeremy noted that she was wearing a simple dark blue skirt but no stockings today. The sight of her bare legs excited him. She also wore a cream-coloured silk blouse. "Shirley was just leaving as I came in," she said, "so I've got you all to myself today." She was wearing dark rimmed glasses which gave her an additional intellectual air and, in Jeremy's opinion, made her look even more attractive than usual.

She poured herself a cup of coffee and walked back to the visitor's chair. She took a sip and looked over the top of her glasses in what Jeremy perceived as being a very sensual manner. "Are you pleased to see me Jeremy?" she asked and crossed her legs in her usual way giving him a clear view of most of her bare legs.

"Seeing you," he responded, "Is the most wonderful surprise imaginable," he said appraising her legs as he spoke.

"I was dealing with another case today which reminded me of you," she said, "Do you remember not long ago I told you about a divorce petition I had drafted and whether you would allow it in your court as evidence of behaviour?"

"I do," he said, "and I remember telling you that there is nothing I would refuse if it came from you or words to that effect."

"Yes," she said, "well I've just received another brief for a second lady whose circumstances are surprisingly similar to the first one. There seems to be a local cluster of women with wicked husbands who do not know how to behave themselves." She took another sip of coffee and then leaned forward to place her cup on the desk. She then sat back and unfolded her legs and then re- folded them again. Jeremy watched them avidly.

"Do you know how to behave yourself Jeremy?" she asked coquettishly.

"Most assuredly," he replied.

"I only ask because I have noticed that you are looking at my legs rather a lot you naughty man."

Jeremy's eyebrows lifted and he sighed, "But how can I help it?" he pleaded, "You have such beautiful legs."

Phillipa stretched her legs out in front of her as if to examine them and then rose from her chair. As she had done before she slowly raised her skirt to give Jeremy a full view of her legs. Jeremy felt an erection growing inside his trousers. "Breath taking" he murmured.

"Shall I tell you a little secret?" she said sauntering around the desk to where he sat.

"Ooh," he sighed sucking in his breath.

Phillipa seated herself side saddle on his lap and whispered in his ear, "I'm not wearing any underwear." Jeremy could hear and feel the blood pounding in his own

ears now. He felt the temperature in his cheeks rising. "You were not appearing in the matrimonial court without underwear surely?"

She giggled and gave a little nibble on his ear. She could feel his erection. "No, no, silly," she said, "I went into the ladies and removed my stockings, panties and bra. Shall I show you?"

She slowly started to unbutton her blouse and after undoing four buttons she eased the blouse to one side to reveal one of her breasts.

Jeremy sucked in more breath and stared at it lasciviously. He leaned forward slightly and took her nipple in his mouth and sucked it gently. He rolled his tongue across it. Phillipa closed her eyes and raised her chin.

"Ooh Jeremy that is exquisite."

He reached his hand up to encompass her breast whilst still retaining her nipple in his mouth. He very gently applied a small amount of pressure with his teeth and once more caressed the nipple with his tongue. She gasped and repeated, "Ooh Jeremy." After what seemed to both to be an unending erotic moment, she got down from his lap saying breathlessly, "I'm getting very hot." She shrugged off her blouse and placed it on the desk next to his wig. She stood over him bare breasted.

"You are astonishingly beautiful," he muttered and reached out both hands to envelope her breasts. He gently rolled each nipple between the finger and thumb. Her nipples were stiffly erect.

"Ooh Jeremy," she breathed, "I do love that. My nipples enjoy the fresh air as well as the attention you are giving them. I think it's time we freed you up a bit isn't it. I know how hard you have been. Let's give you some air shall we?"

So saying she reached down to unzip his flies and unfasten his belt. She then grasped both his trousers and underpants and pulled them down to the floor. "Ooh, my goodness, what have we here?" she said taking his erection in her hands and gently massaging it. Jeremy gave a groan of satisfaction and closed his eyes to enjoy the experience.

Phillipa knelt down between his legs and took his penis in her mouth. Slowly she raised her head up and down the shaft pausing every so often to run her tongue around the tip. All the while Jeremy continued groaning with pleasure. Eventually she ceased and stood up to observe Jeremy who still had his eyes closed. He opened them to see Phillipa standing over him bare breasted with a satisfied smile.

"You are fantastic," he said with a hoarse throaty whisper. He looked at her body and could not believe that he was lucky enough to be in this situation. "Your breasts are magnificent," he said. "They are much bigger than I had imagined they would be."

She smiled again. "So, you have spent time imagining what my breasts would look like?"

Jeremy smiled too and admitted, "All the time. I have thought of little else since I first met you but I never imagined that you would ever consider doing this with me."

"But why on earth not?" she asked "You know that I have always flirted with you. Did you not believe that I wanted you? Did you take me for a prick teaser?"

"I just thought it was an amusing dalliance for you but never thought you would seriously be interested in me. I am so much older than you."

"It's not about age, Jeremy. It's about sex appeal and *je ne sais quoi*. You are a judge with great intellect and good looks. Why would any woman not want you.?"

"Now then," she said in a business-like fashion. It's time to finish this." She turned to the desk and scooped up his wig. "You are a Crown Court judge so I insist that you wear your wig for the job you are doing today." She put the wig on his head and then stood back to observe him. "That's better," she said cocking her head. "To me that is much sexier than a fireman's helmet. Now, I told you that I had no underwear on, didn't I?" She raised her skirt above her hips to show that she had no pants on. "See, no knickers," she said, at the same time releasing her skirt which dropped to the floor, and then climbed up on to his lap again this time straddling him with her legs on each side and facing him. She gently grasped his still erect penis and slowly, slowly, lowered herself on to it. They both let out a groan of satisfaction. She sat very still for a while and then marginally moved her hips to slightly raise her body. This brought another moan from each of them. Next, she leaned as far back as she could go which resulted in a deeper penetration for Jeremy who reacted with a further moan.

Gradually Phillipa increased her movement until she was rocking and rising at a steady pace. "Ooh," she cried out loudly, "Ooh, yes!" Jeremy leaned forward to suck one of her nipples and she cried out again. "Yes,

yes, Jeremy. You're the judge pass a sentence on me."

Jeremy took his lips away from her breast and took the nipple between his finger and thumb instead. As he did so he uttered very loudly and firmly the words,

"I hereby sentence you to a term of life imprisonment in my bed."

"Ooh, yes, Jeremy," she almost screeched and began to increase the speed of her thrusts.

Jeremy responded by thrusting upwards and gently pushing her backwards to increase his penetration. "I hereby sentence you to take part in this activity with me for the rest of your life," he shouted and then reached his own climax, just as Phillipa did the same.

They both sat there, arm in arm breathing heavily and clutching each other tightly.

"Oh, my word," exclaimed Jeremy in disbelief, "I have never experienced anything as wonderful as that. You are the sexiest woman I have ever met.

Phillipa kissed his ear and whispered, "You are the man, Jeremy. I have never had sex like that before. Algie is so dull compared with you. I have never had sex with a judge in his chambers. It was such a turn on."

"I am hugely flattered, Phillipa, but am still trying to understand how I can be so lucky as to attract someone as desirable as you."

"Don't worry about it, Jeremy, just accept that you do and look forward to more liaisons just like today." Jeremy was doing just that and already beginning to feel a further erection coming on. He watched as Phillipa donned her bra and then her suspender belt. She sat on his chair and put on her black stockings. He was surprised to find that watching her dressing was as stimulating as watching her undress. When she had finished putting on her stockings, she stood up to search the desk for her panties.

Jeremy was so aroused at the sight of her wearing just a bra, suspenders and stockings that he grasped her gently from behind and began to kiss and nuzzle her neck. He fondled her breasts meanwhile and hooked his thumbs inside her bra to stroke her nipples which immediately became erect. "Ooh, Jeremy," she exclaimed in mock surprise. "Are you feeling horny again already? You really are a man, aren't you? Algie never asks for more this soon afterwards."

She could feel his erection against her bare bottom and without turning around she reached behind her with one hand to grasp his penis. "I just can't help it," he said, pulling her bra down slightly to release her breasts. He took both nipples in his fingers and thumbs. "You are so alluring, so gorgeous, so enticing that I am unable to resist. I cannot believe how I feel, I have never had this sort of appetite before."

"Well, I'll take that as a huge compliment," she said, still fondling his penis. "Have you never had this appetite for Mrs Fallow?"

"No never," he replied. "Never anything like this."

Phillipa held his hands and moved them down until he was gripping her hips. She then leaned right over the desk in order to present her bare buttocks to him. She then parted her thighs and guided his penis into her vagina from the rear and gave a long sigh of satisfaction as he entered.

Jeremy thrust himself into her two or three times very gently. He found that the rear entry allowed him the advantage of being able to view her bare bottom which further aroused him. His thrusts became more urgent and he realised that this would be no prolonged repetition of the previous episode.

"Ooh, ooh, Jeremy," she moaned, "I can feel that you are close. Sentence me Jeremy. Sentence me!"

Jeremy continued to thrust even more urgently pulling her body towards him roughly on each stroke. "I sentence you to be my sex slave, for the rest of your life," he grunted savagely just as he was ejaculating.

"Ooooooh, yes," she responded, "I accept, I agree, ooh you're so good!" She gave a joyful squeal as she reached a climax just seconds after him. He continued to thrust until his erection subsided. He leant against her and kissed the back of her neck.

"You are exceptional," he whispered, "remarkable, outstanding, superb!"

She giggled and said, "You sound like a Thesaurus, Jeremy, but I have to agree with you that we seem to have something special. It's never been like this for me before."

"Ditto," said Jeremy "Each time I saw you I always fantasised that I could do this with you but, despite your flirting, I never thought it would ever happen. I just never thought you would seriously consider it."

"Well," she said meaningfully, "aren't you glad that I took the initiative and came up to see you without any underwear?"

Jeremy took her in his arms and they both kissed fully on the lips for the first time. It was a long sensuous kiss with tongues involved. To his utter amazement he felt the beginnings of yet another erection. He released her and stepped back. "That is an immense understatement," he said. "This is what I call life changing. I feel as though I am about eighteen years old again."

"Do you mean to say," she asked, with a mischievous glint in her eye, "that when you were eighteen years old, you were having sex with a thirty-five-year-old lady barrister?"

They both chuckled and quickly got dressed. She gave him another wet kiss and said that she had to fly but would definitely be in touch. Jeremy said with a glint in his eye that if she did not get in touch, he would issue a bench warrant and have her held in custody until he could deal with her at his pleasure. "Ooh, Ooh, Jeremy," she said enthusiastically, "that sounds wonderful."

Phillipa then left the chambers and Jeremy found that he still had time to get to the county ground to watch some cricket for the rest of the afternoon. When he got there, he found to his disappointment that his brother was no longer at the crease. He had been bowled out a few minutes before Jeremy arrived. He managed to locate Roger in the members' enclosure and so was able to sit with him to watch the rest of the Gloucestershire innings. His brother admitted that he had been bowled by an in -swinger which he ought really to have dealt with.

After a few minutes Jeremy brought the conversation around to physical fitness and asked his brother for some tips on how to stay fit. Roger was astonished that his brother should express this interest because for all their lives he had never been interested in physical fitness before.

"What's this all about?" he demanded "you've never been interested in physical fitness before, what's brought this on?"

Jeremy admitted that he had met a lady who was younger than himself and he had become conscious as to how his body would look to her. He wanted to firm things up a little.

"Aah, ha," exclaimed Roger. "I might have guessed. How old is this siren?" he asked eagerly.

"Thirty-five," said Jeremy.

Roger whistled, "Wow!" he exclaimed, "You lucky bugger. How did you achieve that?"

Jeremy explained that he didn't really know but that she was extremely attractive and for some unknown reason also found him to be attractive. "I don't really know what she sees in me," he admitted, "I'm forty-seven years old and cannot really understand why she should be interested in me."

"You are missing the obvious," Roger said, "women don't always fancy men on their looks alone so much as their character and position in life. You've been so involved in the academic world that you never realised that men and women are different. Men tend to like young women with big tits and nice bums. Women like men who are powerful and influential. Looks are not so important to them. Anyway, you have always been fortunate not to have put on lots of weight as you have aged. You look OK, so don't worry."

"Well, I'm not so much worrying as wishing to tighten up a bit. Can you give me any tips?"

Roger sighed, "Yeah, OK, but like I said it won't make a lot of difference. Probably none at all. If she is interested in you it's not for your looks. It's the fact that you got a first-class law degree at university, achieved the position of Crown Court judge and have a hefty reputation for being a tough nut if necessary. That's what interests her, take it from me." Jeremy had to admit to himself that his brother was probably right.

"I'll give you a list of a few daily exercises which you can do and which will help you to feel a bit better about yourself, but I don't think you have anything to worry about. You should just take it as a huge compliment and hope that it will last. What about Maud?" he asked, referring to Mrs Fallow.

Jeremy winced and said that his wife obviously knew nothing about it nor did he wish to inform her. He explained to Roger that he and his wife had ceased to have any sexual relations long ago and did not even sleep in the same room any more. "She is after all," he reminded his brother, "nearly five years older than me. As you know, she is a wealthy woman in her own right having been born into a rich family."

"Yeah, I suppose so," said Roger. "So if this affair comes to fruition you can just walk away and reach a settlement without losing too much."

"Yes, well," said Jeremy, "I don't know yet how far it will go. It's only just begun so I would not want to risk everything unless and until I can be sure that something really worthwhile has developed."

"Very wise," said Roger.

"What I was wondering," began Jeremy tentatively, "um, erh, your flat in Clifton is probably empty for half the cricket season due to the fact that you are playing away. Yes?"

"Aaagh," said Roger with a wicked grin. "You want to use it as a pied-a-terre? You randy bugger."

"Well, I was thinking that while you are away it wouldn't trouble you would it?"

"Yeah, sure," said Roger and dug into his pocket and produced a spare key. "Help yourself with my blessing. Any time you want. Just give me a ring beforehand, to make sure that I haven't planned to bed someone at the same time."

Chapter Forty-six
Des on the Case

The International Detective was at the railway station. He had trailed Jimmy Pearce there and had joined the queue at the ticket office behind him. As he waited, he pretended to rifle through his wallet as if looking for money. He overheard Jimmy requesting a return ticket to London and the ticket clerk telling him that the train would arrive in twenty minutes.

Charlie decided not to wait but returned to his office. He gazed longingly at the calendar girl's breasts as he telephoned Des Onions at the CID.

"O'Nighons," said Des.

"It's me, Charlie" he said. "I've just trailed Jimmy Pearce to the station. He's bought a ticket to London which is leaving any minute. So I presume that another deal is on. Perhaps you could let the Special Branch know and they can keep watch and observe the handover."

"OK," said Des, "I'll get on to my contact and have them watch out for Jimmy. They were expecting a transaction about now. It means I think that the swoop on the Nite Club will have to be postponed for one more week. Logistically it is difficult to organise it for this week so next week would be better because it should coincide with the Jimmy Pearce matter.

Charlie said that was OK and he would wait to hear further from him with details. He replaced the phone and dialled the office number in order to speak to Pete who answered the telephone himself and listened while Charlie told him about Jimmy Pearce and the fact that the Nite Club swoop had been postponed for a week. He also told him that he had served the divorce petition on Eddie Sharp. "Perhaps we could meet this evening in the usual place?" he said.

"Fine," said Pete and then hung up the phone. He then told George and Vincent about the change of plan for the Nite Club.

Mavis cocked an ear to what Pete was saying and told everyone that she was taking another afternoon off to travel to Bristol with Freda this time for a conference with Phillipa Fry on divorce matters.

Helen was almost as excited about this as Mavis herself. "Oh, I bet you are looking forward to that," she said brightly.

"I certainly am," confirmed Mavis, "If it goes as well as the meeting with Doris did it will be so interesting." She lowered her voice to talk specifically to Pete, "That information you let me have on Freda's husband. Was there anything else I can give to Phillipa Fry?"

"Sure," said Pete, "there were a few small items and I did check the details of the lady in the bookmakers that he is playing away with." He rose from his seat and indicated, with a tilt of his head and eyebrows that she should follow him. Mavis waited a second or two and then made her way to the basement area.

Pete was waiting for her. He produced a copy of wage details for the bookmakers in question. "There's only one female on the books," he said, "Polly Smith. Here it is," he said, "and this is her address. I also have another couple of items here from a contact in the Passport Office or Border Control Force or whatever they are called which appears to indicate that there might be a discrepancy in his visa, though the fact that he is married to a UK citizen probably overrides that."

"Oh, thanks a bundle," said Mavis, with genuine gratitude. "Nothing else?"

Pete smiled, "You mean that's not enough? Well," he said thoughtfully,

"Yes?" said Mavis eagerly.

"Well, there is of course, the supply of class A drugs which is going on. Although nothing is proved yet and can't or won't be until Friday week at least. What the hell why not include that? It will be in all the papers next week anyway."

"Yes, of course," said Mavis with a bright smile. "You are brilliant Pete." She gave him a big kiss on the cheek and left the basement area to make up some more notes on Giovanni Pettacinni for Phillipa Fry.

Early that evening Pete walked into the Jubilee Inn to find Charlie Chivers located at the bar staring fondly at the photograph of Reg Partridge posing with Jayne Mansfield. Pete ordered a pint for himself and another for the International Detective and they both took a seat at a table. Charlie told him that Des had phoned him back to firm up the arrangement for the swoop on the Nite Club.

"Apparently, the Special Branch are trailing Jimmy Pearce in London even as we speak so Des expects there to be another handover of drugs to Jimmy today. They will observe and video him onto the homeward train and tip off Des for his return."

Pete nodded, "So you served the divorce papers on Eddie Sharp?"

"Yep," confirmed Charlie taking a large sip of beer as he spoke. "Like taking candy from a baby."

"Well, I can tell you that another divorce petition is on the way so I would expect you to get another little job soon." Charlie raised his eyebrows. "Giovanni Pettacinno," said Pete and gave Charlie the gist of the conversation he had earlier had with Mavis.

"She's definitely going ahead with it," he said triumphantly, "which will be really good news for my colleague Ken Carter."

Charlie took another long swig from his glass and said, "Yeah, I've been thinking about that. If Giovanni is divorced by his sister and convicted of the drugs matter Mr Carter should be in clover. Now I've put in a large number of hours on this case and I was wondering if I could invoice Mr Carter for some of them especially if his former brother-in-law is deported as a result of all this."

"No problem," said Pete, "I have already spoken to Mr Carter about all that and I can assure you that when this is all satisfactorily finished you and I will be in clover financially." The International Detective took another large swig and smiled.

Simon Nibble smiled as he completed another invoice to assimilate some more of the funds available in his firm's client account. It was his habit to submit bills whenever the client account was filled, particularly with funds introduced by Eddie. Most of the invoices he created were very general in their description. The one he had just completed was in terms of 'For further work in respect of advice and assistance on the matter of X'. Very few of his invoices were, specific enough, he felt to be married up with any work done. Many were almost entirely fictitious.

There was a knock at his door, and Alice came in looking hopeful. "Oh hello, Allison," he said eyebrows raised in enquiry, "what can I do for you?"

"I've got the date for you when my boyfriend and I would like to go to your apartment in Tenerife," she said. She gave him a slip of paper on which she had written the details of dates and the full names of herself and that of her boyfriend. Simon looked at it and smiled.

"Yes, of course," he said, "I will have to check these dates with my wife before I can book the flights for you. She usually does all the arrangements for the apartment you see. I'll check with her first and then I'll let you know. OK?"

Alice said that it was OK and wondered when he would be able to confirm the date. "Well as soon as possible, Allison. My wife is very busy at the moment but I'm sure it won't be very long. As soon as possible."

"It's just that my boyfriend has to book the time off with his employer and he needs to give them reasonable notice" she said.

Simon smiled. "Yes of course, as soon as possible, Allison. I will let you know."

Mavis and Freda took the train to Bristol on a damp Thursday afternoon. As the train chugged along, they chatted, initially talking about the exercise classes which they mutually attended and their friendship with Doris. The conversation graduated to the subject of divorce generally and thereafter to specific items involved in Freda's potential petition.

She explained again, this time in more depth, how she had first met Giovanni and how he had swept her off her feet with his dark handsome Latin looks and ways. She also told Mavis about her own father's instinctive dislike for the man she had chosen and how long it had taken her to eventually acknowledge that her father was right and that Giovanni was no good. Mavis encouragingly told her how wonderful Phillipa Fry was and how marvellous she had been for Doris. She assured Freda that Phillipa would be just as good for her.

They arrived at Clifton Chambers with ten minutes to spare and took a seat in the waiting room. On the dot they were ushered into the room of Phillipa Fry. She was just how Mavis remembered her. Her hair and make-up were just as immaculate as the first time Mavis had seen her. She sat behind a large desk on which were some papers she appeared to be scanning.

"How do you do?" she said in the same cut-glass tones. "My name is Phillipa Fry and I hope that I will be able to help you with your divorce." She indicated two seats and they both sat down.

"Now, I've just been studying the brief which your solicitor has sent me. I believe you are Mavis aren't you?" she said. Mavis blushed and confirmed that was correct. She was impressed that Phillipa had remembered her name. She was also impressed with the unique and spotless appearance of her facial cosmetics, especially her eye make-up which Mavis thought was perfect.

Phillipa asked Freda a number of questions and made notes. Having satisfied herself on most of the points she enquired if there was any other information available regarding Freda's husband's finances and any activities of which she had already been advised.

Mavis produced her bundle of papers which included the information which Pete had given her the day before plus the notes she had compiled on the matter of the supply of class A drugs. Phillipa studied these papers very closely and at great length. She looked up eventually and said, "Your friend has given me such comprehensive information that I am certain that I can prepare a divorce petition on your behalf which will ensure that all the transfers of your shares in the family business can be reversed by the court and all the shares re-registered into your sole name. As for your husband's status as a foreign visitor, there does seem to be a few inconsistencies with his existing visa which might at present be balanced by the fact that he is married to you a UK citizen. Once you are divorced his status would be very fragile and he would almost certainly be deported back to Malta. In that event you would no longer be troubled by him. How does that make you feel?"

Freda confirmed that she would be pleased if Phillipa would proceed as she had described. Mavis had to contain herself not to break out in a round of applause.

As they rose to leave the Chambers Phillipa promised that she would prepare the petition and the accompanying papers which would be delivered to her solicitor very soon. She advised Freda to move in with her brother for a short while until the dust settled.

Tom Richards had opened the office and was in the process of opening the filing cupboards when George arrived unexpectedly early. "Couldn't sleep, eh?" said Tom, still emptying the final cupboard. "Would you like to put the kettle on while I finish this." George did as he was told and soon returned to the desk with two strong cups of tea. Tom was just unfolding his Daily Mail. They both sipped their cups together.

"Aah," said Tom with great satisfaction, "nothing like the first cup of the day. I wonder what today will bring for us all."

"Yes, indeed," said George, Then contemplatively he said, "There have been a few changes lately. Poor old Bill and poor Lionel. Will Vincent be in today? If so will he manage to get here before Piggy arrives? Will Mavis do a full day or will she go for another meeting?"

"Hmm," responded Tom. "Both Bill and Lionel were very unfortunate but at least Bill is still alive. Vincent is a different matter. If he stays involved with those dodgy drugs he may end up in the same place as Lionel. I saw enough of that with the coolies out in the Far East. Once they got started on the opium they were doomed. They couldn't or wouldn't work, couldn't eat and would just lay there in a stupor."

"How long were you out there?" asked George.

"Oh, best part of twenty years," said Tom. "And as for Mavis, she has changed a lot in recent weeks. She seems to have found more purpose in her life and it suits her. She is very happy helping her friends with their divorce problems and she also appears much happier since she has been going out with you."

"I am very fond of her," said George. As if on cue Mavis herself then arrived closely followed by Helen. As soon as they sat down Mavis began telling Helen about her visit to Clifton Chambers with Freda.

"She was just the same as before," she told her, referring of course to Phillipa Fry. "She was brilliant and her make-up, like before, was perfect. Everything about her is immaculate. She said the information that I had provided was perfect too."

"Did she really?" said Helen. "That was quite a compliment."

"Yes," said Mavis, "she said the information was comprehensive and was of tremendous assistance to her. She also said the information I supplied for Doris was also of the same high standard."

Pete, who had arrived half way through their conversation and who caught the tail end of Mavis' remarks, said, "I'll take that as a compliment then shall I?"

Mavis blushed and admitted to Helen that most of the information had been provided by Pete who smiled triumphantly. He then added with some gallantry, "But I'm sure that the way in which you presented all the facts to her made her job easy. You would be suited to a job like that, you have all the attributes."

Mavis was somewhat overcome by this unexpected compliment and thanked Pete for his generosity.

Vincent arrived just in time to be on the premises before Mr Pigg who entered with a crash and a bang as usual. He went straight to his room without speaking to anyone. Everyone in the office wondered if he were in a bad humour or whether he was concentrating on some aspect of work. Mavis said she hoped that he had not gone back to his former habit of preparing illustrated graphs.

They were all surprised when the door opened as no one else was expected to arrive. They were all even more surprised to see that the person who had entered the office was none other than Bill Butler who looked considerably changed from the last time that George and Mavis had seen him.

Everyone expressed their delight to see him and all congratulated him on his changed appearance. Indeed, Bill had a healthy glow about him and a glint in his eye which gave apparent evidence of full recovery. He explained that he had chosen to call in to see everyone just to assure them of his recovery and also to have a word with Mr Pigg regarding his intended immediate return to work. He then excused himself and went in to see and talk to Mr Pigg.

The general atmosphere of the office was one of great elation in view of the obvious improvement in Bill's health. They were all also looking forward to his return to work. Bill was ensconced with Mr Pigg for a long time during which time the staff talked among themselves mostly on the subject of Bill's impending return. The general verdict was unanimous. The return of Bill would greatly improve the atmosphere of the office.

Eventually Mr Pigg emerged from his office together with Bill who paused to talk to each of them in turn. Mr Pigg made his way to the front of the office and tapped the desk with his pen. "Can I have your attention please," he bellowed. Everyone looked up to see what he would say.

"I just wanted you to know that Bill has confirmed that he is well enough to return to work and therefore will resume his post next Monday. I am sure that all of you will be pleased to hear this. Welcome back Bill." Everyone concurred and all said their congratulations to Bill who thanked everyone.

While this was going on Mavis cornered George to have a private word. She told him that her parents were going away for the weekend the following week. She wondered if he would like to come over and stay with her for the weekend at her house. George told her that nothing would give him more pleasure.

The International Detective lit a Manikin cigar and drew deeply on it. He was reading his paper and gazing at the picture of a topless model therein. He glanced across at the calendar girl on the wall to compare the two. Although the proportions were similar, in Charlie's expert opinion both generous D cups, the girl in the newspaper picture, again in Charlie's opinion, could not hold a candle to the calendar girl.

In his experience young ladies who bared their breasts fell into either of two categories. Firstly, there were the ones that were proud to display what was on show and the alternative were the ones that looked as if they had never meant to display anything and had been ambushed by the photographer, the calendar girl was definitely one of the latter category but in addition she gave the appearance of being only twelve or thirteen years old even though the size of her breasts told a viewer that that was definitely not the case. The model in the newspaper had a look of wanton pride about her whilst the calendar girl still exuded innocence which appealed to the International Detective.

His telephone rang. He picked up the receiver,"Chivers Detective Agency."

It was Duffey Fry & Co solicitors to inform him that they had another divorce petition for personal service on one Giovanni Pettacinni. Charlie said he would be round in about ten to fifteen minutes to collect the papers. He reflected to himself ironically that if he failed to serve this document properly then he could no longer rightfully call himself 'International'.

He pondered on the tactics of serving Freda's husband with the papers. He knew of course that he was sometimes at the Nite Club but he could see difficulties with gaining access to the interior of the club. He did not fancy hanging around outside until the early hours.

The address was of course on the instructions and the petition itself, and although he had never been there, he was confident that he could always serve at the home address. His final alternative was to try to locate him at the bookmakers where Pete had told him Giovanni was often seen due to his preference for the lady who worked there. This was the alternative which Charlie plumped for so having called at the offices of Duffey Fry & Co he made his way to the bookmaker's shop and entered.

He was quite surprised at how many people there were inside the shop. They were all men, mostly seated on stools staring avidly at a horse race on the television. There were several screens positioned on two of the walls. The men all sat around tables in the centre of the premises studying the form of horses either from the TV screens or from newspapers.

At the far end of the shop was a counter behind which two people administered to the customers. One was a young man in his mid-twenties who was taking bets and issuing slips to the punters. The other was a lady of about thirty-five years of age with dark brown shoulder length hair and a generous sized bosom which was enhanced by the fact that it was only partially covered by a white T-shirt with a plunging neckline. She was seated behind the counter talking earnestly with a swarthy looking man who grasped one of her hands with both of his. He held her hand close to his face and occasionally kissed it.

Charlie seated himself at a table close by and observed them for a while. He had never encountered the man before nor had he seen a photograph of him. Nevertheless, he was fairly sure that this was the respondent named in the petition he had collected. When the young lady referred to him as Joe he was certain. He sorted out the papers for service from a shopping bag which he was carrying. He covered these with a newspaper which was folded to show the racing page.

He sidled up to the counter and stood beside his target with his eyes fixed upon the cleavage of the lady across the counter. Eventually they stopped talking and turned to look at him enquiringly. In response Charlie pointed at one of the horses listed on the page. "What are the chances of this horse winning today, Giovanni?"

The target glanced at the name of the horse and frowned. "No chance at all," he said. "Ow you know my name?"

Charlie removed the newspaper from the top of the pile leaving the divorce papers in full view on the counter.

"It's all in here," he said tapping the petition. "All the information anyone could need. And that goes for both of you. You have been officially served, Joe and you Polly. Have a nice day."

With that the International Detective turned on his heel and strolled out into the street and back to his office to type up the affidavit of service. He then went downstairs to the offices of Huw Roberts& Co solicitors to swear the affidavit and eventually back to Duffey Fry & Co to hand back the evidence of service together with his own invoice.

As he made his way back to his own office Charlie whistled a tune "*Love is in the air*," Once he was back in his office he telephoned Pete to give him the news that he had just served Giovanni with the divorce papers. "You'd better let your friend Ken Carter know as soon as possible" he said.

"When and where did you serve him?" asked Pete.

"In the bookmakers about an hour ago," said Charlie. "He was all over some bird with big tits who I presume was this Polly something or other."

"That's really good news," said Pete. "He has always hated Freda's husband. He'll be glad to be rid of him now. The only thing that ever worried him was that Freda would remain obsessed with him. Now that she has seen the light and decided to cut the cord he will be overjoyed. I had arranged to see him this evening in the Plume of Feathers. Would you like to come along? I'll introduce you and you can tell him yourself. "Charlie said he would like that and arranged a time to meet Pete.

His final job that day was to telephone Des Onions to let him know the news. Luckily Des was in the office. Charlie told him that the papers had been served upon Giovanni."

"Well," responded Des, "It couldn't happen to a nicer bloke. That should give him something to distract his mind from the drug dealing going on in his Nite Club."

"What's the position with Jimmy Pearce?" enquired Charlie.

"A deal definitely took place," said Des. "And Jimmy is on his way back. The Special Branch have videoed everything and are poised to arrest his suppliers. It seems to me that everything is now ready for us to arrest Jimmy and the others. As I said before, next Friday certainly seems the right day. All our officers are lined up for it. We will keep a close watch on Jimmy between now and then. I don't suppose he will be going anywhere except round to see the Gibson twins."

Chapter Forty-seven
George and Mavis

On Saturday morning George made his way to Mavis's house. It was a neat semi-detached house with a small front garden and a driveway at the side leading to a single garage. It had a long rear garden the first half of which had a neatly trimmed lawn beyond which there was a large vegetable patch.

He rang the front door bell which was opened by Mavis herself. She ushered him into the front room which contained a three-piece suite positioned around an open brick-built fireplace. In the corner of the room, close to the front bay window, was a large TV set. On the other side of the fireplace was a large floor to ceiling bookcase which was crammed full of books.

Mavis asked him if he would care for a cup of coffee and although he did not really want one, he heard himself accepting the offer and wondering why. She scurried off to make one while he took off the knapsack he had been carrying, and placed it on the floor. He opened it and removed from it a bottle of wine which he had bought in the wine merchants on the way to the house. It was a bottle of Chianti. George was not too experienced at choosing wine and had decided to purchase what they had drunk at La Scala the previous week. He had remembered that both he and Mavis had enjoyed it.

He could not quite understand why he was feeling so nervous. He had known Mavis long enough now to know that he really liked her and he was completely confident that she liked him. Nevertheless, he still felt like an inexperienced schoolboy out on his first date. He had not expected to feel so lacking in confidence.

Mavis came back into the room with his cup of coffee. "Do you take sugar?" she asked putting his cup down on the coffee table.

"No thanks," he said, realising then that although they had worked together for quite a few months neither of them knew if the other took sugar. He picked up the bottle of Chianti to show her and said, "I bought this on the way over because I thought we might like to drink it later. Well actually of course you may prefer to go out for a drink instead and of course if that's what you'd like then it's fine with me."

Mavis took the bottle and read the label and said, "Hmm, that looks lovely. How sweet of you." She leaned over and gave him a big kiss on the lips. "I thought I would cook us something to eat this evening so this will go very well with it. I made an apple pie already," she continued, "together with a smaller one which I made for a lady down the road. I've just got to walk down the road with it now. Would you like to come with me?" she asked

George said he would and waited while she gathered together some papers and the dish which contained the apple pie. They then left the house together and George insisted on carrying the apple pie. Mavis was wearing blue jeans and a white blouse. George yet again thought how pretty she looked. He felt so proud to be walking down the street with her. They only passed three properties and Mavis turned into the next. It was a tired looking semi-detached house in the same style as that in which Mavis lived. The only difference was that in Mavis's house the garden was well cared for. In this house the garden looked like an uncared-for jungle. The net curtains at the windows were grubby and tattered. The paint on the windows was peeling.

Mavis picked up a flower pot near the door and retrieved a door key from underneath. She unlocked the door and they both walked in. "Hello Ethel, it's only me," she called out loudly and walked into the living room followed by George. "This is my friend, George," she said. "I've made you an apple pie which I'll put on the kitchen table for later."

George smiled at Ethel who was a thin elderly lady seated in an armchair with one leg resting on a foot stool. "She's so good to me," she said in a frail voice. Mavis came back into the room and spread out the papers she had brought. "I've had a word with the office and they confirm that you are entitled to the benefit. I have completed the application form for you. It just requires your signature here." She indicated where to sign and gave Ethel a pen and she signed the form. Mavis folded it up and said, "I will drop it off at the office on Monday. You should get quite a bit more money from now on. Is there anything else you need today?"

"No, thank you," she said

"Would you like me to make you a cup of tea while I'm here? It's no trouble."

"No thanks," she said. She looked at George and said, "She is such a lovely girl, I don't know what I'd do without her."

"Well, we'll pop on then. I'll see you later. Don't forget the apple pie which is on the kitchen table. You will need to warm it up."

"Thank you so much," said Ethel who waved them goodbye. As they walked back to her house Mavis explained that Ethel had lived alone for a number of years since her husband had died. "She nursed him for a couple of years before the cancer finally took him," she said.

"Doesn't she have any children?" asked George.

"Yes, she has a daughter but she lives a long way away and she has children of her own to look after. She calls down whenever she can but it is difficult for her."

George reflected on what Tom Richards had said in the office once, that there was more depth to Mavis than was immediately apparent. "You are a really nice person aren't you?" he said.

Mavis smiled deprecatingly and said it was nothing and anyone would do what she did. "But they don't do they?" responded George. "You are making apple pies, filling out welfare forms, and accompanying ladies to their solicitors and their barristers for their divorces. You are a marvel and you should admit it."

When they arrived back at her home Mavis gave George a quick tour of the property including the view of the back garden from her bedroom. The tour ended in the front lounge which was the room that George had first entered.

He occupied himself briefly glancing at the many volumes on the bookcase. He was impressed by the range of literature contained on the shelves. "Who do all these books belong to?" he asked.

"My dad," said Mavis "he's always read a lot. He's read all those several times. While you are looking at those, I'll start the cooking." She went into the kitchen and began chopping carrots and onions and garlic. She put them into a large saucepan with some olive oil and later added some mincemeat. She also added some chopped fresh herbs and a tin of tomatoes. She brought them to the boil and then turned down the gas to the minimum and then left it to simmer. She came back into the lounge to talk to George who was still studying the books

"Have you read any or all of these books?" he asked.

"Most of them," she admitted, "though some of them I couldn't finish. My dad always encouraged me to read a lot, and in some ways, I am glad that he did but I have never been the avid reader that he is."

"What does your father do?" he asked.

"He's a school teacher," she said, "but actually I would say he's a frustrated author or politician."

"Well, he's certainly an all-rounder," said George respectfully, "I've not even heard of some of these. If you have read most of these then you are a better-read person than I am. I'm not trying to be rude, but when I first met you, I would not have judged you to have read any books let alone this many."

"Well, thanks very much," said Mavis with mock severity, "so you mean I looked a bit of an ignoramus?"

"No, no," protested George and then, diplomatically, "I suppose I was concentrating on your physical assets and had completely overlooked your intellectual ones."

"Oh, nicely done," said Mavis, "you got out of that one very well." She held his face affectionately and gave him a big kiss as a reward for his mental adroitness.

"Right," she said determinedly, "let's go out for some fresh air. I forgot to get any milk when I shopped earlier. If we go to the shop, we can get some air as well.

That said they both left the house together and walked hand in hand to a nearby park which was set upon a hill. They stood for a moment to take in the view from near the top of the hill. They then left the park by an exit gate near the top of the hill and walked along a street to a corner shop from which Mavis purchased some milk. They then retraced their steps back to the park.

As they descended the hill Mavis asked him, "What do your mum and dad do then?"

"They are both dead," said George.

"Oh no," said Mavis in genuine dismay, "what happened?"

"They were both killed in a car accident a long time ago, when I was about eight years old," he said.

"Oh no," repeated Mavis, "you poor thing. Were you with them at the time?"

"No, I was at school that day"

"So you are an orphan then?" said Mavis mournfully. She felt almost vindicated in her original instinct about George, that of the little boy lost. He told her that his parents' car had been struck by a lorry and they had been killed instantly. Thereafter he had been raised by his grandmother with whom he still lived. His grandfather who had helped to bring him up had also died just over a year ago. He also explained that when his parents had died, he, as an only child, had inherited everything. His grandparents had sold his parents' house and invested the money for him but now that his grandfather was dead, he did not feel that he could leave his grandmother on her own.

Mavis had more compassion than she could conceal. She had to pause for a moment to wipe her eyes with a tissue. "You poor boy, what a sad story. What a miserable life you have had."

"Not at all" he answered. "I was too young really to appreciate the momentous seriousness of the event. I have always received great love and affection from my grandparents and I have not had an unhappy life with them."

Mavis gave him a big hug and said, "Let's go home and have something to eat."

They made their way home and Mavis immediately put a large saucepan full of water on the stove in order to cook the spaghetti. She also turned on the heat under the meat sauce. Next, she laid the table in the dining room and then searched the kitchen drawer for the corkscrew which she took to George saying, "Here you are, Man of the House," she said, "open the wine bottle please."

George did as he was told and placed the opened wine bottle on the dining table. Mavis said, "Keep an eye on the meat, don't let it boil over, I'll only be a minute." She hurried upstairs. A few minutes later she came back down having applied some make-up and perfume and donned an attractive flowery dress. George was overcome by the transformation. Even though she had looked pretty before she went upstairs, she now, to him, looked dazzlingly, amazingly, beautiful.

"You look really attractive." he said.

"Thank you very much," she said. George grabbed her impulsively and gave her a kiss. "You are very beautiful," he whispered in her ear.

They settled down to eat their meal both sipping the Chianti with it. As they ate, they chatted. She asked George, "So how many girlfriends have you had George?"

He thought for a moment and shrugged, "Well none, really," he said.

"None!" she repeated, no girlfriends at all?"

"Not really," he replied, "I mean I've been out with girls but never had a proper girlfriend. Never been out with the same girl more than once."

"But why not?" she asked, "didn't you like any of them enough to ask them out again?"

"No, not many of them. Also, I've always been very shy and found it difficult to speak to girls just like that. I needed to work up courage and by the time I'd done that the moment was lost."

Mavis looked shocked. She could not believe that George was so inexperienced with women. Given her own vast experience of sexual encounters with men she could not believe that she was dining with someone who had none. "So are you are a virgin, George?" she asked. She thought to herself that she certainly wasn't too shy to discuss such matters.

George gave a wry smile. "Well I suppose you could say that, yes. I have had a few unsuccessful attempts but nothing meaningful."

"Well," she said with great emphasis, "We will have to do something about that won't we?" She smiled coquettishly.

George blushed furiously not because he was embarrassed per se but because his inexperience had been exposed. "Don't tell Helen, or anyone else will you?" he begged. Mavis felt once more that urge again. That feeling when his little boy lost character came to the fore. She wondered if she liked him as much as she thought she did or was it simply that she liked mothering fledglings and orphans.

When they had finished the meal, she suggested that they adjourn to the lounge. George brought the half-empty wine bottle together with their glasses. Mavis drew the curtains and switched on the record player which began playing soft music.

"Would you like to dance?" she asked sensually moving with the music. He stood up and held his arms out in readiness for a formal ballroom hold. She ignored them and pressed her body right up against him with her arms around his neck. They moved slowly and rhythmically together cheek to cheek. He kissed her cheek and then kissed her on the mouth. The music stopped temporarily and they came up for air.

George sat down on the sofa while she dealt with the record player. When the music resumed, she turned to face him. She began to sway to the music again. She walked towards him then stood over him smiling. Slowly she began to unbutton her dress down the front. She slipped the dress off her shoulders and let it fall to the floor. She stood in front of him in her bra and pants still swaying to the music George was nursing an enormous erection and found the sight of Mavis in just bra and pants to be overwhelmingly erotic.

"You are so beautiful," he whispered hoarsely. She smiled and reached behind her and unfastened her bra straps. The bra tumbled to the floor. George gasped at the sight of her generous breasts. She knelt down beside him and slowly unbuttoned his shirt and took it off. She then undid his trousers and pulled them down and off him. She took his penis in her hand and massaged it up and down for a while. She then eased her pants off and straddled him. She hovered above him briefly stroking her vagina with his shaft before easing herself onto him. They both sighed with pleasure at the feeling. Mavis slowly began to rise and fall while continuing to look into his eyes. Gradually she increased the rhythm until they were both gasping in unison.

"How's this for your first proper experience?" she whispered.

"Fantastic!" cried George. She increased the pace of her thrusts and George climaxed almost immediately gasping almost in disbelief.

Mavis felt him climax and stayed on him until his erection subsided. She smiled and leaned forward to kiss him. She said softly, "That was lovely George. Just perfect."

They lay together for a while and then took themselves upstairs to her bedroom and fell asleep.

When the early morning light filtered into the bedroom (the curtains had not been drawn the previous evening) George stirred first and took a moment to realise where he was. He turned to see Mavis asleep beside him. He put one arm around her and lay there marvelling at how wonderful it felt. He breathed in her body scent and kissed her gently on the shoulder.

He reflected on the evening before and felt so ecstatically happy. It was not just the sex alone, which was superlative, but also the togetherness and accord which he now felt lying next to her.

She stirred marginally and lay on her back without opening her eyes. She was in that in-between state before becoming truly awake. He turned on his side to view her. He reached up his hand to caress her breast. As he did this the nipple became erect, as he did himself. He continued to caress and she gradually eased more into the world of wakefulness but still without being wholly awake.

"Hmmm," she sighed as his fingers continued to caress her. She moved her own hand across onto his thigh and grasped his member and began to gently massage him. George leaned over and took her nipple in his mouth and gently moved his tongue around. "Hmmm," sighed Mavis again

He moved his hand down onto her tummy stroking all the while, and then down between her thighs. He gently massaged her with his fingers. Despite his admitted inexperience of having sex with women George found that everything came naturally. Each time he did something which was special Mavis would give a sigh of satisfaction and he would repeat it. She closed her eyes with her head back on the pillow and was temporarily in another world. He increased the tempo of his strokes and she responded more vocally. As her excitement grew, he increased the tempo further until, or so he thought, there was an explosion inside Mavis which arrived at the same time as her tumultuous cry. George was so gratified to realise that he had just given her an orgasm.

They lay there for a second. "Oooh," she cried, "that was so wonderful! All I can say George, is that for a beginner, you are a quick learner. Very few men have ever made me feel like that."

George smiled down at her and kissed her on the lips. He moved his right leg across her until he was between her thighs. His still erect penis slid gently into her. She gave another long sigh of satisfaction and when he began to move, she gripped him lightly whispering, "Just hold it there a moment, my darling. This moment is too good to lose." George did as he was told but after a while felt that he was in danger of ejaculating even without movement. He chanced a very gentle withdrawal followed by an equally gentle thrust.

"Oooh," sighed Mavis, "that's perfect." George repeated what he had done and each time, in response to a sigh of approval from her, increased the power and the speed of his thrusts.

Eventually he got to such a state of ecstasy that he was thrusting faster and deeper. Suddenly he climaxed and cried out with joy. He lay forward with his head on her breasts and breathed heavily.

"Oh God," he said. "That was really something."

Mavis smiled at him and kissed him. "You were good my darling," she said then slipped out of bed and went into the bathroom. While she was gone George lay back with his head on the pillow still breathing heavily and reflecting on how wonderful his first proper experience of sexual intercourse had been.

Mavis came back into the bedroom and took a pair of pants and a bra out of a drawer and put them on. George watched her. "You are so beautiful you know," he said. Then as an afterthought he said, "You do know how beautiful you are?"

She smiled at him. "Thank you," she said. "As long as you continue to think that, then everything is good."

"But why wouldn't any man think that?" he questioned "You look like a page three model girl or a film star. Anyone other than a blind man would find you attractive."

She smiled again and said, "All men say complimentary things to a woman after satisfactory sex."

George felt almost as though he had been slapped across the face. "No, no," he responded, "do you think I didn't mean it. I think I love you that's why I said it."

"Oh, that's so sweet" she said but then she added with a mischievous humour. "You only think you love me?" George was aware again of his own lack of experience and Mavis' greater knowledge on all matters both physical and cerebral.

"Compared to you I am still a child," he said without any malice, "my inexperience shines through doesn't it?"

Mavis moved over to him and grasped his head in her hands and said, "We have just started a journey of 'you and me' and I have no more experience of that journey than you. Any previous relationships are irrelevant. You are as good as me." She kissed him fervently.

George thought about this for a moment and then said, "You are so wise. You are incredible. You make me feel naïve. When I first met you, I so underestimated you. Not that I didn't realise you were a terrific looker, but I now see that you are so much more than that. How can I not love you?" Mavis kissed him again and felt very happy.

They spent the rest of the day just hanging around the house. They felt like an average married couple might feel and were blissfully happy just being together. George eventually said that he would have to go home in the evening to sleep otherwise his grandmother would worry. "I'll see you in the office on Monday morning" he said as he finally said goodbye and left the house.

Pete had picked up Charlie Chivers in his car and gave him a lift to the Plume of Feathers in order to meet up with Ken Carter. When they arrived, Mr Carter was not yet there so Pete and Charlie decided to have an early evening snack from the pub menu. They each had a pint as well. Pete had ordered a burger and chips and Charlie had opted for fish and chips. Just as they were starting their meal Ken Carter arrived. Pete made the introductions and Mr Carter shook hands with the International Detective.

As they finished their meal Charlie described to Ken Carter the service of the divorce petition upon Giovanni Pettacinni. He also told him about the similar service upon Eddie Sharp. Mr Carter had already heard about both events which to him were of equal importance. He was thrilled that his sister had finally decided to exorcise the ghost of her husband who was a man that he had never liked. He knew also that his father had vehemently disliked him. He had always hoped to fulfil his father's dream in achieving the expulsion of the man from the lives of his sister and her father. He was equally thrilled to hear that trouble had been heaped upon Eddie Sharp in the form of a divorce petition which would undoubtedly result in a reduction of his wealth at the very least.

Charlie was able to advise Mr Carter that not only had he served the divorce papers on both men but also had unearthed the drug deals that were going on and which were linked directly to both Eddie and Giovanni. He emphasised his own connection to the local CID who were poised to arrest both men and their cohorts. If the operation went smoothly, he assured him, they would both be guests of Her Majesty for a reasonable period.

Charlie then produced for Mr Carter a photocopy of each of the divorce petitions so that he could see for himself the full array of the forces assembled against Eddie and Joe. As he read both documents, he acknowledged how impressive they were and how totally damning of the two gentlemen.

The International Detective gave credit to Pete for discovering many items contained in the petitions and also to his colleague (Mavis) who had assisted both ladies considerably in the presentation of their cases.

"In the case of your sister, Mr Carter," said Charlie, "she (Mavis) assures us that all transactions and documents drawn up by Eddie and Joe and the former's solicitor are false and fraudulent and will be reversed by the court."

Mr Carter was elated and insisted on buying Charlie another drink. Pete refused another because he was driving but was happy to sit and watch Mr Carter assure the International Detective that all his efforts would not be forgotten and that in due course, he would be financially rewarded.

Chapter Forty-eight
Bill Returns

Monday morning in the office it was business as usual except that when Tom Richards arrived to open everything up he found Bill Butler was already there. For the first time in many weeks, they sat together in Bill's glasshouse and drank their tea. They chatted generally about a number of topics including the chances of Arsenal winning the League title this year.

Tom then moved on to the developments in the office, telling him about Vincent's problems and the involvement of Pete and Mavis. Bill said he was not in the least surprised to hear of Pete's part in recent occurences but was slightly surprised to hear about Mavis being involved. Tom told him the same thing as he had told George earlier, that is that there was more depth to Mavis than a first glance would indicate. Bill agreed wholeheartedly saying that he had always known the potential that was there. He said his only surprise was that it had come to fruition a little sooner than he had expected. "You know she's actually very intelligent," he said to Tom and listed her academic qualifications which had been displayed on her job application. "Not that one would ever think so looking at her. One would think that she was more suited to work in a nail bar or even a strip joint than an office. But underneath it all she is a lovely girl."

"Well," said Tom thoughtfully, "I think you might find that she has turned a corner since you left." He then told him about her involvement with the two ladies with whom she shared exercise classes and her accompanying them each to solicitors' and barristers' offices. He also described to him how she had tracked down Vincent. "She also seems to have coupled up with young George in a serious way which has caused her to alter her appearance and attitude generally."

Bill raised his eyebrows slightly and said, "Oh yes, they came to visit me at home. He's a really nice young man and I should have put two and two together then. She looked as if she had roses in her cheeks."

With that the man in question entered the office and came to say good morning to them both. "Morning, George," said Bill, "we were just talking about you. Nothing bad I hasten to add. I hear that you and Mavis are going out together?"

George nodded and smiled and then panicked slightly inside wondering if Bill could somehow have discovered about his Saturday night with Mavis but then realised that could not be the case.

"Well," continued Bill with mock severity, "you've got yourself a little princess there so you make sure that you treat her right or else you'll have me and Tom after you. That's right isn't it?" he said to Tom who affirmed that it was.

As if on cue both Mavis and Helen arrived together and settled down at their table. Bill and Tom spoke for a little longer on the subject of the unfortunate Lionel before eventually getting down to work.

Helen asked Mavis what sort of weekend she had had and Mavis responded that it had been OK. Her voice gave an upward lilt to the end of her sentence which implied that her weekend had been more than just OK.

Helen held one hand up to her own face behind which she pointed at George and mouthed the words, "Did you see?"

Mavis nodded with a smile and Helen then, in a stage whisper, asked "Where did you go?"

Mavis quietly whispered, "Nowhere, we just stayed in."

"Oh, I see." Helen's whisper was less quiet now. "And what did your mum and dad make of him?"

Mavis blushed and placed one finger on her lips. "They were away for the weekend."

Helen gave a silent, "Ooh!" and placed both her hands on her cheeks. She raised her eyebrows as far as they would go and mouthed the word "Good?"

Mavis nodded emphatically and smiled and blushed again. The vicarious pleasure which Helen always felt when being advised of any of Mavis's lovemaking episodes was unsurpassed at the thought of the occasion being shared with George. She looked as if she had just been advised that she had won the lottery.

George himself all the while was pretending not to overhear anything but knew very well what they were talking about. He was mildly miffed that Helen had managed to extract the information from Mavis so quickly and easily but at the same time was conscious of his own urge to shout about it from the rooftop. He was so besotted with Mavis after Saturday night that he wanted to tell the whole world himself so he knew in his heart that he could not be angry with her for letting Helen know.

Pete and Vincent soon arrived which put an end to the whispered conversation between Mavis and Helen. Pete told Mavis and George about the meeting with himself, Charlie and Mr Carter emphasising that both of them had received recommendations from the International Detective. He also advised them that Charlie had said that the CID were ready to go on Friday. Pete made a point to remind himself to have a word with Vincent to give him a pep talk about the operation on Friday next. He knew how vulnerable and anxious Vincent was and he wanted to make sure that he did not lose his nerve. He wanted to be sure that he would see it through.

Eventually Mr Pigg arrived in a very buoyant mood. He bellowed a cheery good morning to everyone. Before going into his own room, he paused to talk to Bill in the glasshouse. Clearly Bill's presence improved the humour of Mr Pigg who presumably felt that a large proportion of the daily stress or responsibility had been lifted from his shoulders.

In fact, everyone's spirits were lifted by Bill's return. Tom produced some money from his wallet and invited Mavis to go out and buy cream cakes for everyone to celebrate his return. As she left the office with the cake money, she was accompanied by Helen who took the opportunity to take a cigarette break. This was a euphemistic way of getting Mavis to herself for a few moments to gain a few more personal details of how Saturday evening had been. Mavis gave her some titillating details but never mentioned that she had been the one to take George's virginity.

Mrs Balstaff and Penny were genuinely pleased to have Bill back. The former was overjoyed to go back to the old routine. "It is so nice to have you back, Mr Butler," she said. "And looking so well. Did you have Mr Davies, the consultant, as your doctor while you were in hospital?"

Bill said, reluctantly, that he did not.

"He's such a nice man," said Mrs Balstaff, "Ay, play bridge with his waif you know." Penny was simply pleased to see Bill again and was not really bothered about the style of typing which his presence produced.

When she returned with the cream cakes Mavis gave Tom his change and began distributing the cakes to all the staff. She went into Mr Pigg's office to give him one and when she returned, she said to Helen, "You won't believe it but he's started doing those graph things again."

Pete and Gorgon arrived at The Barn for a physical workout later the same afternoon. As they pulled into the car park at the rear, they saw the gym owner, Jim Wild stood next to a car talking to a lady. There was a spare tyre on the ground. Jim was scratching his head. They walked over to him and Pete said hi to Jim and asked what the problem was.

"Hi" said Jim, "it's a flat tyre. I was trying to change it but I can't find the jack." Pete searched the boot of the car but could not find one and shrugged his shoulders. "It's not just me then," said Jim, "I thought I was going mad."

"What about the car lot on the corner?" asked Pete, "They must have one."

"I already thought of that," said Jim. "I asked the twins who work there sometimes but apparently the equipment is in the machine room which is locked because the mechanic has the afternoon off. They are not really very helpful."

Just then, Mavis appeared with her friend Doris. "Hello, Pete," she said, "what's happening Freda?"

Freda, who was the car owner, explained to Mavis that her tyre was flat and they were trying to help her but there was no tyre jack in her car. "That bloody husband of mine," she complained. "He bought me this cheap nasty little car and he swans around in a big luxury car himself."

Pete looked at the problem and picked up the wheel spanner. While the wheel was secure on the floor it was easy to loosen all the wheel nuts. Looking around he spotted a concrete block in the car park. He carried this over to the car and turned it on end next to the vehicle.

"If we lift this side of the car you slide this block under it, OK," he said to Jim. He then nodded to Gorgon and both of them gripped the underside of Freda's small car. "On three, Jake," said Pete, "One, two, three."

They both heaved the car off the ground for a few seconds during which time Jim slid the concrete block under it. Pete and Gorgon then released the car which rested upon the block. Jim quickly slid off the flat tyre and replaced it with the spare and then did up the nuts to finger tightness. Together then Pete and Gorgon took the strain once more and held the car aloft whilst Jim removed the concrete block and the car was lowered. Jim then tightened the nuts.

Everyone was elated that the problem had been solved so easily. Pete slapped his friend on the shoulder and said, "Jake here, took all the strain. I was just pretending to lift."

Gorgon smiled sheepishly. Freda grasped his arm and extended her profuse gratitude. "You are so strong," she said feeling his bicep. "Thank you so much." Jake blushed furiously.

Pete smiled broadly and said, "Well all's well that ends well." Mavis made the introductions all round. "Well," said Pete ironically, "We had meant to go into the gym and lift weights but after that I suppose we can go straight home."

They all chuckled and then said goodbye. Pete and Jake went inside with Jim and the girls went on their way. As they made their way into the gym they passed the Gibson twins and a couple of their satellites walking out. There was a brief eye contact as they passed each other.

The twins moved down the street to the car lot where their cars were parked. They paused for a conversation before moving off. As they stood there a van came into the parking area. It was Jimmy Pearce. He jumped out and cheerfully hailed the twins. "Orlright then? What's happening?" The twins had no enthusiasm for him and neither spoke. Jimmy persisted in his hearty way. "I might have some more business for you gentlemen," he said smiling.

"Didn't you understand?" said one of the twins. "Eddie said last time was the last time. What bit of that didn't you understand?"

"I know, I know," said Jimmy in a placatory manner. "But what about you gentlemen?" he said. "I've got another batch in just as good as the last lot. I've got a guy in Bristol who will take half of it so that would leave the other half for you two, wouldn't it? Only half the price, but just as effective. What do you say?"

The twins went into a huddle to discuss the potential deal. One said, "Eddie is not going to like it if he finds out."

The other said, "He's not going to find out, is he?"

"How are we going to pay for it?" asked the other

"Well," said his brother, "There's that amount we hived off from the last deal. That will pay for half. We could tell Jimmy that we'll pay the second half in a month's time. If he doesn't like it, he can fuck off."

"Right," said the other and on that basis a deal was quickly finalised. Jimmy fetched the stash from his van.

Chapter Forty-nine
More Problems for Vincent

Judge Jeremy Fallow QC was in good humour. In fact, he had been in a good mood ever since Phillipa Fry had visited his Chambers. As a result, the general atmosphere in his court had lifted. The judge's fearsome reputation normally intimidated anyone who appeared in his court. At present the atmosphere was more relaxed. Despite that, Jeremy Fallow's decision making was as decisive as ever.

A trial had just concluded after three days of vigorous cross-examination and submissions on both sides sprinkled with the usual interruptions by Jeremy often thinly disguised as objective interventions but in reality, being pro-prosecution additives.

The defence counsel Mr Augustus Samuel was just reaching the culmination of his summing up speech. "Humph," he muttered, before saying to the jury," Ladies and gentleman, you have listened carefully to all the evidence produced by the prosecution and are possibly saying to yourselves, 'he probably did it'. If that is the case then your duty is clear. You must find the defendant not guilty. It is your duty, ladies and gentlemen, to reach a decision beyond all reasonable doubt. It is my submission that the prosecution has not fulfilled their requirement to persuade you that there is guilt beyond all reasonable doubt. You must find this defendant not guilty." Augustus then sat down.

"Thank you, Mr Samuel," said Jeremy. He turned to face the jury and commenced his summing up speech. "You have just heard a speech by the defence counsel who you have no doubt judged to be a brilliant advocate. The eloquence and the persuasive quality of that speech are of course impressive but beware, in your deliberations, of merely remembering only those eloquent and plausible words. You must also look to the meat of the evidence against the defendant.

You must ask yourselves if, as the defence counsel assured you in his brilliant speech, the defendant could not have committed the crime of which he stands accused today, because it was always his habit on that evening of the week to attend choir practice at the local church, then why was no witness called to confirm that he was at the church instead of at the scene of the crime? That, ladies and gentlemen, is a question which I leave entirely to you."

Jeremy had, as always, spotted the flaw in Mr Samuel's case namely the lack of attention to detail. Although his general good humour was undoubtedly due primarily to the recent liaison with Phillipa Fry it was also accentuated by the pleasure which Jeremy always experienced when he scored a point against Gus.

As he was talking Jeremy scanned the viewing gallery and noted that Phillipa was sitting there gazing at him through her dark rimmed glasses. He paused momentarily and Phillipa gave him her most seductive smile. He continued with his speech for a further twenty minutes or so meticulously referring to all the evidence which had been produced and gently tugging at the thread of each item to emphasise its importance to the jury. Frequently, he emphasised the eloquence and brilliance of the arguments presented by the defence counsel but on each occasion that he did this he reminded them of their duty to examine carefully the evidence which had been produced. When he had finished the jury were led out to consider their verdict and the case was then adjourned.

Jeremy retired to his chamber and shortly thereafter his clerk Shirley Kemp showed Phillipa into the room. As she sat down and formally greeted Jeremy, Shirley busied herself by preparing two coffees for them. Having served them she then retired.

"Well," said Phillipa, "that was as good as any of your summing up speeches that I have heard. I was not present to hear any of the evidence but I certainly know which decision the jury are likely to come to."

"You don't think I was perhaps a little too partial?"

"No, no," responded Phillipa" You were completely objective. Gus is such a moron. He pays no attention to detail. That can work with some judges but never with one as punctilious as yourself. You wiped the floor with him Jeremy which is exactly what he deserved. I doubt if the jury will be out for long."

"But you don't think it was biased in any way?"

"Not at all," she assured him. You repeatedly emphasised how brilliant Gus was which just isn't the case at all. You were superb as always Jeremy. He would have no grounds for appeal."

"It is comforting to hear you say that," he said.

"You knew exactly what you were doing and saying Jeremy. You don't need any comfort from me."

"*Aux contraire*," he said, "a little bit of comfort from you would be exactly what I would like."

"Ooh, Jeremy," she said coquettishly, "surely not while Shirley is in the other room?"

"No, no," he said, "unfortunately not at this very moment. You know my brother Roger plays cricket for Gloucestershire?" Phillipa nodded. "Well, he lives in a flat in Clifton and this week he is playing away all week so his flat is vacant. And I um…." he said meaningfully, "have got the key, so I was thinking I could give you a viewing one night."

"Ooh, Jeremy," she said with an intake of breath which he found very sexy, "is that what you call it?"

"Name the evening," he said, "and I'm all yours."

"Hmmm…". she murmured. Let me see…. Yes, I think I could manage Friday evening very nicely, thank you. Algie is going away Friday evening for a weekend jaunt, so that would be very convenient."

"That's a date, then," said Jeremy and wrote down the details of Roger's flat on a piece of paper and handed it to her.

"It's just around the corner from the Chambers," he added, "I expect you know it, Chalfont Square, the one with a small park in the centre." Phillipa said she knew it and that all being well she would arrive at about six p.m. depending on her diary and possible court appearances.

"What would you like me to bring with me?"

"You mean apart from your scantiest night attire," he said voluptuously.

Phillipa put her index finger into her mouth and looked at him over her glasses, "I have to tell you, Jeremy, that I don't usually wear anything in bed." Then, in a mock baby doll voice she added, "would that be all right your honour?"

Jeremy felt the commencement of an erection and was thankful that it was hidden beneath his desk. "That would be just perfect, Phillipa," he purred.

"Actually," she added, "I meant should I bring any food or a bottle of wine?"

"No," he said, "I can sort out the wine. There is an Indian restaurant nearby who can deliver food. Do you like Indian?"

"Ooh, yes," she said in her huskiest voice. "The hotter the better."

"That's settled then," he said, "so Friday night it is. I cannot wait."

Phillipa then rose from her chair and came over to him and gave him a long sensual kiss on the lips. "See you Friday," she whispered and then left the room.

Tom Richards had always enjoyed arriving at the office early in the morning. He liked the solitude of being there alone before everyone else arrived. He enjoyed it even more now that Bill Butler had returned. Although, now that Bill was back, he was no longer completely alone, he did not resent Bill's presence in the office first thing in the morning. Rather, they shared the solitude together.

Tom relished their early morning conversations over a cup of tea and the Daily Mail. He also acknowledged to himself that only Bill amongst the office staff had a comprehensive knowledge of football in general and the Arsenal in particular. He did appreciate that during Bill's absence George had been an early morning fellow who had striven to provide suitable companionship but nevertheless the latter's knowledge of the Arsenal had never been more than superficial.

When he did arrive, George found them together in the glasshouse. They all said good morning to each other and George retired to his desk. In his head he was still reliving Saturday night which he had spent with Mavis. He had thought of little else since then. He continually revived in his head the sight of Mavis's voluptuous body stood in front of him.

He experienced again the sensual pleasure of lying beside her naked and also the thrill of merely being in her presence and sensing a mutual feeling of gratification oozing from her. Once again, he was reminded of his own lack of experience and he wondered if what he was feeling was true love. He had experienced nothing like it before and therefore had nothing to compare it with. He had read somewhere once that the definition of love was gratitude for pleasure and he had to admit that that was precisely what he was currently experiencing. All he knew was that living together with Mavis was heaven. He realised that it was all he wanted to do. He explored in his mind how he could immediately do that. He could, he thought, ask Mavis to come and live with himself and his grandmother. Alternatively, he could go to live with Mavis at her house but he had never actually met her parents. He marvelled at his own naivety and could already think of many reasons why those two alternatives would be impossible. How could he decide what to do, who should he look to for advice? Perhaps, he thought, he should talk to Pete about it. He was so experienced, so confident. Yes, he decided, Pete would know how to proceed.

Tom and Bill continued their conversation in the glasshouse before settling down to the normal business of the day. As a final afterthought Bill brought up the death of Lionel Witherspoon. "I keep thinking about that," he said to Tom. "I always thought he was a bit odd. He lived in that dead end street, close to the railway bridge, didn't he?" Tom nodded and said, "Yes at the end of the dual carriageway section of the road."

"Yes, that's what I thought. So why did he stop at that old trading post / mini-market which is halfway along that section of roadway. In order to do so he had to park in the pull-in area and walk across both highways which are often full of speeding cars. And yet, a bit further along that road, just around the corner from his street, there is a larger supermarket which would appear to be much more convenient. Why would he stop there?"

"I have no idea" said Tom.

Helen and Mavis arrived almost simultaneously followed shortly by Pete. Mavis began immediately to tell Helen all about the incident at the Barn the previous evening.

"Thanks to Pete and his friend Freda's flat tyre was replaced and she managed to drive home OK. Who was that guy, Pete?" she asked.

"Jacob," said Pete, "a friend from the rugby club."

"He was so strong," Mavis said to Helen. "He lifted up the entire car by himself."

Pete chuckled and said modestly, "Well, I did try to help him. But I agree he is strong."

"I think Freda was quite taken with him," said Mavis, smiling to Helen, "a big strong knight in shining armour."

Pete chuckled again. "Well, he's certainly big and strong but I'm not so sure about shining armour. He works on a local farm and spends every day with pigs and cows. He has little experience with women however."

"Hmm," thought Mavis to herself, "I know the feeling."

As usual Vincent arrived just before Mr Pigg so as to avoid losing any house points. Mavis asked him, "Are you still living round at Lizzy's place?"

"Uh, uh," responded Vincent.

"Have you been home at all Vince?" she enquired. Vincent shook his head. "Well don't you think you should?" persisted Mavis. "When I saw her, your mother was extremely worried about you. Have you been in touch? Just to let her know you are OK?"

Vincent shook his head again. "I don't want to go back there," he said.

"But can't you at least get in touch with your mother to let her know you're all right and where you are?" Vincent shrugged his shoulders but said nothing. "Look," said Mavis, "It's your step-father isn't it? I get that but it need not prevent you from seeing your mother or maintaining some contact with her. Would you like me to go and see her to re-assure her that you are OK?"

Vincent shook his head once more. "She's not really interested," he said.

"Oh, how can you say that, Vince?" asked Mavis. "When I saw her, she seemed genuinely concerned and anxious about you."

"Well," said Vincent "she knows the telephone number of this office. How come she's never bothered to get in touch with me?"

Mavis could not answer that question but she conceded to herself that Vincent had made a good point. Nevertheless, she felt that she could not leave the matter in the air. "I'm sure she loves you and is concerned about

you," she said. "Why don't I go round and see her and let her know you are
OK and tell her where you are living? I could bring her to see you at the
library coffee bar where you could both talk. You could introduce her to
Lizzy and you could talk privately together, without your step-father being
nearby. What do you say?"

Vincent shrugged his shoulders again but still did not speak.

"Right," said Mavis decisively, "that's what I'm going to do this
afternoon, straight after work. George will give me a lift to your house,
won't you George?" He nodded emphatically. "You go straight to the
library, and we'll meet you there."

Just then the conversation was interrupted by the arrival of Mr Pigg
who crashed through the general office on the way to his room. No sooner
had he arrived when a telephone call was put through to him by Penny. It
was Mr Jenkins, the Regional Controller. "Good morning, Arnold," he said
cheerfully, "and how are you this morning?"

"I'm very well, thank you, sir. I've been hard at it for some while. I
was just about to stop for a tea break."

"Good man, Arnold," responded Mr Jenkins "It's the early bird, eh?"

"Indeed sir," said Mr Pigg who had not yet taken off his coat.

"I hear that Bill butler has returned to work," said the Controller.

"He has indeed, sir," said Mr Pigg "he was sorely missed of course but
now we are back to full strength and raring to go."

"Good, good," said Mr Jenkins. "Listen, Arnold, I have some time
available this morning so I plan to pop in and see you all, in about an hour,
OK?"

"Oh absolutely," Mr Pigg assured him. "I'll look forward to seeing
you."

"Just a flying visit," said the Controller. "I'm on route to another office
which I need to reach by lunchtime. So I'll be with you for only a short
while."

Shortly after, Pete made his way to the basement area on the pretext of
wishing to trace a file. George quickly made an excuse to leave the office
and joined him there. He quickly came to the point and explained to him
the problem which he had been wrestling with in his own head since
Saturday night with Mavis. Pete pulled a face as if he had just bitten into a
lemon. After an intake of breath he said, "I don't think you should rush into
either plan. There are so many imponderables that either alternative might
throw up. It is risky enough just moving in with a girlfriend because in no
time at all one can find that both parties do not suit each other and living
together can antagonise difficulties. It is even more risky to expect one of
the parties to move in with a relative of the other. You have not even met

Mavis's parents and nor has she yet met your grandmother. Neither would make any sense just to allow you to get your end away with Mavis, lovely as she may be. "No," confirmed Pete, "You should just allow some time to go by and let your relationship with Mavis grow or expire. If she likes you as much as you clearly like her then she's not going anywhere. Just tread water and see how it goes and at least wait until you've met her parents and she's met your grandmother.

"There is one further alternative which you may wish to consider. Get yourself a place of your own. You've mentioned that your mum and dad left you some money so why not think of using it to buy a property?"

"Oh, I'm not sure," said George. "My grandmother told me that the money had been invested in trust for me and it wouldn't be available to me until I reach the age of twenty-five years which means I have to wait for another year or two."

"So that restricts you a bit," said Pete. "I can only think of one further alternative for you. You've seen my flat of course. It is a nice flat and has three bedrooms which actually is slightly bigger than I really need. If you are interested you could move in with me. You would have your own room and any time it was convenient you could invite Mavis to stay the night. You would have to pay half the rent of course which is not too expensive. The landlord is Fillipo from La Scala downstairs and you've met him haven't you?"

George had not been expecting this and didn't know what to say. He could see that what Pete had said made good common sense. It was definitely not a good idea to move in with someone else's relatives whom one had never met. But he had never before considered sharing a flat with another bloke. He paused to think about it.

"Well, no rush," said Pete, "think it over and let me know what you think." George said he would do that.

A little while later Mr Jenkins the Regional Controller arrived at the office and was shown in to see Mr Pigg who shook his hand vigorously. "As I said on the telephone, Arnold, this is a flying visit so I won't take up too much of yours, or anyone else's time. I was hoping that while I'm here I could have a quick word with Bill Butler. Do you think you could ask him to come in here so that we can both talk to him together."

The rest of the staff, as usual, were interested to learn that their Regional Controller had called again and as before they speculated as to the reason for his visit. Both Helen and Mavis were foremost in the speculation but neither could come up with an answer which could satisfy the other

"What do you think Tom?" asked Mavis.

"I could hazard a guess," replied Tom, "but I really don't have any definite idea."

"But what would be your best guess?" asked Mavis.

"Why don't you just wait and see," intervened Pete "no doubt we'll find out as soon as he's gone. Piggy won't be able to keep quiet about it."

As if on cue a loud crashing and banging preceded the arrival in the general office of Mr Pigg, Bill Butler and the Regional Controller Mr Jenkins. As they took their places at the far end of the office Mr Pigg instructed Vincent to summon Mrs Balstaff and Penny from their room and everyone arranged their chairs in a semi-circle to attend the announcement.

As Mrs Balstaff and Penny arrived Mr Pigg was in the process of asking everyone loudly, "Can I have your attention please."

As always Mrs Balstaff seated herself at the head table whereas Penny sat with the others.

"As you see" bellowed Mr Pigg, "Mr Jenkins is with us today for a brief visit. I would be grateful if you would listen to what he has to say." Mr Pigg then sat down and left the room to his Regional Controller.

"Good morning, everyone," said Mr Jenkins, "I will not keep you for more than a minute. I am sure you are all pleased to see the return to this office of Bill Butler. I trust that you will agree with me that he looks in good health. When I was last here, I made a decision to promote your manager Mr Pigg to the role of roving assistant controller. Due to the very unfortunate death of Lionel Witherspoon that promotion was put on hold for a while. However, now that Bill has returned (in rude good health), there is no reason why Mr Pigg should not take up his new role starting next week. Congratulations Arnold," he said and paused to allow for some 'hear hears' or even perhaps a small round of applause, of which there was none.

"You are no doubt," continued Mr Jenkins, "wondering who the office manager will be. Well, I am able to tell you that that position will now be carried out by Mr Bill Butler. Congratulations Bill" he added.

This time there was a small amount of enthusiastic applause led by Mavis and Helen. Mr Jenkins then took his leave of everyone and headed off to keep his next appointment. Mr Pigg went straight to his room to start telephoning people.

After they had gone the staff discussed the new arrangements. Everyone was delighted that the office would be managed by Bill from now on. "After all," argued Mavis, "he had always done it before without actually being paid for it. "No one thought that Mr Pigg would be missed, although no one actually begrudged him any success which might go with his new role.

"There is a theory," said Tom, "which holds that everybody is promoted to a grade which is one step beyond their actual competence."

"Well, I think that somehow, Piggy managed that at least twice," suggested Pete.

Mavis added, "Too right."

Later that day George and Mavis left the office together and drove to Vincent's mother's house. George parked the car and they both walked up the garden path together. They each marvelled again at the shabby, dingy nature of the property. Mavis pressed the doorbell and they waited for a reply. Eventually the door was opened by Vincent's mother who looked in worse shape than the last time they had called. Her face looked more drained and very pale. She moved and looked like a person ten years older. The bruise on her face had turned yellow and she gripped the open door as if she were unable to stand upright without it.

She remembered Mavis who immediately announced that she had come to take her to see Vincent who was eager to speak to her. "Oh, I'm not sure," she responded, "how long will it take? I'd have to be back to prepare Ted's tea. He likes his food on the table when he gets in and he doesn't like it if I go out."

"It will only take ten minutes in the car," said Mavis persuasively, "you can stay as little, or as long as you like. You do love your son, don't you? He would like to see you. Now you come along with us and we'll have you back in no time."

So saying Mavis grasped her arm to help her through the door. Vincent's mother gasped in pain and grimaced. "What's the matter?" asked Mavis. "Are you in pain? Have you hurt yourself?"

Vincent's mother grimaced again, and said, "It's nothing, I fell over. I'll be all right."

"Right, let's go" said Mavis decisively and led her gently down the path. "It needn't take too long and Vincent would love to see you."

They all got into George's car, Vincent's mother continuing to look in pain. When they arrived at the Library Mavis helped her out of the car noticing that every movement made her wince with pain. "Where is it you are hurting?" enquired Mavis as they walked slowly across the carpark. She held one arm across her midriff by way of explanation. "You say you fell over?" said Mavis hoping for more information. She nodded but did not say anything more.

They came to the door of the coffee bar and Mavis helped her in over the threshold. Vincent was seated at the nearest table and rose to greet them. He attempted to embrace her but could see the pain she was in. "What's the matter?" he asked with some alarm.

She eased herself on to a seat and said, "It's OK, I just had a fall and I'm feeling a bit sore."

"Show me," said Vincent.

His mother shook her head and said, "It's OK, I'll be all right it's nothing."

"Show me!" repeated Vincent with more power and authority. She began to lift her cardigan but was in such pain that she could not manage it properly. Mavis assisted her to raise the cardigan which revealed extensive bruising all across her midriff.

"He's been at it again, hasn't he?" demanded Vincent.

"No, no," said his mother. "I just fell over, honestly."

"And I suppose you banged your head at the same time?" he said. His mother instinctively fingered the bruise on her cheek. She nodded.

"But that bruise was done at a different time," observed Mavis. "I recall seeing it when I last called at your house. I don't like the look of your chest. I think it should be looked at by a doctor."

"No, no," she said with some alarm, "that can't happen. I have to get home to cook Ted's tea."

"Oh, bugger Ted's tea," said Vincent. "You need to get that looked at."

"Absolutely," agreed Mavis. "We'll get you round to the hospital immediately. You are obviously in pain and it must be looked at by a doctor. We can worry about your husband later.

That said, everyone stood up and helped the poor woman to her feet. As they exited the coffee bar she was still trying to argue that she needed to go straight home to cook her husband's tea. No one listened to her. "He won't like it if I'm not there when he gets home."

"So what?" said Vincent "who cares what he thinks?"

"But he gets very angry if I don't do what he says." she added sobbing.

"You are not going back to that man, in that house," said Mavis firmly. "You are coming with us."

"You know as well as I do, that as soon as a doctor sees all that bruising they are going to arrest Ted, and so they should," said Vincent.

"But," said his mother, now sobbing more than ever, "I don't know anyone who could help me. Once the police get involved, and then go away, I'm afraid he will hurt me again."

"Well," said Mavis assuredly, "you may not know anyone but I certainly do. Let's get you to hospital first and we'll think about everything else later."

So it was decided. They all helped her into George's car and made their way to the Accident & Emergency department of the local hospital. While George parked his car the others made their way into the A & E department. Vincent's mother was quickly signed in and due to the appearance of her injuries and her age, given some priority.

By the time George had parked his car, and made his way to the A & E he found Vincent on his own, in the waiting area.

"They've taken her for an X ray," he said. "Mavis has gone with her."

After approximately one hour they had the results of the X rays. The doctor told them that Vincent's mother had three broken ribs to go with the extensive bruising. He also confirmed that she would be admitted to hospital and would spend at least one night there. He then asked how the injuries had been sustained. Vincent's mother, whose first name was April, stayed silent.

"I have to say," said the doctor, "that the information you gave on admission, namely a fall, is not consistent with these injuries. My experience tells me that you suffered several separate blows and I have to ask you did someone do this to you?"

Mavis could not contain herself. "Yes, her husband did it," she said.

The doctor frowned and said, "These injuries are very serious and the outcome could have been much worse. We are going to have to telephone the police and advise them of this. There is no way you can go home to your husband at the moment and in any event, I would not recommend that you do until the police have looked into this."

April began to sob again, and Mavis tried to console her. "What did he hit you with?" asked the doctor.

She continued to sob and eventually, through a choked-up throat, uttered, "A cricket bat."

Mavis and George were aghast, the doctor frowned again and Vincent said, "That old bat of mine, which used to be outside the back door?" April nodded still sobbing bitterly.

"All right," said the doctor, "this has to be sorted out officially. We will telephone the police and get them to send someone round to take a statement. In the meantime, you won't be going anywhere for one or two nights so that we can keep an eye on you."

Within approximately one further hour, April was admitted to a ward and was settled in bed. Soon after, two police officers, one a female, arrived and took details and a statement. They then left, informing them that they were going straight to Vincent's house to arrest Ted and charge him with common assault. They asked if April had a solicitor who could represent her but she said no and further that she had no funds to pay one. They advised her that almost certainly she would be granted Legal Aid which would mean that she would not have to pay any money.

Mavis told them that she knew someone at Duffey Fry & Co, who might be able to help April. The two officers agreed that the firm was a respected firm of solicitors and that the police would be happy to co-operate with them. Thereafter Mavis and George decided to leave Vincent and his mother alone together. They agreed to meet the following day at the office and catch up on information and the progress of the police investigations.

The following morning Tom and Bill were together in the glasshouse both enjoying their early morning cup of tea. Tom had just congratulated Bill on his promotion and asked him if he would be making any changes.

"Not immediately," he said. "What about you, Tom? Have you decided how long you want to go on working?"

"I'm still unsure," said Tom "but certainly no longer than a couple more years." Bill nodded. George arrived next and briefly advised them of the events the previous evening with Vincent's mother. Their reaction was hardly surprising.

"A cricket bat!" said Bill in astonishment.

"Wow!" said Tom, I expect they'll throw the book at him."

Mavis came next shortly followed by Helen and then surprisingly came Vincent who arrived much earlier than expected. "So what happened after we left?" asked Mavis, "how is your mother?"

"She's fine," said Vincent. "They are keeping her in for another night apparently just to keep an eye on her."

"What did the police say?" asked Mavis.

"They arrested him and locked him up. They are taking him to court this morning apparently."

"What are they charging him with?" asked Mavis.

"Grievous bodily harm," replied Vincent.

"Come with me," said Mavis and led Vincent into the glasshouse. She explained the situation briefly to Bill who assisted her by confirming that Tom had already outlined the facts to him. Without more ado Bill immediately allowed both Mavis and Vincent a couple of hours off work this morning or as long as it took. Mavis gave Bill a hug and said, "You're such a brick Bill," and then kissed him on the cheek. Bill watched them leave and smiled.

Simon Nibble also smiled as he reviewed the invoices he had issued over the last month. He savoured the cup of coffee which Mrs Sargent had just made for him and did some mental arithmetic which told him that financially he was doing very well. His telephone rang. He picked up the receiver. Mrs Sargent said, "It's the custody office at the police station, for you."

Simon took the call and spoke to the Custody Sergeant who told him that they were holding a man overnight and were ready to interview and charge him. When they had asked him if he had a solicitor, he had said Huw Roberts. Did he (Mr Nibble) wish to attend and later represent him in the court? Simon asked what the man had been arrested for and the custody sergeant said, "Beating his wife."

"Very well," said Simon. "I'll be round in about ten minutes."

Mavis and George made their way on foot to the local magistrates court where they sat in the viewing gallery overlooking court number one. The magistrates trooped in and sat at the raised bench at the far end. The clerk announced that the order of the day would be slightly altered to allow them to consider an overnight matter.

"Call Edward Hudson," said the clerk loudly and the doorway below the floor of the main witness box was opened and Vincent's stepfather climbed the steps to the box accompanied by a police officer from the custody suite. They both stood together in the witness box.

The clerk read out his name and he said, "Yes," and the head magistrate told everyone to be seated.

The prosecuting solicitor rose to outline the case very briefly explaining that the defendant had been arrested by the police the previous evening for having attacked his wife with a cricket bat. The victim he explained had suffered broken ribs and was still in hospital. He also explained that due to the ferocity of the attack and the serious nature of the injuries suffered the case would be transferred to the Crown Court.

"Who is representing the defendant?" enquired the magistrate. Simon bobbed up immediately. "If you please your worships," he said and sat back down immediately.

"What is the position with regard to bail?" asked the Magistrate.

The prosecuting solicitor rose and said, "Bail will be opposed, Your Worships. The grounds are, the serious nature of the offence, the seriousness of the injuries and the possibility of a repetition of the offence." He explained that the defendant and the victim (his wife), lived in a rented council property and that they had lived there for some time. "When his wife is released from hospital, she will be very vulnerable if the husband is still at the property. She has no other place to live or means to afford anywhere else."

"Mr Nibble?" said the Magistrate.

"Your Worships," said Simon rising to his feet, "My client wishes me to make an application for bail on his behalf on the grounds that this incident is, as yet, unproved. In any event it is most unlikely to be repeated. My client has a full-time job with a regular income and would be unlikely to abscond. If he were to spend time in custody awaiting a trial, he might be likely to lose his job. It would be better to grant him bail so that he can continue to earn money to maintain the matrimonial home. My client has every intention of defending these charges and being found not guilty."

"What job does your client hold?" asked the magistrate.

"My client is a lorry driver for the Sodford Brick Works Ltd, Your Worships. He has held the job for a number of years and is I understand well thought of by his employer. He is a local man who works for a local employer and is held in high esteem by them. There would be no likelihood of the defendant absconding. Bail would be entirely appropriate."

The prosecution solicitor rose again. "Bail is definitely not appropriate in this case, Your Worships. This is not an isolated assault but the latest in a long line of regular habitual attacks. These injuries are very serious and it is only a matter of extreme good fortune that we are not dealing today with a case of murder or manslaughter. Further, there are other items of inquiry which the police are making in respect of this defendant and which may lead to even more serious charges. It would be advantageous to those enquiries that the defendant remains in custody. Further, the property in which they lived together up until yesterday is a council owned property. The tenant is Mrs Hudson not the defendant. Even if bail were granted the defendant could no longer return to this council house because that would be a bail condition. He has no other permanent accommodation and would I submit be likely to abscond.

The magistrates withdrew to decide upon the matter of bail.

Mavis had been making notes on a note pad which she had brought with her. "What other matters?" she asked Vincent.

He shrugged, "I've no idea. The police never mentioned anything to me."

The magistrates soon returned and announced that bail would not be granted. Vincent's stepfather was remanded in custody.

Chapter Fifty
Mavis and Phillipa

Mavis and Vincent left the Magistrates' Court and made their way to the offices of Duffey Fry & Co. Mavis asked if she could see Mrs Robinson who fortunately was free and able to grant them an audience. Mavis quickly gave her the details of the matter while Mrs Robinson made notes. The latter confirmed that under the circumstances Vincent's mother would be entitled to Legal Aid. She gave the necessary form to Mavis for completion and April's signature. In the meantime, she confirmed that she would prepare papers on April's behalf for an application in the matrimonial court in Bristol for either a divorce or non-molestation injunction or alternative process depending on the result of the criminal proceedings in the Crown Court against Vincent's stepfather. "Bring the papers back to me and I'll arrange some representation on the telephone in the meantime," she said.

"You will make sure it's Phillipa Fry won't you," said Mavis.

"I will try," she said, "but I don't know if she is free."

Mavis and Vincent then made their way straight to the hospital to see April. She was sitting up in bed and looking a bit better. The livid bruise on her face, though obviously getting better, was looking at its worst. The yellowness had spread but at the outer area it was still purple. The bruise contrasted with the paleness of the rest of her face which had the brittle appearance of an eggshell.

She signed the legal forms which Mavis assisted her to complete. She thought that the hospital would keep her in for one more night but so far this day no doctor had been to see her. Mavis said she hoped that the doctor would be pleased with what he saw and then excused herself to return to the offices of Duffey Fry & Co. She told Vincent that she would see him back at the office sometime later in the day.

She then made her way back to the solicitor's offices and handed in the papers to Mrs Robinson who confirmed that she would be preparing a brief shortly. Could she (Mavis) call later to get full details of what would happen.

Upon her return to the office, Mavis told the others how she had got on. She also expanded upon what had happened the previous day. Everyone was impressed but nobody was surprised at the depth of Mavis's involvement in the affairs of Vincent and his mother.

"So what happened in court?" asked Helen.

"Well," said Mavis, "in a way it was something and nothing. They just decided to transfer the matter to the Crown Court and that was that really. Apparently, he'll be dragged before them in a few days' time."

"Was that all that happened?" asked Helen in disbelief. "What was actually said?"

"Well," said Mavis, "there was a man from the CPS (that's the Crown Prosecution Service), who told the court what had happened. He said he wanted it to go to the Crown Court because it was serious. There was a solicitor acting for him who applied for bail but they would not give him any so he's still locked up."

"Who was his solicitor?" asked Pete who felt that he would know the answer before Mavis gave it.

"Someone called Nibble," she replied, "he was a bit of a 'flash Harry' in a posh suit. And that was a strange thing," she said, "When they asked him what his job was, his solicitor told them he was a lorry driver for the Sodford Brick Works Ltd. Now that was the vehicle that ran over Lionel, wasn't it?"

Tom said it was but added that there would be a number of lorries in their fleet so it wasn't certain that Vincent's stepfather had been driving the one that hit Lionel.

"Yes, I appreciate that," said Mavis, "but the prosecutor said that the Police were making other enquiries about Vincent's stepfather which were not connected to his mother and that was why they wanted him locked up and they opposed bail."

"Hmm," said Tom thoughtfully, "that is interesting."

Bill, who had come out of the glasshouse to listen, said, "We were only talking about Lionel's death the other morning, weren't we, Tom. I always thought there was something fishy about it."

Mavis then told Bill that she might have to pop out to visit Duffey Fry & Co later and was that OK. Bill confirmed that it was and jokingly suggested that perhaps they could offer her a job there since she had done lots of work for them lately.

Mavis smiled and said, "Well I do enjoy doing things of a legal nature. It does fascinate me. Vincent should be back soon. I just left him alone with his mother for a while. It certainly perked her up to see him again."

Bill smiled, and said, "You are a really nice person, Mavis."

Nothing was seen of Mr Pigg that day who remained in his office the entire day telephoning the managers of every other office in the region to bring them up to speed on his promotion and forewarn them of imminent visits to their offices by himself.

Pete told Mavis that he was familiar with the solicitor Simon Nibble who was the one who acted for Eddie Sharp and also had represented Jimmy Pearce in the Crown Court. "Aah of course," said Mavis, "I thought I should have known him but I didn't recognise him."

Vincent finally turned up and was able to report that the hospital had decided to keep his mother in for one more night. "But where will she go when she leaves hospital?" asked Helen.

"Well home, of course," said Vincent without any great authority.

"But will it be safe for her?" asked Helen again, echoing everybody's thoughts.

"Well, it definitely will be until Friday." said Mavis with assurance. After that it will depend upon the outcome of the criminal court and what punishment they deal out to Vincent's stepfather and as a back-up what legal protection can be put in place, care of Phillipa Fry." Everyone smiled at Mavis's enthusiasm for her favourite barrister.

Both Mavis and Vincent left the office early enough to call at the offices of Duffey Fry & Co. Mrs Robinson was expecting them and had already produced the necessary paperwork and confirmed to Mavis that she had spoken on the telephone to Phillipa Fry who had said that she was free on Friday to lend a hand.

"I have prepared a brief for Miss Fry a copy of which I have faxed to her chambers." she told Mavis. "If you would be good enough to take this original with you on Friday you can hand it over to her."

Mavis confirmed that would be all right without even considering whether she would be able to take the day off work. Subconsciously she had probably assumed that Bill would permit it.

As they left the offices Mavis and Vincent discussed the game plan for Friday. "It partly depends on whether or not your mother is well enough to come with us and whether she would even want to. If she doesn't come then it might be better if you stayed here with her."

"I don't have any more annual leave left," said Vincent. "I used the last few days on that festival I went to."

"Well, in that case I'd better go," said Mavis. "I'm quite certain that Bill will allow it. In any case, I know the barrister and where to go."

On Friday morning everyone in the office was experiencing some anxiety. Tom and Bill had their usual early morning chat over tea and the *Daily Mail*.

"Big day today," said Tom.

"Yes," said Bill "for everyone, more or less. Difficult to know who will be the most nervous today."

Tom nodded, and began to tick off the fingers of one hand with the

314

index finger of the other. "There's Mr Pigg, who's working his last day here today. Secondly, there's Mavis who is probably, as we speak, on her way to court this morning. Next, there's Pete and George who will be involved in a Police raid of a night club where drugs are sold, and finally there's Vince who could be the sacrificial goat in that operation as well as worrying about his mother." Bill agreed, "On balance I guess Vincent will be the most anxious."

George was the next to arrive as usual. He greeted Tom and Bill in the glasshouse and inevitably they all three began to discuss the same topic.

"So," said Bill, "Mavis should be on her way by now."

"Yes," said George, "I think she's really excited about it. She'll be doing something really helpful for Vincent and his mum and meeting her favourite barrister at the same time."

Pete came in next and joined George at the table. They also discussed the same thing. George's main concern was for Mavis who would be on her own at court. Pete discounted this with a wave of his hand. "She'll be fine," he assured George. "She's very capable and she's taken to all this legal stuff like a duck to water. My main concern is Vincent who I'm afraid might even fail to turn up. We'll have to keep the pressure on him not to forget to be there and also re-assure him that everything will be all right. I'm going to bring Jake and a couple of others from the Rugby club who know how to handle themselves. We should be able to protect Vince. In any case, according to Charlie's contact there ought to be a few CID chaps around."

Helen arrived a little later than usual because, in the absence of Mavis, she had been recruited to go shopping first thing to find a gift for Mr Pigg on his last day. When she came into the office, she was bearing a large bouquet of flowers, which Helen thought would be appreciated by Mrs Pigg if not by the man himself, and a 'Good Luck' card for everyone to sign together with a gift voucher which she had purchased from a well-known shop in town.

Despite Pete's misgivings Vincent turned up (luckily for himself just before Mr Pigg) and also confirmed, when challenged that he would be at the Nite Club this evening. Pete was relieved and told him to be in the Jubilee Inn by seven thirty p.m., where Charlie and Des had agreed to meet for a pre- operation briefing. Pete reassured Vincent that some money would be given to him, to purchase the drugs.

Mr Pigg's arrival was, as usual, preceded by crashes and bangs. He went straight to his room which gave Helen the opportunity to scurry around the office with the Good Luck card and obtain everyone's signature thereto with the exception of Mavis whose signature Helen expertly forged. She then crept into the room of Mrs Balstaff and Penny and requested their presence in the general office. Once everyone was assembled Mr Pigg was summoned and he came crashing through trying vainly to appear modestly surprised.

Bill made a short speech outlining his career and wishing him all the best in his new role. He also assured him that he would be sorely missed by those he left behind. Predictably there were no ringing tones of' 'hear, hear' when Bill said this.

Mr Pigg harrumphed his way through an acceptance of the gift and confirmed that his wife would be delighted with the flowers. He ended his acceptance speech with a reminder to everyone that he would, from time to time, re-visit the office in his role of Assistant Controller. There was a barely discernible groan in response to this promise.

In the meantime, Mavis was on the train to Bristol. She reviewed the paperwork which she carried in respect of Vincent's mother. She noted that the one and only item of documentation which she did not have was April's marriage certificate. She had been unable to receive this document because it was, presumably, still at April's house and she (April) had not been home since Mavis had last seen her. She had however made notes of all the necessary facts which she felt Phillipa Fry might ask for.

Once she arrived in Bristol, she made her way to Clifton Chambers and was soon shown in to see Miss Fry who said how nice it was to see her again. She handed over the original brief and then answered, to the best of her knowledge, a few questions which Phillipa put to her. The latter made a few notes and then said, "The case against Mr Hudson, is listed in the Crown Court at ten o'clock. Now, strictly speaking, I am a matrimonial barrister who normally frequents the divorce courts not the criminal courts, but the judge this morning, Jeremy Fallow QC, is a special friend of mine and he probably won't mind me being present as a representative of the victim. You can sit behind me so that you can take notes and answer any queries which may occur to me or the judge."

While she was speaking Mavis marvelled again at the quality and perfection of her make-up. "So tell me," said Phillipa, "I know very little about you. What is your full name?"

Mavis winced slightly, "Mavis Clutterbuck," she replied. "I know, I know, it's a very old-fashioned name. Previously when I came to see you, I was with Doris and then Freda. What an old-fashioned trio, Doris, Freda, and Mavis! I suppose if I were to marry, I could have a better name. The trouble is, the chap I am dating is called George Davies. If I married him, I'd become Mavis Davies."

Phillipa smiled sympathetically and said, "It's not the name that's so important. It's the quality of the character behind it. I can tell you that I have been accompanied into court by many solicitors but none of them has been better than you. You are always well informed and well prepared. Have you ever thought about becoming a lawyer?"

Mavis blushed and modestly said, "Oh, I don't think I could manage that."

Phillipa looked her straight in the eyes and said, "Well, what I think is that there is nothing that you couldn't do. The only thing that is holding you back is your own lack of confidence. My advice to you is to divide everything down into small bite-size chunks and examine each one separately and ask yourself can I manage this? You will find that none of them is beyond you. Put them all back together and tackle them head-on and you may amaze yourself with what you achieve. Now then, before we head off is there anything you want to know, anything you're not sure about?"

Mavis took a deep breath and said, "This will sound really small and stupid. But how do you manage to get your eye make-up to look so fantastic?"

Phillipa laughed out loud. "I so wasn't expecting that," she said. She fished into her handbag and pulled out her dark rimmed glasses and put them on the end of her nose. "Make-up is a bit of an illusion," she assured Mavis. "A bit like these glasses," she confided. "They are very weak, and if I am honest, I don't really need to wear them. However," she added looking over the top of them, "They create an illusion with juries and judges. Make-up is the same. If we have time after the court hearing we can take a cup of coffee somewhere and I'll give you a few tips."

Mavis's face lit up as she sensed a kindred spirit and knew then that her initial infatuation with Phillipa had not been misplaced. They both gathered their papers together and made their way to the Crown Court on foot.

Jeremy Fallow QC was in his chambers at the Crown Court looking at the day's itinerary with his clerk Shirley Kemp. "So what do we have on the menu today, Shirley?" he asked.

"Well, Judge," she said, "The first item is a transfer from the Magistrates court. It is a GBH: a man attacked his wife with a cricket bat. She ended up in hospital with several broken ribs. It is not certain whether she is still there but the prosecution maintain that it is a miracle that she is still alive."

"If that is the case why have they not made the charges attempted murder one might ask?" said the judge. "Who is the prosecutor today?" he asked.

"Mr Sabin," she replied.

"Aah," said Jeremy. "Perhaps that explains the diffidence of the charges."

"Well, it is an initial hearing, Judge, not a trial. Perhaps Mr Sabin will gain some confidence from this morning's hearing."

"Yes, I suppose so," said Jeremy "perhaps we can make a prosecutor out of him after all."

"Another aspect of this case which may interest you Judge is that the victim, the defendant's wife, is represented by Phillipa Fry. She may be in court this morning."

Jeremy raised his eyebrows. He had been in an exceptionally good mood since Phillipa's last visit and this morning his mood was even more cheerful in anticipation of the evening to come. He had not expected to see Phillipa earlier than six p.m. "Really," he said, "and who is representing the defendant?"

"Mr Samuel," said Shirley with a smile. She was well aware of the Judge's aversion for Gus (or Humphrey by nickname) and also his very definite attraction for Phillipa Fry.

Jeremy thought for a moment. "It will be interesting to see what defence Humphrey will put up for a man who attacks his wife with a cricket bat. No doubt he will say that he was merely practising his cover drive and she got in the way."

Shirley laughed. "Perhaps your brother could give him a few tips, eh?"

"My brother is a craftsman with a bat but as far as I am aware, he has never attacked a woman with one. Indeed, the closest he's ever come to such an action is to offer a leg glance." he added with a chuckle.

"Oh," said Shirley, moving over to the coffee machine. "Is he a ladies' man, then?" She had always secretly thought that Jeremy's brother was quite dishy.

"Oh, I think he has his moments. I believe that well-known sportsmen attract females almost as much as rock stars. Not that my brother is in the top echelons of his profession but nevertheless he has his admirers."

"I should think so," said Shirley handing him a cup of coffee, "he's a very handsome man."

"Yes," said Jeremy striking a pose, "it's a family trait" They both chuckled and Shirley shuffled some papers and said, "I am not sure how long this morning's hearing will last. I suppose that depends on how long Humphrey speaks for or should I say how long you allow him to do so. There is, of course the trial, which concluded yesterday and whether or not the jury will come back with a decision or whether you will be required to lecture them on a week-end interruption."

"I sincerely hope they will make a decision by lunchtime" said Jeremy.

"Anyway," said Shirley looking at her watch, "it's nearly time to start. I'll go into court and make sure everyone is ready and then I'll give you a call."

Mavis had seated herself behind Phillipa in the court. To the right of Miss Fry was the prosecution counsel Mr Sabin a thin young man possibly of Indian extract who was wearing tinted glasses. To her left was the defence counsel Augustus Samuel, a man of about forty-five years of age who contrived, due to obesity and hair loss, to look ten years older. Behind him sat Simon Nibble who wore his cream Armani suit and a supercilious smile. The door behind the judge's bench opened and Shirley Kemp came out. She said good morning to everyone and asked if they were ready. Upon confirmation from the lawyers, she asked the usher to summon up the defendant.

Ted Hudson appeared up the steps into the defendant's witness box accompanied by a prison officer. They both sat down together. Mavis recognised him as the brute of a man who had come to the door at Vincent's house. As soon as everyone was assembled Shirley Kemp went back through the door and then quickly re-appeared calling, "All rise."

Judge Jeremy Fallow QC stepped through the door wearing his wig and gown. He bowed and said, 'Good morning' to everybody and then took his seat. The opening formality was dealt with by Shirley who asked the defendant to confirm his full name and then to confirm how he wished to plead. To Mavis's astonishment Ted Hudson pleaded not guilty. While Mavis was striving to understand how he could possibly plead not guilty the case continued.

"Yes, Mr Sabin," said Jeremy. The prosecutor rose and outlined the facts of the case and gave the judge the details of the injuries April had suffered. He explained that she was still in hospital but would be available in due course to give evidence of the assaults.

"Humph," began Mr Samuel, as he got to his feet.

"Yes, Mr Samuel?" said Jeremy. "Your honour," he began with a sigh, "I am at a loss to understand what my friend is doing here today." Here he indicated with an inclination of his head in the direction of Phillipa who rose to her feet. She gave Jeremy a coy look over the top of her glasses and said, "Watching brief, Your Honour. My client is the wife of the defendant. My friend's client nearly killed her the other day. I am here to make sure that her interests are protected. If this court cannot provide this protection then I will make the necessary application in the Matrimonial Court."

"How nice to see you, Miss Fry," said the Judge. "You are always welcome in my court. I will endeavour to afford every possible protection which your client might need. Please carry on, Mr Sabin." The prosecution counsel continued his outline of the case and finally sat down.

"When is your client likely to be available to give evidence in this case Miss Fry?" the Judge asked.

Phillipa stood up. "She is due to be released from hospital tomorrow, Your Honour, and should therefore be well enough to come to court within a couple of days."

"So a conservative estimate might be one week?"

"Yes, Your Honour."

"Mr Samuel, what is the basis of your client's defence in this matter?"

"Humph, the evidence against my client consists wholly in the allegations made by his wife. My client refutes these allegations."

"I understand that, Mr Samuel, but I am asking what your client will allege happened. Is your client saying that someone else attacked her or that it was an accident?"

"Humph, Your Honour. I believe that the mainstay of my client's defence will be, that the evidence given by my friend's client will be unreliable.

"Very well," said Jeremy "We appear to have reached an impasse. The allegations of the wife, are defended by the husband, and are allegedly untrue. However, there appears to be no doubt that the injuries were suffered and I am very concerned by the serious nature of these injuries. I would advise you, Mr Samuel, to talk candidly to your client in order to establish whether or not he has a defence of any substance and that his position is more than a mere denial. On that basis I will adjourn this matter for one week during which time I strongly advise you to speak to your client."

Phillipa Fry bobbed up. She mentioned that April was coming out of hospital tomorrow and had nowhere to live except the matrimonial home. She emphasised that she was the tenant of the property not the defendant.

"There are processes which can be put in place, for example non-molestation injunction, and exclusion orders etc. which could be commenced in the Matrimonial Court but only at expense and inconvenience to the victim."

The judge raised his hand to stop Phillipa in full flow, "Be assured, Miss Fry, there will be no bail granted to this defendant. Your client will be entirely safe in her home until this case concludes. There will be no need for the cost or inconvenience of other measures. That should allow you sufficient time to issue and file divorce proceedings, if your client wishes, and if you need any other directions or restraints you may apply to this court at any time. I am sure that I will see you again soon," he added with a twinkle in his eye. Phillipa inclined her head.

Judge Jeremy Fallow QC then rose to leave the court, having adjourned the case for one week. He noticed, before walking out, the solicitor seated behind Mr Samuel. He saw that it was the same man who had been in his court a week or so earlier. The man wore the same cream coloured Armani suit which Jeremy found quite unsuitable for a court of Law.

Mavis and Phillipa Fry retired to the coffee bar on the ground floor of the court building and shared a small table near a window. "So, what did you think of all that?" asked Phillipa.

"Really interesting," said Mavis, with great enthusiasm. "I've never sat in a court before. I thought it was amazing. But I just couldn't believe it when he said it would be a 'not guilty' plea. How can that be possible?"

"Well, it can't be, can it?" responded Phillipa. The defence counsel, Mr Samuel, is a complete moron and never pays any attention to detail as the Judge knows only too well. Anyway, he's given him sufficient warning and that should be enough to guarantee that he will persuade his client to change his plea to guilty. It's a bit of procedural posturing which often takes place but he won't be allowed to get away with anything with this judge."

"It was lucky for April, that the judge took your side over the facts, wasn't it?" said Mavis.

"Believe me," said Phillipa meaningfully, "luck had nothing to do with it. Now what did you want to know about eye make-up?" She opened her handbag and took out a small case of make-up accoutrements. She looked closely at Mavis' face and said, "You don't need very much at all. Just some of this," holding up a tube, "and also some of this," she said, pointing to something else. "Both of these are quite expensive but they are far superior to any other products. But you don't need much, you are really very beautiful. I wish I had your natural shade and your eyes are amazing."

Mavis blushed. She could not believe that someone as perfect as Phillipa could be so complimentary towards her. She said, "Thank you so much."

"You are very welcome," said Phillipa. "Now, tell me, would you be interested in studying law? It might take a few years but you could, I believe, qualify as a solicitor in about five years and you would be an asset to any firm who was looking for a trainee. What do you say? Might you be interested?"

"I am interested in the law and how it works," conceded Mavis "but I never thought that I could be good enough to do what you suggest, but I will definitely give it some thought."

"Well, good for you," said Phillipa, "and on the point of whether or not you are good enough, take it from me you are!"

They separated and agreed to keep in touch and Mavis made her way back towards the railway station feeling totally elated. She was pleased to note that there was more than enough time to get home and get changed in readiness to meet George at the Jubilee Inn for a pre-operation meeting with Charlie Chivers and the Detective Des Onions.

Before returning however Mavis made sure that she visited a quality department store in town to purchase some of the items of make-up which Phillipa had recommended.

Chapter Fifty-one
The Nite Club

Charlie Chivers the International Detective was seated on a stool at the bar of the Jubilee Inn. He sipped his beer and gazed nostalgically at the picture of Reg, the landlord, with Jayne Mansfield. Reg himself leaned over the bar and asked," How's it going Charlie all right?"

"Yeah," drawled Charlie. "I was miles away. How about you?"

"Fine, fine," Reg assured him. "I'm going to London soon so there might be a new photo on the wall before long." He indicated the wall behind him with a wave of his hand.

"Well make sure it's another photo to match this one," said Charlie indicating the photograph of Jayne Mansfield. Reg gave a wry smile and said, "That one's not too popular with the wife I'm afraid. That's why she tucked it away behind the optics. If I turned up with another one the same I don't know what she'd do with it."

"You could put them side by side," said Charlie, "then they'd be two abreast."

Reg chuckled, "Yes very good."

Des Onions arrived next just as Charlie was finishing his pint. He bought Charlie a re-fill but declined to have anything to drink himself as he was on duty. They sat down together at a table. "So it's just you and me is it?" said Des ironically. "I do hope your friends are going to turn up. My mob are all geared up and waiting round the corner. If your pals don't turn up there will be a lot of wasted expenses and I'll have a lot of explaining to do."

"Oh, I'm sure they'll be here soon." said Charlie without any conviction in his voice. "What about the Special Branch? Are they poised and ready?"

"Definitely," said Des. "That's why it's so vital that your friends arrive."

Charlie could appreciate the importance of what Des was saying but was more anxious than his seemingly casual demeanour indicated. He need not have worried. Pete had made sure that nothing would go wrong. He came into the pub in the company of Sandra and Vincent and Lizzy. Shortly after George and Mavis arrived together.

They all sat together around the table and Des instructed everyone as to what was going to happen and what was required of each of them. He produced some bank notes, which were brand new and which had been finger-printed, which he gave to Vincent along with some specific directions as to what he should or shouldn't do. He also attempted to lecture Sandra about her involvement in the evening's proceedings. She did not try to argue with him but simply assured him that she would not enter the premises.

Charlie wished everyone good fortune and assured Des that he would not be present either inside or outside the Nite Club because as he himself said, "At my age I would stick out like a sore thumb." He advised everyone that he would stay exactly where he was and would see them all later back in the Jubilee Inn to celebrate a successful operation.

The others made their way on foot to the High Street. As they neared the Nite Club premises Des Onions excused himself and said he was going to join up with his CID team. Pete said he just had to check on his pals from the rugby club and would be straight back. That left George and Mavis with Vincent. Sandra had already gone to find her cameraman. When they got to the Nite Club they found a queue at the door. The youngsters were keen to gain entry early in order to pay the reduced entrance fee.

When they were waiting for the queue to die down George spotted the Gibson twins amongst the door staff. He whispered to Vincent, "Where do they do the deals?"

Vincent said, "Upstairs, in a back room."

Eventually they reached the head of the queue, paid their entrance fees and made their way into the main dancing area. Although it was early there were plenty of people in already. George bought some drinks and they moved away from the bar. Mavis and himself secured a table sat down with Lizzy. Vincent wandered over to the DJ centre to say hello to his friend.

After ten minutes Pete re-appeared and joined them at the table. The early evening attendance crowd had settled in and were enjoying the music. No other people appeared to be entering now and so the door staff were reduced to a minimum. George spotted the Gibson twins patrolling around the dance area.

Vincent returned from the DJ and sat next to Pete who told him that now was the time to affect the deal, while there was a lull until the next influx of customers following the closing time at the pubs. Vincent gave a pained grimace and nodded. He rose and made his way across the room to where the twins were standing. He showed them the handful of bank notes which he held and then placed the hand in his pocket. The twins glanced at each other and then indicated with a nod of the head that Vincent should follow them. Pete had risen out of his seat and followed them out of the room into a corridor which led to the toilets area. On the left were the Gentlemen's and, on the right the ladies'. At the end of the corridor was a large private room which the club owner, Giovanni used as an office. It was there that the twins went accompanied by Vincent.

Pete positioned himself by the doorway of the Gentlemen's toilet and waited to see what might happen. He was joined almost immediately by Mavis and Lizzy who both stood in the open doorway of the ladies' toilet. Mavis kept her heel on the door to prevent it closing.

In the office room Vincent handed over the bank notes to one of the twins who immediately counted it carefully and pocketed it. He then nodded to his brother who produced a small plastic bag from his pocket and handed it over to Vincent. As the hand over was taking place the door behind Vincent opened and someone came into the room. Vincent turned to leave and found himself staring into the face of Jimmy Pearce.

"What's he doing here?" demanded Jimmy. Vincent meanwhile slipped past him and closed the door behind him. "Just a little business," said one of the twins to Jimmy.

"But he's a nark," shouted Jimmy. "I know him, if he gets away from here, he'll have the police all over this place."

"What!" exclaimed one of the twins. Then he shouted, "Let's get him quick."

When Vincent had come through the door, he looked ashen and terrified. He got as far as Pete and Mavis and blurted out, "They've sussed me. It's Jimmy Pearce he recognised me. They'll kill me."

Mavis immediately grabbed him by the arm and almost threw him into the ladies' toilet. She pulled Lizzy in after her and just managed to say,

"Keep them busy," to Pete before slamming the door. The office door then opened and the twins emerged looking furious followed by Jimmy Pearce.

"Where did he go?" demanded one of them of Pete, who was still leaning nonchalantly against the door jamb of the Gents' toilet.

Pete shrugged and said, "Don't know, downstairs I think." He pointed into the gents' and said, "there's no-one in here." One of the twins went straight into the gents' to search the room. The other twin looked from Pete to the door of the Ladies and paused for a split second. "That's the Ladies" said Pete meaningfully.

The twin looked back at Pete and said, "Don't fuck with me my friend. You haven't got your giant with you tonight." He then kicked open the door to the ladies' toilet and marched in.

Mavis was seated at a wash hand basin applying some eye make- up and checking her reflection in the mirror. "Do you mind," she shouted in as outraged a voice as she could manage. The twin looked around the room. There was only one toilet cubicle and he walked towards it. "That's my friend in there," shouted Mavis in the same outraged tone.

"I'm looking for a guy who might have come into here," said the twin who began thumping on the door with the heel of his hand.

"Do you mind!" shrieked Mavis, "that's my friend Lizzy in there and she's not well. Leave her alone." The twin got down on his hands and knees and tried to look under the door to see the legs of whoever was inside. Mavis continued with her offended outrage. "How dare you. This is a ladies' toilet. It's an outrage! I'll report you to the police if you don't leave immediately. Are you all right Lizzy?" she asked in a concerned way.

Lizzy responded from within crying out, "Leave me alone. I don't feel well."

This seemed to convince the twin who was satisfied that it was a woman's voice he had heard and only one pair of legs that he could see in the cubicle. Reluctantly he decided to continue his search elsewhere.

As he left the ladies' he met his twin brother leaving the gents' The latter shook his head, and said, "Empty."

"I told you so" said Pete who was still nonchalantly leaning against the door jamb.

The twin who had been inside the ladies' and who seemed to be the one in charge, looked menacingly into the eyes of Pete and said, "I don't have time for you now but I would advise you to stay out of my way." Then he said to his brother, "Let's try downstairs and see if he's still in the building." They both rushed off downstairs closely followed by Jimmy Pearce who had followed them out of the office.

Pete immediately went into the ladies' toilet to find Mavis still in there. There was nothing in the room except for the toilet cubicle and the wash basin. There was a waste bin below the sink and a large fire extinguisher in the corner.

"Quick," he said, "they've gone downstairs. We have only a few seconds before they come back up."

Lizzy and Vincent came out of the cubicle when they heard Pete's voice. Vincent said, "I don't want to go downstairs. They'll see me and catch me and I'm really scared."

"You don't have to," Pete assured him. "This is a fire escape," he said pointing to a door in the corner of the room. He moved over to it and pressed the emergency lever and the door opened to reveal a fire escape stairway to the back of the premises. "Go on," said Pete, pushing Vincent through the door. Almost immediately after Vincent had exited the corridor door burst open and the twins entered. One glance told them where Vincent had gone and one of them went straight out onto the fire escape while the other, advancing on Pete, said, "You just couldn't keep your nose out, could you? I'm going to break your fucking neck!"

He made a lunge at Pete who was too quick witted for him. He eased sideways away from the twin's grasp and tugged at his arm and dashed him against the doorway clearly damaging his shoulder. While the man was shaking himself together Pete stepped forward and lined him up and hit him as hard as he could with his fist in the twin's left eye.

Pete felt an immediate shock of pain to his hand and heard a cracking sound. He was not sure if the sound was his own bones in the hand breaking or the sound of the twin's eye socket disintegrating. In any event he judged that to remain in a confined space with such a muscular man did not make any sense, He also wanted to lead the twin away from the girls. He ran through the doorway onto the stairway and descended as quickly as he could. The twin followed him cursing.

The foot of the fire escape was positioned in an alley which ran down the side of the Nite Club premises. It ended in a tiny courtyard which contained some garages. The alley was very dark and appeared to be completely empty except for the twin who had already descended. He was searching for Vincent who was cowering behind a dustbin and shivering with fear. As the first twin neared the dustbin Vincent lost his nerve and pushed the bin towards the twin and scuttled to the far end of the courtyard.

As Pete and the second twin reached the bottom of the stairway the first twin announced, "Here he is." Looking into the shadowy corner. "I've got him. Let's finish this."

Pete shouted, "Let him go or it'll be the worst for you." Even as he uttered these words Pete knew that he held no threat for the twins. He already realised that he had broken his hand when he hit the second twin who now looked as if the blow had had no effect. The man thrust Pete aside with distain and moved in to assist his brother to apprehend Vincent who now cowered in the dark corner.

"You heard what the man said," shouted a voice from the High Street end of the alley.

The twins turned to face the man whose voice they had heard. "Who are you?" said one of them.

"Just a friend." Was the reply. "Now let him go or else"

The dominant twin appraised the situation. Looking at the man who had his back to the High Street lights which afforded only a silhouette figure. The twin was not impressed by what he saw.

"You don't know what you're dealing with old man. I advise you to fuck off while you can or you'll be sorry."

"I know exactly what I'm dealing with. I know a foul-mouthed bleeder when I see one," he said. He added, "Orl right, Pete?"

"Fine thanks, Arthur," said Pete.

The twin moved in on Arthur who lowered his head and charged the man. To Arthur it was just another scrum and he had experienced hundreds of those. Despite the fact that the twin was twenty-five years younger and pumped up by steroids the canny old prop forward gave the twin a lot more trouble than the man was expecting. He was already under the disadvantage of not being able to see clearly due to the state of his eye which Pete had punched. It had already swollen and puffed out almost entirely blocking his vision. In addition, the old war horse Arthur was gouging the other eye with one hand whilst punching the twin in the ribs with the other.

Eventually the superior muscular ability of the twin prevailed and he threw Arthur to the floor and scrambled on top of him and began pummelling the older man in the head.

Finally, the lights went out for the twin. This sensation was due partly to the High Street lights being blocked by something or someone and partly due to the blow which Gorgon delivered to the twin's head. The latter was poleaxed and slept quietly on top of Arthur who struggled to get out from underneath him.

"Right," came the cry from the other twin who had just caught hold of Vincent around the neck. He held Vincent aloft like a rag doll and warned everyone. "My brother and I are walking out of here, and if anyone makes any attempt to stop us, I will snap his neck." As he delivered this warning Vincent uttered a squeal of pain and fear. Everybody froze for a moment until there was heard a loud cracking sound after which the twin dropped Vincent and collapsed on the floor.

Next, a car's headlights, lit up the alleyway to reveal that the twin had been floored by a fire extinguisher which had been thrown from the halfway landing of the fire escape by Mavis. She had aimed the extinguisher at his head but it had connected with his shoulder which had broken. Colleagues of Des Onions swarmed into the alley and arrested the twins who looked in bad shape. It transpired that some further officers had arrested Jimmy Pearce who had been apprehended by George who had made his way upstairs in search of Mavis.

Des Onions was more than satisfied by the way in which things had gone. The Gibson twins and Jimmy Pearce were all bundled into a police van and taken away. The only thing that slightly irked him was the fact that Giovanni Pettacinni had not been on the premises when the drug dealing took place under the eyes of a number of police officers. However, he thought, there was already plenty of evidence available in lots of other directions.

"Well," he said rubbing his hands together with satisfaction. "That went about as well as it could. Now the long hard work for us starts. We have to make a few more arrests and then we charge them all. If you want to go back to the Jubilee for a celebratory drink you can let Charlie know how well it went. Tell him I'll be in touch with him soon but obviously I'll be fully tied up for the next forty-eight hours or so."

The only member of the remaining group who had any reason to complain was Pete who was nursing a broken hand. Despite this he agreed to accompany everyone to the Jubilee Inn but said that first he would try to locate Sandra who had earlier been talking to customers who were queuing outside the night club. She was still there with her cameraman, having done a piece to camera whilst the police vehicles were in attendance. She was just finishing her work when Pete arrived and whisked her off to the Jubilee Inn for a drink before closing time.

The International Detective was still seated in the Jubilee Inn and wrestling with the Daily Mail crossword puzzle along with his fourth pint of bitter. Since the others had left, he had not left his seat except to go to the bar to get his drink refilled and for frequent visits to the toilet. When they came in, they were all exultant some for more reason than others. Vincent was wholly relieved to have escaped a beating by the Gibson twins and was overjoyed to feel safe again. Mavis was full of excitement. She had not felt any fear throughout the incident but merely the adrenaline effect that the whole episode had had upon her.

George had been, without doubt, excited by the adventure but at the same time always anxious about the outcome of it all. He had to admit to himself that, as with the rugby match which he had recently played in, the presence throughout of Pete had encouraged and re-assured him. Pete himself showed no indication of excitement. He behaved as one who experiences such happenings every day. He was only amused by the sparkle of excitement in the eyes of Mavis.

Arthur treated the whole thing as he would the aftermath of a game of rugby. He played the part of the victorious skipper as he had so often done at the Old Sodfordian Clubhouse. He insisted that everyone should have a full glass and drink to the well-deserved victory. As he had done so often before, he analysed the events retrospectively, "The trouble with these body building bleeders," he confided to all, "is that they have no experience of hand-to-hand conflict. They might be strong but they have no moves. They train by lifting weights on bars and chewing steroids but they're not really fit. They don't know the meaning of the word innovation." George reflected that he was amazed that Arthur himself knew the meaning of the word.

"They don't have a side step or a feint," Arthur continued "they are so bleedin' predictable. Not like Jake here," he added, thumping Jake on the shoulder. "That was a nice right hook you showed that bleeder who was on top of me. Just in time. I was just about to knock his head off."

Everyone laughed including Jake who had been very modest about his own part in the proceedings.

"And the look on the other bleeder's face when that fire extinguisher hit im was priceless," Arthur concluded. "That was a fine shot," he said congratulating Mavis on her aim.

Mavis herself said that the evening had been the most exciting of her life. George whispered in her ear, "But I thought that was last Saturday, not tonight?"

Mavis blushed and gave George a kiss on the cheek. "You know what I mean," she said.

Reg Partridge called, "Time please, ladies and gentlemen." Arthur insisted on buying one more drink for himself and Charlie Chivers. The latter was in good humour having heard not only that the evening had been successful but that Des Onions would soon be in touch with him. He hoped this would mean some financial reward for all the hard work he had put in.

Vincent and Lizzy decided they would go home to bed and said goodbye to everyone. George and Mavis also decided to go home. As they stood to leave Sandra was examining Pete's hand. By now it looked the size of a boxing glove and Sandra was concerned. Pete tried to pooh-pooh her anxiety, but in the end had to agree to let her drive him to the hospital.

George escorted Mavis home and as they walked along hand-in-hand he told her what an amazing person he thought she was. As they reached her house, he embraced her and kissed her passionately, "I do love you," he said.

"I love you too," she replied.

Chapter Fifty-two
Jeremy and Phillipa

On the same Friday evening Jeremy Fallow QC arrived at his brother's flat in Charlton Square having just left his Crown Court chambers. Although he had visited his brother's flat once or twice before he found that he had to do a tour of inspection to familiarise himself with the premises.

It was a generous three-bedroom ground floor flat overlooking a charming Victorian square. It also enjoyed an enclosed rear garden accessed through the kitchen door. The lounge was a very large room which contained two matching leather Chesterfield sofas coloured green. The master bedroom was used by his brother Roger and so Jeremy decided that he ought not to use that room. He inspected the second largest bedroom which was almost as big as the master bedroom. It also overlooked the rear enclosed garden area. He thought it was a very nice room.

On his way he had visited an off-licence property in the neighbourhood and had purchased some wine. He had realised that he did not know whether Phillipa preferred red wine or white and so he bought three bottles of each and decided that anything that wasn't consumed he would leave at the flat for his brother.

The doorbell rang and he rushed to answer it. He opened the door and there stood Phillipa, looking
, he thought, beautiful. She was wearing her blue suit and white blouse which was her usual court attire which she always wore beneath her court gown. Over her shoulder she carried a duffle bag which is commonly seen among barristers who use them to carry their gowns wigs and other accoutrements into court.

They embraced on the doorstep and shared a brief kiss. They both appeared to perhaps be experiencing some nervousness about the meeting which was perhaps surprising in view of the deep intimacy of their last encounter. Jeremy in particular felt anxiety. Perhaps, he thought to himself, their first encounter had been so wonderful and erotic that any subsequent meeting would be bound to be a disappointment.

"I've come straight from court," she said, as he showed her into the lounge. "But I have brought a change of clothes," she said, and deposited her duffle bag onto one of the Chesterfields. She flopped down onto the other with a sigh.

"Hard day?" asked Jeremy.

She nodded and thrust out her bottom lip and expelled air skywards. "Yes. A tough afternoon in the Matrimonial Court," she said. "The easiest part of the day was the brief appearance in your court."

"Ah yes," said Jeremy, "the cricket bat assault. It was a nice surprise to see you."

"Yeah," she said, "yet another example of Gus making a complete buffoon of himself. He must be the only one stupid enough to run a 'not guilty' plea, without a defence. And they voted him Head of Chambers!"

Jeremy smiled and said, "Can I offer you a drink to take away the stress of the day?"

"Oh, yes please, Jeremy," she said, "what have you got?" He showed her the wine which he had purchased which he had placed on the coffee table. "Hmm," she said, "lovely. We can enjoy that later, but right now, I'd love a nice gin and tonic."

Jeremy said he would look and see what was available. He went into the kitchen area and found a bottle of gin and some tonic. His brother however appeared to have no lemons or fresh fruit of any kind. He returned with her gin and tonic and also a menu from the local Indian restaurant. "No lemons I'm afraid, but I've found the menu for the Indian tonight. What do you fancy?"

They both made their choice and Jeremy telephoned the order. As the restaurant was literally just around the corner, he arranged to collect in thirty minutes time. They sat down while Phillipa drank her gin and tonic and Jeremy sipped a brandy.

"Yes," he said. "Humphrey can be monumentally stupid at times. As you say he is not really suited to be a Head of Chambers. Mind you, a counsel is only as good as the brief that is delivered to him. Did you notice the solicitor sitting behind him? The term 'flash Harry' comes to mind. Do you know him?"

"Yes, I do," she said. "His name is Simon Nibble, and I think the term 'flash Harry' is not too far removed. He instructs Algie quite a lot who always complains that the briefs are never fully informative. Furthermore, he had the nerve the other week to offer Algie and I a free holiday in his newly acquired holiday apartment in Tenerife."

Jeremy raised his eyebrows. "Well I never," he said. "Did Algie want to accept?"

"No, not at all," she said, "and neither did I. I think the offer implied that we should go there and share it with them. That makes me shudder to even think about."

"Anyway," said Jeremy, "shall we walk round the corner to collect our food?"

They strolled around the block and entered the Indian restaurant. It was a long narrow premises with tables on either side of an aisle. The reception desk and the waiting area was at the front of the restaurant. Jeremy gave his name and they took a seat while the waiter went to the kitchen at the far end. They stood up as he approached with a large paper carrier bag containing their food. Phillipa hissed, "Oh shit," and turned her back on the waiter and whispered to Jeremy,

"I've just seen Gus. He's sitting at the far end."

"Really?" said Jeremy looking over her shoulder towards the far end of the restaurant. By then the waiter had reached them and so they took the food and he paid the bill at the counter and they then exited the restaurant.

"Did he see you?" Jeremy asked as they walked back.

"I don't know," she responded. "I can't be sure. He might have done." Jeremy sucked in his breath. "Is this a big problem for you?" she asked.

"No," he said, "not at all. I told you at my chambers that this was a life changing event and I meant it. Public knowledge may have come slightly sooner than I anticipated." She leaned forward and kissed him then tucked her arm in his and they walked back to his brother's flat. Once there they busied themselves in the kitchen/dining area unpacking and identifying the items in the bag. They dished up the food onto plates and sat facing each other across a small table. "Oh, I nearly forgot," said Jeremy. "The wine. Which would you prefer? Red or white?"

"Red, please," said Phillipa.

"Well, I've got a rather nice Chianti, or an even nicer Rioja, which would you prefer?"

"Hmm, Rioja, please" she said.

He went into the other room, collected the bottle, and returned to the dining area and opened the bottle and poured two glasses. Phillipa raised her glass and sipped the wine. "Hmm, that's lovely," she said.

"And so are you," responded Jeremy. "In fact, you are ravishing and I still can't believe I'm lucky enough to be here with you."

She smiled at him lovingly, "You are no luckier than I am," she said "this food is delicious, the wine is memorable and the company is perfect. How lucky am I?"

They worked their way through the various dishes and also finished the bottle of wine. As they finished the food she asked him mischievously, "Did you bring your robe and wig with you tonight?"

Jeremy blushed and said, "Why no, I never thought. How stupid of me. I'm sorry. I didn't realise how important it was for your enjoyment."

"It's not at all," she said emphatically. Role playing is exciting and stimulating but by no means essential. Sometimes for me it is just as good to take off all my clothes and simply lie in a warm bed with the man of my dreams." And that is exactly what she did.

Detective Chief Inspector Desmond O'Nighons had a long night after the twins had been arrested and locked up in the local police cells. His first priority was to apply pressure to the weakest element of the suspects in the hope that some information could be obtained quickly which might be used against the other elements. The weakest element he decided, was of course Jimmy Pearce

. Des knew by instinct, and from previous personal experience with Jimmy Pearce that the latter was weak-willed and spineless and more than willing to betray any co-defendants in exchange for a reduction in any charges levelled against him.

His problem was that despite his own lack of fibre Jimmy had, by dint of frequent arrests and police station detentions, picked up some knowledge of police procedures and the rights of detainees. Thus, Jimmy's first reaction to arrest and detention was that he refused to say anything to Des and Co (as he himself put it 'going no comment') except in the presence of his solicitor Simon Nibble.

This was no more than Des expected. He knew that under PACE (the Police and Criminal Evidence Act) he could detain Jimmy initially for a period of twenty-four hours before charging him. He decided that he did not wish to waste an official recorded interview by allowing Jimmy to reply 'no comment' to every question. Instead, he applied pressure by popping into Jimmy's cell to assure him that an interview was imminent. "I can't understand what you thought you were doing getting yourself in with the big boys, Jimmy," he said. "Usually, we would go through the normal procedures. There would be a quick interview, you would go 'no comment' and we would charge and release you. But this time it's different Jimmy. This is much more serious."

"I want my solicitor," protested Jimmy, who was already starting to panic. "I want Mr Nibble here before I say anything."

"No can do," replied Des, with a wry grin. "Mr Nibble won't be going anywhere for quite a while. Even as we speak my officers will be arresting him for conspiracy to be involved with the same sorry adventure which you are part of and other charges over and above that. You can have a solicitor by all means but not Mr Nibble I'm afraid. You won't be getting a bent solicitor tonight, Jimmy, but I can offer you a pucker one, from the duty solicitor rota, who will no doubt advise you to plead guilty and tell us everything you know.

Jimmy was flabbergasted to hear about Simon Nibble. "You're pulling my leg, aren't you?" he said trying to laugh it all off. "I'm not talking to you until he's here beside me."

"I'm afraid not, Jimmy," said Des. "I'm telling you the truth and I'd advise you to do the same. Eddie Sharp is being arrested too, him being the employer of the Gibson twins who were acting under his instructions. Of course they are saying that they were only doing what he told them to do and that they had no idea what you were supplying them with and that basically it was all yours and Eddies' fault."

"That's crap," exclaimed Jimmy with an element of alarm in his voice. "They knew exactly what they were doing."

"I'm sure you're right," allowed Des, magnanimously but of course we've only got their version of the story so far."

"But you can't believe what those bastards say," suggested Jimmy. "They'd say anything."

"Absolutely," said Des, "but as I said we've only got their side of the story so far. In any event, Jimmy, as I told you this is far more serious than the usual pushing of a few harmless drugs. This is big time stuff, Jimmy. The Special Branch in London are on to this one which has connections on the continent with big international dealers. I can't really interview properly until I get the go-ahead from London. Some of this stuff which has already been passed on to you and others has caused the death of at least one young man who was unfortunate enough to use it. So this is not just an ordinary investigation into a small amount of dealing. This is a murder or manslaughter investigation, Jimmy. You just think about that. Now I'm going to have to leave you alone in your cell for a few more hours while I gather more evidence and when I hear from the Special Branch then maybe I'll be in a position to do a proper interview with you. Meanwhile you just stay here and think about things. If there's anything you feel you want to tell me then you let the Custody Sergeant know and I'll be happy to listen but be assured, Jimmy, this thing is bigger than you think. You could be looking at a long stretch here."

Des then left Jimmy in his cell and went back upstairs to supervise proceedings. His second-in-command, a seasoned veteran detective sergeant advised him that the twins had not said a word. Indeed, the one who had been hit with the fire extinguisher had been taken to hospital, under guard, for treatment.

"So," said Des, "I've just left Jimmy Pearce to fester in his cell having planted the seed in his mind that everyone else will be saying that it's all his fault. I am confident that he will soon be singing like a canary. In the meantime, I think it is time to go and arrest Eddie Sharp and his solicitor."

Jeremy awoke early when the first beams of sunlight penetrated the venetian blinds in the bedroom. He glanced to his left to see Phillipa's head resting in the crook of his arm. She was breathing deeply. He marvelled yet again at her astonishing beauty and still had to tell himself that he wasn't dreaming.

He eased himself out from under her and crept gingerly out of the bed. He scooped up the pair of boxer shorts which he had discarded on the floor the evening before and put them on. He then crept into the kitchen and made a pot of tea as quietly as he could. He poured two cups and placed them on a tray and carried them back to the bedroom.

Phillipa stirred as he re-entered the room and placed her cup on the bedside table beside her. She opened her eyes and watched him as he took the other cup to his side of the bed. Then he moved to the window and opened the blinds to allow the full effect of the sunshine into the room. "Hmm, Jeremy you still have a wonderful figure," she said. He gave a silent 'thank you' to his brother for the list of daily exercises which he had devised and which he (Jeremy) had performed daily for a while.

"You are too kind," he said, "and I know that I don't deserve it. You on the other hand are like a beautiful angel and I am still pinching myself."

She sat up in bed revealing her bare breasts to him. He was still standing at the window and looked at her in dumb- struck admiration. "You said you thought my breasts were bigger than you had expected," she said coyly, cupping one of them with her hand. "Do you think they are too big?"

"Oh no, no, no," he replied almost in horror, they are absolutely perfect." As he uttered these words he was conscious of his erection which the boxer shorts were not able to conceal.

"Well..." she said, even more coyly, "would you like to handle them for me. I always think it feels nicer when you do it."

"I'd like to kiss and suck them too," said Jeremy moving round the bed towards her.

"Hmm," she said archly, "I think I would like that too."

He sat down on the bed beside her and leant over to cup one of her breasts in his hand. He leant further and took her nipple in his mouth and sucked it for a while. She reached up and began to fondle his ear almost as if he were a faithful dog. He strayed over to the other breast and took that nipple in his mouth. Phillipa leaned back against the bed head and sighed. "Hmm, Jeremy, that is so wonderful."

She reached down to encompass his erection on the outside of his boxer shorts. Jeremy continued to kiss her breasts and sighed also. He came up for air and sat back alongside her. She massaged his chest sensually and then moved down to his stomach and wormed her way inside the top of his shorts. She gently grasped his manhood and leaned across to kiss him on

336

the ear. As she did so she murmured to him, "Ooh, Jeremy. Does that feel good for you?"

"Oh yes!" he sighed, and reached down to remove his shorts. She gradually moved across and down, kissing and licking him. As she reached his abdomen, he gave a loud triumphant cry.

She took his penis in her mouth and sucked gently for a few moments during which Jeremy was transported to an erotic place. She drew back her head and then straddled him and, taking him with both hands she gently massaged herself with his penis. She gradually became more stimulated by this contact which was very like masturbation. Jeremy meanwhile remained in his own erotic heaven.

She expertly brought herself almost to a climax and then mounted Jeremy with a sensual sigh. Simultaneously he cried out as he himself climaxed. She then brought herself off by giving two or three swift thrusts while Jeremy remained erect. She collapsed onto his chest and continued to kiss and suck his ear whispering, "Ooh, Jeremy, same as before, best ever. We really do have something, do we not?"

He clutched her tightly, "Ooh, yes, superlative. You are miles beyond anything I have previously experienced. In retrospect I realise that the initial attraction that I felt when I first saw you was not a mere fancy which a man feels for an attractive female, but the real thing. For several years I have disciplined myself not to touch or approach you but all the time deep inside I wanted nothing else. My only regret is that we didn't start sooner."

She sat up, still straddling him and said with an enticing smile, "You are right of course. My continual flirting with you was just that. I am not by nature an habitual flirt. Nor am I promiscuous ordinarily. I have never indulged in it with other men. I was only ever drawn to you and flirted with you instinctively. Aren't you glad I did so?"

Jeremy looked up at this bare breasted goddess who was seated on top of him. "It was the most wonderful, stimulating and erotic moment of my life when you came into my chambers without your underwear," he assured her

They lay together for a while both quietly reflecting to themselves how wonderful it was to find another to whom one was so strongly attracted and doubly so to discover that the other felt the same way about you.

Eventually they rose and got dressed and then went into the kitchen area. Jeremy put a pot of coffee on the stove and then went out to the newsagent around the corner to get The Times newspaper. When he got back the coffee pot was simmering and he made some toast. They both sat together at the table eating and drinking. Jeremy attempted the crossword puzzle, something he did every day, and was surprised to note that when she looked across at the clues in an attempt to assist him, she was even more knowledgeable with the question than he was. "Do you do this crossword every day?" he asked

"No never," she said.

"Hmm," he reflected "I always prided myself that one's ability to solve these clues depended completely on getting inside the mind of the clue setter and here you are...." he added somewhat begrudgingly, "never having attempted this puzzle before, and you turn out to be better and quicker at it than me. That is something I would not have expected."

"Ooh" she cried in fake outrage, "is that a back-handed misogynistic compliment?"

Jeremy laughed out loud, "No," he said, "if anything it should have been a straightforward compliment. As well as being very beautiful you are also extremely intelligent. It is just that you do not display that intelligence overtly. Or perhaps it is the case that I cannot see beyond your physical beauty. You would have been a much more suitable candidate for Head of Chambers than your husband and certainly better than Humphrey."

"It's funny," she said, "I was saying similar things to a young girl yesterday. The one who was sat behind me in your court. Did you notice her?"

"Of course," said Jeremy, "a very pretty young lady."

"Yes well..." said Phillipa, as if pretending to sound jealous that Jeremy had referred to Mavis as very pretty.

"She has brought me two divorce cases and has provided comprehensive notes in assistance thereto. She also brought me the case of the poor unfortunate woman who had been attacked with a cricket bat. Her notes and general ability reveal to me someone who is very intelligent and caring and quite passionate about the Law and Justice. And yet her general demeanour conceals her intellectual ability. She behaves as if she is less intelligent than she really is. Or is it ....?" she said enquiringly, "that she is just so very pretty that everyone is distracted from her intellect?"

"Probably," admitted Jeremy ruefully, "but I suspect that with you as her mentor she may begin to show the world how clever she really is."

Phillipa said that unfortunately she would have to go home in order to feed and see to her horses and secondly to ensure that she would be home when Algernon returned.

Chapter Fifty-three
Des Closes In

Des Onions and his team arrested Simon Nibble and Eddie Sharp at their respective houses and on each occasion, armed with a search warrant, Des left several officers to carry out a thorough search of each property. Not that Des necessarily expected to find anything incriminating at either house. He already had chapter and verse from Charlie as to where to locate the files at the offices of Huw Roberts & Co solicitors and knew how incriminating they would be. The private houses Des felt were just the icing on the cake. If they provided anything of interest then so much the better. Otherwise, the following day he would lead a search of the solicitors' offices and obtain the actual documents which he already held copies of.

He had a little more trouble locating Giovanni Pettacinni. His first port of call was his home address but that produced no result since the house was clearly unoccupied when he called. He tried again at the Nite Club but found that the owner was still not on the premises. Enquiries of the staff revealed that Giovanni was expected to arrive in approximately half an hour. Des and those accompanying him duly waited and as soon as he arrived, he was arrested and removed to the police station.

Des knew he had the right to detain all three arrestees for a maximum of twenty-four hours before charging them or applying to the magistrates for an extension of the time for holding them. He was confident that by now Jimmy Pearce would be tearing his hair out but he thought he would let him stew for a bit longer.

Next, he tried Eddie Sharp from whom, initially at least, he was not expecting any co-operation. He visited him in his cell and said, "You know why you were arrested Eddie, because we told you at the time. Is there anything you want to tell us before we have a formal interview?"

"I'm not saying a fucking word to you lot until my solicitor is present" he responded.

"And that would be?" enquired Des.

"Simon Nibble," said Eddie.

"That I'm afraid is not possible," said Des.

"Mr Nibble is not far away but he is unable to help you. He is under arrest for the same reason as yourself. You may have any other solicitor of your choice or one can be provided for you from the court legal aid rota.

I'll leave you alone for a while to think about things. We will be carrying out a formal interview in due course."

Des moved on to Simon Nibble who did not look too comfortable in his cell. He briefly outlined the case against him and suggested that he might be interested in making a statement. "You are, as you know, entitled to the advice of a solicitor If you do not have one then a solicitor can be provided from the rota to which you belong. As you are an experienced solicitor who deals in criminal matters, I would imagine that you would feel confident to be interviewed without legal advice? You let us know if there is any solicitor you wish to be present when you are interviewed, otherwise, I will assume that you feel able to be interviewed alone."

Having said this Des left him alone in his cell. He felt quite happy with the progress so far. In respect of both Eddie and Simon Nibble he still had approximately twenty hours to run on the detention time allowed under PACE. He needed to obtain the original documents from Simon Nibble's office which would provide sufficient evidence of their guilt. He did not wish to rely upon the copy documents which he had already received from Charlie because of the way in which this evidence had been obtained namely Charlie's illegal entry to the premises. Once the search warrant had been used and the original documents seized, Des knew that his hand would be strengthened enormously. He knew that he could not serve the search warrant at the offices of Huw Roberts & Co until Simon's staff had opened up the offices. This would be in a few hours' time which would still allow him twelve hours or so of detention time after the search of the offices. In any event, he assured himself, if time began to run out, he could always make an application to the magistrates for an extension of the time.

Des decided that he would let Giovanni stew for a while in his cell while he liaised on the telephone with the Special Branch in London. In a lengthy call he learned that those in London had successfully completed their end of the deal. They had caught red handed those who had supplied Jimmy Pearce. Having raided the London address they seized a large amount of Class A drugs which were still at the premises. The haul, they estimated to Des had a street value of over one million pounds. They were very elated not only because they had caught the middlemen red-handed but also because they had already given them information in the form of names and addresses and contact details, of those who had supplied them. The line of distribution had already been passed on to their colleagues in Amsterdam who were presently acting on the information. Des made a careful note of all the details.

He now thought that the time was right to apply some more pressure to Jimmy Pearce. He went down to his cell to see him. Jimmy looked very anxious when he opened the door. "Well Jimmy, good news," he said, "your pals in Paddington have been arrested and were caught red handed with the remains of the haul some of which they supplied to you about a week ago. Furthermore, they have given my colleagues full details of all those who supplied them and details of all their customers which includes you Jimmy. So, what does that mean? you may well ask. Well, it means we have enough evidence to charge and convict you without even getting a statement from you."

Jimmy looked even more worried. "You can't take everything they say as gospel. It's only their word against mine."

"Well…" said Des, "It's not so much a question of what I might believe it's more a question of what a jury would believe isn't it? Anyway, if you want to go 'no comment' all the way through, that's up to you but I am one hundred per cent certain that with what we've got already we would achieve a conviction. If you wanted to give us a statement then it might be possible that the court might reduce your sentence but either way you are going down Jimmy. Whether it is for six months or six years is entirely up to you."

Jimmy began to chew on his knuckle and looked even more nervous. "OK," he said, "but I need some assurances from you."

"Concerning what?" asked Des.

"A non-custodial sentence," he said, "in exchange for all information about everyone else."

"But I'm not sure that you know that much about the others that we don't already know and can already prove. Besides Jimmy, a non-custodial sentence for supplying Class A drugs worth up to a million? You've got to be kidding."

"Oh, come on Mr O," he pleaded. "I can give you plenty of information that you have no idea about. If you put me inside and I have to do time in the same place as those twins I'm a dead man. What would you like to know? I can give you chapter and verse. Just keep me out."

"Well, I may be able to help you but only if you tell me everything you know. I will get you a solicitor from the rota who will no doubt advise you to make no comment but if that is the case then the deal is off and you go down anyway along with the twins. It's up to you."

"OK," said Jimmy with immense relief — it's a deal."

On Monday morning Tom Richards and Bill Butler shared their usual cup of tea and thirty minutes of peace and quiet in the glasshouse. Tom was particularly pleased because the Arsenal had achieved an away win at White Hart Lane on Saturday. "You are always so cheerful when they beat the Spurs," observed Bill.

"Of course," said Tom, "north London rivalry. There's nothing quite like it. How does it feel to be in sole charge of the office this morning? I take it that this is Mr Pigg's first day in his new Regional Office post."

"That's right," said Bill "I never thought it would happen. Especially immediately after my stroke. For a while I never expected to return at all never mind end up in charge. Mind you the way things are going I don't know how long this office will remain open."

"What would you do if it closed?" asked Tom.

"I would probably take an early retirement package. I certainly wouldn't consider re- location at my time of life. Still, at least I would retire on a higher salary thanks to this unexpected promotion."

"Unexpected maybe," said Tom, "but not undeserved."

"Thanks very much," said Bill. "I wonder how our colleagues got on over the weekend?"

"No doubt we will hear all about it shortly," said Tom. Almost precisely on cue George arrived next and said his hello's to Tom and Bill.

"So what happened on Friday night?" asked Bill.

George spread his arms and puffed out his cheeks. "Well," he said, "I don't even know where to start. I think I'll make myself a cup of tea then make a stab at it." He wandered off to boil the kettle and make himself a cup of tea which eventually he brought back. As he was placing the cup on his table Mavis and Helen arrived. George was only too happy to sit himself down with his tea and leave the floor open for Mavis. She was still completely excited by what had happened on Friday night and immediately began recounting what had gone on at the Nite Club.

She missed not a single detail of the story and both Tom and Bill and Helen were as fascinated by the exhilaration displayed on her face as by the contents of her tale. Her garrulous gallop through Friday night's adventure was delivered with such breathless excitement that everyone was completely captivated.

"Oh, my word," exclaimed Helen, who was overcome not only by the story itself but the frenzied way in which Mavis had described it. "So they are all in prison now are they?" she asked. Mavis said she thought they were all in the cells at the local police station, but in all honesty, she did not know where they were.

Just then Pete arrived and caused some more excitement when he took off his coat to reveal that he had his arm in a sling and his hand and forearm covered in plaster. His visit to the hospital on Friday night had confirmed that he had broken bones in his hand when he had punched the twin.

"So what time did you get home on Friday night?" asked Mavis.

"Oh, early hours of the morning," he replied. "You know what it's like at the A& E."

"So how long does your hand stay in plaster?" asked Helen.

"About a month, they said," answered Pete.

"So no more rugby for you for a while." said Tom.

"That's right," said Pete, "but at least it's stopped hurting now. Still it was worth the pain just to give that bully boy a right hander. That will teach him to chase poor Vince. Anyway, his brother was in the A & E at the same time as me and he was squealing like a pig while they tried to fix his shoulder where Mavis had hit him with the fire extinguisher."

Everyone chuckled at this and neither Tom nor Bill, were surprised to learn that ultimately Mavis had been the heroine on Friday night. She herself caused more laughter by assuring everyone that she had not meant to hit the twin on the shoulder. She had been aiming at his head.

Vincent then arrived and joined the general conversation. He admitted that most of the time he had been terrified. He had, he said, always had a bad feeling that everything would go wrong and that he himself would end up in the hands of the twins who would have done goodness knows what to him. He said he would be eternally grateful to both Pete and Mavis for the part they played in his protection. He asked what the position was with those who had been arrested and in particular the twins, He was still paranoid that they would be released by the police and return to the community. Pete said that he was intending to contact Charlie Chivers today who would undoubtedly have information about those arrested.

Meanwhile the International Detective was sitting in his office gazing thoughtfully at the calendar girl's breasts. He was wondering to himself whether or not it was too early in the day to telephone Des Onions. He decided to give it a go and dialled the number. He was surprised to hear Des answer. "I was not sure that you would be at work yet," said Charlie, "any news?"

"I've been here all night," said Des, "in fact, I've been here the whole weekend with virtually no sleep. Jimmy Pearce sang like a canary. He's given us so much information mainly about the twins and Eddie Sharp and also a little bit about Simon Nibble. Everything he's told us is invaluable."

"So what's happening now?" asked Charlie.

"Well, all the suspects are still held in custody. We've made an application to the magistrates for an extension of the time they can be held. We've got an extra seventy-two hours which means they will be produced in court on Wednesday morning. Meanwhile we have further time in which to gather evidence. In fact I'm just about to serve the search warrant at Nibble's office so I'll see you in a few minutes."

"How on earth did you get a time extension of that length?" asked Charlie."

"Well…" said Des, "a combination of a few things. Firstly, the nature of the offence. Supplying Class A drugs and the sums of money involved. Special Branch estimated it at over one million. Secondly the fact that at least one person has died from the dodgy drugs therefore the potential charges could include manslaughter. Thirdly the involvement of Special Branch and the international connections of everyone involved. Anyway, I'll see you in a short while and you can show me exactly where the papers were that you discovered in Nibble's office.

The arrival of Des and his crew at the offices of Huw Roberts & Co solicitors came as a big surprise to the staff therein. "Good morning," said Des to Mrs Sargent. "My name is O'Nighons. I am a Detective Chief Inspector from the local Police station and this is a warrant entitling us to search these premises."

Mrs Sargent looked shocked as she read the warrant which Des had handed over. "But I am afraid I will have to ask you to take a seat, Chief Inspector. I do not have the authority to permit this. I will have to ask you to wait until Mr Nibble arrives," she said in her haughtiest manner.

"Mr Nibble," said Des with great authority, "will not be arriving. He is at present in a cell at the police station awaiting some very serious charges. You have misunderstood me: I was not asking for your permission to search, I was showing you my authority for doing so."

"But what are we to do in the meantime?" asked Mrs Sargent.

"Madam," said Des with even more authority, "you should go about your daily business to the best of your ability. My officers and I will carry out our search as quickly and quietly as we possibly can. I have already been in contact with the Law Society and they will shortly be appointing someone to call here and temporarily run this office while the law takes its course. Now, where is Mr Nibble's office?"

"On the first floor," she said, "it's the room immediately above this one."

"Thank you," said Des who left one officer in reception and went upstairs with the others. They met Charlie coming down. "Morning, Charlie," said Des, "I've served the warrant down below. Now kindly show me where I may find the incriminating documents."

Charlie led him into Simon's office and opened the filing cabinets to reveal the papers which he had already photocopied. Des perused these and instructed the other officers to search the rest of the room. He studied one of the documents carefully. He took it downstairs and showed it to Mrs Sargent. "I wonder if you could help me" he said in a tone that implied that there would be trouble if she didn't. "This witness signature, here," he indicated on the land and share transfer document. "The address on it

344

indicates that it was signed in this office."

Mrs Sargent stared at the document long and hard. "I've never seen this document before," she said

"Whose signature is it?" persisted Des.

"That's Alice's, our junior," she said. "But I do not understand why she should have witnessed a document like this. That was never her function."

"Could you ask her please to come up and see me in Mr Nibble's room?" said Des. Although it was phrased as a polite enquiry it was delivered in the style of a firm instruction.

He was seated at Simon's desk marvelling at the luxurious nature of the swivel chair in which he was seated. He reflected that it made him feel like Captain Kirk the *Star Trek* commander. There was a timid tap on the door. Des shouted, "Come in."

The door eased open and Alice crept in. "Mrs Sargent said you wanted to see me," she almost whispered.

"Yes, come in," said Des, "sit down please. It's Alice isn't it?"

"Yes," she said timidly. "I'm not in any trouble, am I?"

"I hope not," said Des. "I am Detective Chief Inspector O'Nighons, and as long as you tell me the truth about everything you know I am sure you will not be in any trouble. Now Alice, what can you tell me about this document?" he asked, showing her the deed which she had witnessed. "That is your signature is it not?" Alice nodded obediently. "Well now, I would like you please to tell me everything about the circumstances in which you signed this piece of paper."

Alice did just that and explained in detail to Des how Simon had persuaded her to sign the deed. She even indicated to him the desk drawer in which Simon stored the brochure concerning his seaside apartment in Tenerife.

"Now let us be absolutely clear about this," said Des. "At no time was Mr Eddie Sharp present when you signed this document?"

"That's right" said Alice looking more and more anxious. "I didn't do anything wrong did I? Mr Nibble said it was completely OK for me to sign, it as I am an employee of this firm."

"And he offered you a free holiday in Tenerife in return for signing it?"

"Yes... Well, no," she stammered. "He said the holiday was for being such a good girl at work, not for signing the document. But it was a reward wasn't it? I see that now and he said that I should not tell anyone else about it. How could I be so stupid? Have I done something really wrong? He didn't even give me the holiday. When I asked him about the dates, he fobbed me off. I should have realised. How stupid have I been?"

"Not to worry," said Des paternally, "you were not to know. You were only obeying instructions. Now, I want you to repeat all that you have told me to this officer who will make a statement for you to sign. At some time in the future, you may have to repeat your story to a judge in court but I doubt very much if that will be necessary. So long as you tell the truth you will not be in any trouble."

So saying Des left Alice with his fellow officer and went downstairs to supervise the rest of the search. In particular he asked Mrs Sargent to locate the paperwork and bank statements for Simon Nibble's client account which she did. Des perused the statements and gave a long whistle. "Check Mate" he said to himself as he gathered up these documents and included them on the search warrant list of seized items which were eventually handed to Mrs Sargent.

That poor lady was quietly reflecting upon her misfortune ever to become entangled with Simon Nibble. She remembered with pride how fastidious and thorough Mr Huw Roberts had been and how disastrous his illness had been both for himself and the employees of the firm.

When Des had finalised the search of the premises, he gathered the statements of Alice, Mrs Sargent and one or two others, in particular the firm's cashier, a white haired semi-retired lady with bottle-glazed spectacles, whose name was Sylvia. The latter had been cashier for Mr Roberts from the start of the business and gave a statement to the effect that in Mr Roberts' day all accounts had been kept immaculately. Thereafter everything had changed, she said, and despite frequent protestations from herself Mr Nibble had run the client account as if it were his own private savings account.

Des was hugely satisfied with the business of the day and before leaving the building he popped upstairs to update Charlie. He confirmed the position regarding all the defendants who were in custody, including those in London whom the Special Branch had assured him were going down for a number of years. He also confirmed, which was of much more interest to Charlie, that all his time and effort in the investigations, would be financially rewarded in due course.

"But what," Charlie wanted to know, "does 'in due course' mean?"

"Well, obviously, upon conviction," said Des, "or," he added, solicitously, "upon receipt of any statement admitting guilt."

"Well, yes," accepted Charlie, "but if they go 'not guilty' it could take months before there is a trial and a conviction."

"Yes, but trust me on this one Charlie. One or two might go all the way on a 'not guilty' plea, but most of them I am sure will accept guilt for a lesser sentence."

Mavis, Doris and Freda had just completed an exercise class. Red faced and heaving they gathered together for a cup of coffee and a cream slice.

Mavis regaled them with a brief summary of her Friday night and urged them to tell her what had happened to them whilst she was having her adventure.

Doris was the first to tell her tale. "My daughter had to go round to our house first thing on Saturday morning because she had a piano lesson. Her teacher was arriving at nine thirty a.m. At about ten a.m. she telephoned me to say that the house had been raided by policemen and her dad had been arrested. I went straight round there to placate her and to see for myself what was happening. By the time I got there they had arrested Eddie and taken him to the police station. I think they were relieved to see me because my daughter was quite upset. The policewoman they had allocated to look after her was I think at her wits end.

"They were in the middle of searching the house and they produced a search warrant which they served upon me. I tried to help them by asking them what they were looking for. They said they were not able to say but did confirm that it was only items in respect of Eddie they were interested in. I told them he had a safe which was hidden in his games room underneath a window seat in the bay window. I told them the combination number and they opened it. And do you know there was thousands of pounds in there as well as some packets of powder which I now presume are the drugs they have accused Eddie of peddling. They also helped themselves to a note book which Eddie kept and which contained notes and information about goodness knows what or whom. The police seemed very interested to have found it. They did not appear to find anything else of interest in the house so they then left and I took my daughter back to my mum and dad's place."

"So what are they planning to do with Eddie?" asked Mavis.

"Well, as far as I can gather, they are holding him, pending the information they have gathered at our house and elsewhere following which they will charge him with all manner of offences and then he will have to go to court.

"And what about you?" asked Mavis speaking to Freda.

"Well," said Freda "much the same as Doris really. The police contacted me to get them into the house. They told me that they had arrested Joe at the Nite Club and that he was at the police station in custody. They had a search warrant which they served upon me and then went into the house and turned it inside out. They did not appear to find anything of interest but they did also have a warrant to search the Nite Club. I went there on Sunday and let them in. They went straight to the safe in the office and found a lot of money in there too. Apparently, he will be held in custody until there is a trial.

"Well, I have a great idea," said Mavis. "By way of celebration and just to cement our new found friendship, I think we should all go out for a nice Italian meal together. I will invite Pete and Sandra to join us and we can all have a jolly good chin-wag as well as a tasty meal. You two can celebrate your new found independence. What do you both say to that? OK?"

Both Doris and Freda confirmed that they would like that so Mavis said she would arrange it. She then had to excuse herself because she had to attend another meeting.

At the Jubilee Inn the landlord, Reg Partridge, was admiring the new photograph which he had just hung on the wall. It was a picture of himself stood in the central lobby of Parliament with the Speaker of the House of Commons. Reg's chest swelled with pride as he looked at it.

The International Detective who was seated on a stool at the bar looked at the new photograph with some distain. "Couldn't you find someone to match Jayne Mansfield?" he asked. "He looks such a diminutive little man."

Reg looked disappointed. "Well, Charlie," he said with some disapproval, "not every snap I take has to have some cleavage in it."

"Hmm," said Carlie grudgingly, "but most of them are all the better for it."

Mavis and George came into the pub followed by Pete. They bought Charlie a replacement pint and all sat down at a table. It was the first time that Charlie had seen them since the Friday night and certainly he had not seen Pete with his arm in a sling.

He told them about the police search warrant procedure at the offices of Huw Roberts & Co and was able to advise them of the success of the Special Branch in London and how informative the guys they had arrested had been. "Des is absolutely cock-a-hoop," he said. "Apparently the whole thing has gone like a dream and they have oodles of evidence against everyone. Jimmy Pearce has made a full statement implicating everyone else."

"And what about the other matter we asked you to look into" asked Mavis. She was referring to instructions which she and Pete had previously given to Charlie concerning the death of Lionel Witherspoon. Following the hearing in the Crown Court when she had sat behind Phillipa Fry, Mavis had given Pete all the details. He was especially interested in the part of her story which revealed that April's husband had probably been driving the truck which had killed Lionel and more particularly that the vehicle he was driving belonged to the Sodford Brick Co Ltd. Pete had discussed the matter with Ken Carter who gave his authority for Pete to instruct Charlie to make enquiries.

"Well," said Charlie methodically, "I made enquiries the same as the police had and initially got the same result. I went to that halfway trading post minimarket, and saw the man who runs it. He's an Indian chap whose English is not great. He was adamant that he had not seen anything. He was in the shop at the time it happened but he was not looking out of the window at the moment of the accident and so could offer no information. He said he had just taken over from his daughter who minds the till while he has his tea. He also told me that that he had told all this to the police. I asked him where his daughter was and he said she was at school. He said she was only twelve years old."

Charlie took a deep breath, "And I guess that's where the uniform branch left it. I did ask if he had a wife and he said yes but she seldom if ever came into the front part of the premises so she too would not have seen anything. And that's where I too almost left things. But having thought about it I decided to go back again, this time about the time of day when the accident took place when I might be able to meet the daughter. When I returned sure enough there was this girl minding the till. She might be only twelve years old but her English was much better than her father's. She recalled your colleague what's his name."

"Lionel," intervened Mavis.

"Yes, Lionel," said Charlie. "Anyway she remembered him only too well. She thought he was creepy. She said he pretended to be perusing items in the deep freezer but was peering at her all the time. She also said that after he left the premises your colleague hung about outside peeping through the window at her. She was then relieved by her father and she was on her way to the back of the premises. She looked out of the front window at the side of the shop on her way to the passageway to the rear. She saw the truck approaching and she judged that it was going far too fast. It was in the process of overtaking, on the inside, a car which was occupying the inside lane. In order to achieve this the truck had attempted to use the slipway area which belonged to the minimarket and struck Lionel who was never standing in the road at all. These are copies of her statement which I have passed to Des for the uniform branch to follow up. Des has arranged for them to go into prison to interview him on this subject and I would expect that he will be facing a further charge of 'causing death by negligent or dangerous driving'. Believe me, this little girl is one smart cookie and her evidence will be crucial."

Charlie dished out copies of the statement which everyone read.

"Well," said Mavis, "that's really good work, well done, Charlie."

"Yeah, I suppose so," he conceded, "but uniform should have picked it up straight away. Anyway, they are going over their facts and figures which I believe will show that he was driving much too fast. Of course, if the driver of the other vehicle had stopped, he could have told them all this but perhaps he genuinely didn't see anything."

"Well, better late than never," said Pete. "Will there be sufficient time for him to be charged for the driving offence as well as the cricket bat assault on April?"

"Oh, certainly," said Charlie. "Des was quite confident of that."

"Wow!" said Mavis that is absolutely amazing. What a difference it makes just being methodical doesn't it?"

"Definitely," said Charlie. "I imagine this information will be especially important for your friend Mr Carter. If this girl's statement is accepted by the court then no actual blame will attach to his company for the accident. That should save him a considerable sum on his insurance."

"That's for sure" agreed Pete, "as I already told you he will be financially responsible for all your costs and expenses so far."

Mavis was jubilant and said that she could not wait to telephone Phillipa Fry to give her this new information. "I will also have to let Vincent and his mother know." she added. Then she thought again. To Pete she said, "I've told Doris and Freda that we should all share a table at 'La Scala' to celebrate the good fortune that we have all experienced with the exception of your arm, Pete," she added with a gentle touch on his plaster.

"Do you think it would be a good idea? I thought you could bring Sandra and what about your friend Jake, I know Freda was quite taken with him (I think she likes them big and strong) and Charlie here of course, oh Vincent and Lizzy. Wouldn't that be nice?"

Pete smiled and nodded. "Well, they don't' come much bigger and stronger than Jake. Shall I ask Mr Carter as well? No one has more reason to celebrate than him. He's not only saved his business but got his sister back."

"OK," said Mavis, "sounds wonderful. This weekend? Will you book the table?"

Pete said he would and that was settled.

George who had remained silent most of the time, said to Pete, "Oh, the answer to your invitation is a resounding 'Yes' I spoke about it with my grandmother who was completely OK about it."

"Right," said Pete "That will be another reason to celebrate next Saturday won't it?"

"What's that?" asked Mavis.

George said, "I'm going to share Pete's flat with him. I will have my own room so any time you wish to stay the night with me you can."

"Oh, yes," said Mavis, with a big wink to Pete, "and what makes you think I would want to do that?" George looked a bit non-plussed for a moment and then realised that the other two were laughing at him. "I think that's brilliant," said Mavis with great enthusiasm. "I can't wait."

"Well," said Pete, "it sounds as if everyone will be celebrating on Saturday."

Des Onions could not have been more pleased at the way things had worked out. True, only Jimmy Pearce so far had pleaded guilty and made a statement but although the others had all made a 'no comment' interview Des knew that this was only the first step on the ladder of success. He knew he already had sufficient evidence in respect of every defendant to obtain a conviction. He also knew that the connection with the London Special Branch and its international connections meant that this whole operation was for him, a real coup.

He relished also some little additional items of evidence which had not been anticipated for example the statement of Alice at Huw Roberts & Co that she had been bribed or cajoled by Simon Nibble to falsely witness a legal document. Also, the fact that one or two of the brand-new bank notes which had been noted and finger printed in advance, had turned up in the safe at Eddie Sharp's house. Such little extras were for Des the icing on the cake. He congratulated himself and promised himself a good night's sleep to make up for the lack of sleep he had experienced over the weekend.

Before going home to bed, he telephoned his counterpart in London firstly to confirm that Jimmy Pearce had made a full confession and guilty plea and secondly to enquire if London (now assured of the convictions at their end) were now able to reward his private investigator for all the work done. The man in London agreed that payment was in order and confirmed that he would send the paperwork to Des immediately so that Des could pay out the cash to Charlie.

Chapter Fifty-five
Phillipa in Action

The next day Mavis popped into the offices of Duffey Fry & Co to advise Mrs Robinson of the recent developments in the case of Vincent's mother. Mrs Robinson faxed a copy of the Indian girl's statement to Phillipa Fry's chambers and followed it up with a telephone call. Luckily Phillipa was in her chambers and answered the call. Mrs Robinson spoke to her for a few minutes and then handed the telephone to Mavis. "Hello, Mavis," said Phillipa. "I see that you've come up trumps yet again. This statement is quite impressive. My only concern is the age of the girl. Would she crumble if she were under cross-examination from a defence counsel?"

"Definitely not!" responded Mavis, "the gentleman who took her statement is a retired CID detective who said she was surprisingly intelligent for one so young and that she was one of the most reliable witnesses he had ever interviewed.

"Good, good," said Phillipa "not that I expect there to be a 'not guilty' plea, but you never know. Are you coming up for the hearing, and can I expect Mrs Hudson to put in an appearance?" she asked.

"Yes, to both," said Mavis without checking to see if she could get time off work. "Good then I'll see you at chambers at about nine thirty a.m. and once again thank you for your invaluable assistance."

Mavis returned to the office and explained the situation about Vincent's mother's case. Bill was very understanding and said he was only too happy to allow both Vincent and Mavis to take a day off for attendance at the Bristol Crown Court.

Vincent confirmed that his mother was now out of hospital and living at home. He said that her ribs were healing nicely and she was supremely happy to be living on her own. He also confirmed that she would be able and willing to travel to Bristol for the trial of her husband. It was agreed that they would all meet at the railway station in plenty of time and Mavis would show them the way and introduce April to Phillipa Fry.

The next day Des awoke refreshed and made his way to the police station. The first thing he did was to check with the Custody Sergeant on the conduct and welfare of the prisoners. The sergeant assured Des that they were OK, "Except to begin with, the two twins were shouting out a lot. I think they were trying to locate each other in the hope that they could compare notes and decide what story to tell. The sound proofing in here is too good to allow them to converse with each other. I think the one who was in the hospital on Friday night would like to have a word with you.

"You think he wants to make a statement?" asked Des.

"I'm not sure," said the gaoler, "but I think it might be possible."

"Good," said Des rubbing his hands together, "divide and rule, eh?"

He then went down to the cell which contained the twin who had been hit with the fire extinguisher thrown by Mavis. Like Pete this twin was heavily bandaged up and had one arm in a sling. He was looking quite sorry for himself. He sat up on his bunk bed and looked up at Des in a rather forlorn manner. Des thought that he looked a sorry shadow of the confident, muscular fellow who had been videoed selling drugs to George on two occasions.

"You all right?" asked Des.

"Wass going on?" demanded the twin, "where's my brother?"

"Well," said Des, "at the moment we are waiting to see what everyone is going to say and what sort of case we have against each of you. In a couple of days, you will all be appearing in court but, as yet we are not one hundred per cent sure what charges we will be making against each of you. If none of you says a word, we will charge you all with conspiracy to supply Class A drugs. If any of you is prepared to make a statement then we would probably think about charging you with a lesser offence. It's really up to you."

"But what sort of sentence does that carry? asked the twin.

Des sucked his teeth, "Hmm," he said, "very difficult to say. Anything up to ten years I'd say."

The twin looked up with a jolt. "Ten years?" he exclaimed, "just for passing on a bit of powder? You're 'avin a laugh, aren't you?"

"Ordinarily of course, you'd be right," said Des, "but I expect you've heard already that at least one young man has died locally and several others have been very ill. We are pretty sure that the death was caused by the stuff which you were peddling. We are waiting for a laboratory report before we can be absolutely certain but it does appear to be the case that the stuff you were selling was either doctored before it came into the country or afterwards. That makes things very serious indeed and at worst it might be a charge of conspiracy to commit murder or at the least a ten year stretch for recklessness etc."

"Whaaat!" exclaimed the twin, "if anyone tampered with the stuff, it'll be that fucking, Jimmy Pearce."

"Well," said Des, "it's funny you should say that, 'cause that's exactly what he was saying about you."

"Whaaat?" echoed the twin again, "that grubby little shit bag. He'd say anything to save his own scrawny neck. You can't believe anything he says."

"Just what he was also saying about you and your brother," Des assured him. So perhaps now that you understand the seriousness of it all perhaps you would like to think again about whether you wish to make a statement."

"What has my brother said?" he asked. "Oh, you know I can't tell you that," said Des.

"But I have to know what my brother will say. I have to talk to him. We are twins for Christ's sake. We will always stick to the same story but I need to check with him exactly what he wants to say."

Des shook his head emphatically, "Really sorry, but I can't let you talk to each other. The most I could manage is to let you know whether or not anyone has made a statement."

"And?" said the twin.

"And what?" asked Des.

"Has anyone made a statement?" asked the twin.

"I can tell you that someone, has given us a full statement." said Des.

"Fucking Jimmy Pearce, I suppose," he said.

"I'm sorry, I cannot confirm that," said Des. "All I can say is that it might be in your best interests to tell us what you know." The twin looked very undecided and chewed on the thumbnail of his good hand. He momentarily weighed up the circumstances and then said,

"OK, but me and my brother were only passing on stuff supplied by Jimmy. We had no idea there was anything wrong with the stuff. We thought it was mild. Just a recreational drug, relatively harmless. Any tinkering with the stuff is down to Jimmy or those who supplied him. Jimmy did all the negotiations with Eddie who gave us instructions and he and Joe decided to move the stuff at the Nite Club and all responsibility is between the two of them. We were just taking orders."

"The Nuremburg defence, eh?" said Des with a knowing sneer.

"What?" said the twin with a puzzled look.

"Oh, nothing," said Des. "But let's get down to it shall we. I'll get the room set up and we will complete your statement in no time at all and then we will see about a possible reduction in charges against you and your brother.

The morning of the trial Mavis met Vincent and April at the railway station. They travelled to Bristol together and Mavis took them to Clifton Chambers where they both met Phillipa Fry. The latter looked at her notes and then asked April if she knew the route that her husband drove when he was at work. Or did he, she wondered, drive a different route each day.

April told her that the company had few drivers and her husband always drove the local route.

"So, Mrs Hudson, would it be fair to say that if a company truck was involved in an incident at that time of day on that stretch of road that your husband would be the driver?"

"Yes," said April.

"Well," said Phillipa, "perhaps this morning we will see the original road traffic report which will reveal who was driving but I have little doubt that it was your husband."

They all then gathered up their papers and walked to the court. When they arrived Phillipa quickly engaged with Mr Sabin the prosecution counsel firstly to enquire if he had seen the statement from the young girl and secondly whether any charge had been made against the defendant in respect thereof. He confirmed that the charge had been made against the defendant of 'causing death by dangerous driving'.

He also confirmed that the original police report had not been thorough enough. He said that the police officer who had attended the scene had failed to take full measurements of the scene. Apparently, he had been distracted by the demeanour of the driver who was overcome by grief. He continually grasped the officer in a hug and wept against his chest telling him repeatedly that the man had stepped out into his path without warning. There were no other witnesses and it appeared to be an open and shut case of accidental death to the officer who left the matter to lie, without taking fastidious measurements. The officer is now the subject of a disciplinary enquiry for negligence.

Fresh measurements had been taken and the whole scene had been meticulously examined and it now seems that the truck had been driving too quickly. Further, and more significantly, the second closer examination of the area had revealed Lionel Witherspoon's warrant card lying on the hard shoulder, not on the roadway itself where the body had been lying when the police officer arrived. This accorded with the statement made by the young girl. Indeed, if her statement was accepted then Lionel's body would have been found in the same place as his warrant card.

This suggested, of course, that Lionel's body had been moved prior to the arrival of the police. As a result, the prosecution had added to the charge list an extra charge of 'perverting the course of Justice '

Phillipa quickly updated Mavis, April and Vincent and then went in search of Augustus Samuel the defence counsel. "I take it you've seen the latest revised traffic report on the accident and the statement of the girl from the Trading Post?" she said.

Mr Samuel confirmed that he had.

"And what will be your client's plea?" she asked.

"Well," he said with a half grimace, "It's all a bit last minute. I still have to speak to my client who I trust has only just been delivered by the prison service. I will speak to him before making up my mind."

"But what about the charge of assault with a cricket bat, Gus? You must have advised him on plea Already particularly in view of Jeremy's remarks last week."

"Yes, I have," he responded. "He's going to plead guilty to that charge."

Phillipa felt a surge of personal victory at this news but this feeling was overridden by her own instincts of justice which demanded a satisfactory outcome to the death of Lionel Witherspoon.

After a further fifteen minutes the court was assembled and Shirley Kemp asked everyone to stand. Jeremy Fallow QC entered wearing full wig and gown and said good morning to everybody.

"Yes, Mr Sabin," he said to the prosecution counsel who rose and outlined the recent events of which he had earlier advised Phillipa. Jeremy listened with his chin in one hand occasionally raising his eyebrows.

When Mr Sabin had concluded his outline and sat down Jeremy turned to the defence counsel,

"Have you had sufficient time to advise your client Mr Samuel?" The latter rose slowly and breathed deeply, "Humph," he began, "yes, I think so, Your Honour. My client is um aware of his own shortcomings and urges and no doubt your honour will give full credit for an early plea."

"Yes, of course," said Jeremy "So perhaps we can have the charges put to your client?"

Without further ado, Shirley Kemp read out the charges and Mr Hudson pleaded guilty to them all. Mr Samuel then got to his feet again. "Humph, this is a tragic case of misjudgement rather than ill intent, Your Honour. Mr Hudson has always been a good hard-working citizen who has never previously transgressed, who quite out of character on a couple of occasions made an error of judgement. You will appreciate your honour that I have had only five minutes this morning to take instructions and in view of the additional items added to the charge list by my friend today I would like more time to consider matters in order to present a speech in mitigation. I therefore seek an adjournment in this matter of say, one further week."

Jeremy looked at Mr Sabin who nodded and at Phillipa who raised her eyebrows hopefully.

"Yes, Miss Fry? Have you any observations?"

"Your Honour, I don't need to describe the relief with which my client has received the 'guilty plea' in respect of the assault upon herself. I am sure your honour will allow whatever lenience is appropriate in regard to that charge. My client is, needless to say, astonished at the additional charges none of which she was aware of. My client had already decided after the very serious assault that she no longer wished to remain married to the defendant and I have been instructed to prepare and issue a divorce petition against him. Whatever happens to this defendant my client needs protection not only from him but also from the normal exigencies of life. She is a frail ageing lady without income and is the tenant of a council property. She has suffered constant beatings by her husband and has only her son (who is with her today) to protect or support her. I will need to serve the divorce petition and other documents, in respect of the property and bank account in order to secure her future."

"Do you have those documents with you, Miss Fry?" asked Jeremy.

"Yes, Your Honour, I do."

"Well, perhaps now would be a convenient moment to serve them, Miss Fry," invited Jeremy helpfully. As Phillipa produced the papers in question and passed them over to Mr Samuel Jeremy added, "Let it please be recorded on the court record, that the divorce petition and accompanying documents were validly served upon the defendant in this court today."

"Humph... oh, please, Your Honour, is this really appropriate for this court? I am not a matrimonial barrister after all, as Your Honour knows."

"Well pass them along to your client, Mr Samuel. The court is not expecting your client to respond officially today and in any event I suspect that he will have more important matters to worry about in the next week or so. Mrs Kemp, please note the court record that the documents have been served. Stand up, Mr Hudson," he continued. April's husband did as he was told and had now begun to sob bitterly.

"I am adjourning this case for a further week to allow your counsel Mr Samuel to talk to you and to prepare a mitigation speech on your behalf which I will hear next week. In the meantime, you will remain in custody and I warn you that when you return you will almost certainly be facing a custodial sentence."

With that Jeremy rose and left the courtroom. April watched as her husband was led away by the prison guards, still sobbing. She felt some sympathy for him and wondered, in view of the life that he had led her, if these feelings were at all appropriate.

Vincent, on the other hand, felt totally elated as he saw his stepfather being led away. He never doubted for a second that the man's tears were shed only for himself and he was so pleased that his mother would never again have to put up with him.

They all went downstairs to the court coffee bar and sat around a table together. Vincent volunteered to get coffees for everyone and while they sat waiting April wiped away a few tears. She excused herself and said she needed to find a toilet.

"What a good result," said Mavis enthusiastically. "I cannot believe it."

"Mostly due to yourself and your friend," said Phillipa, "there is no substitute for good meticulous investigation. And, how are you?" she asked. "I see you've done something to your eyes. They look fantastic today."

"Thank you," said Mavis who was still riding on the 'high' of the court hearing. "He's so nice, the judge, isn't he?"

"Yes, he is," replied Phillipa with some emphasis on the last word.

Mavis looked at her hard and watched as she blushed. Mavis instinctively directed all her worldly-wise experience to that blush. "He's very special, isn't he?" she enquired and watched as Phillipa blushed again.

She returned Mavis's look, and nodded slightly and murmured, "Uh, huh."

Mavis could not stop her face from lighting up with obvious excitement. As a kindred spirit she said to Phillipa, "Oh that is so lovely! He looks so perfect and you are just so brilliant, it was meant to be."

Phillipa coloured again and was beginning to feel embarrassed. She felt that this young girl had seen straight through her and although that made her vulnerable, she was still drawn to her. She gave herself a shake and said, "And have you had any more thoughts about learning more law?"

Mavis said she had been seriously considering it and would let her know if and when she made a positive decision. She then made an instant decision and before she could reconsider, she heard herself blurting out, "Well actually I would like to see you again, not for any legal reason but simply as friends. It was so good of you to give me those tips on eye make-up and I would so like to see you again to talk woman to woman about clothes and things. I just like you so much I couldn't bear not to see you again." Having said all that she instantly felt completely embarrassed and discerned that her outburst had been much more than she should have said.

Phillipa looked her straight in the eyes and gripped both her hands tightly. "That would be so nice, and yes, I feel exactly the same about you. It would be really nice to meet up somewhere and have a drink and a long chat. We must arrange something on the telephone."

The next morning Tom Richards and Bill Butler were enjoying their quiet half hour together with the *Daily Mail* and a cup of tea. "I see," said Bill, "that the reporter on my paper reckons that the Arsenal need a new centre half."

Tom tucked his tongue in his mouth and rolled his eyes. "They haven't let many goals in so far this season," he replied triumphantly.

"No," conceded Bill, "but they are always a bit fragile towards the end of the season, aren't they?"

"Well," said Tom with an air of finality, "success for a whole season depends upon injuries or the lack of them." Bill nodded his approval.

As usual George was the next to arrive. He made himself a cup of tea and stood in the glasshouse doorway taking a sip. "So," said Bill, "how is it going between you and Mavis?" He gave a half wink to Tom.

"Good," affirmed George. "I stayed at her house the other weekend. It was very nice."

"How did you get on with her parents?" asked Tom innocently. "Um… they were away that weekend," admitted George guiltily.

"Oooh," said Tom and Bill simultaneously.

"Well," said Bill affecting a serious tone, "now that you've moved up a level, I trust that you will not be dallying with Mavis, for whom Tom and I, have a high regard."

"No, no, quite the contrary," George assured him. "In fact, I have decided to move into Pete's place to share his flat. It's a big flat with a spare bedroom and we can share the rent. Mavis and I might be able to see some more of each other."

Tom and Bill gave another unanimous 'ooh' which caused George more embarrassment. Bill laughed and said, "Only kidding, she's a lovely girl and we both wish you well."

"Here, here," echoed Tom.

On cue as usual the girl herself arrived followed almost immediately by Helen. No sooner had they shed their coats when Mavis began to regale everyone with the happenings of the day before. Even as Mavis herself was telling the story she found herself having difficulty in believing parts of it.

She laboured heavily the part of the story concerning Lionel's death. In the middle of the tale Pete entered the office and was as entranced by the story as everyone else. "I knew all along there was something odd about him," said Bill.

"Oh, definitely," said Mavis.

"That young girl was absolutely correct," added Helen, "he was certainly creepy."

"Yes, but all the same," added Mavis, "It is such a tragedy that he should die in such a shabby way. And the truth would not have been known if Pete's friend Charlie the International Detective had not made enquiries. He did much better than the police." Everyone agreed.

Just then Vincent arrived, last as usual and everyone told him how happy they were that things had worked out well for his mother. Vincent admitted that it had been an immense relief for him. "I always hated him" he said. "He was a complete bastard and treated my mum rotten. To be honest I was scared of him. When he was drunk, he used to knock me about too."

Mavis sobbed and gave him a hug. "Not any more, Vince," she said.

Des Onions awoke after his second full night of sleep feeling exceptionally well. He reflected how well all the pieces of the jigsaw were falling into place and he tried to make a mental note of all the good points so far.

Firstly, he had a full statement from Jimmy Pearce which pointed the finger of guilt well and truly at all the other defendants. On the positive side this was good evidence supported in some measure by for example the video evidence of the drug dealing by the twins and also the large amounts of unexplained bank notes found in the safes of both Eddie and Joe.

On the negative side he reflected that a defence counsel could well point to the dismal criminal record of Jimmy Pearce and the certainty that everything he might say would be said to improve his own situation. He could envisage in advance a loquacious defence counsel emphasising that Jimmy was a convicted criminal and a congenital liar and not a single word of his evidence should be accepted by a jury.

Secondly, he now had the statement of the injured twin who also pointed the finger at Eddie and Jimmy. In addition, his statement had included the information that most of the drugs money had been deposited by Eddie into Simon Nibble's client account.

Des knew the importance of financial evidence eg. bank statements and profit and loss accounts which always provided indisputable evidence in court proceedings. He remembered reading somewhere that the famous American gangster Al Capone had been convicted due to the evidence of his books and accounts rather than for the violent crimes he had committed and which were more difficult to prove. His jail sentence had been for fraudulent tax returns and under payment of tax rather than for the murder of opponent families. Des knew that it was the evidence supplied by Simon's books and client account records which would convict him rather than statements by Jimmy and the twins, useful though they may be.

With a view to tying up Simon completely he had contacted the solicitor whom the Law Society had appointed to look after their erstwhile solicitor's office. He had an appointment to see the man this afternoon. He had also made a mental note to search his office for the deeds of Simon's Tenerife apartment which had been recently purchased and more particularly evidence of where the money for the property had come from.

He knew that he already had plenty of evidence against the man but felt in his water that this final possible nugget of information would put the icing on his own cake

He thought to himself that prior to the appointment with the lawyer he would have another crack at the second twin. He knew this was the dominant twin who would be a tougher nut to crack than the injured one. This one, he figured to himself, was probably the first born of the twins and therefore more assertive. Nevertheless, Des knew that what he had in his favour was the fact that the other twin cracked under pressure and made a statement. This gave Des some confidence and armed with this he went to see him. The custody sergeant showed him to the cell where the twin was lying on his back reading a paper. He did not look up or get up when Des entered.

"Hi," said Des cheerily, "how's it going?" The twin continued reading his paper and said nothing. "Just thought I'd look in to see that you were OK. Also, to let you know that your brother's shoulder has been fixed by the hospital and that he is now fine. I just thought you'd like to know that." The twin made a sort of tutting sound and rolled his eyes.

"Yes," said Des, "He was fine when he made his statement." The twin put down his paper on the floor and sat up.

"You can fuck off," he said giving Des the evil eye.

"Course," said Des as if he had not spoken, "he was not precise about every little detail but he was most particular to say that he wanted to be in accord with whatever statement you made. You know, being twins like, he wanted to be certain that everything he said would meet with your approval. I told him naturally we couldn't tell each of you what the other might say as the rules don't allow that but he was anxious that you would both 'tell the same story'." Des indicated quotes marks with his fingers.

"And I'm supposed to fall for this bullshit?" said the twin with great distain.

"Well," said Des, "I'm surprised, I thought you were the smarter of the two twins but it looks like I was wrong. It looks as though Jimmy Pearce holds the ace hand, with all the evidence he has given us, and all that your brother told us to try and combat that, in this statement I have here, is wasted if we can't find anyone to back up his statement."

Des threw the copy statement onto the bedside table in disgust. "It's a shame. Your brother's efforts seem to be for no purpose. I am sure, if you were to say anything that is, that you would also confirm that Jimmy and Eddie hatched this up between them."

There was a knock on the door which opened to reveal the Custody Sergeant again. "A quick word if I may chief," he said. Des walked to the door and over his shoulder he said, "Back in a moment." He walked to the end of the corridor with the Custody Sergeant and paused. "I think he might take the bait," he whispered. "We'll see."

He walked back to the cell and stepped inside. The twin was on his back again reading the paper. Des stepped over and picked up the copy statement. "Now, where were we?" he asked rhetorically.

"You must think I was born yesterday," said the twin. "You can fuck off."

"Fair enough," said Des, without appearing disappointed. "I just had to give you the chance to say a few words. We think we have enough evidence here, what with the deals you and your brother made which have been videoed, and the full statement which Jimmy gave us which implicates you fully along with your brother, to put you away for a long time. I did tell your brother that at least one person has died taking the stuff you handled and that elevates the charges from simply supplying to possible murder or manslaughter. There's a lot of difference between the penalty for a bit of simple supplying and a life sentence for murder don't you think? Your brother certainly did."

Des straightened up and walked to the door. He knocked and the door was quickly opened for him.

"Well anyway," he said cheerily, "you have a think about it and let me know if you change your mind. I'm sure that another statement which is similar to that given by your brother would sound quite plausible to a jury." Des walked away with fingers crossed.

Chapter Fifty-five
Mavis Moves On

Arnold Pigg had been settling in at the Regional Office. He was experiencing the euphoria of starting a new job in new surroundings on a higher salary. Despite this general feeling he was still unable to dismiss a small feeling of discontent about his new existence.

His biggest disappointment was the size of the room that he occupied. It was barely half the size of his office at the old building and it only possessed a very small window without a view. He had been anticipating a much larger room with large windows and panoramic views. He had also hoped for thick carpets and curtains but there were none.

He found also that he was afforded no personal secretary to assist with typing and general administration. At the old office he had had the luxury of being able to rely on Mrs Balstaff and Penny to, sometimes miraculously, transform his own thoughts and jottings into impressive looking documents. Penny in particular always seemed to have the knack of producing professional looking graphs with additional charts which made sense of them: here he had to rely on the typing pool.

His new job, he felt, would entail new graphs in respect of the twenty odd offices in the region. This would mean many more graphs than he had ever produced in the old office, probably up to one hundred or more. He was puzzling to understand how he would achieve this without Penny's help.

His door opened following a peremptory knock and in walked Mr Jenkins. "Morning Arnold," he said, "how are you this morning?"

"Very well, thank you, sir," said Mr Pigg.

"Well, you've been here a few days and I expect you are settled in now. Have you decided on your rota for office inspections yet?"

"Yes, sir, I have," said Mr Pigg eagerly. "I have created a map and chart which I have here," he said moving towards a filing cabinet in the corner of the room.

"No, no," replied Mr Jenkins abruptly. "I don't have time I'm afraid, and in any case, I think the order of your visits is something which I will leave entirely to you. I just popped in to say that I shall be away for a few days. I've been summoned to Whitehall. So I will see you next week and look forward to reading the report of your first office inspection." Without further more he took his leave of Mr Pigg who then resumed his contemplation of various graphs and schedules.

Meanwhile in his old office the staff were still discussing the astonishing adventure of the day before experienced by Mavis, Vincent and the latter's mother. They were all agreed upon how astonishing was the coincidence that the lorry which had struck and killed Lionel should have been driven by Vincent's stepfather.

"I cannot believe that," said Helen for the umpteenth time. "I know" responded Mavis. "And to think that he was cunning enough to move the body afterwards. If that had been me, I would have been beside myself with concern. To think that he behaved so cynically and strategically."

"Oh," said Helen, "you're beginning to sound like a lawyer already. Now tell me about Phillipa Fry. How was she this time?"

"Well," said Mavis, her eyes lighting up with enthusiasm, "she was brilliant as ever." She then recounted to Helen the episode in court concerning the service of the divorce petition and accompanying documents.

"Do you think that's legal?" asked George who had no idea himself. "I mean, is it legal and valid to serve a document for one court in a hearing of another court?"

"Well, the judge allowed it," said Mavis.

"A judge is a king in his own court" uttered Tom wisely.

"Well, this judge was very impressive," said Mavis. "He was tall and handsome and I could tell that he was very taken with Phillipa Fry."

"Oh, surely not," said Helen. "How on earth could you assume that?"

"I don't know really," said Mavis, "but I just felt it strongly."

"Oh you're just being romantic," said Helen. "that sort of thing doesn't happen in court."

"But why not?" asked Mavis. "It can happen for example in a hospital. A theatre nurse can fall for a surgeon. A young teacher can fall for her headmaster. Surely it happens everywhere does it not?"

"True," conceded Tom, "but it is unlikely that such mutual attraction would be exhibited in a court of law."

"Precisely," agreed Helen.

"Well," said Mavis, you can all be as sceptical as you like but I had a strong feeling. That's all." What Mavis did not say was that Phillipa had all but admitted it to her. She then went on to describe to Helen how she and Phillipa Fry had declared their intended friendship and had vowed to meet again simply as friends.

"Really?" said Helen in astonishment. "Good heavens!"

"Now, you're just making things up," said Pete, cynically.

"No, I'm not," said Mavis stubbornly. "I thought I would go to court again for the sentencing of Vincent's stepfather and have a chat with her after that. And also of course I could report the outcome to Vincent and his mum."

"You can't expect Bill to give you another day off, surely," said Helen.

"No," said Mavis. "I could take a day's leave. I have plenty of time due to me this year."

Detective Chief Inspector Desmond O'Nighons met Mr Paul Ferguson at the offices of Duffey Fry & Co. Mr Ferguson had been appointed by the Law Society to run the office pending the outcome of the police investigation into Simon Nibble's affairs. He explained to Des that he had formerly been in private practise in this part of the country but on retirement from that position he had been employed by the Law Society generally to cover for such occasions.

Des showed him the client account details which he had seized from the offices and Mr Ferguson confirmed that these showed activities by Mr Nibble which were totally inappropriate and expressly forbidden by Law Society rules. He confirmed that whatever the outcome of the criminal investigation, Mr Nibble would have great difficulty in retaining his practicing certificate upon the evidence of his client account.

Further investigation, with the assistance of Mrs Sargent and the cashier Sylvia finally produced copies of the deeds to the Spanish holiday apartment in Tenerife owned by Simon Nibble. It also transpired that the purchase price of the apartment had been transferred from Simon's client account which coincided almost exactly with some large deposits of cash into the same account. Mr Ferguson confided that most of the large transactions in the client account were highly suspicious and contrary to the Law Society rules.

Des was pleased to hear this, especially from a representative of the Law Society, although of course he always knew this. He requested a statement from Mr Ferguson to the effect of what he had said and that gentleman confirmed that he would be happy to provide one at the normal Law Society rates. Des confirmed that was acceptable and Mr Ferguson said he would draw one up and Des could collect it the following day. He also confirmed his ability to give oral evidence, if necessary, in the Crown Court in due course at the same Law Society rates.

Des returned to the police station and checked in with the Custody Sergeant regarding his prisoners. The sergeant told him that the second twin had asked to see him. Des was excited to hear this and quickly went to the dominant twin's cell. The latter greeted Des with the news that he was prepared to make a statement but it was subject to certain conditions. What were those Des wanted to know.

"Firstly," said the twin, "neither my brother nor I, knew anything about the drugs that were peddled. That was all agreed between Eddie, Joe and Jimmy Pearce. Secondly, we always thought they were recreational drugs not hard stuff, not Class A. The only stuff we have knowingly passed on is the steroids at the gym but those are just for body building purposes. Finally, we never tinkered with any of the stuff that passed between Jimmy, ourselves and Eddie. Any tinkering occurred either before we handled it or after we passed it on. Got that?"

"Absolutely," confirmed Des, "let's get something down in writing, shall we?"

Two hours later the twin signed his statement which looked uncannily similar to that rendered by his brother. Des left the police station that day rubbing his hands together and feeling extremely pleased with himself. He now knew that a guilty verdict was assured against the three main defendants of the case namely Eddie Sharp, Simon Nibble and Giovanni Pettacinni. He was very happy.

Jeremy Fallow QC was in his chambers early on Friday morning. It was the sentencing day for Edward Hudson the man who had pleaded guilty to the charge of assaulting his wife (Phillipa's client) with a cricket bat. He had also pleaded guilty to causing death by dangerous driving, of the man named Lionel Witherspoon who had been shopping at the Halfway Trading Post at approximately five thirty p.m. on the day in question. In order to escape justice, he had moved the body of Mr Witherspoon before the police arrived at the accident and then made a false statement to the police as to what had happened. As a result, the amended charge against him included a charge of attempting to pervert the course of justice.

Jeremy was writing his sentence speech in time to deliver it when the court was resumed. His instinct was to impose the maximum sentence possible upon a man who would thoroughly deserve every year imposed upon him. He was aware that the defence counsel Augustus Samuel would be looking for any points for appeal that might present themselves. He realised that if he imposed the maximum sentence then one ground of appeal would obviously be that the sentence imposed was too severe.

He recalled also that he himself had boxed Gus into a corner in the earlier hearing when he had insisted that his bare denial of the charges was insufficient and would not be accepted by him (Jeremy). He worried if Gus would think to use this as a ground of appeal.

He also knew that when they had shared chambers, and he (Jeremy) had been Head of Chambers, that he and Gus had never got on well together. Now that Gus was Head of Chambers, he might wish to get one over on

Jeremy just to show that he now had the ascendancy.

Lastly and most worryingly there was the possibility that Gus who had been in the Indian restaurant last weekend had seen him with Phillipa. Although he felt no shame or guilt about his association with Phillipa there was no doubt that it was scandalous and very awkward in the circumstances with her representing the victim of the case. He wondered if Gus would be bold enough to mention such a prejudice in his appeal if he made one. He knew that if he did it would make things very difficult for him and might even force him to resign.

He carefully considered all these points and then wrote his sentence speech knowing that he had done the right thing.

Later Shirley Kemp arrived and made some coffee for him. He thanked her for the cup of coffee which he received just as he concluded his speech. He read through the notes he had written as he was drinking his coffee. He wondered if Phillipa would be in court this morning. Technically she did not need to be there because she represented the victim rather than the defendant. He hoped she would be there just so that he could have a glimpse of her.

On the other side of his chambers' door Phillipa was seated, having met Mavis who had walked with her to the court. Mr Sabin the prosecution counsel was present and so was Mr Samuel who represented the defendant.

Shirley Kemp came through the door and ordered everyone to 'please stand', closely followed by Jeremy himself. After a brief summary of where the case stood Jeremy invited Mr Samuel to address him in mitigation.

Gus then humphed and herumphed his way through twenty minutes of near meaningless waffle concerning the defendant's life and his alleged good previous behaviour. There had been two or three previous convictions for violence, all against previous female partners, which Gus attempted to dismiss as unimportant or inappropriate to the present case. He had clearly not gathered any clear points of mitigation and it might be supposed that there were none to have been gathered. He concluded his address by requesting Jeremy to show leniency for the single mistake in an otherwise blameless life.

There was a brief silence before Jeremy launched himself into his sentence speech. He outlined the offences committed and then, having borne in mind the possible points of possible appeal, he emphasised to the defendant how persuasive and erudite his counsel had been when speaking on his behalf. He told him that he had been advised by Mr Samuel that this was a one-off offence and that he had previously led a blameless life. And yet, he told him, there were previous offences of violence recorded against him concerning previous partners. He also reminded him that in the original charge there had been facial injuries caused by him on a separate occasion before the assault with the cricket bat. Finally, he told him, his action at the roadside accident site of moving the body showed extreme deviousness on his part which was indefensible. He had no alternative but to impose the maximum sentence. Mr Hudson got fourteen years imprisonment.

Having delivered this sobering judgement Jeremy rose and left the court. The defendant was sobbing, as before, when he was led away. There was a brief moment when all who were left in the court shared a feeling of shocked silence. Gradually everyone pulled themselves together and packed up their papers and left the court.

Phillipa and Mavis made their way quietly to a nearby coffee house where they seated themselves in a window seat. "Wow!" said Mavis, "I don't know why, but I'm not sure I was expecting that."

Phillipa nodded in agreement. "It is always a sombre moment when a judgement is passed."

Mavis nodded too, "I mean he was a most dislikeable brute of a man who probably deserves every day of it but to sit there and hear the sentence passed is quite a shock."

Phillipa nodded again, "It is a very difficult thing for anyone to have to do. To pass a severe sentence believe me."

"Yes," said Mavis. "It brings it home to me what a difficult and lonely job the judge has to do."

"Indeed," said Phillipa and then, trying to brighten up, she said, "What shall we talk about then?"

Mavis stared deeply into her eyes which looked as if they were filling with tears. "You're concerned about him, aren't you?" Phillipa took a tissue out of her handbag and wiped her eyes and nodded. "It is a lonely job, and he made the correct decision, but often there are consequences. But anyway, let us try to move on and not let it spoil the rest of the day."

"I can't bear to see you unhappy," said Mavis, "previously, you have been glowing with happiness. We come from different worlds that are totally unconnected but there is a chord between us. If you want to unburden yourself on me I would be happy and privileged to listen."

Phillipa looked at this younger woman who she felt was so much more worldly-wise than herself. She leaned forward and wept quietly on her shoulder. Mavis hugged her and stroked her head. "You are in love with him, aren't you?" Phillipa nodded against her shoulder.

Mavis said, "He is a glorious man and you are a brilliant, beautiful woman. You are both so suited to each other, that there cannot, should not, be anything which could prevent you from being happy together. Now come on dry your eyes don't spoil your fabulous make-up."

Phillipa pulled herself together and wiped her eyes. She smiled at Mavis and said, "It's so odd. I feel that you can look into my eyes and know everything about me."

I do," said Mavis, "I am a woman too and I recognise everything you feel because I have also experienced the same thing in my life."

She gathered up her handbag and retrieved from it a glossy fashion magazine. She opened it to a certain page and pointed to a photograph of a model wearing a stylish dress. "What do you think of this?" she said.

Phillipa's eyes lit up. "That is wonderful," she replied, "It would suit you."

"Or you," said Mavis smiling.

They both laughed simultaneously and were immediately back on a sympathetic basis. They chatted for a while about the clothes in the magazine and fashion in general. Mavis asked about her life generally and she told her that she was an only child who had done well at school and studied hard and gone to university in Bristol and then studied for the bar exam in the same town. She had qualified and became a pupil barrister at Clifton Chambers where she met and was courted by Algernon who joined soon after her. She thought her life was perfect insofar as she had acquired all she could ever need in life at a relatively young age. Algernon, she told her, was from a well-off family and was able to afford a nice house in the country. Her childhood passion had always been horse riding and before studying law she had always been idyllically happy attending gymkhanas and stables and being around horses generally. She and Algernon had married young and acquired the country property which had a stable with two horses which she loved passionately.

"So how and why did things change for you?" asked Mavis

"I'm not really sure," admitted Phillipa. "When I joined Clifton Chambers he, Jeremy that is, (the Judge) was the Head of Chambers. He is about fifteen years older than me and I was young and just getting married and concentrating on work and the horses etc and never really gave it any thought. And then suddenly one day it dawned on me how very attractive he was. I used to creep into his court when I had a free moment and watch him in action from the gallery. He is so intelligent and erudite and I gradually realised how dull Algernon was when compared to him. It sounds so childish and spoilt, and in many ways, I succeeded in supressing my inner feelings towards him. I flirted with him for several years when we were in the same chambers and although I could see that he was always attracted to me I could also understand that he would never take the initiative and take things beyond a formal association.

And then he was appointed to be a Crown Court Judge. It was

inevitable that this would happen sooner or later. He is so able, but I realised that once he left the chambers (which he had to do once he became a judge) our contact would diminish and it was then that I realised how much I would miss him. I can't believe that I'm telling you this. So I just took the flirtation to a higher level and he responded as I had always hoped he would."

"And was it as perfect as you had imagined it would be?" Mavis asked.

"Even more than that," she assured her. "I realise now that it is all I have ever wanted and I would be willing to give up everything for it."

"Oh, how wonderfully romantic," sighed Mavis. "But were you certain that he would respond as he did or did you take a big chance?"

"Well both really," said Phillipa. "I always felt that he would but did not really have any evidence. He was always too proper and well behaved to make any advances. I am not naturally flirtatious but felt that unless I made all the running it would never happen. But even when it did, I could not believe how good it was."

"It was meant to be," said Mavis wisely.

"And what about you?" asked Phillipa. "Tell me about the man in your life."

Mavis told her about George and herself. How she had answered the bell at the public counter and seen that little boy lost character who was applying for a job. She said that she too was an only child, that her father was a school teacher and that there were always a million or so books in the house which she read and which her father was always encouraging her to look at. She had never been studious or academically successful at school but at home she was very well read. At school she said, she spent all her time chasing or avoiding boys. She had been the most flirtatious and sought-after girl in the school. She was, sexually very experienced and found that she had more trouble rebuffing men than attracting them. She explained about her mistaken attraction to Lionel Witherspoon and described how the realisation of his proclivities had made her realise how attracted she was to George who she explained was an orphan who lived with his grandmother for years following the death of his parents.

Their time together came to an end because Mavis had to go home. She explained about the evening meal which was booked at the Italian restaurant and the reason for the celebration and its connection to Doris and Freda whom Phillipa knew of course. When they separated Mavis promised to update her on anything of interest concerning not only Doris and Freda but also the saga of the criminal procedures in which she herself had become involved. They each pledged to remain in touch generally as true friends.

Chapter Fifty-six
La Scala Again

The celebration meal at 'La Scala' restaurant was timed for seven thirty p.m. but George and Mavis arrived ten minutes early. He had already moved some of his belongings into Pete's flat which was above the restaurant.

Fillipo was at the door to greet them. "Aah, so good to see you again," he oozed shaking George's hand and then taking the hand of Mavis and kissing it enthusiastically. He looked to George and said, "She's a so beautiful, you are so lucky." He led them straight to their table where Pete and Sandra were already seated together with Jake who looked too big for the chair he was sat on. Sandra and Mavis exchanged greetings and kissed cheeks. They decided to wait for the arrival of the others before ordering drinks and Fillipo left them to chat while he went to greet someone else.

"Nobody else here yet then?" noted Mavis, "perhaps we are a bit early?"

"Yes," said Pete. "Mr Carter is usually punctual but Charlie I guess at this time of day (he glanced at his watch) will be in the Jubilee Inn. I hope he remembers to come."

Even as they spoke Ken Carter arrived and greeted everyone. He was accompanied by his sister Freda and also Doris. Mavis expertly showed Freda to the seat beside Jake. While they were all greeting each other and deciding where to sit Vincent and Lizzy arrived. Fillipo then attended the table and took orders for everyone's drinks. They all decided that it would be fitting if Ken Carter sat at the head of the table and by a process of elimination that left an empty seat at the opposite end of the table for Charlie to occupy as and when he arrived.

Mr Carter made a positive announcement both to the other guests and to Fillipo that he would be paying the bill for the whole table at the end of the evening. Everyone protested but Mr Carter was adamant.

"No, no," he insisted, "this meal is a celebration and financially, at least, I have more to celebrate than anyone. And anyway," he added contentedly, "I can afford it so I don't want any arguments. Tonight, is on me OK?" He looked directly at Fillipo and raised his eyebrows for agreement. The latter inclined his head obsequiously towards Mr Carter and said "Si si of course, whatever you wish."

Mavis was slightly embarrassed by Mr Carter's offer particularly since the idea of a celebratory meal had been her's and she said as much to him." Nonsense" he replied" You have been so helpful towards my sister in her divorce procedures that I feel I owe you much more than this."

"Hear, hear," said Doris, "and she's helped me loads as well. She is an absolute star!"

Mavis blushed but blurted out a thank you and reminded everyone that Pete had been very helpful also. "Absolutely," said Mr Carter emphatically. "So no more objections from anyone. The whole evening is on me."

Vincent and Lizzy in particular were extremely relieved to hear this. Before arriving, they had been nervous about the cost of a meal in this restaurant. In fact, it was the first time that either of them had eaten out in a proper restaurant environment.

Finally, Charlie arrived and seated himself at the foot of the table. Everyone was pleased to see that he had remembered to come. Once he had ordered a drink and been served, he was able to settle down and confirmed to those around him that he had already been to the Jubilee Inn for a drink.

Everybody studied the menu and orders were made. Pete asked Charlie about the latest information on the arrestees. "Well," said Charlie, "I spoke to Des this morning. They've all been produced in court and they've all been remanded in custody to appear in due course in the Crown Court. Full admissions and statements have been made by the twins and Jimmy Pearce all of whom blame Eddie Sharp and his solicitor. Those in London who supplied Jimmy Pearce were all arrested and gave full statements and admissions and gave information about their suppliers. Des is absolutely delighted and congratulates all of us."

Mr Carter, who had already ordered a bottle of champagne made sure that all the glasses were charged. "I think congratulations are in order for all of you. I would ask you all to raise your glasses and drink a toast to each other." Everyone did as they were instructed and drank a toast.

"So," said Doris to Freda, "have you decided what to do about the Nite Club?"

"I shall continue to run it, on my own," she replied, "what else can I do, these places are very difficult to sell. In any case, my brother will be there to help me if I should make any mistakes won't you, Ken?"

"I certainly will," confirmed Mr Carter.

"But do you have any experience?" asked Doris.

"None at all," admitted Freda, "but

how hard can it be? Joe used to do it and he knew nothing about anything. The only difference is I won't be selling drugs."

"Well," said Doris, "I don't know anything much about anything either but if you want any help, I would be happy to assist you."

"What a brilliant idea," said Mavis whose eyes lit up with excitement. "You could go into partnership and run the place together. You are such good friends it couldn't fail to be a success. You are both much superior to Eddie and Joe."

"That's right," echoed Sandra. "You would both be good together."

"I think it could work," confirmed Freda, "as far as I can make out the place runs itself. Joe was hardly ever there but it still functioned. It's a question of knowing the right people to employ. Of course, my most immediate problem is finding a couple of replacement doormen to replace the twins and I believe the DJ has found himself a job in London so I will have to find a replacement for him."

"Look no further," exclaimed Mavis with real glee. "We have here amongst us a DJ with natural talent." She indicated Vincent who looked modestly surprised. "You could do it couldn't you?" insisted Mavis. "The present DJ told me once that you are really knowledgeable about music and would one day be a really good DJ."

"Well yes," said Vincent modestly, "I'd love to do it."

"There you are," said Mavis with finality, "that's sorted. When can you start Vince?"

Lizzy said, "Tomorrow evening," and everyone laughed.

"So," said Mavis archly, "all we need now is someone who is big and strong for Freda." Everyone laughed again and poor Jake blushed furiously.

"Well," said Pete, "nice idea but I think Jake has to start too early in the morning on the farm to be able to work at night as a nightclub doorman. But anyway, there are a few other blokes in the rugby club who could do the job well enough so it shouldn't be too difficult to replace the twins."

"How exciting," declared Mavis with a glint in her eye. "You two together running the Nite Club. As you said, you couldn't make a worse job of it than Joe and Eddie."

"That's right," said Freda, "and I have another idea as well. That room we use at the Barn for our exercise classes is so small and has never really been suitable. The dance hall at the Nite Club is enormous and would make a wonderful venue for a ladies aerobics class. The toilet areas are already in place. All we need to do is install a shower unit in the ladies. We could offer coffee and we have the seating already in place."

"Wow!" exclaimed Mavis enthusiastically, "what a wonderful idea, I'm sure there are a number of extra girls and women who would want to join."

"I've got a plumber who does work for me," said Mr Carter to his sister. "He would be able to fit a shower unit for you."

"That's great," said Freda, "what do you think Doris?"

"Yes, very good," said Doris, "I also have an idea," she said, "my daughter has piano lessons. The lady who teaches her, doesn't have suitable premises for practise. That doesn't matter to us because we have a piano at our house. But other children are not so lucky. If we could install a piano at the Nite Club then the music teacher could take lessons there in the daytime and also singing lessons there. She's really very good and would be able to pay rent. She used to rent the church hall until it fell into disrepair. What do you think?"

"It's a brilliant idea," said Mavis with more enthusiasm. The Nite Cub can work in the night time and in the daytime." Everyone nodded in agreement.

The meals were served and everyone began eating. Mr Carter ordered more wine and everybody was feeling happy. Mr Carter raised his glass and said, "I will ask you all to raise your glasses again. This time I want you all to drink a toast to Pete. I have offered him a job working for me and he has agreed to do so. Therefore, please raise your glasses to Pete if you will."

"To Pete," said everyone.

"My goodness, what a surprise," exclaimed Mavis. "It's certainly a night for surprises isn't it. What do you think of that then?" she asked Sandra.

"I think it is a very good move," she said clutching Pete's hand.

"And talking of work," said Mavis, "how is your job going?"

"Very well, thanks," said Sandra. "And how did the TV programme go in respect of all the goings on at the Nite Club go?" asked Mavis.

"Well," answered Sandra, "we will see won't we. Firstly, we have done a few brief reports as simple News items but in addition we are planning a longer documentary programme which will cover the events as well as all the consequences. Obviously, that will include the trial and the outcome so it will take a month or two to finish."

"Wow how exciting," said Mavis, "so that will be a complete film or programme about the whole story not just the events of last Friday night."

"Quite so," confirmed Sandra, "and I will be hoping to interview everyone to get the background story. So that means you and you." Here Sandra indicated Doris and Freda. "And you of course," she said indicating Mavis.

"Me?" cried Mavis, "but why me?"

"But you were the heroine on Friday night," responded Sandra, "if you hadn't intervened goodness knows what would have happened to Vincent." Everyone agreed.

"And of course, I will hope to interview DCI Onions, who I hope will give me a full official response with detail about the contacts with the drug barons on the continent." Everyone was impressed. "And don't forget Pete," said Mavis. "In fairness, most of the information gathered was down to him and Charlie of course. If you interview Pete now, he will look really heroic wearing a sling."

"Not me though," intervened Charlie, "as a private investigator I don't want my mugshot all over the TV screen or I'll never be able to continue working."

"That's OK," said Sandra, "we can hide your face and disguise your voice so no one will know or recognise you."

"That," said Pete with a chuckle, "would be an inspired idea, to hide Charlie's face. After all we don't want to frighten the viewers, do we?" Everyone laughed heartily even Charlie himself.

"And don't forget Jake," said Freda patting Gorgon affectionately on the knee. "He put paid to the tougher of the twins did he not?" Again, everyone agreed. When they had all finished their meal and had a cup of coffee Mr Carter requested the bill and duly settled it and they all said their farewells to each other.

Mavis and Sandra were going upstairs to the flat which was now occupied jointly by Pete and George. Vincent and Lizzy thanked Mr Carter for his generosity and walked back to Lizzy's flatlet. Mr Carter offered his sister and Doris a lift home but Freda explained that Jake had kindly offered them a lift and so the three of them left together.

In the flat above the restaurant Mavis and Sandra giggled happily over the fact that Freda and Jake seemed to be getting on so well. "She looks very happy," said Mavis, "he is so different, almost the exact opposite to her husband in all ways."

"One thing is certain," confirmed Pete, "he won't court her romantically and persistently like a Maltese lover."

"Perhaps that is what she needs and wants," suggested Sandra, "she strikes me as being a strong-minded woman who prefers to make decisions for herself rather than being led and/or driven by someone else."

"Precisely," said Mavis. They all agreed that it was nice for the two of them to start a relationship when they were clearly attracted to each other. "Has he ever had girlfriends before?" enquired Mavis.

"Yes," said Pete, "he's had girlfriends in the past but the difficulty has always been that he has to get up so early in the morning to work on the farm that it curtails any evening activity which he may wish to indulge in."

"Yes," said Mavis, "I can see that could create problems but I don't think it will be a problem with Freda. I think she was smothered by her husband Joe and would be happy to have a relationship which is less intrusive."

They all agreed that they were tired out and opted for an early night and George experienced for the first time the advantage of living away from home. Curling up in bed beside Mavis gave him such a feeling of well-being that, if it were not for the fact that it would have disturbed Pete and Sandra, he would have whooped for joy.

Chapter Fifty-seven
Time Runs Out

Chief Detective Inspector Desmond O'Nighons was feeling wholly confident but by no means complacent about the matters in hand. He knew from experience that there was no substitute for a job which was well prepared. He was aware that the devil was in the detail and had already scrutinised every detail and tiny document and was taking nothing for granted.

He was just perusing for the third time the written evidence of Mr Paul Ferguson the representative of the Law Society. At first glance it was utterly damning of Simon Nibble and his actions and ordinarily a prosecutor would presumably have accepted the document as completely satisfactory and not have questioned any part of it.

Des however was not prepared to blandly accept any evidence without scrutiny. Having received the report from Mr Ferguson and bearing in mind the evidence of young Alice, the trainee at Huw Roberts & Co there was one small point that niggled slightly in his mind.

He picked up the telephone and contacted Mr Ferguson. "Good morning to you," he said, "thank you for your evidence statement which I have in front of me. Very helpful. One small point that occurs to me. Your statement on the second page concerning the deposits in the client account. I think we need something more concrete than the mere presumption of wrong doing. I know it may seem paranoid but can I ask you please to amend your statement to give chapter and verse of the Act of Law and/or the precise rule that has been breached. Do you think you could assist me? Thank you so much."

Similarly, he had scrutinised the laboratory report which had confirmed the exact nature and content of the drugs seized. On the telephone he challenged the signatory on the report and demanded to know the name of the most senior and academically qualified scientist at the laboratory. The response was that the most senior person at the laboratory was Professor Watkins who was the leading authority in the country in these matters. He was the author of the foremost book on the subject but he did not normally give evidence in court and in any case reports from the laboratory normally carried his implied endorsement as Head Scientist. Des explained that he wanted the professor to give evidence in the court case.

He was reminded that costs of court attendance and waiting time was considerably more expensive in the case of the professor than the standard representatives. Des was aware of this but insisted that he wanted the professor. He knew that any half-decent defence counsel would seek out, as a defence witness, any scientist with impressive qualifications and he did not wish to be found wanting during the trial procedure.

Another aspect of the cases which concerned him were the contents of the two divorce petitions that had been served upon Eddie Sharp and Giovanni Pettacinni. Charlie had supplied him with copies of these documents which, by anyone's standards, could be regarded as dynamite. Each petition was superlative in its narrative. Both documents did a comprehensive job of demolishing their respective respondents. Des knew that whatever the potency of evidence presented in court against these two defendants, that if the two divorce petitions were read by the jury then a guilty verdict would be inevitable. His problem was the relevance of the divorce petitions in a Criminal Law Court. He realised that any defence counsel would argue that they were totally irrelevant and therefore should be excluded. On the other hand, it could be argued by the prosecution that, because they contained some information about the criminal activities of the defendants, the petitions should be allowed. Des knew that the exposure of the petitions to the jury would prejudice the defendants in the minds of the jury members.

His problem was, how the petitions would be introduced during the trial. He was aware that the respective wives of the defendants would hardly be expected witnesses for the prosecution and indeed, if required to give evidence, could validly refuse. He determined that the petitions should be introduced as information of an ancillary nature to a testimony which could be presented by Charlie Chivers. He judged that if Charlie gave evidence of having trailed or researched Jimmy Pearce for supplying drugs and pursued the link with the other defendants, he could also tell the court that he had been employed to serve the petitions on the defendants in court which could then be viewed by the jury. He knew that Charlie would be reluctant to give evidence in court but he was confident that he would be able to persuade him. To that end Des had arranged a meeting with Charlie in their usual agreed place.

The International Detective was waiting for him when he entered the Jubilee Inn. They settled at a table over their pints and chewed the fat for a while. "What's happening with Joe Petacinni?" asked Charlie.

"He's given a 'no comment' interview just like Eddie and his solicitor," replied Des. "But, like the other two, there is enough evidence to convict. We have been in touch with the Border Agency and his days in this country are numbered even, heaven forbid, if he were found not guilty. Once the divorce petition is finalised, he will have no further status for remaining in this country and will be extradited back to Malta either at the end of his prison sentence or immediately if perchance he is found not guilty. But he won't be of course which brings me onto what I wanted to speak to you about."

Here Des reached into his overcoat pocket and produced an envelope bulging with twenty-pound notes. "This is the payment due to you which has been authorised by the Special Branch in London." He handed over the cash which Charlie looked at approvingly.

"What about the local money?" asked Charlie,

"Well," said Des carefully, "as I said before, that can only be released when there is a conviction or a full admission. The guys in London made a full admission which is why this money is available. The local money still depends upon the conviction of Eddie, Joe and the solicitor. It will be influential and necessary for you to make a statement and give evidence in court to ensure that we get those convictions.

"But you said I wouldn't need to give evidence," said Charlie with some irritation.

"That's right," said Des, "but only in relation to the stuff you had obtained by illegally entering Simon Nibble's office. We have that covered by the fact that we got those items by the use of the search warrant. Now if they try to go behind that by asking for example, what made us think there would be something in the offices that we would need a search warrant to discover, we can say that your investigations gave us a strong suspicion and the contents of the divorce petitions that you served confirmed it. Pretty neat eh?"

Charlie grudgingly admitted that it was inevitable that he would have to give evidence in court. Although he did not particularly want to do it he did accept that, when he was on the force, he had vast experience of giving evidence in court. Certainly, Des was very confident about his ability to do a good job and Charlie himself accepted that it was the only certain way of receiving payment for all the hours he had put in. They arranged therefore to meet again at the police station for Charlie to make a full statement.

Arnold Pigg was intrigued and excited. He had not been at the Regional Office building very long and had hardly set foot outside of his own office. This morning however he had been summoned or invited to the office of Mr Jenkins the Regional Controller. He had not been in Mr Jenkin's office before. On each occasion that they had spoken to each other Mr Jenkins had chosen to visit him in his office but this morning the Controller had requested that he go to his office for a chat.

Mr Pigg knocked tentatively on the door and waited. He heard no sound so knocked again. "Come in" hollered Mr Jenkins in a manner that indicated that he had already bidden the person outside to enter. Mr Pigg went in and was amazed by the size of the room. The office was a corner unit with window space down two walls. It seemed to Mr Pigg that the room occupied an acre of space. Mr Jenkins sat in an enormous cosy swivel chair behind a massive leather-topped desk which despite its size looked lost in the huge office space.

"Aagh, hello Arnold," he said, "come in, sit down, how are you today?"

"Very well sir," replied Mr Pigg, seating himself before his Controller.

"Are you nicely settled in now?" he asked. "Yes, thank you, sir," replied Mr Pigg.

"I have some important information for you Arnold. You know that I have just come back from a visit to Whitehall." Mr Pigg nodded and waited for the Controller to expand.

"Well, I'll come straight to the point and tell you that I have been promoted and transferred to work in Whitehall itself." Mr Pigg was astonished by this information. He drew a deep breath and said, "Congratulations sir. When will the transfer take place?"

"In one month" responded the Controller "I must admit it came as a bit of a shock to me. When I was invited to go to Whitehall I wondered if I was in trouble but that was not the case. However..." Here Mr Jenkins paused and drew a long breath, "My trip to London was not all about me. There are some momentous changes in the pipeline of the department. As you are no doubt aware there have been great strides made in the field of computers and automatic transfer devices. The numbers in respect of office buildings and personnel will be reduced. One of those reductions will be of especial interest to you. Your old office is one of those that will be closed soon. It will be a delicate function which will fall to you to carry out the closure of your old office. I am sure that you will be up to the task Arnold."

Mr Pigg was even more astonished by this information and it took a few moments for him to absorb the information and realise the task which he was being asked to undertake. "Well I must say," he responded, "I am very surprised to hear that. Is not a job like that a matter for the HR section to deal with?"

Mr Jenkins pulled a face and said, "Well, not exactly, Arnold. It is a job which requires diplomacy and delicate handling but at the same time requires action by a dynamic person. I thought that it might suit you and I also thought that as you had been previously in control at the office you would wish to deal with the closure. But if you do not feel you are up to the job, I will have to find someone else who can do it."

"Not at all," said Mr Pigg, sensing that to refuse the task would be a mistake. "I will do my best of course."

"Fine, fine," concluded the Regional Controller. He handed Mr Pigg a folder containing papers. "Here is all the information you should need with regard to redundancy rules and calculations. The HR section should be able to supply you with information as to vacancies in other offices and or departments which may be acceptable for one or two of the staff."

"What is the time scale for the closure?" asked Mr Pigg.

"Three months," said Mr Jenkins firmly.

In the Bristol Crown Court Judge Jeremy Fallow QC was going through the motions on a miserable rainy day. A defence counsel, Mr Aloysius Medland, a barrister whom Jeremy had not encountered before, was labouring long and hard on behalf of an obviously (to Jeremy) guilty client who was accused of exposing himself to women and children in a public park.

Mr Medland continually suggested to a series of eye witnesses who positively identified the defendant, that they were mistaken. Each and everyone of them, assured him that they were not mistaken and that the person they had seen in the park was the same person they now saw in the court. Mr Medland responded each and every time by suggesting that they were in fact mistaken. On what appeared to Jeremy to be the umpteenth time he said to the witness in the box, "I put it to you madam that you are mistaken. I suggest that the person you see before you, was not the man in the park."

"Yes, it was," said the witness. "I am certain it was him. I recognise his curly ginger hair."

"But," said Mr Medland forcefully, "I suggest that you were mistaken, and further…"

"Mr Medland," said Jeremy with great irritation, "this witness has already confirmed on several occasions that the man she saw in the park was the defendant. Unless you can produce some evidence to the contrary, I suggest you leave the matter there."

Aloysius Medland paused and gave a look towards the judge which could either have been a smile, a grimace or even a sneer. He seemed to be deciding upon a response but was clearly unsure, not having appeared before this judge, as to what would be the most appropriate. After a moment the grimace or perhaps the sneer developed into a smile. He inclined his head and said, "As Your Honour pleases. No further questions."

"Thank you," said Jeremy with an element of relief in his voice. "I think now would be a good time to adjourn for lunch." He then rose and left the court, retiring to his chamber.

Once there he reflected again on the matters which had been distracting him during the court hearing. These were firstly the possibility of an appeal being lodged by Gus in the matter of Edward Hudson whom he had recently sentenced to fourteen years imprisonment. On the one hand he realised that imposing the maximum sentence in a case when a guilty plea had been lodged was open to an appeal. On the other hand, he reflected, on the first court appearance the man had pleaded not guilty so it could not be argued that he had pleaded guilty at the earliest possible moment. Also, he had moved the body in an attempt to hoodwink the police. Clearly a case of perverting the course of justice. This surely balanced out any credit for pleading guilty.

The other matter that had been distracting him had been the thoughts he had been having about Phillipa Fry. His Friday night and Saturday morning with her had not caused him any misgivings about the relationship. Rather they had cemented the feelings in his mind that everything about her was perfect despite all the obvious arguments which could be arraigned against such an association. Only his brother, he reflected, would not judge him for pursuing this affair.

He wondered yet again if Gus had seen himself and Phillipa in the Indian restaurant the previous week. He also speculated on when the next case would occur when Humphrey appeared before him and if so whether he would be able to discern any indication in his demeanour which would betray the fact that he had been seen. He tried to imagine what his reaction would be if the roles were reversed but he was unable to seriously consider Gus in the role of Crown Court Judge.

There was a knock on the door and Shirley Kemp popped her head around the door. "Visitor for you Judge," she said, and showed his brother Roger into the room. "Shall I make you both a coffee?" she enquired already busying herself at the coffee machine. Roger said thank you and Shirley blushed. She made two cups of coffee and served them up and then left the room.

"You're back then," said Jeremy, "where have you been?"

"Durham," said Roger, "and before you ask, we lost. They've got some excellent bowlers and a difficult wicket to play on."

"Hmm," said Jeremy, "I am old enough to remember when Durham were not in the league."

"So," said Roger sipping from his coffee cup, "How did it go last week?"

"Wonderful," said Jeremy, "I hope we didn't leave any mess?"

"No, not all. So was it as good as you'd hoped?"

"Even more so," said Jeremy, "it was perfection. I know they say there is no fool like an old fool but I have to say she is everything I have ever expected or wanted and I still can't believe that it's happened. How lucky am I?"

"Well…" said Roger carefully, "just take it slowly and allow things to take their own course. It's wonderful that you feel so happy and certain about everything but nevertheless take it gently

and see how things pan out. You don't need to announce it to the whole world until you have tested it out and are absolutely certain about it.

Jeremy agreed wholeheartedly and confirmed that that was the way he had always intended to play it. However, he went on to explain to his brother how it had become a possibility that the affair would become public knowledge sooner than intended. He told Roger how he and Phillipa had gone to the Indian restaurant and may have been seen by the barrister Augustus Samuel.

"Well," said Roger, "that doesn't sound so bad. He surely won't be telling everybody will he? I thought members of the bar were subject to a strict code of confidentiality and honesty. He surely won't let you down."

"Hmm," replied Jeremy, "the problem might be that he might refer to it in an appeal, if it was lodged, on the basis that the relationship between us was prejudicial to his client's case."

"But that's just work, isn't it?" said Roger, "surely that will remain as just a work-related matter. None of it would find its way back to Maud would it?"

Jeremy explained that if the appeal was lodged and accepted or believed by the Court of Appeal then it might be a question of his resignation that would be required. In addition, he explained that Phillipa's husband, Algernon, was a member of the same chambers as Gus. If the appeal was raised and included the mention of Jeremy and Phillipa's relationship then the liaison would definitely become public.

Roger was more avant-garde about the situation than his brother. "Well," he announced, "I don't think it's that catastrophic. If it all comes out will you be really unhappy to spend the rest of your life with Phillipa?"

"No," admitted Jeremy. "Well, there you are then," said Roger with some finality. "If there is an appeal made it won't be the end of the world. If there is none then there is nothing to worry about. What's this Gus character like?"

"Nothing very special," admitted Jeremy. "He is a blusterer who does not possess a real backbone. However, I would not trust him one hundred per cent."

"Well, anyway." concluded Roger, "he does not sound as if he is your equal. It all depends on whether or not he lodges an appeal and even if he does it may not include anything about you and Phillipa and even if it did it might not succeed. Nothing really to worry about I would say. Just enjoy life."

Jeremy had always been more conservative than his brother and was by no means as confident as Roger but nevertheless was always grateful for his brother's opinion.

Chapter Fifty-eight
Mavis Moves On

The next day George returned to his grandmother's house, partly to check on how she was and partly to collect a few more personal items to take to the flat. When he entered the house, he found his grandmother seated in her dining room drinking a cup of tea and leafing through a photograph album. As he came into the room, she wiped a tear from her eye.

"What are you looking at?" he asked standing over her and looking at the photographs in the album. The pictures revealed George's mother and father with a small baby, presumably George himself. As she turned the pages George recognised himself growing up and each photograph brought back a memory for him.

"Ooh," he exclaimed, pointing at one picture, "that was when we were on holiday in Devon that time." He gazed at another picture of himself stood in a garden next to his father. "It's funny," he said, "I look nothing like him, do I?"

"Well, George," she said meaningfully, "there were a couple of things that I wanted to talk to you about. Sit down a minute please." George sat down and wondered what she was going to say, "You know that I've been to the doctors a few times since your grandad died, don't you?"

"Oh dear," said George, "has your indigestion returned?"

"Well not exactly," she said. "I'm afraid that while your grandad was ill everything with regard to my tummy went onto the back boiler. Anyway, to cut a long story short I went back to the surgery yesterday for a further check-up and they advised me that my condition had got worse. Actually, it's cancer and recent tests that have been carried out show that I have only a short time left to live. That was why I didn't mind you going to live with your friend because I will shortly be moving to a hospice where I will spend my final days."

George was astounded and struggled for words to express how he felt. "But I don't understand how a thing this serious should suddenly occur. You had problems with indigestion for several years and now suddenly they tell you it's cancer. How come they did not manage to diagnose it right from the start?"

"Well, actually they did," she said, "they correctly diagnosed it right from the start but that was at a time that your grandad was gravely ill. I could not pay too much attention to it at the time. In any event it was not curable and now it is close to the end."

"But was there no cure at the outset? What is it called, chemotherapy or something?"

"That's right. Well, if they had tried that soon enough there might have been a possibility but I was totally concerned with nursing your grandad at the time. I could not spare the time to attend hospital for chemotherapy."

George was non-plussed and could think of no words of comfort that he could offer. His grandmother continued, "But now that my time is short there is something else that I need to tell you. Before they died your mum and dad had always planned to tell you, at a moment which they judged would be appropriate. When they died unexpectedly your grandad and I also planned to tell you one day but that time was postponed by your grandad's illness and death. Now however I have to tell you, before it's too late, that your mum and dad were never able to have children and adopted you when you were very small."

Yet again, poor George was speechless. Later in the day, when he had left his grandmother's house and when he managed to find some words again, he told Mavis what had happened. She wept openly for George and buried her head in his chest. "Ooh, poor you," she wept, "What a sad story. And you had no idea?"

George shook his head. "She had some paperwork which mum and dad had passed on to her but I believe the rules of secrecy or confidentiality are so severe that it is difficult to trace anyone. And anyway, I'm not so sure that I want to. As far as I'm concerned, my mum and dad are dead so why would I wish to pursue anything further. I wouldn't know how to do it anyway."

"I know someone who would," said Mavis with certainty. If you ever wanted to research further into it just let me know and I will have a word with Phillipa Fry. She will know what to do."

The next morning in the office the day began, as usual, with Tom and Bill enjoying their early morning cup of tea and a friendly conversation. They were discussing the latest news in the office namely the information that Pete was leaving to take a job working for Mr Carter.

"Well, I can't say I'm surprised," said Bill, "he was never really stretched here and he was always capable of so much more."

Tom agreed. "He was only ever functioning in second gear."

"Yes," agreed Bill, "but that was not really his fault. It was the result of the decline in the amount of work which this office had to offer. As you know the work has been dropping off for years and I have been seriously concerned for a long time that this office might be closed, and in all honesty,

I could not defend a decision to do so. Pete was under used. He could do his day's work in approximately one hour. I hope there will be enough for him to do in his new job. He is a very able young man." Tom nodded in agreement.

The next member of staff to arrive was Mavis. Since moving in with Pete George was no longer the third to arrive in the morning due to the fact that he preferred to wait for Pete in the morning rather than leave early without him. As soon as she came in Mavis began to recount to Tom and Bill the news about George's grandmother and the fact that George had been adopted as a baby. They each agreed that it was a very sad story. Mavis herself, even though she knew the story, had difficulty in not breaking down in tears when she told Tom and Bill. Just as she was finishing the story Helen arrived and Mavis found herself once more re-telling the tale to her and, once again, having great difficulty in not breaking down.

Vincent was the next to come in and when he did, he asked Bill if he could talk to him for a while. Bill said he would just see to a few things, opening post etc, and would then be able to give Vincent as much time as he might require.

"Are you going to tell him about your chance to work at the Nite Club?" asked Mavis.

Vincent nodded, "The DJ has had the offer of work in London confirmed and is definitely leaving so I have decided to take up the offer from Freda and work full-time at the Club. So I will be handing in my notice."

"I'm so pleased for you," said Mavis, "I know that you will be so happy doing what you love doing."

"Yes," agreed Vincent, "I believe, I will."

"And how is your mother now?" asked Mavis, "has she fully recovered?"

"More or less," said Vincent, "she still has a bit of pain if she breathes in deeply or sneezes, but otherwise she is fully recovered."

"That's good," said Mavis, "but how is she going to manage financially now that your stepfather is no longer there?"

"Well, she has always had a part-time job working in the shop down the road from where she lives. They have confirmed that she can work some extra hours which will probably be enough for her to live on. Although he earned money while he lived there my stepfather never gave much to my mum. He spent most of it on booze. So she will probably be better off financially without him."

Pete and George then arrived together and settled down at their desks. Mavis asked George if he had thought further about the question of enquiring into the identity of his real mother and father. George replied that he had given it a lot of thought but still had not decided if it was a good idea.

"But aren't you curious to find out who they may be?" asked Helen "I know I would be."

"So would I," said Mavis. "What do you think Tom?"

Tom breathed out long and hard and crinkled up his nose as if there was a bad smell. He shook his head, "It's never that easy you know. Babies are taken into the adoption procedures for all manner of reasons and usually none of the reasons are good for the children themselves. It must have taken George a long time to get over the tragedy of losing his mum and dad. It's a bigger blow to suddenly discover that there may be another pair of parents out there that are unknown to him. It's something he will have to mull over."

"But surely," pleaded Mavis, "It is only natural curiosity which would drive anyone towards an enquiry to discover one's own natural mother and father?"

"Well, I think it must be a gender thing," offered Pete, "I would not want to get in touch or be involved if it were me."

"Why on earth not?" challenged Helen.

"Well, it's simply a matter of probabilities isn't it. The chances of everything going wrong and ending in a complete mess are pretty high. The chances of everything going hunky-dory and ending like a fairy tale are virtually one in a million. Life is hard enough already, why take on more misery?"

"Ooh, that's a bit cynical," said Mavis.

Bill beckoned to Vincent that he was ready to talk to him and they both went into the glasshouse for a chat. Meanwhile in the general office the conversation continued. "Your enthusiasm does you credit," said Tom to Mavis, "but Pete does have a point. As I said, most adopted children come from broken homes where they are often unwanted. To expect to be able to stick together broken homes and relationships is perhaps over optimistic."

"But," said Helen, "it is still surely the right of all adopted children to enquire into their true parents' identity. It is only simple curiosity."

"Of course," responded Pete, "but it should not be assumed that all of them will want to."

The conversation continued thus for a few more minutes until Vincent emerged from the glasshouse. He sat down at the table and was immediately addressed by Mavis. "Well," she said, "What happened?"

"I gave in my notice," he said, "which Bill accepted."

"Good for you," said Mavis,

"Well done," added Helen, "so when do you start the new job?"

"In one month," replied Vincent.

"Well, I wish you the best of luck," said Tom.

"Thank you," said Vincent. Before anymore could be said on the subject the door opened and Mr Arnold Pigg strolled in and with a brisk 'good Morning' to everyone made his way to the glasshouse where he engaged with Bill for ten minutes or so behind the closed door. Eventually they both emerged into the general office. "Can I have your attention, please," bellowed Mr Pigg. "Vincent, could you please ask Mrs Balstaff and Penny to come in and listen to what I've got to say. Gather round please."

Vincent scampered off to summon the typists who duly appeared. Mrs Balstaff joined Mr Pigg and Bill at the front of the room while all the others arranged their chairs in a semi-circle to face them. Mavis placed her chair next to George and when she sat down, she immediately placed her hand on his thigh. George placed his hand upon hers. Mr Pigg cleared his throat and began, "I have called to see you all today because I have an important announcement to make. There are two important items of news. The first is that our Regional Controller Mr Jenkins has achieved promotion and will soon be leaving this region. He will be going to work in the corridors of power in Whitehall itself. At the moment there is no information as to who will replace him. The second piece of news is even more pertinent to yourselves. I can inform you that it has been decided that within three months this office will be closed."

Having delivered this bombshell Mr Pigg paused briefly to allow the information to sink in. It was clear from Bill's expression that this was the most interesting speech that Mr Pigg had delivered in this office for a long time. Usually, when he began talking, after a minute or so Bill always adopted a blank zombie expression which gave the impression of a man asleep with his eyes open.

"There will be arrangements made to find alternative posts for anyone who wishes to remain in service. For those who cannot move, or do not wish to, there are arrangements for redundancy and I have brought with me some leaflets and circulars which give information on the regulations in respect thereof."

Mr Pigg sat down and Bill got to his feet. "Well, thank you, for this information," he said. "I know that you have to journey on to at least one more office in this region with a similar announcement and I am sure that we all have quite a lot to talk about."

Mr Pigg was, as Bill had indicated, keen to leave quickly and without more ado he gathered up his briefcase and papers and left the office with a hearty 'must fly, be back soon'."

Left to themselves the staff all chatted together about the news that Mr Pigg had brought. Both Bill and Tom were unsurprised having discussed the situation on more than one occasion. It was in fact something they had been expecting for some time. The announcement was of no concern to Pete and Vincent who had both already handed in their notice. Bill confirmed for them that it would not be possible for them to rescind their respective notices to quit which had already been recorded, and thus opt for a redundancy payment instead. Even if that option were possible Bill explained they would undoubtedly be found alternative posts somewhere in the UK which it could be argued were comparable to their present jobs.

Bill confirmed that for his part he would not be interested in moving to another office but would opt for an early retirement package. Tom also said that he would do the same. He also had no desire to move house just for an alternative job which at best he would only hold down for a year or so.

Mrs Balstaff also confirmed that she too would opt for an early retirement. "Aye could not possibly think of moving house for another job," she confirmed. "May pension will be enough to live on. Aye have paid into it for many years. Air house is too nice to change. Aye will be able to devote may time to helping our hospital League of Friends."

"Well, that appears to leave you four," said Bill addressing Helen, Penny, Mavis and George. "As I said, there will be alternative jobs found and offered to you all. These may or may not be in this department and may or may not be in this region. When those posts are announced and if you decide that they are not appropriate there is always recourse to the Union who can advise and assist. I know that this information will have come as a big shock to you all but I was wondering if any of you have any plans?"

All four of them shook their heads.

"Well," said Bill, "you will all have a few weeks to think things over. Perhaps in that time a suitable alternative job can be found for you all. Oh, and by the way, Penny, Mr Pigg mentioned to me that he is in need of a secretary at the Regional Office. If you were interested in working for him that could be arranged. You just need to let me know and I will contact him for you.

Penny told Bill that she would think seriously about it.

Later Mavis and Helen were discussing the matter together. Helen revealed that she had always had an interest in working at the computer centre which was situated in the north of England. "They are always advertising in the union magazine for people to work there. The wages I understand are higher than in all the other offices in the country. The property prices are much cheaper up there and I've always had a fancy for working on computers."

"But it's such a long way off," said Mavis. "You won't know anyone up there. Would you not feel lonely?"

"Not really," responded Helen. "My family don't come from around here. By moving up to the computer centre I would be considerably closer to them than I am now. And I don't really have any close friends here. In fact, you are the closest friend that I have in this town. But what are you going to do?"

"I don't know," said Mavis. "I have been thinking about something that Phillipa Fry said to me. She told me that I could become a solicitor if I just studied hard. She said I had the brains and the initiative to make it. I have to admit that I have really been inspired with the legal work I have done and by meeting Phillipa. I am thinking of starting studying and looking for a legal firm where I can start training. Phillipa Fry has told me that she would help me in any way possible."

"That's a wonderful idea," said Helen. "You'd be a terrific lawyer."

"Oh, I'm not really sure I could manage it," said Mavis.

"You can do anything you put your mind to," said George.

"Here, here," said Tom. "You are a remarkable young lady. There is nothing that you cannot do if you really want it."

"Absolutely," said George.

Chapter Fifty-nine
Des Tightens His Grip

DCI Des Onions was still working hard on the preparation of the cases against Eddie Sharp, his solicitor and Giovanni Pettacinni. He had been over the statements of his team of officers who had carried out the search of the offices of Huw Roberts & Co and who also had arrested Jimmy Pearce and the twins. He had reviewed and tweaked all the statements and then been through all of them with each officer. He tried to think of any and all questions which a defence counsel on behalf of the accused might come up with. He felt reasonably happy that any leak holes had been sealed up.

Today he was labouring over the statement which Charlie Chivers would be making. The preparation of the statement was not as difficult or complicated as Des had feared it might be due primarily to the fact that Charlie was an experienced former CID officer. Both he and Des were on exactly the same wavelength in regard to the points of evidence that the statement would cover. It took them just over an hour to prepare the statement which was comprehensive and utterly damning as far as the defendants were concerned. Charlie knew exactly, from experience, how to present his evidence and Des was completely satisfied when the statement was finished.

"Well, I think that wraps it all up, Charlie. I cannot foresee any faults in this which a defence counsel could exploit."

Charlie nodded in agreement. "Yeah," he confirmed. "There's no holes in that. It shouldn't take a jury five minutes to come to a guilty verdict. As long as the members of your team give their evidence in a reliable way everything should go smoothly."

"Oh, there's no problem with them." Des assured him. "They're all well drilled and well-rehearsed."

"Good," said Charlie, getting to his feet. "I'll be off then. When is the trial?"

"Oh, another couple of weeks or so." Des assured him. "I'll let you know."

After Charlie had left Des reviewed again the evidence he had amassed against the defendants. Despite the financial evidence available in respect of Simon Nibble's client account (the figures speak for themselves thought Des), he had obtained a statement from the solicitor's cashier to the effect that she had spoken to her boss on several occasions about what she regarded as misuse of the client account. Her boss, she had told Des, had overridden these criticisms.

Des had also pressed Jimmy Pearce to provide some further information. Jimmy was more than happy to give evidence against Eddie Sharp particularly as there was a huge incentive for him to do so. The reduced charges were sufficient to convince Jimmy to co-operate. Des wondered how Jimmy had financed the first deal of drugs from the London suppliers and suggested that perhaps Eddie had provided the capital. Jimmy had readily agreed to say this and Des knew that if that were believed by the jury then it would be the worst for Eddie in the trial. He did know however that Jimmy's evidence might be regarded with some scepticism by the jury who would hear of Jimmy's past criminal record. Also, he was sure that the defence counsels would do their best to discredit Jimmy.

One piece of evidence which Des had found to be most fortuitous was the note book which had been found in Eddie's safe. This book contained names and telephone numbers together with dates and references many of which were indecipherable. He had checked the names and discovered that all were people with criminal records. He sought to tie these in with information already received from Jimmy Pearce. The latter of course was only too willing to give further evidence to link the entries in the note book with the criminal dealings. Des was aware that in the trial itself a discussion of the entries in the note book would be fatal for Eddie. He knew that Eddie would be incapable of explaining what the entries meant.

With regard to the evidence against Giovanni Pettacinni, Des felt that his hand was not as strong as he would like it to be. True, he had plenty of evidence that Joe had been involved in the fraudulent transfer of family shares in conspiracy with Eddie and his solicitor. He was aware however that Joe could simply deny this and claim that he had left all the technical details to the solicitor and had assumed that all was well. His lack of mastery of the English language would assist him in this defence.

True also was the fact that drug dealing had been going on at the Nite Club and also that in the Nite Club safe had been found drugs and large amounts of unaccounted for cash. In theory this was very incriminating for Giovanni but Des was aware that Joe's defence might be that the items were stored in the safe by the twins without his knowledge. The only evidence to the contrary was provided by the twins which, if their testimonies were believed, would be more than enough to convict Joe. If however, the twins were not believed then clearly the storage of the drugs in the safe together with the money would be attributed to the twins and the defence team would seek to imply that Joe had no idea what had been going on under his nose.

Des was reasonably confident that the evidence against the defendants would be sufficient to gain a conviction but what he wanted was even more evidence. He wanted it to be so overwhelming that there would be no doubt at all. To that end he mused over the papers which he held and tried to think of another angle.

He looked again at the note book which had been recovered from Eddie's safe. Although the entries therein gave reference to a number of names which enquiries had shown were people with criminal records, his problem was that he did not understand the hieroglyphics contained in the book. He knew the note book contained a thread which joined all the criminal episodes together. Each entry referred firstly to a name followed by a figure. Almost every entry was written or underlined in a different coloured crayon. Des scratched his chin and tried to comprehend the thread.

He left the building and drove to Eddie's house. He rang the doorbell and waited until Doris answered. "Hello, Mrs Sharp," he said. "There is something I'd like to discuss with you. Could I please come in for a moment."

Doris led him into the games room which Eddie always used to entertain people. Des flourished the note book and showed her the entries. "I was wondering if you could shed any light on the entries in this note book which we found in your husband's safe."

Doris looked at the entries for some time her brow furrowed, "I'm afraid not," she said, "he never confided in me nor did he ever discuss the note book with me. I'll see if my daughter can help. She's good at puzzles. She's in the other room. I'll just go and get her."

She left the room and soon returned with her daughter who was asked to look at the note book entries and try to explain them. She looked at these and nodded. "Do you understand them?" asked Des.

The girl nodded again, "The colours are the same as the balls on the snooker table," she said. "He always used the snooker table as a desk when he was doing the entries. The black equals seven, the pink is six, blue is five etcetera."

"Aah," said Des softly to himself, "and these notifications here and here?" he pointed to some letters which had been written.

"Snooker again," she said, "R equals red, W equals white and G equals green etc. That reference there," she pointed to the word MAX, "that isn't someone's name, it means 147. That reference there to 'rocket' means someone called Ronnie or O'Sullivan. Also, the reference to Dracula really means someone who is called Ray or Reardon."

Suddenly all the entries began to make sense to Des. As he carefully examined each entry, they all came together. He thanked Doris and her daughter for making everything clear to him. He returned to his office at the police station and summoned two or three of his team and explained the sense of the entries in Eddie's note book.

"Anybody here a snooker fan?" he asked. Two of the team admitted that they were. "Right," said Des handing over the note book to one of them. "All these entries are written with a snooker connection. The coloured entries refer to the value of the balls in snooker. Take this away with you and try to figure out what each entry says exactly. OK?"

Mavis was at home with her father. Her mother was out shopping. She had just made a cup of tea for both of them and while they were sipping their teas she told him that she was thinking of studying law, in order to become a solicitor. Her father was frankly amazed that his daughter was interested in doing this. He had always known that she was intellectually capable. He knew that she had read all the books in the house which he possessed. However, he had never thought that she had the drive or ambition to study something at length. At school she had never excelled academically even though he knew she was clever enough to do so.

He realised now that perhaps he did not know her as well as he thought. She explained to him how recently she had assisted her friends Doris and Freda, with whom she shared exercise classes, in their divorce proceedings and also how she had helped the mother of Vincent, her work colleague, as well. She told him how she had met Phillipa Fry the barrister and how impressed and inspired she had been and how Phillipa had encouraged to take up the studies and how she had now definitely determined to do so. Her father was flabbergasted and realised that his daughter had now turned a corner in her life.

"Well, I know someone at the local college. They run a Law Society course. I could give him a ring if you like and see if they could include you on their course. What do you think?"

"Well, actually, I was thinking of doing it by joining a legal firm and learning from within." said Mavis.

"But I think," said her father, "That most of the people on the course are already embedded in legal firms. They just do college work as well."

"That would be great" she said "thanks very much."

"But ...." said her father sententiously "it's a long arduous course."

Mavis nodded and said, "I realise that but I'm prepared to do it."

"No more time for going out socialising or dancing," he added.

Mavis nodded again. She thought that since her father had raised the subject of social activity it might be appropriate to mention her romantic attachment to George. Her father took the news with delight and insisted that she bring him home to introduce him to her mother and himself.

Vincent's mother had almost got over her broken ribs suffered from the attack upon her by her husband with a cricket bat. She no longer felt any pain when breathing and could now sleep at night in any position. She only ever felt any discomfort if she had to unexpectedly sneeze and that was not too often. Not only did she no longer feel any physical discomfort but in general terms she felt as if an enormous weight had been lifted off her shoulders. She was no longer anxious and pessimistic when getting out of bed each morning. Now each day she felt optimistic and some days even joyful. She reflected on how her life had changed for the better.

Prompted by Phillipa Fry and accompanied by Mavis she had attended the Local Authority offices and made enquiries about the purchase of the council house in which she lived. She was astounded to find that under the 'Right to Buy' scheme she, as a life-long tenant was entitled to buy her house for what seemed to her to be a ridiculously low figure.

Mavis then took her to see a financial adviser who was able to locate a lender who was willing to offer her a mortgage for the purchase of the property. The mortgage loan was for the full purchase price, no down payment was required from April and when all the figures were worked out, she found that her monthly mortgage payment was almost exactly the same as the rent she had always paid. Furthermore, as a result of the agreement to purchase, the Council promised to carry out certain improvements to the property as well. She could hardly believe it.

It was due to these massive improvements in her life and the absence of what had previously been a daily threat from her bullying husband that she was truly happy. In fact, she could not remember how long it had been, if at all, that she had felt so happy.

On top of everything else she felt reassured that eventually she would have her own house to leave to Vincent when her time came. For this reason alone, she knew she would be eternally grateful to Mavis who had made it all possible. In addition, it was she who had saved her son from the violence of the twins at the nightclub when the arrests had been made.

Vincent himself was also very happy. Firstly, he was immensely relieved that his mother's life with the ogre was ended. Also, he was relieved for his own sake as he too had been intimidated and frightened by his stepfather. Now he could visit his mother whenever he pleased. In addition, he was so happy to be released from the obligation to work at the office every day. He had always hated the job and he disliked Mr Pigg who constantly picked on him. Now he was working out a mere fortnight of his notice before commencing full-time work at the Nite Club. He was already working there in the evenings to get to know the ropes and set up his own style of operation and he felt joyous. Lizzie was with him every evening to help and support him.

Mr Pigg, following his visit to his old office, was also happy. He had to admit that he had been dreading the prospect of having to visit his old territory to announce the news that everyone would soon be out of a job. He felt rather guilty about the perfunctory way in which he had dealt with the matter but he excused himself by relying on the fact that he had another important visit to complete on the same day and therefore had to rush off and could not linger to supervise the occasion with diplomacy.

As it happened, the problem had resolved itself in a way in which Mr Pigg himself could never hope to have achieved. He had already heard on the telephone from Bill that both he and Tom and Mrs Balsaff would opt for early retirement and that Pete and Vincent had already found alternative jobs. Also, Bill informed him, Penny had decided to accept his offer to work for him at the Regional Office.

Mr Pigg was ecstatic to hear this. He knew that with Penny beside him he would be able to continue to produce his beloved graphs. These were, he knew, so important to his job and so well appreciated by everybody. Also, he was delighted to learn that the only remaining members of staff whom he had to find a position for, were Mavis, George and Helen. Even the latter, he heard from Bill was considering a move to the computer centre up north provided a vacancy could be found. He was sure that one could be found and so that just left Mavis and George to be sorted out. He couldn't believe how easily the seemingly impossible job had been solved. When he had reported to Mr Jenkins that gentleman had confessed to him that his delegation to Mr Pigg of the task of closing his former office had, in effect, been a test for him.

"I have to admit Arnold," he said, "I did think that you might find the job of closing down your own office to be a Herculean task but you seem to have coped with it without breaking sweat."

Chapter Sixty
More Flirtatious Shenanigans

Jeremy Fallow Q C was in the middle of a sentencing speech in the case of the man who had been found guilty of exposure in a public place, namely a park. The case had been adjourned for sentencing and Jeremy had told the defendant that he was not ruling out a custodial sentence.

The defence counsel Mr Aloysius Medland had, Jeremy admitted to himself, presented a good mitigation speech. Furthermore, he had produced a persuasive character witness, a man of the cloth no less, who had been able to say good things about the defendant who was a member of his flock. Jeremy had been predisposed to impose a custodial sentence on the defendant but had allowed Mr Medland to persuade him to impose a non-custodial sentence.

Whilst passing sentence Jeremy went to great lengths to advise the defendant how fortunate he was both to have such an eloquent and persuasive counsel and also an impressive character witness. He emphasised, when imposing a two-year suspended sentence that if the man did anything further to bring himself to the court's attention then he would be facing instant custody. The defendant who had been weeping copiously in the dock throughout Jeremy's speech, thanked him and assured him that he would not be returning to court again.

Mr Medland inclined his head towards Jeremy in acknowledgement of the leniency which had been afforded to his client, but despite the obviousness of the situation, namely presumed gratitude and pleasure in respect of the sentence passed, he still contrived to wear on his face what looked suspiciously close to a sneer.

Jeremy rose and bowed to the court before retiring to his chamber. He noticed as he turned to leave that Phillipa Fry was sat in the viewing gallery. Once inside his chamber he took off his wig and his robe and settled down to do some paperwork. Shirley Kemp his clerk came into the room and busied herself at the coffee machine.

"You do remember that I have to leave early this afternoon, Judge?" she said, "I have to go to my daughter's school for a parent/teacher meeting."

"Yes, yes, I remember," said Jeremy. "You leave as soon as you wish Shirley. I hope it goes well for you. Is your daughter doing well?"

"Oh, yes, I think so," said Shirley, "but of course I will find out soon won't I?" She left the room and immediately opened the door again saying, "Visitor, Judge. I'll pop off now and see you in the morning."

"Yes, thank you, Shirley," said Jeremy. "Good luck."

Phillipa Fry walked into the room. She was wearing a blue suit with a cream blouse. On her shoulder she carried her barrister's fabric bag in which she carried her wig and gown. "Hello, Jeremy," she said placing her bag down on the floor, "can I help myself to a cup of coffee?"

"By all means," said Jeremy sipping his cup. Phillipa poured herself a cup and sat down on the chair facing him.

"Well Jeremy, a non-custodial sentence, eh?"

"Yes," said Jeremy. "I hope I haven't made a mistake but I was impressed with the mitigation. It's not everyone who gets a character reference from their vicar."

"Hmm," she said, "I suppose that's right."

"Do you know Mr Medland?" he asked. "I have not come across him before."

"Not really," said Phillipa. "I believe he has just recently joined Albion Chambers from the London area. What did you think of him?"

"Well..." said Jeremy with some hesitation, "his mitigation today was very thorough. He has an eye for detail and fights his corner hard. However, in the trial itself he was in danger of spoiling any of his own good points with excessive interrogation of witnesses. Sometimes less is more and he does not seem to have appreciated that yet. Also, I felt all the way through the trial that he was in danger of showing disrespect. He must try to curb that or he'll come a cropper. But enough of that. How are you today?"

"I'm very well, thank you," said Phillipa. She relaxed in the chair, sipped her coffee and crossed her legs. Jeremy noted that she was wearing her black stockings and, as usual, was not afraid to show her legs to him. Jeremy as usual appraised them openly.

"May I say," he said, "that you look particularly beautiful today."

"You may indeed, Jeremy," she assured him. She placed her coffee cup on his desk and leaned back in her chair lifting one leg to brush off an imaginary speck of dust and thus affording Jeremy a further view of her thighs. Once again Jeremy ogled her and already felt an erection growing in his trousers. He was somewhat surprised that although they had on previous occasions established an intimacy and even spent a whole night together in bed, it seemed to him that this subsequent encounter had the feel of an initial meeting. Certainly, he was experiencing an excitement which was not typical between a man and a woman who had the confidence of previous encounters.

Phillipa was wearing her black rimmed glasses which Jeremy always found to be so attractive. She looked at him over the top of the glasses with a seductive smile. "Did I hear Shirley saying goodbye to you as I came in?"

"You did indeed," said Jeremy. "She's gone to a parent/teacher meeting at her child's school. So we are completely alone."

"Hmm, I am so glad," she said. She stood up and slipped off her suit jacket and hung it over the back of her chair before sitting down again. Once more she crossed her legs with some extravagance and once again brushed away the same imaginary fleck of dust from her thigh. Jeremy stared hungrily at her legs.

"Jeremy you really are a naughty man," she said in mock severity "you are looking at my legs again, aren't you."

Jeremy raised his eyebrows and shrugged his shoulders, "They are so lovely, what else can I do?" he asked.

Phillipa stood up and unfastened her skirt at the side and let it drop to the floor. She stepped out of it and stood in front of him wearing only her black stockings and suspenders, with panties and a blouse above them. Jeremy breathed in deeply and made a silent ooh expression with his mouth. The sight of her chorus girl legs in high heels and stockings excited him so much.

Phillipa began to unbutton her blouse very slowly. "Would you like me to show you my breasts, Jeremy?" she half whispered stepping towards him.

"More than anything," he said with a hoarseness in his voice.

She reached the bottom button and then eased her blouse off her shoulders and dropped it on the floor behind her. She wore a red bra trimmed with black. She stood in front of him and reached behind her to undo her bra straps. The bra also dropped to the floor and she eased a little closer so that he could reach out and touch her.

"You are so beautiful" he whispered taking a breast in each hand and fondling her nipples between thumbs and forefingers.

She sighed with satisfaction, "Do you really think so, Jeremy?" she asked. He leaned forward and took one of her nipples in his mouth and gently sucked and kissed it.

"Ooh, Jeremy, that is so wonderful," she whispered, reaching down to fondle his groin area. She felt his erection and stroked it on the outside of his trousers. He stood up and held her head in both hands and kissed her on the lips softly and passionately. She leaned back against his desk as she unbuttoned his trousers which fell to the floor. She then lowered his underpants and grasped his penis which was fully erect. "Ooh, Jeremy," she whispered, "I can tell that you are pleased to see me."

She began to stroke herself with his penis on the outside of her panties and quickly became aroused. Jeremy reached behind her and grasped her buttocks and gently lifted her onto the desk. She meanwhile continued to stroke herself with his penis until they both could wait no longer. She pushed aside her panties and guided him into her and they both gave a loud sigh of satisfaction. He slightly adjusted his position so that he was totally on top of her and then gradually began to push and withdraw.

Phillipa reacted with pleasure each time he fully entered her. "Ooh, Jeremy, so nice, exquisite. Ooh yes that's perfect, ooh, yes, just keep doing that my darling." He nuzzled her neck and continued as instructed.

"You are the most beautiful sexy woman I have ever known."

"Ooh, yes, yes, Jeremy. You are the one, you are the judge sentence me!"

Jeremy who was now thrusting hard said, "I sentence you to be my sex slave for ever!"

"Ooh, yes! Jeremy yes!" she cried and reached her climax with a long joyful cry.

After two more thrusts Jeremy too climaxed and lay on top of her breathing heavily. "I love you so much, Phillipa," he whispered.

"Me too," she replied. They clutched each other for a further moment then separated and got dressed. Phillipa gathered up her bag which she shouldered.

"My brother Roger is back in Bristol," he told her, "I'm not sure when he's away again but I will let you know."

"That would be so nice," she said. They kissed each other goodbye and Phillipa left.

George arrived at the hospice care home to visit his grandmother. He checked himself in at the reception desk, and sat in a comfortable chair in the welcome room waiting for someone to show him to his grandmother's room. It was a quiet room with a warm thick carpet and pastel shaded wallpaper.

A lady with dark, slightly greying hair came to shake his hand and show him to her room. As they walked, she assured him that his grandmother was comfortable but obviously tired at times. She did assure him that although she was not suffering any pain, she was being given morphine.

She ushered him into the bedroom which was bright and cheerful with a French window that looked out over a peaceful garden. His grandmother was lying on her back and looking heavy lidded. The lady patted her hand and told her, "Your grandson is here to see you."

His grandmother opened her eyes and smiled when she saw George. He pulled a chair forward and grasped her hand. "How do you feel?" he asked her.

She nodded and smiled benignly. "Not so bad," she said in a voice that seemed a little faint to George.

"Are they looking after you?" he asked. She nodded again and also smiled. "What's the food like here?" he asked. Again, she nodded as if to confirm that she had been eating well but in truth nothing had passed her lips except a glass of water.

"I've left everything to you, George," she said, "my will is in the drawer of the writing desk in the dining room." she added

"Don't worry about that," he responded. "You just relax and take it easy. They are closing the office where I am working." he told her. "I will have to look for another job soon. I haven't been there that long either. Of course I don't have to find a new job. They will find me a post in another office but that could be anywhere in the country and I don't really want to move. Not now that Mavis and I are a unit. It's certainly something I will have to think about." He looked towards her and realised that she was asleep.

He remained where he was for about an hour and eventually, appreciating that she was unlikely to awaken, he rose from his chair and left the room to find the lady who had shown him into the room. When he found her, he told her that he had decided to leave due to the fact that his grandmother was asleep and did not look likely to wake up. She assured him that this was due to the morphine but that his grandmother was not expected to last more than a day or so.

Mavis had approached Bill first thing in the morning to request an absence from the office for an hour or two to allow her the opportunity to call on some local solicitors to enquire as to whether or not they could offer her a position of trainee or articled clerk. Bill was only too pleased to allow her some time off and wished her good fortune.

Her first port of call was, not surprisingly, the offices of Duffey Fry & Co with whom she was already familiar. She asked to speak to Mrs Robinson who was her contact in the firm. That lady told her that at the present moment the firm had all its quota of trainees or articled clerks and probably would not wish to absorb one more.

She did tell Mavis that she personally would be extremely happy to have her as an ordinary clerical assistant which might be approved by the partners of the firm. Once she was embedded in the firm Mrs Robinson assured her that the firm would almost certainly agree that she could graduate into the post of articled clerk. This however might take slightly longer to achieve any qualifications. She suggested as an alternative that Mavis might wish to make enquiries at the offices of Huw Roberts & Co.

She pointed out that the solicitor who had been in charge at the firm, Mr Nibble, had been arrested and was currently in custody. She knew that Mavis was aware of this because the divorces of Doris and Freda had contained references to Mr Nibble.

"Mr Nibble" she said, "has never been wholly popular with the other lawyers in town. His gung-ho methods and lack of careful preparation on any case he handled has meant that he is not respected professionally. However, it is fair to say that he runs a firm that is commercially quite successful. He also inherited one or two very experienced and respected employees when he took over the firm." "At present," she said, "the firm is being run by a lawyer who has been appointed by the Law Society to run the firm at least until the trial of Mr Nibble is concluded. I am sure that they are in need of an articled clerk and when you think about it there is nobody better to be articled with than a Law Society representative. His name is Mr Ferguson," she said. "Would you like me to telephone him to try to arrange an interview with him?"

Mavis confirmed that she would like that and so Mrs Robinson telephoned Huw Roberts & Co and spoke to Mr Ferguson who agreed to meet Mavis within the hour to discuss things. She then went to the offices of Huw Roberts & Co and met Mr Ferguson who was a middle-aged man with kind eyes and silver hair who reminded her of Bill Butler.

"Mrs Robinson at Duffey Fry & Co was very complimentary about you," he confided. "It would perhaps be superfluous but do you have anyone else who could give you a reference?"

"Phillipa Fry," said Mavis. "She is a barrister at Clifton Chambers in Bristol."

"Yes, I've heard of her," he said. "Would it be all right to contact her for a reference. Would she give you a favourable one?"

"Well, she said she would," said Mavis. "Well, perhaps if you give me your contact details I will contact Miss Fry and then get back to you."

Mavis thanked him very much and went back to the office. When she got back there, she found that the atmosphere was very casual. This was undoubtedly due to the fact that everyone knew that the office was closing. Everything had taken on a temporary feel. It seemed that work had almost dried up so everyone was sat around talking about the future.

Mavis told them of her experience at the solicitors' offices and everyone was confident that she would get the post. Mavis herself was not so confident although she was sure that Phillipa Fry would not give her a bad reference.

She asked George how his grandmother was and he told her what had happened the day before and that according to the hospice care staff today or tomorrow might be her last day. Predictably perhaps Mavis became emotional on behalf of George. Her obvious distress made everybody feel bad for her rather than George and the latter felt so uncomfortable that he had to excuse himself on the basis that he had, once more, to visit his grandmother. His exit produced even more grief in Mavis who had to be consoled and cuddled by Helen. All the others felt uncomfortable for Mavis but on balance they did not feel any criticism towards her because she wore her heart on her sleeve. They simply knew that this was the way that Mavis was.

A little later in the day Mavis received the call from Mr Ferguson at Huw Roberts & Co. He confirmed that he had spoken to Phillipa Fry on the telephone and that she had given him an outstanding reference for Mavis. In view of this he announced he was able to offer her the post of articled clerk.

Chapter Sixty-one
George's Loss

When George arrived at the hospice care nursing home he contacted the lady he had seen the previous day in order to check upon the health of his grandmother. He was told that she was in the same condition as the day before and that she had slept for nearly the whole twenty-four hours since he had last called to see her. She explained again that the tiredness was due to the pain killers, mostly morphine, which were being administered.

He went into her room and saw that she was still asleep on her back. She looked very pale and drawn. He drew up a chair and sat beside her watching her closely as she inhaled with short pants of breath. He reached out and held her hand and she opened her eyes and focused on him. She gave a tired smile and closed her eyes again. He thought that she had gone back to sleep again but without opening her eyes she murmured quietly. "I've left everything to you, George. My will is in the writing desk in the dining room, so is the bank and building society pass books. Go and see Mr Reynolds at Duffey Fry & Co. He drew up my will for me and knows what I want. He will help you to do everything. There is also a funeral plan in the writing desk. Take that to him as well and a life insurance policy."

"Shush, shush," whispered George. "Don't concern yourself about anything. Just rest and get Better," he urged.

She shook her head slightly though her eyes remained closed. "No, no," she said quietly, "my time has come. I've enjoyed having you with me. I know you will be all right." She looked exhausted and continued breathing now more deeply. George stayed with her for approximately one more hour and then decided to leave. He kissed her on the forehead and left the room. He sought out the lady who had helped him and told her he was going. She told him frankly that his grandmother's last moments had arrived. She assured him that she was in peace and would gently slip away. She was unlikely to awake again. She took his contact details and promised to be in touch.

Detective Chief Inspector Desmond O'Nighons read the translation of the entries which had been made in Eddie Sharp's note book. The two officers in his team, who were snooker enthusiasts, had studied the entries together carefully and had very soon interpreted the note book which indeed had snooker references connected to each entry. They had typed up a page which set out the precise meaning of all the entries which showed a record of criminal dealings, mostly connected to drugs and the recipients and the amounts paid.

Des decided that one of those two officers would submit the interpretation of the note book as evidence in the court case. He chose the most experienced of the two at giving evidence in court. He knew that this man was one of his most experienced officers and would present the evidence convincingly. It was obvious to him that the defence would deny the Crown's interpretation of the entries in the note book but Des knew that his officer's version of the entries would be believed by the jury partly because it was very plausible and also because Eddie would be unable to put forward a more bland or straightforward explanation. He knew also that before a jury it was never good enough to simply present a blank denial of evidence. If Eddie did not accept the Crown's explanation of the entries, which of course he could not afford to do, he would have to present a more plausible explanation and Des sensed that he would be unable to do that. Des rubbed his hands together in complete satisfaction.

George had returned to the office even though it was late in the afternoon. His conscience would not permit him to go straight home even though there was slightly less than an hour of the working day remaining. He settled himself down at his desk without talking to anyone.

"Well?" said Mavis staring at him. He looked up and raised his eyebrows. "Well... how is your grandmother?" she repeated.

George inclined his head from side to side and grimaced a fraction. "She's sleeping almost all the time," he said. "They've told me that it won't be long."

"That is so sad," said Mavis wiping a tear from her eye. George nodded and looked down at his paperwork. He did not feel able to deal with grief, either publicly or even at all. This inability was emphasised by the obvious ability of Mavis to display her emotions for all to see.

The other members of staff felt sympathy towards George but there was a feeling of discomfort in the air. No one felt brave enough to break the silence. Mavis eventually brought the atmosphere back to more mundane matters. She said to George, "What plans do you have for tea tonight?"

He shook his head. "None."

"Well, you are formally invited to my house to have tea with my mum and dad."

Pete gave a snort of laughter. "Blimey, he's having a bad enough day already. Don't make things any worse for him."

Tom and Vincent sniggered but Helen turned on Pete with some venom, "Don't be so ignorant," she said.

"Just joking," Pete assured her.

When the office closed Mavis and George made their way to her home where she introduced him to her parents. When he met them George instantly understood one or two things. The first thing he understood was where Mavis got her looks from. Her mother was, he guessed, in her mid-forties but still a very attractive woman. Her facial features were very close to those of her daughter with the addition of a few lines. Her hair was beginning to show a touch of grey which was cunningly disguised with blond highlights. She had also retained her figure and successfully managed to avoid acquiring the usual female forties pear shape.

Her father was slightly older. His hair had more grey in it, but the salt and pepper impression added a wisdom to his appearance which showed George where Mavis's intellectual side came from. They both fully welcomed him to their house and asked the usual formal questions which, ordinarily, would be accepted as normal polite enquiries. Mavis had failed to inform them of the deaths of George's parents nor of the imminent expected demise of his grandmother. She intervened now to advise them that George was an orphan and had, until recently, been living with his grandmother who was now in the hospice care home.

This information rocked them back for a moment after which they expressed their sympathy for his situation. Her mother showed where Mavis got her ability to show empathy for others. As she patted him sympathetically on the shoulder with one hand, she wiped a tear from her eye with the other.

When they had finished the formalities of introduction Mavis's mother instructed them to sit around the dining table and they began to serve the food which she had prepared. They all tucked in and after some small talk the conversation turned to the office in which George and Mavis worked. Mavis had not previously informed them of all the recent happenings at the office particularly the fact that the office was soon to close although of course told her father that she had decided to study law. They talked about this for a while and her parents were gratified to hear that she had found a post at Huw Roberts & Co.

Mavis's father turned to George and asked, "And what will you do?"

"Do?" said George enquiringly.

"Yes," said her father, "when the office closes. Have you found another job or do you know what you will do?" George admitted that he did not have any idea and had not really applied his mind to it. He explained that he had been pre-occupied with the health of his grandmother.

"Yes, of course," said Mavis's mother with a critical glance at her husband. "It is entirely understandable that in the circumstances, you have not had a chance to think about it."

"Yes, I quite understand that," said her father, "but you do have a limited time in which to consider things don't you."

George admitted that he was right and that it was about time he himself did something about it. He felt some guilt that he had not already considered the matter but he also felt embarrassed that he had been caught out by Mavis's father. He had hoped that her parents would like him but he felt that he had been found wanting.

When they had finished their meal, Mavis helped her mother to clear the table and do the washing up. George was left alone at the table with her father. In an effort to fill the silence he said, "What is it you teach at school Mr Clutterbuck?"

"English and Drama," was the reply. George nodded as if he expected nothing else.

"What were your best subjects at school?" he asked George who grimaced and shrugged a bit.

"I suppose I was pretty average and never excelled at anything. I suppose I still don't know what it is I want to do. As soon as he had uttered these words George realised how pathetic they must have sounded to a school teacher and a potential father-in-law. Once more he reflected that he was not making a good impression.

"Just like Mavis," he responded. "When she was at school, she was never inspired by any of the subjects she studied. She also had no idea what she wanted to do. Until now of course. I must say it is very gratifying to see her really interested in something."

George was unable to assess whether or not this man liked him or whether perhaps he was decidedly unimpressed that his daughter should decide to associate with someone who had no clue what he wanted to do. Did he feel that anyone who Mavis chose was good enough or did he feel that George's indecision was inexcusable? He did not have enough experience of the man to make an assessment of his attitude toward him.

Mr Clutterbuck, as if sensing George's anxiety, said "If it's any consolation to you I find that nearly all the students at my school do not have any idea what they want to do when they leave school."

George did not really know what to say but nodded in what he fondly hoped was a sage-like manner. Mavis and her mother returned to the room with cups of tea. "So George," said her mother cheerfully, "Have you decided to contact your real mother and father?"

Mavis gave her mother a furious glance. George was slightly non-plussed by the directness of the approach. He shook his head slowly, "No..." he said carefully, "I have not properly got my head around the news that I was adopted when I was very small. I will have to think carefully about it. At the moment I still feel that my real mum and dad are dead."

"Yes of course," said her mother sympathetically, striving to make up for her non-diplomatic introduction of the subject. "Perhaps when you have had more time to think about it you may feel differently. So where do you live George?" she asked. George explained that he had lived with his grandmother since the death of his parents but had recently begun to share a flat with Pete who was a work colleague.

"But what about your grandmother's house?" she asked. "What's going to happen about that?" George was again taken back by her directness.

Mavis intervened strongly, "Mum!" she cried.

"His grandmother is still alive. It's none of your business."

"I was only showing an interest," insisted her mother. "Poor George will have to consider these points soon enough."

"Well, that's as may be," said Mavis, "but at present he does not need to think about anything other than his grandmother's health." She rose from the table and said to George, "Let's go into the other room for a few minutes." She took his hand and led him into the front lounge where they sat together on the sofa. "Sorry about that" she whispered to him, "She can't help herself." She gave him a brief kiss.

"That's OK," he said and clutched her hand. "I'd better be off," he said, "I wanted to check up on my grandmother's state before going to bed."

She stood up and, still holding his hand, she led him back into the dining room. Her father was doing a jig-saw puzzle and her mother was reading a ladies magazine. "George is going now," she said. He thanked them profusely for their hospitality and said he hoped to see them again soon. They both shook his hand and said it had been a pleasure to see him.

Mavis then showed him out and they kissed affectionately on the front door step. George returned to the flat which he shared with Pete.

Jeremy Fallow QC was taking an afternoon off and attending the county ground to watch some cricket. He knew that the home side were batting and he hoped to be able to watch his brother Roger enjoy a good innings.

When he arrived, Roger was at the crease and, although he was playing nervously, had already made twenty-four runs. As Jeremy watched he noticed the ferocity of the opposition fast bowling. Roger and his partner were having great difficulty in dealing with the speed and the hostility of the attack. Several deliveries caught the edge of Roger's bat but each time the ball raced to the boundary behind the wicket. By the time Jeremy had been there twenty minutes his brother had doubled his score without really getting his eye in.

Jeremy was reflecting how fortunate Gloucestershire were to be eighty-nine for no wickets when Roger snicked yet another ball behind the stumps. This time the wicket keeper held on to the ball and Roger was out. Eighty-nine for one.

When he had taken off his pads and disposed of his bat Roger made his way to Jeremy whom he had spotted as he returned to the pavilion. He sat next to his brother and said, "Well, that was a pig's ear. I just couldn't pick the ball up today. The light is not too good but their bowlers are fearsomely quick. Still, somehow or other we have just about managed to see off their openers and with nearly one hundred on the board for one wicket only is a good result."

"Yes, I think you are right," said Jeremy. "Most of the runs you scored were... dare I say it, a bit streaky."

"Definitely," said Roger. "So how are you? No court work today?"

"No," said Jeremy. "I had a trial collapse so I thought I would take the opportunity of watching you for a while."

"Well, you picked the wrong innings to come and watch," said Roger. "Still, fifty runs, is a reasonable score."

They sat side by side for ten minutes or so without talking further. Eventually Roger said, "Next week we've got another away game. If you wanted to use the flat you could."

"That would be good," said Jeremy. "I will have to check with Phillipa and let you know. I've also got a trial coming up but I don't suppose that will interfere with anything." They continued chatting for about another hour and watched Gloucestershire reach a respectable total for the loss of only three wickets but without showing any assurance in their style of play.

Meanwhile, just along the road from the county ground stood the Bristol prison. Its bleak exterior, positioned as it is in a quiet residential street just off a main road lined with shops, comes as a surprise to anyone approaching it. A visitor is not expecting to find a structure, the size of a football stadium, in a quiet neighbourhood.

Today's visitor was Mr Aloysius Medland who was visiting Simon Nibble. After undergoing the usual rigmarole of the search procedure, similar to a customs inspection, he was shown into a small room, the size of a telephone booth, and was eventually joined by Simon Nibble.

The latter looked terrible. A couple of weeks or so of hospitality from Her Majesty had put paid to his previous supercilious attitude. Attired as he was in prison denim and without the benefit of his preferred Armani suit, he looked dejected and forlorn.

"Good day Mr Nibble. I am Mr Medland, your barrister."

Simon looked puzzled. "But I instructed Algie Phillipson. What are you doing here?"

"Alas, Mr Nibble, the trial in which Mr Phillipson is currently involved is taking longer than expected and he will therefore be unavailable at the commencement of your matter. His brief has been passed to me."

"But I do not know you," said Simon. "I have never even heard of you and have no idea of your suitability for this matter."

"I have just transferred here to Albion Chambers from London. I can assure you that I have ample experience in matters such as yours. Now, there are a number of points that I want to go through with you."

Simon looked even more dejected but realised that, with the position he was in, he had no option but to accept the situation as it was. He endeavoured to assist his new barrister as much as he could but the longer the interview lasted, the more pessimistic he became. On each occasion that he presented Mr Medland with what he himself regarded as a reasonable or plausible point, the latter appeared to adopt what he could only describe as a cynical sneer. This was very disturbing for Simon whose confidence was beginning to diminish.

On several occasions Mr Medland asked him about entries and withdrawals to and from his client account. Each time Simon assured him that he always left such matters to his cashier. The sneer appeared again accompanied by an almost imperceptible snort of derision.

"Yours is the ultimate responsibility in these matters." Mr Medland emphasised with an additional sneer. "I cannot go in front of Judge Fallow with such an inadequate defence."

"Judge Fallow?" said Simon enquiringly. "I've been in his court more than once," he added blandly, "he seemed nice enough. The last case I took before him we managed to get a not guilty verdict. Of course that was with Algie Phillipson."

"Yes, well…" said Mr Medland, with a gratuitous curl of the lip. "Make no mistake, Mr Nibble, Judge Fallow is no push over. If you get on the wrong side of him then woe betide you."

They remained together for another hour or so during which time Mr Medland's sneer became more pronounced and Simon's demeanour grew more despondent. In his heart he was always aware of his own guilt but was even now uncertain as to how it had occurred. He still was unable to believe how cavalier he had been with the management of his own client account. It had started with one or two false transactions which, having seemingly gone unnoticed, enticed him into making further bigger transgressions. On reflection he thought it was similar to the situation where a gambler allows one or two fortunate early lucky bets to tempt him into more and more extravagant wagers until he becomes thoroughly enmeshed in the whole sorry procedure.

Between them he and Mr Medland seemed to come to a half-hearted conclusion that the best way to proceed was to emphasise the criminality of Eddie Sharp and the Svengali influence which this had upon him. The hope was that Eddie could be portrayed as the true villain of the situation and his own involvement in everything would appear to be minimal in comparison. He was not sure how that would dovetail in with a 'not guilty' plea since it appeared, even to Simon himself, to contain an element of admission on his part. He was not confident that Mr Medland could persuade the jury or Judge Fallow that he (Simon Nibble) had been totally duped by Eddie Sharp into doing things which he had not intended to do. He realised that his future was entirely in the hands of Mr Medland.

In the early hours of the morning George received the telephone call from the hospice informing him that, during the night his grandmother had passed away. He was told that he could call into the hospice to see his grandmother before the undertakers were instructed to remove her body. They told him that perhaps first thing in the morning might be the best time to call.

He felt surprised that, although he had always loved her dearly, he was unable to raise a tear for her departure. He wondered if he was at fault for not being able to produce this indication of grief and also whether or not others shared this inability. He felt some guilt that perhaps he was the only one. Surely, he thought, there must be others who experienced the same sense of sterility. He determined to visit the hospice first thing the next day and also to contact a firm of undertakers immediately afterwards.

Judge Jeremy Fallow QC was in his Crown Court Chambers writing up some notes for a sentencing hearing which was due the following day. Shirley Kemp was busying herself in his room with some filing. She also prepared his coffee machine for a cup for him. She heard a sound in the outer room and went to investigate. She returned immediately saying, "Visitor Judge." And was followed into the room by Phillipa Fry who smiled at him and seated herself in the visitor's chair. Shirley Kemp made them both a cup of coffee and then retired to her own room.

Jeremy said, "I spoke to Roger yesterday. He told me that he is playing away again next week. Are you able to come to his flat next week?"

Phillipa looked at him archly over the top of her glasses. "That would be really lovely Jeremy. Algie is in the middle of a trial which seems to be taking longer than expected. He is likely to be another week at least. The trial is in Exeter so he won't be home. I'll be able to come to Clifton to see you as before."

"That's wonderful," said Jeremy. "I'm thinking of staying there the whole week during the trial so you can choose whichever night or nights suits you."

"I might decide to come on Wednesday next week," she said. "I've got a couple of days free then and I thought I might come to watch your trial. You know I have slightly more than a passing interest in the trial, because the prosecution, are intending to produce my two divorce petitions as evidence. Mr Sabin contacted me for my views and permission you know."

"Yes, so I believe," said Jeremy, "and as I have told you before I am always happy for petitions prepared by you to be included as evidence in my court. However, he went on, "I cannot see the defence counsels allowing them to go unchallenged, can you?"

"Not really," conceded Phillipa, "but the ultimate decision is yours of course. Who are the defence counsels?"

"Well…" said Jeremy, "I believe that Mr Medland will be representing one of the accused who is a solicitor. Another is represented by Humphrey and I'm not sure I remember who is representing the third defendant."

"Yes," said Phillipa. "Mr Medland is counsel for the solicitor. I think I told you that he had tried to ingratiate himself with Algie and me. Apparently, he instructed Algie first, but he's involved in a case in Exeter which is taking at least a week longer than expected so the brief was passed to Mr Medland. I made a few enquiries about him. Remember I told you he had recently come from London, well, apparently, he made his reputation there some years ago representing a number of coloured defendants who were involved in the Brixton riots. It seems that his early success coupled with an obvious anti-establishment attitude endeared him to the black rioters."

"Yes…" said Jeremy. "I thought I discerned a certain lack of respect. At times in a recent case I could almost believe that he wore a sneer on his face."

"Hmm, yes," said Phillipa. "His attitude seems to indicate that it is a sneer, but in reality, I believe it is simply an unfortunate tic or spasmodic twitch of the muscles in his face. It hasn't gone unnoticed by those around him and he has already been nicknamed Elvis by some, not because of any good looks or likeness to the King of rock and roll, but because of the curl of his lip."

Hmm," said Jeremy sceptically. "It didn't look like an involuntary twitch to me. More like a sceptical, cynical judgement."

"Yes," said Phillipa. "I agree it can look like that. But could it not be the case that it is nothing more than an expression he wears when he is concentrating on something. Like a classical musician who sometimes has a grimace on his face while playing a demanding piece of music. He still loves the music despite the grimace."

"Yes," said Jeremy. "I accept that that may be the case but I'm still not certain. If it turns out to be disrespect, he may find himself in some trouble. Anyway, as I said, I suspect that your divorce petitions will be the first interesting point in the trial."

"Almost a trial within a trial," added Phillipa almost questioningly.

"Absolutely," said Jeremy. "Humphrey at least will be resolutely opposed to their inclusion. And, although I have little or no experience of Mr Medland, I cannot believe that he wouldn't take any point that was offered. Mind you, I have not heard anything more about the defendant who assaulted his wife with the cricket bat. I would have expected an appeal by now. It looks as if Humphrey is out of time on that one so I can only assume that he did not see us together in the Indian restaurant."

"Good," said Phillipa. "Next time we should take advantage of their delivery service."

"I agree," said Jeremy. "Or perhaps I should go round there on my own while you warm the plates and the bed."

Phillipa looked at him over the top of her glasses. "Ooh you naughty man." She rose and came round the desk and planted a wet kiss on his lips. He grasped her bottom and pulled her towards him. With the other hand he began to stroke her thigh. "Ooh, Jeremy," she sighed huskily. "That feels lovely. But…" she said more brusquely, "Regrettably, I do not have the time today and in any case, Shirley is in the other room." She gave him one last kiss and sauntered out of the room.

Chapter Sixty-two
The Trial Approaches

Arnold Pigg had settled in well at the Regional Office. Although his own office was on the small side, he found the Regional Head Quarters generally to be quite acceptable. The office block was large and spacious with a first-class cafeteria and assembly hall all of which was set in its own gardens and parkland with a man-made lake with swans. Arnold was looking forward to some sunny days which might afford him enjoyable lunch hours strolling in the parkland.

He was also very gratified with the way in which the problems associated with the intended closure of his old office had been resolved. The way in which the whole procedure was fortuitously concluded without him having to make any decision or take any action was very satisfying for him. He was in the happy situation of knowing that only one of the staff, namely George, still needed to be re-situated.

Arnold was now in the fortunate position of being able to concentrate upon the production of his graphs. Now that Penny had arrived at the Regional Office Mr Pigg was fully equipped for graph production. He had discovered in the Regional Office stationery store a supply of large laminated boards onto which he could fasten his graphs. At last Arnold felt fully liberated.

Penny was also reasonably happy. Two or three weeks before she had been looking at the prospect of losing her job. The office in which she had worked all her adult life was closing and she had no idea what she would do next. Thereafter she had received the offer to work for Mr Pigg at the Regional Office which she had readily accepted. At first, she had regarded it merely as an alternative to being unemployed. When she arrived however, she realised that it was much more than that. Instead of sharing a cramped space with Mrs Balstaff and her multitude of indoor plants, she found herself all alone in a room which was twice the size of the one she had previously shared. It was then that she instantly realised how unsatisfactory her professional life, sharing a room with Mrs Balstaff, had been. The latter, Penny now understood, had been overbearing and insufferable. Most of her work she had delegated to Penny who effectively did most or all of the typing work for Bill Butler as well as the graphs for Mr Pigg.

Now, however, she had little or no ordinary typing work to do. Her entire present function, it appeared was to produce the graphs with which Mr Pigg was so pleased and fascinated. Penny herself had no difficulty in producing these although on occasions she knew that the graphs she turned out were sometimes presented upside down. This did not appear to make any difference either to Mr Pigg himself or anyone to whom the graphs were presented.

The additional working space which she now occupied came as a serious luxury to her. She also had a room with a window and a view of the parkland outside. She now appreciated how constant and domineering Mrs Balstaff's opinions on any and every subject in the universe proved to be. Penny now luxuriated in her own spacious individuality.

She had little or no interference from Mr Pigg who had no reason to bother her as he knew that she was reliably producing his graphs at a speedier rate than he himself could assimilate and/ or use in his own demonstrations. Also, lately, he had been preoccupied with a book which he had recently discovered. The volume was a self-help book entitled 'Let's get cracking' It was a do-it-yourself instruction manual on how to take a good look at one's life, analyse all its aspects, give it a good shake and end up with a totally reformed and powerful character. In short it was a 'Charles Atlas' type advice volume on how to improve or alter all aspects of one's life. Ironically one chapter was actually devoted to body-building and physical exercise entitled 'How to turn yourself into Super Man'.

The remainder of the book was divided into separate chapters each concentrating on a single way in which one's character and life could be improved. For example, chapter one was entitled 'How to get other people to do what you want'.

Mr Pigg was completely enhanced by this book which purported to give simple instructions on how to achieve anything in life. In short it contained the very secret of life as far as Mr Pigg was concerned. Currently when he was not producing graphs, he was studying a chapter of his new found book.

This morning he had already discovered that there was one chapter headed 'How to end problems with alcohol'. He was intrigued to see this chapter included in the index and turned the pages to learn the advice which was offered. He was aware that he and Mrs Pigg, by enjoying a bottle of Pinot Noir or Cabinet Sauvignon together each evening whilst watching a soap opera on TV, put themselves in the bracket of society which might be targeted by some as over consuming alcohol. He himself did not believe that their consumption was excessive. He preferred to believe that it was elegant and sophisticated and did them little or no harm at all. Some research, he had already discovered, showed that the consumption of some red wine every day was good for one and that was the evidence that he preferred to accept.

It was with some curiosity therefore that he turned to see what advice the book gave on the subject of 'How to end problems with alcohol'. He was very surprised and, he had to admit, a little disappointed to find that the chapter consisted of only three words:

"Stop drinking it!"

Despite this slight setback Mr Pigg's fascination with the book still persisted and each day he learned a little more about ways in which he might be able to improve himself.

George arrived at the hospice care home and was shown into a different room where his grandmother was laid out awaiting collection by the undertakers. He sat down beside her and held one of her hands which was already quite cold to the touch.

As before he was surprised to note that despite the sombre atmosphere of his surroundings and the presence of his grandmother's corpse, he was still unable to produce a single tear. This problem was becoming worryingly familiar to him. He was even beginning to doubt his own love for his grandmother even though in his soul he ached for her departure.

He was interrupted in his reflexions by the arrival in the room of the lady who had helped him before. She expressed her commiserations for the death of his grandmother for whom she appeared to have felt a genuine affection. She explained to George that unless he had a personal preference, she would arrange for a local undertaker to collect the body and store it in readiness for a funeral. George told her that he was quite content with that arrangement and would be most grateful if she could proceed. He took the name and details of the undertakers. He then took his leave and made his way back to the office.

There, the few that remained were making the necessary arrangements for the office closure. These few were Tom, Bill Butler, and Mavis.

Since the departure of Mr Pigg, the office staff had diminished gradually commencing with Pete who had recently left to take up employment with Mr Ken Carter. He was followed by Vincent who had taken up full time employment as a DJ at the Nite Club and Penny who had transferred to the Regional Office to work with Mr Pigg. Mrs Balstaff had elected to leave the office instantly rather than work out the customary retirement notice period. Helen had applied for and been granted recently a transfer to the computer centre up north, which left only Bill, Tom, Mavis and George himself to work out the last couple of weeks of the office existence.

George told them of his grandmother's demise. Tom and Bill expressed their sympathy and Mavis wept openly. Bill told George that he could take whatever time off work that he may need to sort out his grandmother's affairs. George took this opportunity gratefully and, with Bill's consent, immediately left the office to return to his grandmother's house. There he collected her will from the writing desk together with the bank and building society books and the funeral plan documents.

From there he then made his way to the offices of Duffey Fry & Co and asked to speak to Mr Reynolds, who fortunately was free and available.

Mr Reynolds was fully familiar with George's grandmother's affairs He expressed his sympathy for his grandmother's death and made some written notes. He then retrieved a file from the cabinet in the corner of his room.

"I remember preparing your grandmother's will recently," he assured George. I will need to receive a death certificate from you as soon as possible. You can obtain this by attending the registrar's office which is just around the corner. Once that is received, I can deal with your grandmother's probate. I can tell you frankly Mr Davies that your grandmother was a far wealthier woman than one might have supposed. When her estate has been wound up you may discover that you will not need to work again."

George was astonished and asked how that could possibly be. Mr Reynolds explained that his grandmother had substantial savings which had been left to her by her own father who had himself been a wealthy man. In addition, there were rental properties." There is also the sale proceeds of your mother and father's own house which was left in trust for you upon their deaths."

Jeremy Fallow QC was in his chambers on a day between court matters. He was using the day to catch up on paperwork. Shirley had just made him a cup of coffee. She retired to her own room, and a few moments later she returned. "Visitor Judge," she said and allowed Phillipa Fry to pass her and walk into the room. "Morning Jeremy," she said, seating herself in his visitor's chair.

"Coffee Miss Fry?" asked Shirley making her way to the coffee machine.

"Ooh, yes please, Shirley," she said then, looking at Jeremy she crossed her legs extravagantly. He stared lasciviously at her legs and she, keeping an eye on Shirley, provocatively pulled up her skirt as she sat in front of him. Jeremy gulped and admired the view yet glanced anxiously towards Shirley who was still concentrating on the coffee machine. Phillipa rose and stood in front of him. She looked at him seductively and slowly and gently raised her skirt to give him a full view of her legs clad in her usual black stockings. Jeremy silently mouthed a simulated 'Ooh'.

As Shirley finished pouring her cup of coffee and was about to turn around Phillipa lowered her skirt and sat back down. Shirley passed her the coffee cup and then retired to her own room.

"I only popped in for a moment Jeremy," she said, "I've got a case in the Matrimonial Court in a few minutes. I've just heard from Algernon that the case he's involved in is likely to go short by a day or two. As a result, the brief for the trial in your court has been returned to him as he was the barrister originally chosen by the defendant. Therefore, he will be back in Bristol on Friday. So I will be able to watch the first couple of days in your court and meet you at your brother's flat, say Wednesday and/or possibly Thursday night."

"That is wonderful," said Jeremy. "I look forward to that. But what about the trial itself? I cannot allow the case to start with one of the defence counsels missing surely."

"Well as far as I understand it" said Phillipa "the brief for the other defendant, the Maltese husband of the lady I issued the divorce petition against, has been passed to Mr Medland who I believe is happy to accept it. He is already fully familiar with the case having put in some hours on behalf of Algie's client. As for Algie's late appearance that shouldn't be a problem. After all, the first day is merely preparatory, selecting jury etc. And you yourself said that there will, initially, be an argument as to whether or not my divorce petitions should be admitted as evidence. Those arguments only concern the second and third defendants not Algie's client so he won't be missed for the first couple of days until the trial proper begins. Algie will be back by then."

"Well, that's OK I suppose," said Jeremy, "but already red lights are flashing in my brain in connection with possible appeals based upon the lack of adequate defence in view of the late instruction."

"No, no," said Phillipa with confidence. "It won't be like that. You know very well that the case against them is overwhelming. Even in the court of a pro-defence Judge, they would stand little chance of being found 'not guilty'."

"You are saying that I am a prosecution minded, Judge?" said Jeremy with a wry smile.

"No, I am not saying that," she replied with a generous smile. "It's more what everyone else in town is saying."

Jeremy chuckled, "Well I have always regarded myself as infinitely fair and objective."

"I am well aware of that, Jeremy," she said. "Anyway, I have to go now. I will see you on Wednesday evening." She rose and stepped forward and gave him a big kiss. "I will see myself out."

In the sombre atmosphere of Bristol prison, the three accused, Simon Nibble, Eddie Sharp and Joe Pettacinni reacted in different ways to their surroundings. Simon Nibble, like a delicate orchid which had been plucked out of a greenhouse environment, was declining daily. He had no previous experience to compare with life behind bars and found himself unable to adapt to the harsh interior. He was consumed by a fear of all other inmates, however harmless they appeared to be. He felt the threat of their co-existence.

Giovanni Pettacinni did not experience the same terror with regard to the other inmates. His upbringing in Malta had bred into him an understanding of and immunity to the threat of violence from his fellow man. He had experienced several short terms of imprisonment in the country of his birth and knew how to maintain his equilibrium in such an establishment.

Of the three Eddie Sharp was the most comfortable behind bars. He was not overtly muscular but had always been able to take care of himself and seemed to exude a scent of smouldering animosity which always dissuaded anyone from interfering with him.

Aloysius Medland arrived at the prison armed with his alternative brief which required him to represent Mr Petacinni. Having made himself familiar with the case generally during his foreshortened representation of Simon Nibble he did not feel too disadvantaged by the short notice given with his new client.

He cut straight to the chase by advising Joe that his best chance of acquittal would be to claim a complete lack of knowledge of the drug sales and to blame the twins who carried out the sales on his premises. He also advised Joe that he would be challenging the admission of his divorce petition amongst the prosecution case against him.

"I assume also," said Mr Medland, "that the deeds transferring the family shares into your name were all double-Dutch to you and were all drawn up by the solicitor, Mr Nibble."

"Si, si," said Joe, who was smart enough to realise that a lack of good English on his part would stand him in good stead with the jury.

"Quite so," said Mr Medland with some satisfaction. "I would advise that you speak as little English in court as you can manage. Do not be afraid to ask anyone who questions you, to repeat the question because you have not properly understood. Do you get my drift?"

"Si, si," said Joe again, who understood exactly what was required of him.

Augustus Samuel arrived at the prison on the same day but at a different time of the day. When Eddie Sharp was brought in to the interview room he introduced himself. "Good afternoon, Mr Sharp. My name is Mr Samuel, and I am your counsel for the approaching trial."

"Well," said Eddie in his no-nonsense way, "you'd better be good. How do you suggest we talk our way out of this one? Have you read the papers?"

"Indeed, I have, Mr Sharp. And I will not try to fool you by pretending that it will be easy."

"Well, I could have told you that," responded Eddie, "but how are we going to play it?"

"Humph…" Began Augustus who was not renowned for making pro-active decisions. "It is the duty of the prosecution to prove the guilt of the accused beyond all reasonable doubt. This is a very onerous duty to discharge. I suggest to you that the evidence against you in respect of the distribution of drugs consists entirely of the statements given by the twins who worked for you. There is no direct evidence from any other direction which would point towards you. If we can discredit these twins in the eyes of the jury then the case against you falls apart."

"So we only have to prove that they are liars and we're home and dry. Is that right?" said Eddie.

"In a nutshell," confirmed Augustus. "Now what can you tell me about them? Do either of them have a record?"

"Yeah," said Eddie with absolute certainty. You can check the records which will show that they've been in trouble in the past. Mostly for physical assaults."

"Good, good," said Augustus. "I will check the records and confront them with it when they give their evidence. They won't be able to deny it and will be completely discredited in the eyes of the jury. I seriously have to doubt the wisdom of the police who have chosen to base their case against you on the word of two people who have criminal records."

Eddie was influenced by the confidence being expressed by Augustus and he nodded with satisfaction. For a further fifteen minutes or so Mr Samuel went over a number of points which Eddie felt he dealt with reasonably well. Eventually he mentioned the note book which had been seized by the Police during their raid on his house.

"So what is the significance of this notebook?" he asked.

"Nothing," answered Eddie. "Just some random jottings regarding car sales."

"Good, good," said Augustus. "So nothing for us to fear about that. Our case is that any dealing that occurred happened at the Nite Club not at your premises. Any dealing, if it took place, was carried out by the twins themselves so the jury are not going to believe anything they say.

Eddie nodded emphatically and Augustus felt encouraged. He decided that all relevant points had been covered and that his client's case was fairly secure. "I will see you in court Mr Sharp," he said, as he rose to leave. "I believe that together we will give the prosecuting counsel a bloody nose."

Having said this, he gathered up his papers and left the room leaving Eddie in a confident and cheerful frame.

DCI Des Onions, was reviewing the information he had for the coming trial. He had already been over the statements which his own team would be giving to the court, many times. He was satisfied that all his men were word perfect. He was also sure that, if the evidence of Jimmy Pearce and the twins was believed by the jury, a guilty verdict would be inevitable.

Additionally, he was confident that even if the evidence of Jimmy and the twins was not accepted by the jury, a guilty verdict would be likely. He knew for example, that the figures in the client account records of Huw Roberts & Co would result in a guilty verdict for Simon Nibble.

He knew also that the discovery, in the safe of Eddie Sharp, of the large amount of cash some of which included the notes marked by the police and the note book which had been interpreted as information on drug dealing activities, pointed to definite guilt on the part of Eddie Sharp. He fervently hoped that the defence counsel would not pay too much attention to this volume and will readily accept any general assurances that the entries therein were mere random jottings. He knew that the jury, once the interpretation of these entries was put to them, with the snooker clues, would accept fully the prosecution explanation of the note book. He was aware also that the jury would not accept that a note book full of random jottings would need to be stored in a locked safe.

He was also sure that the documents and deeds in respect of the company shares and their transfers would be judged fraudulent by the court which would mean guilt for all three defendants. In addition, the discovery, in the Nite Club safe, of large amounts of cash which also included some more notes marked by the police would confirm the guilt of Giovanni Petacinni.

All these points Des was aware of. He also knew that, on balance, the evidence of Jimmy Pearce and the twins would be believed. They, after all, had admitted their own guilt and were merely helping the police with their enquiries as required by the law.

He had lived and breathed this case for many weeks and had always searched his mind for more leads which might provide more evidence for him. One or two of his officers had researched youngsters who frequented the Nite Club and also were known to indulge in drug taking. Having been granted immunity in respect of any charges for drug taking some of them were willing to give statements which were duly collected. All confirmed that the drugs had been available at the Nite Club on a regular basis for at least the last three years. The suppliers, they also confirmed were the twins but most of the statements collected contained information to indicate that all buyers believed that the twins were acting merely as agents for Joe the owner of the club.

Further, members of the CID team had researched amongst the gym members and discovered some members who had been willing to give statements regarding the twins' habit of supplying steroid drugs to gym members. As with the Class A drugs supplied by the twins at the Nite Club the gym members all confirmed that it was their understanding that the twins were acting as agents for Eddie who was generally understood to have the money to be able to finance the drug dealing.

Des knew that, in the event that the jury were undecided on the evidence generally, these independent statements would probably hold sway in the minds of the jurymen. Also, he knew that the video evidence of the twins dealing at the car lot owned and run by Eddie was extremely incriminating as far as the latter was concerned

His case against Eddie was reinforced by a statement supplied by an inspector in the Flying Squad who gave evidence to show that not only was there a clear trail from the arrival of the Class A drugs into the country to Jimmy Pearce and subsequently Eddie Sharp, but the profits made from the imported drugs matched the payments introduced to Simon Nibble's client account. The Flying Squad officer was also able to emphasise the quantity and value of the drugs imported and thus show that such transactions could not have been financed solely by people like Jimmy Pearce or the twins.

The most important item of news which Des had received was the information from the medical laboratory that the young man who had recently died in the area was killed as a result of taking drugs from the same batch as those sold by the defendants. This promoted the charges made against them from mere drug dealing to potential murder or manslaughter.

But Des knew that there was no specific evidence to link the death of the young man, who lived within a fifty-mile radius of the defendants, with the actual drugs supplied by Jimmy or the twins. The medical evidence only showed that it was powder from the same batch. There was no evidence to show where the unfortunate young man had acquired the drug.

Nevertheless, Des was certain that the potentially more serious charges raised the bar for the defendants and applied more stress to them. He reflected that this gave a psychological advantage to the prosecution case. He continually racked his brain to try to create more.

He had recently contacted Mr Ken Carter to gather his opinion on the transfer of the family shares into the name of Eddie Sharp. Des knew that he had not, from the start of the case, been able to produce as a prosecution witness, Joe Petacinni's wife primarily because she would not have wished to give evidence against her husband and furthermore could not be compelled to do so.

The recent issue of divorce proceedings against Joe by Freda his wife altered the situation. Des was aware however that the defence counsels would be only too eager to get Freda into the witness box and would try their best to discredit and humiliate her. He preferred to keep her out of the witness box and rely on the contents of her divorce petition which had been drawn up by Phillipa Fry, as expertly as any oral statement by Freda herself could portray.

A statement had been taken from Mr Ken Carter detailing the intimidation of his sister Freda by her husband and the suspect nature of the transfer of company shares. He also gave his account of the meeting he had had with Eddie Sharp and his solicitor Simon Nibble in the Grand Hotel and the doubtful nature of documents prepared by the latter.

Similarly Des knew that the divorce petition of Doris, (also, prepared by Phillipa Fry), was as influential as any oral statement given in the witness box by Doris herself. He was also certain that the information contained in the client account of Simon Nibble's firm was all the evidence that he required for a conviction.

George was back at his grandmother's house trying to sort out possessions and wondering what items of furniture he could reject or retain. He had decided to bag up all his grandmother's clothes and take them to a charity shop. He had already more or less completed that task. He now turned to the writing desk in the rear dining room and began emptying the drawers onto the floor.

One of the first things he unearthed was a large photograph album. He began to thumb through it and discovered many photographs of his own father and mother, some before his own birth but many which included pictures of himself with his parents. Ironically there were very few pictures of his grandmother presumably because of the fact that she herself had taken most of the photographs in the album.

As he leafed through the album, he finally came to a picture which included his grandmother. The picture showed his own parents sitting in deckchairs alongside his grandmother at the beach in Weymouth. George was seated on the pebbles in front of them eating an ice cream. It must have been a sunny day because he was smiling and squinting at the camera which must have been held by a mobile professional photographer. As he gazed at the photograph George found himself transported back to a day when he had been so happy. Beside him on the pebbles stood his bucket and spade with a fishing net which he remembered he had used to collect hermit crabs.

Suddenly the presence of his grandmother and his parents were real and immediate. The joy of the holiday came back to him with all the colour and laughter which it had originally given to him. He looked at their faces and felt his eyes filling with tears He broke down and cried copiously partly form the grief which he had previously felt unable to express, and partly from the pleasure of being again in their joint presence. He set aside the album and realised that it was the first item in the house which he had determined he would retain.

In the early morning at the office the day commenced, as usual, with Tom and Bill sharing a cup of tea and a conversation. Since the announcement of the office closure their conversation had turned, on a daily basis, to their respective ambitions as to how they would spend their time in retirement.

Both of them had always been keen on sport and when young each of them had played a variety of games. As they had grown older each had confined themselves to playing golf. Neither of them, were especially good at the game but they were both equally enthusiastic and had already promised each other that they would meet on the golf course, instead of the office, as often as they could after the office closure.

When George arrived both Tom and Bill asked how he was feeling. He assured them that he was OK and went to make himself a cup of tea. Whilst he was out of the room Mavis arrived. When he returned with his cup of tea she asked him how he was and he confirmed again that he was OK. She asked him how he had got on at Duffey Fry & Co the previous day. George told her that he had met a Mr Reynolds who had prepared his grandmother's will recently. He told everyone what Mr Reynolds had said to him. They were all astonished and all offered their congratulations for his good fortune.

"Well," said Bill. "News like that could not have come at a better time for you in view of the recent office closure notice."

"That's for sure," said Mavis. "So what was the estimated size of the estate?"

George said that he did not know because Mr Reynolds had not given him an estimate. "He did say that her savings were substantial," he told her. "But gave no figure. He also said that she had owned rental properties but did not say how many. Also, of course, there was her own house and the proceeds of my mum and dad's house."

Mavis whistled loudly. "That does sound considerable."

"Indeed, it does," mused Tom who knew quite a bit about house values in the area. "If he described the assets of your grandmother's estate as consisting of 'rental properties' ie, plural, then that would mean there are at least two properties that are rented out. If one assumes that those properties have the average value for properties in this area then that would be an approximate valuation of half a million pounds. If your mum and dad's house and your grandmother's house are also about the average valuation then that would give a total house valuation of approximately one million pounds. In addition, he informed you that your grandmother had substantial savings. If you estimate conservatively I would think you are dealing with an estate value in the region of two million pounds at least."

Bill puffed out his cheeks in appreciation. Mavis whistled again and George himself was even more astonished.

"Well," said Tom with certainty. "The man was absolutely correct in telling you that you will never need to work again. What do you think about that?"

"Wow," uttered George. "I don't know what to think about it. It's all a bit of a shock. I'm not sure I feel really comfortable about never working again. I've always worked and certainly have had no practice at doing nothing."

"But no one is saying that you are not allowed to work," said Mavis, "it is simply the case that you do not need to work. Surely that is a good position to be in?"

"Yes, of course," replied George. "It is just such a shock. When my parents were alive, they used to tell me that grandma was well off but they never went into detail. I just assumed that meant that she owned her own house free of mortgage and had some modest savings. I never dreamed that she was so well off. The house she lived in was not palatial and she never put on any airs and graces. I just had no idea."

"Well," said Tom wisely, "it might be an idea to take some advice from a financial expert who might be able to tell you how to manage your inheritance when you receive it. You will also, sooner or later, have to decide what you would like to do on a daily basis instead of going to work. I am sure that if Bill and I had come into a fortune when we were your age, we would have spent every day on the golf course." Bill nodded emphatically. "Although" he added "I 'm not so sure that our lives would have been any better."

Tom nodded. "But seriously, Bill, as we were saying earlier, our lives would not have been any worse if we had met each morning on the golf course rather than here in this office."

Bill chuckled, "Yes, well," he said. "In a few weeks' time you and I will be able to take advantage of the pensioner's reduced green fees and play a round together once or twice a week. George here will have to find something to occupy himself with every day."

"But that…" intervened Mavis optimistically, "is a welcome challenge not a problem isn't it George?"

"Yes, I suppose so," responded George who was beginning to realise that good fortune almost never came alone.

"Well at least I will be in a position to support you while you are doing your legal studies, won't I?" he said.

"Ooh," said Mavis reaching over and giving him a hug and a kiss, "that is so sweet of you. But this inheritance is yours, not mine. You don't have to give any of it away to me."

"Well, no…" said George in a measured way, "but if we are going to get married and live together then it's only fair isn't it?"

There was a brief moment of silence during which George, as well as everyone else, was surprised by his own words. Only as the words had left his lips did he realise how seriously he meant them. How much he felt for Mavis and had done since the moment he had first set eyes upon her. It did occur to him momentarily that, due to his inexperience with girls, he may be overestimating the value of his relationship with Mavis and may be mistaking that which is ordinaire for something which might appear to be superb. Upon reflection however he knew instinctively that Mavis was the one and that however many girls he had known previously she would always be so.

Tom and Bill remained silent and exchanged raised eyebrows with each other. Mavis was flabbergasted and for once in her life was temporarily speechless. "Can I take that as a backhanded proposal?" she asked.

George smiled gamely, "You certainly may," he said. "If I had more romance in my soul, I would have chosen a better moment but I blurted it out without thinking.

Mavis was not without words this time. "Well my darling" she said "I am more than happy to accept your offer" and with that she put her arms around him and kissed him.

Both Tom and Bill smiled broadly and got to their feet to congratulate them both. They each shook George's hand and gave Mavis a kiss on the cheek.

Chapter Sixty-three
The Flirtation Turns to Love

At the end of the day Jeremy Fallow QC and his clerk Shirley Kemp tidied up their respective desks and left the chambers together. Both had been engaged upon tidying-up work which they had left over from the week before. Both of them wished to clear their desks and minds for the three-handed trial which began the next day.

They both shared the lift to the ground floor and said goodbye to each other. Jeremy watched as Shirley walked down the street and he reflected that he was fortunate to have the assistance of a clerk who was both efficient and agreeable. He regarded her as more of a friend than an employee.

Tonight, instead of making his way home he wound his way to the flat belonging to his brother Roger. He was intending to live in the flat, which was much closer to the Crown Court building than his home, for the length of the trial which was starting the next day. Maud, his wife was away from home staying with her sister and nieces who lived in Surrey and so Jeremy had no reason or need to stay at home.

He accepted to himself that the overwhelming reason why he was eager to live at his brother's flat for a while was that he could spend some time with Phillipa. At the same time, he told himself, even if he were not currently seeing Phillipa, and if Mrs Fallow had been at home, he would still have chosen to sleep at his brother's flat for a week or so. It offered him not just the proximity to the Crown Court but the chance to be alone each evening to concentrate on the details of the trial each day.

On the way to the flat he stopped off at the wine merchants and purchased some wine. He also bought a replacement bottle of gin and some tonic for his brother. Also, he called into a greengrocer's shop and bought some lemons.

When he arrived at the flat there was no sign of Phillipa. He tried to remind himself whether it was tonight that she was intending to call round or whether it was tomorrow. He reflected that this was just another example of a myriad of items which lately had slipped past his memory. He knew that it was only a day or so ago that they had made the arrangement to meet but try as he might he could not recall definitely if Phillipa had confirmed that she would come tonight or tomorrow. Also, he was unsure if she had decided to stay for just one night or for two nights. He busied himself in the flat puffing up cushions and pillows and drawing curtains. When the doorbell rang, he knew instantly that the arrangement made with Phillipa was that she would arrive this evening.

With a beam of delight, he threw open the door to find himself staring into the face of a man of about forty years who looked equally surprised to see him. For a brief moment each of them looked at each other in obvious surprise. Eventually the caller said, "Is Roger in?"

"No, I'm sorry he's not here," said Jeremy. There was another awkward silence.

"I'm his brother, my name is Jeremy. Can I take a message and get him to give you a call?"

"Oh, that's OK," said the visitor, "I'm Malcolm. I've got the next door flat," he said indicating with his left hand. "I expect I can catch him another time."

"Of course," said Jeremy, "but he is away for the week but I will be here for the whole time that he is away if there's anything I can do."

"That's OK," said Malcolm. "I just wanted to have a chat with him. I told him before that I might be interested in selling my flat. I promised that I would tell him if and when I made a decision and he said he might be interested in buying it."

Jeremy raised his eyebrows. "Really?" he said. "Why would he want it? to live in or to rent out?"

Malcolm shrugged. "I'm not absolutely sure. He had a look round and definitely liked it. It has more garden than his and an extra room. I got the impression that he might wish to live in it. Anyway, I have decided that I will be selling it so I will hope to have a word with him when he returns."

"Certainly," confirmed Jeremy. "I will give him a message and no doubt he will contact you on his return. Very nice to have met you."

As Malcolm made his way back to the next-door property, Phillipa arrived with her barrister's robe sack over her shoulder. Jeremy's face lit up. He gave her a hug and a kiss and told her how lovely she looked. "Thank you, Jeremy. Who was that man?"

"Roger's next-door neighbour," he said, "apparently he is going to sell his flat and has given Roger the promise that he can have first refusal on it. Not that I can see what he would need it for. After all, he is not here half the year. Come in anyway."

He led her in and took her coat from her and hung it up in the hallway. She was still dressed in her court suit and wearing high heels. "Do you mind if I change my clothes a minute, Jeremy, I've been working all day."

"Of course," he said. "You know where everything is. I was thinking of making you a gin and tonic. How would that suit you?"

Phillipa smooched up to him and put her arms around his neck. She pressed her breasts into his body and kissed him deeply on the lips. "That Jeremy would be just the thing to get me into the right mood." She spoke in such a sultry manner that Jeremy felt an erection forming. He went into the kitchen and made two gin and tonics in long glasses and put sliced lemon into them. He took them into the living room and seated himself on the sofa.

Phillipa returned dressed in blue jeans, slippers and a tight low-cut white T-shirt which Jeremy thought made her look very sexy. She accepted her gin and tonic and seated herself alongside him on the couch with her legs pulled up underneath her like a young girl. The only compromise she had made with her professional appearance was to keep her black rimmed glasses on.

"Hmmm," she murmured after taking a long sip at her drink. "That's so much better. And how are you my darling?"

"Much better for seeing you," Jeremy assured her. "Have you been in the Matrimonial Court this afternoon?"

"Yes," she said, "but it's been a bit of a dull day altogether. How has your day been?"

"Oh, very quiet," replied Jeremy, "just clearing up some paperwork in readiness for day one of the trial tomorrow."

"Hmm...." she said, sipping her gin again. "I'm looking forward to it. Algie telephoned this morning. He said he might be back on Thursday or Friday at the latest."

Jeremy nodded and took a sip at his own drink. "Yes, well... I think the first day at least will be taken up entirely with challenges against the inclusion of your divorce petitions in the prosecution documents bundle."

"Do you think they will be?" asked Phillipa coquettishly.

Jeremy puffed his cheeks out and gave a little shrug. "Well, it is a crucial point for both sides. If the prosecution win, the point then they almost certainly win the game. If the defence win the point then it makes it a more even contest. Those petitions are so brilliantly narrated that they are crucial to both sides."

"Well, thank you, kind sir," she said with a coy look at him. She noticed him taking a glimpse at her cleavage.

"It depends of course on the nature of the points which Mr Medland and Humphrey put forward," he said.

"Well, we know for certain that Humphrey won't come up with anything. He never prepares properly. I'm not so sure about Elvis though. I think he might give you some more arguments than Humphrey."

"Yes, I think you may be right," said Jeremy. "I, of course, will be only too pleased to include them in the bundle as I told you before. But of course, it does depend entirely on the potency of the arguments made."

"So you might include them?" she said, snuggling up to him. "How sweet of you."

"Of course I would," he said putting his arm around her, "but of course if the vital arguments are put to me I cannot refuse them without giving myself the possibility of a successful appeal."

She nodded sagely and took a final mouthful from her glass. "How afraid of a successful appeal are you at any time?" she asked.

"Well..." he offered in a measured way. "Always aware and moderately concerned, but never ever especially afraid. I always know when I've made the right decision and generally like to believe that my decisions are correct. It's not arrogance. It is merely confidence."

"You are so clever, Jeremy," she murmured snuggling even closer to him. He looked down on her and admired her cleavage. He stroked her upper arm gently and kissed the top of her head. She slid her right hand across his thigh and began to stroke him. He moved his hand from her upper arm onto her left breast which he now began to stroke. His hand cupped her breast and gently squeezed it. He moved his hand up to the top of her T-shirt and slid his fingers inside which enabled him to tweak her nipple which was already erect. She moved her hand on his leg to encompass his erection which she gently stroked. Jeremy was feeling very aroused but did not wish to move at all in case any mere movement might spoil the beauty of the moment.

Phillipa did not mind moving and in one lazy, laconic motion she released herself from his grasp and lifted her T-shirt up over her head. She then expertly reached behind her and released her bra strap.

"There," she whispered, "that's better isn't it?"

Jeremy was, as always totally captivated by the sight of her breasts. "It certainly is much better," he agreed, "they are magnificent."

"You do like my breasts don't you, Jeremy?"

"I adore them," he said. "I think they are the most beautiful breasts I have ever seen. Not..." he added, "that I have enormous experience."

"Ooh, I'm not sure I believe that, Jeremy," she murmured. "I bet you've had lots of experience you randy old dog you."

He chuckled and grasped her to him again. This time he was able to encompass her breast one handed. She snuggled into him again and once more stroked his erection on the outside of his trousers.

They remained like that for several minutes. After a while she undid his trousers and lowered his zip and then slid her hand in to grasp his penis. She began to massage it and Jeremy sighed gently. She leaned over and took his penis in her mouth and began to gently move her head up and down Jeremy continued to sigh with satisfaction. "Ooh, that feels so wonderful," he sighed.

Phillipa continued her motion and increased the pace, fondling his testicles with one hand and gripping his shaft with the other while moving her mouth up and down. Eventually he cried out in ecstasy but she continued her actions until he ejaculated. She did not remove her mouth but continued to stroke him until his erection subsided. He lifted her from his waist and hugged her tightly. "That was fantastic," he whispered, "but I feel guilty that I had all the pleasure while you did not get any."

"Oh, Jeremy," she answered, "my feelings for you are so immense that there is nothing that gives me more pleasure than seeing you satisfied."

"I feel exactly the same about you," he said. They leaned back together on the sofa. He fondled her breast and asked her gently, "Can I do the same for you?"

"But of course," she confirmed and stretched out her legs and put her head back on to the sofa. Jeremy undid her jeans and slid them down to the floor. He drew down her panties and began to kiss her thighs. He fingered her clitoris and moved up her thighs with his tongue. Eventually he ceased manipulating with his fingers and inserted his tongue and began to lick her methodically. In the meantime, he stroked her thighs and buttocks with both hands. Phillipa began to sigh volubly and as he increased the rhythm of his tongue strokes and his fingering of her thighs, her voice lifted until she was clearly close to a climax. "Oooh, oooh, yes, Jeremy," she shrieked "that is exquisite! Oooh, oooh, Jeremy, oooh, fantastic, oooh!" With a final loud long shriek of satisfaction, she climaxed.

"Oooh, Jeremy," she sighed. "That was absolutely wonderful. Sex has never been so beautiful before for me.

"I feel the same," he said. They both lay in each other's arms and marvelled at the strength of their mutual love for each other.

"I've never had sex at this time of day before," he said, "but no matter what time of day it is, whenever I see you I want to have sex with you. I have not felt this way ever."

"That's because you love me, Jeremy" she said, "and I love you."

They lay together for a few more minutes and then got dressed again. They ordered a take-away Indian meal from the same restaurant as before but this time they chose to have it delivered. When it arrived, they sat together in the kitchen-diner and Jeremy opened one of the bottles of wine which he had purchased earlier.

When they had finished their meal, they decided to go to bed even though it was only eight thirty p.m. They lay, naked together and both reflected on how happy they were.

In the morning they awoke early with the dawn. Jeremy rose and went into the kitchen and made a pot of coffee. He poured two cups and returned to the bedroom. They both sat up in bed sipping their coffee and chatting.

"Well today's the day," she said. "The question is will you allow my divorce petitions to be included in the bundle?"

"We will see, won't we," replied Jeremy. "I could of course include them in the bundle without more and to hell with everyone. But of course, if the arguments employed by defence counsels are reasonable and if I reject them, then it would afford a good appeal point." He gave her a kiss.

"I repeat, we will see."

Chapter Sixty-four
The Trial Begins

Mavis and George met early in the morning and made their way together to the railway station. They were on their way to Bristol to view the trial in the Crown Court. There was no problem with them both taking a few days off work primarily because there was little work remaining for them to do. Also, both of them had annual leave due to them which they had not yet taken. In addition, Bill regarded their attendance at the trial together as important for both of them and would have granted them both time off, even if the office had been busy and they had no holiday entitlement left. He knew that himself and Tom would be able to cope with whatever might crop up. He also thought, in a romantic avuncular way, that it would be nice for Mavis and George to spend a day together.

Once they were on the train, they settled down beside each other and were both excited to be in each other's presence. Mavis, who thanks to the advice from Phillipa Fry, had made up her face and looked quite startlingly beautiful. Her eyes which were her most impressive feature were minimally and expertly shaded and high-lighted. A mere sprinkling of freckles across her nose just added to her attractiveness. She shed her coat, as soon as they boarded the train, to reveal that she was wearing a primrose yellow dress superimposed with marmalade polka dots. The dress looked gay and bright and Mavis' facial appearance matched the mood of her dress. Her bright and cheerful disposition was infectious and George was similarly in good humour and revelling in her company.

"So, Mr Moneybags," she said mischievously, "have you made any decision yet as to what you will be doing with the rest of your life?"

He grinned at her humour. "Not really," he said "It's all a bit much to take in. I have however made one decision and I think you might like it."

"Oh, yes," she said, "and what is that?"

"Well," he said, "what I would like to do is get in touch with the local golf club. I want to pay them to upgrade the annual membership of Bill and Tom so that they can play at any time of day and not just at the cheap pensioner's times. I was also thinking of lodging a sum of money behind the bar to allow them to enjoy a free drink for the next twelve months after each game they play."

"Ooh, you sweetie," exclaimed Mavis. She grasped him impulsively and kissed him on the cheek.

"You are so kind," she said. "I think that's lovely and they will so enjoy it."

George grinned. "I hope so," he said, "as to any other decisions I think I will wait until my grandmother's estate is settled before I make any. "Anyway," he concluded, "how do you expect things to go today in court?"

"Well…" she replied slowly, "I have no experience but I would assume that day one of the trial is primarily procedural. You know, swearing in the jury etc. I'm not expecting it to be too riveting today except however we will be meeting Phillipa Fry who will be in attendance. I have been in touch with her by telephone and she will meet us outside the court and spend the day in the viewing gallery with us. The prosecution have included in their evidence bundle, the two divorce petitions which Phillipa prepared in relation to Doris and Freda. I'm so excited about it that I can't wait to see it.

George agreed that it was exciting and that he too was looking forward to watching the trial. He had to admit to himself however that his own input into the events which led up to the trial had not been as significant as that of Mavis and so he could understand her anxiety and expectation in respect thereof.

When they arrived at Bristol they alighted and made their way on foot to the Crown Court building. In the concourse on the ground floor, they encountered Phillipa Fry who had, by telephone, arranged to meet Mavis there. George was slightly surprised to note the mutual joy and excitement with which they greeted each other. Although they came from different backgrounds and had not known each other for long their meeting gave the impression of two life-long close friends meeting after a long separation. George could sense the genuine affection between them.

They all seated themselves in the coffee bar on the ground floor of the building. Phillipa was wearing her usual court attire even though she was not planning to appear in the court itself. She complimented Mavis on her appearance and concluded that she had now mastered the ability to accentuate her eye make-up.

Mavis was grateful for the compliments offered and seemed to grow in the company of her idol. She questioned Phillipa closely about the forthcoming trial. The latter declined to offer many opinions and suggested that everyone would have to 'wait and see'.

Mavis however, was not to be thwarted on the subject. "Oh come on," she urged. "You must have some inside information. What can you tell us? Will our divorce petitions be included in the prosecution bundle?"

"Oh, certainly," said Phillipa, "but of course the defence may object to their inclusion."

"But what if they do?" enquired Mavis. "What happens then?"

"Well…" said Phillipa, "It is then a matter to be decided by the judge whether or not they are included. If he sides with the defence then they will not be included in the bundle and that will be an end of it."

"But surely he will let your petitions be included." said Mavis with some emphasis.

"Not necessarily," responded Phillipa. "If the defence arguments are persuasive then he will exclude them." Mavis was disappointed by this having assumed in her own mind that Judge Fallow would automatically allow any document which had been prepared by Phillipa.

George then excused himself to pay a visit to the toilet. During his absence Mavis questioned Phillipa more closely on the point. "But your petitions are so brilliant and… well, you and the judge are….so close that… well, why would he refuse to include your documents?"

Phillipa smiled serenely, "Perhaps, in view of our relationship there would be more reason to exclude them?" She raised her eyebrows quizzically. "It is also a matter of giving the defence a good appeal point. Mavis nodded gravely and admitted to herself that she had not fully considered the point before.

"Talking of our relationship," added Phillipa. "Have you mentioned that to your friend George who is with you today?" Mavis looked horror stricken.

"Ooh, no, definitely not!" she assured Phillipa, grasping her hand tightly. "I would never dream of it. That was, and remains totally confidential."

"Thank you," said Phillipa. "I did not really doubt you."

"Well, there is something about George that I need to tell you," she said.

She then went on to tell Phillipa about George's news of his grandmother's estate and more particularly his back-handed proposal of marriage. She also confirmed that she had been offered the post of articled clerk at the solicitor's office to whom Phillipa had supplied a reference. She also thanked her profusely for giving them a good reference for her.

Phillipa was overjoyed for her and hugged and kissed her in celebration.

While this was going on George returned to the table and Phillipa congratulated him as well. She also asked what plans they had for a wedding day but both of them assured her that they had not yet decided. They then realised that it was time for the trial to start. Phillipa led them to the viewing gallery of the court and they settled down in the front row.

The court case convened exactly on time. Judge Jeremy Fallow QC entered through the door at the rear of the court, behind the judge's bench. He looked very fetching in his wig and gown. He gave a bow and said, "Good morning," to everyone and then seated himself in his chair.

Everyone in the court who had risen to their feet when he entered the court, replied with a polite 'Good morning' and all resumed their seats as soon as Judge Fallow had sat down. There followed some formalities in which Shirley Kemp read out the charges. During this procedure the defendants had to stand to acknowledge their names and all three of them confirmed that it was their intention to plead not guilty.

The next procedure was the choice of jury members. A group of selected citizens fifteen in number were led into the court by an usher and herded into the jury seating area. Judge Fallow took over and advised them that the process of whittling them down to twelve in number would now take place. He introduced them to the barristers who were seated in the front row with their clients seated in the row behind them. He indicated Mr Augustus Samuel who would be representing Mr Eddie Sharp, and Mr Aloysius Medland who would be representing Mr Giovanni Petacinni. He also introduced to them the prosecution counsel who was Mr Sabin.

Judge Fallow also advised the jury members that Mr Nibble's counsel, who would be Mr Algernon Phillips was delayed in a different court in another case which was in its final day. He assured them that he would be joining them some time tomorrow to represent his client.

"Now ladies and gentlemen," said the judge, "the prosecution will have something to tell you before we can decide which of you will be selected to help us today. Over to you Mr Sabin."

"Thank you, Your Honour," said Mr Sabin getting to his feet, then to the jury members, he said, "If any of you know or recognise any of the defendants then you will be ineligible to sit on the jury. Therefore, kindly let us know if any of you do know them," he paused for a moment to allow them to digest this information. When there was no response he moved on.

"I have here a list of people who might be what is known as 'associated people'. If any of you know or have any connection with these persons then it would not be appropriate for you to be a member of the jury. So if any of you do know any of these people kindly let us know." He passed some copies of the list to the jury with instructions to pass them along and read them.

While this was going on Augustus Samuel was leaning back on the bench, his own eyes fixed on his own lap and wondering to himself what he might be eating for dinner tonight. Gus liked his food and had indicated to his wife, before leaving home, that a plate of liver and bacon and onions would be a pleasant change. He knew that his wife did not like to eat liver but he felt that once in a while it was reasonable to expect her to cook some for himself. He began to wonder which wine he would choose to drink with it.

While he was thus deliberating Mr Medland was scrutinizing the jury members and whispering to his client. He had been closely examining one lady in the jury seats. The lady was middle aged with mauve-coloured hair and a haughty demeanour. She was observing the defendants with what, to Mr Medland's mind, appeared to be a most disdainful look reminiscent of someone who had just detected an unpleasant odour.

When her name was read out and she acknowledged, Mr Medland got to his feet and blandly advised the judge that this lady would not be suitable to serve on the jury.

"Why is that?" asked Judge Fallow. "My client recognises her," he replied. "Obviously they have met at some time in the past and therefore this lady will have to stand down."

The lady in question looked dumbfounded. The judge asked her if it was true that she had previously met or known any of the defendants. "Definitely not," she assured him. "I have never seen any of them before."

Mr Medland curled his lip with great scepticism and said, "Oh, come now. You have surely met somewhere or how else would my client recognise you? Perhaps you have visited his night club on one or more occasions."

"I can assure you that I have never been to a night club in my entire life." she said with distaste.

Mr Medland's sneer was now evident. "Well, nevertheless my client recognised you immediately and so it would only be appropriate for you to stand down."

The lady looked mystified and turned towards the judge. "I don't know them," she assured him.

"I understand," said Jeremy. "Perhaps, in this case, in order to avoid any doubt or mistaken identity we will allow one of the other people to sit on the jury instead. Is that the extent of your objection, Mr Medland?"

The latter remained on his feet, still examining the jury members, still with a curl on his lips. He stroked his own chin slowly and after what must have been at least twenty seconds he turned to the judge and said, "It is, Your Honour." He then sat down.

"Very well," said Jeremy, talking to the lady with the mauve hair, "You are excused. Thank you for your attendance."

The unfortunate lady who had obviously been looking forward to playing her part in the trial, was thus forced to leave the court which she did whilst shaking her head.

Judge Fallow addressed the twelve selected jury members. "Well, now that procedure is concluded the prosecution counsel will now outline their case for you. Mr Sabin, if you please."

Mr Sabin rose and began to describe to the jury the prosecution case and what it would entail. The jury listened attentively. During his summary Jeremy glanced up at the viewing gallery and noticed Phillipa and Mavis sitting together.

After ten minutes or so Mr Sabin finished and sat down. Mr Medland then rose and, with a curl on his lip, he indicated that he had an application to make before the trial could continue. As if not wishing to be left out Mr Augustus Samuel also got to his feet to echo Mr Medland's application.

Jeremy, of course, was not surprised by this development. He glanced at the clock on the wall and then addressed the jury, "The defence wish to make an application which will be heard in your absence. Looking at the clock I think it would be a good time now to take an early lunch. This afternoon we will be starting without you and once their application has been heard you will be joining us again and the trial will formally begin."

At the Regional Office Mr Pigg had just completed a telephone conversation with Bill Butler at his old office. He was delighted to hear from Bill that all the previously potential problems at his old office had been solved. Or rather, he had to admit to himself, that the problems had solved themselves.

Bill had advised him that Mavis had now decided to take up law and had found a post at the office of a local solicitors and, following the recent death of his grandmother, George had now come into sufficient money to allow himself to no longer need a job and had therefore decided to let his Civil Service career lapse.

Mr Pigg could not be more pleased. All the problems, some of which he himself had not envisaged, had been solved without any effort on his part. All the personnel were settled and so that only left the office building and its contents to be sorted out. He knew of course that the office premises were only leased and not government-owned therefore he knew that all that needed to be done was to give a notice to the landlord and this had already been done by Mr Jenkins the Regional Controller as soon as the decision to close the office had been made, or so he thought.

That only left Mr Pigg with the problem of sorting out the contents of the office and he mentioned this to Bill Butler who re-assured him on this point. "There are a number of items, eg. stationery and envelopes etc, together with certain items eg. telephones and keyboards and screens etc which I have already found a home for at another local office. That leaves only the furniture itself which is not particularly valuable, to be dealt with and I have already found a local dealer who will take the lot away for a reasonable price. All that needs to happen is the official closing which Tom and I will deal with."

When the call was concluded Mr Pigg replaced the receiver and gave himself a pat on the back. He wondered to himself what his book would have to say about generating help for oneself. He reached into his desk drawer to retrieve the book and looked in the index.

'How to make things happen' was the title to one section of the book which he judged was close enough to be most relevant. He closely studied the section and discovered that it was essential to first identify and list the problems which were causing difficulty before deciding how to deal with them.

Once identified, he read, a problem could be dealt with either by tackling it head on or by treating it with disdain and pretending that it did not exist. Mr Pigg definitely preferred the latter and decided that that was how he had expertly dealt with the problem of the closure of his old office. As he read further through the section, he learned that it was sometimes possible or desirable to persuade or suggest to others that a problem could be their fault or responsibility rather than your own. This also appealed to Mr Pigg who instinctively felt that this was the best way to deal with any problem. He learned that blaming others was often a useful way of distracting attention away from oneself. He was vaguely aware of a poem which said something about 'keeping one's head while those around you are losing theirs and blaming it on you' and could see what an effective device blaming others could be.

As he was ruminating thus there was a single knock on his office door which was immediately opened to reveal Mr Jenkins who entered with a cheery, "Morning, Arnold." He asked how things were going and Mr Pigg was able to update him on the closure of his old office. "And what about the office lease?" asked Mr Jenkins. "Has notice been served upon the landlord?"

"But…" said Mr Pigg sounding confused, "Surely that should have already been done by the property department, as soon as the decision was made to close the office?"

Mr Jenkins thought for a moment and in that brief passage of time Mr Pigg for the first time since he had met his Regional Controller, felt that he was not quite so decisive as he had always thought.

"Well…" said Mr Jenkins. "See to it, will you, Arnold. I'll leave it to you." And with that he promptly left the room.

Mr Pigg picked up his phone and looked in his inter-office directory for the number of the Property Section. Whilst he was dialling the number, he reflected on how correct his book had been to recommend the importance of blaming others.

The court case resumed after lunch but in the absence of the jury who remained in their own waiting room where they were able to talk and read newspapers and drink tea or coffee until summoned to return to the court.

Judge Fallow entered the courtroom and seated himself and then glanced towards the defence counsels. "Yes, gentlemen," he said,

They both stood up. They had obviously had time to discuss the case beforehand and had decided that the opening salvo would be fired by Augustus Samuel who was senior in years and experience.

"Humph," he muttered, "the, erh, matter which concerns us is the inclusion in the prosecution bundle of the two divorce petitions concerning of our respective clients.

"Yes, Mr Samuel, and what did you wish to say?"

"Humph... well, Your Honour I am addressing you in respect of the divorce petition filed against my client, Mr Sharp, but the two petitions are in a sense inextricably linked in so far as they tend to cover similar grounds and facts and since the defendants are linked anyway. Therefore, it follows that any arguments made in respect of Mr Sharp's petition will almost certainly apply in respect of the petition lodged against my friend's client and vice versa." At this point Mr Medland inclined his head in acknowledgement.

"Furthermore, Your Honour," continued Mr Samuel, "the similarity between the two petitions is not simply confined to facts that were similar but also the narrative of the documents which were of course prepared by the same person namely Miss Phillipa Fry."

"Indeed, they were," said Judge Fallow.

"Humph... .the petition served upon my client is inadmissible in this court, of no probative value and totally prejudicial to my client. A divorce petition has no value or meaning in this, a criminal court, and can only be a distraction for the jury."

"And what do you say to that Mr Sabin?"

Mr Sabin rose "The petitions accurately describe the character and the actions of the defendants, Your Honour. As such they are entirely relevant to the case and should be included in the bundle."

"Has there been any response from the defendants which have been filed in the Matrimonial Court Mr Sabin?"

"None to date, Your Honour."

"Humph..." said Gus Samuel getting to his feet. "It is I believe well known in a Matrimonial Court that a reply to a divorce petition is not always filed. It does not mean that the contents of the petition are true just because no response has been filed."

"Well, that is an argument, Mr Samuel, but no doubt Mr Sabin might say that if the contents of the petition were untrue the recipient would wish to file a response in order to put his side of the case to the world?"

"Indeed, Your Honour," said Mr Sabin, "and furthermore, I would argue that anyone who receives such a petition and decides not to respond probably accepts that the contents of the petition are true or at least understands that the rest of the world would believe that he accepts that the petition is true."

"Quite so," said Jeremy. "And what do you say, Mr Medland?"

The latter got to his feet. Before he spoke his upper lip was already curled. He held up a copy of the petition which had been served upon his client. "This document is completely and utterly prejudicial. It reads almost like a penny dreadful novelette," he announced. Waving the document, he allowed the curled lip to transform into a full-bloodied sneer. "The author of this should be writing for a cheap soap opera programme on TV. No one should have to read stuff like this unless or until…"

"Mr Medland," bellowed Judge Fallow. "Do you have any legal arguments in respect of your client's petition? If so I would like to hear them rather than listening to your literary critique."

Mr Medland was startled by the ferocity of the Judge's intervention and paused for a moment to consider his next move.

"Your Honour, this document is extremely prejudicial."

"I agree, Mr Medland. Did your client respond to the divorce petition?"

"No, Your Honour. My client is a foreign national and cannot be expected to understand the importance of a document like this."

"Did your client seek any legal advice?"

Mr Medland went into a hurried whispered conference with his client and then turned to answer the question. "My client did go to see a solicitor but so far, that lawyer has not taken any action. My client does not fully understand the procedures."

"Do they not have divorces in Malta, Mr Medland?" enquired Jeremy. The defence counsel gave a grimace which might have been interpreted by some as a sneer. "My client's country is primarily Catholic which frowns upon the concept of divorce, Your Honour."

"But in order to frown upon something there is a presumption that the concept is understood surely? In any event your client took legal advice." Again, Mr Medland winced and showed his teeth.

"Your Honour, whether or not my client took any legal advice does not alter the fact that inclusion in the prosecution bundle of my client's divorce petition is still highly prejudicial."

"Agreed, Mr Medland, but what are your legal reasons for excluding it?"

"This is a criminal court," said Mr Medland forcefully, and almost with a jeer, "Not a Matrimonial Court. A divorce petition has no place here particularly one containing so much personal venom directed towards the respondent, full of mere allegations which are, so far, uncontested. It has no relevance in this court and must be excluded. If, which is not accepted, this court decides that these documents should be included then I would respectfully suggest that some of the passages therein should be redacted. In particular, the name of one of the defendants is mentioned several times in the petition served upon my friend's client (here he indicated Mr Augustus Samuel). This is perhaps of much more importance to my friend Mr Phillipson who unfortunately is not here today. If he was, I am sure that he would request that at least his client's name should be deleted from the copy of the petition and may I presume to make that application on his behalf." He then sat down.

Judge Jeremy Fallow cleared his throat. "Thank you, Mr Medland. I have been asked to decide on the point of whether or not the divorce petitions should be included in the prosecution bundle. I have been reminded by both counsels that both petitions are prejudicial for all three defendants. They have also suggested to me that in a criminal court documents that are commonly present in a Matrimonial Court have no business or place in this court and cannot be regarded as acceptable evidence.

I have been asked by Mr Medland to decide that, because his client is of foreign extract and could have some difficulty in understanding the petition that it be excluded. However, I believe that Mr Petacinni has lived in this country for a number of years and must by now have a reasonable grasp of the English language. Furthermore, when he was served with the petition, he took legal advice and must have known what the petition was all about. Also, I do not agree with Mr Medland's opinion of the quality of the narrative of the petitions. I believe that the narrative is superlative. I further believe that it is that quality which most influences the desire of the defence counsels to have the petitions excluded from the bundle.

In their position I too would have made the same application. Upon hearing these words Phillipa smiled down from the viewing gallery and Mavis gave a silent whoop.

"However," continued Jeremy, "I cannot accept that although these petitions are prejudicial towards the defendants, they should be excluded from the prosecution bundle. I rule that the petitions shall be included with the proviso that the name of the second defendant be redacted throughout."

Saying this the judge looked at the clock and noting that there was another hour of daylight remaining he invited the defence counsels to agree 'here and now' what words in the petitions should be redacted. He explained that the trial proper could not start until Mr Phillipson was present to represent Mr Simon Nibble and therefore once the deletions of the wordings in the petitions was agreed the case would adjourn early and with luck, they might be able to catch up some time the following day.

Chapter Sixty-five
George Gets a Surprise

The following day George was unable to accompany Mavis to the Crown Court because he had an appointment at Duffey Fry & Co in respect of his grandmother's estate. He arrived at the office exactly on time and was immediately shown into the room of Mr Reynolds who was ready for him. He had a file open in front of him and several documents upon his desk. He told George that he had quantified the value of his grandmother's estate.

"This firm holds the title deeds and documents for all the properties which she owned." he said. "As well as the house she owned and lived in there was also a property which was rented out. This property which was inherited from her own father is a large Victorian structure consisting of fourteen separate flats all of which is producing an annual rental income of approximately one hundred thousand pounds per annum.

She also owned several shop premises in a terrace in the town, four in number, all of which produce together a total rental income of a further two hundred thousand pounds per annum. There was also, the sale proceeds of your own mother and father's house which was valued at approximately two hundred thousand pounds which your grandmother invested in a building society in trust for yourself.

In addition, there were some premium bonds in the approximate sum of five thousand pounds and a life insurance policy in the sum of one hundred thousand pounds. The main slice of the estate however was the bank savings account which she inherited from her father. These savings amounted to approximately one million two hundred thousand pounds. I have prepared a statement for the Revenue detailing the precise size of the estate and an application for a grant of probate. Kindly sign here, he indicated.

George was so stunned by the total of the sums which his grandmother had left him that he was almost paralysed with shock. He just about managed to sign the document.

"So what happens now?" asked George.

"Well..." said Mr Reynolds. "We will make the application on your behalf and the grant should come through in about two to three weeks. There is nothing especially complex about the estate although it is quite large. Just bank accounts, and the properties, fourteen of which are in one block. All quite straightforward. Once the grant of probate is received, we will transfer all the properties into your sole name. This will not be difficult since we already hold the deeds for them all. Each and every property in the portfolio is mortgage free. We will also get the bank and building society accounts transferred and also transfer the premium bonds into your name as well. That should not take too long, say a month approximately and then the whole estate is yours. At present, we manage all the rental properties for an annual charge which your grandmother was always happy to pay us. You may wish to consider whether or not you wish to consult a financial adviser/accountant who could give you advice on how best to deal with your new-found wealth. If you do then I would recommend that you employ the same firm of accountants who advised your grandmother. I am sure they would be happy to take you on."

George said he would think things over and wait to hear from him regarding the grant of probate. He did say that if the arrangement had suited his grandmother then almost certainly, he too would adopt it.

"So what is the total value of the estate?" he asked.

"Just over four million pounds," said Mr Reynolds.

George left the offices of Duffey Fry & Co in a state of shock and made his way back to the office where Bill and Tom were surprised to see him. He told them what he had heard from Mr Reynolds and they both gasped in amazement. "I just don't understand it" said George "I mean, four million pounds is a serious amount of money but my grandmother never looked or behaved as though she had much money at all. She lived in a very ordinary house and never spent lavishly on anything. My mum and dad always told me she was well off but I never dreamed it was to that extent."

Both Bill and Tom were flabbergasted by the news even though they had previously had a conversation with George which indicated that he might be coming into some money. "When is the funeral?" asked Tom.

"It's two weeks today," said George. "The undertakers have just told me. I will have to go out later to have a word with the priest who knew her and who will be conducting the service. Not that many will be there I suppose. She had no family except my mum and dad and me and theoretically I was not her blood relative. Is it all right if I go out later and do that?"

"Of course," said Bill. "You go on and do all you have to do. There is nothing left here to be done that Tom and I can't handle. Are you going to the court tomorrow with Mavis?"

"Yes, if you don't mind," he said.

"Of course," said Bill again. "You don't need to ask. You've got the annual leave due to you anyway and like I said there's little to do here."

"Thanks," said George.

He left shortly afterwards and made a couple of visits. One was to the local newspaper office to put in a note in the deaths column. Next, he called at the local golf club and saw the secretary who was on duty that day. He was more than happy to take a cheque from George to elevate the membership of both Bill and Tom. He also put some money behind the bar which was sufficient to allow them to have one free drink per round of golf for the next twelve months. The secretary was personally familiar with Bill and Tom and promised to tell them what George had paid for. He told George that what he had done was very generous but George poo poohed it. Then he went off to see the priest to give him the information he would require for the funeral service.

After that he went to the High Street to look in the window of an antique jeweller's shop. The shop had been in the High Street for ever and had always enjoyed a reputation among locals for offering value for money. In the window he saw an engagement ring which he immediately knew was the ring for Mavis. It was expensive but not extraordinarily so but was very charming. It had a ruby stone set in amongst diamonds and as soon as he saw it, he knew that it would suit Mavis. He went into the shop and paid a deposit on it and promised to return in a week or two to pay the balance and collect the item. The gentleman who served him assured him that it was a ring that had a history to it and had belonged to a local titled lady at one time who had fallen on hard times and passed it on. He told George that the ring was worth far more than he was paying for it. As far as George was concerned it was worth every penny and was classy and elegant. He knew it would look perfect on Mavis.

Chapter Sixty-six
The Trial Continues

The next day George met Mavis at the station and they travelled together on the train to Bristol. George told her what had happened the previous day at Duffey Fry & Co. Mavis not surprisingly was utterly astonished to learn what Mr Reynolds had told him. "Four million!" she gasped. "I cannot believe it. That is astonishing. What are you going to do?"

"Well, nothing for the time being at least. Most of the properties are rented out and managed by Duffey Fry & Co. That gives me a regular income without having to do anything. Why should I change that?"

Mavis nodded. "So you are a millionaire?" she said in an expression of disbelief.

"I know," said George. "It's ridiculous isn't it?"

They both laughed and continued to chatter all the way to Bristol. Once they arrived, they made their way to the Crown Court building. They met Phillipa Fry in the ground floor coffee bar. She and Mavis chatted gaily over a cup of coffee. Mavis, having already told Phillipa of her engagement to George now advised her, that her fiancé was a multi- millionaire.

Phillipa was no less amazed than anyone else who had been advised of George's good fortune.

"Well," said Phillipa, "that is truly astonishing. And you had absolutely no idea how wealthy your grandmother was?"

"No," said George. "I always knew she was comfortable but not wealthy. She just seemed so ordinary and never had any airs and graces."

"She sounds as if she was a wise woman. She clearly wanted you to have a regular upbringing."

"Yes," said Mavis, "and if she hadn't done that, I would never have met you."

They all chuckled and then decided that it was time to go into the court. As they made their way there Phillipa told Mavis that her husband, Algie, was back in town and would be representing Simon Nibble in court today.

When the court convened Judge Jeremy Fallow welcomed both the jury and Algernon Phillipson the defence counsel for Simon Nibble. The judge explained to the jury that there had been an application, made by the defence counsels that the divorce petitions in respect of the first and third defendants be excluded from the prosecution bundle. He further explained that the application had been refused by the court. He added that although the petitions were now included the only proviso that the court had made was that some words in the petitions should be deleted or redacted. "In due course when you read these you will find that some words are blanked out but otherwise, they are complete," Jeremy told them. He then indicated to the prosecution counsel, Mr Sabin, that he should proceed.

That gentleman rose and said, "I call my first witness, Detective Chief Inspector Desmond O'Nighons."

Des entered the courtroom and made his way to the witness box. He was dressed in a smart dark suit with a dark blue tie. He was a tall slim man who had the look of a guardsman. Mr Sabin ran him through his evidence in a methodical way. Des answered every question with confidence and with slick professionalism. Both Mavis and George were very impressed with the way in which he gave evidence. Even though they had seen him before they were hugely influenced by his courtroom manner and were certain that he was a witness with whom the jury would be greatly impressed.

Algernon Phillipson was the first counsel to cross-examine. He made a number of points which Des skilfully deflected. Algie persisted but each time on which he might have expected to expose some weakness in the chief inspector's armoury the latter would efficiently extricate himself from any pressure.

Augustus Samuel was the next to rise. "Humph, I put it to you that your evidence is implausible, Chief Inspector."

"Not in any way" Des assured him, looking the jury members honestly in the eye.

Gus Samuel tried again, and suggested that in some ways, the police had crossed the boundaries of legal investigations. Des took the insult in his stride and once more assured the jury rather than Gus that everything had been done properly. Gus hurrumphed his way through a few more approaches to which Des responded expertly. Gus tucked his thumb inside his gown and huffed and puffed a little more and then finally sat down.

Mr Medland rose and without looking at Des said, with some cynicism, "Detective, what gives you the right to break into people's property?"

"Search warrants, legally obtained," answered Des.

"But," sneered Mr Medland, almost with disbelief, "based upon what evidence?"

"Reasonable suspicion," replied Des.

"Hardly, detective," responded Mr Medland with a curl of the lip.

"Most assuredly," said Des, again looking the jury members honestly in the eye.

"Suspicion, I'll grant you," said Mr Medland, "but not reasonable, surely? In your mind alone I suggest."

"Not at all," said Des steadfastly. "When the warrants were executed we discovered overwhelming evidence against the defendants."

"But not with any reasonable suspicion, Detective," persisted Mr Medland with a snarl of suggested contempt. "Just a hunch on your part, I would suggest."

"No sir, not at all, and actually it is Detective Chief Inspector."

"I am not so much concerned with your rank, as how you use, or misuse your authority" sneered the barrister.

"Mr Medland," said Judge Fallow, "where is this line of questioning going?"

"It is going," snarled Mr Medland, "to possible prosecution misconduct."

"Mr Medland!" roared Jeremy with thinly disguised rage. He paused for a moment then said, "Counsels please approach the bench."

All the counsels approached the bench and Jeremy took a deep breath. He then whispered slowly, "This line and style of cross-examination is inappropriate. You will kindly desist from this style and also show a little more respect for the witness and the bench. Do I make myself clear?"

"But there is…" began Mr Medland stoutly.

"Do I make myself clear?" repeated Jeremy fixing his steely gaze upon Mr Medland.

Algie and Gus and Mr Sabin respectfully kept their eyes lowered. Mr Medland, who clearly sensed that he was now backed into a corner, appraised the situation and instantly changed his expression. With a respectful inclination of the head he whispered, "Apologies, Your Honour."

All three counsels returned to their stations, and Mr Medland said, "No more questions, Your Honour."

Mr Sabin rose to re-examine. "Just to clarify, Chief Inspector, the search warrants were all properly and legitimately obtained?"

"Absolutely," confirmed Des, "and the suspicion was completely reasonable and the evidence discovered more than justified the application for the warrants."

"And have you made many applications in your career for search warrants?" intervened the Judge.

"Yes, Your Honour, literally hundreds."

"And have any of your applications ever been refused by the Magistrates?" continued the Judge.

"No, never, Your Honour."

"Thank you, Chief Inspector," said the Judge, and Des then stepped down from the box and made his way to the rear of the courtroom. Judge Fallow glanced at the clock and judged that there was sufficient time for another witness before lunchtime.

"Yes, Mr Sabin," he said.

The latter rose and said, "I call, Sergeant Williams."

Sergeant Williams was Des Onions' first lieutenant and was a vastly experienced CID officer. He had given evidence in both the Magistrates' Court and the Crown Court on countless occasions. He was very good at remaining cool in the witness box and had never previously been flustered by cross- examination by solicitors or barristers. In addition, he now had the advantage of Jeremy rebuking Mr Medland for his robust style of cross-examination.

For approximately half an hour he gave straight bat answers to interrogation and gave information on all the evidence gathered against the defendants. With Mr Medland effectively muzzled by Jeremy neither Gus nor Algie were able to penetrate his business-like exterior. By the time he had finished giving evidence the jury were fully informed regarding all the evidence amassed against the defendants by the police.

Jeremy glanced at the clock again and saw that there was only fifteen minutes to go before lunchtime. He decided to adjourn for an early lunch and instructed everyone to return in one hour.

Mavis and George had lunch in a nearby snack bar with Phillipa. They spoke about the progress so far and everyone agreed that so far, the contest had been won by the prosecution.

"I wasn't sure what went on when the barristers had to go up to the bench for a whispered conference" admitted George.

Phillipa explained that if and when something private or confidential has to be said to or explained by the judge it either has to be done in complete private ie go into another space, or whisper quietly, or send the jury out of the court. "Basically," she added. "He was giving Mr Medland a dressing down because of his attitude. If he is disrespectful again then he is in big trouble. His problem is that he cannot effectively operate in a different style and now he is handcuffed."

"But what can he do about that?" asked George.

"Absolutely nothing," said Phillipa. "Except totally change his style and/or save it all up for a possible appeal."

"So, he could refer to that whispered rebuke in an appeal, could he?" asked Mavis.

"Well..." said Phillipa, with some hesitation, "because it was just a whispered aside in the court itself it will not form part of the official record. The jury were not excluded and there will be no official record of it. If it were referred to in an appeal Jeremy would be able to deflect it with ease. After all, it was not a rebuke as such but merely a threat to impose something unless Mr Medland desisted in his actions. It is therefore difficult to make an appeal point out of it. I am certain that is why Jeremy did not dismiss the jury or invite the counsels into his chambers for a private hearing."

"Hmm," said Mavis. "Very clever then?"

"Indeed," said Phillipa.

"And what about your husband?" asked Mavis, "what would be his reaction to it?"

"Well, I have not had a chance to discuss it with him but I don't believe he would be especially inclined to assist Mr Medland in any appeal points. His major problem will be the same as both other counsels, namely the strength and quality of the evidence against them. I personally doubt that there will be any valid points." They finished their meal and made their way back to the court and it's viewing gallery.

The first prosecution witness after lunch was Charlie Chivers. The International Detective, as expected, gave a good account of himself having had the advantage of personal coaching from Des Onions and a vast amount of experience as a former CID detective. His performance in the witness box was impressive. He never faltered at any time even though, when Gus Samuel was cross-examining him, the latter blustered and harrumphed his way through Charlie's offered evidence. At no time did the International Detective put a foot wrong especially when detailing the personal service of the divorce petitions on Eddie Sharp and Giovanni Petacinni. In respect of the latter, he went into intricate detail regarding the co-respondent whom he simultaneously served with a copy of the petition as well as Joe himself.

At the back of the court, DCI Desmond O'Nighons (who having given his own evidence was able to sit in court) congratulated himself and Charlie on the standard of prosecution evidence given so far. Before Charlie Chivers actually retired from the witness box Mr Sabin got him to verify the copies of the divorce petitions which he had served upon Eddie and Joe. Charlie duly confirmed these documents which were then identified to the jury as items X and Y in the bundle which each jury member had been given.

The next witness called by Mr Sabin was the professor from the laboratory who gave evidence regarding the drugs which formed the case primarily against Eddie and Joe. Mr Sabin, when taking him through his evidence, laboured the point concerning his qualifications and went to some trouble to ask him, "And so, professor, you are the leading authority in the country on this subject?"

The professor modestly confirmed that he was indeed.

"And I believe, professor, that you have published the only book that has ever been written on this subject. Is that correct?"

Again, the professor modestly admitted that it was. He then went on to give his evidence which was exactly how Des Onions had rehearsed with him. Whilst watching and listening Des himself was so glad that he had taken the trouble to upgrade his witness from the normal laboratory assistant to the leading expert professor in the country.

All three defence counsels struggled to cross-examine him in any effective way. The professor was far too knowledgeable for them and Des could feel how enamoured with him the jury were. When he stepped down from the witness box and left the court Des gave himself another hearty pat on the back.

He knew that the only vulnerable witnesses for the prosecution were Jimmy Pearce and the twins. The doubt in the minds of the jury, he knew, would be caused when they heard of the criminal element to these witnesses' characters. However, he also knew that despite their record these witnesses would probably be convincing enough to persuade the jury that most of what they would say would be true.

The first witness called was Jimmy Pearce who took the stand with much more confidence than anyone who knew him would have expected. He was kitted out in a new dark suit and his hair was slicked back with gel.

Mr Sabin was wise enough to steal the thunder of the defence counsels by asking Jimmy if he had a criminal record and then asking him about the recent circulation of drugs obtained from a contact in London. To both questions Jimmy gave full and honest answers admitting his part in the drugs circulation. Thereafter his evidence was not entirely truthful. In effect he blamed Eddie Sharp who, he assured the court had master-minded the drug dealing. During cross-examination, when it was suggested that his evidence against Eddie Sharp was untrue, he plausibly responded that he himself had insufficient funds to be dealer whereas Eddie was wealthy enough to finance the deals.

Jimmy was well rehearsed by Des Onions who knew full well that the jury would only believe him if he fully admitted his own guilt. Jimmy was astute enough to grasp his own role to perfection. In true Uriah Heap style, he adopted an ever so humble self-critical character fully, admitting all previous guilt and in effect begging the jury to believe him.

Des judged that Jimmy had played his part very well. Each time he was challenged, primarily by Gus who was after all Eddie's counsel, Jimmy would readily admit his own guilt but emphasise that he was only an agent for Eddie. Gus harrumphed and blustered on many occasions but each time

Jimmy stole his thunder by admitting more guilt but always adding that Eddie had put him up to it. On balance Des was wholly satisfied with the evidence offered by Jimmy.

There was not much time left in the day for further witnesses and Mr Sabin chose to fill that time with the evidence offered by an officer on the Flying Squad. This was a chief inspector who had been the contact with Des when they were trailing and observing Jimmy Pearce and the dealers in London.

The chief inspector was equally as impressive in the witness box as Des had been and his evidence mainly emphasised the size and nature of the drugs haul which the Flying Squad had detected. He explained how, with tip offs from police in Amsterdam, his team had tracked the drugs into this country and observed some of them being passed on to Jimmy Pearce. He confirmed also that the size of the haul had a street value of several million pounds. He also gave it as his opinion that, due to the immense value of the drugs, the dealer in this area would have to be someone of more substance than a mere Jimmy Pearce type.

Due to the fact that none of his evidence directly incriminated anyone other than Jimmy Pearce, his cross-examination did not take too long. Both Mr Medland and Algernon Phillipson decided not to ask any questions other than to obtain confirmation from the chief inspector that the only person who had had any contact with the London criminals was Jimmy Pearce.

Gus cross-examined with more vigour. "Humph, Chief Inspector, you suggest that the dealer/organiser in this region is a 'Mr Big' (here Gus gave a fingered interpretation of inverted commas), but that is no more than a guess on your part is it?"

"An educated guess," corrected the Flying Squad man. "I have dealt with cases like this for over fifteen years and it is always my experience that the dealer is a man of substance."

"Humph... So you have no evidence that anyone other than Jimmy Pearce was involved?"

"Only my instinct, which has served me well all my career," replied the chief inspector.

"Humph... So no evidence whatsoever?" persisted Gus.

"Nothing definite," he said with a sceptical edge to his voice.

"Thank you, chief inspector," said Gus who then sat down. Des, who was still at the back of the court, was very satisfied with the way his colleague had presented his evidence. He judged that he was slick and very experienced and that the jury were impressed by him.

Jeremy glanced at the clock and announced that the day's work was at an end. He reminded everyone that they should return at the same time tomorrow.

Des was wholly satisfied with the way the day had gone for the prosecution. He was especially gratified that the final item of evidence which the jury would take home with them was the testimony of the Flying Squad officer.

The next day Simon Nibble was not smiling. Overnight at the prison he had reflected on the prosecution case so far and concluded that it had not been a good day for himself, Eddie or Joe. Although he was not a specialist in criminal law he knew enough to realise that the evidence offered so far had been fairly damning. He had even been quite impressed with the way that Jimmy Pearce had given evidence. He knew of course that Jimmy was a congenital liar but still appreciated that his evidence had been proffered expertly. It was almost as though he had been tutored by someone he thought.

The food in the prison canteen was dire and it made him feel even more despondent. He knew that unless he could come up with some startling evidence that he would have to get used to the prison diet for many of the coming years. In the prison van on the journey from the court back to the prison he learned from Eddie that the main plank of his defence would be that the distributers of the drugs were Jimmy Pearce and the twins. He (Eddie) would be arguing that they alone had been the drug pushers and he had had nothing to do with it. When he had passed on the money to Simon's client account, he had no idea that it was illegal drug money. Although he had not said it Simon could imagine that the second layer of his defence would be that, having handed over the money to Simon he had trusted him to invest it wisely and honestly and knew nothing about solicitors' client accounts. Simon realised then that it was every man for himself.

The following day George and Mavis made their way to the Crown Court. Whilst enjoying a cup of coffee in the ground floor café they were surprised to meet Sandra Pete's girlfriend. She joined them for a coffee and confirmed that she had come to watch the trial. She told them that she had been unable to attend the previous day but was hoping to be able to watch the proceedings for the rest of the week. Mavis quickly gave her a precis of what had happened the day before. There appeared to be no sign of Phillipa and so the three of them made their way to the viewing gallery.

As the court convened and Judge Fallow entered the courtroom viewers in the gallery were able to see that Algernon Phillipson was not in his place. There was a brief moment of startled panic when those present noted the absence of Algie. Whilst they were looking to each other enquiringly there was a scuffling sound as Algie arrived in a rush. Looking up at the judge he muttered, "Apologies for my lateness, Your Honour."

At the same time Phillipa arrived upstairs and squeezed her way along the seating area to sit next to Mavis and George. "OK?" asked Mavis and Phillipa rolled her eyes to the heavens and sighed, "Algie was absolutely impossible this morning."

Meanwhile the court case commenced with Mr Sabin calling one of the twins as a witness. He had chosen the dominant twin having decided that he might be more proficient at giving evidence. He could see no advantage in calling both twins.

The dominant twin was sworn in and Mr Sabin took him through his evidence. As expected, the twin confirmed that the drugs were all received via Jimmy Pearce but that Eddie had been in charge of the operation and had funded the purchase of the supplies and had profited more than anyone. He also confirmed that any dealing which took place at the Nite Club had occurred under the eye of Joe Petacinni. All profits from such dealings were deposited in the Nite Club safe and all contents of the safe belonged entirely to Joe. The twin also told the court that Eddie had told him that all profits from the drug dealings had been paid directly into the client account of Simon Nibble which dovetailed neatly into the evidence which was to follow.

The first to cross-examine was Augustus Samuel who in his usual blustering way started with an accusatory, "Would you call yourself an honest man, Mr Gibson?"

The twin gave a sort of a shrug and replied, "Yes, as far as possible."

"Oh, really," blustered Mr Samuel quoting back the words "As far as possible, eh? The only reason I ask is that previously you have been convicted of a criminal offence, haven't you?" Gus made some display of checking notes on a piece of paper and then quoting an offence and date.

The twin raised his palms and said, "That was a misunderstanding. My solicitor persuaded me to plead guilty. He told me that a 'not guilty' plea would be too long winded and expensive, whereas if I pleaded guilty, they would give me a conditional discharge which was the same as not guilty."

"Oh, I see," said Gus, with heavy irony. "So really you were not guilty but your solicitor told you to plead guilty because it would be a lot easier. Is that right?"

"More or less," said the twin.

Mr Sabin got to his feet and intervened. "Your Honour, the offence to which my friend referred, was primarily one of assault rather than dishonesty."

Gus appeared to startled by this remark. "Humph," he observed, "the point is it is a criminal conviction registered against this witness who was also involved in the dealing in this case. This witness is a convicted criminal your honour."

"But not," intervened Mr Sabin, "convicted of dishonesty."

"Yes, thank you," said Judge Fallow, "have you any further questions for this witness Mr Samuel?"

"Humph, why on earth should this jury believe any evidence given by a convicted criminal?"

"Because I was there, and because I am telling the truth," said the twin.

Phillipa whispered to Mavis in the gallery, "Gus is such a moron. No attention to detail, no preparation."

Gus continued harrumphing for a few more minutes but the twin steadfastly maintained his position.

Eventually Gus sat down, and Mr Medland stood up. Despite the whispered earlier rebuke from Judge Fallow, he could not resist the urge to revert to type and before he uttered a single word his lip had curled into a contemptuous snarl. "Tell me, Mr Gibson, you have been videoed and observed by police officers selling drugs to people and yet you are asking this court to believe that someone else is to blame?"

The twin looked thoughtful, "It's like I said before, Eddie Sharp was in charge. He had enough money to finance it, and I was simply obeying orders."

"Oh, I see," sneered Mr Medland. "The Nuremburg defence." Then with a mock German accent, "simply obeying orders." The twin said nothing.

Algernon stood up and shouted to the twin in a challenging way. You are asking this court to believe that Mr Sharp told you about my client's client account at his office. Now why on earth would he want to discuss that with you?"

"Well, he did," insisted the twin. "I didn't make it up."

"Well, somebody surely did," suggested Algie.

"Why would I lie?" asked the twin.

Algie raised his hands and his eyebrows in complete astonishment. He looked around the court and eyed the jury. "Well," he said sarcastically, "Let me see, perhaps the chance of a reduced sentence might be one possibility.

The twin looked Algie in the eye and shook his head. For a further ten minutes or so Algie harangued the twin with an array of insulting questions but the twin maintained an implacable resistance. Finally, Algie sat down.

Mr Sabin stood for a moment and asked, "Please confirm, Mr Gibson. Have you ever been convicted of a crime of dishonesty?"

"No sir," was the firm reply.

The next witness called by Mr Sabin was a further member of the CID squad led by Des Onions. This man was another detective sergeant who described himself to Mr Sabin as a backroom boy who was an expert at examining and analysing paperwork and computer records. Most of what he had to say was merely a back-up for the information already offered by Des. In particular Mr Sabin alighted on the note book that was obtained from the safe in Eddie Sharp's house. He took the witness meticulously through many of the entries in the note book.

The detective sergeant carefully explained each entry. "They were," he said, "all connected to the game of snooker." Which he also explained was a favourite pastime of Eddie Sharp. He described how they had found, in the room where his safe was located, a snooker table. He described to the jury how the entries in the note book were all a record of Eddie's criminal deals which were all recorded in a secret code which referred to names or descriptions used in the game of snooker. He further explained that entries in the note book made in certain colours referred to the points value of the balls in the game of snooker eg a red ball equals one, yellow ball equals two, green equals three, brown equals four, blue equals five, pink equals six and black equals seven.

There were also names which he explained. In the notebook were certain names or terms which had connotations with snooker. For example, the word hurricane referred to the name of Higgins after a famous player. Similarly, the name Dracula represented the name Reardon after another famous player. The amounts recorded against the names showed the volume of drugs supplied and the value thereof in accordance with the units and the colours in which the entries were made.

Further, when the names were checked they corresponded with the names of criminals known to the police. The CID, he told the court, were able thus to deduce the people to whom the drugs had been supplied and how much money was received by Eddie. Furthermore, the totals shown in the note book matched almost precisely the sums of money which were paid into the client account of Mr Simon Nibble solicitor. Each of the jury members was supplied with a bundle which included not only the note book entries but the names also of the criminals with whom Eddie had been dealing. The evidence was presented by the sergeant in a very professional way. Des, who was still seated at the back of the court was extremely pleased with the way his officer had given his evidence.

Gus was the first to cross examine as his client was the one most implicated by this evidence. "This theory, that all the entries in the note book are connected to the game of snooker, is ridiculous isn't it?"

"No sir," responded the sergeant.

"These entries are simply random records of contacts made by Mr

Sharp with people he knows and have absolutely nothing to do with the game of snooker, do they?"

"No, sir," relied the witness once again. "All the entries make sense once you apply the snooker connections. The quantities and amounts by value are quantified according to the points score of the snooker balls and the totals equal the amounts paid into the solicitor's client account."

"I put it to you that all this snooker ball value or score is just a figment of your own rich imagination."

"No, sir, it all makes sense."

"My client will say that they are just some random notes made by him which may or may not have any great meaning. However, to imply that they are all connected to the game of snooker is just smoke and mirrors isn't it? There is no grand connection is there. The entries are all just random. That's right isn't it?"

"No, sir," repeated the sergeant.

Mr Medland got to his feet and gave the Sergeant a vicious sneer, "Really, Sergeant! Do you really understand what you are expecting this jury to believe? A note book with some random jottings therein, are actually a journal of drug deals and all based on the value of snooker balls?"

"Yes, sir," he replied resolutely.

"But why not a record of football results over the past twelve months, eh?"

"Those would not need to be locked in a safe would they, sir?"

"Indeed, they would not" agreed Mr Medland "but perhaps neither did this one. Perhaps Mr Sharp just dropped it in the safe by mistake. How long have you worked in the CID officer?"

"Fifteen years, sir."

"Well, perhaps you would be better suited to working with M15 or M16 tracking down spies who use secret codes?" he added in a mocking jeer. The sergeant remained implacable.

Algie had a few questions of similar ilk regarding the note book entries but no further progress was made by the defence.

Judge Fallow then decided that it was appropriate to adjourn for lunch. He told everyone to return in one hour and withdrew to his chambers. George and Mavis retired for lunch to the same snack bar they had used before and they were joined by Phillipa and Sandra.

Sandra commented that the twin had given his evidence in a more impressive way than she had expected. Having come across him and his brother at the gym she said that she was expecting him to look very furtive and disreputable. Phillipa agreed that in the circumstances both the twin and Jimmy Pearce who were both admitted participants were unexpectedly plausible. She gave it as her opinion that they had been expertly rehearsed probably by Des.

Mavis asked her why she had arrived so late. Phillipa raised her eyes to the heavens and sighed. "Oh, Algie was so difficult this morning that I despaired that we would ever arrive at all. I think tomorrow it might be easier to drive in separately, which we often do anyway, otherwise we may be doomed never to arrive at all. He's always bickering about something."

After the lunch break the court case resumed and the first witness called by Mr Sabin was Alice the young girl from Huw Roberts & Co. She looked very nervous, even terrified.

Mr Sabin took her gently through her evidence about the deed she had witnessed at work. He also led her through the offer of a holiday which Simon Nibble had made to her. She confirmed his offer of a week in his newly acquired apartment in Tenerife. Mr Sabin produced the brochure which Simon Nibble had shown her and asked her to identify that it was the apartment which he had said he owned. Alice confirmed that it was.

As the evidence tendered was against Simon Nibble his counsel, Algernon Phillipson was the first to cross-examine. "I suggest to you that you may be mistaken regarding the deed which you signed." Alice looked surprised but said nothing. "There was I believe at least one other time when you went into my client's office when Mr Sharp was present. Is that not right?"

"Yes," said Alice.

"I put it to you that it was upon that occasion that you signed the deed."

"No," said Alice. "When I signed the document, it was just Mr Nibble who was there."

"Well, I put it to you that you are mistaken," said Algie. Alice stood her ground and insisted that she had signed the document only in the presence of Simon Nibble. Neither of the other two counsels had any questions.

The next witness for the prosecution was the legal cashier of Huw Roberts & Co. Mr Sabin led her gently through her evidence establishing that she had commenced her legal career with Mr Hugh Roberts himself when he had started his practice many years before. She told the court that Mr Roberts had been a conscientious and outstanding solicitor who had been scrupulous about the management of his client account.

She moved on to say that since Mr Nibble had arrived at the office Mr Huw Roberts became sick and gradually relinquished authority to him and finally died. Since his death Mr Nibble had run the business in an entirely different way. Hugh Roberts had been careful and painstaking. Mr Nibble was cavalier and reckless.

Mr Sabin then led her through a number of entries in the client account pages copies of which were all included in the jury's bundle. She explained that not only were all the entries controlled entirely by Mr Nibble himself but also on all occasions she had reminded him of the Law Society rules in respect of such entries and the fact that on each occasion he was breaching those rules.

The defence counsels were all reluctant to cross-examine this witness but presumably felt they had to. Algernon was the first to make an attempt. As it was his client who was under pressure from this witness, he sensed that the jury would expect him to cross-examine. He did feel however that the character of this witness would be difficult to crack. He sensed also that prolonged cross-examination of a witness who was obviously unapproachable only highlighted to the jury the usefulness of the evidence given by the witness.

He confined his questions to the qualifications and experience of the witness. Even though her experience was greater than that of Simon Nibble himself he endeavoured, by excessively polite questioning, to somehow imply that the witness was less than convincing but he had the good sense not to persist too long with his cross-examination. He suggested with a final thrust that the witness had simply a dislike for Mr Nibble whom she compared unfavourably with Mr Huw Roberts whom she had clearly admired. She admitted that she had admired her original boss but denied that her evidence was prompted by a dislike of Mr Nibble as a person. Algernon tried to gain the upper hand by implying with a final thrust that, "I suggest to you, that your dislike of Mr Nibble shines through the evidence which you have given here today." The witness denied this again and Algernon then with a sceptical glance sat down. The other two counsels declined to cross-examine the witness at all.

The next witness was the expert from the Law Society, Mr Paul Ferguson. His evidence was quite straightforward. He had examined the client account records of Simon Nibble's firm and categorically confirmed that the entries which were highlighted in the copy documents in the jury's bundle were all prohibited by the Law Society rules. His evidence was merely factual statements about those rules concerning the administration of client accounts.

Algernon tried to do his best but was aware, before he got to his feet, that the man's evidence was largely unchallengeable. He suggested that possibly, due to the fact that the entries in the books had been made by the legal secretary and not Simon Nibble himself, the blame for any or all irregularities in the books could not all be aimed at Mr Nibble. The witness confirmed very definitely that the blame lay wholly with the solicitor who was in charge of the office not any of his employees.

The other two defence counsels declined to ask any questions.

The last prosecution witness of the day was Mr Ken Carter. He strode into the court witness box with a ramrod straight back and wearing a Harris tweed jacket with a red tie. He was an ex-guardsman and a Cambridge blue still with a full head of hair albeit white. He looked ten years younger than his age and had a pair of steely grey eyes.

Mr Sabin took him through his evidence shrewdly dwelling on Mr Carter's history and situation. He knew of course that the more the jury learned about the witness the more likely they were to believe anything he said.

Ken Carter laboured upon how unsuitable a partner Giovanni Petacinni was for his sister Freda. He detailed the dismay that his father had experienced when Joe had been courting his daughter, (Ken's sister), He explained how his father and sister had gone on holiday to Malta where Joe was the waiter in their hotel. He told how, despite his father's opinion of the man, his sister had developed an obsession for Joe. He further explained that Joe had followed them back to England and in the words of his own father, continued to 'pester' his sister. Against her father's wishes Freda had married Joe and Ken Carter explained what a disappointing husband he had been. He told the court how Joe had bled the family coffers trying to establish a business of some variety for himself. Due to his laziness and lack of business acumen, nothing he tried really succeeded.

The witness then moved on to the transfer of family shares in the businesses previously owned by his father. He explained how Joe had achieved by fraud a transfer of all Freda's shares in the family business. He moved on to the meeting at the Grand Hotel in Bristol where further papers were signed and exchanged. He emphasised the extravagant manner of a hotel lounge meeting held by Simon Nibble, whom Mr Carter referred to as a flash Harry.

Under cross-examination from Algernon, Mr Carter held firm. Des Onions, who was still watching at the back of the court was pleased with how impressive Ken Carter was as a witness. He felt that the jury completely admired and believed him.

Mr Medland, on behalf of Giovanni Petacinni could hardly contain himself. Despite the previous rebuke from the judge, he addressed the witness with a definite sneer on his face.

"Mr Carter, what evidence do you have of any wrongdoing by Mr Nibble, apart from your obvious dislike of the man?"

"He dealt with the transfer of my family's company shares fraudulently," he answered. "It's true I don't like him," he continued "he did not behave how a normal solicitor would behave."

"In what way?" demanded Mr Medland.

"Well, as I already said, he held meetings in the private rooms of a five-star hotel. He wore a flashy suit, quite unsuitable for a legal office, which gave him the appearance of an ice cream salesman."

"So, because he wore a smart suit, you assume that he was a fraudster. Is that right?"

"No," said Mr Carter, "the deals he made were fraudulent. The fact that he looked like a spiv, was largely immaterial."

"Oh," responded Mr Medland showing his teeth. "so if he had worn a pin striped suit the deal would have been perfectly legitimate?"

"No, of course not," responded the witness "a fraudster is always a fraudster: it's just that he did not look like a typical lawyer."

"Oh, really, and what does a typical lawyer look like?"

"Mr Medland, where is this going?" asked Judge Fallow in a slightly exasperated tone.

"I was merely seeking to reveal this witness' prejudices, Your Honour."

"Well, I think you have already achieved that, Mr Medland. Have you any other relevant questions for the witness?"

Jeremy himself, felt that Mr Carter's attitude was reasonable. In fact, he recalled that he himself had not been favourably impressed, when he first saw Simon Nibble in his court.

"You say the deals were fraudulent but when you attended the meeting in the Grand Hotel you did not mention the fact that you thought the share purchases were fraudulent did you?"

"Well, I always knew they were suspicious but at that time I did not realise how fraudulent they were. At that time my sister was still infatuated by the man but since then she has admitted that she never agreed to sign any documents nor did she ever do so. It's all in her divorce petition, just have a look at it."

"But you never actually made any accusation of fraud, did you?" said Mr Medland.

"I made my views plain at the Grand Hotel meeting," responded Mr Carter.

Gus Samuel rose to cross-examine, "Humph. My client's acquisition of the shares in your family business was completely regular and legal, wasn't it?"

"No, definitely not," said Ken Carter. "The share transfers were fraudulent."

"I put it to you, Mr Carter, that there was nothing illegal or improper about the transfers. They were all properly conducted deals."

"No, sir," said Mr Carter emphatically, "take a look at my sister's divorce petition. All the details of her husband's wrong doing are in there."

"You cannot expect the jury to believe a document like that. It suits you to believe what is written in your sister's divorce petition doesn't it? As Mandy Rice Davies would say, 'she would say that wouldn't she'?"

"Not at all," insisted Ken Carter. "Everything in the petition is true."

Gus blustered on and on for another ten minutes or so and then finally sat down. Mr Sabin then announced that the prosecution case was concluded. Judge Fallow then advised everyone that the day's work was done and the case was adjourned until the following morning.

Chapter Sixty-seven
An Engagement

George and Mavis made their way home on the train. They talked eagerly about the day's trial that they had just witnessed. Neither of them was experienced in any way in such matters but both were firmly of the opinion that the prosecution case had been effective and impressive.

"I cannot foresee that there will be any verdict other than guilty." predicted Mavis. George agreed.

"Wait until the jury reads the divorce petitions prepared by Phillipa," Mavis continued, "that I am absolutely sure will clinch the matter."

Again, George agreed. He looked at his watch and said, "It's still early, the shops will still be open when we get back. There's something I want to show you." Mavis looked curious but George said no more.

When they alighted from the train George led her to the jewellers in the High Street. He pointed out to her the ring which he had already chosen for her. When she saw it, her eyes lit up. They went inside and the same gentleman served George as the day when he had paid his deposit. He remembered George and reached inside the shop window to retrieve the ring. He took the ring from its velvet case and Mavis slipped it onto her finger. It fitted perfectly and Mavis admired it and instantly fell in love with it. There was absolutely no question of Mavis choosing a different ring or even wishing to consider a different one.

George was delighted and produced his credit card to pay the balance. They left the shop together and walked hand in hand down the High Street, both of them idyllically happy.

"Let's go to the Italian restaurant and have a celebratory meal." said George. Mavis agreed and they made their way to the flat which he still shared with Pete. They arrived at almost the same time as Pete who had just finished work. George explained that they were intending to go to the restaurant downstairs and suggested that Pete join them. He explained that he was awaiting the arrival of Sandra who had agreed to call round after her day in court.

George and Mavis decided to retire immediately to La Scala and occupy a table and wait for Pete and Sandra to arrive. This they did and were greeted on arrival by Fillipo who, as usual, kissed the hand of Mavis and remarked about her beauty. They asked for a table for four and advised him that Pete and Sandra would soon be joining them. They chose a drink each and Fillipo brought them some bread sticks and olives to chew on.

Pete and Sandra soon turned up and sat down at the table. They ordered drinks for themselves and Fillipo presented them all with a menu. While they studied the menu, they chatted happily. The number one topic of conversation of course was the trial. Sandra apologised for rushing away when the court had closed but explained that she had to get back to her offices in Bristol to record a report of the day's proceedings.

"We saw your boss giving his evidence," said Mavis to Pete. "He was very impressive." Sandra and George agreed. They all continued to discuss the trial for about another ten minutes until Fillipo returned to take their orders.

It was at this moment that Sandra spotted the finger of Mavis holding her menu. "Oh, my goodness," she said. "I've just noticed your ring. It's beautiful."

Mavis proudly informed her that it was her engagement ring which George had just purchased. There was great jubilation from everyone including Fillipo who suddenly produced a bottle of champagne which he expertly opened. They all drank a toast after which George announced that he would be paying for the meal for everyone. Both Pete and Sandra objected but George insisted and said also that he had something else to tell them.

It was then that he told them of his visit to Duffey Fry & Co and the details of the size of his grandmother's estate. Sandra covered her mouth and nose with her hands to indicate her astonishment at George's good fortune. Pete merely whistled and muttered, "Jesus Christ, four and a half million! As you were George," he said, "perhaps I will allow you to pay for this meal after all." They all laughed and chattered away all evening with Fillipo bobbing back and forth like a mother hen.

Mavis quizzed Sandra about her job with the T.V. company. Sandra told her that everything was going well. She did say that she would not be able to spare any more time to attend the trial. She hoped to return for the final day when a verdict would be announced but could not spare any more time for viewing. She explained that she had already spent some time recording information for a programme about drug dealing generally including some regarding the young man who had recently died.

"Well," said Mavis, "I look forward to watching the programme when it is finally finished and broadcast. For my part I shall look forward to tomorrow and seeing the defendants in the dock though I cannot imagine what defence they will raise."

Chapter Sixty-eight
The Defence

The following morning Gus had an early morning conference with Eddie at the court building. "Humph," said Gus. "Just a few points that I wanted to go over before you give evidence this morning."

"Do I really have to?" asked Eddie. "Can't I just continue my 'no comment' defence, and remain silent?"

"I'm afraid not," responded Gus. "It is no longer quite like the good old days where one could remain silent and the judge would advise the jury that they should not interpret silence as guilt. Nowadays a judge can advise the jury that choosing to remain silent does indeed imply guilt. And make no mistake, this judge would do precisely that. No, you will have to give evidence otherwise the jury will assume you are guilty. I suggest we stick to the story we previously discussed ie, any dealing was carried out by the twins who have already admitted as much. Any money handed to your solicitor was profits from your various businesses. All transfer deals with regard to the shares etc were all drawn up by the solicitor and nothing to do with you. Is that understood?"

"Perfectly," replied Eddie. "But what will he say? Presumably that everything was my fault, eh?"

"Yes, probably," said Gus, "but I believe it may be more difficult for him to plead ignorance or innocence than you." Eddie nodded and Gus rose to leave. "I will see you later" he said and left the room.

Mavis and George took their usual places in the viewing gallery alongside Phillipa Fry who was also in attendance. Jeremy Fallow QC entered the courtroom and everyone stood up. He bowed briefly and said, "Good morning" and sat down. After a brief pause, he said, "Yes, Mr Samuel, have you advised your client about giving evidence?"

"Humph. I have, Your Honour. I would like to call my client Mr Sharp." Eddie stood up and was escorted to the witness box by the court usher.

Gus took him through the opening part of his evidence establishing his name age and profession etc. He expertly coaxed from Eddie the information that he was a self-employed car dealer who bought and sold second hand cars and who also had a dealership for one or two manufacturers of new vehicles. He also established that Eddie invested in properties in the town where he lived either with a view to renting them out or selling them on, after refurbishment, at a profit.

"Mr Sharp," he enquired, "you heard the evidence given by Mr Gibson?"

"Yes," said Eddie.

"Now, I believe you employed him and his twin brother did you not?"

"Yeah, that's right," said Eddie, "but I wouldn't call them employees as such. They just used to do various jobs for me, mainly around the 'car lot' premises. They would do lifting and transporting work and sometimes buy or sell second hand cars for me and deliver them if required. But they weren't employees. They were self-employed. I used to pay them cash. They worked in the evenings at the Nite Club as bouncers. Most of the daytime they would be hanging around in the gym next door to the car lot."

"I see," said Gus, "so they did not work for you directly? Any money they earned was on an add-hock basis?"

"That's right," agreed Eddie.

"And what about Mr Pearce?" asked Gus. "How well did you know him?"

"Hardly at all," said Eddie. "He was a friend of the twins."

"So he was not employed by you either?"

"No," confirmed Eddie.

"And the money that you gave to Mr Nibble, the second defendant, what was the source of that money?"

"It was just cash which some people gave me when buying a car, I would save it up and give it to him every so often. It was more convenient than putting it in the bank."

"And he put it into his client account, did he?"

"Yes, I wasn't aware which account he paid it into. I trusted him completely and left all that to him."

"And the note book that the police found at your house? You heard the police officer, when he gave evidence, suggesting that it gave details of drug deals. Is that the case?"

"No, definitely not!" replied Eddie. "It was just a book with a few random entries concerning deals I think, about cars I had bought and sold."

"And the different coloured entries? Were they significant?"

"Not at all," said Eddie. "They were all pretty casual notes most of which I have forgotten. The colour of the entries depended upon which pencil, pen or crayon was available at the time."

"Humph…. just wait there a moment, Mr Sharp" said Gus, before sitting down.

Mr Sabin rose and looked down at his notes. "The colour of the entries and the quantity of each Entry, were carefully explained by the police officer in his evidence. Are you telling this court that the explanation of the entries given by the police officer were entirely fictitious?"

"Certainly, they were," said Eddie, "I don't know anything about any drug dealing. They're just random entries which have been interpreted by an ingenious mind inside the CID."

"So, you handed over considerable amounts of cash to Mr Nibble rather than placing it in your bank. You said it was more convenient. In what way was it more convenient?"

"Well, his office was only a short walk from my business premises whereas my bank is on the other side of town."

"And did you get a receipt from Mr Nibble each time you deposited money with him?"

"No," said Eddie. "I just gave him the money."

"So there was no record of it. Did that not seem risky or unbusinesslike to you?"

"Not really," said Eddie. "I trusted him completely. He was a solicitor after all."

Algernon got to his feet and said, "These twins who you implied you knew little or nothing about. You said yourself that they spent most of every day at your car lot premises or at the gym next door. They were a bit more than casual workers, weren't they?"

"Not really," said Eddie wondering to himself where this line of questioning was leading.

"They worked for you as muscle men, didn't they?"

"No," insisted Eddie, "they spent most of their time in the gym. They were building up their muscles because they worked as bouncers at the Nite Club."

"You used them to collect debts for you, didn't you?"

"Only sometimes," admitted Eddie. "If a tenant of mine was behind with the rent they would go round and ask him to pay up."

"So, strong-arm tactics was it?"

"No, not at all," insisted Eddie. "Just legal debt collection."

Mr Medland rose and barred his teeth. "These men, the twins, were your well-paid muscular hyenas were they not?" Eddie merely shook his head

"If, as you say, they did not work for you but merely hung around your premises without actually earning any wages, where did they find the money to drive the expensive cars which they owned? Or did the cars belong to you?"

"I don't know," said Eddie, "it was none of my business."

"You...." said Mr Medland, with an enormous amount of vindictiveness in his voice, "used them as resident thugs who did your dirty work for you and you rewarded them by supplying them with fancy cars."

"No not at all," repeated Eddie. "I had nothing to do with their cars nor did I ever employ them. They worked for Joe not me. They were bouncers at the Nite Club."

"That's as maybe," sneered Mr Medland, "but everyone knows they were working for you. They peddled their drugs to young people at the Nite Club passed on the profits to you and were handsomely rewarded by you. My client only employed them as doormen and had no idea what was really going on."

"No, no," insisted Eddie. "I had nothing to do with anything that went on there. If anyone was responsible it would have been Joe."

Mr Medland's lip curled even further as he said with finality, "Mr Sharp, I suggest to you that you are an unconscionable liar, and that the facts speak for themselves."

Eddie's sneer equalled that of his inquisitor, "Is that a question?" he pleaded, palms held upward.

Jeremy interjected. "Mr Phillipson, is your client going to give evidence? Have you advised him of his rights?"

"I have, Your Honour. I would like to call him now to give evidence."

Simon Nibble made his way to the witness box. As Jeremy Fallow watched him take the stand, he reflected that there was little resemblance between the pale, nervous, individual wearing plain non-descript clothes and the brash confident person dressed in the cream Armani suit who had recently appeared in his court.

Simon himself felt nervous and deflated. Despite his own considerable experience of appearing in courts of law he felt truly inadequate today. A few days in the nearby prison had taught him how unpleasant life could be as a guest of Her Majesty. He reflected how only a couple of days ago his life had been so different. He knew now that it was likely that he would not be driving his beloved Mercedes car for quite a while. He knew in fact that it would have to be sold to finance this court case. He knew also that his two children, Noah and Jucinda would no longer be able to continue attending their expensive private school. He tried to imagine how they would manage to adjust to the local state school atmosphere.

Algernon Phillipson began his examination. "How long have you been a solicitor Mr Nibble?"

Simon thought for a moment then said, "Fifteen years," he then quoted the year in which he qualified.

"I believe that you are the principal of your firm?"

"Yes, that is correct," said Simon. He went on to explain how he had become an articled clerk at the firm of Huw Roberts & Co and described the sad death of Mr Roberts and his own succession to the ownership of the firm.

Algernon asked him about the size of the firm and the number of employees and established the fact that it was a financially successful business.

"And so you have fourteen people who depend upon you for their livelihood?"

"Yes."

"And have you ever been previously accused of any faults or discrepancies or misdemeanours?"

"No, never," replied Simon.

"So how would you explain the discrepancies in your client account detailed by the prosecution witnesses we have heard from?"

"The money was banked for my client Mr Sharp. He brought me several tranches and insisted that I invest it for him. I told him that it wasn't entirely appropriate for my client account but he insisted."

"But could you not simply tell him to deposit the money in his own bank?" asked Algie.

"No," said Simon. "He brought me bags full of the cash and before I could argue the point he just walked out after threatening me. He said it was only for a few weeks and then I could write him a cheque and he would put it in his bank."

"In what way did he threaten you?"

"He said it would be the worst for me and my family if I didn't do what he asked. He said he would send the twins round to break my arms and legs and injure my family. I was very frightened. But I honestly did not know that any of the money was the proceeds of any criminal activity. I just thought it was cash he had accumulated from car sales."

"Just wait there a minute" said Algie who then sat down. Mr Sabin challenged Simon on all the points he had made and insisted that he must have been aware of Eddie's activities and where the money came from. Simon held firm and repeated that Eddie had threatened himself and his family with violence.

Gus got to his feet. "Humph... my client, Mr Sharp, never threatened you and you know it. You did very well out of the money that he gave you, didn't you?"

"No, no," insisted Simon. "I had no idea what he was up to."

"He was not up to anything," harrumphed Gus. "My client, Mr Sharp, was never involved in selling drugs. I put it to you, that the drugs were sold by Mr Pearce, and the twins."

"Who worked for Eddie," said Simon.

"No," said Gus. "They were free lancing, weren't they?"

"I'm sure I don't know," admitted Simon.

Mr Medland got to his feet and surveyed Simon Nibble with some contempt. "Mr Nibble," he enquired with a sneer. "What car do you drive?"

"A Mercedes," answered Simon.

"And how much did you pay for it?"

"I can't remember," said Simon. "How much did you pay for the holiday apartment in Tenerife, in which you offered your employee, Alice, a holiday?"

"I can't remember," said Simon again. "What has that got to do with anything?"

"How did you pay for it?" demanded Mr Medland.

"From the profits of my business," answered Simon stubbornly.

"From your client account you mean?"

"No, no," said Simon, "the profits of my business."

There followed some more to and fro questioning during which Simon Nibble stuck to his story that he was intimidated by Eddie Sharp into banking the money in his client account.

Jeremy Fallow decided that it was time for an early lunch. He adjourned proceedings for one hour.

George and Mavis retired to their favourite snack bar for lunch with Phillipa. While he was ordering the snacks and drinks at the counter Mavis was showing Phillipa her engagement ring. When she saw the ring Phillipa was so impressed. She hugged and kissed Mavis and told her that she thought the ring was wonderful. While they were waiting for George to return with the snacks and drinks, Mavis told her the news about his inheritance. Phillipa was both astonished and delighted for them both.

When the snacks arrived Phillipa gave them both hearty congratulations. She wished them all the happiness they could wish for themselves.

As they consumed their food the conversation turned predictably to the court session of the morning. "I am still slightly in shock about what went on in there," said Mavis. "I mean, I never expected that all the defendants would blame each other. I was expecting them to present a united front. Surely it is a dangerous ploy to try to pass off blame onto someone else?"

"Well yes," agreed Phillipa, "but it is not at all uncommon. They are each trying to escape the worst consequences."

"But what are the jury supposed to think?" persisted Mavis, "how can they distinguish who was or wasn't blameworthy?"

"Actually," said Phillipa, "it's not that difficult. Generally, most of each jury usually have a clear idea of who is guilty before they go into a huddle to decide. It is often just one or two who are undecided. As often as not they can be persuaded by the others. If not, then generally it is possible to achieve a majority verdict."

"And what do you think about your husband's client's defence?"

"Well, it is I suppose, the best he can do in all the circumstances. His problem of course is that you cannot argue with figures on a bank account statement. If the figures on his client account statements are incorrect, which the prosecution say is the case, then the finger points at him. It is a black and white situation. Duress is only a partial defence but it is, I suppose, better than no defence at all."

"Perhaps," said Mavis, who was always keen to show Phillipa that she had done some reading up on things legal, it was a matter of necessity that caused Mr Nibble to deposit the money in the client account?"

"Hmm," murmured Phillipa, "so spake the fiend and with necessity, the tyrant's plea, excused his devilish deeds."

Mavis was intrigued, "What was that?" she enquired.

"That was Milton, *Paradise Lost*," replied Phillipa. "Neither necessity nor duress are entirely convincing defences."

"You are so well read," said Mavis in admiration.

Phillipa smiled at her and gripped her hand. "And so can you be," she said with certainty.

They all finished their snacks and returned to the viewing gallery. From their vantage point they could see that Mr Aloysius Medland was having a whispered conference with his client Giovanni Petacinni. It was obvious that there was a difference of opinion between the two. Mr Medland was forcefully telling his client something but each time Joe would toss his head and give a Latin refusal. Whenever this happened Mr Medland would engage with him again even more forcefully, even, on one occasion slamming his fist down on the table. Joe looked away in a melodramatic fashion and crossed his arms in a petulant way.

The door behind the bench opened and Jeremy Fallow QC entered and gave a brief bow. Mr Medland was briefly distracted by Jeremy's entrance but returned again to his client with added venomous whispering.

"Is everything all right, Mr Medland?" asked Jeremy.

"Yes, Your Honour. I was just giving my client some last-minute advice."

"Would that advice perhaps be on the subject of your client giving evidence in the witness box?"

"Indeed, Your Honour," confirmed Mr Medland. "Previously it was assumed that he would give Evidence, but now, Your Honour, Mr Petacinni is firmly of the opinion that he should not."

"Perhaps you would like to tell me, before the jury returns, have you advised him fully on the consequences of not giving evidence?"

"I have indeed, Your Honour, but I am afraid that the situation is not as straightforward as it might normally be."

"Oh really?" remarked Jeremy with a raise of the eyebrows, "how so?"

"Well," said Mr Medland, pausing to choose his words carefully, "My client is of Maltese extraction and his grasp of the English language is less than perfect. I fear that in the witness box he would be at a great disadvantage under cross-examination."

"Are you seeking an adjournment in order for the court to provide an interpreter, Mr Medland?"

"Hmm... not really, Your Honour, interpreting the words is simple enough. The problem is the intimidation of the moment, a foreign person in a strange country trying to understand a foreign concept and being under pressure etc. What I was looking for was perhaps something more bespoke. I was hoping, Your Honour might be able to assure the jury, as in days gone by, that the fact that Mr Petacinni is unable to give evidence would not prejudice his case."

"How long has your client been in this country, Mr Medland?"

The counsel checked momentarily with his client, "Twelve years your honour."

"And we heard from Mr Carter, when he gave evidence, that your client worked as a waiter in a hotel that catered for English guests. Was that not the case?"

Mr Medland merely inclined his head and already his lip was starting to curl.

"Well, Mr Medland," said Jeremy "last summer, my wife and I stayed in a hotel in Italy and the waiter who served us spoke excellent English and as far as I was aware had never set foot in this country. I believe that a twelve-year period is sufficient for your client to be able to deal with the problems of giving evidence. Now, before we call the jury in your client will have to make up his mind whether or not he wishes to give evidence."

There was some more whispered conversation between Mr Medland and his client. "Very well," said Mr Medland.

As the jury was ushered into the courtroom Mr Medland was making notes in a book and looking at his watch. Jeremy could not help reflecting that he was probably making notes for a possible appeal later.

The jury settled down looking expectantly at the court and the bench. Mr Medland and his client were both still involved in a whispered discussion. The counsel continued to snarl and grimace while his client persisted with flounces of head and shoulders.

"Yes, Mr Medland," said Jeremy enquiringly, "have you advised your client of his rights?"

Aloysius Medland threw an irritated glance over his shoulder at the bench. With the grimace still on his face he said, "I would like to call my client to give evidence your honour."

With a nonchalant Latin toss of the head Joe made his way to the witness box. Mr Medland led him through his evidence in an exaggeratedly considerate fashion which emphasised his extreme lack of understanding of the English language.

"Mr Petacinni," he said slowly, "before you owned the Nite Club where did you work?"

"I worka for a while at La Scala," he said.

"Is that an Italian restaurant?"

"Si."

"And then you purchased the Nite Club?"

"Si."

"And did you employ the twins to sell or circulate drugs on the premises?" Joe purported not to understand the question.

"Did you pay Mr Gibson and his twin brother, to sell drugs to your customers?"

"No, no, I pay them to operate the doors."

"Did you know they were selling drugs?"

"No, I know nothing about that."

"And the transfer of the family shares, did you arrange those yourself?"

Again, Joe feigned a misunderstanding of the question. "The shares, who arranged them and how?"

"Eddie," confirmed Joe. "He get his solicitor to do them."

"I see. Please wait there."

Mr Sabin got to his feet, "You are the sole owner of the Nite Club?"

"Si."

"So any money found on the premises, say for example in the safe, must have belonged to you. Is that not true?"

"No, no, I no put that money in the safe. Eet must ava been the twins."

"But who had the key to the safe?"

"The key was in the drawer of the desk They ava to putta the money in the safe at night."

"I put it to you that you did know that the twins were selling drugs at the Nite Club and you were receiving a share of it."

Again, Joe appeared to struggle to understand.

"You knew," said Mr Sabin, very slowly, "that the twins were selling drugs."

"No, no, I avva no idea."

"I think you do, Mr Petacinnin. In your wife's divorce petition, she says that you did know about it."

"No. no, she no tella the truth. She only try to getta more money from me."

Mr Augustus Samuel stood up. "Humph… my client, Mr Sharp, did not organise the transfers of the family shares. That was your own idea. You did it all yourself."

"No, no, Eddie he do it. He getta the solicitor to do all the papers. I just sign them but I donna understand them."

"Oh, come now, Mr Petacinni. You cannot expect the court to believe that." blustered Gus.

"Si, si," protested Joe. "Eetza true."

Algernon Phillipson took a turn at cross-examining the witness. "You say that you own the Nite Club premises, and that you hired the twins to act as bouncers or doormen."

"Si."

"And yet you had no idea that they were peddling drugs?"

"No."

"And you never thought to ask where all the money in the safe came from?"

Joe looked puzzled again. "The money, in the safe," said Algie, more firmly, "Why did you not ask where it came from?"

"I never see no money," replied Joe.

"And the share certificates and transfer deeds, you claim that these were all drawn up by the solicitor, my client, and you had no idea what they were?"

Joe, as usual, purported not to understand the question.

"The family shares," repeated Algie, "why could you not understand them?"

"They were legal documents," he said. "I no understand them."

Mr Medland came back. "Mr Petacinni, did you spend all your time at the Nite club or did you leave things to other people?"

"Si, I trust the others. My wife did the books for me and the manager would do other things."

Mr Medland said, "No more questions." And sat down.

Jeremy Fallow QC glanced at the clock on the wall of the courtroom. He judged that there was just sufficient time for his summing up but only just.

"Ladies and gentlemen," he said addressing the jury. There is barely sufficient time for me to sum up this case for you before the court is closed for the day. I believe therefore that the appropriate time for my summing up speech would be first thing tomorrow morning. That should not take too long, approximately half an hour following which you can retire to consider your verdict. You will then have a complete day for your thoughts and deliberations. I am therefore adjourning this case until tomorrow morning and would ask you all to return then at the usual time.

George and Mavis said their goodbyes to Phillipa outside the court building. The latter assured them that she would be able to attend court the following day and she hoped therefore that the jury would be able to reach a verdict in one day. If not, she told them, she would be unable to come again to the viewing gallery because she would be tied up in the Matrimonial Court.

Mavis and George made their way home and on the train journey, discussed the court case. They both agreed that if they were members of the jury their verdict would be guilty on all counts.

Chapter Sixty-nine
Summing Up

The following morning, Judge Jeremy Fallow QC, began his summing up. He started by reminding the jury of the charges listed against each of the defendants. He told them that they could decide whether all of the defendants were innocent or guilty. Alternatively, if they so decided, they could decide that all or any of the defendants were innocent of all or any of the charges.

He examined with them the prosecution witnesses that they had heard from starting with Detective Chief Inspector O'Nighons. He reminded the jury how the suspicions arose and the facts that some evidence was collected on video film of the drug transactions at the first defendant's car lot premises.

"You will remember," said Jeremy, "that the defence counsels suggested that the search warrants were obtained without sufficient evidence of any suspicious activity. DCI O'nighons told you that the warrants were properly obtained by providing a local magistrate with sufficient reasonable grounds for a search and that the magistrate decided that those grounds were properly shown. In some totalitarian states where secret police forces operate you may feel that the state rigs evidence against innocent people. I would suggest however, in a democratic state such as ours, the system of checks and balances involved in applications for search warrants is fair and reasonable. That is a decision for you ladies and gentlemen."

He then moved on to the evidence of Charlie Chivers the International Detective. "You may have been impressed with the manner in which this witness presented hie evidence." said Jeremy.

"You have been told that he was a respected and experienced CID officer for a number of years. His evidence was challenged by the defence but you must decide whether that evidence was given in a plausible way or whether it was in any way doubtful. You must ask yourselves if there is any reason why a respected former police officer would give doubtful evidence to a court of law."

Jeremy went on to discuss the divorce papers that Charlie had served upon two of the defendants. "You may be asking yourselves ladies and gentlemen what these two documents, which are of course documents of the Matrimonial Court,are doing in this Criminal Court. Apart from being superbly drafted documents they are of course descriptive passages in respect of defendants one and three and as such, are relevant to both the character and activities of both defendants. It has been suggested by the defence that both documents are untrue and are, in effect the fictitious ramblings of two bitter women. The defence has also suggested that because both defendants have not challenged them in the Matrimonial Court, that they are nevertheless untrue. You ladies and gentlemen must ask yourselves if you had received such documents whether, if you felt that they were completely untrue, you would have denied their contents. You must also decide whether the lack of any response is in fact an admission of the truth of these documents. Would an ordinary man or woman who had been served with such papers have left them unchallenged unless he or she knew in their hearts that the documents told the truth? That is a question for you to decide ladies and gentlemen."

He then referred to the professor from the laboratory. He reminded them that this witness was the leading authority in the country and so cautioned the jury against any of the doubts or criticisms voiced by the defence in respect of his evidence.

In the alternative the evidence given by Jimmy Pearce and the Gibson twin merited some doubt or disbelief in view both of their criminal past and their involvement in the present activities.

"On the other hand," prompted Jeremy, "one could ask oneself why would either of them tell lies about what happened? True, they will both receive a lesser sentence for their involvement in this affair but you must resist the automatic assumption that anyone who has previously transgressed is therefore a liar. It might be that Mr Pearce and Mr Gibson are both more plausible because of their background and experience. That is a matter for you to decide upon. You must make up your minds whether you believe them or not."

On the subject of Eddie Sharp, the judge was a little more circumspect. He conceded that it was the duty of the prosecution to prove its case and that Eddie's mere denial of everything that had been said was not in itself proof of guilt.

"However," said Jeremy with slight scepticism, "you are entitled to ask yourself how the twins, who spent most of every day at or near his premises, would have acquired expensive motor cars without some knowledge or input by him. Also," he added, "with regard to the entries in the note book found in his safe, you will have to decide if these were a record of drug dealings as suggested by the prosecution or whether as Mr Sharp himself suggests, merely random jottings about car sales and thus relatively unimportant. You may ask yourselves why someone would lock in a safe a note book containing unimportant random entries. This is a matter for you to decide."

He turned next to Simon Nibble and reminded the jury that the expert from the Law Society had confirmed that the entries and records in his client account register were improper. No evidence had been tendered by the defence to challenge that.

"It follows therefore," Jeremy told them, "that if any of the allegations which he has made against the first defendant regarding threats of violence etc, are true then this would not render him innocent of the charges made against him but merely act as mitigation. Ladies and gentlemen, you must decide."

When it came to Giovanni Petacinni the judge was less objective. "You may have thought that this defendant understood more English than he led you to believe. You may feel that after twelve years living in this country, he should have much more knowledge of the English language. It would be reasonable to ask yourselves why a defendant would pretend to understand little English. Again, that is a matter for you ladies and gentlemen."

Having finished with the witnesses Jeremy then moved on to the law generally in respect of drug dealing and employment and agency. He also gave them some instruction as to their deliberations when they left the courtroom. He assured them that if they had any problems or queries, they could send him a message and he would endeavour to help them. Finally, he instructed them that they had to reach a verdict on all three defendants and in respect of all charges.

The jury filed out and were led to their own deliberation room by a court usher.

George and Mavis retired to the coffee bar on the ground floor: Phillipa hurried away to have a brief meeting with her husband Algernon. She assured them that she would soon be back to check in with them. Left to themselves George and Mavis found a table and settled down to drink their coffees. Eventually Phillipa returned and joined them.

"So," said Mavis to Phillipa, "what did you make of the judge's summing up?"

Phillipa gave a kind of grimace, "Hmm, it was more or less as expected. I suppose that I thought it was nearly reasonable whereas the defence counsels almost certainly regarded it as biased in favour of the prosecution."

"What did your husband think about it?" asked Mavis.

"Well," said Phillipa, he was averagely outraged but not I suspect as much as the other two counsels. Did you not see them all writing hurried notes during the summing up speech. They will be pored over and possibly used in any appeal hearings."

"But," said George, "that was the first summing up speech I have ever heard. It sounded OK to me. What was wrong with it?"

Phillipa breathed in deeply. "Well, there you have it. A speech which primarily sends a message of 'probably guilty' but sprinkled heavily with lots of 'but that is a question for you'. In the end it is probably fair."

"But what is your husband's view?"

"Well," said Phillipa choosing her words carefully, "his view has always been different from mine. He has always regarded Jeremy as a pro-prosecution judge, who should have had more experience of defence work before taking his place on the bench."

"So he disagreed with the summing up then?"

"That, my dear, is putting it mildly. He was ranting and raving about it. I did not help the situation of course by taking Jeremy's side."

"You had a row then?"

"That's also putting it mildly. He was already disgruntled that my divorce petitions were included in the prosecution bundle. On top of that the summing up speech was overtly biased, in his opinion, and then to cap it all I had to remind him that the discrepancies in his client's own client account records was irreversibly damaging to any of the arguments he had presented. He was not a happy bunny."

Mavis could understand the difficulty of Phillipa's position.

Meanwhile, in the courtroom itself a message was passed by the court usher to Shirley Kemp who took it into the judge's chambers.

"A message from the jury, Judge," she said passing the note to him.

He opened the note and read it. "Hmm," he said, "the jury are asking to be told the name of the individual whose name is redacted in the divorce petition of the first defendant. I think we had better advise all the counsels of this request. Perhaps you would be good enough to ask them all to come to my chambers, Shirley."

His clerk popped out to deliver the request and shortly returned to the chambers. "On their way, Judge," she said.

All the counsels soon shuffled into the judge's chambers. "Gentlemen," said Jeremy, "the jury have asked me to reveal to them the name of the individual which is redacted in the divorce petition served upon the first defendant. That name, as we all know, is the name of the second defendant and so I wanted to advise you of their request."

"And what will be your reaction?" Algie asked.

"Well to reveal the name to them of course," replied Jeremy, "after all, in matters like this I am the servant of the jury. They have demanded this information and I must provide it for them."

All four counsels mentally sucked their teeth. They all realised the importance of this item of information becoming known by the jury. Each defence counsel was no doubt assessing the chances of a successful appeal if Jeremy acceded to the jury's request.

"I am not sure that the jury must be given this information," said Algernon thoughtfully. "Aside from the basic point that the petition itself ought not to be included in the bundle and given the fact that the jury are bound to be curious about deleted details, why are they absolutely entitled to see such a detail?"

"They feel that they need that information to help them reach a verdict," said Jeremy. "I have checked the point and believe me they are entitled to request it."

"But are you, as a judge, obliged to provide it?" questioned Mr Medland with a half-smile/sneer.

"I believe I am," said Jeremy with great surety.

There was a further intake of breath by all those in the room. They all knew the consequences. Jeremy exhaled long and hard. "Believe me, gentlemen, no one is more aware of the consequences of this decision than myself but I am certain that it is a correct one."

The jury were supplied with the answer to their query. Soon after that they relayed a further message to the Judge to confirm that they had reached a verdict. This was only two hours after they had retired. The court was re-assembled and the jury filed back in. Shirley asked them if they had reached a decision and the foreman confirmed that they had. They found all three defendants guilty on all counts.

For the final time George and Mavis and Phillipa retired to the nearby snack bar of their choice. Over lunch they discussed the drama that had unfolded in front of them.

"The jury must have been unanimously decided on their verdict right from the start," said Mavis. "They took such a short time to reach their decision."

"Well," said Phillipa, "it was entirely predictable."

"How long will it be before the judge passes sentence?" asked Mavis.

"About one week," said Phillipa.

"Will it take him that long to decide what sentence to pass?"

"Not at all," replied Phillipa. "I expect he has already made up his mind. It is just that he has a diary which is always quite full and a week is the soonest that he will be able to fit it in. Besides, there have to be reports first from the Probation Service for the judge to consider and the defence counsels have to be allowed to prepare their speeches in mitigation. All these things take some time."

As they finished their snack, they all left the café and stood on the pavement outside to say goodbye to each other. Mavis and Phillipa gave each other a hug. Mavis was very aware of the poignancy of the moment. She realised that it might be the last time she met Phillipa and said as much. The latter gave her another hug and assured her that she was always there for her especially if she needed any advice on her legal studies. Mavis felt relieved to hear this and gave Phillipa a final kiss and promised or threatened that she would soon be in touch with her.

George and Mavis made their way home on the train together. All the way they talked excitedly about their arrangements for their wedding day. They were both so happy that they both smiled continuously.

Simon Nibble, upon his return to the Bristol prison at Horfield had nothing to smile about. Although no sentence had yet been passed, he knew that in a week or so he would be receiving a sizeable sentence which would deny him any daylight for a number of years. He visited the toilet area which was dirty and dingy. Simon recalled the beautifully tiled bathroom at his own house. There was one other occupant, a thin wiry man with tattoos on his arms. Simon gave him a smile as he passed him to visit a cubicle and failed to notice that the man held in his hand a home-made blade (a shank) with which he took a vicious swipe at Simon. The blade sliced across his throat and opened his carotid artery. Simon fell to the floor clutching his neck. His assailant immediately left the toilet area consigning the blade he had been carrying to a drain near the entrance to the toilets. The assault was intended merely as a punishment but Simon Nibble quickly bled to death before anyone found him.

Arnold Pigg was not bleeding but at his work place the storeroom was haemorrhaging the plastic sheets which he had found so useful for his graphs. He managed to establish that another department had been using them for demonstration purposes at MOD bases. Mr Pigg, though temporarily frustrated by this lack of supply, thanks to Penny, (who knew someone in the supply department), obtained his own private delivery of two hundred items, which he estimated would last him for approximately four years. Mr Pigg was thus a very happy man.

Tom and Bill now met every morning at the Golf Club instead of the office. After their round of golf, they would go into the club bar and enjoy a drink, usually a coffee, but occasionally they would enjoy an alcoholic drink and raise their glasses in a toast to George and Mavis.

Pete and Sandra were still together both now living in Pete's flat above La Scala restaurant. George had moved out and was now in the newly purchased house with Mavis. They were both blissfully happy.. Both couples met now at least once every week for a meal at La Scala. Pete had proposed to Sandra and she had said yes. Both couples were toying with the possibility of enjoying a joint wedding ceremony.

The End